Inheriting Stars

Eowyn A. Stephenson

Inheriting Stars

Paperback edition—ISBN 979-8-9880556-0-0

E-book edition—ISBN 979-8-9880556-1-7

Cover design by: Damonza.com

Interior design by: Eowyn A. Stephenson

To Mom. Thanks for the adventure.

And to Dad. It may never be a bestseller, but here it is.

Eowyn A. Stephenson

"Praise be to the Lord my Rock,
Who trains my hands for war,
My fingers for battle.
He is my loving God and my fortress,
my stronghold and deliverer."

Psalm 114:1,2

Prologue

What do you make of it?"

Averendier clicked the spyglass shut in his hands. His lips curved into a grave frown, he gazed thoughtfully into the water lapping at the ship's hull. Beside him stood his father, Austinian, awaiting an answer to the question he had asked.

Andrald, Averendier's twin, slipped the spyglass from his brother's unusually slack fingers and propped his elbows on the ship's railing. Though it was nearly midnight, the full moon's light illuminated the sea and its gently bobbing occupants as brightly as if it were day. The clear sea stretched in plain view for miles before fading into the indeterminate horizon.

Sliding the spyglass out to almost its full length, Andrald put the instrument to his eye and squinted through the lens.

Sweeping the glass to the left, he saw through it a convoy of ships, shrunken from that distance, just skirting the horizon.

Behind him, his father said, "They're not merchants."

"No," agreed Averendier grimly.

Andrald frowned as he shifted his gaze to the distant ships' masts. The brisk night winds tugged out from it a red flag. Although it could not be seen over the great distance, Andrald knew—just as surely as he knew his own name—the image blazoned across that field of red. Two battle axes, their shafts crossed to form an *x*. A black serpent, winding its sinister body around the gristly weapons.

An involuntary shudder threatened to shake the young man's shoulders. Tirendria's flag. The enemy's emblem.

The banner of death.

It streamed above those nine ships, ships distinctly built for war. Tirendrian vessels, sailing through Monarian waters as if they had a right to do so. Andrald's eyes skimmed over the nearest ship's side. The name *Vengeance* stood stark against the sun-bleached wood. The one after that bore the title *Tarian* in letters as bold as the ship's movements. The others were too obscured in shadow to be read, though Andrald knew they were no better—if not worse—than the first.

He dropped his gaze to the name carved in the hull beneath him. With sailorly reverence, he whispered, *"Vanguard."*

"If only we could know where they're headed," said Averendier thoughtfully, his gaze still fixed on the wraith-like forms gliding effortlessly through the forbidden waters.

"If they keep their present course, they're heading home, where they belong," Austinian replied. Deep lines creased his forehead as he continued, "But I'm afraid that isn't what we should ask ourselves."

Andrald looked quickly back at his father; the tone of Austinian's voice twisted his stomach with unease.

"Rather, boys, what are the devils leaving behind them?"

Averendier bent his head a moment, his blond hair almost silver in the moonlight. His lips moved barely as he quietly calculated something. The silence around the three men was utterly complete in those terse moments—not even the waves lapping against the hull, or the canvas sails flapping overhead seemed to make their usual noise.

Finally, Averendier looked up, his face grayer than moonlight. "The Tinannakin Islands," he said.

Austinian's jaw noticeably tightened. "I pray not," he murmured. "But if so…"

Quickly, he turned and shouted over the silent deck, "Hrapps!"

The officer summoned ran across the *Vanguard's* deck. "Yes, sir?" he asked, drawing himself up and saluting smartly.

"Signal the *Dermain's Folly*. Tell them to follow us to Starr Island."

Hrapps looked questioningly at his admiral, but since Austinian offered no explanation, he simply saluted, with another, "Yes, sir."

He checked himself before he turned and asked, "What about the *Venture*, sir?"

"Tell them to follow those ships at a good distance," Austinian said, pointing to the Tirendrian convoy off the port bow, "and to keep following them until they leave our waters. Tirendria may be playing its old tricks again."

"Very well. Anything else, sir?"

"No, that is all. Carry on."

Hrapps fell back a step and saluted. He hurried back towards the stern, shouting orders to the dormant crew. At the commands, sailors sprang from their berths and gathered on deck. The *Vanguard* bustled with their sudden, eager response.

"If only I had brought my men," muttered Averendier, fingering absently the captain's medal pinned to his tunic.

Andrald hardly heard his brother. His eyes, round with a wondering fear, were fixed on his father's grim face.

"Starr Island?" he questioned. "Do you think the fort could be in danger?"

Frowning, Austinian probed one temple. His eyes followed his sailors' actions.

"It could be," he said. "Twenty years ago, Tirendria broke the treaty just to get a crack at it. Now that the treaty has expired for good…"

Andrald's stomach churned with sudden nausea as he silently finished his father's sentence. The entirety of Ontaria—Tirendria included—had been locked in a peace promise for the past hundred years. During that time, the civilian population on Starr Island— within and without its legendary fort—had thrived. It was no wonder. Time and time again throughout history, Fort Starr has proved itself unconquerable, even by Tirendria's elite.

But the treaty had expired a year ago. Unhampered by political agreements, Tirendria was free to wage war. There had been rumors of it stirring trouble in the east. Was the black serpent now rearing its head north-west…to Monaria?

To make matters worse, it was cider season. Starr Island was covered in orchards, and every year people trekked there to pick apples and use the cider press there to make cider and bring it back home with them. They had family who went there ever year.

Andrald had to clear his throat once before he could whisper, "I pray not."

The admiral's face grew still more drawn. He turned his face into the briskly blowing wind. "So do I," he murmured.

The setting moon's glow washed the woods, filtering through branches lush with late summer and casting weird and fantastic shadows on the ground.

A unit of sailors, fifty strong, wove in and out of the shadows. Weapons were in their hands, fear beat in their hearts. Yet overriding fear and confidence alike was disgruntled curiosity.

"What are we doing here anyway?" grumbled one sailor, who trudged belligerently beside Andrald. "We're sailors. We don't go wandering in the woods like this. What does Austinian think we are? Deer?"

Andrald chuckled softly and pushed a branch aside.

"No," he said. "Not quite."

It was funny, he reflected, how people could be so oblivious of possible disaster, that they would complain of anything out of the ordinary. Didn't the man know they were creeping towards Fort Starr under the cover of the trees and the darkness they harbored? Could he not feel the fear hanging in the air, thick enough to choke a man?

Yet was not there some sense in the man's complaints? Was it possible that Austinian was being overcautious? Andrald frowned at himself. His father *had* been more than a little on edge over the past year, ever since they had received word of strife in the east.

But that was halfway around the world. Could the east have bent so quickly that Tirendria was already slipping into Monaria?

Andrald knew his father was right. Something was wrong. The night was too still, holding its breath.

Andrald forced himself to breathe deeply. Yet how could he, when none among them knew what lay beyond the line of trees ahead?

The thick foliage suddenly thinned. It seemed sufficient cover against eyes that might be peering, searching for parties like his own. He glanced furtively behind himself, but saw nothing more than his father's men picking their way along the forest floor.

"What then?" demanded the disgruntled sailor, startling Andrald out of his musings. "Foxes, maybe?"

Andrald was thoughtfully silent a moment. Finally, he suggested, "Owls?" He motioned up to a blue and gray feathered bird perched on a limb above them.

The man cocked his head to peer up at the bird. The owl blinked one eye with a superior air.

"Nah." The man shook his head in disgust. "They're out now, sure. But we don't fly. If we did, we might be like one." He silently ducked a low branch. "And that's just odd," he added mildly.

"Shh!" hissed Averendier in sudden warning.

Andrald looked swiftly up to see his brother motioning him to come forward and stand with him. Dread curled in the pit of Andrald's stomach as he joined his brother at the wood's edge.

Under some silent command, the brothers peered through the screen of trees at the same moment.

Beyond the tree line lay a short stretch of open land, through which ran a road. The path led straight up to the fort, a structure surrounded by walls as tall as the trees.

As tall, and just as silent.

Andrald's eyes darted over the darkened walls and the looming hulks of sentry towers standing sentinel at the corners.

"Where is everyone?" he murmured, his low voice drifting under the stillness. He lifted his eyes to his brother's.

Averendier had eyes only for the fort.

"I think we'd better scout it out," he said finally, meeting his brother's gaze. "Just you and I."

Turning slightly, Averendier motioned for the rest of the unit to remain hidden behind the wood line. He ventured out into the open,

Andrald close at his heels. Just as they passed from beneath the trees' shadow, a cloud passed over the moon, darkening the landscape.

The world was silent as a tomb, and just as dark. Not even a breath of wind blew from the shore. The brothers cautiously crept up the road and to the silent fort.

In front of the gate, they hesitated. Andrald stared up at the tall doors, made of iron-studded oak. Awe joined the fear fluttering within him.

Averendier glanced at his brother, then fixed his gaze on the guard towers looming above.

"Stirling," he called, his strong voice ringing through the stillness, echoing against the pressing walls of silence.

No voice from above answered the password. No flicker of lantern or torch betrayed the approach of a sentry. Only a moan sounded, as low and long as the wind soughing through the woods.

Andrald shivered and glanced furtively over his shoulder, half expecting to see some monstrous beast sneaking up on them both.

"Maybe they changed it," he suggested nervously.

Averendier frowned. "It's not an old code, Andrald," he said. "It should work."

"It does," came a voice, still low and groaning, but close at hand.

Andrald jumped back, his hand flashing to the short naval sword he wore at his belt.

Averendier turned coolly towards the voice. "Who are you?" he demanded. "Show yourself."

For one eternal moment, there was no answer. No sound at all but the lapping of distant waves, and the thin, tentative breathing of both young men.

"Easier said than done," said the voice at last, ending in a weary chuckle.

His head cocked towards the sound of the voice, Averendier took a step forward.

Instantly there was the sound of steel swishing across leather as a sword was drawn from its scabbard. Averendier froze.

"Not another move, if you value your life!" exclaimed the unseen man.

Though he could not see it, Andrald sensed his brother's frown.

"Who are you to say so?" Averendier asked.

Just then, the cloud scudded away from the moon. Once again, the ghostly light streamed down, revealing a man propped against the base of the sentinel tower. A blade quivered unsteadily in his right hand, his face was pinched with pain, his breath came in audible gasps. Looking down, Andrald immediately caught sight of the man's leg, twisted grotesquely beneath him.

The man's eyes widened with understanding as they lighted upon the two figures before him, both clad in the green military tunics worn by all Monarian soldiers. His head drooped with relief, and he immediately lowered his sword.

"Fort Starr's guard is who," he answered. "At least," he added, coughing, "what's left of them."

Andrald's gray eyes grew keen as they took in the deserted, blood-soaked man, obviously too hurt and weak to stand.

Averendier touched his brother's forearm quickly. "Talk with him," he whispered. "I'll go get a *meddyg.*"

Andrald nodded. Before he had even finished, his brother strode off into the night.

"Who are you?" pressed the soldier. He let his head roll back against the rough wall.

Andrald offered the man a faint smile. "Andrald Peterson, the admiral's son."

"The navy. Thank God!" breathed the man, momentarily looking up at the stars. His tragic eyes dropped back onto Andrald. "But you only just missed them. They were here a few hours ago."

"We know," Andrald replied softly. "We saw their ships while we were on patrol. That's why we came here."

The soldier pushed himself as high up as his injured leg would allow. "Did you attack them?" he asked breathlessly.

Andrald looked away. "No."

The man's face fell.

"There were only three of us on patrol," Andrald added. "The best we could do was send one ship to follow them to make sure they leave the Tinannakin. The other two sailed here to check things out."

"Don't let them leave!" the soldier harshly exclaimed. He started forward, as if he had half a mind to jump up and run after the ships himself, broken leg and all. "Those hulks are packed with prisoners from here!"

Andrald's head snapped up, his eyes kindled. "Prisoners?" he repeated, his hands involuntarily knotting into fists. "How many?"

"Whoever the brutes didn't kill," answered the soldier, almost spitting. "Men, women, children—goodness knows they don't care who they take! My wife and son likely among them."

"Why didn't they take you?" Andrald asked.

The soldier shrugged, in dismissal or despair. "That's what I'd like to know," he said. "Too broken down, I guess. Or maybe they thought I was dead. I got knocked down from up there." He tipped his head back, squinting up at the tower. "I must have blacked out."

Before Andrald could say anything more, he felt a tap on his shoulder. He glanced back into the tired face of the Vanguard's *meddyg*.

Nodding, Andrald rose out of his crouch and started to turn around.

"Wait!" the soldier called.

Andrald bent over him. "What is it?"

The man grasped Andrald's hand urgently. "My name's Selvahn," he said quickly. "My wife's Mara. And the tyke's named after me. If you ever find her, or him…"

Andrald tightened his grasp over the man's hand before letting go. "If I find them, I'll bring them to you. I promise."

Andrald was hardly confident he would ever have the chance to fulfill such a promise, but Selvahn seemed content to cling to that slim chance. He sank back to the ground, eyes closed. But some of the tense lines on his face had smoothed away.

Andrald left the man to the *meddyg* and joined Averendier, who now stood in front of the fort gate along with the rest of the landing party.

Averendier sent a meaningful glance in the *meddyg's* direction. "Did you learn anything?" he asked.

Andrald drew a slow, deep sigh that lifted his broad shoulders. "Yeah. It's just like Dad thought. I don't think this place has a single living soul left in it."

At these ominous words, a hush descended upon the whole group.

Averendier pressed his mouth into a tight, grim line. "We'll go in anyway," he said. "I want to search this place top to bottom before I say it's empty."

Immediately, the sailors pushed open the gate's heavy double doors. As a body, they cautiously entered the fort.

They worked their way down the wide streets. Nowhere was there any sign of life. Of the many previous inhabitants of Fort Starr, there remained only the occasional dark splotch of half-dried blood upon the cobblestones and stray weapons scattered wherever their owners had dropped them.

When they reached the square set in the fort's heart, the only moving thing was a solitary fountain, weeping down many tiers into a basin. Behind it stood the chapel. The once beautiful structure now displayed jagged teeth of smashed stained-glass windows, their glass glistering like jewels in the moonlight. The sailors murmured with anger.

"If they dared touch the tabernacle…" muttered one threateningly. Steel whispered against leather as the man drew his sword. In agreement, Andrald slung the crossbow from off his shoulder and held it at the ready.

Averendier reached the fountain and turned to face his men.

"Split up," he ordered. "Search every building. But don't touch anything unless it's a person. If you do find anyone, living or dead, bring them here."

"Good luck with that," someone behind Andrald muttered. "Anyone can see they've wiped the place clean."

Notwithstanding any doubts they may have had—thought or spoken—the sailors obediently saluted their commander and scattered towards the silent buildings.

Andrald's fingers curled tight over his crossbow's trigger as he ducked under the doorway of the first building he came across.

He had entered a kitchen, one so small he knew he was in someone's home. At least, what had been their home. It was a disaster. Table and chairs were overturned. Crockery was smashed and scattered on the floor. Pieces of it crunched underfoot as Andrald moved across the room.

The main room was equally destroyed. Embers from the fireplace had been thrown across the room, charring black holes into the green and brown patterned rug that covered the floor. Tattered ribbons of curtains hung limply from the splintered curtain rods (which, by some miracle of balance, still stretched across the window frames). A bed in one corner had been hacked to pieces; its slashed mattress spilled feathers out onto the floor.

However terrible the destruction, it was not what Andrald was looking for. He didn't need to linger over it. He would get more than his fill before the sun rose.

With a soft sigh of disappointment, Andrald turned back towards the door.

A sudden sharp cry broke the stillness. Andrald jumped and whirled, his finger involuntarily squeezing the crossbow's trigger. His eyes followed the flash of crossbow bolt as it slammed into the wall.

He blinked, rubbed his eyes, and looked again.

Sure enough, directly underneath the still-quivering bolt, was a shaft of light, thrown onto the wall from… the floor?

As a small child's wails continued to fill the air, Andrald's eyes followed the beam of light down from where it slipped through a crack in the floorboards.

Feverishly, Andrald lay his crossbow aside and moved to the crack. Something like hope thrilled through his fingertips as he stooped and pulled the bits of charred rug away. Just below him was a trap door, its form framed with light. With trembling hands, Andrald seized the carved handle into the door and flung open the trap door.

Out of the opening, pure light flooded. From inside the cellar, eight frightened faces gaped at him. Six children and a mother who clutched a wailing baby to her chest. A joyous smile broke out over Andrald's face.

"Come on out," he beckoned, reaching into the cellar. "It's all right. The navy's here."

The woman bowed her head and muffled a sob in her infant's shoulder. "Thank God!" she cried.

"Climb on up," Andrald repeated. One child, who had been watching Andrald and sucking her thumb, suddenly held out her little fist. Ignoring the sogginess of her hand, Andrald grasped it and hoisted her up into the room with him.

Seeing their comrade's courage, the other children clamored to be lifted out as well. Andrald helped each one out of the cellar, lasty holding the baby while its mother climbed up a ladder into the room.

"Sweet fellow," Andrald murmured as he restored the babe to its mother.

The woman nodded and tucked the infant's blanket tighter around its body. "His name is Selvahnson, after his father," she said. She bowed her head and planted a kiss on her son's forehead to conceal the tear slipping down her cheek.

Andrald startled violently. He peered intently into her face. "Mara?" he queried, disbelievingly.

The woman froze and stared wonderingly up at him. "How…how do you know my name?" she murmured, white-lipped.

"I'll explain in a moment," Andrald answered. As he spoke, he reached down and slung the littlest child onto his back, wrapping her little hands around his neck. He handed his unloaded crossbow to the oldest child.

"Right now, we need to get these youngsters to the square. Come on, everyone. Keep together!"

The still-frightened children obeyed, snatching each other's hands, the woman's skirts, and Andrald's pantlegs—anything loose to clutch that radiated safety. Andrald tried to offer them each the same encouraging smile as before, but it felt so false sitting there on his face that he quickly gave up altogether. That such innocence should be haunted with such fear!

They left the house and started briskly towards the square, the children and the woman following in an almost straight line behind him.

One searcher passing Andrald in the street stopped to gawk at this strange rendition of goose and goslings.

"Search the cellars!" Andrald called before hurrying on.

Immediately, the man turned and shouted the news to the other searchers.

"It's too late," Mara murmured, her voice choked with tears. "They're all gone."

"Don't be so sure," Andrald answered.

Even as he said it, several women and children trickled out of a house. Out of another building, two sailors bore a wounded man away in their arms.

But Mara only shook her head, her arms tightening around the soft form of her baby.

When they reached the square, Andrald turned to the children. He slung the girl off his back, pried tight fingers from his pant legs, and took his crossbow from the oldest child (who seemed all too happy to give it back).

"Stay here," he said to Mara. "I'll be right back."

Less than an hour later, Andrald walked into Fort Starr's hospital, the young mother Mara trailing uncertainly behind him.

"Sir," began Mara, just as she and Andrald entered one of the wards, "I don't see what we're..." She glanced to the side and suddenly noticed whose bed she was beside. All words failed her.

Her husband, Selvahn, winced as he sat up in his bed. Then he smiled and spread his arms wide.

Andrald stepped back as Mara ran up beside the bed and dropped on her knees beside him, her shoulders shaking, silently sobbing. The baby was laid between them on the bed. Andrald smiled slightly. One family reunited.

Just one.

How many others would never know a moment like this? How many women and children had become widows and orphans?

The smile wiped from his face, Andrald turned away. He collided with a *meddyg* who was hurrying past.

"Sorry," Andrald apologized. Dropping to his knees, he scrambled after the rolls of bandages the doctor had dropped.

"Not at all," answered the *meddyg* as he scooped up the last few rolls. "This happens all the time."

As Andrald bundled the bandages back into the doctor's arms, his gaze drifted back to Selvahn and his family.

"Will he live?" he asked.

The *meddyg* nodded his chin over his armload of medical supplies. "Give him a few months of rest for that bone to knit, and he'll be back on his feet. Still..." He sighed and looked down at his burden. "There are others..."

"I know," Andrald said quietly. His gaze swept the length of the long ward, crowded with cots ready to receive the wounded. At least a fourth of them were already filled.

The *meddyg* followed his gaze. "It's a sorry sight, lad. One I'm afraid we'll get used to. This won't be the end of anything."

Andrald's mouth seemed to fill with cotton. Turning his face away, he forced himself to choke out an answer.

"I know."

1

light breeze blew, relieving some of the oppressive late summer glare. The wind played with a flag—a creamy flag flaunting a tree in full summer foliage with two burning tapers crossed over its trunk. The flag's well-sewn edges were tugged this way and that, the cloth furling and unfurling above the stately building.

The flag stretched its shadow beside that of the building across the streets and cobblestoned square below. The square overflowed with people milling around stalls and tables of all sorts. It was market day in the town of Bryn.

Out of the main body of people, Engrelin emerged. Casually, he wandered up to a weaver's stall. After glancing idly at the racks of cloths and yarn on display, he picked up a spool of white thread and plunked it down in front of the weaver.

"How much for this?" he asked.

"Huh?" The weaver cupped a hand riddled with needle pricks around his ear. "Speak up, boy. I can't hear you through all this." He waved at the surrounding throngs.

He would have been wise to notice the few people who were watching his stand— or, rather, watching the boy with whom he was preparing to haggle. Engrelin was lowborn—he never struck anything but a hard bargain, even over something as trivial as a spool of thread.

Barely refraining from rolling his eyes, Engrelin repeated his question. He knew well the sly gleam lighting the monger's eyes.

"My price stands at six *firlas*," stated the weaver, leaning back on his stool.

Engrelin's eyes widened. "Six!" he exclaimed indignantly. He fingered the meager store of coins in his pocket. "Do I look rich? One-half."

"O…one…" stuttered the weaver. He tugged at the neck of his tunic, as if the suggestion of such a price strangled him. His other hand tightened over the spool Engrelin had selected. "I have to eat, you know." He was silent a moment, as if deeply considering something. Finally, he said, "Five and a half."

"Want the tunic on my back to go with it?" Engrelin added dryly, though his eyes glowed with suppressed merriment. "I'll give you one."

"I won't go below five!" the weaver exclaimed desperately. "One for me, and the others for the wife and children."

Engrelin let out a short laugh. "Right. You've got a family, and I've got a kingdom. My price stands. One *firlas*. No more, no less."

"Five," insisted the monger.

"You might as well ask me for the moon! I said one."

The weaver's broad chest swelled with indignation. "If I sold everything here at that price, I might as well move there!" He looked quickly around. "All right, all right. I'll lower it to four. But only for you."

"One," Engrelin repeated evenly. "I know when I'm being cheated." He angled his body away from the stand, as if to leave. "I can always get my thread somewhere else. Thanks for your trouble."

The weaver snatched Engrelin's wrist and pulled him back. "Fine! I'll give it to you for one," he grumbled.

Engrelin flashed the monger a brilliant smile and tossed the *firlas* onto the table.

As the man handed Engrelin the spool, he added mournfully, "And I'll go without supper tonight!"

"Sure you will." Slipping the spool into his pocket, Engrelin turned and strode back into the crowded street.

The moment he left the shelter of the stall's awning, the sun's rays burned his close-cropped hair. Engrelin scrubbed one hand through it, pulling the brown strands on end.

"Engrelin Peterson," a voice scolded from behind him.

Engrelin quickly turned. His cousin, Mary, stood on the other side of the road. She waded through a flock of loudly protesting geese to join him, her fine linen skirt brushing against their white feathers.

As Mary dusted off her dress, Engrelin smiled widely. "Mary! What in Ontaria are you doing this end of town?"

"Watching your performance," she answered. She rested one hand on her hip. "I'm a little disappointed. I was ready for another hour-long showdown."

Engrelin shrugged. "He's new to the business, I think. Gullible."

"Obviously. Otherwise, he would have closed his stand the moment you came into view. Your reputation of victimizing innocent mongers must not have preceded you this time."

"I'm not that bad," Engrelin protested laughingly. "It's them that cheat us. But, unlike some people around here, he's still too soft to wring every scrap of money out of my pocket." He patted the pocket holding his small store of coins.

"Mm-hmm." Mary looked unconvinced. "And may I ask what it was you stole from that poor man?" She cocked one eyebrow superiorly. "Hopefully, it has something to do with a new tunic?" She straightened her own blouse meaningfully.

Engrelin followed her skeptical gaze to the long rip in the hem of his tunic. "That's what the thread's for," he replied. "Grandmother ran out a little while ago, so she's a bit behind on the mending."

She lifted her eyebrows significantly. "A *bit?*"

"All right, really behind," Engrelin said, smiling wryly. "I wouldn't be here otherwise."

"I was wondering when I saw you at that stall. I didn't think you were going to leave your home at all until your parents got back—at least, not until Elmera was well."

"I hadn't intended to," Engrelin affirmed. "But when your grandmother tells you to go to town to get something for her, you go."

Mary nodded with understanding.

"Any word about the cider pressing?" Engrelin asked.

She shook her head. "I haven't heard anything. I've never been to the cider pressing, so I don't know how long it's going to take."

Engrelin nodded slowly, slightly disappointed, though he was unwilling to show it. Nearly three weeks ago, three of his siblings and his parents had sailed north to Starr Island for the annual apple harvest and cider pressing. Starr Island boasted some of the oldest and largest apple orchards in Monaria, and the Peterson family owned several acres of the orchards. Usually, the whole family made the yearly trek to oversee the harvest. Only this year, his little sister had fallen ill. Since a substantial amount of the family's income depended on the harvest, they had gone, leaving Elmera's grandmother to nurse her, and Engrelin, their youngest living son, to care for and protect them both.

"How is Elmera?" asked Mary, twisting a pleat of her skirt around her finger.

"She's all right now," Engrelin replied quietly. "We had a *meddyg* out just the other day to see her, and he said that she was on the up and up. She ate her whole breakfast this morning," he added brightly.

"By that, I'm guessing your grandmother cooked it?" Mary teased.

Engrelin shrugged. "She did."

"I'm glad everything at your place is all right." Mary sighed. "Father's been gone on patrol for two weeks now, and Averendier and Andrald went with him. They even missed the annual singing at Lord Gwane's!"

To the salvation of everyone's ears, Engrelin thought. Aloud, he said, "I was wondering why you decided to grace a peasant such as myself with your presence."

Mary swatted his shoulder. "Don't start that. Peasant or not, you're my cousin. And Aaron's descendant. Besides, I needed someone livelier than Mother and the servants to talk to."

Engrelin bowed. "Well, I've been talking. I hope I'm lively, ma'am."

"You are, thank you," returned Mary. Eyes dancing, she continued, "When my father gets back, are you going to ask him for another fencing lesson?"

Engrelin dragged the back of his hand across his mouth, stifling a groan. This again! What was it with his highborn relations and their insistence that he learn swordsmanship? Besides, the world was at peace, and he had a bow he knew how to use well. His father had never needed more than that to protect and provide for his family.

"Really, Mary," he said. "I'm a farmer, not some sword-swinging knight. The only things I'm ever going to fight in my lifetime are bugs, weeds, and weather."

"Unless the bugs learned how to fence," Mary pointed out mischievously.

"Then—and only then—would I take your dad up on his offer."

"You might be knighted one day, and have to save a fair maiden's life," Mary continued.

Engrelin smiled incredulously. He? A knight?

"No," he said. "I can just see me falling the moment I take the fair maiden's hand. I'll pass."

"*Myself*," Mary corrected, one hand fluttering with irritation at her side "You can see *yourself.*"

Engrelin shrugged affably. He had as much use for proper grammar as he did swords.

"Mary!" he heard someone calling from down the street. "Where are you, you exasperating girl?"

"Oh no!" Mary groaned, spinning around to scan the street. "I thought I'd lost her."

Engrelin glanced past his cousin to see a woman in well-to-do servant's clothes storming towards them, her swinging body radiating fury.

"Getting into the habit of running away, Mary?" Engrelin asked his dismayed cousin.

"You're horrible!" the girl exclaimed. She immediately softened her words with a quick hug. "Just be glad you were low born and can wander at will," she whispered into his ear.

Engrelin squirmed. Hugged, right here in the square! Had she no sense of discretion?

"I'll try to get away and visit once Mom and Dad get home," he promised.

Mary backed away and nodded a resigned farewell. With a parting wave of her hand, she ran to rejoin her enraged guardian.

Engrelin watched until he was sure his cousin had gotten into the proper hands. Once she was with the servant, he turned and jostled his way down the road, back the way he had come.

Dust hung in a haze over the crowd, which stirred it constantly from the hard-beaten road with every move they made. The parched ground was as hot as a clay oven beneath Engrelin's bare feet as he hurried along. He had one last place he wanted to stop before he started home.

He finally halted in the shadowy doorway of a blacksmith's shop. From inside, the ring of a hammer pounding metal could be heard above the weary wheeze of bellows. Engrelin ventured one step within the shop. A wave of suffocating heat greeted him, accompanied by the stench of sweat and hot metal. Shielding his face with one hand, Engrelin peered into the dim room. He could barely make out the blacksmith's brother, Walche, hammering away with vengeance at an iron stake. Every stroke he made sent orange sparks exploding in every direction.

Despite the heat, Engrelin leaned further into the room. "Lance!" he called.

No answer came from the gloom.

Engrelin turned to the laboring blacksmith. "Walche, have you seen Lance?"

"Why should I tell you?" demanded Walche, letting his hammer clatter onto the anvil one more time before he turned to look at the boy standing in the doorway. "You've probably come to steal my nephew from his work again, haven't you? Well, you're going to find it a lot harder to get him away from me. I never understood why my brother let Lance waste his time with you when the boy could be working. You too, for that matter."

Engrelin let his breath out slowly. "Do you know where he is?"

Walche shrugged his muscular shoulders and weighed his heavy hammer in his hands. "Why should I know?" he asked. He slammed the hammer down on the red-hot stake.

Engrelin scowled. Even though he knew the man could not hear him over the racket, he said, "Because he's your nephew."

Somehow, Walche must have heard him, for he roared back, "I don't know!"

"I'm right here!" called someone from deeper inside the forge. "I'll be out in a minute."

The muscles in Walche's neck bulged with suppressed anger, but he only continued his work.

Containing a smile, Engrelin stepped back into the cooler street to wait. At almost the same time, Lance hurried out of the forge. Charcoal smeared his face and arms, and fairly blackened the thick leather apron he wore.

"Whew! Uncle's fit to burst!" Lance exclaimed with a low whistle. He grasped Engrelin's forearm in rough greeting. "Sorry, I didn't hear you at first. I was at the bellows, and you know I can hardly hear a thing then. You're lucky Uncle stopped hammering when he did."

"I guess I am."

"But what're you doing out here today?" Lance asked. He raked his hands through his blond hair, which was so limp with sweat and full of ash flakes that it had lost its usual wave. He held up one hand, as if to ward something off. "Don't tell me that draft horse of yours threw its shoe again. Do you remember how hard it was to shoe that thing?"

Engrelin smirked. "If I remember correctly, it broke my leg."

"Exactly."

"No, I didn't come for that. If I had, I would have shown up in a suit of armor."

Lance chuckled. "Then why are you here? Nothing bad, I hope."

"Nope," Engrelin replied. "Elmera and Grandmother are both fine. I just came down today to get some thread."

Lance looked at Engrelin wonderingly and shook his head. "Man, Engrelin. I didn't know you were into sewing."

Engrelin shoved Lance hard. "Not for me. Grandmother needs it."

"Okay, okay." Lance rubbed his shoulder where Engrelin had playfully struck. "But you know, this is a forge," he added. "We don't sell thread here."

"I know that," Engrelin said, chuckling at Lance's smirk. "I stopped by to ask if you're coming over Monday to help out. Unless your uncle doesn't give you Mondays off like your dad." He looked back at the forge doorway.

"I think he'll let me go, as long as I tell him how hard we'll be working." Lance's face screwed with distaste.

"If you can make it, that'd be great. I'd promised Dad I'd have some of the harvesting done by the time they got home, but Elmera was worse than we thought. I've got next to nothing done."

"I'll be there," Lance promised. "Only…" He looked at Engrelin sidelong. "You're not planning on trying to preserve anything we're picking, are you?"

"No," Engrelin chuckled, knowing what Lance was thinking. "They should be home any day now, and then Mom will get all the preserving done. All we have to do is pick things."

"Thank. Goodness," Lance breathed in mock relief. More seriously, he continued, "Like I said, I'll do my best. Uncle's been a real crank recently, since Dad left."

"Recently?" Engrelin gave him a look.

"All right, longer than recently. But with Dad gone, it's just…" He shrugged. "Worse. Maybe it's because everyone's up at Starr Island."

"It shouldn't be," Engrelin said thoughtfully, frowning as he noted the weary slump of his friend's shoulders. "Practically half of Bryn is there right now."

"I know, right? Sometimes, I think Uncle isn't meant to be understood, just put up with."

"Lance!" Walche bellowed from within the forge. "Are you planning to socialize your day away? This fire's getting low!"

"Coming, Uncle!" Lance shouted. He turned quickly back to Engrelin. "I'll come Monday, if I survive that long." He jerked his head meaningfully back towards the shop.

"It'll only be for a few more days. Everyone will be home soon," Engrelin said.

Lance's shoulders tightened. He nodded shortly.

"Lance!" roared Walche. "Do I have to drag you in here myself?"

"Coming!" Lance yelled. He gave Engrelin's hand a firm squeeze before rushing back into the misery of the forge.

Engrelin, a troubled frown marking his forehead, gazed at the doorway for a long moment. "Only a few more days," he murmured to himself. Uttering a parting prayer for his friend, he turned and struck off out of the town, into the mountains beyond, to his family farm.

2

"*When are Mom and Dad coming home?*" Elmera asked. She twisted the edge of her quilt around her thin fingers. "I miss them."

Engrelin turned away from the open window. "Just Mom and Dad?" he asked.

"And Damien and Ouen and Reigna," she added, smiling.

"I miss them too," he said, crossing the room to sit on the edge of her bed. "We just have to be patient." Gently, he rumpled the girl's mass of dark, tangled curls.

Elmera hooked her spindly arms around her knees and puckered her pink mouth in a thoughtful frown. "Father Colby told me that patience is a virtue," she said. "But virtues must be hard to keep. Patience is."

Engrelin chuckled. "You think so?" Restlessly, he rose and returned to the window, thinking he'd heard Lance's familiar tread outside. But his friend was nowhere in sight. Engrelin lingered a moment, just to make sure, scanning the countryside spread out before him.

Beyond the window lay the barn and a corner of the garden. Behind them sprawled wide fields and pastures. The farm, Traeth Euriad, had been in his family for generations, leading directly back to its founder, Aaron himself. Pride surged through Engrelin—honest pride as uplifting as the warm breeze blowing in through the unglazed window (glass windows were a luxury the Petersons could hardly afford).

"But it's true!" Elmera exclaimed behind him. Her eyes flashed with indignance at her brother's seeming indifference of what she considered an important matter. "Patience is awfully hard to get. Dad says that every time you lose your temper—and Grandmother said it would be too hard for you to get at all. So, if it's hard to get, it must be even harder to keep."

"You've got that right," Engrelin muttered, his lips quirking despite himself.

Elmera dropped the subject for the moment, and simply scrunched her shoulders in delight as a warm sunbeam fell across her bed. She basked in the warmth a moment and glanced at him. "What kind of box do you keep your temper in?" she asked.

"Box?"

"Well, if you *keep* a temper, you have to have something to put it in," she reasoned.

A persistent grin tugging at his mouth, Engrelin perched on the edge of her bed again. "I probably should put a lock on that box, shouldn't I?" he asked.

Elmera nodded solemnly. "So that it can't get out." She bent closer to him and whispered confidentially, "I think patience is afraid of tempers."

"You bet it is," Engrelin said. She giggled, and he tweaked her chin, trying, as he did so, not to notice the dark bruises of lost sleep under her eyes or the web of veins showing beneath her translucent skin. Her illness had left her so emaciated that her nightgown swallowed her thin frame. She had been so sick for so long—worse than any of them had expected, or surely at least one of his parents would have remained behind. The *meddyg* who had been seeing her throughout her illness had not said whether she would ever fully recover. But she had to recover. He'd done everything he could to save her. And she was only six years old, too young to have such a burden put upon her.

Speaking of burdens…

Heaving a small sigh, Engrelin pulled himself to his feet and headed for the door.

"Engrelin!" Elmera called, her voice sharp with dismay. "You're not leaving already, are you?"

He paused in the doorway. "I have to," he said. "Grandmother's going to town today, and Lance is coming over to help with the chores."

"Will you fiddle for me, before you go?" she begged. She batted her long lashes over her big blue eyes, which she knew few would resist. "Please?"

Engrelin sighed. "Maybe when I come back."

Elmera's lower lip trembled.

Engrelin pondered a moment. Being the youngest in the family, and the survivor of several illnesses—a few of which had taken previous family members—Elmera was extremely delicate and more than slightly spoiled. But it had to be tiresome to have to lie in bed all day, with only their grandmother to sit with her and occasional visits from him, or perhaps just remaining alone altogether. He hated to leave her disappointed, but if he didn't get to his work soon, he wouldn't get everything done.

"I'll play a really long one. Any one you want," he compromised. "But later."

"A really, *really* long one?" Elmera pleaded.

"So long, you'll be bored out of your wits by the end," Engrelin promised.

"I'll never be bored of anything you play," Elmera declared. Satisfied, she snuggled down under the covers and pulled the quilt up to her chin.

Favoring her with a final glance, Engrelin left the room, shutting the door quietly behind himself.

At his entrance to the *ystafell fyw*, Engrelin's grandmother, Vera, looked up sharply. She continued to stab a threaded needle through the tunic resting on her lap. Engrelin realized, with an inward grimace, that it was his.

"Torn clean down the back," she scolded, skillfully launching into a tirade as if she and Engrelin had been having an argument for the past few minutes (likely the unfortunate garment in her hands had already received quite a chastising). "How do you manage to do these things,

Engrelin? Do you think you have all the tunics in the world at your disposal? I nearly had to patch your Sunday one!"

Engrelin stood behind the woman's rocking chair to view the tunic in his grandmother's lap. Though badly torn, the dexterous old woman's needle was working its magic. Soon, it would look almost new.

"I just fell out of the hayloft," he said softly. He planted a kiss on his grandmother's snowy head as a peace offering.

"Humph!" Vera scowled and jabbed her needle at him—a formidable weapon, smooth with wear, sharp as a sword. "You *just* fell out of the hayloft? It's a mercy you didn't break your neck. Where would you be today, I wonder?"

"I'll watch my step up there today," Engrelin said. He edged away from her chair towards the back door.

"Like enough you'll be dancing on the roof tomorrow!" continued Vera, hardly finished.

Engrelin struggled to maintain a straight face. "I'll try not to, ma'am."

Her needle still poised in the air, she opened her mouth to continue.

But Engrelin quickly added, "Love you, got to go," and slipped out the back door, knowing the first words would warm her heart enough to him that she would not call him back inside to hear her finish her lecture.

Smiling to himself, he turned to walk down the path, and collided with Lance, who gasped with surprise and wildly clutched Engrelin's shoulders.

"What are you doing?" Engrelin exclaimed, as Lance stepped back and dusted the front of himself off. "Do you realize that this is the *back* door?"

"Since when have I ever used the front?" Lance demanded.

In reply, Engrelin only grinned. "How'd you get here so early?" he asked.

"Father Colby brought me in from town," Lance explained. "He's picking up your grandmother right now, I think. What's she going to town for? Run out of thread that quickly?"

"A ladies' quilting of some sort. I'm honestly not quite sure."

Lance's face grew long with boredom. "Oh. I'm sure that's going to be real interesting."

Engrelin punched Lance's shoulder lightly. "Come on. You came here to work, right?"

"Last I heard, yes." Lance yanked his dark work tunic securely under his belt, and rolled his trouser legs up to his knees. "What's first?"

Engrelin turned and swept an arm out towards the immense garden that lay a short distance away.

"I hope we're just watering that," muttered Lance, as he wrung out the bottom of his tunic, already anticipating the sweat with which it would soon be drenched.

"Oh, we are," returned Engrelin breezily. "Just after we finish weeding it."

Lance uttered a mock groan. "How did I know you were going to say that?"

"The mighty blacksmith bends before the weed," Engrelin chuckled, and struck out towards the garden.

So, the boys spent the morning crawling beside the Peterson's extensive garden beds, rooting up every weed in sight for hours until they had tugged up the last standing blade of grass. It was with aching bodies, dusty clothes, muddy knees, and a clump of weeds in each hand that they finally stood to survey the neat rows of vegetables.

"Hopefully, it'll stay like that for a while, since summer's nearly over," Lance said over a dipper of water, still ice cold from the well. After taking a sip, he handed it to Engrelin. "What's next?"

"Picking fruit," Engrelin said.

Lance sighed. "Peachy."

3

After filling several bushel baskets with orangey-red peaches, the two stopped for lunch—though not before also filling their pockets with fruit. Engrelin ducked back into the cool, dark house and shuffled together a simple meal for his sister. Though all the jam jars in the cellar were labeled, he struggled to figure out which contained strawberry jam, which was Elmera's favorite. Finally, he shrugged to himself and opened a jar holding the substance which appeared to be strawberry jam. He tasted it once to be sure, then spread the jam thickly over a slice of bread. Placing it on a plate along with a sliced peach, he carried it to his sister's room.

Emera sat up quickly as Engrelin entered.

"Will you fiddle for me now?" she asked excitedly, clasping her tiny hands.

He shook his head as he set the plate down on the bedstead. "Not yet. I still have work to do."

Elmera slumped with disappointment and hugged her sides. "Why not?" she asked.

Engrelin mussed her hair gently. "Work's not doing itself," he said. "I'll have time to fiddle later."

"And I get to stay in here where it's boring," Elmera whispered. A tear trickled down her cheek. "I'll never get out of bed for the rest of my life."

Engrelin pinched his lips tightly together and glanced out the window. Through it, he saw Lance sauntering toward the barn, his tanned arms swinging freely as he walked.

"Engrelin, would you take me outside with you?" Elmera implored.

His gaze shifted from her to the bedside table and supplies the *meddyg* had left. Among the tonic bottles was a piece of paper which contained written instructions for Elmera's care. Did it say Elmera had to stay inside?

"Are you sure you're well enough to go?" he asked. "I'm not sure the *meddyg* wanted you to."

"Maybe if you brought the bed outside, he wouldn't mind," Elmera suggested hopefully. "Just long enough to eat my lunch. Please?"

Engrelin looked at her hopefully. "You're hungry?"

She nodded and peered at the plate on the bedstand. "Especially if that's strawberry jam."

"I'm pretty sure it is."

Elmera looked at him askance. "Didn't you read the label Mom put on the jar?"

"Yes, I…I did," Engrelin ended awkwardly, heat prickling up his cheeks. How could he explain it to his little sister?

He left the room for several minutes. When he returned, he scooped Elmera up, quilts and all, and carried her outside to a bench he had set up against the side of the house and padded comfortably with blankets. Beside it stood a stool, crowned with Elmera's lunch.

"There," Engrelin said, settling her onto the bed. "How's that?"

Elmera looked around herself, snuggling down into the sun-warmed covers. "Perfect! Thanks."

"You warm enough?" he asked, fingering one of the quilts. The last thing he wanted was for her to catch a chill and get sick again.

"One more blanket, and I'd be an *arth wen,*" she said with a mock glare.

Engrelin smiled. He was seeing, more and more, the happy, energetic Elmera beginning to shine through the lingering fog of her illness.

"Just remember…" He jabbed a finger at her plate. "Eat your dinner."

Elmera giggled, clutching her sides as if to keep even the gentle laughter from busting her at the seams. "Yes, sir."

Leaving her luxuriating on the bench, Engrelin strode off toward the barn. He soon found Lance, who was lounging on a mound of marsh grass stacked against the barn's side.

"Hey," Engrelin called.

Lance looked down and pulled a chewed stalk of grass from his mouth. "Hey yourself," he retorted.

Engrelin grinned and scrambled up to the top of the stack, sinking down in it beside Lance. The sweet-smelling stalks crackled beneath his weight and poked through his coarse clothing, tickling his back and arms.

Lance pulled out his pocketknife and sliced thin slivers out of a peach. Following his example, Engrelin crossed his ankles and pulled out a peach and his *cyllel*.

"You couldn't have chosen a better day," said Lance contently. He waved toward the surrounding countryside with his knife.

Engrelin smiled in agreement. *Traeth Euriad's* fields, rippling gold with ripe wheat, sloped down into a sea of swaying marsh grass. Through gaps in the reeds stole glints of the *Tawelich* creek.

"Remember this?" Lance asked suddenly. He tossed Engrelin his closed pocketknife.

A reminiscent smile touched Engrelin's lips as he ran his fingers down the inscribed handle, ignoring the sticky peach juice dripping off it.

"I remember," he said. Lance's father had commissioned the knife from him just before Lance had turned ten. He had forged the knife, then given the Petersons a sketch of what he wanted the handle and its inscription to look like. Engrelin and his father had carved the handle together, following the letters on the paper carefully, with some help from Engrelin's mother.

"I did this one. Dad did the rest." Engrelin reached back and held it out to Lance, who took it.

"You carved those?" Lance squinted at the letters. "No wonder they're hardly readable."

"I wasn't *that* bad," Engrelin protested.

"How would you know?" Lance asked, a wicked smile tweaking the corners of his mouth. "You can't write your own name, much less carve mine."

"Give that here!" Engrelin lunged forward.

Lance stretched his arm far behind him, dangling the knife out of Engrelin's reach. Engrelin started scrambling to his feet. He slipped on the slick hay and fell forward onto Lance. Together, they tumbled down the haystack, landing in a heap at the bottom, Engrelin astride Lance.

"Ow!" Lance exclaimed sharply. He dropped the knife and struggled to push Engrelin off.

"Engrelin!" someone exclaimed behind them.

Both boys turned to see Engrelin's cousin, Averendier, standing beside the haystack. His usually impassive expression displayed astonishment on the brink of disapproval.

Lance and Engrelin exchanged looks and hidden grins. They knew the short tussle hadn't improved their appearance in the least. Stray bits of hay stuck straight out of Lance's dusty hair.

"*Pryntawn da*!" Engrelin said cheerfully. "I thought you were still at sea, Averendier."

A shadow passed over Averendier's face. "I was," he said shortly. "I'm on my way home, but I decided to stop here first. Elmera told me you two were over here… working?" He raised his eyebrows high.

"Lunch break," Engrelin explained.

"And *me* break," Lance groaned, rubbing his torso. "Seriously, Engrelin, you're skinny and all, but that hurts."

"Sorry." Engrelin slid off Lance and yanked him to his feet. Then he turned back to Averendier. "What did you say you stopped by for?"

"Actually, I haven't told you," Averendier answered, lacing his fingers behind his back.

Engrelin and Lance stared blankly at him in the silence that followed.

"So…are you going to tell us now?" Lance asked finally.

Averendier glanced furtively around. "Not out here," he said.

Engrelin looked askance at his cousin. What was wrong with him?

"Okay," he said. "Why don't we go into the house?"

Averendier nodded curtly and swiveled. Dirt crunched under his feet as he marched to the house. No one would know by the way he walked he was a sailor.

"What's eating him?" whispered Lance as they followed Averendier to the house.

Engrelin shrugged. With Averendier, he never could tell.

At their approach, Elmera sat up on her bench, but Engrelin shook his head at her and pressed a finger to his lips. Elmera frowned. Lance bent quickly and gave her chin the gentlest tweak. With the sunshine renewed on her face and shining on their backs, the three filed slowly into the house, the sole members of a solemn procession, the reason for which only one among them knew.

The house's normally inviting coolness had frozen frigid. Its shady interior deepened to gloom. Fighting against the swelling knot in his chest, Engrelin leaned up against the stucco wall to face his cousin.

"All right, what is it?" Engrelin demanded.

Averendier stared hard at him a moment, as though punishing him for desecrating the silence.

"We may be going to war," he said finally.

Lance and Engrelin startled simultaneously.

Averendier held up one hand, as if to check some outburst. "Maybe," he repeated.

"What about the treaty?" Engrelin asked.

"It expired over a year ago," Averendier explained. "Tirendria has been waging war in the east since last year."

Engrelin's hand curled reflexively. Only one year, and already Tirendria had shed its neighbor's blood.

"But it's only been a year since we lifted the restrictions on weapons manufacturing and boat building as well," Lance pointed out. "Could they possibly have built up enough to invade anyone within that time?"

"They had enough time to build a fleet," Averendier answered quietly.

"A fleet?" Lance echoed in disbelief.

"Mm-hmm. We saw what we think was a portion of it while we were on patrol. It seems they found a way to continue their work on the sly."

Lance's eyes darted over to the half-open door, as if he expected a whole armada to come sailing in at that moment.

"Mary told me you'd gone on patrol with Austinian," Engrelin said carefully, "but I didn't think you would be going anywhere near Tirendria."

Averendier, recognizing the probe, pressed his lips into a tight line. After a moment, he asked, "Have you ever heard of Dermain's attempt to break the treaty twenty years ago?"

Engrelin frowned. "Dad might have told me once." *But what does that have to do with anything?*

"Dermain, king of Tirendria then, attempted to throw off the treaty once and for all by attacking the Tinannakin islands. But he was killed in battle, and all efforts stopped there." Averendier paused to lean against the wooden table behind him, carefully avoiding the large bowl that rested on it. Engrelin realized for the first time how tired and stooped Averendier looked. The journey must have worn him out. Yet he'd never seen his cousin like this. Tired…yet, not tired. Engrelin couldn't think of the right words for it.

"After we killed Dermain," Averendier continued, "relations with Tirendria went back to normal. Hengar, Dermain's son, ascended the throne. He reigned for nearly a month until he was assassinated. His brother Vendar took his place. It's said that on his coronation day, he swore to avenge his father's death by attacking Monaria. But nothing ever came of it."

"What does all that have to do with your coming here?" Engrelin asked sharply. Apprehension cruelly knotted his stomach. He took a step away from the wall. "I didn't ask you for a history lesson, Averendier."

"You must understand what is happening," returned Averendier. "The treaty has expired. Vendar took that oath in earnest. We've been attacked."

Hearing that was like running full tilt into a wall. A wall that should have been obvious. It hurt all the more for it.

For a few moments, his lips refused to move. Somehow, he managed to say, "Where?"

Averendier closed his eyes.

Engrelin took one step forward, almost threateningly. "Averendier, where did they attack?"

Averendier gazed at him levelly a moment. "We were patrolling the Tinannakin when we spotted their ships, eight of them. Dad sent one of our ships to follow them and make sure they left out waters. We and the *Dermain's Folly* sailed to see what they were doing in our waters."

"You said they had attacked us," Lance broke in. His ice-blue eyes were fixed on Averendier's blank face. His strong hands doubled at his sides. "Where, Averendier?"

Engrelin glanced at Lance, whose face was as tense as his hands.

"They got their vengeance," Averendier said quietly. "They hit Fort Starr."

The air squeezed from Engrelin's lungs. He forced himself to draw one breath, then another.

"Did we drive them off?" Lance demanded, his tunic rising and falling above his heaving chest.

Averendier sighed and slowly dragged his hand over his hair. "From what we've gathered from survivors—"

Engrelin jerked forward. "You mean—"

Averendier speared him with a sharp, meaningful glance. "From what we've gathered from survivors, the defense was a disaster from the beginning. Most of the soldiers were out in the orchards or working at the press. A minimum guard was left in the fort. No one was ready. When the ships were sighted, everyone on the island ran to the fort. Fort Starr was designed to hold soldiers and the island's inhabitants, but not also the people of Bryn, Mynydd, and Cedruydd Cefren. The overcrowding hampered the soldiers and... increased casualties."

"Why didn't they run into the countryside?" Lance asked. "I've been there a dozen times. There are plenty of places to hide."

"There was no time," Averendier replied. "The Tirendrians scaled the fort's walls within the first hour of attack. They took prisoner anyone who hadn't been killed in the fight. We found a few people hiding in cellars and in the church, but they were the only ones who escaped. The rest are...gone."

4

Frozen, *Engrelin stood and stared at his cousin's drawn face. This was a dream. An evil, wicked dream from which he would soon wake. He had to wake up. Now.*

"What do you mean, gone?" Lance said.

Engrelin heard it through a fog. Muffled, distant, yet every breath as distinct as if he himself drew them.

"They're human beings, Averendier. They don't just evaporate. Didn't you find out what happened to them, chase down their ships—something?"

Engrelin caught his breath and waited in silence for Averendier's answer. He starved for one scrap of hope. But something in that silence denied him even that.

His family had been at the harvest, like every year he had ever known. They had run to Fort Starr to safety. They were gone. Captured, or worse.

"We tried chasing the Tirendrians down, but the *Venture* only had orders to follow them to the edge of their waters. They had no idea what was on the ships. The *Folly* has picked up where *Venture* left off, but we haven't found a sign of them so far. Dad plans on sending more ships—"

"Plans?" Lance burst out angrily. "What do you mean your father *plans* to send more? Send them all! Put every ship in your blasted navy on their track!"

"He's trying to call up reserves, but it's taking time," Averendier tried to explain. "We've sent all the ships we can to track down the raiders and patrol the Tinannakin. We haven't been at war for so long, everything's rusty." He paused, his expression lengthening. "But I don't think we'll ever find those ships. Not if we had all the sailing power in Ontaria. They're in their own territory now, and they'll whisk themselves off to some secret nook until things quiet down. Even if they didn't, it's nigh impossible to attack them without having all Vendar's fleet breathing down our necks."

Engrelin clenched the hilt of his *cyllel*. If only he could use it to fill the gaping emptiness within him. Gone…and never to be recovered?

No. Only a few weeks ago, his family had been in this house, stood in this very room. Living. Breathing. Belonging to themselves, not bundled in the hold of some warship or embraced in a grave's clammy arms.

"Averendier." Lance's voice—stark, cold, and unreal—jerked Engrelin back to the room, to his cousin, to the real world where disaster had struck and nothing would ever be the same. Engrelin looked once at his friend. He grabbed Lance's arm.

"Lance," he warned. "It's no good. We can't do anything about it."

It tasted so bitter, so sharp, so wrong falling from his own lips. Lance shot Engrelin a wild look. He shook off Engrelin's grasp. The veins in his neck stood out like ropes against his skin. Turning, he advanced towards Averendier.

"What are you even doing here?" he demanded. "You should be out on the ocean right now looking for them. You can't just stand here, talking, doing nothing. You can't—"

"Lance," Averendier warned.

Lance lunged to grab Averendier's collar. Quicker than sight, Averendier's hand shot out. Catching Lance's arm, he twisted it. Lance stumbled back into the table. The bowl fell and smashed on the floor. Peas skittered to all four corners of the room.

Engrelin jumped forward, grabbed him by the front of his tunic, and shoved him against the wall.

"Lance, what in Ontaria do you think you're doing?" he demanded.

Lance glowered at Averendier over Engrelin's shoulder.

"Lance!" Engrelin shook him hard.

"They were all I had left," Lance gritted, slowly lifting his eyes to Engrelin's.

Grief clawed Engrelin's heart. He nearly shivered at the pain. Until now, he had been too numb to feel. His hand tightened around Lance's shirt as he fought a dark mist of anger from his vision. He had to stay calm—had to keep Lance calm.

"Me too," he said simply.

Lance jerked his tunic free from Engrelin's hand. "You don't understand," he snapped. "I have no one. The epidemic killed everyone else."

Engrelin nearly stepped back, his eyes riveted to Lance's. Never, never had he seen anyone with such a look. With murder in their eyes.

Lance shoved Engrelin and swung sharply around. "Where'd he go?" he cried, in a voice not his own.

Engrelin glanced quickly around the room. Averendier was gone. Likely, he'd left out of respect.

"Just wait 'til I catch him," muttered Lance, striding towards the door.

Engrelin yanked Lance back. "What do you mean?" he asked angrily. "You can't hold him responsible for this. None of us can."

"How do you know what he did?" challenged Lance, wheeling savagely on Engrelin. Grabbing him by the neck of his tunic, Lance shook him violently. "He was there, Engrelin. He could have done something. But he didn't. He let them die."

Engrelin twisted Lance's hands away. "He didn't, Lance. He did what any of us could have done. It's not his fault—"

"Don't start that!" Lance exclaimed. He was shaking from head to toe.

"Lance, calm down," Engrelin ordered.

"Calm down?" Lance laughed. "Both our families are dead, and you're telling me to calm down? You don't care at all, do you?"

Engrelin froze. Didn't care…The emptiness within him yawned for space. Nothing could fill it. And Lance thought he didn't care.

Lance glared at him for one furious second before turning on his heel. Engrelin started after him.

"Lance!"

"Where'd Averendier go?" Lance asked hollowly, still walking away.

"Lance, nothing you can do will bring them back," Engrelin said. "Leave him alone."

Lance halted. He turned his head slightly toward Engrelin. Engrelin saw the flush on his cheek. "I'm going home," he said.

"I'm coming with you," Engrelin said hurriedly. He couldn't let Lance go home by himself. Not in this state. Who knew what would happen?

"You stay here," Lance replied. "I'm going home."

"But Lance—"

"You can't leave Elmera."

Engrelin sucked his breath in quickly. Lance was right. He couldn't. "Why don't you wait until Grandmother gets home, and I—"

"No. I'm going now."

"Lance…"

Lance stepped out the door and shut it firmly behind himself, leaving Engrelin alone.

Averendier crossed the yard quickly. Passing the barn, he moved on toward the road. His brother, Andrald, jumped up from where he had been sitting in the shade, slowly eating a peach.

"Did you tell them?" Andrald asked, wiping the peach juice off his mouth on the back of his sleeve.

"I did." Averendier wanted to be irritated with Andrald. Eating a peach at this moment seemed nothing short of sacrilege. But they had walked all the way from Cedruydd Cefren that morning and afternoon, and had eaten nothing but a hasty breakfast. His strides quickened as he and Andrald reached the broad main road. He still had to make it to Bryn before dark to give a full report of what had happened to Lord Gwayne.

"How's Engrelin?" Andrald asked awkwardly.

Averendier lifted his shoulders in a slow shrug. He didn't want to talk about it. Didn't want to think about the look in his cousin's eyes.

"I picked one for you," Andrald ventured. He fished a red-golden peach out of his pocket and handed it to his brother.

Averendier took it gingerly. His hands were icy against his brother's skin. He scowled inwardly but refrained from rubbing his hands to warm them. He held the peach absently. He should eat it. But he didn't have the stomach for it.

They walked in silence for a long time. Andrald wasn't humming like he usually did when he walked. Averendier's steps gradually slowed. His feet were sore, chafing against his tall boots. He could have ridden to Bryn, but he hadn't been patient enough to wait for horses to be found. When had he ever not been patient! He flexed his free hand thoughtlessly. Had this been how his father had felt, twenty years ago, when Dermain had attacked Fort Starr during a time of peace?

Only he had won that time. Now…

"If those fools had just listened to Dad," he growled aloud.

Andrald glanced at him, but quickly returned his attention to his feet, kicking up little puffs of dust from the hard-packed road.

"They weren't expecting anything so soon," Andrald said.

"Dad did," Averendier replied. Why else had they been patrolling the Tinannakin and the northern sea for the past year? Why else had Austinian followed the suspicious ships to the edge of their waters? Why else did he immediately sail for Starr Island, when there were dozens of other islands in the area which he might have checked?

"I heard some scuffling," Andrald said.

Averendier's hand went to his short sword.

Andrald waved him off. "Not here. Back at *Traeth Euriad.* Something happen?"

"Engrelin had a friend who was upset by the news," Averendier replied stiffly.

"Wouldn't you be?" Andrald tilted his head quizzically.

Averendier nodded his assent. "Yes. But he blamed Dad and us for what happened." Would they have blamed him so vehemently if they had been with him when Averendier had brought the report that his uncle Everen and his family were not among the survivors?

Andrald blew his breath out slowly and wiped his sleeve across his forehead. "Why do they keep doing that?" he asked aloud.

"They need someone to blame," Averendier replied. He glanced at the surrounding countryside, at men climbing ladders to reach fruit in their tall trees. They passed a man who was laying new thatch mats on the roof of his home. A wagon laden with squashes rattled past. It was all so busy, so mundane, so predictable. As long as he had lived, his home had been this way. Now one night, one catastrophe, would alter this forever. These men would leave their trees and roofs and squashes and take up arms only their great-grandfathers had carried. Many of them would never return.

"Do you think Lord Gwane will put a stop to it?" Andrald asked.

"Hmm?" Averendier looked at his brother.

"Everyone blaming Dad. He doesn't deserve it. After all, he's the only one who thought this might ever happen, except Julian. Do you think Lord Gwane will stop it?"

"I don't know," Averendier said. His eyes swept the brilliant blue sky, searching for the low bumps on the horizon that would herald Bryn. "I just hope he comes home soon."

5

Engrelin *jerked awake. Cold sweat plastered his tunic to his back* and shoulders. The stutter of his heart filled his ears. His eyes darted over the familiar features of the room around him—the fireplace, the rocking chair drawn up in front of it, the loom and the wheel lining the wall, the scarred, ancient grain of the table in front of him. It was like having a bucket of frigid water poured over him. He slumped onto the bench in relief.

Only a dream.

He let his head fall back onto his arms, which were folded on the table in front of him. The dream should not have terrified him as much as it had. It had only been an image. A serpent, more real than life itself, its lithe body glistening with black scales.

Even as he thought it, another spike of terror thrilled through him, shivering down his spine. Sitting up straighter, Engrelin clenched his head in his hands, willing the unexplainable fear away.

What is wrong with me? Strange dreams and...falling asleep at the table?

He started. Though the nightmare had awoken him, that thought jarred him to true consciousness. Why was he sleeping here?

His roving eyes caught a glimpse of the shattered crockery on the floor. Reality roared back, talons digging deep.

Clenching his jaw so hard it hurt, Engrelin dropped his head back onto the table. He wasn't sure if he would ever pick it up again. Every muscle in his body ached. Could he not even find reprieve in rest?

Averendier's visit…Lance's unexpected reaction…being left to his own thoughts…

His jaw tightened. That was the worst part. He could stop people from talking or acting, but there was no way to dam the thoughts that flowed through his mind and heart.

They were gone. Dead.

For the first time since he'd received the news, he allowed himself to think that word. He let it churn sickeningly through himself. They were dead. They would never come home. He would never see them again.

A soft sound wafted into the room, touching his deaf ears several times before he turned his head to one side without lifting it from the tabletop, and glanced at the closed door. He raised his head as his gaze roved to an open window. A thick swath of afternoon sunshine fell through the open window and cast a broad beam across the earthen floor.

The sound came again, clearer this time. Someone was singing softly.

Elmera!

Engrelin staggered to his feet and rushed outdoors. He had left his last living sibling alone outside—sick as she was—and slept?

He tore the door open and rushed outside. His darting gaze fell on Elmera, who was sitting up on her makeshift bed, cuddling a hen in her lap.

Relief washed over him. Yet it carried unexpected anger in its wake. Here was his little sister, toying with a chicken, when the rest of her family was dead or captured?

Fresh grief seized the anger like a parchment, crumpled it, and tossed it aside. Engrelin reached out one hand to steady himself against the side of the house. They were now two orphans among hundreds. And she oblivious of it all!

And when she learned? The thought of telling Elmera filled Engrelin's throat with bile. He had only just freed her from the grave.

Would she want to continue her sweet existence if she knew the majority of her family's had ended?

His shoulders bent. No. Not her also. He wouldn't waste one breath of his life telling her. Not yet. He would wait until all danger of a relapse had passed. He glanced at her again, and his jaw tightened. That he would never have to tell her at all!

At that moment, Elmera looked up and saw him standing by the doorway. Her bright eyes clouded. She shooed the chicken off her lap and shook out her skirt.

"Engrelin?" She peered at him anxiously. "Are you okay? You look awful."

"I'm just tired, okay?" Engrelin could hardly believe the words that had tumbled out of his own mouth. Now was he lying to her? Yet how different was that from withholding the terrible truth?

"I called you a lot, but you didn't come," said Elmera. She folded her hands daintily in her lap—just as Mom always had, thought Engrelin, with a stab of reminiscence.

"I'm sorry," he said gruffly. "I didn't hear you."

"That's all right." Elmera waved her hand dismissively. "I had lots of fun playing with Henny while I waited."

"Henny. Is that the chicken's name?" asked Engrelin, in a dismal attempt to be cheerful.

"Yep." Elmera tilted her head, bird-like, and gave him an odd look. She propped her folded arms across her knees. "I called you because I wanted you to fiddle."

"Fiddle!" Engrelin burst out bitterly. Their whole family moldering in their graves right now, and all she cared about was hearing him play that stupid fiddle!

Glancing sideways, he caught her wounded expression. He forced himself to swallow the lump that had once again risen to his throat. Even if he was the only one who knew, he wasn't the only one hurting.

"When Grandmother gets home," he said, reaching down to touch her softly curling hair.

Elmera looked down, shoulders hunched. "Why do you keep putting it off?" she mumbled.

Engrelin groped for an answer other than the truth—he couldn't play now, not after all that had happened.

"I…" He stopped. "Don't you think Grandmother would like to hear me play too?"

Slowly, she nodded.

"Besides," he added, reaching down and gathering her in his arms. "I think it's time for you to come in and get some rest now."

Elmera wriggled in protest. "Engrelin, please! I want to stay outside!"

But all protests—even eyelash batting—were in vain. She had already spent too much time outside already. Engrelin carried her inside and tucked her in bed.

"I'm not sleepy," murmured Elmera as he drew a quilt over her.

Sleepy or not, she was out in five minutes, her dark hair flowing over her pillow.

He sat beside her for an hour or more, gazing out the window for a long time before his eyes were drawn to his sister's face. He let them rove over her, as if he were memorizing her features, so prominent after her prolonged illness. Her blankets gently rose and fell with each breath she drew.

She was so innocent. How little she knew of the storm gathering thick around her, its stabs of lightning striking even her own family.

Engrelin let his balled fist fall onto his thigh. How long could he shelter her from it?

The whole world had been sheltered with peace for so long, ever since Juran had written the hundred-year treaty at Highlynn. They had spent one hundred years rebuilding their destroyed cities and churches and farms. Save for the scant fighting of pirates and rebel Tirendrians, the world had not known war for three generations.

One year since that treaty had expired. Already, the blood-thirsty beast was on the prowl. The serpent had struck Fort Starr, a place only three day's sail from Bryn.

Engelin gritted his teeth and bent protectively over his slumbering sister. So long as he was here to protect her, no hostile being would touch one hair on her head. Not one.

"Engrelin?" his Grandmother called from the *ystafell fyw*. She was home.

"Engrelin Everen Aaron Peterson, come here and explain this outlandish mess!"

Engrelin slipped away from his sister and joined his grandmother. Vera had seized a broom and was furiously whisking the pieces of crockery and scattered peas into a pile. In the late afternoon sunshine slanting through the windows, he saw the dark patches of sagging skin beneath her eyes. Her bent shoulders, stooping more than usual. Frowning, Engrelin strode across the room and gently took the broom from her.

"I'll get it," he said.

Vera glanced at him fleetingly, then released the broom and sank into her nearby rocking chair. Both shared terse silence, listening to the willow-bough broom scratch across the dirt floor as it raked up shards of bowl and skittering peas.

"I saw Averendier in town today," said his grandmother finally.

Having swept the broken bits out the back door, Engrelin deliberately placed the broom in its corner. He felt like snapping it in half instead. "He stopped here too."

Vera's rocking chair creaked as she leaned forward. "You know, then?" she said. "About Fort Starr?"

Engrelin's hands instinctively curled into fists. "Yes."

The old woman sighed and sank back in her chair. Taking a pair of knitting needles and a ball of yarn out of the basket beside her, she knit furiously.

"I'll be making supper tonight," she said briskly.

Engrelin made no comment. He knew, just by looking at her, that she had done most of her grieving in town. She had probably gotten to talk it over with Father Colby.

"All right." He glanced nervously out the open window. Racks of dark clouds were building on the horizon, emitting ominous rumbles. Engrelin pulled the shutters over the windows and latched them shut.

When he turned, Vera was watching him, her eyes bright with something like pity, her needles seeming to move with a mind of their own.

"Quite a storm brewing out there," she remarked quietly. "The lamp's in the cupboard, dear."

Nodding, Engrelin rifled through the shallow cupboard where they kept the lamps in the summer. They were only needed when a storm such as this blew up and the shutters had to be closed.

"We're going to have to hire someone to help with the harvest," Grandmother said suddenly, but still in a low tone.

Engrelin nearly dropped the oil lamp he had just found. Steadying himself, he rose, shutting the cupboard behind him. Deliberately, he placed the lamp on the table.

"I can try, but I won't find many people. Everyone else around here is going to have the same problem. Not enough hands to go around."

He struck a match and touched it to the lamp's wick. At first, the flame sprang to life. But under Engrelin's intense stare, it guttered and burned low, as if it couldn't bear to have been brought into such a cruel world.

Engrelin turned away.

6

Though it was Elmera's first time eating at the table since the day_ she had fallen ill, supper was a quiet affair. Elmera picked at her food like a bird and chattered just as endlessly. Engrelin stared down at his plate, saying nothing and eating nothing. Grandmother attempted to squeeze in a few words between Elmera's conversation and a bite of supper between her answers. It seemed Vera was the only one with something of an appetite that night.

Finally, Engrelin could bear it no more. Thrusting his plate into the center of the table, he pushed his chair back. "I'll be in soon," he mumbled.

Elmera started. "But aren't you going to play for us?" she asked.

He paused, his hand resting on the doorframe. "I will," he replied, without looking back at her. "I just have to get some chores done before this storm hits."

Elmera slumped in her chair.

Though still early in the evening, it was as murky as twilight outside. Every glimmer of blue overhead had been chased away by a heavy sheet of gray. The marsh grass was a tumultuous golden sea swirling on the creek bank. The strong wind whirled Engrelin's hair in front of his face as he hurried through his numerous chores. Mixed with the usual scent in the air of spicy cedar and rotting marsh grass was the thick, wet smell of impending rain.

Engrelin made sure the animals were cozily bedded down in the barn and their numerous sheds. The two cows were milked, and the milk set in the springhouse to chill. He fastened down all the house and barn shutters. Once everything was finished, he leaned against the barn door and looked out at the storm.

Thunder growled discontentedly overhead, belligerently answering the blue lightning streaking through the masses of clouds. Nothing is more disconcerting than blue lightning. The dark clouds reflected and intensified their light, plunging the word momentarily into a surreal blue glow. The humidity rolled over Engrelin in waves, pressing him down and dampening his clothes with sweat.

Shutting his eyes, he tilted his head back against the door and pushed his hair away from his forehead. It was as if the Tirendrians had gotten a hold of the weather itself and was throwing even that into turmoil.

A few fat raindrops splashed onto this face. His eyes flew open. A gray sheet of rain swept over the fields towards him. Engrelin gave the barn's crossbar a final push into place and ran for the house.

He burst through the doorway just as the heavens broke open with a rending crack of lightning. Dashing the droplets off his hair, he shivered with the sudden cold the drenching had brought.

"Close the door, Engrelin," his grandmother said, looking up from clearing the dishes.

Elmera shuddered in the draft. He quickly shut the door.

As she warmed back up, Elmera looked hopefully at Engrelin. "Now will you fiddle for me?"

"I have to do the dishes first," he said, starting for the kitchen.

Elmera's face darkened. "Chores, chores, that's all you do," she muttered, crossing her arms sulkily across her thin chest.

"Elmera!" Vera rebuked as she handed the stack of dirty dishes to Engrelin. "What a thing to say! Your brother has been working hard all day, and for you. Wait until he's ready."

Elmera bowed her head, though her shoulders twitched with underlying rebellion.

Lips clamped with frustration, Engrelin gladly welcomed the kitchen's dusky solitude. Yet as he slid the few dishes into the tub, thoughts and doubts plagued him.

Poor Elmera was frustrated with how little time he had for her today... How would she feel when the harvest began in earnest? He couldn't just not work the farm. *Traeth Euriad* had been in his family for generations. Giving up was unthinkable. He would just have to work harder. With a lot of determination thrown in, he would be somewhat successful. He would work through the night if it meant keeping the farm together.

Up to his elbows in dishwater, his features hardened. He was used to a hard life. Surely, he could push through this.

He rinsed the last dish, turned it upside down on the kitchen table to dry and returned to the *ystafell fyw*.

Grandmother rocked Elmera in her chair, snuggling the girl curled in her lap. Elmera spotted him. She sat up and smiled.

"Please?" she said.

Is that all she cares about?

Forcing a smile, Engrelin reached down and tucked the wool blanket tighter around his sister's shoulders. "I'll fiddle now," he said. "You ready?"

Elmera gave him a look.

He chuckled. "I'll take that as a yes." He turned and lifted a fiddle off its hooks on the wall, sliding his hand down the instrument's smooth, familiar neck. It was the only instrument the family owned, and only then because it had been passed down from his grandfather. The memories of the kindly old gentleman came to his mind through a sweet lens. It was so unlike the ache now surrounding a similar picture of another man playing the instrument: his father.

His hand tightened around the neck. Even though the fiddle would always hang on the wall, as it had for three generations, two people it waited for would never play it again. How much longer would he use it?

Shaking the thought away, Engrelin fixed his attention on the two familiar faces turned expectantly on him. Very suddenly, he saw them as they really were: frail and helpless in a world whose troubles none of them could even begin to comprehend. An old woman with hardly any strength left in her body, save her tongue and her hands, and a pale wisp of a girl, just pulled from the jaws of death, fairly drowning in the enormous blanket she hugged tightly around herself.

Elmera lifted her chin out of the blanket's folds. "Engrelin?"

"Right." Engrelin tucked the smooth instrument under his chin and took a deep breath, struggling to clear his mind of troubling thoughts. He drew the bow experimentally across the fiddle's strings, listening to them hum and shrill in response.

"What would you like first?" he asked Elmera.

She cocked her head thoughtfully. "How about 'Lily'?" she suggested.

Of course. A cheerful nursery rhyme. But he had promised her she could choose whatever she wanted. "Sure," he said.

"You play, and I sing," dictated Elmera, sitting up straight on Vera's lap.

After a few false starts on Engrelin's part he finally wrestled the slipping bow into submission. The fiddle sang in unison with Elmera's trembling warble:

> "Oh fairest lily of the valley,
> Why do you always dilly-dilly-dally?
> Through the sunshine and through the snow,
> Still you stand so still. You just won't go!
>
> "Oh pretty violet, you're so small!
> Why won't you ever grow really tall?
> Why choose to be so close to the ground,
> Where only beetles can be found?"

At the last moment, Engrelin's rebellious bow slipped, producing an unmelodic screech. Elmera looked at him askance.

"It wasn't supposed to end like that," she observed.

He didn't answer. He knew he had played horribly. No matter how hard he had tried, the music wouldn't come as freely as it used to. But he had to try. He couldn't let her think anything was wrong. Not yet.

"Now could you play 'Hen on the Wall'?"

Inwardly, Engrelin cringed. Even in his best moods, he hated playing that song. But he dutifully plucked the fiddle's strings. Despite all efforts, he concluded with a sour twang that made both him and his sister wince.

"I'm sorry, Elmera." Engrelin shifted his grip on the bow to relieve his cramping fingers. He'd been holding it far too tight. He flexed his arm. "It's been so long since I played."

"Why don't *you* pick a song?" Elmera suggested.

Engrelin looked swiftly at her. Pick a song? He shook his head. "No, it's your pick, Elmera."

Elmera drooped. "But I don't know which ones you like. One that makes you happy."

"I'm supposed to be cheering you up, not the other way around," he said, too forcibly to convince anyone.

Elmera gave him a fleeting look. Before he quite knew what she was doing, Elmera slipped off Vera's lap, ran across the room, and wrapped herself around his leg.

"Elmera?" Engrelin quickly set the fiddle and bow aside and stooped to her level.

"Something's wrong," she said. Looking earnestly into his face, her eyes glistening. "You're sad. You weren't this morning. Did something happen?"

Engrelin drew a thin, shivering breath. It was lost in the bravado of the storm outside, crashing against the house. With his curved knuckle, he traced the profile of Elmera's face, sliding his finger from her temple, down her jaw, to her chin.

"I…had a lot of work today, Elmera. I'm tired," he said.

"But—"

Engrelin pressed his hand over her mouth. "No more," he said. He couldn't let her ask anything more. He wasn't going to lie to her again.

Dear God, why did You let this happen?

"I want to help." Elmera squeezed Engrelin's hand.

Smiling faintly, he squeezed back. "You know how to help? In the best way?"

Elmera's gaze intensified. "How?"

"By being good, resting until you're better, and staying patient. And telling me what song you want next."

She looked doubtful, perhaps because she was still curious, perhaps because she had never seen or heard Engrelin this way. "Really?" she said.

"It'll help more than you know," Engrelin replied. It would help more than himself—she had to get better. Well enough so he could tell her.

He nearly prayed the recovery was slow.

Engrelin picked Elmera up and set her in Vera's lap. Picking up the fiddle, he asked, "Thought of one yet?"

Elmera smiled. "The bumblebee song."

"The bumblebee song?" Despite himself, he chuckled and dragged a droning double-stop. Elmera clapped her hands over her ears and pealed with laughter.

Engrelin sang over the fiddle's throbbing tones.

> "Bizz, bizz, bizz,
> Buzz, buzz, buzz,
> Little wing'd men
> With jackets of fuzz."

Elmera shouted the next verse louder than her brother.

> "A little black collar
> And a yellow waistcoat!
> They snatch their satchels
> And off they float!
>
> Bizz, bizz, bizz,
> Listen to them sing.
> Just don't get too close
> Or you'll listen to them sting!"

Engrelin spun tune after tune out of the old fiddle, fighting it into obedience, making it laugh when it wanted to cry, his fingers flying feverishly when they should have clenched.

It was all wrong. But seeing the joy lighting Elmera's face pushed him to greater efforts. There were so few days left for her happiness. Only so long for her to snuggle down in a blanket and feel safe. He would give her tonight. Something for her to cherish and cling to during future grief. He would let her clap and chortle and collapse with laughter. One night couldn't hurt anyone. Not most, anyway.

Later, he lifted Elmera's slumbering form off Vera's lap and carried her to bed. She hardly stirred as he laid her down on the straw mattress and rustled the quilts over her thin body. But she was still smiling.

"When are you going to tell her?" asked Vera when Engrelin slipped out of Elmera's room.

He looked at her almost defiantly. "One night," he said. "Can't she have one more night without knowing?"

His grandmother laid aside the knitting she had just picked up. "And when you give her just one more night for weeks on end?"

Engrelin turned his back and stretched his hands out toward the empty fireplace, as if it could provide warmth.

"Not yet," he said. "She's still too weak. New like that..." He stopped and bit his lip.

"I know," said Vera softly. "I'm sorry. I just..."

"Want to get it over with." Engrelin laughed a low laugh. "I know."

"She may never regain her full strength," Vera pointed out.

His hands tightened. *Please, no. Let her get well.*

"Engrelin?"

"I'll tell her when I think she should be told," he said.

Vera's look sharpened. "And when do you think that will be?" she asked. "There never is a good time for bad news. I would wait no more than two weeks. If she is better then, I would tell her. She will be wondering by that time why they haven't come home."

The storm still raging outside swallowed Engrelin's silence. Rolling thunder rattled the shutters. Moaning wind scourged the walls with driving rain. Lighting flickered, revealing the contours of the shutters.

"Maybe," he said finally.

7

"*Engrelin? You in here, son?*"

Engrelin turned sharply from his work, nearly dropping the pitchfork he gripped in both hands. He half expected to see his father coming through the barn doors to help him muck the stalls. But the figure framed in the barn doorway was not his father's. It was the village priest. Keenly disappointed, Engrelin dropped his gaze and turned his back to Father Colby. Why had he gotten his hopes up? Exactly one week had passed since he had learned about the attack on Fort Starr. Why couldn't he just accept the fact that his father was dead? Couldn't he stop startling at every corner of the farm, expecting to find his father? Why couldn't he just move on?

"Your sister said you were in here," said Father Colby. He stepped forward, the hem of his cassock rustling across the straw-strewn floor.

Engrelin plunged his pitchfork into a deep mound of straw. "Do you need something, Father?"

"Not at the moment," answered the priest. "I just came to check on you."

"You didn't have to," Engrelin said shortly. The moment the words left his mouth, he bit his lower lip. He'd never spoken to any priest—especially Father Colby—in that manner before.

"I thought I should, especially after I didn't see you in church yesterday," replied Father Colby, hinting at neither anger nor disappointment at Engrelin's failings.

Engrelin tossed his fork load of straw onto a stall floor and paused to lean a moment on his tool's handle.

"Elmera's not well enough to be left on her own, and the cooler weather is taking the sap out of Grandmother," he said slowly. He brushed his hair off his forehead. "I might be able to make it next week. Maybe."

"Everyone tends to get a cold around late harvest," Father Colby said. On cue, he sneezed into the crook of his arm, turning his face away from the clouds of chaff hovering in the air.

Engrelin turned back to forking straw. He couldn't help thinking that the recent loss of her son, daughter-in-law, and grandchildren had his grandmother laid up.

In silence, Father Colby watched him spread a thick carpet of straw on the stall floor. Engrelin's breath sounded loudly in his ears. He knew the priest was holding back from picking up a spare pitchfork and coming to help him, as he had always done in the past. The new restraint only made Engrelin more awkward and uncomfortable—and therefore brusque—in his presence. He continued forking straw, pausing only to pull his itching, sweat-drenched tunic away from his body. If only a breeze would blow through the barn's open doors!

As Engrelin turned to get another fork of straw, several stalks fell out of his hair. Father Colby frowned at Engrelin as the boy picked the straw out of his hair.

"Are you sure you're not working yourself too hard?" he asked. Despite his earlier reserve, Father Colby picked up an extra fork and dropped a dollop of straw into a manger.

Engrelin didn't answer, appreciating and resenting Father Colby's assistance all at once. There was no honest answer that he was willing to give. He knew he was working himself too hard. How could he not know, with his grandmother commenting on it every spare minute he spent in the house?

Yet what did they expect him to do? Stop? Didn't they realize that if he did stop, even for a moment, they would lose everything?

Father Colby nodded to himself once. Setting down the pitchfork, he exchanged it for a shovel which had been leaning against a wheelbarrow half filled with manure. As he strode purposefully into a dirty stall, he asked offhandedly, "How is Elmera doing?"

"Much better," Engrelin replied. "Like I said, I'm hoping that she might be able to take care of Grandmother so that I can go to mass this Sunday."

"I'm glad to hear that," Father Colby said. "We've missed you there, son."

Engrelin only nodded and gave the straw on the floor a final swish before he exited the stall, shutting the door behind him. Wearily, he scrubbed a grimy hand across his face and swept his eyes down the half dozen or so stalls left to be cleaned. As his eyes traveled back, they met Father Colby's face. The priest's peppered black eyebrows bent in a fierce frown.

"Are you *sure* you're all right, Engrelin?" he asked.

Other than being an orphan... Aloud, he said slowly, "I'm okay." He paused and searched the priest's expression. His stomach dropped uncomfortably. "Is something wrong, Father?"

Father Colby's frown deepened, his eyebrows drawing more closely together. He leaned on his shovel's handle.

"Nothing that concerns you. Not yet, that is—" He checked himself, almost scowling. "Just some trouble in town, Engrelin," he said. "I wanted to be sure nothing had spread out here."

"What kind of tro—" Engrelin began, but the priest stopped him with an uplifted hand.

"Nothing you need to be worried about, I think," he said firmly. "I just wanted to be sure no one was bothering you."

Engrelin eyed Father Colby suspiciously. "Why would anyone want to bother us?" he asked.

Father Colby only waved the question off. "I told you, it's nothing you need to worry about, Engrelin. Though," he added, fixing the boy with his keen black eyes, "if you do end up coming to town this Sunday—or at any other time—don't go unless someone you trust is with you. Never try going alone."

"But why?" Engrelin asked, exasperated.

"Just don't," was the priest's unsatisfactory reply. Setting his shovel down beside the now-full wheelbarrow, Father Colby turned sharply and headed for the barn door.

Engrelin stared after him a moment, then ran on the priest's heels to the doorway.

"Father Colby, what do you mean, don't go anywhere alone?" he shouted after the retreating figure.

Father Colby didn't answer. He didn't even look back.

"Engrelin!" someone shouted behind him.

He whirled to see Elmera sprinting towards him, her loose brown hair streaming behind her like a banner.

"Elmera, what is it?" he asked, grabbing her shoulders before she ran straight into him.

Elmera, panting, leaned her hands on her knees.

"Elmera, you knew you shouldn't be running yet," Engrelin admonished, feeling his sister shake beneath his fingers.

"I know!" gasped Elmera. "But I had to. I think the oven's on fire!"

Without waiting for a further explanation, Engrelin grabbed his sister's hand. Together, they sprinted across the barnyard and towards the house. Just to the house's right stood the Petersons' summer kitchen; outside it was a clay oven. It belched smoke into the sky.

"Not again!" Engrelin groaned. He dashed up to the oven. Releasing Elmera's hand, he told her to stand back from the kitchen. He seized a pair of tongs that had been hanging on a hook and thrust them into the oven, shielding his face from the heat and smoke with his bent arm.

Elmera stood on her tiptoes beside him, despite his orders, trying to peer into the oven's hellish interior. "Engrelin, what's in there?" she asked.

Engrelin drew out a charred lump that had once been a ball of dough and dumped it on the ground. Then he grabbed a near-by bucket of sand and tossed its contents onto the sizzling coals within the oven.

"What is it?" Elmera asked again. Crouched down beside the burnt wreck, she poked it experimentally with a stick.

Engrelin glared at the ruined loaf. If it had been stone, it would have melted. But since it was only bread, it did not follow the colloquialism, and merely sizzled apologetically.

"It *was* your dinner," he said.

Elmera looked up. "And what was that?"

"Bread."

Elmera wrinkled her nose. "Eww."

Engrelin nudged the wreck with his toe. Why couldn't anything he baked turn out slightly edible?

Elmera's eyes grew round. "What are we going to eat now?"

He dragged his hand through his sweat-damp hair. "Let's see if Grandmother has anything in the house."

"Please, not more peaches!" Elmera pleaded. She climbed to her feet and followed her brother into the house.

Engrelin descended into the cellar. He scowled as he scanned the jars' various labels. After a moment, he turned away. No luck there. Maybe once the oven cooled some, he could roast potatoes in the ashes…

As Engrelin's quest for something to eat for supper stretched on, Father Colby's visit—and his warning—completely slipped his mind.

8

"I *shouldn't be gone long,"* Engrelin said. *"I'm just going to church and back."*

From her lofty position in Vera's rocking chair, Elmera nodded, lips pursed in a manner she must have thought grown up.

Engrelin hid his amusement behind his cloak as he slung it over his shoulders. The week had brought keen autumn chills with it; the cloak was a welcome addition to his simple wardrobe.

Elmera pulled her own shawl tighter around her thin shoulders and glanced nervously out the window.

"What if they come back while you're gone?" she asked.

Engrelin's chest tightened, his fingers faltering at his cloak clasp.

"If they do, I'm sure everything will be all right. They'd know what to do," he said quietly. She was still waiting for their family to come home. Though, he told himself, while he continued keeping the secret, it was impossible for her to not ask questions. She simply didn't know any better and wouldn't until he worked up the courage to tell her.

"Grandmother will probably be in bed most of the time," he continued. "But if you get hungry, I've set some food out in the kitchen."

Elmera's face brightened. "Thanks! I'll be okay." Standing precariously on the rocking chair's seat, she leaned forward and planted a wet kiss on her brother's cheek. Manfully, Engrelin refrained from scrubbing it off. "You be good in church," she added innocently.

Engrelin rolled his eyes. "And you be good here," he ordered as he headed for the door. "Don't let anyone in unless it's me."

"Or Mom or Dad," Elmera reminded.

He looked down. "Yeah."

After a moment of hesitant silence, Elmera said timidly, "Tell Father Colby I said hi."

"I will," Engrelin answered. He opened the door, took one step out, then looked back into the room. "Bye."

Elmera flaunted her hand dismissively. "Bye!" she chirped.

With a small sigh, Engrelin closed the door and started down the long lane.

Above, the sky was overcast; the sunlight filtered through the gloomy screen, touching the drab countryside with varying hues of gray. Harvesters had already shorn the fields to a dull golden stubble. Brown tints in the grass, the heralds of winter, already crept up the hillsides. Gardens once bursting with the colors of a hundred different vegetables were now sullen gray plots of dirt.

Engrelin hurried past them, his head bent against the brisk wind that knifed through the folds of his cloak and swirled fallen leaves at his feet. He passed so few people on his way that it seemed at times he was the only person left alive in the bleak world. And those he did see averted their eyes from his and hurried past. Even those standing on the chapel steps stopped talking to one another to stare silently at him as he mounted the steps. Heat prickling his cheeks, Engrelin swept past them into the church and slipped into the very back pew.

What was wrong with everyone?

All through mass, the conspicuous glances followed him, noting his every move. Engrelin rested his elbows on the back of the pew in front of him and pressed his folded hands to his forehead. He stared at the floor, striving to focus on his first mass in weeks.

But every prayer that he had ever learned evaporated under the stares. When the bells first rang, announcing Canon, he startled, then ducked his head under the congregation's consequent scowls.

As the last notes of the recessional hymn faded, Engrelin made his thanksgiving in a hurried genuflection and tried to slip out the front door.

But the moment he set foot off the church steps, Father Colby snagged his arm and pulled him close.

"Engrelin, stay with me a moment," he said, just as serenely as ever save for a strange light in his eye.

Reluctantly, Engrelin stood beside the priest and silently watched as Father Colby greeted each person who left the church. It was another unsettling exercise for Engrelin. Though everyone smiled at the priest and readily returned his greeting, their attitude towards the boy beside him was too arctic to be called cold.

Finally, Engrelin leaned toward Father Colby, who was talking intently to a parishioner. "Father, while I'm waiting I'm going to visit the Smith's for a little," he murmured. "If you need me, I'll be there."

Father Colby waved distractedly at him. Taking it as a dismissal, Engrelin slipped away down the street, attempting to lose himself among the pedestrians enjoying their Sunday stroll. Maybe it was the vagabond way Engrelin carried himself, but despite all efforts, he couldn't seem to stop attracting the darker notice of all he passed. Pairs walking hand in hand, lover fashion, veered widely around him. Those relaxing at storefronts and on front porches stared as he hurried by. Children whacking wooden hoops up and down the rutted street saw him and missed their mark, their toys rattling unguided for several yards before teetering to the ground.

Like some giant bubble spanning the width of the street, the silence and the stares followed Engrelin. Cheeks burning, he yanked his hood over his head and fixed his gaze on the toes of his too-small boots. He took bigger and bigger strides.

What was wrong? Normally, no one in Bryn would have given him a second glance.

Engrelin slipped down the first alley he passed. Now he really needed to talk to Lance. Lance would know what was happening.

Finally, he mounted the steps leading up to the Smith's front porch. He tapped the door knocker against the door, which bore a smooth indent worn there by previous centuries of knocking.

No answer came. Frowning, Engrelin knocked harder.

Still nothing.

Shading his eyes, he tried to peer through the front window. But the curtains there were drawn tight against prying eyes.

Engrelin took a step back and stared hard at the door. It was Sunday. The Smith's hadn't been at church. Working on Sundays was against the law. And he knew well that Walche never went visiting anywhere but the taverns—where Lance certainly wouldn't accompany him. Besides, no tavern was open this early on any day of the week. Lance had to be home. So why didn't he answer?

Sudden movement near the side of the house caught his eye. He looked over just in time to see a man rounding the corner of the house. He watched him for a moment. What was he up to? Slipping off the porch, Engrelin silently followed him.

The man beelined for the forge which stood just beside the house. He knocked once on the door and entered, closing it behind him.

Engrelin hesitated in the street. Beyond the forge's blackened windows, lights glimmered faintly, mixing with the occasional shadow. His heart pounded against his rib cage. What were people doing inside the forge on a Sunday?

As he drew closer to the forge, he heard the low murmur of voices from within. Just as he stepped into the building's shadow, everything within fell quiet. Engrelin stopped in his tracks. What now?

The door in front of him swung slowly open, grinding Engrelin's heart to a sudden stop. Walche appeared in the doorway, smiling in an almost friendly manner.

"Engrelin!" he exclaimed, stepping forward to clasp Engrelin's hand. "It's so good to see you!"

Engrelin simply stared at the smiling Walche and let his hand be shaken. He couldn't have been more surprised than if the belligerent man had just sprouted a second head.

"It's nice to see you too?" answered Engrelin.

"Come in, come in!" Walche urged. He yanked Engrelin into the dusky forge. Engrelin barely caught himself before he tripped on the doorstep.

"Thanks?" He quickly took in his surroundings. He had seen this forge many times, but never like this. Every shelf and table in the shop was laden with candles, though their light barely penetrated the gloom.

The many men who stood along or leaned against the forge walls met Engrelin's glance. None smiled, but they all watched him with an expectation that made his palms grow slick with sweat. Instinctively, his hand moved down to grip the *cyllel* hanging from his belt.

Walche's eyes followed the movement. "There's no need for that," he said smoothly. "We're all friends here."

Engrelin took another look at the men around him—they looked anything *but* friendly.

"I just came to see Lance," he said, turning to Walche. "I didn't see him in church this morning, and I was wondering—"

"He couldn't come to church, sick as he is, poor lad," Walche interjected. "Been sick since he came back from your place last week." He cocked his head, looking at Engrelin with one eye while watching his guests with the other. "That was the same day your uncle came home from patrol, wasn't it?"

"Yes, I believe it was," Engrelin answered tightly.

At this, the men standing against the walls murmured angrily.

Engrelin wrapped his fingers more tightly around his *cyllel's* hilt. "Lance just came over to help on our farm, like he always does on Mondays," he continued, though he hadn't the least idea *why*. What was he trying to convince these men of anyway?

"And is this the kind of help you give in return?" Walche demanded, turning sharply on Engrelin. "Driving innocent people onto sickbeds!"

Engrelin held one hand out defensively. "I never dreamed of hurting him!" he exclaimed. "Why would I? We've been friends for years!"

"And a fat lot of a friend you turned out to be!" Walche snarled. "Two weeks he's been a-bed now, and how many times have you visited him?" He waved a closed fist in Engrelin's face. "How many fingers am I holding up?" he demanded. Without waiting for an answer, he continued, "None! That's right. That's how much you care about your *dear* friend Lance."

Engrelin clenched his jaw so tightly it hurt. "That's not true, Walche," he said, his voice low and dangerous. "You know that."

"Oh, it isn't, is it? So, I'm a liar now, as well as a cruel uncle! Tell me, and the rest of the gentlemen here—" He swept his arm out, motioning to the silent watchers "—tell them just how often you have come to see my nephew since he came home from your farm last. And please be honest," he added, in a mocking croon. "We hate lies almost as much as we do Tirendrians."

"Especially if it's a Peterson telling them," someone growled directly behind Engrelin.

He jumped and glanced swiftly behind himself. The swarthy blond man, leaning against the closed forge door, smiled sweetly at him, though the expression hinted towards a derisive sneer. "Uphold the family honor, lad."

A general grumble rolled through the room. Engrelin turned back to face Walche, who plainly tried to mask his triumphant smile.

"I hadn't been able to visit him before this because both my sister and my grandmother are sick," Engrelin ground out. "What matters is that I'm here now. If you're so worried about him," he continued accusingly, "why don't you let me into the house to see him, instead of keeping me here like this? He might like to see a friendly face—for once."

Walche's face alternated furious shades of red and white. Turning away from Engrelin, he held his hands out to the gathered men in an imploring gesture.

"Do you hear how he speaks to us?" he exclaimed, his harsh voice jarring through Engrelin. "So much for the most honorable family in Monaria! They expect us to treat them like gold, even while they rub us in the dirt!" He jabbed a finger towards Engrelin. "And in my own home! Soon to be all our homes. We've put up with this for centuries, treated like trash by this boy and his family. And look at him! Lower than me in age and trade—"

A hot flush burned Engrelin's cheeks.

"—and yet he demands entrance into my home! Can we endure this much longer?"

Indignant cries broke from several lips, punctuated by fists thrust into the air.

Engrelin was too astonished to move or to even breathe. Walche's sidelong glance and silky smile came to rest on him. A surge of anger drowned Engrelin's surprise.

"What do you think you're talking about?" he demanded. The vehemence of his voice stunned the room into an unsettled silence, though several still glared menacingly.

"What would have happened to Justinian's line if it hadn't been for Aaron? He kept Tirendria from conquering the world. Since then, every Peterson I have ever known tries to live with the same honor, respect, and reservation as Aaron. If you have a problem with one of us, take it out on that one man, and don't touch the other good people of his line."

Every mutter in the room died. A few men even looked down at the floor, their expressions sullen. A tiny root of triumph sprouted in Engrelin's heart, but Walche deftly ripped it out by saying,

"As to Aaron's importance, any other man could have done that just as easily." He jutted his chest out proudly. "You forget James, of *my* bloodline. Even if Aaron had not been there, James was, and Anna would have been rescued in the end."

Engrelin's free hand clenched into a fist. "It's not about the ancestry of any man, great or not. I don't know what you all have against my family. But if you do bring it to that, Aaron and James could not have done what they did without each other. Anna wouldn't have been able to escape without either one."

Walche snorted. "Never mind. What happened in the past will never make up for what the Petersons have done now. To us. All Petersons are accountable for your uncle's mistakes. We must have restitution. He won't get away with our lives this time."

Engrelin hesitated. What were they arguing about anyway? It all seemed a disconnected muddle of accusations, and he hardly felt capable of defending his family without knowing the reason behind the men's anger. Still, he murmured, "If we begin with the Petersons, the Smiths will follow."

Walche's sharp ears caught the words; his eyes burned with barely suppressed hatred. "How dare you speak like that in my home?" he hissed

"Technically, it was your brother's," Engrelin retorted. "Now that he's dead, it should belong to Lance."

Walche glowered, emanating malice. Hatred hung in the air like smoke, blinding and choking, charged with flickers of danger. Several men straightened from their former leisurely positions. With a shrinking feeling, Engrelin realized he had better make himself scarce, or face all these men with nothing but a knife and his fists.

Giving the room one final glance—favoring Walche with a significant glare—Engrelin turned sharply on his heel.

"Hold on a minute!" cried Walche, springing forward. Grabbing Engrelin by the front of his tunic, he wrenched the boy back around. Shaking him once, Walche hissed, "You think I'm going to let you humiliate me like that, then walk away without paying for it?"

Engrelin clenched his teeth to keep them from clacking together. His hand darted back down to his *cyllel's* hilt. Jerking the weapon out of its sheath, Engrelin spilled forward in a jab.

Walche bought the feint. He stumbled back, crying out as loudly as if Engrelin had run him through, and tumbled back against a table covered in tools and candles.

As files and candle stubs flew every-which-way, the door connecting the forge to the house burst open. Lance's slight frame filled the doorway. He glanced down at his uncle among the table's wreckage, then lifted his eyes to meet Engrelin's for a single moment.

Someone's fist smashed into Engrelin's mouth. Sparks danced across his vision. His *cyllel* fell from his slack hand and clattered to the floor as he staggered backwards. Ducking another blow, he turned and rushed for the closed door. The swarthy man leaning against it tensed for a fight. Engrelin made as if to dive for the window. As the man rushed to that one side, Engrelin tripped him, grabbed the door handle, and wrenched the door open.

Once outside, he slammed it shut against the men surging towards him. He cast wildly about for something to hold the door shut. He spied a heavy bench that stood just beside the door. Pressing his body up against the door, which resounded with blows, Engrelin reached out and snagged the edge of the bench. Dragging it over, he braced it up against the door.

Then he ran. Behind him, he heard the opening door smash against the bench. A volley of oaths rang out.

Engrelin dashed down the nearest alley. He had hardly turned the corner when grim cries and the thud of pursuing boots on the hard-packed dirt sounded behind him. The bench had delayed them for only so long. Engrelin glanced fearfully over his shoulder, but he saw no one… yet. The sounds of pursuit drew closer by the second. He sprinted down one alley and into another. His tight shoes pinched his feet mercilessly, crippling him to a limping run.

"Over here! I see him!" He heard the dreaded shout from behind him.

Engrelin's heart leapt into his throat. Without a backwards glance, he whipped around another corner, seized a gutter trailing along the wall of a near-by house, and swung himself up onto the roof. He pressed low into the musty thatch and lay perfectly still, his breath pounding in his ears, his heart hammering in his chest.

Running feet clattered harshly across the street below. They seemed to come right below the roof where Engrelin crouched and stopped.

Fear thrilled through Engrelin, intensified by the metallic tang of blood in his mouth. Had they spotted him? He willed himself smaller.

"Drew, I thought you said you saw the kid run down here," someone yelled in disgust.

"I did!" exclaimed Drew between labored gasps. "He ran right down here!"

"And just disappeared?" said the first scornfully. "Like magic?"

"Magic's only in fairy tales to scare little kids," a third scoffed.

"And in the devil's dealings," growled the first.

"I wouldn't put it past the Petersons," exclaimed another. "As if treason wasn't bad enough."

"Julian better set Austinian straight. My son was at Fort Starr. I'm not letting that go lightly."

"Will any of us?"

"Let's get away from here," whimpered Drew fearfully. "I feel like someone's watching me."

Engrelin's breath strangled in his throat, and he tried to press himself flatter against the cottage roof.

"Probably that kid," the first man snorted. "Don't worry. If he likes his skin, he won't come out while we're here."

Engrelin risked a peek over the edge of the roof. The four men in the alley below weren't looking up, but around the alley, in corners, and beneath an overturned crate. All except the third man. He turned in a slow circle, unaware that he was putting his back to his prey, and shook his curled fist at the empty alley.

"You better stay out of my way, Peterson," the man yelled. "You hear me?"

Like I'd be fool enough to respond. Engrelin sank back out of sight. But a cold chord still struck his heart as the sound of the men's retreating tramp echoed against the alley walls. What had that whole thing been about, anyway? Petersons…and treason? Why had all those men gathered in the Smith's forge, and what had Lance been doing out of bed? Had Walche been lying to him? Had Lance been well all along?

Sighing wearily, Engrelin dragged a hand across his face—he drew it away streaked with blood. Muttering, he yanked his handkerchief out of his pocket and pressed it to his split lip. How was he going to explain *that* to those at home?

After a moment, Engrelin stuffed the handkerchief into his pocket, took a final wary glance around, and slipped back down to the alley floor. During his frantic run, he hadn't noticed the stench of waste and rotting trash that filled the alley, but now it was overpowering. Breathing only through his mouth, Engrelin set off through the web of alleys running through Bryn, limping over puddles of stale dishwater and stepping around heaps of trash. He determined not to take the road home; Walche knew where Engrelin lived, and he might set an ambush on the road. He couldn't go back to the church, not with the marks of a struggle plain on his face. There was only one other way home he knew.

Engrelin stopped short in the crossroads of four equally filthy alleys. Father Colby. He'd come to *Traeth Euriad* specifically to warn him. About what?

Trouble in town.

Engrelin drew his breath in sharply. Had the priest known about Walche all along? Guiltily, he recalled how distracted Father Colby had been when Engrelin had left him. Would the priest have merely waved him off if he had heard Engrelin's words more clearly?

And what had one of his pursuers said…about treason? Merely thinking the word brought a bitter bile to Engrelin's throat. Had a

Peterson committed treason? Was that why everyone had either avoided or glared at him the whole day?

Never walk to town alone. Would having someone with him have changed anything? He was sure Walche wouldn't have cared, much less let it stop him. His men searching all over Bryn for Engrelin right now probably wouldn't either. What were two against so many, fueled with hate as they were? All the people in Bryn—in all Monaria—would they really care about what happened to one boy, especially if that boy were related to a traitor?

The thought lent speed to his aching feet, and he flew through the last few alleys. Gradually, the reek of rotten fish added to the overall stench. Engrelin turned a final corner, and Bryn's docks spread out before him, completely deserted according to law. All except for one person.

Engrelin hastened towards the familiar figure. "Irydd!" he called.

The fisherman spun around, a broad grin lighting his ruddy face. "Engrelin!" he boomed. Striding forward with a speed surprising for his heavy frame, he crushed Engrelin in a hearty embrace. Engrelin gasped in the man's bone-crunching hold and gave Irydd a few hard thumps on the back in return.

"Good to see you too, Irydd," he said, backing out of the man's arms. "But I can't stay long. I just came to ask a favor of you."

"Anything for Everen's son!" Irydd declared. Engrelin inwardly winced at the mention of her father's name.

The fisherman gestured towards the crafts moored at the docks with a broad sweep of his arm.

"I just need to borrow a dugout," Engrelin said. "I'll bring it back next time I come to town."

"I'm not worried about it," Irydd laughed. He gave Engrelin's arm a squeeze, nearly yanking it out of its socket as he tugged him over to one of the boats. With a playful flourish, he pulled the cover off a four-person canoe.

"Will this do?" he asked. "It's a little big for just you, but it's the smallest I have."

Engrelin smiled faintly. "As long as it floats, I'm good."

"I'd let you keep it, but I need it next spring," added the fisherman jovially.

"I don't think I'll need it that long." Engrelin climbed into the canoe and accepted a long pole and two paddles from Irydd. "Thanks, Irydd," he said, as he lay the paddles in the boat's bottom. He dug the pole into the creek bed, pushing the boat away from the dock.

The fisherman swept his huge hand in an arch over his head. "You're welcome, Engrelin. St. Nicolas guard you!"

9

The sunset was already fading from the sky when Engrelin rounded the final bend in the creek, which opened onto *Traeth Euriad's* familiar slopes. The bayberry trees bent to the water's edge trembled with the songs of the birds twittering in farewell to the dying day. Frogs wallowing in the shallows thrummed the angelus.

The canoe bumped against the dock pilings—the most wonderful sound Engrelin had heard all day. He tied the boat to the dock with practiced hands. The motion helped ease the tension cramping his limbs. He had never had reason to be cautious in the marsh; he had traversed it since he was knee-high. He knew its every treacherous bend and sandbar. But a new fear, the dread of the pursued, had pressed him closely during the long hours home. Every shadow cast by a shrubby tree or a clump of weeds could have hidden an enemy. Every ripple of a water beetle or the splash of a fish could have been the stealthily dipping oars of a pursuing boat.

Engrelin clambered up onto the dock and stood there a moment to look out over the serene fields and the deepening purple of the sky, the serenity and normalcy of it all. He reached up and touched his swollen lip to assure himself that what had happened in town wasn't all a dream.

He started towards the distant house; chores could be done after he checked on his family.

The falling twilight deepened almost to night's blackness. Engrelin reached the well-worn path that led from the barn to the back of the house. Movement near the house's back door caught his eye. Engrelin froze.

A sentinel shadow flitted back and forth. Then it stopped pacing. It had seen him. Scowling, Engrelin marched up to the stranger.

"Who are you?" he demanded harshly.

In answer, the figure waved a dim hand. It swatted in and out of the slender beams of light that slipped between the cracks in the shutters. "I could ask the same of you," he retorted.

"But this is my property," returned Engrelin sharply. "You'd better tell me who you are and why you're here, or I'll go straight to town and get one of Lord Gwane's men to make you."

The man chuckled. "I'm afraid you'd have no luck there," he said. "I *am* one of his men."

Prickling with sudden fear, Engrelin drew his head back slightly to scrutinize the man as best he could. Did this have anything to do with what had happened in town?

"What are you doing here—at this hour—instead of sleeping in your barracks?" Engrelin asked.

"I'm afraid I can't say," answered the soldier vaguely. He leaned casually back against the doorframe.

Engrelin bristled. "If you can't tell me anything, get out of the way so I can go inside."

"Can't do that either," sighed the soldier. He glanced down at a blade of grass he had been fiddling with and flicked it carelessly away. "Orders."

"Orders from who?" Engrelin demanded, barely able to hold back the surge of helplessness that engulfed him. Yet even as he asked the question, he knew what the soldier's answer would be.

"Lord Gwane himself."

The overlord of Bryn. Engrelin glared at the soldier a moment, as if he could change the lord's instructions merely by defying one of his men. But the soldier only stared languidly back, as if the whole affair rather bored him.

"Why won't he let me in?"

The soldier shrugged. "Goodness knows why. He's been here, there, and everywhere this week, all on account of the Petersons."

There it was again. Engrelin's stomach tied itself in knots. What could have happened for a noble to visit their home?

"If he's here on my account, shouldn't I be allowed inside to speak with him?" Engrelin reasoned.

"If I wanted to make sense of the whole mess, yes," answered the soldier. "But my orders are to say 'no'. I'm sorry," he continued, his voice turning, for the first time, slightly sympathetic. Engrelin begrudged that more than the earlier devil-may-care. "Don't worry about the ladies inside. They'll be all right."

Gritting his teeth, Engrelin spun on his heel and strode quickly away, until his blistered feet painfully reminded him to walk. Could this day possibly get any worse?

Just as he rounded the corner of the house, his foot caught on something, and he nearly went sprawling. Catching himself against the wall, he peered down to see what had tripped him.

Outlined against the ground was the raised cellar door. One of two. The other one opened in the *kitchen* floor…

Gingerly, careful not to make a sound, Engrelin grasped the handle, fingers tingling with apprehension at the thought of the sentry just around the corner. The door opened easily—and silently. The corners of Engrelin's mouth twitched with a smile. Opening the door a little more, just wide enough to squeeze through, he dropped noiselessly into the dusky cellar below.

Pitch blackness enveloped him, mixed with the light, earthy scent of vegetables. Engrelin felt around the dirt-filled bins that held their potatoes and other root vegetables, bushel baskets of fruit and squash, and shelves stocked with canned goods, until his hand brushed up against the worn wood of a ladder. He eased himself up it until the top of his head scraped against the closed trap door above.

A moment later, he was standing in the center of the tiny *kitchen*, facing the closed door that led to the *ystafell fyw*. From the other side of the door came a jumble of voices. Engrelin took a few cautious steps closer, until he could have leaned against the door if he had wanted to, and stood still to listen.

At first, all Engrelin could hear was his own breath rasping anxiously in his throat. Then he heard someone in the adjoining room sigh impatiently.

"How long has he been out there?"

Engrelin pulled a swift step away from the door. Did they mean him?

"I don't know," someone else answered wearily.

A door banged open and shut. The newcomer's footsteps were soft on the earthen floor.

"Who was it, Dylen?" asked the first voice.

"The young Peterson, my lord," answered someone. Likely Dylen.

Engrelin moved back over to the door, his ears straining. So Lord Gwane *was* here. And two others. Dylen and another whose voice had been too faint to recognize.

"He must have run into trouble," said the second man, raising his voice a little this time. "I had wanted to walk home with him, but he must have slipped off while I was talking to others."

"More than a little trouble, Father," Lord Gwane muttered. A chair creaked loudly. "Dylen, what did Haydric do with him?"

"Said the boy ran off before he could even tell him to," replied Dylen in crisp, military tones. "We're not quite sure where he's gone, sir."

"Poor boy," a feminine voice wavered.

Grandmother.

"This will all be a world easier without Engrelin trying to shove his oar in, Vera. He can hear what we have to say once everything is decided."

Engrelin started. There was no mistaking that voice. But what was his uncle doing here?

"He'd more than shove," observed Averendier's voice flatly. Murmurs of agreement rippled in different tones through the room. A prickling heat crept up Engrelin's cheeks, mingling with the burn of curiosity. What were so many people of high status doing in his home at this hour?

Why did they need him out of the way?

"Can't you just leave us alone?" asked Vera. "I don't see what any of this has to do with us."

"It started that way, Vera," Austinian said gravely. "But it's become about more than just me. The blame for what happened at Fort Starr and Highlynn are being hung around the neck of every man who has the misfortune to have Peterson clapped to the back of their names."

"But you did the best any man could have done!" Vera exclaimed.

"The rest of Monaria doesn't share your opinion," Austinian said drily. "They all seem convinced that I bore some prophetic sense that told me the Tirendrians were going to attack, and that I purposefully didn't go to Starr Island until too late.

"And then, while practically a prisoner in my own home, the Tirendrians took advantage and attacked Highlynn. Here, they blame me for the attack itself, even though they were the ones who kept me here, unable to help. In their eyes, I'm a traitor. A few have been bold enough to say that I'm in allegiance with Vendar."

"But it's not true!" Vera burst out. "And they should know it's not true. You're the reason Dermain didn't capture Fort Starr in the first place. And now they tell themselves you're trying to pawn it off on his son?"

"The people need someone to blame," put in Father Colby sadly. "There's no true villain here but Vendar, and he's too far away to see the insults they throw at him. So they chose someone who could."

"Austinian, as your mother-in-law, I can't begin to say how it pains me to see you treated this way. And by your own people, who you've given your life to for these twenty-odd years. But..." Vera hesitated a moment. "What does this have to do with us...and Engrelin? You came to see me about him, didn't you?"

Everyone fell uncomfortably silent. Engrelin pressed his ear to the crack between the door and its frame.

"Vera," said Lord Gwane finally, "I've been receiving reports for two weeks now that your grandson has been causing trouble in the city."

"Absolute lies!" Engrelin's grandmother objected, her voice spiced with anger.

There was the sound of someone shuffling through something. "If they are lies, Vera, tell me that you don't recognize this."

Vera was agonizingly silent. Engrelin pressed his whole body against the door, desperately wishing he could see into the room.

"Is this not Engrelin's knife?" demanded Lord Gwane.

Vera's silence reigned for a moment longer. Then she whispered, so low Engrelin could hardly hear, "Yes."

Engrelin's hand flashed down to his belt and closed over the empty air. His *cyllel!* He must have dropped it during the scuffle at the forge!

"This afternoon, a local blacksmith was storming at my gate. He declared that your grandson had attacked him in his forge with this very knife. He had a pretty nasty gash on his arm, too."

Engrelin squeezed his hands into such tight knots, his fingernails bit into his palms. Walche must have hurt himself when he fell into the table of tools. If only he hadn't dropped his knife! Walche wouldn't have had any evidence to back his lie otherwise.

"Lord Gwane," said Vera shrilly, "are you suggesting my grandson stabbed someone?"

"I am more than suggesting, Vera," said Lord Gwane severely. "This knife is clear evidence that your grandson was in contact with the smith some time today. Whether or not he attacked the man, I can't say. I am only repeating what I have seen and heard."

"I saw the smith as well," piped Dylen. "And, if I may say so, my lord, I'm a soldier, and I know my trade fairly well. And if memory serves me right, this knife probably was not the cause of that man's wound. The cut wasn't clean, all jagged. And this knife is as sharp as my own sword."

"Thank you, Dylen," Lord Gwane said crisply. "But whether or not he is guilty of assault doesn't change matters any. Austinian?"

Austinian cleared his throat. Engrelin's skin crawled with trepidation. Only on rare occasion, when he was extremely uncomfortable, would his uncle do that.

"Vera," he began in a strained voice, "because of what's been happening, I've decided that it would be safest for me to go to the *Pwynt,* where I've found the most support of my innocence. Get some hard work done and, hopefully, reinstate my good name here and elsewhere."

"What kind of work?" asked Engrelin's grandmother.

"Anything in the fighting or diplomatic realm," Lord Gwane cut in briskly. "Hero work. Something to prove his worth to the people."

"He's already done that countless times! What is there left to prove?"

"Everything, it seems," muttered a new voice.

Andrald.

"It's something similar," said Lord Gwane, with particular care, "to what your grandson will be doing."

"What?!" Engrelin and Vera exclaimed simultaneously. Engrelin clapped his hand over his mouth and waited with a frantically beating heart for one of the speakers to tear the kitchen door open and jerk him into the room. They would know now that he had heard everything they had said—everything that they had taken such pains to keep from his ears. Another scar against his name. Engrelin nearly groaned into his palm.

But no one had even heard him. His low cry of dismay had been drowned out by Vera's louder sob of anguish.

"It's all for the best, Vera," Father Colby tried to soothe, though he sounded as if he wanted reassurance himself.

"All for the best!" Vera cried. "Sending that stripling off to war? Is this Monaria's justice, Lord Gwane? Exiling the innocent while the guilty stay snug in their homes? My grandson could be killed!"

"He will be killed—by the villages of Bryn if we don't send him away," argued the lord.

"No, they wouldn't," faltered Vera. "My great-grandfather was the founder of this nation. How could they turn on us now?"

"Woman, haven't you been listening?" Lord Gwane roared. There was the sudden clatter of a chair overturning. "We are at *war!* And we can't win even the smallest skirmish if we are divided against ourselves! We must send every male Peterson away from Bryn—and maybe from other cities throughout the country—so that we can have some peace, and bend our efforts towards fighting the real enemies that are out there. Engrelin must go, and he will! Tomorrow morning, I expect to hear he has straddled a horse and left Bryn for Northern Florenth!"

Engrelin recoiled from the door, the words slamming into him like a punch in the gut. Tomorrow! He wouldn't have been ready to leave in a month, much less tomorrow!

"No! Please, let him stay!" his grandmother pleaded. "We need him here. We have the last of the harvest to bring in, stock that needs caring for. The loft still must be filled for the winter! He's harmless. Please."

"This knife—" something clattered loudly; the knife being dropped onto the table "—tells me he is less harmless than you claim. And again, whether he was defending himself or not, it's no matter. I'm not concerned about looking into it any further or pressing charges. What matters now is that I have a royal order, signed by King Julian, in my pocket. It alone commands that if your grandson is not ten miles away from Bryn by sundown tomorrow, he will be arrested and kept in custody until all this kerfuffle about the Petersons dies down."

10

Engrelin *tried to breathe, but his mouth and lungs strained* uselessly. A royal order? Signed by Julian himself? How could he resist that?

His grandmother sobbed softly in the adjacent room. What would happen to her if he were arrested? What would happen to the farm? They couldn't spend the winter there, on their own. His eyes narrowed with anger at the thought. The only thing that kept him from bursting into the *ystafell fyw* and throwing that order into the fire to be reduced to ashes was the possibility—no, the likelihood—of Lord Gwane's arresting him a day early. The overlord probably wouldn't bat an eye at doing so.

The thought made him retreat across the kitchen. The conversation in the other room had swung into a lull. What if someone decided to come into the kitchen at that moment? What would happen if they found him there?

Engrelin quickly retraced his steps into the cellar and back out into the open night air. He limped over to the barn, giving the sentry at the back door a wide berth and sticking to the shadows. Once inside the barn's murky, dusty interior, he climbed up into the hayloft and sat on the edge, feet dangling, to think things over.

They were making him leave. The thought made his breath catch in his chest. Making him leave Bryn because people blamed his uncle for what had happened at Fort Starr—blame that had spread like pall to cover every Monarian Peterson. And so they were being sent out to do work for Monaria to prove themselves loyal patriots to Julian's crown and their country.

Hero work? What in Ontaria? Did he have to prove to the whole world that he wasn't a criminal or a traitor before he could continue living his life out in peace? And what about his grandmother and little Elmera? Who would care for them while he was gone? If everyone hated them all as Lord Gwane had made out, would any of their old friends and neighbors be willing to come and help, even if it were a feeble old woman and a sickly little girl they would be assisting?

As far as he knew, it would be about a three-week trip to the Northern Florenth border below them. And goodness only knew where he would have to go from there! He probably wouldn't have a chance to come back to Monaria until long after the first snowstorm had struck. Would those left at home have to struggle to care for the stock alone under such conditions? Engrelin rubbed his aching temples. He didn't doubt his grandmother knew how to run the farm. She wouldn't stand by while *Traeth Euriad* crumbled to pieces.

But she was so frail. She would kill herself trying to do all the chores. Why did he have to leave? He needed to be here helping them.

Gritting his teeth in frustration, Engrelin flung his head back to rest it against the rough wall behind.

The livestock in the barn must have heard him, for from below came one mournful bellow, followed by another. Engrelin jerked to his feet and scrambled down the ladder as the cows continued to vent their frustration and pain. It was way past the time they were usually milked!

He was soon beside the first cow with his pail. The creature rolled its eyes and stomped when the boy touched her tight udders.

"Easy now, Bonesig," he murmured, easing himself onto a stool. "You just eat your hay. Don't mind me."

The cow looked suspiciously at him. And though her muscles twitched as Engrelin began working, she resignedly turned her attention to the mound of hay in the manger before her.

The rhythm of the streaming milk zinging into the metal pail beneath was almost mesmerizing, momentarily dulling the sharp ache of troubled thoughts. Once Bonesig was stripped, he moved on to their other milk cow, Dant y llew (name compliments of Elmera). She was more skittish than the dignified Bonesig, and always aimed a few kicks at Engrelin's head and the pail beneath her before she submitted to her fate. Tonight, however, she was too uncomfortable to do more than stamp.

"There's a girl, nice and easy," Engrelin said, sliding the pail beneath her and warming his hands beneath his armpits. "Just eat, and I'll have you fixed up in no time."

"Nice conversation."

Engrelin swiveled his head to see Andrald leaning up against the milking stall, watching him with some amusement. Although every farmer Engrelin knew talked to their cows during milking, he flushed— though from anger or embarrassment, he wasn't sure.

"Keeps her quiet," he said, resuming his chore.

Andrald said nothing; for a while, the only sound was the milk zinging into the pail.

"Engrelin," the older boy said finally, "I didn't come to watch you milk a cow. I've got to talk to you."

"What? You going to explain why you shut people out of their own homes in the middle of the night?" Engrelin couldn't contain the outburst. It flowed from his lips as cleanly and painfully as a stream of hot wax.

Andrald shifted his position uncomfortably. "Well, you see—"

At that moment, the barn doors slid noisily open, admitting Austinian and Averendier. Both hurried quickly over to the milking stall.

"Have you told him yet?" Austinian asked in a low voice.

Andrald shook his head, as if Engrelin were not sitting right in front of them, hearing every word they said. The tips of his ears grew hot. He could feel the burn of their pitying gazes on his back.

"Engrelin," Austinian said carefully. "we've got something to tell you."

Stop stalling and spit it out, thought Engrelin, his hands shaking a little as he milked harder. Dant y llew lowed in protest and stamped dangerously close to the milk bucket.

"To cut to the chase, you're going on a little trip with your cousins."

"Little trip?" Engrelin echoed icily. He couldn't help it. To him, a little trip was walking down to the docks, or to church. He'd never been more than five miles away from home in his entire life.

"Not so little, Dad," Andrald muttered.

Austinian frowned. "You're going to go to Northern Florenth on an errand for King Julian, starting tomorrow."

"Tomorrow," Engrelin repeated flatly, playing on their ignorance of his knowledge.

"Yes, Engrelin. Tomorrow," Austinian affirmed. "So you should probably head inside now to get some rest."

That's already out of the question. "I have chores to do," he said evenly. The sheer number of them marched an endless parade within his head. He had avoided thinking of them, until now.

He was sure he wouldn't be finished with them until dawn.

"You need to be able to come to church in time for morning mass," Austinian continued. "Bring your grandmother and Elmera as well. Father Colby has offered to let them stay at the rectory with him until you return."

The words brought a wave of relief crashing onto Engrelin's shore of troubles. At least they'd be safe. But Engrelin only nodded curtly.

"What about the farm?" he asked, keeping his eyes fixed on the little streams of milk whizzing into the pail. "I'm not going to leave unless there's a man here to take care of it."

Austinian gave him a small smile, the first one of that whole conversation. "Lord Gwane has already thought of that," he said. "He has several willing gardeners and a couple stable hands who will be coming out daily to check on and care for the crops and livestock. The harvest will be brought in, and the hogs slaughtered when the cold sets in."

"The workers can't stay in the house," Engrelin said sharply.

"No, they can't," Austinian assented with a nod. "They'll be staying in their present quarters at night."

Engrelin dropped his gaze into the pail of foamy milk and scrambled for another excuse. There had to be something he had forgotten. Another reason to stay! A loophole somewhere in the royal order, maybe. He frowned at himself. Was there even such a thing?

"Engrelin."

The gentle, measured tones of his uncle's voice drew Engrelin's gaze over to him. Austinian's eyes were glassy with exhaustion, his face drawn with constant stress. Even his hair seemed more gray than blond. Pity twisted Engrelin's heart. What was it like, to be one of the most important men in Monaria, second in rank—below the king himself—only to have the whole country suddenly turn against you. And none of it his fault!

Engrelin didn't feel that he was important to many people. Only a precious few now.

Yet no matter how few or how many people cared for either of them, all were going to be left behind tomorrow for "greater things." Hero work.

Poor Mary. How little she got to see of her father and older brothers. Now there would be no end date for her to mark, no countdown for the day they would return. Only days of anxious, weary waiting.

And all for the sake of the glory the world demanded of them. Because of the accusation of one innocent man, others were being turned out of their homes to prove themselves in a way they shouldn't have to. Of what worth were forced heroics? Engrelin's expression darkened. It was all right in stories. But not here.

"Engrelin, this isn't easy for any of us," Austinian continued softly. "Most of all for you. You've already lost so much."

The corner of Engrelin's mouth spasmed. Did they have to bring that up now?

"But you're not helping anyone by pushing yourself the way you are. Go to bed and get some rest so that you can be fresh and ready to go tomorrow. Averendier and Andrald will be waiting for you there. They're going with you."

It should have been reassuring—at least he didn't have to travel alone. But Engrelin could do nothing but stare at his uncle, a strange tumult of hatred, anger, and heartbreak raging within him.

Austinian reached down and grasped Engrelin's shoulder firmly. "Son, finish that up, and go inside."

Engrelin sprang back out of his uncle's reach, upsetting the milk pail as he did. "I'm not your son!" he exclaimed. "I don't need you to tell me what to do. How do you know what's best for me?"

Austinian reached forward, concern etched on every feature. "Engrelin, you really should—"

"I don't care what I should do," Engrelin growled, his voice so low and forced it cracked. "This is what I *have* to do. So leave me alone to do it."

Austinian drew back a step, still staring intently at his nephew. Engrelin looked away from him to the startled cow, who was jerking at the snubbing rope attached to its halter. Painfully conscious of his uncle's and cousin's eyes upon him, Engrelin smoothed Dant y llew's neck. He stooped to pick the empty pail out of the sodden straw.

"We could help you," Averendier offered quietly.

Engrelin straightened and studied Averendier a moment to see if his cousin was joking. Engrelin was confident Averendier had never touched a live cow in his life or pitched a forkful of hay into a manger.

"No," he muttered, looking away again. "Go home and get your precious rest."

Not waiting to hear their response, he grabbed Dant y llew's halter and pulled her out of the stall, putting her broad, tall body between himself and his relations. He didn't look any direction but forward as he led the cow to her stall and bedded her down for the night. By the time he was finished, and dared a look around, his uncle and cousins were gone. Sighing softly under his breath, he turned back to continue his chores.

Trapped in a sort of dream, Engrelin worked steadily through the night, struggling to make sure everything would be perfect before he left. Confronting his cousins and uncle had drained all the fight he'd had left in him for the night. He knew only that he was bone tired—his mind was otherwise blank as he moved mechanically from place to place on the farm.

When he finally dragged himself into the house, the sky blushed rosily. He didn't even notice it. He only collapsed into his grandmother's empty rocking chair in front of the banked fire. He stared at the ashes through a blur, too tired to summon the strength to stir them and wake the blaze. The only thing that slightly pierced his mental fog was the smart and throb of his blistered feet as he automatically pulled off his too-small boots.

The moment the second boot hit the floor, he was asleep.

11

*S*unlight *flitted across Engrelin's face. He stirred, then groaned,* scrubbing a hand across his face. There wasn't a bone in his body that didn't ache.

Something cool and wet caressed his bare feet. He flinched again and jerked his leaden eyes to open. Lingering exhaustion stubbornly pressed them shut.

"Hold still, dear," his grandmother chided.

Pushing the final clinging cobwebs of sleep aside, Engrelin forced his eyes open a crack. But even before he saw anything, he heard the musical tinkling of water. Once his vision cleared, he saw his grandmother kneeling on the floor beside him, gently bathing his feet with a strip of wet flannel.

"Grandmother, what are you doing?" He sat up, wincing as his neck and shoulders cramped in protest. "You don't have to—"

"And what? Let you galivant across Ontaria without a scrap of skin on your feet?" Vera eyed him sternly over the rims of her spectacles. Sternly, but with tears glistening through. Engrelin looked away and stared absently at a wall until she had finished washing and bandaging his feet.

"There," she said finally, setting Engrelin's swaddled feet down on the floor. "Now I won't feel so terrible about your going."

He forced a feeble smile. "My new skin certainly feels better," he remarked halfheartedly. Rising stiffly out of the chair, he helped his grandmother to her feet. He picked up the bowl of water she had used and dumped it out the back door. The warmth of the newly risen sun made him blink, then shiver. Groaning inwardly, he hurried back into the house. Vera had already settled back into her chair, looking a little pale, but satisfied.

"Keep those bandages on for a week, at least," she ordered briskly, her knitting needles clacking together. Those needles always seemed a part of her—especially when she was trying to distract herself. "You can wear your stockings and shoes over them. It won't hurt them any."

"I won't be able to fit my feet in my boots," Engrelin replied. "They were too small in the first place."

"I found an old pair of Ouen's lying around," said Vera quietly. "You're a bit smaller than he was, but at least they're something."

He looked down again. Wear his brother's shoes…But did he have a choice?

"Where are they?" he asked.

Vera gestured with her needles. "On the table, with your other things."

He moved over to the table, where the boots stood vacant. A stuffed leather pack sat beside it.

"You packed my things already?" he asked, touching the pack's strap. "You should have been resting." Not that his packing would have taken much effort. Three sets of tunics and trousers—including the one he was already wearing—a cloak, and some stockings were all the wardrobe he owned.

"You're one to talk," retorted Vera, looking up from the stocking that was forming at an alarming rate. "I heard you coming in just as I woke. It would have been near sin to tell you to get back up and pack your things. What a state you would have been in!" The sharpness of her voice suggested that she thought the whole affair sinful, an explicit breakage of the seventh commandment: theft of grandsons.

"The only thing I didn't pack was your clothes for today," she continued. "I left those on your bed. Now go get changed, and give me the ones you have on. I might be able to save them."

Engrelin climbed up into the loft. As he changed, he looked at his worn clothes with surprise. He hadn't noticed how wrecked they were—torn from his struggle and run, filthy from the climb through the cellar and late-night chores.

The doze in the chair had left him so sore he could hardly lift his arms above his head. But he somehow managed to wriggle out of his old clothes and tug on his fresh ones. He had retrieved his *cyllel* from his pack, and now fastened it to his belt. Its familiar weight against his hip was comforting, but there was a hint of wickedness in wearing it, since it had been used to testify against him.

The moment his feet touched the earthen floor downstairs, Elmera threw herself against him.

"Grandmother said that you slept in a chair last night!" she exclaimed, clinging to one of her brother's legs as he shuffled around the room. It was a game they often played, and despite her age, Elmera was still small enough to do it. "Was it fun?" she asked, her eyes sparkling at this new novelty.

"No," Engrelin answered, looking at her askance. Since when had falling asleep in rocking chairs been a pleasant experience? He rubbed the back of his aching neck with a hidden grimace. Obviously, it hadn't been dreamed up by someone who had done it before.

Elmera released his leg and twirled in a circle until she was too dizzy to stand. She collapsed on the bench, giggling through labored breaths. She truly rejoiced in her new-found energy. Engrelin cast about for his grandmother, but though her knitting lay on the rocking chair's seat, she was not in the room.

"Elmera, where's Grandmother?" he asked.

"She said she's getting ready to go to town," Elmera called from where she dangled upside-down on the bench. Her face was turning beet red. She waved a hand. "In the kitchen."

"Thanks," he said, adding, "now sit up, before you get a headache."

Elmera obeyed, smiling broadly. "Please put your boots on, Engrelin!" she cried. She ran across the room and snatched the inherited boots from off the table. "Grandmother said that we could all go to town this morning! It's been so long since I've been!"

Engrelin's face clouded as he took the boots from his sister. How excited would she be if she knew the reason they were going to town?

He gingerly pulled his boots on, Elmera watching him impatiently all the while, hopping from one foot to the other.

"I like them," she commented, referring to the shoes. "They're just like your old ones."

Engrelin smiled briefly. Yes, they were. Made of dark brown leather, knee high, and worn around the edges. But they fit nicely, even over the bandages, and that was all that mattered.

"I got to go get something!" Elmera suddenly declared, jumping up and bounding into her room. Shaking his head, Engrelin strode into the kitchen.

Vera was just slowly climbing up the cellar ladder. Engrelin hurried over to help her.

"You should have gotten me to get it," he said, relieving her of several jars.

She harrumphed and took the jars back. "The way you read, you would have grabbed beet juice instead of preserves," she said, with unusual severity. She shoved the jars into Engrelin's hands. "Cranberry and raspberry," she added, hurriedly looking away.

Engrelin set the jars on the kitchen table to wrap an arm around his grandmother's shoulders. She turned into his embrace, throwing both arms around his neck, her shoulders tense.

"Engrelin, what are we going to do without you?" she whispered.

Engrelin's arms tightened around her. "You'll be eating decent meals."

Vera lightly smacked him. "Be serious, for once!" she admonished.

"I'm trying," he murmured. "But we've got to be careful—Elmera might hear us."

"That poor girl. You haven't told her yet?"

He pulled away. "She knows we're going to town this morning," he said quietly.

Vera gave him a sharp look. "No, Engrelin. I mean about your parents."

Engrelin turned, putting his back to her intense look, and pressed his curved knuckles against the kitchen table.

"She's perfectly healthy now," Vera reminded him. "And now that you're leaving… I think you should be the one to tell her. And now's the time."

"Health doesn't make telling her any easier!" he exclaimed bitterly. "Especially with the way she moons around, sure they're going to be back any moment."

"I wouldn't call it mooning," Vera said. "You would do the same thing if you were that little and didn't know any better." Her eyes seemed to be forging themselves into daggers. "You told me last week that you were going to tell her when she had recovered." Her frail hand fell on Engrelin's shoulder, gentle but firm. "I think it's time you told her."

Engrelin pulled sharply away from her grasp and abruptly left the kitchen.

In the main room, he found Elmera bending over a piece of paper on the table, scribbling furiously with a homemade pencil. His stomach twisting, Engrelin slowly approached the table and glanced over her shoulder at the paper. How anyone ever made sense out of those scratches, he would never know.

"What are you doing?" he asked, as he moved away from the table to take the fiddle off the wall.

Elmera looked up, and her face brightened. "Are you going to play?" she asked.

Engrelin shook his head as he carefully wrapped the instrument in a wool blanket. "We're taking this with us," he said. "I don't want it to get messed up or anything."

She twisted around on the bench. "But it's only a quick trip to town," she said, suddenly suspicious.

Engrelin bit the inside of his cheek as he set the fiddle down to rumple the top of her head. "We'll be there for a little while."

Why did I say that? He immediately asked himself. *You'll be there, Elmera. You and Grandmother. But not me. I must go. Don't you realize that life isn't all chickens and fiddling?*

But his grandmother was right. His sister would never understand until he told her.

He scrunched his shoulders. He just…couldn't. Not yet.

"For how long?" Elmera asked breathlessly, her eyes widening more than Engrelin had thought was physically possible.

Engrelin's hands tightened over her silky brown hair. "I…I'm not too sure," he said stumblingly. "Maybe more than a… a month. I don't know."

"A month! I'd better include that too." And she hunched back over her paper.

Something inside him wrenched. But he had to ask. "Include it in what?" he asked.

"My note to Mom and Dad," Elmera explained, motioning to the paper in front of her. "Because what if they came back when we're gone? What would they do?"

This was the perfect time to tell her. *They're not coming back, Elmera. Not ever. They're dead, don't you see?*

Engrelin turned quickly away and wearily drew his arm across his eyes. Why couldn't he just out and say it? It wasn't half as hard as he was making it out to be, was it?

He looked back down at Elmera who, oblivious of her brother's distress, had resumed scribbling, humming a cheery tune all the while.

Yes, it would be hard. Too hard. How could he crush her hopes like this? How could he darken her smile, pale the roses just blooming on her thin cheeks?

No, not yet. He wanted to let her dream on, even if it was for just a few more hours.

"Engrelin!" called their grandmother from the kitchen. "Elmera! It's time to go!"

"Coming!" Elmera shouted back. She turned to Engrelin, who was busy slinging a quiver, bristling with arrows and his unstrung bow, over his shoulder.

"If I left the note on the table, do you think they'd find it?"

Engrelin's hands faltered on the quiver strap. "I'm sure they'd find it," he answered thickly. "Now come on. Grandmother's waiting for us."

Leaving the note on the table, Elmera jumped up and skipped into the kitchen.

He stared down at the note on the table. For once, he was glad he couldn't read.

"Engrelin?" Vera called questioningly from the kitchen doorway. "Elmera's already heading down to the boat."

"Coming. Just a moment."

Snatching the note off the table, he crushed the paper in his hand, and thrust it deep into the banked ashes within the fireplace. The moment it touched the dying coals, it caught. A moment after, it was a thin film of ash.

A moment after that, it was nothing more than a wisp of smoke.

12

Engrelin stood in one of Bryn's almost empty streets, staring across it at the white-washed chapel. He clutched one of Elmera's hands tightly in his. It was the last time for who-knew-how-long that he would be with her. But unknowing Elmera strained against his hold, excitedly swinging her small bundle of belongings in her free hand.

Mass had been over an hour ago, and the sun had nearly climbed to its zenith. But Vera had said that Father Colby had promised to stay in the rectory all day, so whenever they chose to come, he'd be there to receive them.

All they had left to do was cross the street over to the rectory. Other than the hateful looks occasionally speared in their direction, there was nothing to stop them from doing so.

Nothing except Engrelin. He wasn't ready.

The rectory door swung open, and the cassock-clad figure of the priest stepped out. Engrelin's heart sank to the soles of his hand-me-downs as Father Colby swept his arm in an arch over his head, motioning the trio over. Elmera shouted back—what she said, Engrelin never knew. Wriggling free from his grasp, she was across the street and being swept up in the priest's hug before he was quite sure what had happened. He followed her mechanically, Vera trailing after.

Where had the time gone? The two hours it had taken to paddle to town had hardly seemed more than the blinking of an eye. The walk through Bryn's streets less than even that.

And here he was at the fork in the road. He stood in front of Father Colby now, feigning a smile. Smiling, at a time like this. It sat there on his face like a lie, false and uncomfortable.

"Engrelin, are you ready to go?" asked Father Colby, snapping Engrelin out of his trance.

"Go?" Elmera sang out, swinging the priest's hand with her own. "Where are we going now?"

Father Colby gave Engrelin a stricken look.

Vera, seeing it, turned sharply on Engrelin.

"You didn't tell her?" she demanded under her breath.

Engrelin didn't answer. He hardly saw or heard either of them. He could only look down onto his sister, whose mile-wide grin quickly shrank to an inch.

"What's wrong, Engrelin?" she asked, tilting her blue eyes up at him. "What didn't you tell me?"

At some unspoken order, both Vera and Father Colby retreated several paces. Drawing a shuddering breath, Engrelin crouched to come to Elmera's level.

"Elmera," he whispered, "I have to leave."

"Leave! Why?" Elmera asked. She slipped her tiny hand through his. Against his rough, tanned skin it looked like a piece of fragile pearl. He squeezed it gently.

"Just… because," he murmured.

"For how long?" Elmera asked, pressing his hand to her rose-petal cheek.

Oh goodness, did she have to make it harder by being so pathetic? Engrelin resisted the urge to shut his eyes and answered, "I…I don't know."

A sob escaped the girl's lips; a single tear dripped down onto his hand. "You've got to promise to come back as soon as you can," she said. She squeezed so tightly that she left white handprints on his palm. "I don't want everyone to keep leaving!" she cried. "I just want them to stay home. Why don't any of them come home!"

Engrelin's heart lodged in his throat. "Elmera. There's something I have to tell you—"

His voice broke. He couldn't. He just couldn't.

"Engrelin?" Elmera's eyes were bigger than ever.

Taking her head in his hands, Engrelin brushed one of her tears away. "Elmera, I'm just not sure," he murmured, in so low a voice he doubted for a moment that she had heard.

"Not sure of what?" she asked, a little fearfully.

Engrelin drew his breath in sharply. No. It was too much.

"Mom and Dad… Mom and Dad love you more than all of Ontaria, you know that?"

Elmera nodded tearfully.

"And Damien, and Ouen, and Reigna?"

Elmera nodded again.

"And me… I love you too, okay? And you know that, even if they can't come back ever, they still love you? They'll always love you, even if they're far away?"

Elmera, perhaps understanding what Engrelin insinuated, perhaps not, nonetheless flung herself against him and clung to him as if she would never let go.

"I'm going to miss you most of all," she sobbed. "I'll even miss your burnt bread. I want some right now."

A short laugh broke through his threatening tears. "Yeah?"

Despite herself, Elmera also smiled. "Yeah."

"You want to know something else I'll miss?"

Elmera pulled away, her curiosity piqued. Engrelin shoved into her arms a blanket-swaddled object.

She hugged the bundle tightly to her chest. "Your fiddle? For me?" she breathed.

"Keep it safe for me, okay? I'll play it for you the moment I get back."

"I will," promised Elmera, tracing a cross over her heart. "I won't let anyone touch it. Not Grandmother, not Father Colby, not anyone."

"Good. I'll hold you to it." Engrelin got to his feet and led Elmera back over to where Vera and Father Colby stood waiting, along with Engrelin's cousins, who had seemingly materialized out of nowhere.

Taking Elmera's fingers, Engrelin wrapped them around Vera's hand. Elmera ducked her head into the bundled fiddle, stifling a sob.

Father Colby stepped forward. "Boys, may I give you a blessing before you go?"

Engrelin, Averendier, and Andrald knelt as the sweet Latin words rolled over them. As the blessing was still being pronounced, Engrelin tilted his bowed head, sneaking a glance at the church. If only he could have had a few moments inside to kneel in front of the tabernacle, to be permeated by the scent of incense and roses, to gaze upon the winking red light that so gently and joyfully reminded the world of the Presence within.

But the next minute only found him swinging his leg over a horse's back and wheeling out of the rectory yard onto the street.

Soon, they were out and beyond the city gates.

As Engrelin crested the top of a hill with his cousins, he took one last glance at the buildings of Bryn, clustered together on the mountainside above the winding valley that led to home.

I'll come back, he promised silently. *I'll do what they've asked and come back.*

The horses trotted down the opposite side of the hill. Bryn, and everything Engrelin had ever known, sank out of sight.

13

The hatchway above slammed violently open. *At the sudden sound,* Berwyn startled and looked up. A sailor thrust his red race through the opening and bawled, "All prisoners on deck!"

Stupid thing to say, Berwyn thought, *since the only people down here are prisoners.*

People including herself. She shivered a little as she slid off the narrow bench that had been her home for the past few weeks. She was lucky to have gotten even that, she reflected as she scanned the sea of dirt-smeared faces around her. They all crowded towards the ladder that led out of the hold and up onto deck. They ascended its rungs willingly.

A soft whisper of fresh air brushed Berwyn's cheeks, and as she inhaled its clean tones, savoring them. She couldn't blame those desperate to get out. What lay in store for them up there certainly couldn't be worse than their time down in the belly of this ship.

Berwyn's hand tightened around the satchel strap that crossed her chest. She had lived a nightmare for weeks. As far as she ever knew, nightmares never improved as they went on—they always got worse and worse until she finally woke.

There was no waking up here.

"Get up there."

Berwyn strangled a gasp of surprise as a rough hand grabbed her shoulder and shoved her towards the ladder. Trembling with rage,

Berwyn hiked up her brown skirt and climbed the ladder's unsteady rungs. Never, never had she seen a human being treat another with such contempt. They made antagonizing an art. If only her father were here! She hadn't seen him since that awful day on Starr Island…

Tears burned in the back of her throat. She quickly swallowed them and pushed all thoughts of her father aside. Never would she let her captors catch the trace of a tear on her face.

Her head broke over the edge of the deck, and a wave of fresh air greeted her full in the face, so welcome after the rank air below. A scarlet-clad soldier extended his hand to help her up onto the deck. Berwyn jerked her hand away and pulled herself up onto the rough deck unaided. It was far better than accepting *his* help.

With the soldier's chuckle still resounding in her ears, Berwyn plunged herself into the throng of gaunt people crowded on the deck, hoping her face would be lost among all the others, though she wasn't exactly sure from whom she hid. Eventually, she found herself on the crowd's far outer rim, looking out over the harbor.

Four huge ships were moored to a dock dwarfed by the ships' sheer size. Four ships, including her own. Berwyn frowned. Hadn't there been eight when they left Starr Island? What had happened to the other four?

Commotion across the ship snatched her attention. Obeying the sharp orders of meticulously dressed officers, gaunt, ragged men lowered the gangplanks to the dock. Overhead, sea birds wheeled and screeched, adding their harsh voices to the anxious murmurs that rose from the prisoners' lips. Berwyn shut her eyes against it all and hugged herself tightly. From what she had seen of the drab countryside beyond the docks and the coolness of the air, she knew that she had not been brought to the place she had feared most. From the strangely relieved gleam in the eyes of those around her, she knew they had been expecting the same thing as she. Yet another worry festered in its place. If not there, then where had they been brought, and to what purpose?

The sudden, clear tolls of the ship's bell made her eyelids fly open. The crowd around her stirred, a murmur rippling through them. Beside her, a young Monarian soldier let an apprehensive breath hiss through his clenched teeth. He must have noticed her swift glance at him, for he muttered to her, "They're all out."

No doubt he meant the prisoners in the hold. Berwyn had never been particularly tall, but the man was a head taller than she and could see over the crowd.

"What is the bell for?" Berwyn whispered the question, though she couldn't imagine why. The bell seemed to have summoned a silence, one which settled taut over many hearts, including her own.

In answer, the prisoner shrugged. He gazed ahead now, tilting his head ever so slightly, watching something. Berwyn moved to the soldier's other side and leaned far out over the railing.

Only then could she see the stern deck and the man who stood on it—the man everyone seemed to be watching. Berwyn's fine eyebrows drew slightly together as she studied the man, who was presently speaking to a lieutenant. He was stocky, tanned, Blond—the most startling feature—and undeniably handsome. He didn't look like someone plotting the darkest future of the hundreds of prisoners spread out on the four ships. Yet he had to be, in some way. No man would hold himself erect in that scarlet tunic unless he were proud of it.

Everyone around her stared in the same way, the same apprehension creeping desperately towards hope as they gazed upon the embodiment of their fate.

As the last tones of the bell faded, the sea birds silenced their harsh voices and continued their eerie rounds about the mast and rigging. They, too, by some freak signal, knew to be quiet and listen to what the smiling man on the stern deck had to say.

"Friends!" The unexpected warmth of the man's voice jarred through Berwyn as he swept out one hand in a welcoming arch. "After much trial and tribulation, you have finally reached your destination."

The soldiers hemming the prisoners in goaded those on the outside into a spattering applause. The young soldier beside Berwyn shoved his hands deep into his pockets and stared defiantly up at the man. Several others around him followed his example. Lacking pockets, Berwyn latched her hands around her satchel's strap instead. Friends? Did this man think he could conquer the people of Monaria with words alone?

"We have brought you here to Kepspell to begin new lives," the man continued. He flashed a bright smile. "After all, Tirendria is truly your native soil. Your country, even! Despite what your usurper king Julian may say, Monaria and Tirendria are still one. A separation never occurred. Even now, his Majesty, Vendar, is working to restore Monaria to its rightful position within his kingdom. Until then, we have brought you here, where we hope you will wait patiently and productively for the restoration of Western Tirendria.

"We will build a community. We will work together to construct shelter and produce food! We will hunt and create. We will fill this time of war with the work of peace to advance us into a new age!"

Berwyn locked her teeth. The young soldier beside her stiffened. If looks could kill, and with the way many Monarian men were glaring, all the Tirendrians within the vicinity would have been stricken dead.

"Please, do not think of this as a captivity or an oppression! We know that you expect from us all forms of abuse. You expect to be starved, separated from your families, slaughtered without reason. But if we work together in harmony, nothing of the sort will ever happen."

"Good luck with that," a young mother beside Berwyn whispered.

Berwyn nodded in silent agreement.

Their comments were not the only ones, and for a moment the deck droned with the low hum of whispered and muttered words. The man on the stern deck held out one hand, indicating silence.

"You will be given assignments as to where you will work, according to your past skills or occupations. We will do our utmost to please everyone." His smile broadened, displaying rows of perfectly straight teeth. He stood there, hands clasped leisurely behind his back, a wolf contemplating which prisoner to kill first. A shudder coursed up Berwyn's spine.

"Kepspell is looked upon with such hope that the king himself has proposed to visit here in the winter," the man went on enthusiastically. "Let us work to make it a place worthy of his approval—"

"How dare you!" exclaimed a woman in the crowd, shaking her fist above her head.

"We're Monarians. We don't pay homage to any other than Julian," grumbled a man, shaking his head angrily.

"We'll never turn our backs on our country!" cried the young soldier beside Berwyn. Catching the rigging above his head, he sprang lightly up to stand on the railing, raising himself boldly above the crowd. "Bringing us here won't change our loyalty to our king! There will be no peace here—no working for Vendar—while that faith remains true. We will not submit to this tyranny, this mercy of our forefathers' murders. Never will—"

He got no further, for a furious Tirendrian soldier, finally rushing up behind him, brought his dagger hilt crashing against the man's head. The soldier, cut brutally short, fell to the deck. Berwyn rushed forward, instinctively reaching for her satchel, eyes already scanning the freely bleeding gash on the man's head. But as she went to sink to her knees beside him, a Tirendrian grabbed her by both shoulders and roughly shoved her back.

"Don't touch him!" ordered the soldier harshly, his voice resounding over the silent deck. "He will be seen to soon enough."

"Please, I am a *meddyg*," Berwyn pleaded quietly, though she was aware of the burn of many gazes on her turned back. "I can save anyone the trouble of tending him later."

"You will not touch him," repeated the soldier coldly, motioning her away with his dagger. "Back away."

Shaking, Berwyn obeyed, sinking back into the silent people behind her. Her gaze remained riveted on the unconscious soldier's crimson-stained hair, remaining there until two Tirendrian soldiers hurried up and bore the limp burden away. She looked back up at the man on the stern deck. He smoothed his hair back and breathed deeply.

Seeing he had the crowd's attention once more, he flung a hand towards the guards who retreated with the prisoner's body.

"See the result of rebellion and discontentment!" he cried, his voice as smooth and as unruffled as before. "We shall not be able to live peacefully together if we continue this. We must have harmony. You must respect me, Lord Warwick, as your leader, and the esteemed Lord Rees as your overlord. You must thank Captain Gatian—if he ever dares show face here—for bringing you here, to Kepspell. You must accept the jobs assigned to you willingly and carry them out efficiently. And you must accept Vendar as your sovereign!"

Another angry murmur spread through the crowd. The image of their felled fellow soldier was still as fresh in their minds as the small splatters of blood upon the deck. A sick knot tied itself in Berwyn's stomach. Was he bringing them to this already? The choice between treason…or death.

Warwick flashed them another smile, this one of understanding.

"But this is all too sudden for you," he said. "We will begin small and build upon it, just as Kepspell will be built with the work of our hands.

"To start, as you leave the ship, you will be assigned a house and a job, along with a mess number. You will join the group you are assigned to on the mainland. Do not protest your assignment," he warned. "If we see you are unable to carry it out, we will give you another. Otherwise, stick to it. There will be consequences if you do not." He motioned towards a small table that had been set up by the gangplank. The thin soldier sitting at it nodded deferentially when Warwick's gaze fell on him. Warwick clapped his hands twice, briskly. "That is all," he announced, before turning away.

"All right, you heard him. Form a line!" a sailor bellowed.

Immediately, Berwyn was jostled from all sides as the Tirendrians tailored the throng of prisoners into a line leading up to the gangplank. Once the crowd settled, she found herself sandwiched between a young couple holding each other's hands tightly, and two young men, who sheltered a little girl between them. Berwyn clenched her satchel's strap in both hands and closed her eyes tightly. If only *she* had a hand to hold. Then maybe she wouldn't feel on the verge of collapse as the wait to get off the ship stretched on and on.

Yet her turn to stand in front of the table came all too soon.

The soldier rustled a sheet of paper overtop an already large stack. Without even looking up at her, the man dipped his pen in an inkwell and inquired flatly, "Name and age?"

"Berwyn Sirman," Berwyn answered, her voice quavering slightly. She frowned at herself and gently cleared her throat, feeling conspicuous all the while. "I'm seventeen, though I'll be eighteen soon."

"Hmm." The man's pen scratched along the paper. "You're young, but I reckon you'll work hard. Reing wasn't built on the backs of sluggards, and neither will Kepspell."

The mention of Reing filled Berwyn's mouth with sawdust. Was he truly comparing Kepspell with the monstrous prison the Overthrower had constructed after defeating Justinian? Her skin prickled with fear. No man who entered that prison a prisoner ever came out unless it was feet first. That reputation had stood for hundreds of years. Her gaze drifted out at the distant landscape beyond the dock. Would it be the same here—a place no man, no matter how determined, could ever escape?

"Miss Sirman," continued the soldier, his stolid voice bowling bluntly through her thoughts. "Did you have any former occupation?"

Berwyn nodded slowly.

The man made an impatient gesture with his pen. "Would you kindly tell me what it was?"

"I was a doctor. Well, almost. My father was the head *meddyg* at Fort Starr, and I'd been training under him since I was six. I was just about to complete the course when I was…captured," she concluded haltingly.

"Transferred," returned the man smoothly, as he scribbled out this new information.

Berwyn stared bleakly at the top of his bowed head. What was the difference between either word? Both meant that she had been separated from everything—and everyone—that she had ever loved.

"But I'm afraid you won't continue that practice here," the man continued. "We have no need for doctors in Kepspell."

Berwyn's mouth dropped open to protest, but she snapped it shut before she could utter a sound. Saying something would only get herself into trouble. But her mind was in turmoil. What about the young soldier who had been knocked out? Was he to be left without treatment? Perhaps they felt that they could easily pass up one man. But hundreds?

"You have to have at least one doctor," she found herself hoarsely whispering.

The man looked up briefly, an almost amused smile playing about his lips. "Of course we do. For our soldiers."

Berwyn clamped her right arm tightly over her twisting stomach and somehow managed to say nothing she would later regret. Her shoulders rigid, as if she expected a physical blow, she asked, "What am I going to do, then? I've worked at this my whole life. I never learned to do much else."

Still staring at the paper, the man asked, "Nursing people includes making up soups and tonics and such, yes?"

"Yes," Berwyn answered uncertainly.

"Good." The man gave her a thin smile and plunked his pen back into its stand. "You'll be the director of kitchen five. Report there tomorrow morning, early, to be shown your duties. As a kitchen worker, you don't need a mess number, you just eat after all the meals have been served. You will be staying with the Artiz, Rowell, and Sirman families in cabin three." He waved his hand dismissively and turned to receive the couple, who had both turned a sickly shade of gray.

Berwyn joined the line that slowly shuffled down the gangplank to the dock below. But within her heart, a little candle of hope had been lit. The Sirman family. Did that mean only her, or was it possible...

Had her father survived the attack? Was he somewhere in that mill of people, searching for her? She swept her gaze over the sea of heads, searching for a brown one with gray just beginning to show at the temples and in the close-cut beard. It was all whirling confusion as people milled on an open stretch of ground between the docks and what appeared to be hovels, searching for loved ones. Loved ones they might never find.

She prayed she could find her father.

But what to tell him? Her heart sank at the thought. They, the elite of the medical world, were being shoved into a primitive world, a work camp filled with hovels, back-breaking work, exhausting hours, and poor food. A world where work was put before health.

A world without doctors.

"Berwyn?"

At the sound of the familiar voice, Berwyn whirled. She slumped with relief, a sob nearly escaping her lips. Something, even in this nightmare, could be good.

14

ngrelin had been on many trips, for hunting or trading.
But never one like this. Grim silence accompanied Averendier and Andrald for the first several hours. Nonetheless, Andrald—who had never been known to be blue longer than five minutes—shook his depression away with a few of his hearty (if tuneless) songs.

But as long as Averendier remained grim, Engrelin and Andrald resigned themselves to cold silence. Any attempts at cheerfulness froze the moment their eyes lighted upon Averendier's figure, stoic and upright as a statue in the saddle. Engrelin wondered if someone had forgotten to put emotions in Averendier before his cousin had been born. Or maybe, being his twin, Andrald had just absorbed all of it from him. Being exiled seemed to have not ruffled him in the least.

Strangely enough, while Engrelin resented his cousin's silence, in a way, he was grateful for it. In all the tangle and hustle of the past twenty-four hours, he'd had next to no time for thinking. Everything had happened too fast, and any decision making had been done for him.

He wanted to go back. Yank on his horse's reins and turn it around. Kick his heels into the horse's sides and gallop the whole way home. Rejoin his grandmother and Elmera. Refuse to ever leave again.

But then he would be arrested, and he was just as useful to them in jail as he was out here. Probably less. The people were demanding proof of him, evidence that he truly had his ancestor's heroic blood pumping through his veins.

Engrelin's brow creased with a frown. He wasn't the hero type. Of average height, rather poor, neither dashing nor extremely intelligent, and certainly not patient. Of course, he didn't have to be any of these things to do what Julian wanted. At least, he hoped he wouldn't.

His frown deepened. Come to think of it, he couldn't remember if his uncle or cousins had specified what they were going to do at all, only that it meant going to Northern Florenth.

Someone smacked his shoulder. Engrelin looked up in time to see Andrald settling back in his saddle, looking slightly amused.

"You know I've been talking to you and not your horse, right?" he asked.

Engrelin's cheeks tingled. "Sorry, I didn't."

"You didn't even hear a word I was saying that whole time?"

Engrelin shook his head. "Not a word."

"Head in the clouds?" Andrald asked teasingly.

Averendier glanced back at Engrelin. "Is that bow the only weapon you brought?"

Engrelin squared his shoulders, more conscious than ever of the quiver bumping lightly against his back. "Yes, it is," he said.

Averendier frowned and turned back to face the road, making no further comment.

Andrald nudged Engrelin. How did he do that without falling off his horse? Andrald looked at his brother. He leaned more towards Engrelin. "Hey," he said quietly, "Just give him a break, will you? I haven't seen him this bad since—" He broke off, catching himself before he revealed some incident locked away with the sacred key of brotherhood. "Just be easy on him today, okay?"

"Sure." Engrelin shrugged. "But if we all acted like that, because of this…"

Andrald nodded. "I know. Don't worry. We're in this for the long haul, so we need to keep cool and wait. He'll probably snap out of it in a day or two. But you know," he added, quieter, "he hates traveling by land."

Engrelin glanced back at Averendier's stiff frame. One wouldn't know that from his bearing. He was a good horseman, his body moving lightly even with the tired horse's clopping.

He turned back to Andrald and asked, "What was it you wanted to tell me in the first place?"

Andrald smacked his thigh lightly, venting his astonishment. "I clean forgot!" he exclaimed. "Averendier wanted us to look out for a good camping place. We need to stop soon." He raised his eyes meaningfully to the swiftly deepening shadows around them.

Engrelin frowned. In the past five minutes, he had seen several places he had thought worth looking into. If he had only known Averendier was preparing to bed down.

"What is his idea of a good spot?" he asked.

"This looks good," Averendier said, catching his brother with his mouth open to answer Engrelin.

Engrelin looked doubtfully at the copse Averendier had pulled his horse up beside. It was too close to the road, and the glade didn't go back far enough.

Andrald, unaware of Engrelin's disapproval of the place, leaned forward and whispered, "Does this give you an idea?"

Engrelin snorted. It gave him an idea, all right. His cousins may be fluent in several different languages, have met a king or two in their lifetimes and even captained their own ships, but they knew precious little of woods life. He burned to say so, but one look at Averendier's taut face checked him.

He slipped off his horse and led it into the tree line after Averendier, biting his lower lip as his stiff legs reminded him of how infrequently he rode.

Andrald grinned. "Been awhile since you took a ride?"

"Usually, when I'm with horses, they're pulling something, and I'm behind that," Engrelin answered, as they tied their horse's reins to a horizontal branch.

Andrald cocked his head as he lifted his saddle off his horse's back. "Funny how we can go anywhere and everywhere, and not care a whit, and you're just..." He stopped, flushing a little—perhaps at what he had considered saying next.

"Happy as a farmer to stay home and just do what I love?" Despite himself and the horrible day, Engrelin's mouth tugged into a smile. "There's a lot of good in staying home, you know. It's what most people do. Besides," he added practically, "What would all you nobles do with yourselves if we all decided to leave our farms and didn't give a single turnip to the manor?"

A broad smile broke out on Andrald's face. "Take hoeing and plowing lessons from you guys," he chuckled.

"There's a whole lot more to farming than that," Engrelin said, shaking his head. "And you'd have to learn *cymraeg* to understand what any of us are saying half the time."

"I'll pass," Andrald relented with a sheepish shrug. "I'd be old and gray before I learn that gibberish."

"Pass me the tinder box?" Averendier spoke up from behind them.

As Andrald hurried to get the fire-starting kit for his brother, Engrelin finished pulling the horses' tack off and picketed them inside the tiny clearing Averendier had decided upon. The openness of the place made him uneasy, even if the clearing was small—hardly fifteen feet in diameter. He should have been paying more attention to Andrald in the first place. He could have pointed out a better place before Averendier lost patience with him. He glanced over at his cousins, who both crouched on the ground, attempting to start a fire. Already, he saw the flickering of young flames, destined to die in a few seconds. Inwardly, he sighed and stooped to break some small twigs from the bottom of some scrubby bushes.

Wordlessly, he walked over to the struggling fire, knelt beside it, and slipped the thread-like twigs onto a smoldering pile of needles. As they burned in the fire's last desperate reach for life, he rearranged the logs set around them to protect the small flames from the steady breeze that was blowing. He sat back on his heels to watch the fire climb eagerly up its shelter.

Engrelin felt the burn of Averendier's gaze on his turned head. The look clearly said, "I could have done that myself" and maybe more, if Engrelin had chosen to meet it for longer. His cheeks and throat burned, though not from the smoke blowing in his face. All this telling himself he didn't have anything to prove to anyone, and here he was doing exactly that.

"Are the horses settled for the night?" asked Averendier. Pointedly, with great care not to burn himself, he shifted the logs back the way he had originally placed them, much to the pain of the fire, which sputtered again.

Engrelin's fingernails dug into his palms. His cousin's eyes, cold and gray and condescending, made everything in him squirm angrily.

You should see to your own horse, he thought, though he had already picketed and rubbed the horses.

"Yes," he said shortly.

Andrald silently plucked some of the browning moss at his feet, tossing the bits restlessly into the fire.

Engrelin got up from the fire (which, despite Averendier's adjustments, still burned), retrieved his pack and sat back down with it open in his lap.

It broke the stiff inactivity, and soon they sat around a small but cheerful blaze, eating their cold supper.

"I could probably catch a rabbit or two along the road tomorrow," Engrelin commented as he pulled a wrapped hunk of bread from his stores.

Averendier frowned but said nothing against the proposal as he continued to eat indifferently in the stifling silence.

Engrelin watched his stoic cousin a moment, struggling with the questions he had wanted to ask for so long but had never been given the chance to ask. However, as he watched Averendier, Engrelin decided that no matter what happened in the world, it could never be more puzzling than this cousin of his.

Giving up on Averendier entirely, Engrelin shifted towards Andrald and asked quietly, "Andrald, what exactly happened at Fort Starr?"

Surprise flashed across Andrald's face. "Fort Starr?" he repeated.

Engrelin nodded. It hurt like a knife-cut to even mention the place, but it was growing into an almost fear of the unknown. Besides the fact that the place had been routed and gutted, he knew nothing. And he had to know. There was always the chance his family still lived.

"You were there, right?" he pressed, while Andrald still hesitated. "Why did the Tirendrians abandon it instead of using it for their own base?"

"The only reason it was overwhelmed in the first place was the impediment of civilians," Averendier spoke up. He was staring into the fire as he spoke, though a deeper and hotter fire burned within his eyes. "The Tirendrians knew the same thing would happen to them once we launched our counterattack."

"*If* they kept the prisoners," Engrelin pointed out, though his stomach turned at doing so. "If they hadn't, they could have just defended it. From what I remember Dad telling me, it was well stocked."

"They obviously had some use for the prisoners themselves," said Averendier, decidedly grim.

A chill prickled up Engrelin's spine as he tried not to think of what those reasons were.

"But there were also the people in the cellars," Andrald reminded.

Engrelin looked questioningly at them both. "People in cellars?"

Andrald looked over at his brother. But he only pulled his supper out of his pack.

"Some were soldiers," said Andrald with a small sigh. "But only about a dozen of them."

"Fifteen," Averendier corrected. "Along with forty-one women and children. But the soldiers were all badly wounded."

Engrelin's eyebrows knit. "How did they get down there in the first place?" he asked. "Did the women drag them?"

Averendier shook his head. "The men were always alone in the cellars. None of the civilian survivors have any idea what happened to them, and the soldiers have been too sick to tell, if they even know themselves."

Engrelin fell quiet. He had already caught snatches of hearsay that had managed to reach *Traeth Euriad*. But he still wanted to talk about Northern Florenth, especially now that Averendier seemed to be in a slightly better mood.

"Where are we going now, exactly?" he asked, tracing his finger through the ashes edging the fire.

He could already feel the tension return slightly. But he felt it was a fair question that Averendier couldn't refuse answering.

"We're going to Northern Florenth," Averendier said quietly.

Engrelin stiffened with irritation. "Yes, I know that," he said shortly. "I mean *where* in Northern Florenth. It's huge."

"Elstar," Averendier replied.

Engrelin's forehead puckered thoughtfully. His uncle had pointed out that city to him before on one of those big maps he kept. The string of details with which Austinian had filled the lesson muddled Engrelin's understanding of the place. However, one thing stood clear in his memory.

"Isn't that where…" He groped for a name and finally gave up altogether. "Where the king of Northern Florenth lives?"

"If you mean Wilelm, then yes," Averendier said.

Engrelin sat forward. "Are we going to him? And how would that help things at home?"

Even Andrald looked a little surprised. A slight heat rose to Engrelin's cheeks. It was a naïve question, he knew, but he wasn't going to get the answer to anything unless he was point-blank about it.

"We have an alliance with Wilelm," Andrald said.

Engrelin shot him a dark look. "I know at least *that* much," he said. "Do alliances expire?"

Again that horrified look from Andrald.

But Averendier only said quietly, "Not expired, Engrelin. Uncertain. We've heard rumors that Wilelm is considering terminating its alliance with Monaria."

"Rumors?" Engrelin echoed dubiously.

"Even rumors have to have some seed of truth to grow," Averendier said. "We're learning—sometimes the hard way—to pay some attention to them. Like Vendar's oath of vengeance."

Engrelin looked down and absently flicked a twig into the fire. If this rumor turned out to be true… Wilelm was their closest ally besides Alinar. And Alinar took longer to reach—they would have had to skirt the Anailwch mountains that stretched across Monaria's southern border before they could be of any assistance to Julian. Monaria was the smallest country in Ontaria; compared to Tirendria, it was miniscule. Without Wilelm's protection, it wouldn't take long for Monaria to be reduced to ashes.

And how will we help? he wondered, his hand curling with frustration. Did Julian think they could simply talk Wilelm out of his decision?

He realized Andrald had been watching him closely.

"I have a map, if you would like to see our route on that," he offered.

Engrelin perked. Though illiterate, if people read out the names of places on a map to him, he could read the legend and landscape fairly well. Seeing the journey on paper would make him feel a whole lot less like he was plunging blindly into the unknown.

"Sure," he agreed.

"Hold on." Andrald scrambled up. "It's in my saddle. Let me get it."

When he returned, the boys spread the large map out on the uneven ground, pinning the curling edges down with stones.

Engrelin sat back on his heels beside the map and soaked the whole thing in. Deserts, bodies of water, mountains, and forests glimmered in varying shades of gold, blue, gray, and emerald. The compass rose set in one corner was adorned with painted precious stones. Scrolls rolled out along the map's edges.

Engrelin gingerly touched one corner of the map, almost afraid it would disintegrate beneath his fingers.

"You brought this with you?" he breathed in wonder. "I bet it cost a *tunell* to make this thing."

"More, probably," Andrald said, not without a hint of pride, but so jovially that no one could accuse him of bragging. "But if a man's got a good map, he'll never be lost. That's what Dad's always saying."

Engrelin gave a little nod of affirmation.

Andrald cleared his throat importantly and bent over the map. Picking up a slender pine needle, he began using it to point things out on the map, starting in the hills set in Monaria's far north. "This is where we are right now," he said. The pine needle's point skimmed along the painted canvas. "This is Bryn. And this is *Traeth Euriad*."

They had been pointed out to him before, but never on a map this large. Engrelin squinted down in disbelief at the pinpricks that marked those familiar places. They were puny compared to the rest of the world.

"Where's Fort Starr?" he asked.

Andrald pointed to a cluster of tiny dots in the middle of the Northern Sea: the Tinannakin Islands. Engrelin nearly shook his head. Those were even punier.

"What about Highlynn?"

It turned out to be another tiny island, nearer to the point that jutted out from Monaria's northwestern shore.

Engrelin sat back. How big would he be on this map? He shifted uncomfortably. To his family and friends, he was something that could be seen and heard and touched. He could be hurt and loved. Compared to a world this size, what was he? His existence hardly effected anything. His life—and death—was simply another drop in the ocean. He was one of millions, maybe even billions, of the lower class. He was just there to provide food for the nobles and scrape out a life for himself in between.

Yet here he was now, amid something he'd never dreamed of doing—which he certainly didn't want to do. He was going to go help renew an alliance. Engrelin stared at the map, skimming over all its jumbled landscape and castles, finding his eyes drawn to the area he knew to be Tirendria. It dwarfed all the countries around it; the only one daring to rival it was the untamed Southernlands. How could any of them even dare to stand up against it?

He shook the thought away. "Where's Elstar?" he asked.

Andrald let his pine needle pointer drift down to a solemn gray fortress painted close to the southern border.

"That's not too far," Engrelin murmured.

"Only three or four days' riding, once we get out of Tirendria," Andrald agreed, nodding.

Engrelin's head snapped up. "Tirendria?" he repeated sharply.

Andrald sighed. "There's no other way through, unless you want to die trying to pass over the *Anailwch*."

"And we won't die in Tirendria?" Engrelin countered.

Andrald shrugged. "Julian declared war on them only yesterday, after he got word about the attack on Highlynn. I don't think any of the patrols on the border have heard of it yet, so they won't be too hard to slip past."

"Men guarding the border?" Engrelin gave his cousin the look.

Andrald waved dismissively. "Details."

"I happen to like details," Engrelin returned, scowling slightly. He bent thoughtfully over the map again. "But what about on our way back? News will have reached them by then."

Andrald only waved his hand again. "Don't try to cross bridges until you come to them," he replied.

Pursing his lips, Engrelin continued to scan the map. There were many places he didn't recognize, but he didn't feel like asking his cousins what they were. Averendier had completely drawn away from the conversation, and even Andrald was beginning to stare off into the distance, his head resting in his cupped hand.

"I'm going to bed," Engrelin said softly.

Andrald didn't seem to hear him. His eyes were riveted to the map.

Engrelin crawled to where his pack lay, yanked out his woolen blanket, and tucked it under his head. Huddled close to the fire and wrapped in his cloak, he found himself surprisingly warm and drowsy. The sharp ache in his legs subsided. Even his blistered feet succumbed to the powerful waves of sleep washing over him. Drowsily, he murmured his prayers, the final "amen" slurring on his deepening breaths.

15

Sometime later, Engrelin drifted out of a dreamless sleep. He knew from the blackness beyond his eyelids that it was still night. He stirred and settled down further into his cloak. Moving seemed almost impossible, but pleasantly so. He couldn't imagine what might have woken him; the only sound he heard was the steady, even breathing of his sleeping cousins. His head nodded back into the crook of his arm, and everything started slipping back into a fuzzy darkness.

Crack!

Startled, Engrelin's eyes flickered. He lay frozen, his muscles aching with tension as he listened. He could hardly hear a thing over his ragged breathing. But he knew he didn't have to listen so hard. Whatever had broken that stick was heavy and close.

Something shuffled through the litter of leaves on the ground. Another stick snapped. An oath muttered through the darkness.

Ever-so-slightly, Engrelin turned his head and sent his gaze darting around camp. His thin breath caught in the back of his throat.

Over Averendier's slumped form bent a dark figure. The campfire's low-burning embers threw a lurid sheen onto something clutched in the stranger's hand. Engrelin's heart stuttered to a halt, and he shifted his eyes wildly about, searching for his quiver. It lay on its side, a couple yards away. He threw another glance towards the figure, who moved soundlessly to Andrald and bent to inspect him. As the stranger turned, the firelight glinted on a knife clutched in his right hand.

Engrelin grit his teeth and scooted back across the root-ridden ground towards his quiver. His eyes remained fixed on the stranger's turned back.

Engrelin's fingers just brushed his quiver's leather strap when the stranger turned. Engrelin froze and closed his eyes, struggling to keep his breathing steady even while his heart galloped out of his chest. So close! If only the man would pass him up, just as he had the twins…

For a few agonizing seconds, everything was dead quiet save the stranger's stealthy, advancing tread. A rough, warm hand pushed his hair back from his forehead. It was everything Engrelin could do to keep striking.

A voice, harsh even in a whisper. "Here you are."

Engrelin tore away in a swift roll to one side. His hands flashed to snatch up his quiver. Behind him, he heard the thud and felt the tug of the knife being buried in the empty folds of his cloak.

Spitting a curse, the stranger sprang back as Engrelin sprang onto one knee and frantically nocked an arrow. The intruder streaked past, his silhouette dark against the light the fire cast. Another form detached itself from the shadows and fled after the man. Engrelin started violently, and his first shot went awry. Two of them! He recovered quickly and, snapping his bow back in their line of flight, he fired a second arrow. The second person screamed and stumbled, the arrow protruding from his shoulder. The first man caught him by the wrist and yanked him into the woods.

At the cry, Engrelin's whole being numbed. The bow slipped from his hands which were slick with sweat. *Angel with me and Lord have mercy. I didn't just kill someone, did I?*

A hand fell on his shoulder. Engrelin spun away from it with a sharp cry, falling to the ground and doubling both fists for a fight.

But instead of attacking him, the person shook him vigorously. Engrelin clenched his teeth to keep them from clacking together.

"Engrelin? Engrelin, can you even hear me?" a wonderfully familiar voice cried. "Are you even awake? Snap out of it and answer me!"

"Stop, stop!" Engrelin exclaimed, grasping his cousin's hands and trying to pry them off his arms.

Andrald released Engrelin, letting him fall a few inches back onto the ground, and bent to peer anxiously in his face.

"What in Ontaria was that for?" Engrelin demanded.

Andrald only bent closer. "Are you sure you're awake?" he asked. "Do you do this all the time at home?"

"Do what?" Engrelin asked, sitting up and rubbing his elbows. "Shoot intruders who are trying to murder me? No, I never had to."

"Intruders?" Andrald looked around quickly, then back at Engrelin. The boy was surprised to see doubt lining Andrald's brow.

"You don't believe me?" Engrelin sat up all the way.

"I didn't see anyone," he said. "Only you, shooting at nothing."

Engrelin passed a hand quickly over his eyes. "You didn't see anyone? Hear anything?" The wounded person's scream still resounded in his ears.

Andrald thought a moment. "I thought I might have heard a taegr. That's why I woke up. All I saw after that was you shooting thin air."

Engrelin shook his head. "No, it wasn't a taegr. I shot someone." He nearly shivered at the words. He had never felt like this after shooting an animal. Or even after getting into a scrap. He hadn't felt any guilt when he heard Walche had been hurt when he'd pushed him into that table.

But that scream. It had sounded deeper than pain.

Andrald stared directly into his eyes. "Engrelin, I have no idea what you're talking about," he said. "I was awake, and I didn't see a soul. You must have been dreaming or something."

Engrelin's mouth fell open in protest. "I wasn't dreaming," he insisted. "I saw someone. They looked at you two, and at me. He had a knife."

Andrald shook his head. "There haven't been highwaymen in these parts for years, Engrelin," he said. "And the horses are completely quiet. You must have been dreaming."

"If you'd just—"

"Really, Engrelin, that's enough," Andrald said. "We're not going to get any sleep at this point, and we have an early start tomorrow. Everything will be clearer in the morning, I'm sure."

"But…" Engrelin stopped, realizing from the steel in Andrald's eyes that he was not to be convinced. He muttered an apology, and Andrald stumbled back to his cloak. As Engrelin watched, he saw Averendier sit up and quietly say something to Andrald.

Engrelin looked away and awkwardly stretched himself back out on the ground, tucking one arm beneath his head. He knew that Andrald would tell his brother everything. By morning, Averendier too would be convinced that Engrelin shot arrows in his sleep.

Gritting his teeth, he rolled over, putting his back to them both. Had it been a dream?

Don't think about it, he told himself viciously. *Just go to sleep and forget about the whole thing until tomorrow.*

But sleep was just as evasive as the truth. The poor campground Averendier had chosen proved itself truly horrible. The cramps returned to his limbs, and every root and lump beneath him vied for how uncomfortable they could be. He found himself tossing, then freezing to listen tersely to the slightest noises around him. The low hoot of an owl jarred through him like the roar of an explosion. The wind rustling the leaves muttered over and over, *here he is, here he is,* alerting the whole world of his presence, flying the message on whispering wings through the forest.

Dawn came as pink light slipping and twining through the tree branches, followed by a timid peach glow on the eastern horizon. Engrelin sat up on his torturous bed, his cloak falling from his shoulders and pooling around him in a crumpled semi-circle. Sighing wearily, Engrelin scrubbed a hand through his tousled hair. He rose to examine the campsite.

He could find no unusual markings on the ground. No blood where he thought he had shot the man. After a long and fruitless search, he gave up and joined his cousins in saddling up the horses. Neither said anything to him. He said nothing in return. He knew both were thinking about last night. After his failure to find any evidence, he didn't want to discuss it.

He lifted his saddle from the branch on which it had rested overnight and turned to place it on his horse's withers, when he felt a tug of resistance from his cloak. He looked back and saw a branch sticking through a tear in his cloak. Slowly, he lowered the saddle to the ground and reached back to free himself from the clinging branch. His fingers felt the slash, exploring its even edges. A clean cut. No branch could have made that.

Only a blade.

16

"Tore that on a branch this morning, didn't you?" Andrald asked as he leaned over Engrelin's shoulder, watching him stitch the rent in his cloak closed.

"Don't think so," Engrelin answered, looking up briefly from his work,

"I saw it catch on that branch, Engrelin," Andrald said quietly, before moving away.

Engrelin made no reply. He knew a mere branch wasn't enough to tear his cloak this badly, unless he had snatched the saddle off it and ran. Besides, the cut was too clean. But he wasn't going to push anything. His cousins hadn't spoken about last night's incident all day. He certainly wasn't going to bring it back up. Best let sleeping dogs lie. What did it matter if Averendier and Andrald thought he raved like a lunatic in his sleep? Let them believe it, so long as it didn't harm their mission and they got home safely.

Engrelin snapped the tail end of his thread from the finished patch and tucked the needle away in his pack, sealing the repair.

The following week passed pleasantly enough. Though Engrelin was frustrated with his cousin's discussions about things he hadn't heard of, or the poor camping grounds Averendier always chose, he enjoyed their company. The traveling itself was easy—born and raised in the mountains, he thrived off the winding roads and steep climbs.

The countryside itself made every bend they turned beautiful and exciting. Valleys sunk in mountains' midst held villages in their wide bowls. Forests were aflame with autumn. Willows wept over mossy creek banks. Waterfalls hurled their glistening waters down mountainsides into silver ribbons of rivers below.

The only thing missing was Lance, Engrelin thought sadly as he rode through a scarlet strip of woods. Yet another thing he wished he hadn't been forced to leave behind. Lance would have loved something like this, even more than Engrelin. Lance had always been the one seeking out adventure, concocting a thousand different ways to keep Bryn on its toes.

Next time, he told himself, without thinking whether he would actually do anything like this again. In his heart of hearts, he prayed not. For though the scenery he passed was stunning, and the goal he strove to reach was good, nothing would satisfy him until he had once again glimpsed the rolling hills of his home.

Tirendria was everything Engrelin had imagined: a dark, gloomy conifer forest, entangled with vines that twisted and strangled the life out of the gray trunks that shot up at the unguarded northern border and stretched on. And on.

The trio pressed cautiously forward into the tangle. A day passed beneath the dark canopy—a day in which Engrelin was sure he spoke no more than ten words. A darkness, the cause or source of which was unexplainable, hung heavily in the air. The only comfort with them was that the journey through the cursed land would only last a few days.

Engrelin glanced nervously at the shadowy trunks hemming the path in, then looked up into the billowing green clouds of conifer needles above. Though nearly noon, an eerie twilight reigned, as it did every day, sunup to sundown. The thick conifer branches blotted out almost every trace of light. Engrelin pulled his cloak tighter around his shoulders. He had seen a few places like this in Monaria, but never had they stretched for so long, or been too dense and foreboding.

"I wonder what this place was like, before the overthrowing." Whether he murmured it to Andrald, who rode beside him, or to himself, or to something else entirely, Engrelin didn't know.

For several long seconds, Andrald didn't answer. He only nodded. "Probably not like this," he said. "Justinian was a magnificent ruler. Though," he added, shooting a few glances around, "I doubt that would affect the landscape much."

"Do you think Tirendria could ever return to that?" Engrelin asked in a hushed voice. Nothing above a whisper could be spoken in this place. That would simply be asking for trouble.

Andrald hesitated. "Well..."

"Not just for Monaria, though," Engrelin plunged on. "I mean for all of Ontaria. Regain the Tirendrian throne, even. After all, Julian is of Anna's blood. By all rights, the throne is his to take."

"Easier said than done," Andrald said. "Vendar and his men would have to be wiped out before we could consider putting someone good on that throne. As long as any of them are alive, we'll have no rest."

"But Anna was Tirendrian," Engrelin persisted. "Don't you think—"

"Engrelin, Anna was of *Old* Tirendria," Andrald exclaimed in a whisper. "They don't think of her as one of them. All the Tirendrian kings nowadays are of the Overthrower's bloodline."

"Could we get it by force?"

"No," said Andrald flatly. "It would take a miracle to get rid of Vendar and clear the way. The man's a monster."

Engrelin clenched his jaw. "I'd like to fix him myself," he muttered.

"I'd like to see you try," Andrald laughed. "But it'll be impossible for anyone to get close to him. He isn't going to be out fighting with his soldiers like his father was, and let himself get killed. He let his soldiers do the dirty work for him." He paused. "Has anyone told you about what happened in Eastern Florenth?"

"If it has to do with what the Tirendrians have done there, I don't want to hear it," Engrelin said, gazing uneasily ahead.

"I think you should. We learned something new just before we left Bryn. Last month, the Tirendrians completed the campaign over there. All through last year, they've been bringing back every able-bodied man they've captured, and are pressing them into their own armies." Andrald scowled fiercely. "The Eastern Florenthians make up a third of Tirendria's army now. How long do you think it will take Vendar to swallow us whole, along with the rest on Ontaria, especially if Wilelm no longer backs us?"

Andrald spoke as if their terrible fate were already sealed, and doom hovered on the horizon. Engrelin shifted uncomfortably in his saddle, darting glances into the thick foliage surrounding them. With his free hand, he fingered the contents of his quiver and stared bleakly at Averendier, who rode several yards ahead. The waving branches around them seemed to be steadily encroaching on the road. Shifting in his saddle again, he turned back to Andrald.

"You sound too much like Averendier," he remarked gloomily.

Andrald looked up quickly, startled. Then he chuckled and shook his head. "Maybe I did," he admitted. He frowned again. "It's just this place. I can't get over it. It doesn't *feel* right."

"No kidding." Engrelin threw back his head to view the branches overhead, which waved in warning.

"Averendier said that we should be crossing the border today," Andrald continued, still casting about uneasily. "Thank goodness. This place gives me the creeps."

"Yeah." Engrelin let his hand travel down to the limp water-skin hanging from his saddle's pommel. It was stone dry, and had been since he had woken up that morning. Not because they had failed to fill them—they had been stretched to their fullest when the boys had lain down to sleep. Something capable of twisting the caps off and on without puncturing the skins had drained all the water out of them. If his cousins had thought it unusual, they hadn't said so. They probably thought the caps had been put on too loosely, letting the water leak out overnight.

Engrelin thought the intruders he had seen their first night out were responsible. But knowing what his cousins would think of that theory, he had kept his mouth shut. A mouth as dry as the empty waterskins.

"I wish this place would give us less creeps and more creeks," he muttered.

Andrald chuckled and patted his own empty water-skin. "Me too."

Just as they rounded a bend, Andrald stood in his stirrups. He smiled back at Engrelin. "Looks like we got our wish," he said.

Just around the next bend stood a rickety bridge, which spanned a wide creek.

"Are we crossing that?" Engrelin asked skeptically.

"Yep."

"Shh," Averendier warned. With an expert twitch of his reins, he pulled his horse off to one side of the road, out of the bridge's sight. His companions followed his example.

"Here's where it gets tricky," said Averendier, dismounting.

"The bridge does look old," Engrelin agreed as he slid off his mount, "but I don't think it's bad enough to have a conference."

Averendier shook his head. "Crossing is easy," he said. "This creek marks the Monarian/Tirendrian border. Just on the other side is a Tirendrian guard post. They'll stop us to hear our business, and once they hear that…" he trailed off meaningfully.

Engrelin gave Averendier a look. "You're just telling me this now?"

"I told you when we first started that there might be a patrol," Andrald reminded.

"But you said that there wouldn't be any trouble."

"We still don't think there will be," Averendier said. "As far as I know, there's hardly anyone stationed out here to guard the road. Not many people come this way. But to be safe, we came up with a plan to get around it without notice."

"A plan?"

"Yes."

"That 'we' came up with? 'We' meaning you two…without me?"

Averendier's expression hardened. "Yes, without you. Your tactical skills are—"

Andrald elbowed his brother sharply, giving in to a fit of coughing.

"—are… doubtful," Averendier amended

Engrelin glared blackly. *I wish you would have at least talked it over with me first.*

"We need you because you can speak *cymraeg*, and neither of us can," Averendier continued. "And since we're better known, being admiral's sons, we're more likely to get recognized if the Tirendrians see us. We're carrying papers meant only for Wilem's eyes. If they suspected us, they'd search our things and find them. We'd never reach Northern Florenth."

"Because I can speak a peasant's language?" The words tumbled sarcastically from Engrelin's mouth before he could stop them. "I'm touched."

"Touched or not, you're going to do this," Averendier said sharply, his tone making Engrelin long to rebel more than ever. "If the Tirendrians find these papers, we're through."

Averendier's plan wasn't as bad as Engrelin had thought it would be.

It was worse. Much, much worse than anything he thought Averendier capable of concocting.

For his part would require him to come face-to-face to the thing he dreaded most.

But his cousin was right. This was the only way to cross the border without being searched for the papers.

Moments before, they had crossed the rickety bridge. It lay just behind them now, swaying precariously in the gentle breeze.

Averendier and Andrald slipped into the screen of trees with their horses, bearing Engrelin's pack and his mount's tack with them. Gripping his horse's rope bridle in his hand, he tore his eyes from his cousins' backs and looked down the fearful stretch of road ahead.

His horse, sensing Engrelin's uneasiness, pawed the road and tossed its head restlessly. Engrelin reached and patted its neck, murmuring soothingly to it under his breath as he counted the three minutes it would take for his cousins to get deep enough in the woods without being heard at the guard post.

Once he finished counting, Engrelin guided his horse down the road, keeping it at a slow walk.

With every step the horse took, his throat swelled larger and larger. Did his cousins really think something like this would work? If the Tirendrians realized there were people sneaking through the woods past their patrol, they wouldn't care a gnat for the peasant-ish boy using the road like every respectable being in creation.

Engrelin forced himself to take a deep breath. Then he laughed weakly. His first real scrape with Tirendrians, and he was this scared? Good luck to him if he ever met anyone on the battlefield.

It was all rather simple, really. He had lost his horse in the woods and had to go after it. He lived around here. The Tirendrian post was just as unexpected as the trees around him. What if they'd never seen him before? He knew they were there.

Engrelin smiled to himself. Next time, he would help develop the plan, at least for believability's sake. What fool didn't think a Tirendrian guard post a threat?

Suddenly, a bird burst out of the brush along the roadside. Engrelin's horse whinnied and sprang to one side, nearly jerking the reins out of his hands.

Engrelin grit his teeth as the spooked horse charged forward. He leaned forward towards the neck. The horse's mane lashed his face. He didn't dare call out to stop it. He would just let it run itself out. Hopefully, the Tirendrians didn't think he was trying to speed past them.

The horse tore around a bend. Yells and curses greeted it. The horse jerked to a sudden halt. Engrelin, clinging with his hands and knees, kept his seat

"*Nos da!* And what's this?" someone exclaimed in *cymraeg*. Hands seized the horse's dragging reins.

Straightening, Engrelin quickly took in his surroundings. Five Tirendrian soldiers in scarlet military tunics stood around him, staring at him. Not hostilely, Engrelin noted with relief. They actually looked amused.

"Is this yours?" One of them asked, motioning to the horse.

Engrelin nodded and wiped his forearm across his forehead. "My *ceffyl* was startled by a bird coming out of the brush," he quickly explained. Inwardly, he thought, *that bird must have been an angel!* But he made no move to regain his horse's reins.

The Tirendrians exchanged glances. "Hadn't Cuthrell wanted a horse?" one of them asked the others.

A shot of panic surged through Engrelin.

The Tirendrians shoved their companion. "Come on, stop fooling," One, obviously the leader, ordered. "We're not going to waste all our time on a kid and his horse. Let him have it, just pat him down first." He looked up at Engrelin. "Get down."

Engrelin stiffened, but slipped from the saddle. Resistance would only arouse their suspicion. He nearly recoiled as one of the soldier's ran his hands roughly over his body. He drew Engrelin's cyllel out of its sheath, inspected its razor-sharp blade, and slid it back into its sheath.

"Let me see your quiver," the soldier ordered.

Wordlessly, Engrelin slid the quiver off his shoulder and held it out for inspection.

"Check his boots," ordered the soldier as he poked among Engrelin's arrows.

"You heard him," said another soldier, motioning at Engrelin with his drawn sword. "Off with them."

Good thing Averendier and Andrald went through the woods. Engrelin pulled his boots off his feet. While the Tirendrians groped inside them, the leader returned Engrelin's quiver.

"You're clean," he grunted grudgingly. "Take your horse and go."

Feeling contaminated, Engrelin drew on his boots. He took his horse's halter from the Tirendrians, all too glad to turn his back to them and continue his way down the road. Though everything in him urged to run, to get away from the soldiers as soon as possible, Engrelin forced his legs to slowly move forward, one casual step after another, as if he hadn't a fear in the world.

They'd been almost too gentle for truth. Perhaps, even now, they regretted letting him go, and were slipping their fingers in their crossbows' triggers. Engrelin's spine tingled. He could barely keep himself from looking back over his shoulder.

Finally he rounded a sharp turn in the road. He slowly let out the breath he hadn't realized he'd been holding. Out of the Tirendrians' sight at last.

He continued leading his horse down the road, just in case the Tirendrians were still watching him. A few yards ahead lay a small path which branched off the trail. The conifer-flanked path led to a building set far back from the road. Engrelin could barely see it through the screen of branches. He didn't need to see it clearly to know it was the guard post.

He turned away, his steps quickening. The place was probably empty right now, with all the soldiers he had seen on the road. But he couldn't be sure.

Engrelin reached over his shoulder, drew his strung bow out of the quiver, and nocked an arrow on its string. Just in case. Every nerve in his body straining, he pressed on down the road.

Something rustled in the underbrush beside him. Whipping around, Engrelin tremblingly pointed his bow towards the patch of woods.

"Who's there?" he called.

No answer. Only more rustling. Engrelin swiftly pulled the string back and fired an arrow into the brush.

"What on—Really!" someone exclaimed.

A pale but indignant Andrald broke out of the tree line, branches and brush crackling loudly as he shoved them aside. One of his loose sleeves was slashed from the passage of an arrow.

The warmth drained from Engrelin's face. Yet he couldn't help feeling an inkling of satisfaction, for the arrow had struck right where he wanted to. From the lack of blood, he knew the arrow had merely passed through Andrald's shirt without wounding him.

"That's what you get for sneaking up on me like that," Engrelin said.

"I didn't sneak," Andrald retorted.

"You didn't answer me either."

"I was busy trying to get this stirrup untangled." He held up the offending object. "These things weren't designed to be carried long distances, or they wouldn't have made them so grabby."

"Sorry."

His hand dropped to his sleeve, feeling the slash. Something like admiration shone in his gray eyes. "You could shoot a bullseye in the dark, couldn't you?"

Unease rippled through the warmth of praise. Engrelin took the arrow from his cousin's hand and tucked it back into his quiver. Of all his accomplishments, a certain shot in the dark was not one he liked to recall.

One thing was sure: if Andrald knew of it, he would be commenting on more than mere skill. Engrelin's hands grew slick at the thought.

Andrald's eyes narrowed with concern. "You all right?" he asked. "You're a bit pasty."

"Wouldn't you, if you'd just come face to face with a Tirendrian?" Engrelin returned as he unstrung his bow.

Andrald grinned sheepishly and shrugged. "So, since you're here, I take it you survived?"
"Stroke of luck," Engrelin muttered. "Horse got spooked and ran. The patrol caught us both. Other than a frisking, I'm fine."

"Glad to hear that," said Averendier, as he emerged from the brush, leading the other two horses. "Now that everything worked out pretty well, I think we will be able to agree on plans from now on without any fuss."

Hot color rushed back to Engrelin's cheeks, but he kept his lips pinched tightly shut. Andrald silently transferred Engrelin's bridle back onto his mount.

The remainder of the day passed sullenly. Save when he gave orders, Averendier was silent. Andrald only hummed under his breath now and then when Averendier looked preoccupied enough not to rebuke him. Engrelin's silent fuming only intensified with every second that passed. Completely bereft of appetite, he skipped his supper when they set up camp that night, simply wrapping himself in his cloak, hollow and sick to his stomach. His cousins, after a quiet meal, followed suit. The soft, steady wheeze of their breathing soon told him that they had both fallen asleep.

With a sigh, Engrelin turned onto his side and stared aimlessly into the low-burning fire. Though he had spent little time with his cousins before, Averendier had never been so cold or irritable as he was now. Was it because of something Engrelin had done? Or was it merely the result of Averendier's pride being crushed after being so ignominiously treated by his own country? A country that had only, weeks before, lauded him as a splendid captain and promising future Monarian admiral.

A root dug sharply below Engrelin's shoulder blade, so he turned again. The higher you were, the harder you fell. How much more painful was it to be pulled down through no fault of your own?

Engrelin stared up into the charcoal sky, his thoughts warping with exhaustion, yet sleep tarried. If he shut his eyes, the darkness pressed lightly on them, but not enough to send him into unconsciousness.

At some point in the night, a soft sound broke through his drifting. Rolling his head to one side, Engrelin quickly cast about the camp. Near him, beneath their blankets, his cousins were twin gray humps. A dark shadow wavered across their forms, trembling in the light the dying fire cast. Shivering with a sudden, keen chill, Engrelin followed the shadow up to its source.

Someone bent over the fire, stretching their shaking hands out towards the warmth. Engrelin shut his eyes and looked again. Still there.

Not again.

Groaning softly under his breath, Engrelin reached for his quiver.

The person by the fire sprang up and whirled. Engrelin held perfectly still. The stranger's shadowed eyes burned through him. Then the figure turned and sprang away, melting into the darkness beneath the trees.

Engrelin sat up stiffly, his brows knit, and drew his strung bow into his lap, keeping his quiver close at hand. As he sat there, the sun rising in the east blushed to see that there was someone awake to see its shy entrance. However, Engrelin's mind was not on his lack of sleep. Getting up, he searched the camp for signs of a visitor last night. But there were none. He stood by the burned out fire, clenching his hair in one hand. Did he keep imagining things…or was the intruder skilled at hiding all traces of himself? Why was he following them anyway?

17

Riding for the next few days was hard, eating was done in the saddle, and the moment they fed their horses for the night, Engrelin and his cousins hit the sack like dead men. None of these nights were disturbed by mysterious visitors with murderous intents (even if they had, the boys would have been too busy sleeping to notice). Tonight, however, they wouldn't have to worry about that at all if what Averendier had planned worked.

"How do you know her?" asked Engrelin, still breathing heavily from their recent gallop. They now trotted easily through a shaded lane, wider than most they had yet ridden—a sure sign they were nearing civilization.

"Aunt Ruth?" Averendier asked.

Engrelin raised both eyebrows. "Aunt? I didn't know you had relations down here."

"My mother is from here," Averendier answered, motioning to the winter-bare trees around them.

"So, this Aunt Ruth is her sister?"

"No."

"So how is she your aunt? Your dad's sister?"

"No."

Engrelin looked at his cousin askance. "Then why do you call her 'aunt'?"

Averendier shifted the reins impatiently from one strong hand to the other. "She's my mother's aunt," he explained.

"Ah." Rather disgruntled, Engrelin fixed his gaze down the road, making a mental note to ask Andrald even technical questions in the future. Attempting to ease the tight silence, he asked Andrald, "Have you guys seen her any?"

"Of course," said Averendier stiffly, catching his brother with his mouth open. "Coming down here a couple times a year is no problem at all."

Engrelin stared at Andrald helplessly. The older boy only shrugged.

"Does she know we're visiting now?" Engrelin asked, again directing this to Andrald.

"No," Averendier replied.

Engrelin nearly pulled his horse up short. "She doesn't know?!"

Chuckling, Andrald shook his head. "Don't sweat it, Engrelin. She won't mind our dropping by for the night. If she had mind to, she'd house a whole army at her place at an hour's notice."

Engrelin looked down doubtfully.

"Just one thing," Andrald added earnestly, as they turned their mounts down a short lane that would lead to the aunt's house. "Tell her that her flowers are pretty."

Engrelin nearly turned all the way around in his saddle to stare at his cousin, whose face was stony with solemnity. "What?"

"Aunt Ruth's just crazy about her flowers," Andrald explained, the twinkle in his eyes battling the confidentiality of his tone. "Especially her snow drops. But complement just about anything in her garden, and she'll float to the moon and back."

"And if I don't peep a word about them?" Engrelin challenged.

"She won't care one red cent that you're here," Andrald declared firmly.

Engrelin grinned. "Nice joshing. But I'm not going to do it."

Andrald smiled back with a mysterious air, making Engrelin's smile broaden, even as the path in front of him did, opening out of a channel of holly trees to a wide clearing. In the middle of the clearing stood the biggest house Engrelin had ever seen—save perhaps his uncle's manor.

A maze of flower beds wove around it, in full bloom despite the oncoming winter.

"One little old woman, keeping all that and a huge house?" he whispered to Andrald, respect seeping through him.

Andrald nodded proudly. "She won't hire any servants, even after her husband died when I was little. She's got a lot of spunk for a little lady."

The clopping of their horse's hooves must have traveled far over the many, many garden beds, for from beside one of them rose a small, petite form, crowned with snow-white. As she hurried forward, the boys dismounted, just in time for Aunt Ruth to rush straight up to Averendier, such a smile beaming on her face that all Engrelin's fears of being unwelcome evaporated like steam.

"How lovely to see you boys again!" she exclaimed as she clasped Averendier's hands in hers. It was like holding hands with a giant. Engrelin's and Andrald's heads hardly reached the tall man's shoulders—her nose nearly pressed against his broad chest. "And at such a time of year!"

"And you!" she continued, moving on to Andrald, who didn't dwarf her quite so much as his towering brother. "I think you've grown an inch or two since I saw you last!"

"I'm afraid I can't say the same for you, Aunt Ruth," Andrald replied with a laugh and a hearty clasp of her hand.

Aunt Ruth laughed back, a sweet, low sound, trembling only slightly with age. So much like Vera…

The little woman bustled over to Engrelin, and even with his normal height, she tilted her head back to look at him.

"My, I don't believe we've had the pleasure of meeting before," she said, extending her small, thin hand.

Engrelin took it gingerly in his own, afraid he'd snap her hand to the wrist if he squeezed.

"I'm Engrelin Peterson, ma'am," he said.

"And I'm Ruth, Aunt Ruth as all the folks around here call me, whether I'm related to them or not. I'd like it if you'd do the same."

"If you like," Engrelin said. "Thanks for letting us stop by."

Aunt Ruth's hand flew to her mouth. "Thanking me! When here I stand, keeping you boys out here in the cold, when you've come to get a warm roof over your heads and a homecooked supper for at least one night." She waved them to move towards the house.

"Mind the flowers now, don't let the horses nibble them. We'll take them to the north barn; they'll be plenty safe there. My father built it, and whatever he built, it was built to last. And it's still standing!"

And so her cheerful voice followed them to the barn, accompanied their chores with the animals, and hustled them into the house, all without seeming chattery or irritating. Aunt Ruth's home seemed to have absorbed some of her cheer over the years and now shed it onto the weary travelers as they settled heavily into seats around the dining room table, content to sit idle while someone else cooked.

It wasn't long before Aunt Ruth bustled into the dining room bearing a loaded tray on each arm. She made several such trips back into the kitchen and refused all the boys' offers to help. Soon, they were all gathered around the table. Averendier quietly led grace.

After eating camp food the past few weeks, the simple meal of meat, potatoes, and gravy tasted like a Christ Mass feast. To Engrelin, it betokened so much of his usual fare at home, he felt as if he might look up to find himself back at *Traeth Euriad*. Andrald devoured his first three servings ravenously. Engrelin wouldn't have been surprised to see his cousin dive head first into the serving bowl instead of dishing the portions out onto his plate.

The conversation moseyed along at a contented hum. Engrelin ate most of his meal in silence, his eyes wandering across the pink painted walls with their shelves of books and knick-knacks and maps tacked up, over the blue-spread table and the large lamp flickering in its center, to the fireplace with its sociably crackling flames and a small statue of the Virgin and Child standing on the mantle.

He had nearly finished his first serving when Averendier, polishing off his second, pushed his plate towards the center of the table and leaned forward with that dead earnest look that Engrelin had learned to despise.

"Aunt Ruth, have you heard what's been happening up north?" he asked.

Engrelin's stomach lurched. Quickly, he laid his fork beside his almost empty plate, his appetite seized in the clenching ball of his stomach. He hadn't traveled hundreds of miles to hear *this*.

"No, I haven't," returned Aunt Ruth mildly. "With the cold weather coming, I haven't made many trips to town. And you know how little news we get this far out." She reached to replenish Engrelin's plate, but he motioned her hand quickly away. She drew back, looking slightly wounded. The look only tightened the knots in Engrelin's stomach.

Andrald stared hard at his plate—obviously trying to draw a fifth helping onto it if he could. He looked up and said, "It's Tirendria. They're at it again."

"Dear goodness, no!" gasped Aunt Ruth.

"They attacked Fort Starr and completely cleaned it out," Averendier said gravely. "Thank God, we caught them before they destroyed Highlynn as well."

"The demons!" Aunt Ruth muttered fiercely, her hand curling into a fist on the tablecloth. "They just can't leave decent people alone!"

"What's more," continued Andrald, picking up his fork and stabbing with vengeance the helping Aunt Ruth had spooned onto his plate. "They're blaming Dad and us for it. Just about everyone in Monaria is against us now."

Engrelin stood abruptly. "I'm going to check on the horses," he said. "Thanks for supper," he added, before turning and exiting the dining room out onto a roofed back porch.

"Are you sure?" Aunt Ruth called after him. "I—"

She was cut short by Averendier's firm, "Aunt Ruth. Let him go."

Clenching his teeth, Engrelin closed the door most of the way behind him. His legs shook, ready to give out beneath him at any moment, so instead of retreating out to the barn as he had intended, he sank onto the porch steps and propped his chin in his hands, staring longingly out into the dark. He wanted to be angry with himself for leaving like that, but he couldn't. He had heard the story told one too many times. Why must it be brought up at every turn?

"Did he get driven out of house and home as well?"

Aunt Ruth's muffled voice wafted out to him through the partially opened door. Engrelin's fingers curled with frustration. He could still hear them! But he didn't budge to close the door; his body was too much of a dead weight.

"Yes," Averendier answered. "But he drags around like that mainly because he lost his parents and some siblings at the fort."

Aunt Ruth clucked softly with pity.

Engrelin hardly heard her. He didn't drag around! Maybe if Averendier let some emotion other than disgust into his life, he would realize it was only natural to be a little upset. Engrelin knew now that he shouldn't have left the table as he had, but there was also no way he was going to go back in, not now!

Lifting his chin, he stared defiantly out into the darkness. He thought he saw a shadow dart across the barnyard. Starting, he sat forward, squinting as he peered to catch any further movement. After a few minutes of intense staring, he sat back with a sigh, letting his face drop into his hands. Had he actually seen something, or were his eyes simply playing tricks on him? He sighed wearily. Hopefully, the others would finish soon, or he would fall asleep right where he sat.

Tomorrow pressed heavily upon him, more heavily even than his exhaustion, forcing him anxiously awake once more. Monaria's fate rested on what was said and done in Elstar tomorrow. Maybe even the fate of all Ontaria. Would Wilelm even try to help Monaria? Or, like a cobweb hung too long in one corner, would he simply brush them aside?

18

They took leave of Aunt Ruth's hospitality quickly the next morning—too quickly, it seemed. The frigid mountains and small villages flashed past in a swirl of scenery and faces The assurance of Wilelm's fortress standing solidly just ahead on its island steadied all. Time grated along. The horses seemed to drag their hooves across the stone bridge that spanned the river flowing between the city of Elstar and its fortress.

Engrelin stood in his stirrups and squinted. Through the writhing fog twisting up from the rushing river and around the arched bridge, he could see nothing of the fortress in front of them save the occasional pinnacle stabbing through the fog. He sank back into his saddle, his silence drowned in the grumble of the twin rivers flowing around the fortress and beneath the bridge. The water rushed and roared angrily. On a clear day, the sight had to be magnificent. Engrelin shifted uneasily in his saddle. It would have been so much easier to approach something he could see. Now, confusion and powerlessness wound through the blinding fog.

"State your business!" A voice rang out in front of them from unseen heights.

The three boys pulled their mounts up short. Some of the fog thinned ahead, disclosing a portion of gray stone wall and a looming gate.

"We bring an urgent correspondence from His Majesty Julian of Monaria to His Highness Wilelm," Averendier called into the mist.

For one long moment, the unseen challenger did not reply. A few grumbling murmurs drifted down from the battlements to Engrelin's ears, but no matter how he strained, he could not form them into words.

"Wait there," the voice ordered finally. Was it harsher than when he had first spoken or was he simply imagining things?

The boys fidgeted in their saddles, their mounts moving uneasily beneath them and pawing the stone pavement. At last, the creak and groan of a protesting gate resounded through the mist. A dark maw twenty feet high opened before the travelers. Several soldiers' silhouettes advanced through the opening, the light thrown from lanterns in their hands glinting on their drawn swords and the smoothly cut archway.

"Dismount, lay your weapons on the ground, and advance with your hands on the back of your head," commanded one of the soldiers, motioning with his naked blade.

Keeping every motion he made as smooth and as natural as possible, Engrelin slid off his horse, lifted his quiver from his back, and placed it deliberately at his feet. He folded his hands against the back of his head. Though low born, and certainly not a frequent visitor of monarchs, the commands struck Engrelin as odd. Did Wilelm's men treat everyone who came to his gate like vagabonds?

As the faint clank of Averendier and Andrald disarming themselves faded into the mist, the soldiers motioned the Monarians forward into the gateway. Several other guards stepped forward to grasp the horses' bridles and lead them through the gate. Engrelin watched pensively. Even if they needed to, there would be no getting away quickly.

Suddenly, a blinding light was thrust in Engrelin's eyes. As he threw his hands in front of his face to shield it, the cold touch of steel pricked his neck.

"The knife. In your belt. Take it off!" the harsh man ordered.

What knife? Engrelin wondered, squeezing his eyes shut against the painful brightness that made dark spots dance in his vision. He had nothing in his belt but...his *cyllel*. Were they really making such a fuss about that?

The sword pressed harder into the hollow of his throat.

"Now."

Blindly, Engrelin groped for his *cyllel*. His fingers found the familiar wooden hilt; with fumbling fingers, he unfastened it and let it clatter to the ground.

Immediately, the light was withdrawn, and the sword was removed. Engrelin blinked painfully at the misty evening, now disfigured with dark splotches.

"Come," the soldier continued, passing under the gateway as he spoke. "We will take you to His Majesty."

Engrelin followed, eyes averted from his cousin's stares. Averendier's heavy hand rested on Engrelin's shoulders. Engrelin winced and attempted to lightly shrug it off. It wasn't his fault the soldiers considered his *cyllel* a weapon. *He* certainly didn't; it was just another piece of his everyday dress.

"Are you all right?"

Engrelin blinked hard as they passed into the courtyard, but not to clear his vision. Had Averendier really asked him that? He canted his head and looked at his cousin out of the corner of his eye. Yes, it was Averendier. Engrelin dropped his gaze to the cobblestones beneath his feet as they crossed the spacious courtyard.

"I guess," he muttered, shrugging again. "Just can't see without spots."

"They'll clear up," Averendier replied, his voice regaining its staleness. "Just try to remember your knife next time."

Brushing the comment aside, Engrelin squinted at his cousin. "Are all palace guards like that?" he asked.

Averendier gave Engrelin a fleeting glance and strode forward without answering.

Engrelin stared wonderingly at Averendier's back as the spots on his vision faded to a dark gray. Was that a yes or a no? Or… perhaps Averendier was just as confused as Engrelin.

They were led through a large door into the fortress's tapestry-hung passageways. The ceiling soared up into great, gloomy heights. Glass bowls encompassing large lamps jutted from the walls, filling the dim hallways with warm light. The light reflected off the elegantly carved mahogany doors that stood on either side of the hallway.

They passed through a door made entirely out of stained glass and guarded by six men. They walked down a more elaborate hallway before they finally reached another guarded door. The boys' guide halted outside it. Opening the door, he motioned them inside. The boys obediently filed inside the room. One guard entered behind them and shut the door.

The Monarians now stood within a moderately large library. Three of its towering walls were covered floor to ceiling with shelves crammed full of books. A fireplace—so huge, Engrelin could easily have stood upright inside it without knocking his head on the mantle—dominated the fourth wall. The fire dancing within it tossed out light and shadow, burnishing the precious stones embedded in the books' spines. Engrelin stared, but he didn't say a word.

"Wait here," the soldier ordered. "I will inform Wilelm of your arrival."

Turning on his heel, the soldier crossed the room and opened a door on its far side. He stepped into the room beyond and shut the door behind himself.

Engrelin let his eyes rest on the door a moment, then turned his gaze onto the shelves looming around him. So many books! Hundreds, maybe thousands! How had someone gathered them all in one place? What did anyone do with all of them anyway?

The door across the room opened and their guide stepped out, the grimness of his face not in the least softened.

"Wilelm will see you now," he announced.

"My brother and I will go in," said Averendier quickly, motioning to Andrald. "But he," he added, waving towards Engrelin, "will have to stay in here."

Surprise and indignation choking him, Engrelin turned swiftly on Averendier. Andrald gripped Engrelin's shoulder warningly.

"I'll have to lock the library door," replied the soldier, frowning and disinterested. Shuffling across the room, he exited through the door leading out into the hall. The sound of a key turning in the lock echoed through the hall outside.

Rigid, Engrelin ground his heel into the lush carpet beneath his feet. "Stay here!" he exclaimed in a harsh whisper. "What in Ontaria is that supposed to mean?"

Andrald looked down at his feet and snuck his brother a helpless glance.

"It's Lord Gwane's orders," Averendier coldly explained. "He didn't want a… a peasant in the audience."

"So," Engrelin hissed under his breath, "I'm going to be safe when I get home because of the diplomatic work that I came all this way to do and never actually did?"

Averendier's lips set in an iron line. "This is the way it's going to be," he said firmly.

Before Engrelin could protest any further, someone poked their head out of the study door and motioned for the boys to come in. Engrelin's cousins left the library without a parting glance. Engrelin glared at their retreating backs until the door shut behind them, obscuring them from view.

His fists curled with frustration. He'd been dragged halfway across Ontaria…and for what? To sit in a library in Wilelm's fortress while his cousins did all the work? He might as well have stayed home. He honestly wouldn't be able to say he had any important part in the mission. Only the riding and perhaps the success of getting over the border. Compared to what they had come to accomplish, he'd done nothing.

Absolutely nothing.

The whole reason he had traveled hundreds of grueling miles during the harvest season was to help convince Wilelm to renew his alliance with Monaria. But he couldn't do that because he was low born? If Lord Gwane hadn't intended for him to be a part of the audience, why send him on this mission at all?

Bang!

The door behind Engrelin flew open. He whirled, poised for a fight.

A tall, middle-aged man stood in the library entrance. A decorative vase on a table beside him quivered with the violence of his entrance. When the man's dark eyes fell on Engrelin, they narrowed.

"What are you doing in here?" he demanded, closing the gap between them with a few quick strides.

"I'm waiting," Engrelin replied testily.

"Waiting for what?" the man pressed. "Answer quickly, I haven't all day."

"Nothing of importance, apparently," Engrelin retorted.

The man raised his eyebrows higher than Engrelin thought physically possible.

Who cared what the man thought? There was no reason act as if everything were well.

To his surprise, the man suddenly smiled broadly. "You're a smart fellow," he remarked.

Engrelin stared in disbelief.

"Name's Newfield. *Captain* Newfield, to be precise," said the man, extending his large hand.

"Engrelin," answered Engrelin, taking the man's hand uncertainly.

"You must forgive my interrogative conduct, Engrelin, but we've had quite the problem with spies recently, and seeing you in here gave me quite a turn. I wanted to be sure you weren't one of them." Newfield stepped back a moment, looking Engrelin over with such keen eyes that Engrelin wanted to squirm uncomfortably. "Hmm, stuck up pretty well," he muttered, almost to himself. "Should have expected it out of at least one of them."

Engrelin's eyebrows drew slightly together with confusion. Had Wilelm been expecting them?

Before he could ask the captain, someone exclaimed behind Engrelin, "Captain Newfield!"

Engrelin whipped around in surprise, every nerve in his body jangling. A fellow couldn't turn his back to a door without getting snuck up on and scared out of his wits, could he?

"I was about to come in, Brent," said Captain Newfield calmly to the man who stood in the study doorway. "I was delayed."

Brent scowled, though that was hardly necessary to express his displeasure. His mouth already appeared to be fixed in an eternal pout.

"*About* to come in? Captain, the King desired your presence fifteen minutes ago," he rasped accusingly. "Instead, you prefer to bide your time exchanging small talk with a peasant when we have the world's business to discuss. Get in here. "

"In a moment, Brent." The captain turned to Engrelin, who was scarlet with embarrassment and anger.

"Peasant or no, I am glad to have met you, Engrelin Peterson." He turned to head for the study, stopped, and glanced back over his shoulder. "I hope we might meet again."

Engrelin, disconcerted, lips parted to form the question that burned upon them, stared after the man until the study door closed on him also.

How had the captain known Engrelin's last name?

The door clicked shut behind Newfield, sealing more than a mere meeting.

Engrelin paced the brightly colored carpet covering the floor, thoughts tumbling over and over in his head. Why wouldn't they let him in? He had to help somehow, be useful in some way, or how else would he earn a safe life back at home for himself and his family? Didn't they realize what this would be doing to him? Would he have to be sent further into Ontaria to accomplish whatever 'hero work' was out there for one as ignorant in the ways of the world as himself?

Worn out by his frustration, Engrelin sank onto a nearby couch, his head cradled in his hands. The bottom seemed to drop out of the furniture. With a smothered cry of surprise he sprang up. He hadn't broken it, had he?

A short inspection proved the couch whole and intact, just soft and squishy. Why it had been designed to sink like that, he wasn't sure. He didn't find it comfortable. He certainly wasn't going to be found sitting on it or any other piece of furniture in the room, for that matter.

He was left to aimlessly wander the library or glance out the window. Time passed slowly, marked only by the dusk and thicker fog wrapping around the bridge. Longer shadows stretched across the bookcases and the portraits hanging above the fireplace. Firelight flickered, mixing with the shadows. A servant entered, lit the wall sconces, and disappeared again.

Still, no one had emerged from Wilem's study.

He soon found himself staring at the towering bookshelves and the books' elaborate spines. Except for the few of his grandmother's, and the dozens at his uncle's, Engrelin had rarely seen any books. He'd never opened one in his life. Complete and utter boredom compelled him to wonder what lay within the bound sheets of paper that held the literate spellbound for hours on end.

He paused in front of a book near the study door. Gingerly, he drew it off the shelf. It was heavier than he had expected, as tall as his forearm was long, and a little more than half as wide as that. Slanting silver threads crisscrossed the dark-blue leather cover. They framed the dark sapphire set in the cover's center. Engrelin scanned it wonderingly. The cover alone must have cost a fortune!

Keenly curious now, he slowly opened the book. Just inside the cover, in blue and silver pigments, was a sword. Strangely enough, the painted sapphire set in the sword's pommel had a tiny white dot dabbed in its center. Fancily curling script flowed beneath. Engrelin couldn't comprehend a single stroke. Gazing longingly at the page, he wished for the first time in his life that he could read.

He had no idea what the purpose of a book was exactly. But this one seemed to have been made for mere looking and admiring. The pages glowed with paintings of knights, ladies, kings and their queens, castles, villages, fields, battles (with details done in vivid crimson), all twining in and out of the silver pigmented script which were nothing but meaningless scratches to Engrelin, but a crook-necked scribe somewhere understood. A few figures from the illustrations reappeared on different pages, each shown doing something different. And the sword on the inside of the cover appeared often in the hand or at the side of a richly clothed man, whom Engrelin assumed was a king.

One thing in the background of one of the illustrations caught his eye and piqued his interest. A white flag with two lit tapers crossed over the background. A furrow formed on Engrelin's brow. It must be a story about old Tirendria, before the overthrowing. But who was the man? Was there something special about the sword he always appeared with?

"What are you doing?"

The demand, loud and sudden, jarred through Engrelin. Before he could catch it, the book fell from his hands and fell closed on the carpet with a muffled *thump.* He looked up to see Brent scowling at him from in front of the shut study door.

"Were you told you could touch the books?" inquired Brent sharply.

Engrelin stiffened. "I wasn't told I *couldn't* touch them," he countered.

"But you weren't permitted to touch them in the first place," Brent snapped. "Therefore, you shouldn't have laid a single finger on them."

If they hadn't been trying to heal and restore the friendship between their two countries, Engrelin would have given his answer to that with a good, solid punch. But since he couldn't, he only clenched his fists until his knuckles showed white.

Brent bent to pick up the book and rose swiftly, almost brandishing the heavy object. Engrelin took a quick step back, out of striking range. Brent slammed the book down onto the nearest side table.

"You're not to touch the books," Brent said, coldly and deliberately. "Do you understand?"

"I won't damage them," Engrelin said. *Or bang them around, like you.*

Brent's face darkened several shades of purple. "I'm sure you'll have worse things to trouble your dreams soon enough," he spat.

Flushing, Engrelin threw his shoulders back. "What did you come in here for anyway?"

"Oh! So it's your library now, is it?" Brent sneered. "I must apologize for being so im-po-lite in *your* library."

Engrelin looked at Brent askance, which seemed to irritate the man more than smart retorts had.

"If you must know," continued Brent scornfully, "I was sent here to tell you that you may have to wait awhile for the meeting to be over. *Some people* like to drag out the inevitable." He rolled his eyes and scrutinized Engrelin a moment, head to toe, just as Captain Newfield had done. He grunted. "Just don't touch the books."

Brent turned sharply on his heel and stalked back into the study. He banged the door shut behind himself.

Engrelin stared at the door a moment. The man thought peasants were unrefined? Had he ever listened to himself?

He shook his head at himself. No, he shouldn't think that, even if he had nothing else to think of. It was growing dark outside, twilight curtaining the outside from his view. Shadows fell like a pall over the pictures above the fireplace. Books were forbidden. Engrelin hated sitting around and doing nothing. He glanced wryly at the couches. Not that he wanted to sit on those anyway.

After staring at the furniture a moment, Engrelin ventured over. Maybe they wouldn't be that bad…

He pushed down on the cushioned seat several times, feeling it spring beneath his fingers. He stepped back. Nope. Someone would have to pay him a lot of money to rest on those.

He unclasped his cloak, wrapping it around himself like a blanket, just as he had every night of his journey so far, and lay down at the couch's foot to rest. There was no need for the couch at all—the carpet was practically a mattress. And right there in front of that enormous fireplace the plushy fibers were warm to the touch. In fact, to his aching body, the room seemed warmer than any he had ever been in.

Engrelin's head nodded forward. Snapping it back up, he fixed his eyes determinedly on the study door. He was going to stay awake until his cousins came out. Still, he curled into a more comfortable position, watching the door all the while. His head began to sag forward again. He jerked and tucked one arm beneath his head to prop it up. There. Now there was no way he would fall asleep before they came back. No way at all…

19

T*he alliance cannot be renewed. It just isn't possible."*

Engrelin stared blankly at Wilelm. He wished the king hadn't asked him to come alone to receive the news. Averendier and Andrald could have told him that it was all just a joke, just as locking him in the library last night had been.

But one glance at Wilelm's drawn face told Engrelin that he was anything but jesting.

"We have better things to do than help a country swarming with peasants and beggars like yourself," rasped Brent, who stood beside Wilelm.

Engrelin's stomach churned with sickening anxiety. "But if you don't renew it," he said desperately, "what will we do? We need your help."

Wilelm shook his head, his circlet slipping to one side of his head, though he hardly seemed to notice it. "I'm so sorry," he said, "but I'm afraid it just can't be done." He waved a hand at Brent, who stepped forward and took Engrelin by the arm, steering him out of the study.

Engrelin walked towards the door in a haze. This had to be a dream. It just had to be!

Finally, he summoned the strength to speak. But instead of all the important questions he had intended to ask, he found himself saying numbly, "Where are my cousins?"

Brent shrugged indifferently. "I don't know. Why should I?"

"But I don't know my way home!" Engrelin gasped, stopping to extract himself from the man's vise-like grip. Brent, however, only tightened his hold.

"The library is your home now," he growled.

With that, he shoved Engrelin into the library and banged the study door shut behind him.

Engrelin staggered back several steps, then rushed back at the closed door. He pounded its flawless surface with his fists and, when that would not budge it, threw his whole body against it. The wooden door might as well have been made of iron. Engrelin battered himself black and blue, and still it didn't give an inch. A sob tore his chest. Exhausted, he slumped against the door, his legs threatening to buckle beneath him.

This can't be happening, he thought wildly. *It just can't be!*

A breath of air brushed the back of his neck. He rubbed the spot slowly, vaguely wondering where in Ontaria the breeze could be coming from. Had someone, by some miracle of chance, left the library window open? He shivered with excitement. From what he'd seen earlier, it would be a long drop. But at least he could try!

Engrelin started turning and froze. The book he had looked at the night before, which lay on the table by the door, was wrapped in something venomously red. Slowly, the thing drew the book off the table. Engrelin's eyes followed the red line to a gaping maw of a mouth.

He stumbled back against the study door, eyes wide with incomprehensible horror, lips parted in a silent scream.

The giant serpent looked calmly back at him as the tongue drew the book into its mouth. Engrelin, overcoming his first shock, started forward in a futile attempt to save the book. But before he could reach it the monster snapped its jaws shut.

It reared up its huge head, towering over Engrelin. Engrelin's shoulder blades strained against the door, his eyes fixed upon the horrible creature, the blood in his temples throbbing with alarm. The serpent's body, thick as a tree trunk, lay in coils around the room. Beyond it, Engrelin saw the rest of the library—or rather, the remains. The polished bookshelves were empty, their sheeny surfaces reflecting the serpent's black scales. The pictures above the fireplace were piles of ashes resting on the mantle. The floor was bare stone.

Then he saw her. Twisting back and forth frantically, as if searching for something or someone. A little girl with nut-brown hair. Fear as hot and potent as poison coursed through Engrelin's body.

ELMERA!!! He couldn't force his lips to move, but the core of his being screamed it.

As if she had heard him, Elmera turned to face him. Recognition dawned on her face. Stretching out her arms, she tripped toward him.

The serpent snapped its head toward Elmera and let loose a terrifying, furious shriek. The sound shook the library to its foundations, sending Engrelin to his knees. He staggered back to his feet, just in time to see Elmera crumple to the floor, the serpent lunging with gaping mouth behind her. Engrelin sprang forward to put himself between her and the snake.

The serpent's tail lashed out to meet him. The blow thundered across Engrelin's body, hurling him against the study door. He hardly had time to grit his teeth for the jarring impact. He slammed against the door and slid limply to the floor.

Gasping for breath, Engrelin's eyes flew open. His head knocked against something, and he hit a carpeted floor with a muffled *um-fff!*

"Not again!" someone exclaimed from close by. Hands gripped Engrelin's shoulders, shaking him. "Engrelin? Wake up, right now!"

"Stop! I'm already awake," Engrelin exclaimed, struggling.

Andrald's breath whooshed out in audible relief. He released his cousin. Engrelin, shaking his head to clear it, propped himself up on one elbow and rubbed the lump rising on the back of his head. As he did, he sent darting glances throughout the room. The books stood in soldierly ranks upon their shelves. The pictures hung somberly above the mantle. He had just tumbled off one of the many couches (though how he had gotten onto it in the first place was beyond him). Lush carpet lay beneath him.

No sign of giant reptiles anywhere. Not even normal-sized ones.

Engrelin sank back onto the carpet, a relieved sigh hovering on his lips, though his heart still pounded and his muscles were so taut they ached.

Only a dream.

Andrald had put a hand to his forehead. "Engrelin, I'm beginning to wonder what exactly you think you are once you fall asleep. First, you shoot arrows. Tonight, you fell off that couch twice. What in the blazes do you dream about?"

"You don't want to know," Engrelin replied with a dry laugh. He frowned. "Second time? Far as I can remember, I only fell off once. Got the bump to prove it." He rubbed the back of his head meaningfully. "But, to be honest, I don't even remember getting on the thing."

"When Averendier and I got in here, we found you sleeping on the floor next to the couch. So we just lifted you back on. You didn't even stir. That's mainly why we're still in here, instead of having a proper room to spend the night."

Engrelin smiled, though with a tinge of color on his cheeks. "I didn't mind the floor, after sleeping on the ground for weeks. I'm sorry you fellows had to miss out on a bed, though."

Andrald wiped his arm across his eyes. "I doubt we could have slept well even if we had feather mattresses," he said, his face unusually drawn.

"Last night didn't go so well?" Engrelin commented with a frown.

Andrald looked down at his feet. "They've severed our alliance."

It was no surprise, but that did not lessen the punch in the gut Engrelin had. He almost wanted to go back to sleep, to escape the reality otherwise unavoidable. But this was one nightmare he couldn't wake up from.

Laughing mirthlessly to himself, Engrelin rubbed the back of his neck. "You know, I kind of knew you would say that."

"Oh really? Did you also know that we stayed up most of the night trying to talk him out of it?" Andrald asked.

"No." Engrelin sat forward. "But I am still wondering," he said. "Why wasn't I allowed to be in there with you two? I doubt it was because I'm low born, or else Lord Gwane wouldn't have sent me here in the first place."

Andrald shifted uncomfortably. "Averendier just said that thing about your rank to tide you over, I think," he said.

"What was the real reason?"

"Just Lord Gwane's orders. He didn't give any particular reason, other than that he heard you were a little…" Andrald cleared his throat with a hidden wince "…explosive. I think he may have overheard you in the barn that night or something--"

"He thought that was explosive?" Engrelin interrupted.

Andrald shrugged. "I didn't think so either. But he did, and that's the problem. He didn't want you in there. I think he thought you might mess something up, trying to be persuasive."

"Not that there was much to screw," Engrelin muttered. A prickling heat spread across his shoulders. "But he's probably right. I wouldn't have been too happy in there. In fact," he added, hoping to lighten things up, "I probably would have burned the place down."

"That's too tame. Decimation." Andrald flung his arms out wide. "You'd be the first person in history to take out a fortress in one blow."

"First person to seal my death sentence that way too." Engrelin rolled his eyes. "Though I would love to have seen the look on Brent's face."

Andrald's mouth quirked. "You should have seen him when he came back in from telling you we were going to be a while. His face was so red, I thought for a moment you'd tried to strangle him."

"I did want to rearrange his nose a little," Engrelin admitted.

"That's mighty Christian of you, Engrelin," Andrald snorted.

"At least I'm honest."

"And so am I," Andrald returned, "when I say I don't blame you."

"Ahem." Someone loudly cleared a throat behind them.

Both boys turned to see a young maid standing in the library doorway. A slight line of confusion ran across her brow at the sight of the two visitors sitting on the floor *beside* the couch instead of *upon* it. Perhaps the sight of Averendier slumped in a chair was of some consolation, for when her gaze fell upon it, the line smoothed somewhat.

Dusting the front of her starched apron, she cleared her throat once more.

"Pardon me, gentlemen," she said, "but there is a man here who wishes to speak with you. He claims to have come a long way but is willing to wait if you would like a few moments to prepare yourselves."

Andrald frowned but replied, "Tell him to come back in an hour. We'll be ready."

The maid nodded. With a polite, practiced bob, she left with a crisp rustle of skirts.

"Wonder what that's all about," Engrelin murmured, his eyes on the closed door.

"In an hour, we'll find out," Andrald returned.

Engrelin looked swiftly at him. "Will I be able to be in this meeting, or will you lock me in the king's study?" he asked.

"Lord Gwane said you couldn't talk to Wilelm. He didn't say anything about anyone else," Andrald said musingly. "As long as Averendier says yes, I think you're okay to stay. It's not like we can put you in any other room anyway."

"But what about the man himself?" Engrelin thought aloud as Andrald rose to rouse his brother. "She didn't even give us a name. All we know is that he's from somewhere far off."

"And that could be anywhere, considering what you think is far." Andrald stretched a little, then groaned and stooped over. "Like that chair Averendier's in. It's miles away right now. You'd think I slept on a pile of rocks."

Engrelin smiled. "And that is why I slept on the floor."

Andrald threw a mock glare over his shoulder as he shuffled across the room to his slumbering brother. "I'll wake him up, and let's see what he thinks about the whole thing."

20

Engrelin *leaned against the cool marble side of the library* fireplace, watching with interest and slight amusement as Averendier offered their visitor a seat in the library, as if it were the Peterson parlor back in Bryn.

He himself chose to stand against the fireplace for two reasons: one, the furniture was uncomfortable, and two, he thought standing a little way away from the rest would keep him from talking too much. He couldn't recall saying anything particularly smarting or harsh around Lord Gwane, but either the lord had heard other things, or Engrelin was unaware of how vehement he could be. Either way, he wasn't going to display his apparently undiplomatic skills before a man who, though a stranger, had requested an audience with them.

The visitor sat down heavily on the proffered couch, his shoulders slightly hunched. "Thank you," he said. "I will not take much of your time. I am sorry that you did not have any earlier notice of my desire to meet with you. But I only just learned you were here. It's rather…fateful, I find."

"You're all right," said Averendier. He offered his hand, which the man shook firmly. "I'm Averendier Peterson, and this is my brother, Andrald, and my cousin, Engrelin Peterson."

The man nodded to Andrald, but raised his eyebrows ever-so-slightly at Engrelin. He looked the boy quickly over, up and down, with the scrutiny Engrelin now expected and resented from strangers.

"You're definitely a splinter of Aaron," he muttered, more to himself than Engrelin. Though his voice was low and tired, his sea-green eyes shone keenly. Engrelin shifted from one foot to the other, wishing the man would just get on with what he came to say.

As if reading his thoughts, the man turned his eyes away and folded his hands in his lap. "I am Johnathan," he said abruptly. "Johnathan only. I have traveled nearly a month from Alinar to come here. I am a close friend and advisor of King Bendekahn. I came here to seek help and advice from Wilelm, but he had none to offer. So now I come to you."

"What can we do for you that a king can't?" Engrelin asked. His whole body had jerked forward at the mention of Alinar, the desert country south of Monaria. They were allies, yes, but the place was so far away!

Besides, Johnathan didn't look anything as Engrelin thought an Alinar should. He'd always been told they were dark skinned. He was as fair skinned as Engrelin himself, and his light brown hair was heavily streaked with gray.

Johnathan gazed calmly at Engrelin. "You can do much more than even a king, if you agree to my proposal," he said quietly. "I am afraid I cannot tell you much now. But once we reach Alinar, I can explain everything."

Engrelin started forward, but Averendier spoke first.

"What do you mean?" he asked, rising from his seat, "coming here... to ask us to go with you to Alinar without any explanation why?"

"Humbly, yes," replied Johnathan, folding his hands in his lap.

Engrelin sucked in a sharp breath, watching the muscles in Averendier's jaw spasm.

"Is this a joke?" Averendier demanded stiffly. "If so, we have a long way home, and the snow to beat."

Johnathan rose partially out of his chair. "Don't go," he pleaded, putting out one hand as if to stop Averendier (though it was obvious who would have won that contest). "I need you. No one else will listen to me. You're the last ones I have. The last Alinar has."

Averendier didn't move to sit down, but neither did he move to leave.

"And why's that?" Andrald asked.

Johnathan smiled wryly. "For the same reason you just threatened to leave. I don't give enough information about myself and my mission."

"You are asking people to travel a month at the beginning of winter simply because you're asking for help," Averendier said.

Johnathan's smile grew more wry still. "So everyone else has told me. And you all have a point."

Averendier resumed his seat. "You're ready to explain yourself?"

Johnathan's jaw twitched. He looked down at his folded hands. Engrelin watched him carefully, hardly daring to breathe lest he miss what the man said next, though he hardly knew why. There was no way they could agree to travel to Alinar. Not with winter just around the corner.

"If I said," began Johnathan carefully, "that we are in trouble..."

"Quite a few countries are in trouble at the moment, Johnathan," said Averendier.

Johnathan's lips pinched together. "Yes, suppose they are," he said. "But if I said the trouble...was similar to Wilelm's?"

Andrald started visibly. Averendier leaned further forward. Engrelin bit his lower lip. What did Johanthan mean? His cousins certainly understood. It must have something to do with the meeting last night.

"Bendekahn's children?" Averendier asked.

Johnathan nodded curtly.

Andrald went white.

"Not quite so bad," Johnathan added hurriedly. "They're not gone yet."

"What do you mean, 'yet'?" Averendier demanded earnestly.

"I..." Johnathan stopped. He canted his head suddenly to one side, listening. Easing himself silently off the couch, he crept toward the closed door leading to the hall.

Engrelin watched the ambassador as a sane man watches a lunatic. What in Ontaria was he doing?

When he reached the door, Johnathan paused a moment. Then he grabbed the handle and wrenched the door open. It banged against the wall. Engrelin thought he heard the scuffle of running footsteps. Andrald, hearing it also, jumped to his feet.

Shaking his head with disgust, Johnathan shut the door and returned to the couch.

"You see why I cannot divulge," he said wearily. "Vendar's spies are everywhere, even here."

"It might have been a curious maid," suggested Andrald half-heartedly.

Johnthan eyed him sharply. "A maid in boots? No, they're here. How else to you think Vendar got Wilelm's eldest children?"

Engrelin's brow furrowed. "I wasn't at the meeting last night," he said. "What's this about Wilelm's kids?"

Andrald smiled thinly. "I meant to tell you—"

"Perhaps not here," interrupted Johnthan hoarsely, glancing at the door.

Averendier jerked his chin at Andrald. Understanding the motion, Andrald checked the hallway, then stood guard beside the closed door.

"You might as well tell him—and all of us—something, sir," he said. "I doubt the eavesdropper will come back. And if he does, my brother will hear him."

Johnathan drew a long breath and swept his hand over his graying hair. "I'm still not sure..." He glanced swiftly, keenly and Averendier. "Are you considering my proposition?"

Engrelin's mouth went dry. He fixed his eyes on Averendier, who thought Johnthan's words over only a moment.

"Possibly. I would like to hear more."

Johnathan dropped his hand. Leaning forward, he whispered earnestly, "Bendekahn's children need to be hidden before Vendar infiltrates the Alinar court as he has done here."

Averendier drew back slightly. "You want us to go to Alinar to help take Bendekahn's children away? Where to?"

"Monaria, first. Then south. Alinar's southern border is sealed by Vendar's spies."

"The southern border?" Averendier repeated. "You don't mean to take the children into the Southernlands, do you?"

"Not quite. To a safe, secluded Alinar fort near the border. It's unreachable now."

Engrelin leaned back against the fireplace. The cold of the stone seeped through his tunic and into his shoulder blades.

"You're not making any sense," he said.

Johnathan smiled wanly. "I guess I'm not. I haven't quite worked all the kinks out myself."

So you're trying to get people to agree to a plan you haven't finished concocting? Engrelin thought. No wonder no one had offered to help him.

Johnthan sat forward. "What you boys need to know is this: Because of Vendar's threats, Bendekahn's children's lives are in danger. He has threatened that if Bendekahn moves to help Monaria in any way, he will abduct and kill Bendekahn's children. And even though Bendekahn has not decided either way, attempts have been made against the princesses' lives. Before Bendekahn can help Monaria, the girls have to be safely out of Alinar."

"Bendekahn says he will help us if his children are out of danger?" Averendier asked. His hand clenched excitedly over air.

Again, Johnathan hesitated and glanced at Andrald, who smiled to reassure him.

"I have proposed this plan to Bendekahn. I haven't convinced him yet, but I think bringing you to Alinar may tip the balance."

"You think?" Engrelin repeated skeptically. He didn't know much about kings, or Bendekahn, but he doubted anyone would want a plan like this sprung on them.

"Bendekahn has his heart set on helping Monaria," said Johnathan in a low voice. "He and Julian have been good friends for years. Alinar has been Monaria's ally for centuries. But he won't risk his daughters' lives in the bargain. He doesn't think sending them anywhere is safe. I think it will be, if we can get them in and out of Monaria quickly enough and down to one of Alinar's strongest and most secluded forts in the western sea, though there will be some pirates to purge before the voyage..."

Johnthan shook his head to get himself back on track. "It will be arduous to take such a roundabout way. But it is the last thing Vendar will expect, and the safest route in the long run. Once the children are safely away, Bendekahn will be free to help Monaria without Tirendria's hinderance. I assure you, if the heirs are taken successfully into hiding, the war will be over by next Christ Mass."

Engrelin smiled slightly. Everyone in history always seemed to say that. But as far as he knew, no war ended that quickly, especially when Tirendria was involved.

"Are you sure Vendar won't find out about the plan and try to stop it?" Andrald whispered worriedly

Johnathan smiled. "What he doesn't know can't hurt him, or us. Besides, if he did hear we were taking the heirs away, naturally, he would think we would head south, or even east. I doubt it would ever cross his mind that we were taking them right past his own country."

"There couldn't be a better plan," said Averendier quietly, his eyes sparkling with animation.

Which was bad.

Worse still. Engrelin had to admit Averendier was right this time. This might be the only chance left to get help for their tiny country before Vendar's armies crushed it. The brooding fact that Wilelm had refused—even broken off—his alliance only added bruise to bruise. The boys themselves had no acclaim to protect them if they tried returning home. Bryn would make sure the boys suffered for their failure. This was not only the only option to help their country, but also guaranteed their stay home. Engrelin swallowed hard. He'd be gone for so long, far longer than he had ever anticipated. Alinar was at the very least a month's riding away. And with winter almost upon them…

"By the time we get back around here, it'll be winter," said Andrald, so perfectly mirroring Engrelin's thoughts that the younger boy gave him an odd look. "There would be enough snowfall to keep most Tirendrians off the roads. We could stay in Monaria until spring, then sail south."

Johnathan nodded. "That's what I'm hoping," he said. "I still need Bendekahn's confirmation on this. And yours," he added, gazing quietly and confidently at them.

"I'm all for it," Andrald declared, slapping his thighs enthusiastically.

Averendier considered a moment, his mouth a straight, tight line. "It would be acting outside of orders," he said at last.

Andrald's face fell. Johnathan's forehead creased.

"If you have orders to return straight home, I won't keep you from it," he said slowly.

"I don't," Averendier admitted. "But we do have news that should reach home as soon as possible."

Engrelin looked swiftly at his cousin. He could see nothing of any sort of struggle in his cousin as there was in himself. Go home? As much as he wanted to, for personal reasons, what home would there be to return to if the Tirendrians took over after all? After all this travel and worry, just give up? Give up on Monaria? Here was an opportunity for success, for assistance, and they would have to turn it down because they had to inform those at home about their failure?

"Couldn't we send word to someone?" he blurted. "Like Aunt Ruth, maybe? And she could send word along to Lord Gwane about Wilelm's refusal. And we could still make it to Alinar and back before the snow closes off the roads."

Averendier stared at Engrelin, an almost amused smile quirking his thin lips infuriatingly.

"If you put it that way," he said, "and if we could spare the extra day to drop by her house, then yes, I think we could go to Alinar, sir."

Johnathan smiled. "Good. I think I can count you in as well, young man?" He nodded toward Engrelin, who curtly returned it. Johnathan stood. "Meet me in the courtyard in an hour," he said. "I'll have fresh horses ready for you."

The boys nodded, exchanged another round of handshakes, and saw Johnthan out of the room. Then they glanced at each other. Engrelin shrugged.

21

Berwyn *shoved the last wooden bowl into the cabinet and* slammed the door shut with a vengeance, thus ending the daily routine—with her own personal inflections—which she had adopted upon her arrival at Kepspell.

How long ago had that been? Wearily, she rubbed one hand across her face—a hand roughened by the crude soap used to wash the endless stacks of dishes in the monstrous washing tub. Telling time here was almost impossible. Every tomorrow reflected yesterday as the redundant cycle of chores churned on. Her assistants remained the same silent, frightened people. The menu consisted of gruel, beans, black bread, and thin soup. The sky stayed eternally drab. Every little thing, down to slamming that rickety cabinet door every night before she left, was all a measure in the most monotonous and grinding symphony ever composed.

She slumped up against the cabinet, only to remember that she also did this every evening once the fires had been banked for the night and the last dish had been dried and put away for the morrow's use.

From when she woke before dawn to stoke the fires, to when she crumpled exhausted onto her bed long after the sun had set, she was in the kitchen. The moment one meal had been served and cleaned up, it was time to start the next. A never-ending grind enough to drive any person stark mad. Especially since had spent the other parts of her life on different things, things she loved…

Berwyn pushed her straggling hair away from her face. Through it all, she had only managed to bind up a sliced finger here or soothe a scald there. All the training she had undergone, all the things to which she had previously dedicated herself—would it all end in this frightful kitchen?

She slammed her curled fist against the cabinet behind her. Never! Nothing would end here!

"Tired?"

Berwyn raised her head slowly to meet her father's soft eyes. Doctor Sirman stood in the kitchen doorway, one hand resting on the frame. She dropped her gaze and stared at the scuffed toes of her shoes.

"Kind of," she answered listlessly.

"It's not like you to go around hitting things," he continued gently. Crossing the room, Doctor Sirman pulled himself up onto the edge of one of the massive kitchen tables, sighing softly beneath his breath.

Berwyn snuck a glance at her father's slumped figure. No matter how full Fort Starr's hospital, how demanding his work, She had never seen her father as worn as he was after his daily hunts. She had been overjoyed to find that he was with her—a joy tinged with bitterness, because Warwick and his men had refused to let her father carry out his practice.

Instead, they had assigned him to a group of men designated to hunt for the camp. Her lip curled slightly. Not that the kitchens saw much of what was caught. She guessed most of the meat went to the soldiers. But no one, not even her bold father, asked what happened to the carcasses they brought back. It was safest not to ask. Her eyes hovered for a moment on a dark splotch staining the front of her father's tunic before she looked away.

But the stain—that blot against the profession they shared—was branded on her memory.

"How was today?" she asked quietly, hoisting herself up beside her father. She rested her head on his shoulder.

"The usual," answered the doctor shortly, his eyebrows meeting in a scowl. "Got three deer today. If I don't see a scrap of venison in tomorrow's stew..."

"They'll just say that it is all for our greater good," Berwyn concluded. Putting her hand over her father's, she lifted her eyes to meet his. "But, Dad, don't they ever think that the workers might need it too? Can't they see how thin the field workers are getting? And the men building the barracks…"

"That's more like my Wren," Doctor Sirman whispered, tenderly brushing his knuckle against her cheek.

Smiling, she tucked her arm around her father's sturdy waist. In return, he draped his arm around her shoulders, pulling her even closer. A warm glow spread through her, a glow that not even Warwick himself could take away from her. If only there could be such security outside her father's arms. Then she could be brave always.

"You ready to head back now?" Doctor Sirman asked, his voice muffled in Berwyn's dark-brown hair, fallen loose of its bun.

Reluctantly, Berwyn pulled out of the embrace and smoothed back her hair. "I have to put that tonic for Reilah in my bottle," she said. "Then I'll be ready." Slipping off the table, she shuffled over to a saucepan she had left simmering over the coals.

"You've been doing so well taking care of that little girl," said Doctor Sirman, his voice smiling.

She colored slightly with pleasure and turned long enough to flash her father a bright smile. She poured the tincture into a small phial, stoppered it, and dropped it into her satchel, which always hung at her side. She glanced at a cauldron of wheat soaking for tomorrow's breakfast, then straightened before her father.

"Ready, Dad."

With a small smile, Doctor Sirman tucked Berwyn's arm in his. "It's dark out—past curfew," he warned as he steered her towards the door. "Hendric let me come to make sure you got back safely."

"Nice excuse, Dad," Berwyn replied as they stepped out into the inky evening, shutting the kitchen door behind them. "He knows I'll always be out after dark, with all the cleaning up and prep I have to do. But I like you coming out anyway," she added, affectionately squeezing his arm.

"I figured I might as well, since we're not hunting tonight," Doctor Sirman said. He veered around a dead branch littering the muddy path.

"He's a good man, probably a father himself at one point. He sees what they're trying to do to you. You need a little uplifting now and then, when it can be just you and me."

Berwyn instinctively moved closer to her father. Privacy did not exist in Kepspell. You lived and slept with at least two other families in a cramped cabin, you ate as a group, you worked under watchful eyes. She knew that, even now, someone watched them, though the thought that it was friendly Hendric took the keen edge from the disturbing knowledge.

"Hendric is one of the Eastern Florenthians, isn't he?" she asked in an undertone.

Her father nodded. "Torn away from his family to serve Vendar's army, just like ourselves, Wren," he murmured, not without a furtive glance around.

"But we aren't soldiers," Berwyn said. "And we wouldn't have fought anyway. At least, I wouldn't have."

"We fight in our own way," replied Doctor Sirman softly. "Not just with swords and bows, but bandages and tonics. Every soldier we healed back at the fort was one more to eventually return to the ranks and defend our country against tyrants like Vendar. Planting us here as a cook and a hunter instead of doctors takes care away from hundreds of soldiers. So those hundreds will die untended. And that is just those hundreds less to stand between Vendar and Monaria."

She frowned thoughtfully, shuffling her feet through a pile of dead leaves. Her hand moved up to the satchel strap crossing her chest and closed protectively over it. She knew she was being bold, practicing her skill as much as she did. If Warwick found out, might he decide banishment wasn't enough to keep a doctor from performing their duty? Would he determine a more…drastic measure must be taken?

Shivering involuntarily, she clung to her father's arm. She felt as if the image of the tonic phial concealed in her bag had been branded on the leather flap for all to behold.

"Is that why he brought you, even if they sent away the other men?" she hardly dared believe she had said it until she saw her father's frowning face.

"I can only think so, Wren," he replied quietly. "I can't see how else I escaped being sent away with the others. Warwick made it clear that he wants only young people and young families here. But we're smattered with more important people who are safer to keep close."

"Everything's so fragile here," she murmured. "Our very lives on the delicate balance of their pleasure. It's awful. If it weren't Hendric on watch, I might sleep in the kitchen rather than set foot out here. I feel like someone might just put an arrow in our backs for sport."

Berwyn threw a glance over her shoulder as she spoke. Her father followed her gaze. He quickened his stride.

"The only thing we can do is pray to God for deliverance," he whispered to her. "And trust He will show us the way out. Meanwhile, we must stay quiet, and bring as much healing and hope to these people as we can."

Berwyn had no time to reply, for at that moment they reached the threshold of their cabin. Silently, they opened the door and slipped inside.

Several of the cabin's occupants were sitting in the middle of the cabin's floor. When the door opened, their heads jerked up. They relaxed when only Doctor Sirman and his daughter entered. Doctor Sirman nodded briefly. They resumed bending over the paper spread out before them on the earthen floor.

As she crossed the room to where Reilah lay ill, Berwyn noted that men from other cabins were present.

Reilah managed to smile weakly as Berwyn pushed the girl's stringy hair away from her forehead.

"How's the fever?" Berwyn asked gently.

"Still hot," answered Reilah. She watched Berwyn closely as the young doctor opened her satchel, pulled out the phial, and struggled to uncork it. Reilah's nose crinkled.

"What do you put in that stuff anyway, Miss Sirman?" she asked. "Stink-weed?"

"Please, call me Berwyn," Berwyn reminded her for what seemed the hundredth time. Wryly, she continued, "And I don't think there's such a thing as stink-weed."

"What about yuck-weed?" Reilah drew her thin blanket over her nose.

Pursing her lips against a laugh, Berwyn shook her head. "No, not that either. It's an extract of lilan root, willow bark, and a tiny bit of worm moss, all boiled up into something that'll get you back on your feet, even if it is bitter."

"Well, maybe you should look for plants that heal people *and* taste good. That way, you won't have so many unhappy patients," Reilah declared.

"Maybe," Berwyn said. "But I can't promise anything. Now, quick." She pressed the phial to the girl's mouth. Reilah took a few obedient swallows and gagged. Berwyn made her drink the whole small bottle, then tucked the blanket gently under Reilah's chin.

"Sleep now, and I'll check on you in the morning."

"It'll take me an hour to fall asleep after drinking *that* stuff," Reilah moaned. Nevertheless, she fell back onto her pillow with an exhausted sigh.

Chuckling under her breath, Berwyn skirted around the men clustered in the cabin's center and crawled into her narrow, cramped bunk, which was nothing more than an alcove carved into the wall with a thin mattress thrown on the floor. Her father had tacked up an old blanket in front of the opening for privacy—she drew them shut against the men and the dull glare of the dying fire. After whispering her prayers to herself, she stretched out as much as she could and shut her eyes, pursuing ever-evasive sleep.

Despite the cabin's many occupants, dead silence reigned for several minutes. Berwyn even heard the logs in the fireplace settle gently into the ash.

Someone asked in the lowest of low tones, "Doctor, do you still have *it*?"

The emphasis he put on *it* almost made Berwyn sit up.

"I do, Dustan, but I don't want to take it out," replied Doctor Sirman slowly. "I'm not comfortable telling anyone where it is. It's not that I don't trust you men, but there may be others listening, and I wouldn't want to give its hiding place away."

The other men murmured in agreement. Berwyn pushed herself up onto her elbows. Her father gave the word particular weight as well. What was he referring to? And why had he said nothing to her about it. He told her everything! What here could be so important, so secret, that her father hesitated to tell even her anything about it?

Maybe it was best not to know. Snuggling back against her pallet, she drew her patched blanket over her shoulders.

"As long as it's safe, we should be fine. Our only other worry is Damian Peterson. We, among others, are still wary of him," another man growled in his deep bass. "His schemes are still too risky."

"I'm surprised he even made a suggestion at the meeting last week," Dustan chimed. "He's got younger siblings here to take care of. I wouldn't mind risking myself like he does if I didn't have a wife and family back home. For their sake alone, I'm going to wait this out."

"Not all of us agree," Doctor Sirman said quietly. "I'm afraid the men of Kepspell aren't going to be the only ones making sacrifices in order to destroy Tirendria's hold on us. Though we may not want to be involved now, you may find yourselves jumping to action when the time is right, and possibly giving your lives in the process."

"Better finish your sermon, Doctor," one of the men whispered. "You're already on their list. If I were you, I'd wait for that moment and not risk yourself and your little girl."

Berwyn buried her head in her scanty blanket.

A plan? Risks? The list?

As the manager of kitchen five, she made weekly reports to Lord Rees, the overseer of Kepspell and Warwick's only superior officer. Every time she had finished listing the week's accomplishments and needs, he would always ask her if she had noticed "any unusual activity within the kitchen." She had never reported anything.

Though this wasn't the kitchen, Berwyn knew this was something Rees considered reportable. He wouldn't know if she withheld anything, would he?

She shuddered involuntarily at the thought of the lord's cold yellow eyes staring at her out from under his dark hood. No matter how she tried to steel herself against them, they always seemed to penetrate to her soul, to read her darkest and inmost thoughts. If he smelled a rat, he wouldn't rest until he had flushed it out of her. Was that what her father, and the other men, meant by protecting her?

The nagging thought circulated back through her mind. What was *it*?

22

The towering forests of Northern Florenth stretched on into the rolling plains of Western Florenth. The three boys and Johnathan galloped through both, never stopping longer than a night's rest. Soon, the grass around them became riddled with rocks lying haphazardly about, as if some giant had tossed them there at his leisure.

Quickly, the rocks increased in number until they composed the ground beneath the horses' hooves. The grass around them withered down until only a few shriveled patches here and there remained to break the monotony of the landscape. Trees were seldom. Even when they passed one, it was low and twisted, stunted by the heat shimmering in waves on the horizon. In that desolate, roasting country, Johnathan announced they had crossed over Western Florenth's border into Alinar.

They had been traveling across the barren, rock-strewn plain for nearly a week when they struck sandstone cliffs. Engrelin reined in his mount, Glorien, a little doubtfully, but Johnathan pressed on, unruffled by the sheer orange walls jutting to the sky.

"There's a path ahead," Johnathan assured them. "Beyond these cliffs is one of the prettiest sights you'll ever see in Ontaria."

The boys followed Johnathan to the foot of the cliffs, where a narrow, steep path wound up the irregularities along the cliff's face.

"You'll want to dismount," Johnathan said. He slid from the saddle, seized his horse's reins, and started leading it up the path.

Averendier followed fearlessly, leading his horse by the bridle. Andrald and Engrelin followed. Engrelin—mountain born though he was—forced himself not to look over the sheer edges.

After a few nerve-wracking minutes, they reached the cliff's level top. Engrelin scrubbed the gritty sweat from the back of his neck as he joined his companions, who stood at the cliff's opposite edge looking out and saying nothing.

He didn't have to ask why they were staring. The moment his eyes fell on the sight beyond, he knew.

A wide valley opened in the basin of sandstone cliffs. The sun broke over them, striking the shimmering sand below into blinding gold. At the valley's bottom stood a palace, the pastel of the sunrise bleeding onto its otherwise snow-white marble walls, glowing violet, rose, pale blue, and gold. A thin waterfall cascaded down a cliff nearby, feeding the moat that encompassed the palace before flowing on in a thin rivulet through the rolling sand.

The palace itself, even as seen from this distance, was enormous, resplendent, and like nothing Engrelin had ever seen. It seemed to have been built entirely for aesthetics, without a thought towards defense. Engrelin's shoulders slumped with relief. After over a month of traveling, rough riding, and broiling desert sun, they had made it. They were finally here.

"There's another trail leading down," Johnathan said. He turned abruptly from the scenic view, tugging his mount along with him. "Lead your horses slowly, boys."

This path was steeper than the one up and overgrown with a tangle of stunted shrubs. But, Engrelin reflected, as his foot sent yet another loose stone skittering down the path ahead of him, the bushes might be the only things holding the path together.

The travelers slipped and slid down the slope. Once they reached the bottom, they breathed a collective sigh of relief. Engrelin took one step forward and sank to his ankles in the soft sand covering the ground.

If we didn't have horses, we'd have to wade to the palace, Engrelin thought as he swung back up onto Glorien's back.

The horses trotted lightly through the waves of golden sand. They were desert horses Johnathan had exchanged for their old mounts. Their gait was impeccably smooth as they trotted, unhampered, across the stretch of sand to the palace gates.

Guards challenged the travelers at the gates, but Johnathan only had to say one word before the doors swung open. Engrelin braced himself as several dark guards appeared on the drawbridge, but they neither told him to dismount nor frisked him or his cousins. They simply waved them under the looming archway into the courtyard beyond.

The horse's shod hooves rang on the courtyard's marble floor. Leaning over in his saddle, Johnathan murmured something to the stableboy running beside him. Nodding quickly, the boy darted off towards the palace doors, which were not of wood but of bursts of stained glass set in a gilt frame.

Johnathan dismounted and motioned for his companions to do likewise. Engrelin's foot had hardly left the stirrup when a boy, probably no older than thirteen, took Glorien's bridle and jogged off across the courtyard with the golden horse in tow. Other boys, smiles flashing pearl white against their hazelnut complexions, took Johnathan's and the twins' horses. Engrelin looked from them, to Johnathan, to the retreating boys once more, his brow slightly furrowed. He had bedded Glorien down every night since leaving Elstar. It felt strange to have him taken away and have the other boys tend him.

"Right this way," Johnathan said. Crossing the courtyard in a few long strides, Johnathan ascended a marble staircase up to the stained-glass doors. The stairs looked as slippery as the frozen lakes back home. Gingerly, Engrelin put half his weight on the first step. His feet didn't fly out from under him, as he had expected. He found himself mounting the stairs with as much ease as if they had been roughly-cut granite.

They entered the palace through the elegant doors. The whole structure seemed to have been carved out of one enormous, shimmering block of flawless white marble. Rich blue and scarlet carpets ran down the hallways, muffling the boys' steps. Vines and flowers tangled in a web of regal gold paint adorned the ceiling and the inside of pearly domes, which were held up by smooth, icy marble pillars. The occasional gold or blue tapestry hung on the walls, but these were few. For the most part, the walls were crowded with high, arched windows. No glass or shutters stood in them; the only thing standing between the inside and the outdoors were sheer, flapping curtains. So much light flooded through these walls of windows it seemed to Engrelin that they were just walking down one long, pearly balcony, cool despite the broiling heat outside.

Johnathan brushed past all these splendors, leading the boys far into the palace before he stopped in front of a heavily guarded curtained opening. Stepping forward, Johnathan whispered a few things to the guard. The dark, burly man snatched a look at the three Monarians, nodded curtly, and drew back the light curtain behind him. Smiling slightly, Johnathan ushered his guests back into the open air.

This time, they really were on a balcony, at least two stories up in the air. Engrelin squinted against the glaring sun. However, it did not prevent him from seeing a woman rising from a cushioned lounge set at the balcony's opposite end, her arms outstretched in greeting.

"Johnathan, at last!" she exclaimed, her voice soft and remarkably low. She moved towards them, her gait so smooth she seemed to be rippling like running water across the marble, her silk skirts trailing and rustling behind her. Her jet-black hair, hanging loose to her waist and bound only with a thin circlet of gold around her head, blew gently about her shoulders in the morning breeze. The diamond set just above her forehead in the circlet caught the sunlight and threw out small, scattering sparkles.

Just as the woman reached him, Johnathan dropped onto one knee and kissed the slender hand she extended.

"And who are they?" asked the woman, turning to survey the three boys. Much to his irritation, Engrelin's palms grew irrationally slick with sweat as her firm gaze rested on him.

Johanthan climbed back to his feet. "Three boys from Monaria: Averendier, Andrald, and Engrelin Peterson," he answered.

The woman turned her head, rather slowly, a small line etched between her fine eyebrows. She said nothing, to Engrelin's growing apprehension.

Johanthan cleared his throat quietly. "If you would permit me…" he said, motioning to the boys.

The woman nodded.

"Boys," Johanthan said, "This is Bendekahn's wife, Zacara."

Averendier and Andrald instantly went down on one knee as Johnathan had done. Engrelin, unsure of what to do despite his cousins' blatant example, nodded in a clumsy sort of bow.

Zacara smiled briefly—rather, her dark brown, almost black eyes smiled with a golden twinkle at them all. "There's no need for over formality," she said. "I see no need for constant obeisance while you are staying with us. I'm grateful you have come, and I'm sure my husband will be also, in time. Hopefully, you will be able to speak with him shortly."

She looked back at Johnathan. "In the meantime, Johnathan, perhaps you can show them their rooms? I'm sure they'll want to get settled in, and perhaps even be measured for something suitable for the table. I'm sure coming all the way from the North," she added, with another twinkling smile, "you'll be wanting a few additions to your wardrobe."

Engrelin refrained from looking down at his clothes, though there was no need to do even that. He knew how dusty and weather-stained they were. The sand lay in a gritty, unremovable layer between his clothes and his skin, chafing constantly.

Johnathan tipped his head. "I'll see to it that they do. Should I have them made in time for supper?"

"If that is possible," Zacara said. "We will hopefully be able to talk more then."

Johnathan, taking this rightly as a dismissal, bowed. The boys were hardly able to follow suit before Johnathan hurried them back into the palace.

But not before Engrelin caught a glimpse of Zacara's troubled face. Engrelin's heart sank as he trudged behind his companions down the hallway. Had Johnathan been wrong to bring them to Alinar? Were they unwanted here as well?

Once the disturbing thought embedded itself in Engrelin's mind, he could think of little else. Johnathan took them to be measured for more palace-worthy clothing, but Engrelin took in little of the visit. Only one thing broke momentarily though his thoughts—the sight of lace being sewn onto a men's tunic by one of the many tailors who filled a room already crowded with tables and fabric and humming with the chattering of the tailors as their needles clacked against their thimbles.

"You'd have to kill me before I wear lace," Engrelin muttered.

Averendier gave him a sharp look. Andrald quickly hid a chuckle behind his hand. Johnathan said nothing—though perhaps he didn't hear the comment. He watched a portly man poke the three young men into different positions, run a yellow ribbon around what seemed every part of their bodies, and finally step back with a satisfied air.

"I'll have them ready by this afternoon," said the tailor.

Johnathan thanked him and hurried the boys to a different section of the palace, just as elegant and airy as the rest, and stopped before three doors.

"These rooms are for you boys," he said. "Choose whichever you like. I would like to show you around some, but I have business to attend to. It's been a while since I've been in Alinar. But I will send someone else up to give you a tour of a few places. You won't want to be spending your entire visit in your rooms, after all."

"Thank you," Averendier said. "We'll stay in our rooms until then."

"Also, I'll send up a girl to bring your dinner, and perhaps draw some water so you can wash some of the journey off," Johnathan added, already beginning to move away down the corridor.

"Thank you," Averendier repeated. "You can have all the meals sent up to the middle room."

Johnathan waved at them in either dismissal or acknowledgement and disappeared around a bend in the corridor.

"Why the middle room?" Engrelin asked.

Averendier tried the door and pushed it open. "Because this one's mine," he said. He motioned his companions inside.

All the furniture in the room was white, even the sheer curtains flapping in the windows, the bedspread, and the towel hanging by a pitcher and basin. Averendier sank onto a white wicker chair and immediately eyed Engrelin.

"Just a few things, Engrelin. If you see someone as prestigious as Johnathan kneeling to someone, you should too."

Engrelin's shoulders tightened. "You didn't either, until he introduced you to Zacara."

"We had to wait to be introduced," replied Averendier. "And that comment about the lace..."

Engrelin's cheeks flamed. "I was…preoccupied. And I don't think anybody but you two heard it anyway."

"You think, but you don't actually know," Averendier admonished. "Next time, keep that to yourself."

Engrelin's whole body went rigid, but at that moment a knock sounded on the door, and a dark maid bustled in, bearing in her arms a tray laden with three plates.

"You can set them on the table," Averendier indicated.

The maid smiled at him, slid the plates onto the table, and bustled out of the room.

Averendier looked back at Engrelin. "I don't want any more insolence," he said. "A great deal relies on completing this mission for Bendekahn. Everyone's going to be watching us. And you. Just think of that before you do anything. Don't ruin this for us. I don't care how badly you want to go home."

Engrelin bit the inside of his cheek so fiercely that the tang of blood filled his mouth. His churning mind could grasp nothing worthwhile and truly biting to say that wouldn't cause further argument or start a fight. What about all the faulty camping grounds Averendier had picked on the way up? The plan that had made Engrelin risk his neck for the whole group? All the countless other small actions he had performed on the trip that Johnathan wasn't even able to do. For all their courtly training, they knew little of rugged living. The many instances he could fling back in Averendier's face!

Above all, Engrelin inwardly fumed, he didn't want to go home. Not without Bendekahn's children there with him. He didn't think he would ever make a good soldier; there seemed little he could help with in this war. But he could bring some important people to safety through the wilderness. He would. None of Averendier's picking and condescension would drive him from it.

n   Engrelin angrily stabbed his food off his plate. He could taste nothing but resentment. Averendier ate without saying anything more, impassive as always. Andrald munched quietly, not daring to cut the silence binding the argument.

Finally, a bold knock at the door cracked the silence. Carefully, Averendier set his plate down on the table beside him and began to stand. But Engrelin was already at the door, turning the brass handle.

A bronze-skinned solider stood in the hallway just outside. He flashed his white smile at Engrelin.

"Advisor Johnathan sent me to take any of you boys who wished on a tour," he said, in a rich voice that was not quite tenor but not quite bass.

Engrelin looked back at his cousins. Andrald was half-asleep in his chair, his plate teetering dangerously on his knee. Averendier, his expression unreadable, stared steadily back at Engrelin.

"I'd prefer to wait a little while to get washed up," Averendier said. "And I don't think Andrald is going to get up and about without a nap first." He leaned to the side to look at the soldier in the hall. "Perhaps later—"

"I'm up for it," Engrelin cut in. He glanced back at the soldier. "If you're okay taking only me."

The soldier nodded. "That's perfectly fine. I can perhaps show you others about once you're rested."

Lips pressed into a tight line, Averendier only nodded curtly.

Easing out a sigh of relief, Engrelin divested himself of his pack and quiver, and joined the soldier out in the hall, shutting the door against Averendier's piercing eyes.

23

The soldier immediately turned and started down the hallway, his gait measured and precise.

"What would you like to see first?" he asked.

Engrelin shrugged. "Don't know. I don't know much about this kind of place." He gestured to the high, arching ceiling and the pillars flanking the walk.

The soldier smiled. "That's fine. It was a stupid thing to ask anyway. I'll just swing you around to what I know best." He extended his hand. "Name's Xavien, by the way."

Engrelin clasped the dark hand heartily. "Engrelin."

Xavien smiled and turned off towards a set of double doors.

"This is the library," he said, flinging one door open.

Without much interest, Engrelin glanced into the room beyond his guide's shoulder. The room looked similar to the library in Elstar, only there was a whole wall of the arched windows, these ones sealed with glass (to protect the books from the elements, Engrelin supposed). The shelves were carved from marble.

Xavien glanced back at him. "I don't know if you want to go in and have a look…"

Engrelin frowned. "I can't read," he said.

Xavien shut the library door firmly. "Neither can I," he replied easily. "On to the next?"

A few halls down and a hundred rooms later (or so it seemed to Engrelin, whose head spun with the enormity of the place) Xavien ushered him past a large, arched opening in which wispy orange curtains hung.

"The gardens," Xavien explained hastily. "You'd better have a closer look at them later. We've got just a few more rooms to do, then I have to get back to my duties."

"Sorry if this was a bother," Engrelin apologized, though he couldn't feel entirely repentant. He was enjoying the soldier's company.

Xavien waved him off. "Not at all. It gives me a break from the grind. But I do have to be back in time to stand guard outside the family's dining room. And I need to get you back in time to get cleaned up for the meal as well."

Engrelin shook his head slightly in disbelief as he followed Xavien up a short staircase. It seemed hardly any time had passed since he had eaten his tense dinner with his cousins, and already the whole afternoon was almost gone? And he had only seen the parts of the palace visitors were permitted to see. It must take a week for a resident to get through every room and corridor!

Yet it was strange they would show him around at all. Why would he need to see all these things, if they were only staying for a short while?

Xavien hurried Engrelin through a parlor meant for any visitors in general, and a room hung all about with instruments (to his disappointment, he saw no fiddles among them). Finally, Xavien peered out of one of the open windows and turned smilingly back to Engrelin.

"How would you like a glimpse of the girls?" he asked.

"The girls?" Engrelin repeated, puzzled.

Xavien's shoulders shook with silent laughter. "Bendekahn's daughters, I mean. They're playing down here in the courtyard."

Engrelin shrugged. "Sure, why not?"

Xavien pushed aside a curtain and the two stepped out into the glaring afternoon sunshine. The sun's rays were intensified against the shining white marble walls and the marble staircase the two stepped out onto. Engrelin squinted against the brilliancy and shielded his eyes with his hand.

Engrelin's gaze traveled down the spiraling staircase to the bottom where a brawny Alinar guard stood, as stiff and stoic as if he had been carved out of the very stone he stood against. He lifted his frowning gaze slowly to the newcomers, saw Xavien among then, and resumed watching his charges.

When Xavien had said 'the girls were playing,' Engrelin had automatically assumed that Bendekahn's daughters were little. What he found in the yard below him, however, were three young women, the youngest perhaps a year behind himself. They were running back and forth inside a partitioned circle, batting a ball riddled with feathers back and forth over the nets separating them into their sections. Their every move set their silk garments fluttering and streaming out behind them. Their gilded belts shone and the sun danced through the jewels studding their hair, arms, and throats. Their laughter rang as merry and swift as birdsong, echoing lightly against the marble walls encompassing them. Strangely enough, they seemed to take no notice of the near dozen soldiers posted around the courtyard, watching them attentively.

Engrelin's eyebrows knit. Bendekahn certainly took great pains to keep his daughters safe. The excessive number of guards was staggering. His thoughts flitted nervously to the small force his cousins and himself made.

Equally baffling was the girls' appearance. Of the three, only one had her mother's dark hair, and none her soft brown skin. And the other girls' hair was as fine and as pale as flax!

The world that had begun to slip in place when he had seen Zacara was spinning out of focus once again.

The dark-haired girl glanced up at the balcony upon which Engrelin and Xavien stood. She held her racket loosely at her side, arms akimbo, and pinched her ruby lips together, locking gazes with Engrelin. She scowled black as midnight.

Engrelin took a startled step back.

Hello, and good riddance to you too, he thought, as she resumed the game.

"Hopefully," Xavien was saying. Had he been talking the whole time? "You'll have the chance to get better acquainted with them at supper tonight."

I'm not so sure that I want to, Engrelin thought, glancing back down at the girl, who was thankfully too distracted playing to glare venomously at him again. *For that, they don't either.*

Xavien tapped Engrelin's shoulder. "Come on. There's one last thing I've got to show you."

Engrelin retreated gladly back into the palace's cool interior. Xavien led him excitedly up to a door and tugged it open.

"This is our fencing room," he said, walking to the middle of the floor which, unlike the rest of the floors in the palace, was solid wood and scarred with many grooves. "It's for the residents here, and guests, to practice. Even the princesses receive basic lessons here." He motioned to a rack against the wall, holding several slender rapiers, each with a handle more ornate than the one below it. Engrelin looked at them skeptically. Using one of those must be like sticking someone with a giant pin. He glanced over at several other racks, each holding a unique style of sword, pike, bows, and other weapons.

"It's so different from the rest of this place," he remarked, motioning to the panes of amber and cobalt glass that filled the windows, the mahogany paneling covering the bottom three feet of the wall, and the far end of the room, where a heavy velvet curtain covered the wall ceiling to floor.

"Our instructor here, Lamar, had things fixed up this way when he first came here," Xavien explained. "That was before I was posted here. I don't know what it looked like before. But it is rather different." He scratched the tip of his chin thoughtfully. "Well, Bendekahn's rich enough to transform every room in this place if he wanted to. Probably didn't want to lose Lamar; wants him to train the princesses, I suppose. The man's a wonder." He chuckled at Engrelin sidelong. "If you ever want to be perfectly black and blue from head to toe, ask him to go through a routine with you. He'll be happy to oblige."

Engrelin glanced at the racks of weapons, flexing his right hand. "I've got a bow, but thanks."

Xavien brightened. "In that case, you might want to see the range we have. It's just beyond the gardens. It's free for any visitors as well."

Engrelin looked slightly askance at Xavien. "You just have everything set up for visitors here? Does Bendekahn's family get *any* privacy?"

"This is their winter home," Xavien said, shoulders shaking again. "Every Alinar builds their winter homes for guests and frolics. It's the only time cool enough to stick your head outdoors. That, and Zacara loves being a hostess. We wouldn't have over forty guest bedrooms if she didn't!"

Engrelin wheeled sharply to search Xavien's face. "Forty? You're kidding me."

"I'm not," Xavien answered. He gestured vaguely around. "You're in the home of Ontaria's wealthiest monarch!" he exclaimed. "You're expecting this place to be small?"

"Smaller," replied Engrelin wryly.

Xavien cast one final glance around the room before motioning to the door. "We'd better head back to your rooms now," he said. "If you are interested in ever using the range, it's just through the garden's eastern corner, through the gate. You can't miss it."

Engrelin glanced at the sun through the tinted windows. "It doesn't seem so late," he murmured.

"There might be time if you don't mind going to supper looking like a ruffian," Xavien said.

Engrelin glanced down at his travel-worn self. "I wouldn't mind," he answered mildly. "But I'm sure the family would."

Nonetheless, it was good to get back to his room to wash off the grit and sweat of weeks and don the fresh clothes that had been spread across his bed. They were light and soft, unlike his heavier woolen clothes which had made the desert country unbearable at first. The tailors had copied his style of clothing perfectly: simple tunic, trousers, and broad leather belt, stiff with newness. (And, to Engrelin's inmost relief, not a hint of lace anywhere.)

However, he hardly had time to marvel at the tailor's speed and skill. Xavien had already warned him that supper was soon, and he likely wouldn't be on time if he wanted to make himself presentable.

Hastily, Engrelin splashed more water across his face, scrubbed it dry with the towel hanging by the basin, and hurried out of the room, combing his unruly hair back with his fingers as he went.

Halfway down the corridor, he realized he had no idea where the dining room was. Groaning under his breath, he chased down one of the many servants, (there seemed to be thousands running all over the place, and no wonder!) who gave him hasty directions.

Flushed and irate, Engrelin finally spotted the dining room's curtained doorway, Xavien standing just outside it. The guard's face was set in iron lines—every genial crease of earlier had vanished. When he spotted Engrelin coming down the hallway, he stepped to one side and drew the filmy curtain back to admit him. As Engrelin walked past, Xavien leaned towards him.

"I told you you'd be late."

Engrelin snorted softly and stepped into the hallway leading to the dining room. Chuckling, Xavien let the curtain swish back into place behind him. Engrelin strode briskly down the short hall, which opened into the dining room.

It looked much as he had expected: large, open sided with fluttering curtains, dominated by a long table. He stared rather hard at the strange seating, if one could call it that. There were no proper chairs at all, only the long, cushioned, almost couch-like things he had seen throughout the palace. His cousins, the three princesses, Johnathan, and Zacara all reclined on them, propped up on one elbow. And they were all looking at him.

Clearing his throat uncomfortably, Engrelin straightened. "I'm sorry I'm late," he murmured.

Zacara smiled at him and motioned to one of the empty lounges. "You're fine. Xavien warned us."

Engrelin dipped his head in a nod. Resigned to his fate, he approached the table and lowered himself awkwardly onto the lounge, propped on his elbows and laying not quite on his side, as the others were doing. A hint of color burned his cheeks. This was absurd. Who in the world ate lying on their stomachs?

"I dare say Micael needed more time for the fowl," Johnathan remarked easily.

Engrelin forced a small smile, and the hum of conversation resumed around him. Just across the table, the dark-haired princess scowled blackly at him. Engrelin averted his gaze, only to meet Averendier's eyes. His look clearly conveyed, 'we'll talk about this later.'

Pressing his lips together, Engrelin looked down at his plate. He stiffened and slowly corrected himself. Plural. *Plates*. Four of them.

Not to mention the other four cups, three knives, three forks, and two spoons that all swarmed on the table before him. The only singular thing in the whole bunch was a bowl set placidly off to the side. He even had two napkins, both folded into birds with wide-spread tails.

Quickly, he scanned the others' places. They were all the same— the incredible number of dishes, the exquisite bird napkins.

What kind of joke was this? How in Ontaria was he supposed to use all of them?

Even as he thought it, several servants filed into the room, each bearing a tray or a pitcher. The others at the table continued chatting pleasantly as the servants moved around the table, piling one plate at each place high with salad greens and drenching it with a pink dressing. Instinctively, Engrelin's stomach churned. Yet he still began his string of mental notes.

All right, that's the salad plate. Now, which fork am I supposed to use?

He had to wait a moment to figure this out, for Zacara led grace. Only then did everyone start eating. By closely watching Andrald, who reclined beside him, Engrelin finally decided which utensil to use.

Eating was an entirely different dragon to slay. Engrelin had never been a fan of trying new foods, especially not ones swimming in bright pink liquid. The dressing trickled off the crimped edges of the salad greens and pooled in the center of the plate.

Oh well. He nearly shrugged to himself. There was a first for everything. Determinedly spearing one of the dripping leaves, Engrelin put it into his mouth.

The first burst of sweetness made the back of his throat burn. Thankfully, one of the servants had just filled his cup. He pressed it to his lips to conceal his grimace as he swallowed and took a long sip. It was wine (something he didn't particularly enjoy), but he downed half the glass to wash out the dressing's sickly flavor.

"Young man, I'm afraid you weren't in here in time to be properly introduced to my daughters."

Engrelin glanced up to see Zacara looking expectantly at him. Straightening as best he could in his unfamiliar position, he set his cup gently down.

Zacara motioned to the three girls reclining on the opposite side of the table. "These are my daughters, Lilac, Isalinia, and Elvera."

The girls nodded in turn, the black-haired girl last. Engrelin studied her curiously. Her name sounded so much like Elmera's, and certainly not Alinar-ish.

Elvera caught him staring at her, glanced at her mother to see if she was looking, then screwed her face at Engrelin.

"And yourself?" Zacara asked. "I'm afraid, with all that happened this morning, I misplaced your name."

"Engrelin, ma'am," he answered, stopping from smiling at the last moment. "Engrelin Everen Aaron Peterson."

Averendier's eyebrows lifted ever so slightly, but Zacara simply nodded. No doubt she heard such a list of names (and doubtless much longer ones) on a regular basis. Engrelin, however, was anything but accustomed to rattling the lot off; his cousin's evident disapproval made him stare down at his plate. His stomach still churned, but the salad couldn't just be left there. Engrelin stabbed another small forkful and chewed it with a vengeance that Dermain himself might have admired. Around him, Zacara and her oldest daughter, Lilac, continued the conversation pleasantly. Few questions were directed to Engrelin, leaving him to silent battle with the salad.

Eventually, the salad plates were cleared (despite all efforts, most of Engrelin's salad remained). Other plates were heaped with what looked like sweet potatoes in gravy. Engrelin took a cautious bite, then subtly reached for his cup. Thankfully, it had been filled with water this time. He took a long sip.

So the meal dragged on, full of useless chatter and overly seasoned dishes. Engrelin was far too accustomed to a simple menu to enjoy anything served, but he ate what he could, and shifted more and more onto his side to escape lying on his rolling stomach. He could only hope that the meal was like this to welcome them. But if all meals in Alinar tasted like this…

"Now, boys," said Zacara, straightening and folding both arms against the low arm of her lounge, "Johnathan told me he brought you here to speak to my husband."

Engrelin's ears perked, and for a moment he could ignore his nausea.

"But," she continued quietly, "I'm afraid he left for Methicayn, a city several day's ride from here, a couple days ago on business."

Engrelin's eyes riveted to the queen's drawn face. Bendekahn was gone?

"It was urgent business," Zacara continued, "And he had no idea when Johnathan was returning, or that you would be with him. I'm truly sorry. I know you came a long way to see him." She was silent a moment, her fine lips pressed firmly together as her gaze swept over her visitors. "Are you willing to stay here and wait for his return?"

"Of course we are," Averendier affirmed. "How long do you think it will be?"

"A month. Perhaps two," Zacara said. "The time was uncertain when he left."

Engrelin inhaled slowly and painfully. Two months. It was an awfully long time to be away from home. At that rate, he would get no winter crops in. His grandmother and Elmera would have to spend the whole time at the rectory.

Yet he had no choice but to stay. What was the point in going home when failure to remain might risk everything he and all other Monarians held dear?

"Why do they need to talk to Father?" asked Elvera. Everyone turned their heads to look at her. It was the first time she had spoken throughout the entire meal.

"They have some business to talk over with him," replied Zacara, voice smooth as glass. "You girls will learn soon enough. Now, off to your rooms, please. I'll be with you after we escort our guests back to their rooms."

Elvera immediately stood, favored Engrelin with a glare, and flounced out of the room.

What would she say if she knew she might be coming with us on a long journey? Engrelin thought as he swung his legs off the lounge and stood as the remaining girls left the room. Lilac, the oldest girl, cast a probing look at her mother before she followed her sister beyond the sheer curtain. No doubt she suspected her mother was hiding something from her.

His brow knit, Engrelin trailed out of the room behind Andrald. Why was Zacara hiding it from them anyway?

"Two months?" Andrald hissed to Averendier as they followed Zacara and Johnathan through the palace halls. "What are you thinking?"

"Are two months too much for you?" Averendier asked.

"I'm fine," Andrald replied. "But what about him?" He jerked his head back towards Engrelin. "Tomorrow is the last day of the harvest. We'll be here past Christ Mass!"

Averendier glanced quickly back at Engrelin, who flushed cherry red.

Turning back around, he answered coolly, "He's just going to have to put up with it. I'm not leaving until we've done what we came to do."

As he strode along, Engrelin simmered. Did Averendier still think he was upset about having to come? When would he stop thinking that all Engrelin cared about was going home? He certainly would have liked to be back in Bryn by now, but that didn't mean he wasn't willing to wait in Alinar. Two months or two years, he didn't care, so long as he could aid his country and perhaps live in peace.

They had reached their rooms and Averendier was bidding Zacara and Johnathan goodnight when it hit Engrelin. Andrald had said tomorrow was the last day of harvest. Which meant today…

Bowing hastily to his hosts and murmuring goodnight, Engrelin retreated woodenly into his room. He eased the door closed behind himself and leaned heavily against it, one hand clutching the doorhandle. How could he have forgotten?

Exactly eighteen years ago, he had been born.

"Do you think it will work?" Zacara's voice was muffled through the door, but nonetheless discernable. "Johanthan, they're—"

"I know," Johnathan replied. "But it is the last thing he will suspect."

"Still, Bendekahn will have to give his approval," Zacara reminded, her voice growing fainter as she moved down the hall. "Though I have no doubt he will. Alinar is no longer safe…"

Before Engrelin heard anything more, the two drifted out of range.

Engrelin sighed and glanced around at his room: the bed with filmy curtains hanging about it, the curtain standing between the room and the balcony outside, the lounge in one corner, the ornately tiled floor. This was the last place he would have expected to spend his eighteenth birthday, an occasion which would have been celebrated hugely at home—his entrance to manhood. It was something every Monarian child looked forward to for seventeen years and three hundred sixty-four days.

Here, in the lonely darkness of his room, it hardly seemed anything important. He could hardly think of his own small steps in life when the peril and destruction of nations hovered overhead.

Eighteen years he had waited. All for a troubling, painful day in a strange land.

And more waiting.

He could only hope that this time, the wait would prove fruitful.

24

o you understand any *of it?"* demanded Andrald, exasperated. "No," Engrelin admitted grudgingly. He glared down at the speller lying open on the table in front of him: his nemesis of the past few afternoons. In a final burst of anger, he swept the thing shut and shoved it across the table towards his cousin.

Andrald clutched his head in his hands. "Do you even *try* to understand it?"

"Yes, I do," Engrelin gritted. He had tried so many times! But how was anyone supposed to figure out how all those lines and squiggles and dots represented the words they spoke daily?

Another thing he needed to understand: Why had he let Andrald drag him into this?

Sighing heavily, Andrald kneaded his temples with his fingertips. "Engrelin, I'm sorry, but I don't think I can take this anymore."

"That's fine by me. I can't either," Engrelin replied, pushing his chair away from the table. "It's not like I need to read anyway, unless I really want to know what's stored in the pantry."

Andrald shook his head. "It isn't funny, Engrelin."

"I hadn't meant it to be."

Andrald frowned. "I was hoping to give you something to do besides target practice and walking in the gardens."

Engrelin frowned. "I want to be prepared," he said quietly. "A little practice never hurt anyone. As to the gardens…" He shrugged. "I've never seen anything like them. I think they're interesting. You might like walking there instead of trying to teach a hopelessly stupid farmer."

"Maybe I should," said Andrald drily. "But maybe you should give up spending all your time over plants and arrows and eat breakfast every once in a while."

Andrald did have him there. Engrelin hardly ever joined the family for their breakfast. Accustomed to rising with the sun, he couldn't eat hours after dawn as the family did, so he ate his breakfast in his room.

"I tried the first few mornings," he said. "But they serve it too late. Besides, Zacara told us that we could eat in our rooms whenever we chose. Dining with them is just an option."

"You might want to try harder," Andrald remarked. "Besides risking starving to death, you missed what Zacara told us about Bendekahn this morning."

Of course I did. "Bad news?" Engrelin muttered, fiddling with a loose thread on his tunic's hem.

"Sort of. It's not anything that we didn't already know. Bendekahn affirmed he'll be gone awhile. Nothing we can do but wait."

Engrelin looked down at the floor. As Andrald said, it was nothing they hadn't expected. But it was disappointing to get yet another confirmation.

They were in for the long haul.

Whatever Andrald might think, the gardens were truly a beautiful place to be. Plants strange and exotic to Engrelin filled every bed and corner, waving large, fan-shaped leaves and brightly colored flowers.

One section of it wasn't filled with plants. Instead, the beds contained remarkably life-like imitations of plants, all twisted and carved out of precious stones. They sparkled in the sunlight as if perpetually drenched with dew. Even whole trees had been constructed, with dark roots glinting through the sand and topaz leaves rattling in the wind overhead.

After Engrelin's conversation with Andrald, however, these splendid creations seemed to have lost their luster. Even the water spouting from the classic three-tiered fountain in the garden's center seemed to spray less than usual. Engrelin wandered up and down the paths, glanced at a few plants (both real and stone), and sighed. Soon he found himself pacing up and down the wide paved area around the fountain.

Andrald was right. Engrelin desperately needed something to do. Something physical. He was so used to working hard all day long, the sudden inactivity was grating. His consent to reading lessons was proof enough! To sit around all day, waiting, wandering, but never actually doing anything truly purposeful…

In one aspect, Andrald was wrong. If Engrelin died before Bendekahn came, it wouldn't be from missing breakfasts. He would first waste away from complete and utter boredom.

His face darkening, Engrelin turned sharply on his heel and strode back into the palace. Marching around outside wasn't helping anything either.

In the hall, he nearly walked straight into Xavien.

"Hey, are you blind?" exclaimed the guard, catching Engrelin by the shoulders and shoving him back.

Engrelin laughed ruefully, scrubbing the back of his neck with his hand. "No, just bored out of my wits," he admitted. "And not watching where I'm going."

"You try out the range yet?" Xavien suggested.

"Every day, for hours," Engrelin replied. "But even that gets old, especially when I'm the only one out there."

"Fair enough," Xavien acknowledged. "Not much else here to interest you, is there?"

"It's an amazing place," Engrelin said, waving towards the highly vaulted ceiling above them. "I'm just not…used to it all," he concluded lamely.

Xavien nodded. "Took me a few years to get used to it myself."

"No offense, Xavien," Engrelin said, "but I hope I won't be here for that long."

"So do I," Xavien said, in a way that made Engrelin wonder if he knew why the three Monarians had come. Brightening up, he added, "There's not much time before supper, but I just came back from the fencing room. Lamar, our instructor, is back. You might want to meet him. Maybe you two can practice together, if you don't mind getting banged up."

Engrelin shook his head. "I wouldn't mind, but I can't swing a sword to save my soul."

"I'm sure if it were that desperate, you could," Xavien chuckled. "But you may just want to talk to him. Give you something to do other than bumble around in the halls, impeding royal guards."

Engrelin was still uncertain, but what else was there to do? His feet adopted minds of their own and dragged him away from Xavien, down the halls, and up the short staircase to the fencing room. He stood uncertainly outside the door a moment, then grabbed the handle and pushed himself inside.

The clash and ring of a mock battle greeted him. In the center of the room, two men were fighting with dull scimitars. The blades flashed in the colored beams of light that shone across the room. The men moved so quickly Engrelin could hardly follow their fight.

One of the men must be Lamar. There would be no talking to him, Engrelin decided, relief mingling strangely with disappointment. At least he could watch the fight. Creeping along the wall, he settled to watch in a corner filled with ancient-looking blades.

The curved swords were mere blurs in the fighters' deadly dance. The clash and whizz of the blades filled Engrelin's ears. Every now and then, the larger of the two men called out some sort of instruction to his comrade. Sometimes, it would be to pull apart for a few moments, just long enough to catch a breath before resuming the fight.

Finally, when the two blades swung so swiftly that they seemed to have welded into one, the larger man gave a curious flick of his wrist and his opponent's scimitar flew out of his hand in a neat arch to the far end of the room, where it clattered to the floor.

"Wonderful job, Mirtael!" the master exclaimed, heartily thumping his disgruntled student on the back.. "You stuck at it for a while that time!"

"You still got me, Lamar," returned Mirtael, looking down. However, he couldn't conceal a grin as he walked across the room to retrieve his sword.

Smiling, Lamar turned. His eyes locked with Engrelin's.

Engrelin stiffened. As Lamar opened his mouth to speak, an unexplainable apprehension tore through Engrelin. Not waiting to hear what the man had to say to him, he slipped from his hiding place and left the room.

Now why'd you do that? he berated himself, even before the door swung shut behind him. *You could have at least listened to what he had to say, instead of skulking out of there.*

A glance out the nearest window told him that he didn't have time to go back in, however badly he wanted to. Supper had probably begun by now.

Besides, he told himself as he descended the stairs two at a time, what use would he have for lessons? Even if Lamar went so far as to teach him a couple things, Engrelin had no sword. He might as well stick to his bow.

"Late again?" asked Xavien, eyes twinkling, as Engrelin approached the curtain.

"When aren't I?" Engrelin asked, flinging his hands up hopelessly.

Chuckling, Xavien drew the curtain aside. "Don't worry," he whispered, "I don't think they've eaten everything yet."

Shooting the guard a mock glare, Engrelin passed through the doorway and walked down the short, carpeted hallway.

He had nearly reached the dining room when he heard Averendier's voice distinctly asking, "Zacara, if I may…"

Instinctively, Engrelin paused in the doorway, hands clasped behind his back, waiting to be noticed and welcomed to the table. But all heads, even Elvera's, were turned towards his older cousin.

Zacara made a small, indulgent gesture. "Of course."

"It's about my cousin, Engrelin," Averendier began quietly.

Engrelin's gaze sharpened on the back of his cousin's head.

"You received the confirmation this morning that we will have to wait a couple months to meet with your husband. But Engrelin has a grandmother and sister whom he takes care of back home. He's already been away from them longer than he counted on, and I'm not sure that he's willing to wait so long to finally get back to them."

An all too familiar flame seared Engrelin's frame, but he did not move a muscle. When had he ever complained of the wait? What was Averendier thinking?

"And…" Zacara prompted, her brow creased.

"I was wondering," Averendier said quietly, "If it would be all right if he went home ahead of time, with one of your men, or even my brother. He doesn't know the way himself and would need a guide back."

Engrelin's jaw spasmed, his fists balled at his sides. This couldn't be happening. Averendier was not doing this to him.

Next thing you know, he'll be telling them what an idiot I am because I can't read. And that I need to be defended because I can't lift a sword correctly—arrows probably wouldn't count to him.

Zacara looked down at her plate in the long silence that followed. Finally, she looked up and asked, "Have you spoken to him about this? I wouldn't want to consent to anything he hasn't."

"No, I haven't mentioned it yet," Averendier replied. "I didn't want to get him excited about anything before I had your permission."

Since when was I excited to back down from anything?!

"If this is what he wants, I won't stand in his way. You are guests, after all, and free to leave when you please." Zacara's voice was painfully brittle, her movements jerky. "But I would like to talk to him also, if he wouldn't mind."

"He doesn't," said Engrelin starkly from the doorway.

At the sound of his voice, everyone turned to stare at him. Everyone including Averendier, who seemed to be—for once—a trifle pale.

Engrelin took one step into the room. "May I join you?" he asked. "I'm sorry for being late."

"Of course! Please, sit down," Zacara offered, extending her hand graciously. The twinkling of triumph in her dark eyes nearly made Engrelin smile.

Engrelin moved slowly to his place, carefully breathing the air thick with the mental darts Averendier shot his way. He settled just as carefully onto the lounge, propped both arms beneath himself, and smiled at the servant who moved forward to fill his glass with water instead of wine. Though filling his cup was hardly necessary. The air was so thick, he could easily have drunk it.

"I assume you heard what we were discussing," said Zacara smoothly. She seemed to be the only one at the table completely at ease, except perhaps her daughter Lilac. Then again, Zacara always seemed that way. Comes of being the wife of the richest monarch in Ontaria.

"I did, ma'am," Engrelin said (forgetting yet again how improper it was to address a queen so familiarly. But Zacara didn't seem to mind it in the least).

"If going home is what you truly want to do, I will not stand in your way," she said quietly.

Averendier's gaze bored into his young cousin. Struggling to ignore its burn, Engrelin replied, "I do have family at home, but they're in good hands. I'm sure they'll be fine until we've all met with your husband and are ready to go back." His voice hardened a little as he repeated, "I don't intend on leaving until we've spoken to Bendekahn, ma'am."

Zacara smiled warmly, her right cheek dimpling. "Thank you, Engrelin. I'm glad to hear that."

It was her last comment on the subject. She said nothing to Averendier, only gave him a look. Andrald hastily switched to commenting on some poem he had recently read. This captivated the princesses and scholarly Johnathan instantly. Under the lively discussion, the flames of the situation quickly faded in all of them.

In all except Averendier. He was far from quenched. There was nothing else to say at the table. Watching his silent cousin sidelong, Engrelin wondered how long after the meal Averendier could contain himself.

He wouldn't have long before he found out.

Engrelin was lying sprawled out on his stomach across his bed, spelling primer in hand, when someone rapped sharply on his door. Shoving the book beneath his pillow, Engrelin rolled onto his side.

Before he could even call out "Come in," the door opened and Averendier stepped into the room.

For a moment, he stood just inside the doorway, staring at Engrelin, who struggled to hide his dismay. He had hoped Averendier might take time to cool off before he came.

But dinner had ended only a few minutes ago, and here was Averendier already, jaw locked, eyes burning.

"You need something," Engrelin said. He didn't even try to sound surprised.

"A little talk might be nice," Averendier returned. He shut the door behind him with the finality of an executioner.

Engrelin's mouth tightened as he watched Averendier cross the large room and retrieve a chair. Even if Averendier hadn't wanted to calm down, Engrelin had. He still felt capable of biting off someone's head. At the very least, give them a good drubbing.

"Averendier," he said haltingly, "I really don't feel up to this—"

Averendier set the chair down beside Engrelin's bed with a deliberate *thunk.*

"No, Engrelin" he said severely. "This can't wait. We have to talk."

"Talk about what?" Engrelin asked, rubbing his forehead between his eyes.

Averendier stared at him. "Engrelin, don't act like you don't know."

Engrelin sat up and swung his legs over the edge of the bed. "I don't think I do," he said. "You're acting as if *I'm* the one in the wrong. When did it occur to you that planning other people's lives behind their backs was okay? What in Ontaria made you think I wanted to leave?"

Averendier drew back in his chair. "I only thought—"

"Thought I wanted to go home. I wonder why? Especially since I haven't said a word about returning since we got here," said Engrelin, plowing forward with abandon. "Do you want me to go home?"

"We all want to help with this, Engrelin," Averendier said quietly. "But you don't have to hide the fact that you're homesick."

Homesick! Engrelin reeled to his feet.

"Stop hedging. What is it really?" he demanded. Though a full foot shorter than Averendier, Engrelin felt as if their heights had evened. Averendier kept his seat, exaggerating the sensation. "Do you hate me, Averendier?"

Averendier chuckled, somewhat bitterly. "It's not that—"

"Then what?" Engrelin asked. "From the start of this trip, you resented my coming with you. You never listened to me, even when what I said was worthwhile. You lied to me about the reason Lord Gwane wouldn't let me see Wilelm. And now this?"

Averendier's features were immovable. "Engrelin, it's not what you think."

"Of course not. It's never what *I* think, is it? Just you and your schemes and commands," Engrelin said sarcastically. "This isn't your ship. You don't have absolute control over everyone and everything around you. You can't shove me away from my duty because you don't like me. I know I'm low born, and I can't read or swing a sword. So what? At least I have the manners to talk to a fellow before I rub his face in the dirt in front of a queen." Engrelin banged his fist against his thigh, wishing he'd smashed it into Averendier's grim smile instead. Angrily, he tugged his hand through his hair. "How could you be so stupid?"

Averendier rose, his hand shooting forward. Grasping Engrelin by the front of his tunic, Averendier shook him.

"Enough!" he growled, balling his hand into a fist.

At that moment, the bedroom door burst open. Andrald rushed into the room. Averendier glanced up at his entrance.

Siezing the opportunity, Engrelin drove his fist into Averendier's middle. Averendier, coughing, released his hold and doubled back. Engrelin jumped a step back, gathering himself defensively. Recovering, Averendier doubled his fists and charged at Engrelin.

Andrald sprang between them. He caught Averendier's fist and jerked him back. Engrelin lunged after Averendier, but Andrald's flying fist caught him on the jaw, flinging him back on the bed.

"What are you two doing?" Andrald demanded angrily, gray eyes flashing.

Engrelin jumped back to his feet, breathing heavily, watching Averendier reflexively clasp his wrist. Engrelin's' hands curled. Why had Andrald stepped in? He'd waited too long for this. The fire in Averendier's eyes told Engrelin this was a language Averendier understood.

"Do you have any idea what this might do to us?" Andrald turned sharply on his brother.

Averendier gripped the back of his chair; the cording in his arms rippled, his knuckled showed white. He was stubbornly—infuriatingly—silent. Engrelin's jaw spasmed.

Andrald turned to Engrelin. "What—"

"Ask him," Engrelin jerked out. He crossed the room and retrieved his quiver, slinging it's strap over his shoulder.

Averendier started forward, as if to stop him. But Engrelin was already striding out into the hallway. He shut the door carefully behind himself.

Engrelin grunted softly as he pulled his billionth arrow out of the target. Two hours of shooting and he was still frustrated. And angry, once again. Not just at Averendier, but at himself.

I shouldn't have lost my head, he thought, sending the billionth and first arrow thudding into the target. *I did more than chew his head off* (billionth and second arrow). *I've just about wrecked any goodwill he had left in him* (billionth and third). *It'd just be* (billionth and fourth) *so much easier* (billionth and fifth) *if he wouldn't be* (billionth and sixth) *so difficult!*

Sending his last arrow quivering into the crowded target, Engrelin strode forward and ripped them all out again. He yanked them out so violently, he was lucky they were fletched out of sturdy wood, or they might have splintered.

After filling his quiver, he stalked back to the painted white line that marked where an archer should stand as he shot. He nocked an arrow, sighted swiftly down the shaft, and fired. The arrow leapt towards the target and smacked into the edge of the center circle. Scowling at himself, Engrelin tugged another arrow out of his quiver.

"You know, if you angled your bow a bit more, it'd hit more true," said someone behind him.

Engrelin turned slowly to see the weapon's instructor, Lamar, leaning against the garden wall.

"Change it how?" Engrelin asked aloud, though that was not truly the question burning his mind. *Just how long have you been watching me?*

"Here. I'll show you." Stepping forward, Lamar drew a bow out of his own quiver, strung it, and nocked an arrow. Tilting his bow ever so slightly, almost imperceptibly, he swiftly shot three arrows in succession, his hands mere blurs. The shafts thudded into the target in almost the exact same spot, their orange feathered tips quivering in the target's dead center.

Lips parted ever so slightly, Engrelin nodded his admiration.

"You're pretty fast."

Lamar, seeming to ignore the compliment, asked, "Did you see how I did it?"

"I think so."

"All right. Try it."

Engrelin attempted to imitate Lamar's angle and shot a single arrow. It struck the target only a few centimeters away from Lamar's.

The man's brow puckered slightly. "Try again," he said.

So Engrelin shot again, and again, the heat of the challenge rising within him until one of his arrows finally clipped the feather off one of Lamar's.

Only then did Lamar nod and hold up his hand, signaling Engrelin to stop.

"You'll pass," he said, adding, "You pick it up pretty quick." Biting his inner lip thoughtfully, Lamar gazed at Engrelin a moment. "How old are you?"

"Eighteen, just two weeks ago," Engrelin replied, looking at the man askance.

Lamar's eyes sharpened. "And you're a farmer by trade? From *Traeth Euriad*?"

Engrelin's eyes narrowed. "Did Johnathan tell you that?" he demanded.

Lamar didn't answer. He just looked Engrelin up and down. "How'd you like to try using a longsword?" he asked.

Engrelin blinked at the abruptness of the question. A longsword?

"I've never tried my hand at swords much," he said slowly.

"You'll learn," Lamar replied. "You're quick, and you'll be here a while. It would give us both something to do."

Without another word, he swiveled and strode back towards the garden gate. "I wouldn't skip breakfast tomorrow morning if I were you," he added over his shoulder. "You'll need it for tomorrow. I want to see you by eight sharp."

Engrelin watched Lamar disappear into the garden. *What in Ontaria was that all about?* He shook his head, as if he didn't quite believe what had just happened. He glanced back at the target, at his arrows and Lamar's orange trio, almost as if to reassure himself. One of Lamar's was split, driven completely through by another of his orange-crowned arrows.

25

The following morning, Engrelin lay on his back for a few moments and blinked at the high ceiling. His whole body ached because he'd slept on the lounge in his room instead of in the voluminous, canopied bed (which was too soft for comfort). Groaning softly under his breath, Engrelin sat up and recited his morning prayers. This done, he shuffled over to his basin of water and sloshed it over his face and neck. The icy water stabbed him fully awake. As he pulled his tunic on, someone knocked on his door.

"Door's open," he called, tightening his leather belt around his waist.

The door opened, and the smiling little maid who had been serving him since his arrival entered. She balanced a breakfast tray against one hip.

"I'll set it right here on the table," she said. She arranged the tray and a small vase—into which one single flower had been thrust—on the table. Then she straightened and smoothed the front of her skirt.

"Anything else I can get for you?" she asked.

He waved her off. "No, that's fine. Thanks."

Bowing slightly, the girl left the room, leaving Engrelin to stare at the tray.

He had nearly forgotten. Lamar expected him in the fencing room by eight. At least, he supposed the fencing room. He wasn't entirely sure—Lamar hadn't said exactly where to go. His proposal had been too sudden. Sudden and strange. Engrelin wasn't quite sure how to feel about it. Excited, nervous, and apprehensive all at once.

Quickly, he plunked down in his chair and lifted the lid off his plate. He was sure of one thing—he had to eat fast if he wanted to get all the way across the palace in time.

"I see you decided to come."

Whether Lamar was pleased about this or not, who could say? But Engrelin had rightly assumed that they were to meet in the fencing room, and he had gotten there on time, so he was at least satisfied with himself.

"There's not much else to do in this place," Engrelin said, with a light shrug.

Lamar eyed him sharply. "There's plenty to do, for those who look for it. Only sometimes, those things must find you. Did you eat?"

"Yes," Engrelin answered irritably.

Lamar nodded curtly. "Good. I've had far too many students faint on me in my time." He scanned Engrelin briefly, then wheeled and marched across the hall to a rack of weapons. Engrelin followed silently.

"These dull blades are for training," Lamar said, motioning to the near dozen swords lying horizontally on racks up the wall. "We'll find one the right weight and get started."

Engrelin wondered exactly what Lamar meant by the "right weight." Every sword the man thrust into his hands felt heavy and clumsy to Engrelin, a lanky obstruction. Finally, however, Lamar was satisfied with the way Engrelin held one.

"Usually in books one describes it as being an extension of one's arm," Lamar observed as he watched Engrelin weigh the weapon in his hand with growing confidence.

"A very long, very sharp extension," Engrelin said. It didn't feel quite like that, he thought. It was still clumsy, but maneuverable.

"Today, I don't want you to think of it quite as an extension," Lamar continued. "Rather a shield. It can protect you from every blow. It can be taken from you at any moment. Once we've got that down, you can start thinking about the extra length."

"Why just a shield?" Engrelin asked. This was nothing like what his uncle had tried to do with him.

"A shield for now," Lamar said. "I'm going to attack you."

Without further ado, the man seized a sword from the rack and sprang at Engrelin. Engrelin jumped back a step. Seeing the blur of metal swooping down on him, he flung his sword up to protect himself.

A jarring impact, the scrape of metal, and his weapon shot out of his hands and onto the floor.

"Pick it up!" Lamar shouted, advancing with his own sword poised. "And never be so loose!"

Engrelin scrambled after his weapon, snatching it up just in time to deflect a slash at his head. Lamar's sword glanced off Engrelin's shoulder and rounded for another blow. Wincing from the bruise, Engrelin tensed, holding his weapon diagonally in front of himself, both hands wrapped around the hilt. Lamar's next slash sent ribbons of fire jarring through Engrelin's hands. Engrelin uttered a strangled gasp as his sword fell from his numb hands.

"Never tense up so much!" Lamar barked. "Right hand on the grip, left supporting the pommel. I'd have broken every muscle and bone in your arms if I wasn't being gentle."

Gentle was not the word Engrelin would have used to describe Lamar's strokes. But there was no time to argue vocabulary. Lamar was moving back in. Engrelin shifted his hold on his weapon according to Lamar's instructions.

Lamar thrust, jabbing Engrelin in the ribs. He doubled back, his sword thwacking down a moment too soon, striking the floor. He now knew why the ground was riddled with so many grooves. Too late to lift it. Lamar was already gripping his arm, striking forward with the round pommel of his weapon. Engrelin ducked, and the blow landed on his shoulder. He stumbled back another step.

"You anticipate my every move!" Lamar exclaimed, sounding exasperated. "Move to block a strike as I prepare or as I make it. Strike after and you're dead. Build a wall—a steel wall, and don't let me through."

"A wall?" Engrelin wondered aloud as he sprang temporarily out of Lamar's range. Or so he thought. A smart rap on the side of his head sent him reeling.

"I mean never let your blade outside your defense," answered Lamar. He followed his rap with a blow to Engrelin's knee. Engrelin tried to jump back but moved one second too late. Lamar's sword sent Engrelin sprawling backwards. Instantly, he felt the dull steel against his neck. Lamar stood calmly over his outstretched body.

"Usually you won't use defense as your main tactic," he said. "I wanted to feel you out first thing this morning. You did well for being green. But I expect better next time," he added sharply. "Stop falling back. Defense does not mean retreat. You always want your opponent at easy striking distance. They should be the ones moving to get to you. And don't be afraid to grab me or my sword to keep me from striking. If you see me stumble, take advantage of it. Especially with me, chances are few and far in between." He smiled grimly and honestly. "You have a lot to work on. Better get off the floor."

Engrelin grasped Lamar's extended hand and regained his feet, though not before retrieving his fallen sword.

Engrelin lost count of how many times Lamar flung his sword out of his hand or knocked him to the floor. Training proceeded like that for a week. Engrelin despaired at times at his seeming lack of improvement. He and Lamar spent hours in the hall. Sometimes they paused for meals. Sometimes they forgot them in the thrill of a new thrust or defense. Gradually, Engrelin improved.

The training intensified with each day. It was brutal.

Engrelin loved it.

Agile, Blond, middle-aged Lamar enthralled him. His mastery brought Engrelin back every morning even after going to bed bruised and bleeding the night before. Every stroke the man made captivated Engrelin, gave him something to strive for even if it seemed he never would attain it. Lamar was neither a mysterious, grumpy old codger nor a dashing duelist. He was a master—no more, no less.

For that, Engrelin continued to train on. And on. Days bled into weeks, and weeks into months. Engrelin felt he had improved his swordsmanship somewhat.

Meanwhile, the nights were getting nippy. Christ Mass was only one week away. Spiky fruits called pineapples adorned the doorways. A stuffed peacock with outspread feathers presided in the parlor where the Monarians occasionally gathered to socialize with the royal family. Huge red flowers with tapering petals were scattered throughout the palace and would soon drown the chapel altar.

And still, no word had come from Bendekahn.

"We'll all be old men by the time he returns," Engrelin muttered. He was sitting on the fountain's edge, holding in one hand a sweet cake that Averendier had given him for having missed supper (he and Lamar had lost track of the time, yet again, and had been sparring long after supper had ended). Ripping off a small corner of the cake, Engrelin dropped it into the fountain's bowl. Several ornamental goldfish swam up and nibbled elegantly at the floating crumbs

It seems they can't even bake a decent potato around here, he thought. *With the Christ Mass approaching, it's only getting worse. I miss a meal, and they give me desert. Then I have to feed it to you fish.*

A rather bloated fish dragged itself up to one of the crumbs, gulped it whole, and promptly spit it back out.

Even the fish don't like it. Engrelin probed his bruised temple and watched the unbelievably fat fish nose another crumb before flailing its puny fins in the tremendous struggle to propel its scaly bulk a few inches through the water. Training that day had been difficult, followed immediately by a long, sharp lecture from Averendier about missing yet another meal. Engrelin didn't mean to skip meals. It just…happened.

By then, a veritable swarm of goldfish churned around the cake crumbs. The water's surface frothed as they snatched at the tidbits.

Their orange scales briefly flashed black. Their darting bodies contorted to lithe, writhing tails.

Engrelin dashed his hand through the water, scattering the fleeting vision. Clenching the fountain's rim, he forced himself to breath steadily as he gazed down at the rippling water and fleeing fish.

Already, his nights were plagued with nightmares. He didn't need to start seeing things in the day.

As he watched, the water smoothed, reflecting another picture. A face. A face not his own. Fair, fine eyebrows curving above violet eyes. Thin lips pursed with a question. A long, flaxen lock dipped suddenly into the image, sending little ripples running across the reflection.

Engrelin turned his head slowly.

Even though her lips barely moved, the princess's eyes smiled. A fine line of confusion arched across her forehead. Prickling heat spread across Engrelin's shoulders and crept up his neck. Hopefully, she hadn't been standing there long. This whole thing with different people sneaking up on him was getting creepy.

"Are the fish…bothering you?" Lilac asked. Her voice was soft, and though tinted with amusement, it was in no way contemptuous. Engrelin relaxed slightly.

"No, they weren't," he replied. *Actually, they were doing me a favor.*

"If you were trying to catch them," she pursued lightly, "it won't work that way."

Engrelin's mouth quirked. "It wouldn't," he agreed. He pointed at the bloated fish (which was attempting to swim lopsidedly). "Unless I aimed for that one."

Lilac smothered a horrified gasp in her hand. "Oh, that poor thing! It's fit to burst! What have the gardeners been feeding them?"

Engrelin's smile shifted to a frown. Thank goodness he had smacked the water's surface; otherwise, the crumbs would still be floating on top. He glanced at the fat fish and racked his brain. How many times had he fed these fish a pastry of some sort? Surely not enough to stuff a fish like that…he hoped.

"I'll have to tell Varel about it," Lilac murmured to herself. "It must have eaten something it shouldn't."

The girl dipped her slender fingers into the water and stirred them gently about. A few brave fish swam up cautiously to nibble her fingertips. Finally, she sighed and lifted her hand out, letting it drop slack at her side. She turned to Engrelin, a penetrating—almost burning—stare searing the laughter from her eyes.

"Johnathan tells me you three came to speak to my father," she said.

Forcing himself to meet the girl's sharp gaze, Engrelin replied, "We wouldn't still be here otherwise."

"If you knew he was going to be gone so long, why didn't you three and Johnathan just go to Methicayn and meet him there?" Lilac queried.

Engrelin couldn't tell her the deep truth—they stayed where they were because of the girls. As soon as Lilac heard that, she would know for certain that the Monarians' business there in Alinar had something to do with her. More than a little something.

Lacing his fingers around his knee, Engrelin stared into the fountain's water.

"None of us were quite sure how long your father will be away, Lilac," he answered slowly, turning each word over in his mind as diligently as he had furrows with his plow. For whatever reason, the girls didn't know about Johanthan's idea, and he certainly didn't want to be the one who revealed it to them. "Imagine if we left and passed him on the road."

Pinching her lips together, Lilac looked away. Engrelin watched her thoughtfully. Had she been puzzling over this since he and his cousins had arrived? Why wouldn't her mother tell her and save all the fuss?

Slightly disturbed, Engrelin rose and paced the path around the fountain.

"Where exactly did you travel from?" Lilac asked, as if to hold Engrelin's attention and so prevent him from leaving. She perched on the fountain's edge and folded her hands in her lap.

"Northern Monaria," Engrelin answered shortly.

Lilac's eyebrows arched. "Johnathan told us he found you three in Northern Florenth," she remarked critically.

Engrelin drew a quick breath. "That's where he found us, yes. But it's not where we live. We were just…visiting there."

"On business?" She twisted a fold of her silk skirt nonchalantly around her finger.

Engrelin hesitated before he said, "Yes."

"Of what kind?"

"I can't say," Engrelin answered in clipped tones.

Lilac bent her head, as if scrutinizing a single thread in her skirt. Engrelin watched her silently. Trying to piece all this together was no easy task. He should know—he had been living the puzzle for the past few months, and still he didn't have all the pieces!

"So…you're a diplomat?" Lilac asked.

Engrelin laughed shortly and shook his head. "No, not at all. I'm a farmer."

"Do you live in the mountains?" Lilac fiddled with a slender gold bangle clasped around her wrist. "I'd like to visit there some day," she added. "See snow."

Engrelin stopped pacing to stare incredulously at her. "Never seen snow?!" he exclaimed. He lived a third of his year waist-deep in it!

"Yes, never seen it," Lilac said. "But I've read about it. We've got several poetry collections containing poems about it. They're upstairs, if you ever want to read them."

"I don't think I'll need to, since I've seen it," Engrelin replied stiffly. She and her sisters were the last people he wanted to know about his illiteracy.

"There's so many places I want to go," Lilac continued quietly. "We girls have always tried to talk it over with Father. But he—oh!" She rose, dusting off the front of her immaculate dress. "I nearly forgot. Mother wanted to send a servant to bring you to the parlor. But I said I'd rather fetch you."

Of course you did. How else would you have gotten to talk to me privately?

"Did she say why she wanted me?" Engrelin asked.

Lilac dipped her chin in a quick nod. "Yes. I think it's about news from Father."

26

So Bendekahn says he'll be home within the week?" Lamar asked.
"That's what Zacara told us last night," Engrelin answered. He jumped up over a sword stroke that might otherwise have taken his feet with it if he hadn't developed quick reflexes over the past two months. In turn, Engrelin bore down on Lamar, intending to punish him with an overhead stroke, but it was blocked, as always, by the trainer's swifter blade.

"You don't sound thrilled," Lamar observed. His blade played with Engrelin's a moment, then darted under. Engrelin slashed away not only Lamar's sword but also a terrific bruise under the ribs to add to his collection.

"Not terribly. I mean, I could get excited over nothing. For the past two months we've all said he could come any day. It's still the same thing for me, though it is progress." Seizing a rare opportunity, Engrelin swiped at Lamar's legs.

Lamar leaped out of the way and swung his own sword around. Engrelin lifted his blade and caught it.

"At this point," Engrelin continued, "he could be gone for years, and everyone would be expecting him the following morning. It grates after two months, I guess."

"That's why we're all still expectant," Lamar said, his blade flashing in front of him almost faster than a human eye could follow. "But he is a king, Engrelin. He comes and he goes as he pleases. Still, even kings have their limits. He'll be home soon—within the week, if that's what he said."

Engrelin said nothing to this. Ridiculously, he almost didn't *want* to go. There would be so much he left unfinished. His training would be incomplete.

Something jabbed swiftly into his side. Engrelin jumped and brought his sword smashing down. That only earned him a whack on the side of his head.

"Ow!"

"Better watch that wandering mind of yours!" Lamar rebuked. He punctuated his words with thrusts, which Engrelin was wise enough now to parry. Blade against flat, striking tiny sparks that vanished as quickly as they burst. "I always get you with that one. You're lucky it was just this dull mock. A chance like that against an enemy with a real sword in his hands, and right now you'd be either spitted or in multiple pieces."

"As you said—luckily, I'm not," Engrelin retorted.

"True. Your head's too thick to be cracked in one blow." Lamar knocked Engrelin's blade neatly aside and cracked him sharply across the head once more.

Engrelin retreated a few paces long enough to shake the stars from his vision. "Sometimes I wonder why I even do this to myself," he said.

"You wanted to learn how to fight," Lamar said, clanging his blade against Engrelin's.

"Funny. It seems all you're teaching me is how to take a beating," Engrelin snorted. The two locked blades a moment. Engrelin shoved forward, knocking his instructor back several paces and following him before he could recover.

"The point," Lamar grunted, "is to escape with as few bruises as possible."

Engrelin lunged to lock blades once more, but Lamar stepped neatly aside and flicked his blade towards Engrelin's leg. Engrelin deflected the blow and aimed one for his instructor's momentarily exposed shoulder. Lamar brushed the stroke aside just in time.

"You must be learning. You don't look so bad this week," Lamar remarked. "Or maybe I'm just not hitting hard enough."

He followed his words with such a series of blows that Engrelin had to back away, on the defensive yet again. The room reverberated with the ring of steel meeting steel, punctuated once by another low exclamation from Engrelin, who finally sprang out of the shower, only to wade back in, driving Lamar before him.

"You're bleeding," Lamar remarked casually.

Engrelin barely refrained from rolling his eyes. Like he couldn't feel it! "What do you want me to do? Stop?"

"We could," Lamar offered, still taking gradual steps backwards, his blade only bantering with Engrelin's.

"I'd rather not," Engrelin said.

"We've been at it since this morning," Lamar reminded.

"I know, I know." Engrelin side-stepped an awry stroke. "But this gives me an excuse to skip other things."

"Like what."

"Reading lessons, for one."

"I appreciate being chosen over reading," Lamar said dryly.

"I might change my mind," Engrelin said, with mock thoughtfulness. "Words won't beat me black."

"Like I said," Lamar said, "the point is to learn how not to get beaten. Or disarmed," he added, with a sudden flick of his wrist. His sword shot forward several inches. At the same time, Engrelin reached out and grasped the hilt of Lamar's sword between the master's gripping hands. With a painfully jarring impact, both swords seemed to get tangled within each other and shot away onto the floor, leaving Engrelin and Lamar weaponless and panting. Both gazed uncomprehendingly at the two swords lying a short distance away.

"I've never had that happen before," Lamar said, rubbing his wrist.

"Is that good or bad?" Engrelin asked laughingly.

"The truth is, Engrelin, you're an exceptional fighter," said Lamar slowly. "I know it doesn't seem like it, but that's because you're only fighting me, and you're only following everything I've taught you."

This was the first inkling of praise Engrelin had ever heard Lamar utter. It stunned Engrelin into silence.

"I've trained kings, Engrelin, Bendekahn among them. But I didn't teach even him everything I know." He raked one hand through his hair, which Engrelin realized was flecked with gray. How had he not noticed that before? Everything about Lamar seemed to have forwarded well beyond his age.

"Where I came from, I was the best of the best. And a man only lives so long. I'm trying to show you everything I know. Absolutely everything. Cramming it into two months was harsh, but you've done better than I dared hope. I don't think I could have asked for a better student."

Uncomfortably, Engrelin shifted his weight from one foot to the other. Then he smiled wryly. "There's one thing you still haven't taught me," he said.

"What?" Lamar asked innocently. Mischief and guilt gleamed in his eyes.

"The way you disarmed me…or, let me disarm you…whichever we did…"

"We disarmed each other, Engrelin. May I remind you, that's not ideal in battle. You want to keep your sword and not resort to fisticuffs."

Engrelin smiled. "Your sword seemed to grow. I've never seen anything like that."

"Ah. It's a simple trick. Old and forgotten, but simple. You could do it in your sleep once you got the hang of it."

Considering what his cousins already thought of the way he behaved in his sleep, Engrelin didn't think he needed to add a sword maneuver to the list. But he wasn't going to let a single trick of Lamar's go unlearned.

"So, take your sword," Lamar instructed, "and thrust. Yes, like that. Now, watch."

Lamar thrust forward, his hand flashed, and the sword's tip extended several inches beyond its normal reach.

"I didn't see it," Engrelin said. "You went too fast."

"Any slower and I'd drop it on your toes," Lamar snorted. "Here. Take your sword, make the thrust, and mid-stroke let go of the grip. When the blade slides forward, catch it by the pommel. And there you have it. A longer sword."

"Huh." Engrelin looked down at his sword in fascination.

"All right. Now try it."

Engrelin thrust forward and let the momentum slide the grip through his fingers. Then the *pommel* slipped through his fingers. Desperately, he stumbled forward. Lamar, who had been anticipating just this, stepped neatly aside. The sword flew out of Engrelin's reach and clattered to the ground at Johanthan's feet.

Engrelin viewed Johanthan with surprise. He hadn't even heard the man enter.

Engrelin glared at Lamar. "Simple trick?" he hissed.

Lamar shrugged. "Simple once you get the hang of it," he said. "After years and years of practice, that is."

Rolling his eyes, Engrelin returned his attention to Johanthan.

The scholar cleared his throat quietly. "Lamar, the king is at the gate."

Engrelin startled. *Bendekahn? Here? Already?*

"Does he want them to come and meet him now?" Lamar jerked his head towards Engrelin.

"No. Zacara doesn't want to trouble Bendekahn with anyone until after dark. Have them take their meals in their rooms."

Lamar nodded tightly. 'I'll see to it, Johnathan."

Johanthan turned to leave and hesitated. Picking up the sword, he pressed it back into Engrelin's hands. "Keep it up," he said. "You'll need it."

His eyes drilled into Engrelin before he turned quickly and strode out the door, leaving Engrelin clutching tightly his sword's hilt and staring after him.

"Don't look like that," Lamar admonished, with forced cheerfulness. "We're not dead yet, Bendekahn's finally back, and we have a new trick to pound into you. What's the worry?"

"The part about pounding it into me," Engrelin replied with a grimace.

"No bruises, nothing to show for what you've accomplished!"

"And nothing left of me to help Bendekahn," Engrelin added in a mutter.

"I'm sure there'll be something left," Lamar remarked. "Now begin."

27

*E*ngrelin spent the supper hour lying on the lounge in his room with a cool, damp cloth plastered over his bleeding head. A fierce headache pounded against his temples, but worse still was the anxiety throbbing in his heart. They were going to see Bendekahn that night. The awaited moment had finally come. Now what? Would they be assigned to escort the three princesses back to Monaria, or would they have to return home empty-handed? And what of home? What would happen to it if Alinar wasn't able to help drive the Tirendrians back?

Someone rapped on the door. Snatching the cloth off his head, Engrelin shoved it into the basin of water on the table beside him.

"Come in," he called.

The door opened just enough to let Lamar shove his head and torso into the room. "Bendekahn's ready for us," he said simply. He squinted at Engrelin and frowned. "I thought I told you to put something on that head of yours. That bump may be small now, but it'll be the size of your fist tomorrow morning if you don't listen to me."

Engrelin lifted the dripping cloth above the basin so that Lamar could see it before letting it slide back in. "I just took it off when you knocked. I'm not going to Bendekahn looking like I just came out of a hospital."

"It might have helped keep that hair of yours from sticking up," Lamar remarked.

Engrelin grinned and scrubbed a hand through his thick hair, making it stand more on end than ever. "That better?" he asked.

"You're lucky you're out of reach," returned Lamar. He swung the door open wider. "Come on. The others will begin to wonder what we're doing."

Engrelin got up and walked with Lamar through the palace halls to the fencing room. Once there, they crossed the long room, their dull footsteps resounding against the walls and vaulted ceiling. Lamar paused in front of the long velvet curtain hanging at the room's far end and drew one corner back, disclosing a plain wooden door set in the wall.

"We decided to meet in my quarters, for security reasons," Lamar murmured in explanation. Out of his pocket, he drew an ornate brass key. He thrust it into the lock, turned it, pushed the door inward, and ushered Engrelin inside. Lamar stopped in the dark, narrow hallway just long enough to lock the door behind himself. The grate of the key turning in the lock lodged a lump in Engrelin's stomach. The last time he had heard that, he had been locked out of a secretive and crucial meeting.

This time, he was locked into one.

Inhaling slowly, Engrelin followed Lamar down the hallway and into a warmly lit sitting room.

The first thing he saw was Zacara seated on a northern style sofa. Beside her, with his arm across her shoulders, was a man. Engrelin didn't even have to see the man standing to know he was tall. He turned his blonde head at Engrelin and Lamar's entrance, his expectant— almost terse—gaze held by unwavering violet eyes. He wore no mark of distinction, not even a circlet like Zacara always wore. Yet Engrelin knew he was Bendekahn.

"Sit down, please," said Bendekahn, motioning to another sofa. "Then we can begin."

Engrelin glanced swiftly at Johanthan, Averendier, and Andrald, who were also seated on the remarkably northern furniture. He sat down on a sofa beside Lamar.

Bendekahn sighed softly. The man let his eyes rove over Johnathan, Lamar, and the three Monarians. His eyes seemed to linger on Engrelin longer than on the others. Engrelin wanted badly to shift in his seat, but instead forced himself to hold the king's gaze. Behind the monarch's mask of indifference, Engrelin thought he detected a flickering frown. But before he could be sure, Bendekahn looked away and down at his wife.

"You all know who I am, and I know who you all are, so there is no need for further introduction," Bendekahn said. His quiet voice rolled through the room's unsettling stillness. He pulled his arm away from Zacara and sat forward, resting his forearms on his knees. "Johnathan brought you here to me in hopes I might finally take his advice concerning my daughters' safety. When you three arrived here and found me gone, he sent a cryptic message to me explaining the situation and asking me to reconsider yet again."

The king paused a moment, letting his forehead rest against his folded hands. "I've had nearly two months to consider now. I had nearly a year before that when Vendar's letter first reached me, threatening to harm my children if I tried to help Monaria in any way. Fellow monarchs around Ontaria received similar letters. None of us understood quite what they meant. Eastern Florenth was under attack at the time, and, if anything, Vendar should have been insisting that we not help *them*. Only after the attacks on Fort Starr late this summer did we understand Vendar's intention to wage war across Ontaria, starting in the east to build up his armies and moving on to the north to wreak his vengeance."

On the table beside Bendekahn stood a stack of papers. He drew one off the top and set it in his lap, glancing once down at a paper crammed with writing before continuing.

"Just before I left Methicayn, I received this letter from your king, Julian. One of his men managed to smuggle himself aboard a merchant's vessel to deliver it to me. In it, Julian refers to the most recent battle in Monaria." He motioned to the letter lying in his lap. "Monarian and Tirendrian forces clashed at the Pwynt. Monaria was victor, but with heavy losses. Among the severely wounded were his highest officers, including Monaria's admiral, Austinian."

Out of the corner of his eye, Engrelin saw Andrald jerk in his seat. Even Averendier's face contorted momentarily with dismay.

Engrelin's jaw tightened. Lord Gwane and all of Bryn had their hero now. Only Austinian might have paid for that title with his life. And the rest of the navy? What would they do with their commander and many of its officers out of commission or—God forbid—dead? Monaria had ruled the northern seas for years. It was imperative that they continued to do so.

And what about his cousins and himself? What would "clearing their names" cost them and their families? Were they also expected to prove themselves so drastically? Of course, the discontented people of Bryn would pity the boys if they died doing their duty. As long as the boys' deaths didn't affect anyone else, Bryn couldn't care less.

"This letter," Bendekahn pursued, not noticing the boys' distress, "is the fifth one Julian has sent, asking me to come to Monaria's assistance. The request itself is short. Julian's patience with me has been long surpassed. He wants action. His friendship—and Monaria's people—means a great deal to me. But so do my daughters. Vendar has threatened their lives, and even though I have said neither yea nor nay to helping Monaria, several attempts against my girls have already been made, even within the walls of my own home."

"Exactly three attempts, your Majesty," Johnathan said. "And, if I might add, the most troubling thing about them was though we captured the assassins twice out of those three times, they managed to get away somehow. That can only mean help is coming to them from among those here in the palace, those who *claim* to be faithful to Alinar.

"I myself witnessed one of these escapes. I blame myself for it," the scholar added, bowing his head and scowling with shame. "I, along with two guards, were taking the assassin into custody when someone snuck up behind us. He attacked the guards first, knocking them both unconscious. I was spared the same fate for only a moment. I managed to catch a glimpse of the attacker before he took me out. If the passage hadn't been so dimly lit, I might have been able to identify him. No one else saw anything happen, though a few other prisoners testified that they heard a scuffle. But by the time another guard reached the scene, there was nothing to be seen but we three, unconscious on the floor."

"That scoundrel would have seen a thing or two himself if I had been there," muttered Lamar.

Engrelin's lips quirked. He knew exactly what maneuver Lamar would have used too. The man was skillfully trained in perceiving even the most muffled footsteps behind and gauging how far away they were from himself. He had drilled the same thing into Engrelin until the boy was so stiff with bruises he couldn't turn around fast enough to meet Lamar's attack. Out of all the tactics Lamar had taught, that was the hardest to learn.

Bendekahn, meanwhile, pulled different sheets of paper from the stack and scanned them quickly before also laying them on his lap.

"Wilelm wrote me also," he continued. "His eldest three children were kidnapped the same day he sent a letter to Julian asking him for particulars on Fort Starr. Vendar has threatened to kill the hostage heirs if Wilelm makes any more friendly moves towards Monaria. I sent Johanthan to ask him about all that had happened concerning the children. That is why he happened to be in Elstar at the same time as you boys."

"That, and Divine Providence," Zacara interjected.

Bendekahn nodded in acknowledgement. "Through Johnathan, Wilelm was able to send me a letter. In it, he begs me to take Johanthan's advice concerning my daughters so that I can help Monaria unhampered. He said, right here…" He held up one of the letters to the light of a guttering lamp. "… 'If you do not assist them [Monaria], it will fall, valiant to the last, and all the more shattered for their bravery. Vendar—just as he has done with the men of Eastern Florenth—will push and pull, and even torture the Monarian men into his army. He will move on to destroying all other countries in Ontaria in his mad and terrifying scheme to bring the whole world under his sole rule. And who will be strong enough to oppose him? Unless we make a stand now in Monaria, the matter of Vendar's supreme rule will have already been settled and sealed.'"

Bendekahn looked up from the letter, his lips fixed in a determined line. "I intend to exert myself and this whole country to its utmost capacity to assist Monaria," he said. "It will be over my dead body if they ever reach beyond your country's shores. But I will never permit it to be done over my daughter's corpses. And this way," he added heavily, "Lilac will be able to succeed me if I fall."

Zacara looked away but nodded slowly to herself.

Bendekahn leaned still further forward, meeting each boy's gaze in turn. "I am willing to let you carry out Johanthan's plan for my daughters to take refuge in Southern Florenth. But are *you* willing, even after hearing all this?"

Without even exchanging looks with each other, the three boys nodded simultaneously.

Bendekahn sat back. "Good," he said softly. "That's good." He sat silent a moment, gazing out at nothing. Then he resumed.

"Do not speak about this anywhere to anyone at any time. When you think you're alone, you aren't. Those in this room, Wilelm, and soon Julian, are the only human beings in Ontaria who now know of this plan. Not even my daughters have been told. For their own safety, the letter is never to be mentioned to them. The true intent of this mission is to be concealed. It is best for them to remain completely ignorant of everything involving this plot. What they don't know can't be extracted from them."

"What are we going to tell them we're doing?" Averendier asked. "I doubt they'll believe that this is just a pleasure trip, and I know you won't want us to feed them lies."

Engrelin's eyes swiveled back to Bendekahn. The king was scowling with frustration.

"That's the only real kink in this plan," he admitted. "They won't believe anything but the truth, I know. I'm afraid I'm just going to have to tell them to go with you and not ask any questions. We have no alternative. We've put this off long enough."

Engrelin's thoughts flew back to his encounter with Lilac at the garden fountain the previous day. Lilac, for one, wasn't going to be pacified with mere orders. But Bendekahn was right, the time for waiting was over. The girls would just have to keep wondering.

"Our course is still the one Johanthan first discussed with us—to Monaria, then back down?" Averendier asked.

Bendekahn nodded. "We'll arrange with a frontier fort while you journey north. We'll send information to Julian's court once everything is settled. It should all be waiting there for you by the time you arrive."

Engrelin looked askance at Johanthan. "I thought you said the southern border was sealed off from here," he said.

Johanthan smiled ambiguously. "I have my ways," he said. "Not ways for three princesses. But I do have some." He cleared his throat. "Averendier, I was thinking about the route we discussed the other day, and I just remembered that it passes through a portion of Tirendria. Is it wise go through there with the princesses?"

"I think it's best." Zacara said. "If Vendar gets wind of our girls heading north, leading our daughters through his territory is the last thing he will suspect. All his eyes will be turned towards the Anailwch."

Bendekahn nodded. "It would also be prudent to avoid large towns. The fewer people who see you, the better."

"And when do we leave?" asked Andrald practically, speaking for the first time.

Bendekahn sighed. "Here's where it gets difficult for you and my girls," he said gravely. "Every eve of the Christ Mass, we have midnight Mass at the chapel here, proceeded by a celebration in our grand hall. That night, we will all attend Mass. While we head to the hall, you three boys will get last-minute packing done and saddle the horses. Towards the end of the feast, just as everyone begins to leave, Lamar will bring the girls to you at the stable. By then, the other guests will be packing up, so when you ride through the gate, the guards will let you pass without question.

"Then ride like the wind for the border. I will provide you with our fastest horses. Leave as few tracks as possible. And may God and St. Christopher guide you."

Bendekahn and Zacara stood. Johnathan, Lamar, and the boys followed suit.

"Goodness knows you'll need all the prayers in Ontaria to help you on your way," Bendekahn said. "I can't give you those, but be assured of mine."

Zacara grasped her husband's hand. "And mine also. But for now, get some rest. It's already past midnight, and this next week will be a full one. For all of us," she added, looking concernedly up into her husband's face.

"Thank you," Averendier and Andrald said simultaneously.

"Thanks," Engrelin echoed. Everything inside him squirmed with excitement and anxiety. He ran his fingers hurriedly through his hair, feeling as he did his collection of cuts and bumps. He smiled. Lamar had prepared him well.

With whispered farewells, Bendekahn and Zacara withdrew from Lamar's quarters, accompanied by Johnathan. Averendier and Andrald immediately followed them out, Andrald murmuring something to his brother. Engrelin was left alone with his instructor. He turned and wrung Lamar's hand.

"Thanks. For everything," he said.

Lamar only nodded towards the door. "You heard Zacara," he said. "Go rest. You need it just as much as they do."

Smiling wryly, Engrelin turned to leave when a blue glimmer of light in an adjacent room caught his eyes. Curious, he stared at the closed door and the surprisingly bright blue light flowing out from under it. He threw a questioning glance at Lamar.

Seeing the strange light, the instructor's expression shifted from startled, to pleased, to stoic. Pulling his gaze away from the closed door, he jerked his head towards the exit.

"Goodnight, Engrelin," he said, almost sharply. "Sleep well. No lesson tomorrow."

Engrelin had no choice but to obey and leave the room. The scrabbling grate of the key turning in its lock told Engrelin just how quickly Lamar had locked the door behind his student. Engrelin frowned as he traversed the palace's vacant halls back to his room. Lamar had always been rather curt, but never mysterious. And what could let off such a bright blue glow that seemed to startle Lamar, even if for a moment? A blue lantern?

Engrelin had to smile at himself. His guess was probably far from the truth. But the glow had been there.

When he entered his room, Engrelin drew up short. Averendier rose from where he'd been sitting in a chair. Engrelin caught himself before he scowled, though he couldn't keep from inwardly groaning. *What does he want now?*

"Engrelin," Averendier said quietly, "I have an apology to make."

Engrelin stared, dumbfounded, at his cousin, who was still impeccably composed despite the sincerity in his eyes.

"Apologize for what?" he asked with a nervous laugh.

"For everything," Averendier said. "The way I've treated you on the road…and here. I'm sorry."

"You didn't have to apologize," Engrelin said awkwardly, though relief broke over him in waves. The last thing he had wanted was to set out on a perilous journey with their quarrel still hanging heavily over their heads. "I wasn't exactly an angel either," he added.

"I needed to," Averendier replied.

He started towards the door and Engrelin stepped aside to let him pass. At the last moment, however, Engrelin called out, "Averendier!"

Halfway out the door, the older boy paused but did not look back.

"What made you do it?" Engrelin asked.

Averendier's shoulders visibly stiffened. "There's no use making enemies of each other right now, Engrelin," he answered starchily. "Unity is the only thing that will keep us strong."

"I'm sorry about your dad," Engrelin said quietly.

If possible, Averendier went more rigid. "Good night," he said starkly. He marched out into the hall and shut the door firmly behind himself.

28

I've never seen so many flowers in a church at one time," Andrald murmured to Engrelin as the two pushed through a throng of richly clad guests down a hallway, leaving the palace chapel behind them.

Engrelin shrugged. "It's Christ Mass. But I didn't think so many flowers grew in Alinar, especially in the winter." He looked at his cousin askance. "But why are you coming this way?" he asked in a hush. "Aren't you supposed to be getting our things?"

"I am. But we go somewhat in the same direction, so I thought I'd tag along. Besides," he added, screwing his mouth to critique Engrelin, "Yours won't be hard to get. You're wearing half your stuff. Why didn't you accept the extra sets of clothes we were offered?"

"I like traveling light," Engrelin replied. "I'm used to it. I didn't get my way with all my wardrobe." He gestured to his torso. Upon Lamar's insistence, Engrelin now wore over his tunic a brown leather jerkin.

"Why that?" Andrald asked, looking at the jerkin askance.

"Something about needing it for the trip. It's supposed to stand up well against—" Engrelin broke off before he said *weapons*. "Well, it's supposed to be pretty sturdy," he concluded lamely.

"Honestly," Andrald chuckled. "I don't know what made Lamar take such a liking to you after that meeting last week."

Engrelin walked on in silence. He had never told either of his cousins about his training sessions with Lamar and he didn't intend to. In this, at least, he was content to be underestimated. The less people who knew about his skill, the better for all their safety. No one would expect any threat from Engrelin.

"Well, here's where we part ways," Andrald declared cheerfully, stopping before two intersecting hallways. Fewer people were around them now, and those were mainly scurrying servants. Clapping Engrelin heartily on the shoulders, Andrald struck off down one passage, whistling as he went. As the off-key notes floated back to him, Engrelin grimaced. Shaking his head, he continued out to the palace stables.

Alinar boasted the finest horseflesh in Ontaria. Engrelin was slightly disappointed that the steeds Bendekahn assigned them weren't the pure desert stock, but as the king wisely pointed out, Alinar horses would be horribly out of place in the northern wilderness, especially during the winter. The king had instead chosen six horses that were a cross between northern mountain horses and the desert creatures. The result was a horse with the fleetness and beauty of a desert mount, but the endurance and slightly heavier build of a northern beast.

When Engrelin reached the stables, he took the six horses out of their stalls and led them outside, where he hitched them all to one long marble hitching post. Glorien, the palomino that Engrelin had ridden to was among them. Engrelin let his hand run down the stallion's silky neck as he skillfully wound its lead around the post.

"Night ride tonight," he whispered. "It'll be just like old times." He lifted his light saddle onto the horse's back, pushing it up near the stallion's withers and reaching down under its belly to tighten the girth. "Sometimes," he grunted as he tugged the leather strap tight, "I wonder if we were born to do all this sneaking around and dangerous stuff, whether we like it or not."

Glorien tossed its pale mane and whinnied. Engrelin moved away from the powerful beast, watching it as it stamped the sandy ground with a hind hoof. Jerking on the rope that secured him to the pole, the horse pricked its ears toward the open stable door.

Shushing under his breath, Engrelin reached out to stroke the stallion's mane. "What's wrong with you?" he asked, still speaking gently as he twisted to follow the horse's gaze. Through the open door, he saw a tiny light bobbing through the stable. Engrelin frowned. The party guests' horses had been stabled hours ago before Mass began. The princesses shouldn't be arriving for another hour at least. Who would be skulking around during the celebration inside, which even the stable hands had been invited to attend?

He glanced once more at the bright pinpoint of light and absently patted Glorien's neck.

"Stay here, fella," he murmured, as if the horse could move from the post. Throwing one final glance around the deserted stable-yard, Engrelin slipped back into the barn.

His breathing sounded loudly in his ears as he crept down the passageway towards the light. He could only guess it was a candle, or perhaps a small lantern. Had one of the stable hands left it on by mistake, and had he only just noticed it?

The thought was reassuring. But it did not last long. Engrelin heard footsteps crunching against the sandy floor. The light extinguished, plunging the inner stable into semi-darkness.

"You're late."

The voice couldn't have been more than a yard away. Strangling a gasp of surprise, Engrelin ducked into the nearest empty stall and flattened himself against the cool wall. Every hair on the back of his neck prickled. The coldness emanated more from within himself than the frigid stone around and beneath him.

"I can't be punctual all the time," hissed a different voice, this more deep and rough than the first.

"If I had ever let myself make pitiful excuses like that, Mirtael, we'd all be in very different places right now," returned the first speaker coldly.

"At least be thankful I was able to get away from Lamar. You know how the old man is."

The other man laughed an icy, grating laugh that made Engrelin clench his teeth.

"Did you take care of everything?" the man demanded sharply.

"Jaarmon," Mirtael grumbled, "I didn't get everything. You should know it's impossible for me to do *everything*. I'm not as high in this place as you are. I can't get around too easily."

"Can't get around?" Jaarmon spat. "Don't tell me you 'can't get around.' You're a common guard; you're free to do just about anything you please, and no one will be watching you. I have Bendekahn to work around, along with all his advisors and now those Monarians. I never want to hear again that you can't accomplish the simple, easy tasks I assign you."

"Little!" Mirtael laughed nervously. "They're little better than—" The soldier lowered his voice, "Aren't you aware what the penalty for treason is?"

"Mirtael," Jaarmon said, with a sigh that would have been fatherly had it not been so keen, "I, of all people, ought to know that. I, of all people, have the right to be most frightened about the discovery of the least of our secrets. And yet do I look frightened to you now? Am I going to let that fear get in the way of carrying out Vendar's mighty will? No. I expect you to do the same, to live up to the oath you took last year, and to carry your every duty without shirking. If you don't, you'll have more than just Bendekahn after you."

Mirtael grumbled something under his breath that Engrelin couldn't make out.

"You know very well how much I would have just liked to slit the throats of the whole lot," Jaarmon snarled. "But Vendar has other plans. He says it would be crossing the borders of honor to do that. Bah! As if he ever cared about honor!"

"But that is beside the point. You must deliver that message."

"Do your filthy business yourself!" Mirtael snapped.

"I might," returned Jarman mildly. "But what will his Highness think if I told him that I did all he assigned us alone, when I had underlings who were supposed to assist me?"

"At least I have the brains to actually fear for my own life!" exclaimed Mirtael vehemently.

"I have brains enough to know that whenever I risk my neck, it is for my country and the rewards that any such actions will gain for me. It's the pain-shirking pipsqueaks like you who skulk on the corners of danger, waiting for the worst to be over before you crawl out to bask in the glory. It's also those spineless saps who are most detested by the rest of our kind. Queen Zacara herself has a hundred more times more courage than you!"

Engrelin's hand crept up to his chest, feeling for the familiar quiver strap that hung across his chest. However, his fingers met nothing but the cool leather of his jerkin. *I must have left it in my room when I went to mass,* he thought. He stared out into the darkness without seeing the disputing figures. He didn't dare move for fear they'd see him. If they did, he had no doubt they would kill him on sight. If only he could slip out unnoticed and bring someone to capture these men! But he had no idea where exactly they were standing, or if they would see him if he tried to sneak out. He had no choice but to stay hidden until they left.

"But I don't think you'd ever make a double betrayal," Jaarmon continued smoothly, almost cajolingly. "You made the right choice when you joined us. Only you're a little nervous. That's only natural. I just wouldn't want to see it continue for long. You don't want people to think you're unwilling to serve your country."

"Unwilling? I'm more than willing!" Mirtael said. "I'm a single man. I've got nothing tying me down."

"Then why do you fight every single assignment like this?" Jaarmon demanded. "Going soft?"

"No," Mirtael protested. "I'm just—"

"You know, I've always thought softer flesh easier to pierce," Jaarmon remarked. "Of course, you wouldn't want me to have to test this theory on you, would you?"

"No," Mirtael ground out.

"Good. You will take this message to the agent waiting in Daron. It's urgent. I expect it safe in our agent's hands by tomorrow."

Parchment crackled loudly as Mirtael snatched the letter out of Jaarmon's hand. The furious man stormed out of the stable. Jaarmon chuckled softly under his breath. A soft, warm glow illuminated the aisle—the man must have lit the lamp or candle again. The soft shuffling of sand underfoot and the dying light told Engrelin of the man's exit.

Engrelin crouched in the stall even after the footsteps died completely away. Finally he rose and crept out of the barn. He glanced once around the deserted yard and took off towards the palace, using the servant's entrance to slip inside unnoticed. He had to find Lamar or Johanthan.

The sounds of the party were a distant hum reverberating through the palace. Engrelin ignored it as he rushed through several deserted halls towards the fencing room. Perhaps Lamar would be in his quarters.

Before he reached the short stairwell, however, he ran slap-bang into Johanthan.

"Engrelin, what are you doing here!" Johnathan exclaimed, catching himself. "Aren't you supposed to be..." He jerked his head meaningfully in the direction of the stables.

"I had to come tell someone," Engrelin gasped, resting his hands on his knees. "I overheard some men talking in the stables. They may have been spies or something."

"Spies!" Johnathan echoed. "In the sire barn?"

Engrelin shook his head. "No. Bendekahn had me get some of the northern stock from the eastern barn. They were in there."

Johnathan gripped Engrelin's shoulders with trembling hands. Johnthan. "How many of them?"

"Two, I think," Engrelin answered.

"What do you mean, *you think*?" Johanthan exclaimed harshly.

Engrelin took a step back. With a sigh, Johanthan released him, letting his hands drop at his sides.

"I'm sorry, Engrelin," he murmured, putting a hand to his head and looking suddenly old. "To hear this, at the last moment..." he broke off, his brow knit. Finally, he looked up. "Did you catch anything they said?"

"Pretty much all of it," Engrelin replied. "They were arguing because one seemed unwilling to carry out an assignment, to carry a message to a city called Daron. Nothing else was really talked about."

"I'll send someone to intercept the messenger," Johnathan said. "And I will speak to Bendekahn about this as well. It's too late to change any of our plans for tonight, I think. I can only assume that they know nothing about the trip."

"They didn't say anything about it," Engrelin admitted. "But I wish I knew what was in the letter."

"We'll do everything possible to find out," said Johnathan firmly.

Engrelin watched Johanthan's terse face a moment. "Should we continue as planned?"

"Yes, unless I give further notice," Johanthan said. "But before you go," he added, "did you hear any names? It may help me track them down. From your uncertainty of their numbers, I take it you didn't see any of them?"

"I didn't."

Johnathan exhaled slowly and nodded. "Well, the names will have to do, if you caught any."

"Mirtael and Jaarmon," Engrelin said. "Mirtael's a guard here. I'm not so sure who Jaarmon is."

"He's an official of Bendekahn's, a diplomatic officer. He should be in Methicayn right now, dealing with the troubles there." Johnathan's mouth set in a tight, firm line. "I'll start looking into this at once," he said. "I won't let this spoil our hard work. Please," he added, looking sternly at Engrelin, "don't mention this to anyone. At this point, I doubt we can safely trust ourselves with a secret. It's bad enough we're talking openly like this." He glanced warily up and down the empty corridor. "Go back to your preparations now, and…thank you."

With a parting nod, Engrelin swiveled and started walking back to the stables. He'd hardly taken a few steps when he heard his name being called from behind. He turned. Johnathan was gone. Lamar was in his place, hurrying down the hallway.

"Engrelin, what are you doing in here?" Lamar demanded. Behind the man's severity, concern glimmered.

"A little trouble," Engrelin said. "But Johnathan's taking care of it."

"What kind of trouble?"

For the briefest moment, Engrelin hesitated. Johnathan had told him to tell no one. But Lamar was so close to Bendekahn, it probably would not hurt to tell him. Quickly, he related to the instructor what had passed in the barn.

"Well, if there's anyone who can take care of something like that, it's Johnathan," Lamar said once Engrelin had finished. "He's been dedicated to Bendekahn since—for a very long time. He'll know what to do."

"But now that it's settled, I need to get back to the horses," said Engrelin, turning to leave.

"Wait." Lamar caught Engrelin's arm. "Come with me."

"But I have to get to the—"

"It can wait," Lamar urged. "I'm the one bringing the girls anyway. You'll have time for the horses. This… this can't wait."

Engrelin shrugged uncertainly and cast a final glance over his shoulder. "All right…"

Lamar hurried Engrelin down the corridors, up the short staircase, and into the fencing room. Then beyond the curtain into his quarters. He locked the door behind them, then stood stock-still in the middle of the sitting room, as if waiting for something. Engrelin watched him with growing apprehension.

"What are we doing?" he asked.

Lamar didn't answer, only stared at him.

Engrelin was about to ask again when a familiar blue gleam sprung up in his peripheral vision. He turned towards a door, the seams of which were all outlines with the cold blue light pouring through.

Lamar chuckled softly, almost wonderingly. "So I was right after all," he murmured. "It *is* you."

"What is me?" Engrelin asked, still transfixed by the strange light.

Lamar waved the question off. "Come in here," he ordered, moving to open the door.

Engrelin followed. A flood of blue light washed over him as Lamar opened the door and they entered. The light wasn't blindingly bright; Engrelin took in the contents of the room at once.

There wasn't much. The first and only thing his eyes lighted upon was a long glass case standing in the room's center. And in that case, resting on a bed of dark velvet, was a longsword. Its blade shone with an almost crystalline blue glow, illuminating the entire room. Set in its pommel was a large sapphire, slightly smaller than a plum, rimmed with steel. Curiously enough, in the stone's center was set a sparklingly white diamond, giving the impression of a star in a midnight sky.

Engrelin glanced wonderingly from the sword to Lamar. "Why are you showing me this?" he asked.

Lamar's eyes remained fixedly on the sword. "Pick it up, Engrelin," he ordered quietly.

"Pick it up?" Engrelin's eyes widened. He shook his head. "No, I...I..."

"Pick it up," Lamar repeated, lifting his eyes to Engrelin's.

Obediently, Engrelin advanced towards the case. For a moment, he simply stared down at the sword. Below the sapphire setting, the hilt ran, big enough to be wielded with two hands, and wrapped around and around with worn blue leather. Its bare blade was flawlessly smooth, not scarred or nicked anywhere. Some sort of script flowed down the blood-groove.

"Take it out, Engrelin," Lamar commanded.

Engrelin slid the case's glass lid back. After a split-second hesitation, he reached down and grasped the sword's hilt. Slowly, he lifted the heavy weapon out of its case. It seemed to him that the blade shone a little brighter. Or was he just imagining that?

"How do you like it?" asked Lamar, watching him intently.

Engrelin weighed the sword carefully in hand. He smiled gently, almost wonderingly. "It feels like it was made for me," he said softly.

"Beautiful, isn't it?" Lamar admired.

Engrelin nodded slowly, brushing over the gemstone's smooth surface. "I've never seen one like it," he said.

Lamar smiled fiercely. "It's yours."

Engrelin's head snapped up to meet his instructor's calm gaze. "Lamar! I can't take this from you."

"You can and you will," Lamar said sharply.

"But, Lamar, isn't this yours?"

Lamar shook his head slowly. "No, Engrelin. That sword hasn't belonged to me since the day you were born."

Engrelin frowned. That was...strange. "Then who did it—"

"It doesn't seem to belong to any certain person," Lamar interrupted. "It isn't mine to give or yours to take. You're meant to bear it. You're not going to leave Alinar without it."

"Meant to have it?" Engrelin laughed nervously. He tilted the sword in his hand, watching its blue light shift the shadows along the wall. "What in Ontaria is that supposed to mean?"

"The way it glowed when you and I were alone in here last week was extraordinary," Lamar said. "I've never seen anything like it outside of battle. All swords of its kind do something like it. Kingswords, anyway. But the fact that you can hold it says it all."

"Because I can hold it?" Engrelin stared down at the sword. It was light in his grasp, felt almost a part of him. Yes, that overworn description was nonetheless true—it most certainly seemed an extension of himself. In almost more ways than one. Something prickled up Engrelin's spine, and he shivered. Carefully, he laid the sword on the floor. The light on its blade dulled to a barely discernible glow.

"Here, Lamar, you try," he said.

Lamar sighed deeply, in a way that suggested he *had* tried, many, many times. Nevertheless, he bent, wrapped both hands around the sword's hilt, and yanked quickly upwards. He had hardly lifted it a foot from the floor when the sword sprang—literally sprang—from the man's hands. It clattered to the floor, its light extinguished like a snuffled candle. The room was thrown into darkness. Engrelin cried out and jumped back, flinging one arm in front of his face to shield himself from he knew not what.

"You see?" Lamar's voice echoed through the darkness.

Engrelin wiped a hand across his eyes. "Actually," he said, "I can't see anything at all."

Lamar snorted. "Arrian seems to have a mind of its own, literally."

"How?"

The glow sprang to life on the blade, casting its beams onto Lamar's figure.

"Arrian is ancient—a Kingsword," Lamar said. "It's a strange weapon. Even in all the years I had it, I never quite understood why it does the things it does. But it's good and has worked only for good when I had it."

Lamar smiled encouragingly. "I know it takes a while to get used to. I had it for years until on your birth date eighteen years ago, it leaped out of my hands, just like it did a moment ago. It only let me pick it up long enough to place it in this case. It hasn't let me touch it since."

"Arrian is its name?" Engrelin asked. Bending cautiously, he lifted the sword. The light in its blade blazed up.

"Yes. It's *cymraeg* for—"

"Stirling, the South star. I know." Engrelin continued turning the blade over in his hands, a little uncertainly. "Lamar, I still don't think—"

"Engrelin," Lamar said seriously. He placed a heavy hand on Engrelin's shoulders. "You have to take it. Arrian is yours. It isn't an easy burden. None of ours are. But as long as you let this be your light, let the star guide you north, and keep hope burning in your heart, you will bear it well. Are you ready?"

A rueful smile tugged at the corners of Engrelin's mouth. "All except one thing," he said. "Where's the scabbard?"

Engrelin slipped back to the horses, Arrian slapping his left thigh with every step he took. He found the horses where he had left them, stamping restlessly at the hitching post. As he passed Glorien, Engrelin let his hand slide down the stallion's satin shoulder. "Almost ready," he muttered to himself.

Even as he spoke, Engrelin heard a low murmur of voices nearby. It gradually increased as the speakers drew closer. Engrelin turned to see his cousins and the princesses emerging from the midnight gloom. Lamar, behind them all, nodded to Engrelin from a distance before turning and heading back towards the brilliantly lit palace.

"Everything ready?" Averendier asked.

"Yes," Engrelin replied. Out of the corner of his eye, he watched Andrald sling their meager baggage across their mounts' backs. But Averendier held Engrelin's full attention for the moment, inspecting him with tightly pressed lips. This time, Engrelin couldn't blame his cousin for his scrutiny. He knew he must look like some sort of assassin with a sword at his hip, his *cyllel* at his belt, and a quiver of arrows protruding from behind his shoulder. To Engrelin's relief, however, Averendier made no comment. Instead, he turned to address the princesses, who stood bunched together, looking rather confused and (at least in Elvera's case) fiercely displeased.

"It's time to mount. We have a long road ahead of us," Averendier said.

At once, they all mounted their steeds and turned them towards the gate. They were all silent, except Andrald, who kept up a quiet but cheerful banter that was part of their cover.

The guards at the palace gate wasted no glances on the party of Monarians and the disguised princesses. They simply opened the gate and uninterestedly watched the group ride across. One even grumbled about the tiresome business of opening and closing the bridge "starting already."

The thought that it was their beloved princesses riding past them, towards their shelter or their doom, never even crossed their minds.

29

Though the Monarians were forbidden to tell the princesses of the purpose of their journey, they were allowed to give them details such as the route they were going to take. After the night ride away from the splendid Alinar palace, up the sandstone cliffs, and into the flat, rocky plains, Lilac requested a full explanation of their route. Bendekahn had left details of the trip to the boys, since it was best spoken of outside the palace where spies would be less likely to hear. Averendier was more than willing to give it, perhaps to dispel any fears the girls had. Engrelin doubted it would ever reduce the number of questions Lilac would ask. She overflowed with them.

"We're here," Averendier began, spreading a map out of his lap and pointing to the midst of the Alinar wastes. "We're trying to make it up here, to Monaria." He traced the rough path of their journey north across the map, up to the Pwynt. "Depending on the weather, we'll get there in roughly two months."

Elvera scowled. Engrelin watched her, suppressing his own frown. Hadn't he and his cousins waited in Alinar for several months for her father's return? They had survived. His eyes drifted momentarily down to Arrian. He smiled slightly and looked back up at Averendier. The wait had even been worth it.

"Old Finick—he was one of the farmers down the road from us— he told me this summer that he thought we'd have a mild winter this year," Engrelin said. "And Finick was always right about that sort of stuff. If we're lucky, we won't have any real trouble with snow until later."

"Why not just cut through these mountains?" suggested Lilac, motioning to the ragged chain of the *Anailwch*.

"If there was actually a road going through those mountains, it might save us some time," said Averendier gently. "But since there isn't, it's much faster to cut through the south-western tip of Tirendria."

"*Anailwch*? What kind of a name is that?" Elvera snorted.

Engrelin stared at her. Couldn't she keep those thoughts to herself?

Lilac's eyes darted across the map; she searched its every detail as if the canvas held the answers to her many questions. Finally, she tore her eyes away.

"Two months of travel?" she repeated.

"Only if the weather is bad," Averendier reiterated. "Moving quickly, we can make it in a month and a half." He whisked the map off his lap and swiftly rolled it into a tight tube. "Everyone understand what we're doing now?"

Whether or not they understood, everyone nodded.

"Good. Now get some sleep. We have a long day ahead of us tomorrow."

"A long, miserable day, if it's anything like last night," muttered Elvera as she climbed to her feet.

Only if you're there to make it so, thought Engrelin. He couldn't help it.

The girls settled beneath a canvas shelter the boys had rigged for them against a stunted desert tree. Engrelin moved to start unpacking his own things to lay down by their banked fire. But Averendier caught him by the arm.

"Stay a moment, Engrelin. There's something I want to talk to you about."

Engrelin glanced apprehensively at his cousin. He relaxed when he saw no trace of anger or indignation on Averendier's face. He waited until the others had reached their blankets and were talking among themselves.

"What's up?" he asked quietly. "Did I do something wrong?"

"No, not at all," Averendier replied. "But we need to have a plan, in case any of us get separated."

Engrelin immediately frowned. "I hope we never do."

"So do I. But we should be prepared, just in case," Averendier said. "One never knows what can happen on a journey like this, especially in the winter."

Engrelin nodded uneasily.

"I have an idea. I talked it over with Andrald before we left, but I wanted to run it through you as well."

Engrelin shrugged, though surprised satisfaction seeped warmly through him. "Thanks. Fire away."

"The route we're taking home is the same we took here, Elstar and all," Averendier explained. "You can read the landmarks and legends on a map, right?"

"Yeah. Your dad taught me," Engrelin said.

Averendier pulled a folded map out of his pocket and smoothed it out over one knee. Though smaller than the one he had just shown the girls, this map was more detailed and was—strangely—marked all over with red curved lines. The markings started at many different places on the map, but all flowed into the drawn fortress representing Elstar.

"This one should be easy to read," Averendier said. "It has almost all the smaller landmarks along the road laid out."

Engrelin bent closer to review the map. "That's nice," he admitted.

"Good. Now you want to know what to do with it?"

Engrelin nodded. He listened as Averendier explained his plan. Gradually, Engrelin's stomach knotted. Once Averendier finished, he handed the map to Engrelin, who folded it and stuffed it into his pocket.

"They won't like it," he said. "The girls, I mean."

"Do *you* like it?"

"I think it's as good as that sort of thing gets. I just don't know how the girls would react to it." Engrelin jerked his head towards the reclining princesses.

"They probably won't like it," Averendier assented. "Which is why we're not going to tell them about it. We may never have to resort to this plan in the first place. I don't want to get them all worked up about something that might never happen. But if it does happen, and we must employ this, I'm sure they'll realize it's for the best."

"I guess so." Engrelin let his hand creep back down into his pocket, letting his fingers curl momentarily over the folded parchment. "I'll pray we never have to use it."

Averendier stood. "We all will."

"If she complains about one more thing, I'm going to dismount and walk the rest of the way home without her, even if it takes me the rest of my life," Engrelin muttered darkly to Andrald.

His cousin, riding beside him, chuckled. "It hasn't been that bad, Engrelin," he said. "You've already survived two weeks."

"Two weeks too many," Engrelin retorted. "It feels like years."

"She isn't that bad," Andrald said.

Engrelin gave his cousin a look. "That's the first lie I've ever heard you tell, Andrald."

"For goodness sake, would this wretched wind just stop!" Elvera exclaimed behind them. Engrelin glanced back to see her jerking her flyaway cloak tightly back around her shoulders, scowling black as the night all the while. Hardly more than a gentle breeze stirred.

"Correction," Andrald said ruefully. "I thought it was true." Smirking, he added, "I hope the soles of your boots are thick. You've got a long walk ahead of you."

"Forget it," Engrelin said, easing into a small smile. "I'll deal with her to have my horse. She just grates."

Besides Elvera's steady flow of complaints, the past two weeks hadn't been so bad after all. Lilac's and Isalina's cheerfulness made up somewhat for the thundercloud that was eternally hovering over Elvera's head. The musty scent of dead leaves wafted on the breeze; no sharp smell heralded snow yet. Glorien, despite his size, maintained the smooth gait of the Alinar horses. The road stretched on like an even brown ribbon under the arching canopy of mottled branches above them.

Andrald began humming softly under his breath. Engrelin glanced at him, hoping that that was all his cousin would do.

His hope was in vain. Soon enough, Andrald threw back his head and sang:

> "Before me bends the hard-packed road,
> Where many-a traveler bore his load.
> Before me, twists and turns unfold
> And they're all leading me home.
>
> "It is a troubled, winding trail
> Where few unseasoned shall prevail
> Still I'll trod on through hill and vale
> For my soul's a-pulling me home."

Though Engrelin cringed at the sound of his cousin's voice, he nonetheless joined in, quietly murmuring the tenor words to himself, as if mulling over them.

> "Strife and pain and grief abound
> Just turn a bend and they'll be found,
> But beyond it all is that sweet place,
> That everyone knows as home.
>
> "So down this weary road I'll tramp
> Caring not for dew and damp
> Just for one glimpse of that dear lamp
> Which I know is lit at home."

Gray eyes shining, Andrald sat back in his saddle, perfectly content with his performance despite being totally off key the whole time. He made up for it with passion. Maybe a little too much passion, Engrelin thought smilingly.

"Know any other songs?" Andrald asked the inevitable question. Once he got singing, there was no stopping him until he couldn't think of any more songs.

"A few," Engrelin admitted reluctantly.

"How about…that chicken one Elmera is always asking for! Andrald exclaimed, as if he had hit upon a brilliant idea.

Engrelin flushed crimson. "I don't know, Andrald. That one's—"

"Come on, it always cheers a body up!" Andrald persisted.

Flinging his cousin a glare, Engrelin jerked out the song.

"A big, fat hen sat on a big, tall wall.
Carefully, carefully, so she'd not fall.
She spied some crumbs: some big, some small,
So she flew to the ground and et them all!"

Andrald's whole frame shook with suppressed laughter.

"Usually, after that, you're supposed to count as high as you can to say how many breadcrumbs the hen ate," Engrelin added stiffly. "That only works with Elmera, though. She can only count to twelve."

Andrald howled with laughter and slapped his thigh. Engrelin only scowled.

"My turn again," said Andrald, wiping at his eyes.

Engrelin shook his head. Maybe he *should* sing more nursery rhymes—anything to keep Andrald from singing!

"Though the night be clear and bright
And the moon be silvery sheen.
The waves be lapping, and the wind be sobbing
Calling me back to sea.
Calling me back to sea!
Woe for you and me!
And I'm sorry to say
This'll be the last day
You'll ever be seeing me—"

"Too sad," Engrelin cut in sharply. That song was, by far, the worst Andrald had ever mangled. He wouldn't survive the next ten verses.

"Huh! Obviously, Engrelin, the guy who wrote it wasn't happy at that moment." Andrald rolled his eyes. "Well, *sir*, is there anything you want to sing, since you ruined my song?"

You already did that the moment you opened your mouth, Engrelin thought, but said nothing.

"I know quite a few songs," said a feminine voice behind them. "If you don't mind my joining."

Engrelin turned to see Isalinia, who had urged her horse up to be with theirs. She smiled shyly but eagerly.

He shrugged. "Sure. I don't mind."

"I heard both of you singing from all the way back by Averendier," Isalinia continued. "It was very nice."

Smiling modestly, Andrald straightened in his saddle. Engrelin looked away to keep from bursting out laughing. Usually, if anyone said anything to Andrald about his singing, they were screaming at him to stop while mashing their hands over their ears to preserve a portion of their hearing.

"Do you have any song in mind?" Andrald asked graciously.

Isalinia dipped her chin. "I do. It's rather long, though, and more poem than song. Chant, I think you call it up north. I hope you don't mind."

"We don't," Andrald answered readily.

Engrelin smiled in agreement. *Anything to keep him from singing, please.*

Drawing a deep breath, Isalinia began.

"Lights in azure,
Twinkling bright.
Diamonds purest,
Winking slight.
Gems of heaven,
Sparkling light.

"Surreal sheen,
Silvery glow.
Midnight velvet,
Pale beams flow.
Lunar charm to
Land below.

"Radiant sear,
Scorching ground.
Brightest flame,
Piercing stare.
Shooting rays from
Burning glare.

"As I said, more of a chant, compared to your songs earlier," Isalinia concluded. "But it's three riddles put to music. Nursery rhymes, really." She smiled at Engrelin, who colored.

"It was nice," he said. He snuck a glance over at Andrald. His blond head was bent, his brow furrowed. Likely, he was trying to consider which song to murder next. "Can you think of any others?" Engrelin hurriedly asked the princess.

"I know hundreds!" exclaimed Isalinia, brightening.

"What about poems?" Andrald asked.

"Those too. I can think of a good one that I memorized just recently. It's long, though."

"Long is fine," Engrelin said. To his relief, Andrald nodded amiably.

Isalina closed her eyes and was silent a moment, her lips just barely moving. Finally, she murmured,

"Jewel of desert,
Hope and light.
Balm to many
During blight.
Of noble blood,
Hildrael:
Beam of laughter,
Sorrow well.
Ebony hair,
Raven eyes.
Smile sweetness;
Laughter cries.

Inheriting Stars

Virtue crowning
Charity.
Love with perfect
Clarity.
Purest meekness,
Light and shine
Even through
The darkest time.

"Alas, alas, for what shall pass.
Alack, the storm is brewing!
Woe, woe, to those who go
Their way in ignorance.
Flee, flee, away with thee,
Leave this growing darkness!
Away, away, gone are the days
Passed in thoughtless bliss.

"So troubles come,
Swift and sure,
Off land and shore,
Vengeance due.
Many were lost,
Bloodlust, storm.
Ever the rose,
Pluck the thorn.
Of her soldiers
So gallant,
She by far most
Valiant.
Though not as knights,
Battle tested,
She prevailed, with
Virtue vested.
Against the foe,
She stood strong.

No despair in
Pain or wrong.

"Foe was pushing,
Lines weaken.
Grim death; soldier's
Worry steepens.
Till Kahn cried out,
'Wife, anon!
Coming night shall
See you gone!
Tonight depart,
West to float.
Seek relief in
Sea remote.

"Alas, alack,
For while at sea
A gale would rise,
Great fury.
'Neath great sheets of
Green sea foam
Hildrael perished,
Ne'er come home.
The beloved rests
Beneath waves
Buried in deep,
Wat'ry grave.
Our brightest gem
Departed far.
Farewell great queen
Of Alinar."

Once Isalinia finished, she sat silent in the saddle, and the boys with her. Finally, snapping out of her trance, Isalinia asked timidly, "Did…did you like it?"

"Like it!" Andrald exclaimed. "It was better than anything I could have done!"

That wasn't saying much. Swallowing a smile, Engrelin nodded. "I've never heard anything like it," he said softly. Though the stanzas had in one way seemed disjointed, Isalinia's voice polished and smoothed them into a flowing, haunting stream of phrases that swirled around her.

"It's a ballad about the queen who lived during the overthrowing of Old Tirendria," Isalinia said, mentioning the grave moment in history as lightly as if it did not now put her life at risk, even more than Hildrael's had been. But of course, she couldn't know that. Engrelin looked away, as if his thoughts would be written on his face for her to read.

"I know a ballad," Andrald cried, saving Engrelin from having to answer the question blooming on Isalinia's face.

This time, as he roared out another grating tune, Engrelin was grateful enough to not grimace.

30

W*ho's on watch tonight?" Averendier asked. The party had* pitched camp for the night, far away from the road, beside a small glade. The girls had already bedded down in the bough shelter the boys had erected. It was the girls' first night camping in the woods. After the flat stretches on Alinar, they sat up talking about nothing in particular to delay falling asleep beneath the deep, ever-shifting shadows.

"I have first shift, Engrelin second," Andrald promptly replied.

"I could always take—"

"No, Averendier," Engrelin said firmly. "If we let you have one of the watches every night, you wouldn't get any sleep. And then where'd we be?"

Averendier opened his mouth to protest, but stopped. He looked down and frowned. "It's the quiet," he said. "It doesn't feel right. Makes me nervous."

"It was just as quiet on our way here," Engrelin said.

Before Averendier could respond, Lilac walked up out of the darkness, her fingers laced behind her back, her eyebrows slanting in a frown.

"Averendier, may I have a few words with you?" she asked.

"Of course." Averendier stood and walked with Lilac over to the glade where the horses were picketed for the night. Andrald and Engrelin followed the two with their eyes. Andrald sighed softly.

"She's always wondering how far we've gotten and what we're going to do next," he said.

"Probably all the queenly training," murmured Engrelin, thinking of Zacara. "She'll make a fine one, like her mother." Silently, Engrelin added, *if she lives*. His hand moved to grasp Arrian's hilt.

It seemed he had hardly drifted off when Andrald shook him awake.

"Your watch," he whispered, before moving silently to his own blanket.

Engrelin sat up and raked a hand through his hair. He glanced down at Arrian, placid on the blanket beside him, its sapphire pommel gleaming in the faint moonlight. Engrelin considered the sword a moment, then threw his blanket over it to protect it from the dew. He had his *cyllel* at his hip. That should be sufficient for a night's watch.

For a while, Engrelin stood by the fire, occasionally shoving a log deeper into the coals or glancing around at the girl's bower and his cousins' slumbering forms. The warmth and the smoke blowing up into his face lulled him. Shaking himself awake, Engrelin threw off his cloak. The chill evening air knifed into his clothes, stabbing him awake. Now shivering, Engrelin took a step closer to the fire.

Crack!

At the sound, Engrelin jumped and whirled towards the tree line. A pair of bright red eyes gleamed back at him, blinked, and gleamed again. Relaxing, Engrelin smiled at himself. He wasn't sure what he had expected, but it certainly not a harmless racoon.

He watched the pudgy creature waddle around the edge of their camp, sniffing the ground. Engrelin's expression shifted to a frown as the racoon snuffled at the base of the tree where the group had hung their food and stores in the branches out of most creatures' reach. The animal lifted its pointy nose in the air and sprang into the tree. The packs slung on a near-by branch swayed. The racoon scrambled higher.

"Get down from there!" Engrelin hissed. Catching up a long, sharp branch from the brush, Engrelin ran over to the tree. He jabbed at the thieving creature which scrabbled toward the bags as fast as it could.

"That food needs to last us a few more weeks and you're not going to get any of it," Engrelin growled. He made one last swipe at the racoon.

His stick collided with the creature's furry body. Hissing and spitting, the racoon rushed back down the tree's truck.

Another blow from the stick knocked the creature to the ground several feet away from the tree. Still swearing, the racoon retreated across the clearing. Falling silent, it skidded to a stop. It glanced back at Engrelin, bared its fangs, and promptly trotted back towards the tree.

Oh no, you don't! Engrelin rushed the racoon, swinging his stick close to the ground. Hissing again, the racoon turned tail and scampered across the meadow as fast as its short legs would carry it. Once it reached the tree line, Engrelin slung his stick at the animal. It caught the racoon on the head. Yelping with surprise, the racoon scampered into the underbrush. Engrelin slid to a stop, breathing heavily through his gritted teeth. Of all the things to happen on his watch—

A rough hand clamped suddenly over his mouth. At the same time, one strong hand caught his wrists and wrenched them behind his back. Engrelin gasped in surprise. The broad, warm hand covering his mouth smothered it. The bitter tang of dread filled Engrelin' mouth. Behind him, his assailant breathed heavily. The hot breath prickled down Engrelin's neck. His skin crawled. He wanted desperately to shrug the sensation away, but his captor gripped his arms too tightly.

"Not a sound," the man whispered in Engrelin's ear.

Engrelin shut his eyes and forced a deep breath into his lungs. He let his legs buckle. He dropped like a stone in his attacker's arms, the flung himself forward, straining to break free.

Cursing under his breath, the man wrenched Engrelin's right arm savagely, jerking him backwards. Engrelin cried out, but a hand slapped over his mouth, cutting him short.

"Think you can get away, huh?" the man demanded. He jostled his prisoner. "Forget it. I'm not going to let you slip away like last time."

Last time? Engrelin ceased struggling for a moment to think. The man's voice was growing maddeningly familiar. But where had he heard it before?

"Having trouble?" someone whispered coolly.

Engrelin tried to turn his head to see the newcomer, but his captor held his head firmly in place. The new voice contrasted remarkably with the attacker's, whose very presence blazed.

"Thinks he can get away." The man crushed Engrelin's arms tightly against his chest. Engrelin twisted slightly and grimaced.

The newcomer laughed softly and cruelly. "It happens," he murmured. "Lads his age are usually headstrong." His words sharpened to a meaningful point.

"Save your breath, Linford," the man growled. "May I remind you who commands here?"

Linford muttered something under his breath.

"Get back to work," ordered the man holding Engrelin. Again, he tightened his grip around Engrelin's arms. "I'll fix things here."

Linford's footsteps crunched away across the leaf-littered ground. Though unable to move, Engrelin inwardly strained against the man's hold as his mind scrounged through every word Linford had spoken. Was the man holding him prisoner young? He might have a slight chance against him if he was. Engrelin clamped down hard on his lower lip. If only he hadn't left Arrian on his blanket!

"Fix you indeed." The man chuckled darkly, disrupting Engrelin's thoughts. The hand slid away from Engrelin's mouth. His relief was momentary, however, as he felt his *cyllel* being slipped out of its sheath.

Something sharp pricked against his back. Engrelin stiffened.

"What are you doing to me?" he demanded.

"Quiet!" the man ordered. He pressed the tip of the knife into Engrelin's spine. A tiny, keen thrill of pain shot through Engrelin; he felt a few drops of blood trickling down his back.

"If I hear one more peep out of you," the man threatened, "I'll have just found myself a new pincushion. Do you understand?" He gave the boy another sharp jab, punctuating his words with pain.

Engrelin remained silent, though the blood simmered in his veins. What was this man doing anyway? Why was he even here? Was he after the princesses?

That had to be it. Who would have a reason to target him?

The man grunted at Engrelin's silence, in satisfaction or irritation. Did he *want* Engrelin to fly out in a rage, just to have a reason to stick him with steel?

"All the horses, sir?" Linford asked. Engrelin jolted at the unexpected sound.

"Yes, all of them," the man answered impatiently. "And take some of their provisions while you're at it. Let's make these people suffer."

"Yes, sir." Linford's crackling footsteps marked his retreat once more. Engrelin's frown deepened. The horses? Were these men just ordinary horse thieves? Yet the man had spoken as if he had seen Engrelin before. And as far as Engrelin could remember, he'd never associated with highwaymen. That was something he wouldn't have easily forgotten.

"We'll make them suffer alright," the man muttered behind Engrelin. His hot breath stirred the boy's hair. Engrelin barely resisted a shudder. "But none of them will suffer as much as you. Once my men finish with your horses, you'll meet your end on your own knife. And after all you've done, no one in all Ontaria deserves it more."

"What did I ever do to you?" Engrelin demanded.

"Shut up!" the man hissed. The *cyllel's* tip twitched across Engrelin's back but did not pierce. Engrelin sucked in a thin breath. The man's impatience to kill sent panic slamming through his chest. Yet, if he was so eager, why hadn't he stabbed Engrelin in the back the moment he'd caught him? What was the use of dragging it out?

"We're done," came Linford's eerily hushed voice. Engrelin's gut wrenched.

"Good," Engrelin's attacker said, his voice smacking with satisfaction. "Now, take the men to the crossing. Wait for me there. I have a little business to finish here."

Wordlessly, Linford left to carry out his orders. Engrelin's blood pounded so loudly in his ears, he did not hear the other men mounting the Alinar horses and riding off into the night.

The man heaved a sigh of mock sympathy. "You behaved so nicely," he said. "It's a pity you can't be spared. No, wait," he growled. "I lied. I'm not sorry. You deserve this."

"Why?" Engrelin demanded.

Sparks flew across his vision as the man struck the *cyllel's* hilt against Engrelin's temple. Engrelin reeled slightly, sucking in a swift breath.

"But I'm not totally unfair," the man continued. "I did want to give you a warning, for a while there."

For a while? Engrelin's mind spun. "On the way here?" he wondered aloud.

"When else?" the man spat. "I've been watching you and your cousins this whole time, boy."

"No more a boy than you are, Tirendrian," Engrelin grit.

The man flung Engrelin against the trunk of a tree and pressed the cyllel to Engrelin's throat.

"Don't you ever call me that again," snarled the boy. "I'm not one of them. They're next, after you. This is my reprisal."

"Been reading the dictionary recently?" Engrelin demanded.

"It's better than you ever could have done, Engrelin," the boy shot back. "You couldn't even read the labels on the jars back home."

The words kicked Engrelin in the gut. He froze, the breath choked out of him. He peered directly into his antagonist's face. Awful reminiscence coursed through him. Icy blue eyes glared back at Engrelin under wavy blond hair. Incomprehensible hatred twisted the familiar, tanned face.

Engrelin's lips moved wordlessly several times before he could force any sound beyond them.

"Lance?" he faltered.

"The one and only," replied Lance coolly.

Engrelin's eyes widened with horror. "But Lance…why…what…We've been friends for…"

"Maybe that was a mistake," Lance rebuffed.

Engrelin shifted his shoulders against the tree trunk, boring his gaze into his former friend. "Lance…you don't actually want to kill me, do you?"

Lance pressed the knife harder against Engrelin's throat. "You want to test that?" he demanded.

Reaching up, Engrelin grasped Lance's wrist and strained it back so that he could at least breathe. "What's happened to you?" he asked angrily.

"I just realized what a fool I was to think you were my friend," Lance snarled. "I can't believe I even let you live this long. I should have killed you when I had the chance."

With that, Lance jerked his hand and the knife free from Engrelin's. The blade slashed through Engrelin's palm and wrist. Gritting his teeth, he sprang forward. He smashed into Lance, sending them both sprawling.

Almost instantly, Lance regained his feet. He snatched up the *cyllel*. Jumping up, Engrelin snatched wildly for the knife in Lance's hand. Lance kicked Engrelin's feet out from under him, then slammed his foot into Engrelin's ribs. Coughing hollowly, Engrelin looked up to see for one startled second the cold steel gleaming in his adversary's hand. He rolled quickly to one side, hands outstretched to grasp anything that would help him pull up. A spear of agony pieced his right hand, stopping Engrelin short with a startled yell. Rolling back slightly, he made himself look at his hand. The *cyllel* had been driven straight through its back.

"Never thought this could happen, huh?" Lance taunted. Deliberately, he stepped down on Engrelin's awkwardly twisted arm and drew the short sword that had been hanging at his side. Engrelin clenched his jaw against a roll of nausea and glanced swiftly at the *cyllel* once more. It as crudely made, but it still had a cross-hilt. It might just work...

"Hero work. Really, Engrelin?"

Engrelin's tense left hand ached. He'd only have one shot.

"Someone's got to put an end to that. And you." Lance's hateful eyes roved ravenously over Engrelin's face.

Engrelin locked gazes with him for one fleeting moment. He rolled to the side. Grunting behind his gritted teeth, jerked the knife out of his hand and slashed at Lance's leg as the older boy sprang forward to destroy him. Lance yelled with pain and anger.

Staggering onto one knee, Engrelin braced himself for the inevitable sword stroke, his slick fingers gripped around the *cyllel's* hilt, already sticky with his own blood. Roaring with rage, Lance brought his blade smashing down. At the last moment, Engrelin twisted to one side and surged up. He caught Lance's blade on his own, binding them fast.

"I should have just stabbed you in the back," muttered Lance, pushing hard against Engrelin's *cyllel*.

"You already did that, thanks," Engrelin retorted. He clenched the *cyllel* tightly in both hands to keep Lance from shoving it aside.

Lance scowled. "I should have done it harder!"

He pulled his sword away so violently that Engrelin stumbled forward, the *cyllel* falling from his hands. Lance screamed and charged, knocking Engrelin to the ground. Engrelin grunted as his shoulder blades hit the dirt.

But no blade fell. Engrelin looked up at Lance, who stood poised above him, sword raised for the stroke. His broad shoulders heaved with passion. His eyes glowed with hatred. But he did not move. He merely stared.

A harsh thud broke the stillness. Lance jerked and toppled forward onto Engrelin. Engrelin lay perfectly still for a moment, breathing heavily, and waited for Lance to get up.

But Lance didn't move a single muscle.

Running footsteps crackled through the fallen leaves.

"Engrelin? Dear God…"

Engrelin's whole body slumped with relief. It was Averendier.

"I'm not dead," Engrelin called out.

Lance's slumped form was pushed off him. Engrelin found himself blinking up at his cousin. Averendier met his gaze a moment, then glanced down at Lance.

"I see I arrived just in time," he said simply.

Engrelin sat up, holding his bleeding hand away from himself. "What did you do to him?" he asked.

"Rock," Averendier answered. "It was the only thing on hand I could throw in time."

"Did you kill him?" Engrelin asked anxiously. He turned Lance onto his back and dragged the sword away from him. At least neither of them had been hurt by its fall.

Averendier grasped Lance's wrist to feel his pulse, then felt all over the unconscious boy's scalp. "No, he'll live," he said finally. "But I don't envy the headache he'll have when he wakes."

Engrelin sat back on his heels and breathed a sigh of relief.

Averendier looked up quickly. "Who is this, anyway?" he asked. "And what is he doing here?"

Engrelin's jaw tightened. "This is Lance Smith. From Bryn," he said.

Averendier's gaze sharpened. "Lance, the blacksmith's son?"

Engrelin nodded slowly. "The one and only."

"I thought you two were friends."

Engrelin looked away from Averendier's searching eyes and down at Lance. Revulsion rose within him. What had induced Lance to do such a thing?

"We were," he said softly. "I don't know what happened to him. I can't believe he followed us all the way out here."

Averendier stood and wiped his hands on his trousers. "Thank goodness he didn't wake anyone but me," he said. "If this is connected with Tirendria in any way, it's the end of Bendekahn's secret."

"And of me. But I don't it's connected," Engrelin answered. "Lance denied being connected with them. He even claimed to want to take revenge on them next."

Averendier wiped his arm across his forehead. "At least we don't have to worry about that," he breathed.

Engrelin frowned. "No, but we still have Lance."

"That's no problem. We can hand him over to the authorities at the nearest town."

Engrelin's head jerked up. "Hand him over!"

"Engrelin, he tried to kill you. And—why is he here anyway?"

Engrelin smiled a hard, small smile. "Look in the glade."

Averendier started and whirled to face the now empty glade. "Were there more men here?" he asked.

"And they took the horses," Engrelin concluded. "Didn't you see they were gone?"

"I was too busy saving your life to take in the scenery," Averendier said. He rubbed the heel of his palm against the bridge of his nose.

"We'll just have to take Lance along as a prisoner until we reach a town—" He held up one hand, cutting Engrelin's protests short. "Let me finish first," he commanded. "We'll have to tell the girls about the horses, and that we captured one of the thieves, which is perfectly true. You don't need to tell the girls that you know Lance, or that he tried to kill you. Especially not that. I don't want them to worry any more than they must. Missing the horses will be bad enough."

"Then how do I explain this?" Engrelin demanded, thrusting his wounded hand at his cousin. "It just so happens that though the thieves carried no weapons, one of the horses had a sword. Right. This is brilliant."

Gently, Averendier took Engrelin's hand in his. He drew a slow breath and carefully probed the gashes, spilling more blood all over Engrelin's hand.

"Pretty bad, for a hand," he commented. Quickly, Averendier doused the wounds with the stinging contents of a small phial. Engrelin clamped down on his lower lip. Averendier glanced swiftly up at him, then bound the handkerchief tightly around the wound.

"You're lucky," he concluded, dropping his cousin's hand. "It went all the way through your hand but didn't hit any bones or anything. It'll take a while to heal, though. A month, maybe longer."

Engrelin smiled grimly. *It had to be my sword hand too.*

"Meanwhile, we'll just have to stick with our first explanation, and try to avoid questions about your hand. They can assume to their hearts' content. One of the other thieves were just as likely to have attacked you as the one we captured. They don't have to know it was Lance."

Engrelin glanced down at the clumsy bandage. "Okay." He looked up quickly. "But we're taking Lance to Monaria."

"What?"

"You're not giving Lance to the authorities," Engrelin said deliberately.

"Engrelin, are you nuts?" Averendier demanded in a whisper. "We can't keep him. He tried to kill you. Think of the girls!"

"I am thinking," Engrelin argued. "I'm the one he wants, not the girls. He said so himself."

"And you believe him," Averendier said flatly.

Engrelin squared his shoulders. "I do," he said. "And I believe the worst he wants to do is kill me, then skip town. That's the worst that could happen, right?"

"The worst…" Averendier shook his head. "I can't allow it, Engrelin. We need you. You're no use to us, or to Monaria, dead."

"But if you just—"

"No, Engrelin," said Averendier sternly, sitting back as if he had put in the final word to the conversation. "He's not coming home with us. It's too dangerous."

"But he's my friend. I can't leave him."

"Your friend," Averendier echoed, fires lighting in his gray eyes. "Murder is a token of endearment now? Engrelin—" Averendier paused to look back at camp once again. "I know what you're trying to do. It's noble. You want to spare Lance from the justice he deserves and spare his life. At any other time, I might help you. But he just tried to kill you. Something in him has snapped. He's dangerous. He's going to the nearest town so the authorities can take care of him. I'm sorry."

"And if he were Andrald?" Engrelin demanded.

Averendier looked at him sidelong. "I don't see what—"

"You know perfectly well what I'm saying," Engrelin replied. "If Andrald were in Lance's position, if he had nearly killed you, would you turn him over to complete strangers to be tried for theft and murder?"

"Engrelin, this isn't about my brother—"

"No, it's about mine," Engrelin interrupted. "The only brother I have left. I couldn't save Damien and Ouen. But I'm going to save Lance, and nothing you say will stop me. I'll use the map you gave me to bring him home myself if I must. But I won't leave him to be judged and sentenced by strangers who don't care a whit about him or his soul."

Averendier stood silent, a dark, somber tower wrapped in his own thoughts. The silence stretched on, dragging breath after painful breath from Engrelin as he waited.

"You may keep him," Averendier said finally. "But you'll be solely responsible for him. And," he added sharply, "if he tries anything like this again, or moves to hurt someone, or spirits them away like he did the horses, we will turn him in."

"Yes, sir," Engrelin replied quietly. His heart stuttered with relief.

"Now check his pockets and make sure he isn't hiding anything," Averendier directed. "I'm going back to camp for some rope."

Averendier hurried back to camp. Meanwhile, Engrelin rifled through Lance's pockets. Reaching beyond bits of string, a strip of dried meat, and a rather battered compass, Engrelin's fingers closed over something cold. He drew out a hunting knife, its wicked blade concealed in a leather sheath. Engrelin nearly shivered to think what might have happened if Lance had used that on him instead of the cyllel.

Averendier returned.

"Here." Engrelin tossed him the hunting knife.

Averendier caught it. "Anything else?" he asked.

Engrelin reached into Lance's other pocket. His fingers found steel and smooth wood. Another knife. Engrelin drew it out and cradled it towards the moonlight.

Lance's clasp knife.

"This all?" Averendier asked.

A lump lodged in his throat, Engrelin nodded. His fingers curled protectively around the inscribed handle.

"Yeah," he said. "That's all."

"Good. I'll tie him up and watch him tonight. You sleep this off and take charge of him in the morning."

"Yeah, sure. Thanks."

Rising slowly, Engrelin crossed the glade and picked his way back to his outspread blanket. He sank heavily onto it and shut his eyes, his fingers traveling up and down the knife he still clenched. He thought he could still feel the sticky peach juice from that long ago summer day slathered over the handle. But it was his own blood, seeping through his crude bandage and soaking the hilt.

31

E *ngrelin?"*
Slowly, Engrelin's eyelids fluttered open. He stared groggily up at Andrald, who hovered over him.

"Engrelin, Averendier says he wants you to come see him in the glade. What's the big idea? Did you seriously let him take your watch after all?"

Andrald's demanding tone snapped Engrelin's clinging threads of sleep and brushed them aside. He sat up and raked his hand through his hair. Lance's knife fell into his lap.

Andrald pounced on it.

"What's this?" he asked. He held up the knife for all the world to see.

Engrelin snatched the knife from Andrald's hand and jammed it deep into his own pocket. "Nothing," he said quickly.

Andrald's eyebrows shot skyward. "And what's this?" He took Engrelin's bandaged hand and stared at the bloodstains that had formed overnight

Engrelin jerked it away (not without a wince). "Nothing."

Andrald gave him a look.

"What is this, an interrogation?" Engrelin demanded, irascible.

"Nope," Andrald retorted. "It's nothing."

Engrelin rolled his eyes. "All right, you win. They're all something. But if Averendier wants me now, I'll have to explain it all later." *Not like you won't learn soon enough anyway, with no horses to ride and Lance on our hands.*

"Ooo-kay then." Andrald stood. "If you two need me, I'll be making breakfast."

Engrelin grimaced, but Andrald had already turned his back, so he didn't see it.

Slowly, Engrelin slung his quiver over his shoulder and buckled his sword belt around his waist. He rested his hand a moment on Arrian's cool pommel. He wasn't going to leave his sword behind this time.

Lance glowered as Engrelin approached the tree. Averendier moved into the glade to meet Engrelin.

"He hasn't said a single word since he woke about an hour ago," said Averendier.

"That's not bad," Engrelin whispered back. "It's when he opens his mouth we've got to worry."

Frowning, Averendier threw a glance at Lance, who slouched against the tree, muttering to himself.

"How are you going to break it to the girls?" Engrelin asked.

"Just bring him into camp and tell them what happened to the horses last night. There's so much brush between camp and this glade, I doubt they've noticed the horses are gone. Just keep our explanation short and sweet. It's all we can do."

Short and sweet…like peaches. Engrelin's hand traveled down into his trouser pocket and closed over Lance's clasp knife.

Averendier jerked his chin towards Lance.

"He's all yours. I'm trusting your judgement in handling him, but you must always keep his hands tied. You may want to lay a few rules out, so he knows his boundaries. Though I doubt it will do much." Averendier didn't say anything more, but his thoughts might as well have been pasted on his face. *If a guy is obsessed enough to chase another guy halfway across the world…*

Engrelin's jaw tightened. "I'll think of something," he promised. "And…thanks."

Averendier looked at him askance. "For what?"

"Letting me bring him."

Averendier jerked his head in a nod. "Just remember our main duty is to Bendekahn and his daughters. Anything—and anyone—else is secondary."

Engrelin smiled thinly. "I won't forget."

"Also, I discovered this morning we're missing some of our supplies," Averendier said. He took a step towards camp. "I'm going to check that now. Have fun."

"Thanks!" Engrelin called sarcastically after his retreating cousin. He wiped his hand wearily across his eyes. Lance probably hadn't expected to be captured, or he might have let his goons leave the food alone. And now Lance was an extra mouth to feed…

Despite all his earlier aspirations, Engrelin's hand groped for Arrian's hilt. He shut his eyes briefly.

Think of the girls, he told himself. *Don't do anything that'll put them in danger.*

Engrelin drew a deep breath and swiveled to face Lance. He watched the sullenly bent figure for several silent seconds.

'Well?" he demanded. "What do you have to say for yourself?"

Lance threw his head back. "Fine," he growled. "Kill me! Get it over with."

Engrelin dropped Arrian's hilt. "Is that all?" he asked.

"No," Lance muttered.

"I'm not planning on killing you—" Engrelin began.

"Getting someone else to do the dirty work?" Lance sneered. "Huh! Typical of you." His eyes scanned Engrelin until they fell on his injured hand. "But I guess that's just because you can't do it yourself."

Mouth set, blood burning, Engrelin strode forward, grabbed Lance's collar, and shoved him up straight against the tree.

"Looks like I hit the nail on the head," Lance taunted, his eyes wildly mixed with fear and hatred.

"Just the opposite," Engrelin gritted. "I never dreamed of laying a hand on you, Lance."

Lance snorted derisively. "Right. And what're you doing right now?"

Engrelin dropped his hand sharply, clenching his teeth as a warm spread of blood on his bandage reminded him he had used the wrong hand. Quickly, he jammed it into his pocket.

"Lance, being your guard doesn't make me an executioner," Engrelin said quietly. "You're coming with us. We're giving you a few rules to live by—"

"You mean *you're* going to lay down some rules," Lance snarled.

Engrelin's good hand curled into a fist at his side. "All right. *I'm* going to give you a few conditions. If you accept them, you'll come with us. If you refuse them, I'll leave you at the base of this tree until someone comes back here and finds you. And I don't think many people around here find horse thieves pleasant company, unless they're highwaymen themselves." He paused for a moment to let his words sink in. "If I were you, I would just accept the conditions."

"If I were you, Engrelin," Lance spat, "I'd be afraid to look at my own reflection. But," he continued smoothly, "let's hear your conditions, and I'll decide whether they're humane enough to accept."

Engrelin let his breath out through his teeth. "Fine. I'm a hangman and a monster. But these are the conditions. Reject them, and I leave you to fruitlessly reconsider."

Lance looked down and cursed under his breath.

"That's the first," said Engrelin sharply. "None of that ever, especially when you're around the girls we have with us."

Lance grumbled but didn't look up.

"Second condition," Engrelin continued. "No touching any weapons. Sword, bow, arrows, the like. If it's sharp, leave it alone. No murdering anyone—that should be obvious anyway—and no fisticuffs, either."

"You sure know how to take the fun out of things, don't you, Engrelin?" Lance sneered. "It's not like I can do any of those things anyway, trussed up like this."

Engrelin nodded. "That's another thing. As long as you behave, those ropes are the only kind of restraint you'll have. But break any of the conditions, you'll get more."

His final words slid into the nothingness of Lance's expectant, brooding silence. After a few seconds, the suspicious prisoner looked up.

"What else?" he demanded.

"Nothing," Engrelin answered simply.

"That's all?!" Lance exclaimed.

Engrelin held Lance's bewildered gaze steadily. "Yes, Lance. That's all."

Lance looked down in utter confusion. The bandage that Averendier had wound about his head was all Engrelin saw for nearly a minute. When Lance finally looked back up, the fierce defensiveness had returned to his eyes.

"All right," he said. "I'll enslave myself to your rules for a while. But with conditions of my own."

Engrelin groaned inwardly. *Here we go now…*

"I won't take orders from anyone but you," Lance said. "Unless you have to leave me—then put me under one other person's charge. I'm not going to live with you guys if a million people are telling me what to do."

Engrelin nodded. "Fair enough—"

"I wasn't finished!" Lance growled. "I don't want anyone asking me about my past. Or the present. Or anything. And I don't have to answer any questions anyone asks me either."

"Is that all?" Engrelin asked dryly.

"Yes, if you're ready to shut up."

Engrelin pressed his lips in a tight line. *Same goes for you.*

In the silence that followed, Lance looked down, blowing out of the corner of his mouth. "How long will I have to submit to all this?" he asked.

"Until we reach Monaria," Engrelin answered.

Lance let his breath hiss out.

"I could always turn you in to the nearest authorities for horse theft and attempted murder to save you the trip," Engrelin added. "It was your choice, Lance."

"My choice!" Lance exclaimed. "If I had my choice of this—"

"Averendier!" someone called from across the meadow.

Engrelin scowled and peered around the tree. He saw Lilac on the edge of the glade, headed in his direction (though she hadn't spotted him yet).

Rats, what does she want now?

Couldn't she have chosen a better time to bug Averendier about the day's plans?

"Lance, don't make a sound," he whispered threateningly. "That's an order. I don't want Lilac to see you."

Lance drew back in mock offense. "Don't want her to see me? Have you looked in a mirror recently?"

"Shut up!" Engrelin hissed. He speared Lance with a warning look before darting out from behind the tree. He nearly collided with Lilac.

"Oh!" the girl exclaimed, her hand flying up to cover her heart.

"Sorry," Engrelin apologized quickly.

Lilac slowly dropped her hand. "You're fine." She smiled. "Have you seen Averendier?"

"Yes, just a moment ago," Engrelin answered. "Why, do you need him? Is something wrong?"

Lilac twisted a pleat in her skirt around her finger. "Oh, no, nothing's wrong. I just wanted to talk to him about schedules and such. Though is he saddling the horses already?"

A terrible, gurgling snarl sounded from behind a tree. A little line of confusion crossed Lilac's forehead.

"Averendier's over checking our supplies," Engrelin said causally.

"Thank you," said Lilac.

Another unearthly burble met their ears.

"Good luck," Engrelin said hastily. Why wouldn't she just leave?

"I don't believe in luck," answered Lilac. She leaned ever so slightly to one side, subtly attempting to peer beyond Engrelin's shoulder. Engrelin followed her gaze. To his relief, the broad-trunked tree hid all sings and sights of Lance.

"Do you know what that sound was?" Lilac asked, looking expectantly at Engrelin.

"Nothing, probably," Engrelin said slowly.

"Liar," Lance choked.

Engrelin scowled and dealt himself a mental slap. He might as well try to hide a horse under a drinking glass

Lilac raised her eyebrows slightly. What Engrelin wouldn't have given for a rag to clap over Lance's mouth at that moment!

"I'll explain later," Engrelin muttered. "You should probably find Averendier now."

Lilac gave him a long look and nodded slowly. Then she turned and walked back across the empty glade in search of Averendier.

Engrelin waited until she was out of earshot, them whipped back around the tree.

"What about 'be quiet' do you not understand?" he demanded.

Lance's lips twisted in a maddeningly insolent grin. "The quiet part," he replied.

Engrelin dragged his hand across his face and up through his hair, though he really felt like yanking it from his scalp. He was going to have to live with this for the next month? But it was his own choice. Given the chance to relive last night, he wouldn't have altered his decision.

Engrelin reached down and grasped Lance's arm.

"Come on, get up."

"Where are we going?" Lance asked, not budging an inch.

Engrelin pulled him to his feet. "We're going to camp to get breakfast," he answered.

"What if I don't want to eat breakfast?" Lance challenged.

"You're coming anyway," Engrelin said. He motioned to the curl of smoke that indicated the near campfire. "Come on."

They crossed the glade to camp. The two younger princesses didn't notice Engrelin and Lance's entrance; the girls were sitting on logs with their backs turned to the glade. Engrelin hoped to escape their notice for as long as possible. Propelling Lance before him, Engrelin quietly made his way over to the fire, where Averendier and Andrald stood discussing something in low tones. Andrald, scrubbing a pot vigorously, also had his back turned to the newcomers.

"Andrald, did you save anything for us?" Engrelin asked.

"Yep." Andrald handed Engrelin a bowl without even glancing back at him. Engrelin looked down into the bowl. He grimaced. At one point and time, its contents had been oatmeal. All he saw now was a blackened mess.

"Did you make any for Lance?" Averendier asked quietly.

Andrald looked sharply at him. "Lance?"

Averendier motioned subtly behind his brother.

Andrald jolted and whirled, knocking into Engrelin's still-outstretched hand, flinging the bowl to the ground. Wincing, Engrelin bent to retrieve his bowl, which had flipped face-down.

"Is this the thief you caught last night, Engrelin?" Andrald asked. He eyed Lance suspiciously.

"Yeah," Engrelin answered distractedly. "That's the something I told you about earlier."

He snagged the bowl's rim and flipped it upright. Besides the addition of a single dead leaf, not one clump of the burned oatmeal had fallen out. Averendier, who had just picked up his own bowl, took one glance at Engrelin's and quickly set his own down.

"The other men took about half the provisions, Engrelin," he said in a low voice. He glanced swiftly at the seated princesses to be sure they weren't hearing anything. "We'll have to make an unexpected stop at the nearest farm or village to get more. We won't last until Elstar."

Setting his bowl on the ground, Engrelin sank down onto a log beside it, making sure Lance sat down beside him. He tugged his map out of his pocket and smoothed it over his thigh.

"It's too late to try any of the small places," he said thoughtfully. "We're in a poor area. No farmer for miles will be willing to sell anything from their cellars this season. Our best bet would be here." He placed his finger on a tiny etched dot set at a crossroads. He tilted the map so Averendier could read the village's name.

"Hyke's Crossing?" Averendier's lips bent in a tight frown. "That's nearly a week out, on foot. Food will get tight."

Make Andrald cook for that week, and you won't have to worry about any shortages. No one will want to eat a crumb, thought Engrelin, bemused.

"We may fall short," Engrelin said. "But no sensible man with a family under his roof is going to sell an ounce of flour during the resting season. This village may be our best and only bet."

"Then let's set our course for there," Andrald declared.

"Remember, Zacara told us to avoid villages and cities as much as possible," Averendier reminded.

"It's not like we can help it, Averendier," Engrelin said. "We're of no use to anyone dead from starvation."

Averendier nodded tightly. "All right," he said finally. "But don't tell the girls about the shortage. I don't want them to worry."

"If we need to, I can hunt evenings," Engrelin offered.

Averendier nodded again. "We'll need it, especially with no horses to carry anything. We'll have to take things in smaller hauls." His jaw visibly tightened again as his eyes roved back towards the empty glade. Which reminded Engrelin of something.

"Averendier, did you get to talk to Lilac?" he asked. "She was looking for you a few minutes ago."

Averendier opened his mouth to answer but was overridden by a quiet voice from behind.

"I did get to speak with him some, Engrelin. Thank you."

They all turned to see Lilac, standing rigid with her hands clenched tightly behind her back. A deep frown ridged her forehead. "Averendier, where are the horses? I thought you might be saddling them somewhere, but now you're here, and I can't find them anywhere."

Engrelin drew his breath in gradually. Here it was.

"I was wondering when one of you would ask that," said Averendier carefully. "Your Highness, several men came into camp last night during Engrelin's watch and stole the horses."

"During Engrelin's watch?" shrilled Elvera from where she sat.

"Yes," Averendier replied evenly.

Engrelin glanced at her. She scowled back. Engrelin looked quickly away. Why in Ontaria did she always look at him like that?

"Is this young man one of the thieves?" asked Lilac. She motioned to Lance, who had—somehow—remained either unnoticed or unmentioned until now.

"Yes," Averendier answered. "He was the only one we managed to capture."

"Are we going to turn him over to the authorities?" Lilac asked.

Averendier glanced at Engrelin. Lance intently followed the look, watching his guard with hostile expectancy. Engrelin quietly cleared his swelling throat.

"No, Lilac—I mean, your Highness," he said. "We're taking him with us to Monaria."

"All the way to Monaria!" Elvera cried. Springing off her log, she took several swift steps toward Engrelin and his prisoner. "We're going to lug that—that vagabond with us all the way north? Whose idea was that?!"

"Mine," Engrelin said dryly.

Elvera snorted and threw a glance upwards. "Why am I not surprised?"

Engrelin colored. He couldn't tell them of his past connections—his friendship—with Lance. But neither would he ever let them convince him to dump his friend in the nearest town to meet some awful fate alone. He would never leave him.

Isalinia, who had been sitting silently this whole time, now spoke up (perhaps to change to a slightly more pleasant topic). "Are we going to buy new horses?" she asked.

Everyone turned to look at Averendier, who wiped his hand wearily across his forehead.

"I'm afraid we can't," he said. "We don't have the time or the funds. We'll just have to push the rest of the way on foot. It may take a little longer, but it's not much worse than bumping around in a saddle for hours on end. And this way, we can set up and break down camp faster."

With a despairing groan, Elvera crumpled back onto her log and buried her face in her hands.

"If that's what we must do, I am willing," Lilac said quickly.

"So am I," Isalinia agreed.

Elvera remained motionless for a moment. Then she lifted her head and nodded bleakly. She stared at Engrelin for several seconds, her eyes drifting down towards his crudely bandaged hand. Her hand shot to the pack lying on the ground beside her. Drawing it into her lap, she hugged it tightly to her chest.

Engrelin rammed his injured hand into his pocket. Did she have to stare? Or maybe she was staring at his sword. He looked down at Arrian and bit his inner lip. He still couldn't believe that after all his work, all his training with Lamar, he was completely unable to use his sword until his hand healed. By that time, they'd be back in Monaria, and what need would he have for it then? Clenching his teeth, he ran his left hand through his hair. Mid-swipe he froze and slowly drew his hand back down. He stared at his good hand for a long time.

Slowly, he smiled.

Averendier began organizing the departure and separating the supplies evenly into their packs. Engrelin trotted over to Andrald, who was cramming the detested oatmeal pot into his pack.

"Hey, Andrald, would you help me with some sword practice tonight?" he asked.

Andrald scratched the back of his neck and looked at Engrelin askance. "I mean, sure, if you want. But you're not too good at it, you know."

Engrelin blew out the corner of his mouth. "That's why I practice, right?"

Andrald shrugged and turned back to his packing. "Sure, I guess. Hey, Engrelin, didn't Averendier want you to make a bundle for that Lance guy to carry?"

"I'll get it," Engrelin said. He couldn't help smiling grimly as he retrieved his pack, dragging Lance along with him. Who ever said you could only use your dominant hand for fighting?

32

B*erwyn?"*
Berwyn turned towards the timid voice. Lednora, one of her kitchen helpers, shivered in the woodshed doorway, clasping her shaking hands before her. Berwyn returned her attention to her armload of wood. Lednora was always freaking out about something or other in creation. Undoubtably, she presently suffered from another panic attack. Lednora was lucky Doctor Sirman managed to gather herbs in the woods during his hunts, or her hysterics might have killed her long ago.

"Lednora, how many times have I told you to wait to ask me a question until I passed you in the kitchen?" Berwyn sighed, straightening and hefting a cord of wood into the crooks of her elbows. Just above the high stack, she glimpsed Lednora's blanched face.

"I know what you told me, Berwyn," Lednora gasped. "And I was just at the quartermaster's to get that portion of yeast we needed."

Berwyn frowned. "Did he refuse?" *How am I supposed to make bread without yeast?*

Lednora shook her head. "He gave the yeast to me, Berwyn. But he also told me that Lord Rees wants you right away. There's a boat waiting for you at the creek."

Berwyn nearly dropped the wood. Shards of fear stabbed her stomach like broken icicles. Lord Rees wanted to see her now? Today? But she'd given her weekly report only a couple days ago!

"Did he say what he wanted me for?" she asked Lednora.

A sob tore Lednora's voice. "I don't know, Berwyn. The quartermaster wouldn't tell me! Is it because you stitched my finger last week? Did I get you killed?"

"That's nonsense." Berwyn shifted the bundle of wood awkwardly under one arm to wrap her free arm around the girl's shuddering figure. "I'm sure it has nothing to do with you," she added softly. "It was the quartermaster who told you, right?"

Tearfully, Lednora nodded.

"Well, then," Berwyn said, forcing cheer to bolster Lednora. Her own courage seemed to have broken through, like the bottom of a rotten bucket. "Maybe we're finally going to get a change in the menu."

Lednora shivered and pressed her hot, wet cheek against Berwyn's shoulder. "That's not why he wants you. It can't be! Why would they change the menu now? They haven't since we got here. It's something worse." Her tears seeped through the shoulder of Berwyn's thin bodice. "What will all of us do without you? You're the only person who ever really did anything more than tell me to shut up. And if they take…if they take…" She choked off, gulping for breath.

Berwyn grasped Lednora's shoulder and held her an arm's length away. Meeting the girl's swollen eyes sternly, she asked, "Did you say Alton is waiting at the creek already? If he is, I must go before I'm late."

Lednora gaped at her but managed a nod. Her hands clutched at her chest as if she were suffering from a heart attack.

"Good." Berwyn dumped her load of wood onto the floor. "Tell Mariana that she must come get the wood for the fires this time. And Rebeka is in charge while I'm gone. I have to go."

Digging into her satchel, Berwyn drew out a small pouch sewn of tightly woven fabric. Crushed herbs crunched pleasantly inside it as she pressed it into Lednora's trembling hand. "Steep it for five minutes in boiling water, then drink slowly," she whispered. "That's an order."

Smiling faintly, Lednora's fingers curled protectively over the sachet.

"Everything's going to be all right," Berwyn continued reassuringly (though she could have used some assurance herself). "I'll be back in an hour to help with supper."

"How do you know that?" Lednora whispered as Berwyn headed for the door.

Berwyn turned to squeeze Lednora's hand. "I don't know. I just hope," she said. "It's all I can do right now."

Not giving Lednora any more time to protest, Berwyn strode out into the open air.

Sheets of gray clouds brooded over Kepspell. To Berwyn, it seemed they had never ceased since her arrival, casting their gloom and the occasional drizzle onto the huddled hovels and the people below.

Berwyn's steps lagged as she passed the extensive fields where sailor, merchant, and soldier worked alike as farmers, preparing the soil for the spring planting or tending the short green shoots of winter wheat that bravely poked from the drab soil. Berwyn heaved an inward sigh and pushed on down the muddy path, bending her head to the brisk wind that cut through her threadbare clothes.

"Hello, Miss Sirman."

At the greeting, Berwyn jerked her head up to smile the passerby. When her eyes lighted on the person, her friendly smile shifted to a frown. The man beside her was none other than Damien Peterson. He smiled amiably, almost shyly at her. But she couldn't help noticing the bluish-green tinge around his right eye, where serious bruising had been only a week before, and the scabbed split in his lip. Berwyn offered him a reserved nod. In her mind, there was gaining their freedom, and there was Damien Peterson. A wide chasm lay between.

"Good day, Mr. Peterson," she returned icily.

Damien frowned and did exactly what Berwyn prayed he wouldn't—he stopped in the middle of the road to study her confusedly.

"Miss Sirman, I don't understand your attitude towards me," he said. "Every day, just a nod and a greeting. Have I done something to offend you?"

Had he done something? Berwyn stared at him in disbelief. He was the only one in the entirety of Kepspell with enough gall to organize secret meetings in the prisoners' cabins at night. He was planning sedition. Something that might free them…or bog them down in further oppression. All the Tirendrian guards constantly kept their eyes, as well as their fists, upon him (as his bruises clearly testified). Her eyes caught a gleam of scarlet in the brush beside the path, and her heart hammered against her ribs.

"Miss Sirman?" Damien turned his head to follow her gaze. A bright red cardinal burst out of the thicket and swooped out of sight among the trees. Berwyn's breath escaped her in a soft sigh.

"Are you afraid of them, Miss Sirman?" Damien asked her.

Berwyn looked at him sidelong. She knew he wasn't talking about cardinals. "*Am* I afraid of them?" she echoed in a fierce whisper. "I think I should be, don't you?"

Damien's brow creased. "Maybe a bit," he replied. "But we can't let fear paralyze us."

"You just think I'm scared because I don't like being around you," she hissed. "You're trouble, Damien. You don't care what happens to yourself or the rest of us, so long as you get your taste of precious freedom."

"You're free to distance yourself from me if that's what you wish, Miss Sirman. But I am grateful that you finally answered my question," said Damien. But instead of looking grateful or even relieved, as Berwyn thought he should, concern clouded his dark blue eyes. "But sometimes we're called to do what seems out of line and downright dangerous, especially in a place like this. What I'm doing isn't wrong."

"Isn't wrong?" Berwyn choked. "Something that will cost dozens, if not hundreds of husbands and brothers and fathers their lives? I've overheard your men talking when they thought I was asleep. I know what you're plotting. You may not be worried about dying; you don't have a wife or children to worry about. But what about the others you're entangling in this? What about their families?"

"So instead we're to let them rot away here, and that will do them a fat lot more good?" Damien exclaimed in the lowest of whispers. His eyes penetrated Berwyn like fire for a moment. He dropped his gaze to the ground.

"Berwyn, a man cannot love in any greater way than to lay down his life for others," he said softly. "I'm not saying I don't fear the consequences. I do. And I could lose the sister and brother here in my care. I don't want anything to happen to them. But I can't fear. God is with me. Whether I succeed or not, He is with my siblings as well, and He will care for them if I'm killed."

Damien lifted his gaze to Berwyn's, his eyes brimming with such serenity that Berwyn looked away. Her own eyes prickled with tears and guilt. Here was Damien talking about death—and smiling! She nearly shuddered.

"I…I still don't think it's right," she faltered.

Damien's smile grew almost amused. "Think what you like," he said.

Berwyn glared at him.

"It's not that I think you're funny," he hastened to assure her. "You just reminded me of my stubborn little brother. He'd always end arguments that way, even when he knew he was wrong."

Berwyn blushed a deep, angry red. "Maybe you should go get him," she snapped, "So with combined stubbornness we can talk you out of this whole thing."

She regretted the words the moment they flew from her mouth. But there was no taking them back—they were dandelion down on a breeze. Some inner pain contorted Damien's face.

"Miss Sirman," he said tightly, "My littlest brother wasn't brought here with us, and I'd never bring him here even if it was to get one last glimpse of his face before I died."

Berwyn averted her eyes and scuffed her toe through a rut in the dirt. What to say? But there never was and never would be something to answer that anger and pain and love.

"I have to go now, if you'll excuse me," she mumbled, pushing past him and down the path, head hung low. His gaze burned her back until she walked down a bend in the path and was hidden from his sight. Just ahead, the trees parted to display a slice of the creek, its bank, and the flat-bottomed boat that bobbed patiently in the water, waiting to carry her to Reing.

Drawing a shaking breath, Berwyn rewound her hair in a knot at the nape of her neck. She started down towards the boat. She couldn't think any more about Damien Peterson and his dangerous schemes. She needed to gather all her strength and composure for her unexpected meeting with Lord Rees. The thought of the man made her shudder and lengthen her strides. It was best to get it over with, and quickly.

"According to your report, everything seems to be going rather well in sector five's kitchen, Miss Sirman," said the Lord Rees coldly. He braced his shriveled palms on the stack of papers in his lap and leaned back in his chair. In front of him, Berwyn stood at rigid attention, her hands clasped behind her back, her head high. No matter what, she would never let this man know how greatly she feared him.

"I'm glad you think so," Berwyn answered carefully. She had given that same answer at the end of every report, following the customary comment he had just made.

"So am I." Rees nodded once, his amber eyes fixed on Berwyn, seeming to drill into her soul as they stared from beneath the shadow of his voluminous hood. Berwyn's breath strangled in her throat.

"But tell me," he continued, leaning forward. "You are troubled. No, don't try to hide it. I can see it plainly." As he paused, Berwyn groped to retrieve her scattered wits. Why did he always have to talk like that and stare at her so intently as he did!

"You wonder why I summoned you now, instead of at our usual weekly mark? That frightened you. I didn't intend it to." He drummed his fingers (which seemed to be made of mere bone and sinew with yellowed skin stretched over them) on the papers in his lap and peered at her in his unsettling manner. Berwyn nervously clenched and unclenched her hands behind her back.

"I summoned you here because I am leaving Reing tonight, and I will not be back for several weeks. You will give your reports to Warwick in Kepspell during my absence." He stared at her for one long, terrifying moment. "You are absolutely sure that you have nothing unusual to report?"

"Nothing whatsoever," Berwyn replied. Her voice trembled slightly.

Lord Rees' chair creaked as he leaned still further forward. "Miss Sirman," he said coldly, "I find it quite unusual you have never reported any forbidden or suspicious activities in all the months you have been here." His eyebrows knit in a scowl above his glaring yellow eyes. "By which I mean *very* unusual, Miss Sirman. I can see you're hiding something from me."

Berwyn's palms grew slick with sweat. Never had he gone this far. Always before, she had given her list of supplies that had been used, what had broken during the week (this list was often the longest), and what was needed in the next week to keep the kitchen functioning. Never had she mentioned the barrage of cuts and scalds she soothed, or of any whispered rumors she heard.

"Sir, if I had felt that something needed to be reported, I would have reported it," she said evenly.

"That's an easy thing to say," Rees replied. "But exceedingly difficult to believe."

Berwyn's heart faltered several beats, but she forced herself to hold Rees' gaze. He let the silence and the stares eat away at her for a moment. Then he suddenly sprang to his feet. Amid the flurry of displaced papers, he struck Berwyn hard on the mouth. Berwyn jumped back with a startled cry, her hand flying up to cover her stinging lips.

"I have had contrary reports, Miss Sirman," Rees continued coolly as he sank back into his chair. "One arrived today just before you did. One of my men saw you stop on your way here to speak to Damien Peterson, the young rebel. We haven't found anything stark against him yet. But he and your father are not shining examples of what we would like to see in the citizens of Kepspell."

Berwyn drew her hand away from her swollen mouth and stared at the blood smeared across her fingers.

"Is your mouth sore, Miss Sirman?" inquired Rees.

Slowly, Berwyn lifted her eyes to meet his taunting gaze.

"I assure you, Miss Sirman," said Rees quietly, "If you and those around you do not shape up to our standards, there will be far more blood spilt than from a mere lip."

He looked down at his scattered papers, scowled at himself, and looked back at her. He waved his hand dismissively. "You may leave."

Berwyn had no choice but to turn and obey.

33

It had been another sleepless night. Since he had settled on his blanket, Engrelin had watched the moon drag itself through the field of sluggishly winking stars. Engrelin dug the heels of his hands into his gritty eyes.

Had it really been a week already? It had passed so quickly. Lance had been fairly well behaved throughout, especially over the past few days. He'd hardly let a threat or insult fly.

Engrelin frowned and shifted onto his side. It was relieving and concerning all at once.

The morning dawned with a knife in hand, slicing its chill straight through the huddled figures on the ground. Engrelin jerked his aching body to its feet and glanced tentatively up at the sky. Dark swaths of batting-like clouds hung close to the treetops. He drew a deep breath. The frosty air stabbed his lungs. Engrelin winced, blinked several times, and scrubbed his face with his hand. He was awake now.

Not bothering to rouse Lance, who still sprawled face down on his blanket and snored softly, Engrelin strode off to join Averendier, who was dousing their banked fire.

"Did you make breakfast already?" Engrelin asked, surprised.

"No." Averendier grunted as he shoveled some soil over the still-smoking embers. "We're eating on the road today."

Engrelin jerked his head meaningfully towards the sky.

Averendier nodded.

"The girls won't be able to handle a white-out," Engrelin said.

Averendier scowled slightly. "I know."

"We're going to have push hard to reach Hyke's Crossing today instead of tomorrow morning like we planned."

"I *know*." Averendier sloshed a kettle of water over the smoking heap of dirt that had been their fire. "Really hard." He set the kettle down. "If we reach the crossing before it snows, we'll try to get supplies, and then maybe hole up somewhere in town. But what are we going to do about Lance? Do you want to wait on the outskirts until we're done bartering and join us later?"

"Averendier, this village is tiny. Probably everyone there, except maybe a tavern keeper, speak only *cymraeg*. You'll need me to translate."

Averendier's eyebrows knit. "I hadn't thought of that," he murmured.

"Besides," Engrelin continued, "It could start snowing at any moment. We should stick together."

Averendier looked at him sharply. "You still have your map, don't you?"

Engrelin's stomach twisted, and he reached involuntarily to finger the creased edge of the map in his pocket. "Yes, I do."

"Then we won't have to worry if one of us does get lost."

Engrelin's eyes narrowed. "I don't want to use it if I don't have to," he said. "Anyway, Lance has been pretty okay for the past few days. I think we could safely take him into town. I can keep his hands tied behind his back. With a cloak thrown over them, no one's the wiser."

"All the same," Averendier replied, "I think you should keep a pretty sharp eye on him. Goodness knows what he might do in a crowd."

"He's behaved fairly well, Averendier."

Averendier turned sharply on his cousin. "And how trustworthy is he?"

Engrelin averted his eyes. "Not very," he admitted.

"Like I said," Averendier said evenly. "Keep your eyes on him. And expect anything."

By trekking hard all day on the narrow road, baring their shoulders to the biting wind, the group reached the brink of a valley by late afternoon, sooner than Engrelin had dared hope. The valley opening below them looked as if it had been scooped out of the surrounding mountains by a giant spoon. The slopes bristled with mildewed stubble: all that remained of last year's crops. Here and there, a cow or horse grazed, turning its haunches to the wind. A thatch-roofed village clustered around the two intersecting roads that drew a bold, brown cross in the valley's bottom. Engrelin let his gaze drift back upwards to the darkening clouds kissing the mountain peaks, too heavy with snow to rise higher.

Engrelin remained silent as his group descended the sloping road to the village. (Elvera made up for his silence by complaining loudly about the steepness and the iciness of the road the whole way down.) As they neared the village, Engrelin placed his hand lightly on Lance's upper arm. Lance scowled at him but said nothing and made no move to shake his guard's hand off.

The villagers cheerfully hailed them from their porches and doorsteps. Though secluded, the village crossing probably brought a few visitors. Engrelin darted a glance over at the girls and nearly grimaced. They walked as they had been taught to walk: like princesses. Though dressed in typical northerner's traveling clothes, he wasn't sure if everyone around them would be convinced that they were travelers only. But it wasn't like he could approach the girls and tell them to slouch their shoulders a little and not walk as if they had pikes thrust up their backs.

"*Edrych ar ef!*" called a childish voice close by. Engrelin glanced over to see a grinning child jabbing a chubby finger at him. No, not at him… at the tip of Arrian jutting out from beneath his cloak. Coloring, Engrelin jerked his cloak farther over to his left side to conceal the sword as much as possible. There was no harm in the child pointing the sword out, he reasoned. The kid probably hadn't seen anything bigger than a *cyllel* at someone's hip.

A large splinter of wood thudded against Engrelin's boot.

"*Hi,* lad! What you think you are?"

Engrelin stopped walking and looked up (still gripping Lance's arm) to see several men lounging on a tavern's front steps. A sign adorned with a maple leaf and some writing unintelligible to Engrelin swung over their heads. The man who had called out grinned in a not-unfriendly manner and motioned to Arrian; its tip still stuck out from beneath Engrelin's cloak.

"*Hwn*?" Engrelin returned. He pulled his cloak back slightly, though he curled his fingers around the gemstone pommel so the men wouldn't see it. "I heard you had a pest problem around here," he said. "Thought I'd come take care of it."

The other men on the porch roared with laughter, while the one who had spoken tugged his beard and stared at Arrian in wonder. Engrelin ground his teeth. It wasn't every day one got to see a longsword—a Kingsword, at that (though these men wouldn't know what Arrian was). Engrelin wished he could have walked on, but that would arouse the suspicion of not only these men but also the other villagers.

"Better stick to a *cyllel*, boy," another called out.

One of the men, a gnarled, older man, who had been thus far silent, now opened his heavy-lidded eyes. He glanced briefly at each of his companions before resting his gaze on Engrelin.

"He will need more than a *cyllel* to defeat the serpent," he said, quietly but distinctly, his clear eyes shining. "What he bears is sufficient."

Everything within Engrelin jolted; snippets of his constant nightmares flashed before his mind's eye. His hand instinctively tightened around Arrian's hilt.

The men congregated on the steps did not notice Engrelin's violent reaction. They only darted confused glances at one another, then at the elderly man crouching at their feet.

"A little early to be at the bottle, don't you think, Grandfather?" suggested one of them nervously.

The old man did not reply. He gave Engrelin one final look, potent with sagacity, before letting his eyelids droop closed over his pale eyes.

Suddenly, Lance kicked Engrelin in the shin and jerked out of his loose grasp. Engrelin cried out sharply, staggered a step from the blow, and whirled. Lance was already dashing around the tavern's corner into an alley. Gritting his teeth, Engrelin sprinted after him.

He should have known Lance would take advantage of any distraction! He skidded into the alley just in time to glimpse Lance disappearing around the other corner. Scowling, Engrelin pumped his legs in pursuit. For a guy whose hands were tied behind his back, Lance was fast. Arrian dragged at Engrelin's hip and slapped against his thigh. Seizing its hilt, he tried to hold the blade clear of his leg. Who knew a sword could be such a nuisance!

Engrelin flew into the street behind the tavern… and smashed into someone carrying a basket of apples. Amid a cascade of apples and the monger's colorful exclamations, Engrelin stumbled back and sat down hard.

"Ruined!" wailed the monger. He scrambled to his knees to snatch a few apples that were rolling past. "Totally ruined!"

"Sorry," Engrelin murmured hastily. He caught up the apples closest to him and dropped them back into the man's basket.

The man's face turned purple. "Sorry? These were the best from my cellar. Now they are ruined! Squashed! Bruised!" He clenched his fist around the pulpy remains of a fruit he had (unfortunately) sat upon. "Pick them up and pay!" He shook the pulverized fruit in Engrelin's face.

Engrelin shot a glance down the street. Lance was gone.

"Sir, I have to—"

"No 'but's! Pick them up!"

Engrelin scrambled around in the street, gathering all the damaged apples and heaping them in the man's basket. Groping in his pocket, Engrelin scooped up a few stray coins. He pressed them into the monger's hands and sprang down the street in the direction he thought Lance had taken. He couldn't be sure, though. There were so many alleys and side-streets and yards that he hadn't seen when standing on the ridge, looking down on the village. It almost seemed a labyrinth built especially for Lance's getaway. Where had Lance gone?

Stumbling into a narrow alley, Engrelin rested his hands on his knees to catch his breath. Where would Lance have run once he realized Engrelin had fallen behind? Engrelin tipped his head back against the building's side. Through the gap between roofs, he saw a sliver of the surrounding hills. At once, he straightened. Of course. Lance would have run for the closest shelter.

Darting from alley to alley through the village, avoiding people as much as possible, Engrelin finally reached the village gate he had walked through only a few minutes earlier. Pausing just outside it, he squinted up at the hills. Barely discernable against the winter-bare slopes moved a gray form. Engrelin smiled grimly to himself.

There you are.

He drew one deep breath, then charged up the hillside. His eyes remained fixed on Lance until the escapee plunged into the woods amid a whiplash of branches. Marking the spot in his mind, Engrelin struggled up the final stretch of the slope and mounted the summit. There, he paused.

Dense branches loomed, a seemingly impenetrable wall, waving and hissing menacingly in the rising wind. Lance's reckless entrance hadn't left even a dent in the springy undergrowth. Engrelin paced up and down the wood line, scrutinizing the brush for an entrance. Once through the first wall, he knew the forest floor would be clear of debris and vegetation. But he had to find Lance's entrance site. And quickly. Lance knew too much now to be loose.

"Engrelin?" demanded a shrill voice from behind.

Engrelin jolted, wrenched Arrian from its scabbard, and spun.

With an undignified screech, Elvera leaped beyond the bare blade's path. As Engrelin stumbled back in surprise, Elvera quickly collected herself, planting her hands on her hips, curving her lips in a scowl.

"Engrelin, what are you doing over here?" she demanded.

Engrelin didn't answer, sheathing his sword with fierce precision. Any embarrassment he might have felt evaporated in a blaze of irritation.

"Well?" Elvera impatiently tapped her shoe's pointed toe on the dead turf. She glanced back and forth.

"Where's Lance?" Her eyes stabbed Engrelin accusingly. "Isn't he supposed to be with you?"

"He is," Engrelin returned. "And aren't you supposed to be with Averendier and the others? You shouldn't have followed me. Now I have to take you back to the village to be with them before I can go look for Lance." He extended his right hand to the girl. "Come on."

Flushing crimson, Elvera slapped Engrelin's hand away. Engrelin snatched back his hand, now burning with pain (he'd forgotten his healing wound). He clamped it tightly under his left arm, as if to protect it from further assault.

"I'm not a baby," Elvera hissed. "You have no right to order me around, especially now that you've lost Lance. I had to follow you to make sure you brought him back."

"Who told you to do that?" Engrelin demanded in furious disbelief.

"I told myself," Elvera answered coolly. "And I'm glad I did. You can't do anything on your own."

Anger prickled across Engrelin's cheeks and spread down his shoulders. *I'd like to see you handle Lance for a day,* he thought.

Elvera made a shooing motion, as if herding a flock of witless poultry forward. "We'd better hurry. Lance will probably be gone by the time you get back, so there's no sense in standing here arguing while he gets away."

Engrelin's jaw spasmed. She was so lucky she was a girl and a princess. He hadn't even heard the peasants in Bryn speaking to each other that way. His thoughts flitted to Lance and Walche, and he frowned. All right, *most* of the villagers hadn't. But she was right about something. Sharply, he turned on his heel and waded into the brush.

"Where are you going?" Elvera's snippety voice floated to him like a nightmare refusing to be forgotten.

"I'm going to find Lance," Engrelin called back, his voice edged with anger.

"What about taking me back to the village?"

"Like you said, Lance would be long gone by the time I got back," Engrelin said. "I can't take you. You found your way here, you can find your way back."

"But I—"

Engrelin turned fiercely to face her. The trailing vines he had just pushed through framed her every indignant feature, hands still on her hips, scowl darker than ever. "You can come with me if you're afraid to go alone," he said.

The girl's face screwed. "No!"

"Then walk back yourself," Engrelin said, turning back to face the forest ahead. "I'm not going to carry you."

He heard her snort behind him, but nothing more. Shrugging off her glare, Engrelin fixed his eyes on the ground. They lighted on a crushed pinecone lying near the base of a sapling. A yard away from it, a snapped vine told of a violently forced passage. Setting his jaw, Engrelin followed the path of trampled brush that would lead him to Lance.

Still at the wood line, Elvera paced back and forth, muttering to herself. Of all the stubborn blockheads she'd ever met, Engrelin was the worst. Stubborn, *unchivalrous* blockhead, she fiercely corrected herself. Who would have imagined that a young man would refuse to escort her down a strange hill and into a strange town because he wanted to chase down a good-for-nothing highwayman? She, for one, would be pleased if she never again saw Lance, that vile, incorrigible youth she had endured for a whole week.

One week, and no longer. If Engrelin had come with her back to the village, Lance's track would have grown too cold to pursue before the pending storm. Engrelin would have to return scorned and empty-handed. And Lance would be gone forever.

Elvera clenched her hands and ground her teeth. And here she was, standing alone, letting Engrelin chase the vagabond and bring him back.

She threw her dark hair back off her shoulders. Not on her life. She turned, surveyed the tangle of vines and thorns that Engrelin had just disappeared into, and plunged viciously after him.

34

Engrelin moved swiftly, mere glances at the ground leading him deeper into the forest. Something crushed here, another splintered there, even the most subtle clues caught Engrelin's trained eye. He trotted onward, shaking off the branches and thorns that snatched at his face and clothing. At one point, Engrelin came upon a ledge of earth, below which tangled a mass of thorns, all matted down by a sudden and heavy fall. Engrelin winced as he picked out a safer descent. That must have hurt.

After nearly an hour of searching, Engrelin spied a human footprint. He bent eagerly to examine it. It was deeply embedded in a bed of thick moss along the creekbank. Beside it sprawled a discarded length of rope. His heart throbbing with excitement, Engrelin picked up the rope. Lance had been here! And not so long ago. A print wouldn't have stayed long in such lush, springy moss.

His gaze drifted back down to the moss to inspect Lance's footprint more carefully. His eyes lighted upon another, much different print. He froze.

Near Lance's footprint, sunk in the frozen mud, was an even larger print, larger than Engrelin's outspread hand. Four cruel claw marks dug deep into the mud. Automatically, Engrelin stooped and brushed his fingers around the print's perimeter. A thin film of ice crackled onto his fingers. He rubbed them together slowly. At least the print was old.

But age did not alter its maker. A taegr cat. Knowing the animal, it might still be lingering close by.

Engrelin glanced apprehensively around. He had his sword and his quiver. To assure himself, he reached up and brushed his hand over the shafts bristling with feathers. A spear was the ideal weapon to hunt a taegr, a huge beast that could reach ten feet from nose to tail. Engrelin stared down at the print in the dirt. That cat had been no small creature.

And Lance had no weapons. The thought stirred something flutteringly like panic in Engrelin's chest. Lance was completely defenseless. Against a beast that size, he'd have no chance.

Something small, white, and dainty settled gently inside the print; a six-pointed flake of crystal perfection cupped within that monstrous print. Engrelin threw his head back and frantically scanned the roiling sky. A soft flutter of flakes brushed against his face. His blood rushed sickeningly through his veins. No, it couldn't be snowing. Not yet!

Several more flakes drifted noiselessly down, settling at Engrelin's feet. One lighted on Engrelin's wrist. He stared down at it for one long moment, then shook it off. Reality crashed down around his ears. The snow would cover Lance's tracks!

Engrelin rushed away from the creek bank, tugging his cloak tighter about his shoulders and Arrian. At the base of a pine tree, he found among the scattered cones several that were crushed and broken, their scales scattered about. The other cones around them were already curling shut against the oncoming storm. Engrelin hurried past.

Almost immediately, he broke into a clearing. The rocky ground buckled beneath the weight of rocks and boulders scattered across it. A few stunted trees pushed their way through the barren soil. Beyond, a wall of sheer cliffs loomed, casting a deep shadow over the landscape below. Engrelin gazed out at it, dismayed. He wiped the snow from his face with the back of his hand. No one could track across that terrain!

A sudden blast of icy wind ripped his cloak out of his hands and whipped it out behind him like a brown banner. The chill struck him like a wave of arctic water. Around him, the swirling flurries thickened. Snatching his cloak back around his shoulders, Engrelin turned in a slow circle. There had to be some shelter somewhere where he could wait the storm out!

His darting eyes fell on a splotch of crimson, brilliant against the quickly whitening landscape. He blinked. A girlish figure stood with her arms wrapped around a stout tree trunk, clinging to it as if her life depended on it. Engrelin blinked again and dashed a hand over his eyes. No, she couldn't have followed him all this way. He'd told her to go back to the others.

Yet there she stood.

"Elvera!" he yelled. The wind snatched his words and hurled them along the tearing wind. Engrelin stumbled forward, holding one arm out in front of his face to protect it from the stinging pellets of snow hurtling through the air. The crackle and groan of thrashing branches filled his ears as he struggled over to the girl cowering against the tree.

"Elvera!" he shouted over the tumult.

The princess didn't answer. Her eyes were squeezed tightly shut and her face was pressed against the tree's rough bark.

Grabbing Elvera by both shoulders, Engrelin shook her hard. "Elvera, can you hear me?!"

The girl's eyes fluttered open. She stared glassily at Engrelin for a second. Then her lips moved feebly, but whatever she whispered was lost in the wind's shrieking. Several tears streamed down her cheeks. The sight of them softened the anger broiling within Engrelin. She had been foolish to follow him, Yes. But she had had no idea of the danger.

"We've got to get you to shelter!" Engrelin yelled, his lips almost pressed against her ear. He groped blindly through the whiteness until his right hand found hers and latched tightly onto it, despite the pain. Elvera squeezed it weakly.

"Are we close to anything?" she tremored.

Engrelin bit his inner lip but smiled wanly. What was the point in smiling? It wasn't like she could see him through the whirling snow.

"We're going to make it, all right?" he yelled. "You just have to trust me and keep hold of my hand. Don't let go!"

Elvera's hand tightened around his. Engrelin winced. At least he wouldn't lose her.

He stood inside the tree's slight shelter long enough to whisper a prayer. It, too, was lost in the howling wind. Stretching one arm in front of himself to feel his way, he struck out into the storm, dragging Elvera with him.

The snow drove like red-hot needles against Engrelin's skin as he struggled forward. The looming cliffs were branded on his memory. Which direction had they been? Even if he had known, it didn't matter now. North, south, east, and west were all one in this whirling white madness. Hopefully, he would get lucky and wander into them before he wandered over.

Even as he thought it, his fingers met the broken surface of rock just in front of him. Tingling with triumph, he drew Elvera closer to its rough salvation. The cliff sheltered them from some of the driving wind. Not much, but enough that he dimly made out Elvera's crouched form where before there had been nothing. Engrelin pulled her even closer to himself.

"We're going to walk along this cliff and see if we can find a crevice or a cave where we can wait this out," he shouted. "You okay?"

"I wish I were dead," Elvera whimpered.

Engrelin smiled wryly to himself. If she was well enough to complain, she was well enough to walk a little farther. He tried to clasp her hand a little tighter, but he couldn't feel her hand at all. But he knew he held her hand—he could see it gripped tightly in his own. His eyes narrowed as he swung them both around, putting their backs to the wind and himself beside the wall, his free hand grasping the rocks. They had to move quickly, or their hands wouldn't be the only thing without feeling.

Together they waded through the ankle-deep snow, Engrelin keeping Elvera as close to himself as possible while feeling his way along with his other hand. The wind fought with him over the princess; there were times when he thought he had lost her completely. Engrelin held her hand tightly, his heart clogging his throat. If he lost her, after all they had done to get the girls this far…

His left hand, instead of running over the uneven stones, shot out into space. Engrelin stumbled, then groped in the snow-filled air. The wall! He'd lost the wall!

Unless…

Engrelin stepped cautiously to the left. When he didn't bump into the wall, he took another step. Then another. And another. The snow ahead seemed to be thinning against a backdrop of deepest blackness.

"What are we doing?" asked Elvera. She clung onto his whole arm.

Her voice struck Engrelin with astonishment—he could actually hear her!

"I think we've made it to a cave, Elvera," he said quietly.

Elvera immediately straightened. "What?!"

Engrelin pulled her farther into the cave until no more snowflakes fluttered around them. The cavern's welcome darkness reigned. The hellish shriek of the wind now moaned distantly Though chilly, the cave held nothing of the driving cold outside.

"It's so dark in here." Elvera shuddered, hugging her sides and shivering.

Engrelin pulled his snow-crusted pack off his back, swiped a good five inches of snow off its top, and rummaged inside for a moment. He drew out a stout stick, swaddled with fabric on one end.

"What are you doing?" Elvera asked. She crouched down near him. Engrelin could just barely make out her profile against the blackness. "Is that a stick? Do you seriously keep firewood in your bag?"

Engrelin sighed and struck a match. He touched it to the stick's cloth end. The fabric blazed up for a moment before sinking to a small but steady glow. Engrelin stood, holding the torch aloft, chasing the nearest shadows into corners and crevices.

"I don't keep firewood in my pack," he told Elvera. "But I do carry torches."

"Looked like firewood to me," Elvera grumbled.

Engrelin chuckled softly as the girl came into the light. Head to toe, she was covered in snow. It was in her hair, heaped on her shoulders, and even caught in her eyelashes.

"You may want to brush some of this off," he said. He reached to dust her shoulders off. "Someone'll think you're a snow monster or something."

Elvera scowled, batted his hand away, and proceeded to knock the snow from her shoulders herself.

"You're a worse mess," she snapped. "Clean yourself off."

Engrelin grinned and ran his hand through his hair. The melting snow came off his head like globs of icing off a cake. Rolling her eyes, Elvera continued to beat her clothing clean.

Engrelin, seeing she didn't want any help, shrugged and pulled his cloak aside to check on his sword. Arrian was hardly touched. Only a little of the hilt and the scabbard's tip bore snow. A tiny sliver of the blade showed above the scabbard. To Engrelin's trepidation, the sliver shone a clean, cold blue. Engrelin sucked back a groan. It hadn't done that since the night Lamar had given it to him. Why did it have to go and glow now? Elvera was freaked out enough as it was.

Ramming Arrian the rest of the way into its sheath, he draped his cloak over it as best he could.

"Lucky sword, it gets all the love and care," Elvera huffed.

Engrelin looked up sharply. "I thought you didn't want my help," he said.

Elvera glared at him. "You never asked."

Engrelin drew a slow breath. "Well, are you okay?"

"I'm not, thank you for asking," Elvera replied. "I'm stuck in a cold, wet cave in the middle of a blizzard with the worst person imaginable."

"Besides that, you're all right?" Engrelin concluded dryly.

Elvera shrugged. "If I'd had my way, I wouldn't be stuck here with you, that's all."

"But beggars can't be choosers," Engrelin reminded with an edge.

"Are you calling me a beggar?" Elvera demanded angrily.

Engrelin dragged a hand down his face. *It's just a figure of speech!* He thought, exasperated. From the way she was talking, one never would have guessed he had just saved her life!

"Me, a beggar!" Elvera muttered

"You could be stuck with worse people."

"Huh. I can't think of anyone," Elvera huffed. "Name one."

"How about me?" suggested a voice from deep within the cavern. The words echoed, mulling over themselves until they were distant whispers. Gasping with fright, Elvera jumped towards Engrelin. At the same time, he pushed her behind him and drew Arrian, turning to face the unseen presence. Irritatingly enough, Arrian's blade threw off a brighter light than the torch in his right hand.

"Who are you?" he challenged, taking one step forward.

In answer, a rock whizzed past their heads and shattered against the wall behind him.

"Get down!" Engrelin hissed. He shoved Elvera to the floor behind a boulder. Taking his stance in front of the huge stone, he held Arrian protectively in front of his body.

"Who are you?" he repeated.

"If I were you, I would put that thing down," said the voice, echoing less than before. Someone emerged from the gloom into Arrian's circle of eerie light which, mixing with the torch's beams, seemed almost green. Engrelin took a startled step back. He hadn't realized the person was so close.

"I never can seem to get rid of you, can I, Engrelin?" the person growled.

Engrelin's jaw tightened. Of course. Who else had he expected?

"You'd think, after all I've done to you, you'd have sense enough not to follow me," continued Lance, edging forward. "I was planning to have this cave all to myself."

Lance moved just close enough so that Engrelin could see the boy held another large rock in his strong hands, ready to throw at any moment.

"Everyone has to have unexpected company now and then," Engrelin returned tersely. His hand tightened over Arrian's leather-bound grip.

"You're not welcome," Lance snarled. "I hate being a host. I prefer making my guests leave, quickly." So saying, he reared his hand back for a devastating throw.

"Lance, don't you dare," Engrelin warned, his eyes riveted to the rock.

"Who's stopping me?" Lance jeered.

Engrelin moved to retort when something above Lance's head caught his eye. The blood that had been burning within him only moments before froze as solid as the world outside.

They were not alone.

35

W here are they?" Isalinia wondered aloud. She glanced nervously up and down the village's hard-packed road. "It's been a while since you let Elvera drop back with Engrelin and Lance. Why did she want to go with them in the first place? That thief gives me the creeps. She should have stayed safely here with us."

"She said something about helping Engrelin… I'm not sure," Lilac answered slowly. "And I didn't let her go. I heard her saying something about leaving, and when I turned around, she was gone. I was busy trying to help Averendier translate at the time."

She motioned to their guides, who were attempting to barter for supplies and were having a difficult time. Lilac had thought for a moment that she knew the language these northerners spoke. But once she had engaged in conversation with one of them, she realized she couldn't understand a word the man said. If only Engrelin hadn't taken off with Lance (for the former was apparently their translator). Her gut twisting, Lilac followed her sister's tentative glances up and down the road. Where had those two gone? Where was Elvera? Was she in any danger?

"'What is taking Averendier so long?" Isalinia wondered despairingly. "Don't they know Elvera's gone?"

Biting her lip, Lilac looked back at the merchant and her guides. Both parties were disputing, gesturing wildly. It had been going on like this for an awfully long time. Elvera had been gone too long. And the temperature was plummeting. Shivering, she pulled her cloak tighter around her shoulders. Why hadn't Elvera stayed with them?

"Here they come!" Isalinia waved her hand high over her head. "Any luck?" she called.

"A little," answered Andrald wearily as he joined them, hefting a large crate filled with provisions. "It might have gone faster if we'd known what that guy was saying, and vice versa. It didn't help that he wanted to sell us out of house and home for a couple crumbs."

"Still, we got what we needed," said Averendier, head bent as he marked something off a slip of paper. "Now we just have to find out where Engrelin took Lance." He stuffed the paper into his pocket and looked up. Immediately, his eyes narrowed. "Where's Elvera?" he asked.

Lilac and Isalinia exchanged looks. Lilac, struggling to swallow the knot in her throat, stepped forward, like a prisoner up to the bar.

"Averendier, just after you and Andrald stepped over there to barter, Elvera slipped off almost without our knowing to join Engrelin."

Averendier frowned. "We can only hope she actually made it to him," he said. "She must have left you two at least five minutes after Engrelin. Though," he added, seeing Isalinia's frightened countenance, "the people around here seem rather friendly. If she loses her way, someone will surely direct her back to us."

Again, Lilac bit her lip to restrain the worries crowding her brain and blocking her throat. She knew he was only trying to comfort herself and Isalinia. But even if Elvera did find someone willing to help her, how would she know where to go? She had no idea where the group was headed. *It's a small town,* she told herself fiercely. *It'll be easy to find us.*

Lifting her eyes, she met Averendier's troubled gaze.

"This doesn't mean we're not going to look for her," he added. "We're all going to find a central meeting place, then I'll start asking around; that way—"

A sudden blast of arctic wind cut him short. As Lilac's cloak was torn back, she clutched at her clasp and dragged it forward to keep it from sliding back and choking her. Lilac shot a glance at the sky and was momentarily blinded by the white flecks driving down from the heavens.

"Everyone!" Averendier shouted over the howling wind. "Double back to that tavern we passed on our way. Quickly. Keep together!"

Andrald struck out at a run, and the princesses followed. Averendier dropped behind to ensure no one strayed from the group in the quickly thickening snowfall. Lilac's pack bumped lightly against her back as she ran. The snow whizzed past her face. She had read often about snow. She's always longed to see it. But no poem had mentioned this screaming white monster that buffeted her with each step she took, pawing at her like an amused, abstract giant.

Out of the storm, the tavern's dark shape jutted. Lilac could barely make out the tavern sign, swinging crazily in the wind. The copper maple leaf engraved upon it was already frosted white. Lilac rushed up the stairs behind her sister, springing up them two at a time in a manner that would have shocked herself at any other time but this. She dashed through the tavern's door into a welcoming wave of warmth. Behind her, Averendier entered and slammed the door against the wind. After the bravado of the storm, the large room they had all just entered seemed strangely quiet.

Andrald threw a hasty glance around the room. Several long tables, hemmed in by benches, stretched across most of the floor. At the far end of one of these, two men were playing cards. (One man, nibbling on the edge of his cards and groaning whenever his opponent made a move, was obviously—and sorely—losing.) A huge fireplace dominated the far corner, hosting a roaring fire. Above the mantlepiece, a huge set of antlers branched out like giant coat hooks. Browned maps, sketches, and trinkets were scattered on various hooks and shelves along the dark-paneled wall. At a small counter near the kitchen door, a large, heavy man—probably the tavern keeper—leaned over his counter. His multiple chins rested in his hand as he fixed his piggish, mildly interested eyes on the newcomers.

Other than the tavern keeper and the card players, the room was empty. The townspeople had holed up in their homes.

"Do we have everyone?" Averendier asked, glancing over his depleted group.

Andrald followed his brother's sweeping gaze. Other than those who had already been noted missing, they were all there. Discomfort rolled in his stomach. After being seven strong, four seemed too few.

"Now all of you stay here with Andrald," Averendier ordered. "I'm going out to look for Elvera."

He turned towards the door, and Lilac's lips parted in hopeful astonishment. But Andrald caught his brother by the arm.

"What are you thinking?" he demanded in a whisper. "Do you think you'll be of any more use to us dead in that storm? If Elvera went with Engrelin, she's in good hands. He won't let anything happen to her. We'll only be throwing our lives away trying to find her out in that."

"We don't even know if she made it to him," Averendier returned angrily. "Engrelin never should have left the group without telling us in the first place."

"Maybe not," Andrald agreed uncertainly. He didn't think it likely that Engrelin had wandered off for no reason. Something must have gone wrong. Something with Lance. He shook the thought away. Saying that wouldn't help his cause any.

"But what's important right now is to stay here," Andrald continued. "Blizzards like this can last for days, and we don't know where any of them have gone. We'd have a heinous time trying to find them on a clear summer day. You don't have a chance. None of us would! No one's asking the impossible of us. We should stay here and take good care of the girls we have left. The only thing we can do for the others is pray they found somewhere to hole up until this blows over."

Averendier hesitated, hand still partially outstretched to clutch the doorknob. He glanced back at Lilac, who smiled bravely. Andrald looked at his brother askance. Was he doing all this…for her?

He shook his head again. He was just thinking things. Lilac was the oldest, the one Averendier would expect the answers from most.

"At least Engrelin still has that map," Averendier murmured. Still, he hesitated before stepping away from the door.

Andrald smiled tightly; it was so forced it almost hurt. He knew how much Engrelin had dreaded a moment like this. It was hard to think that he would ever voluntarily split up.

"We'll talk later," Averendier added. "Right now, you get the girls something to eat. I'm going to find the tavern keeper and see if he has any vacant rooms. We'll have to stay put until this stops."

Andrald nodded. Resigned to his fate, Averendier crossed the room in a few quick strides and said something to the man at the counter. The man merely gestured to an open doorway at the room's far end, which Averendier entered.

Andrald, forcing another smile, steered his charges to one of the long, empty tables closest to the blazing fire and sat them there.

"Now, I'm going to get us some supper. You girls okay here?"

Lilac nodded, then turned to exchange a whisper with her shaken sister. Nodding again (more to himself than anyone else), Andrald strode over to the counter.

The fat tavern keeper had retreated through a low doorway that no doubt led to his kitchen. But on the counter sat a bell. Beside it sat a little note that read, *ring for service*. Andrald picked it up and rang it quietly. Then a little louder. After several more vigorous rings (Andrald worried for a moment that the bell's clapper would fly off) the tavern keeper finally returned.

Red-faced and perspiring, balancing a loaded tray on one hand, he emerged.

"Just a moment," he wheezed as he lurched past Andrald. He crossed the room and laid the tray in front of the two card players. Waddling back to the counter, he leaned his bulk against it.

"What do you need now?" he demanded, his voice startlingly crude.

Andrald nearly drew back. Never, in all his traveling days, had he met a tavern keeper like this.

Sensing the boy's disgust, the keeper extended his flabby hand across the counter. "Name's Clane," he grumbled.

Andrald took the hand and shook it gingerly; it was overly soft and plump, fingers as thick as sausages.

"Adrian," Andrald replied, not untruthfully. Adrian was his middle name. Aliases were another of Averendier's ideas, just in case Vendar somehow learned their real names.

"Well, Austain, what would you like this evening?" Clane attempted a smile, which only creased his chins grotesquely.

"Tea for four," Andrald answered. He doubted the girls would want to eat much more than a light meal. He slid a gold coin across the counter.

Instantly, Clane straightened, snatched it up, turned it over in his hands a few times, and polished it on his sleeve.

"Twenty *saris*," he muttered to himself. "Are all travelers suddenly rich?"

Andrald's ears perked. "What do you mean?" he asked, leaning forward against the corner. His short sword slid forward and knocked gently against the wood counter.

Clane glanced down at the weapon. His eyebrows rose. "Armed too," he murmured. Gulping slightly, he pocketed the coin. "I shouldn't wonder…" He adopted a thoughtful expression, which seemed out of place on him. He shook his head, smiling falsely once more.

"Quite all right," he chuckled. "But do you want anything to go with your tea, or should I give you your fourteen in change?"

"What kinds of pies do you have?" Andrald asked, though his thoughts were far from food. What exactly had Clane meant?

"Mince and sparrow tonight," Clane answered.

"Sparrow sounds good," Andrald said.

"I've got one cooling now. I'll send it to your places once your tea has steeped," said Clane. Squinting over at the tables to mark the girls' place at the table in his memory, he nodded to himself and wheeled to puff back into the kitchen.

Andrald remained standing at the counter. He wanted more than just a hot meal from Clane. What he had said about other wealthy guests, guests that were apparently armed…

He listened intently as Clane clattered about in the kitchen, banging pots together and yelling at his unseen helpers.

When Clane stepped back out of the kitchen and saw Andrald still standing there at the counter, surprise flashed over his face. He wiped his hands off on his greasy apron and dragged himself back over to the counter.

"Anything else?" he asked, unable to keep his voice from jittering. Yanking a rag out of his apron, he swept it across the already shining countertop.

"How much change do I have left, after the pie?" Andrald asked.

Clane's shoulders slumped with relief. "Twelve *saris*," he said.

"What if…" Andrald leaned a little closer to the man, despite his revulsion, "…what if I told you to keep it?"

"What!" Clane furrowed his brow. "You're crazy," he muttered, shaking his head. But a hungering light sprang in his eyes. "What for?" he demanded.

"What you said earlier," Andrald said quietly. "I'd like to know a little more about it."

Clane's hand went down into his apron pocket where rested the large gold coin Andrald had given him. "What do you want to know?" he asked finally, his voice a dry rasp. "Speak quickly, boy. I haven't all day."

"You mentioned you'd had a few wealthy guests," Andrald said carefully.

"What, can't a fellow make a little honest money now and then?" Clane demanded.

"Sure," Andrald shrugged. "But I didn't want to know about the money they gave you. I'm more interested in the people."

"Ah." Clane rubbed his blubbery hands together. "Well, if you insist on knowing, two men came in here about four or five days ago. They were kind of like you, counting the money and the swords." He eyed Andrald's weapon suspiciously. "If they hadn't had them, you know, I wouldn't have paid so much attention. Men with swords need watching. And men with money." He drew himself more upright and tucked his thick hands into his apron pocket. "Other than that, I thought they were pretty average customers. That was, until I saw their horses."

Andrald drew a swift breath; his heart kicked up several gears. "Horses?" he echoed.

"Yes, three of them," said Clane. "Prettiest things you ever saw."

"What colors?" Andrald asked quickly.

Clane looked at him askance, but after reassuring himself with a glance that Andrald did indeed have a sword, he swallowed and continued.

"If I remember right, one black, one gold, and one white." He choked on each word that left his mouth. "I'm no horseman, but I've seen quite a few horses just keeping this place of mine. And these were the most impressive horseflesh I've ever seen."

The horses matched the Alinar horses, though the colors were common for any horse. That Clane thought the breed remarkable was all Andrald needed to know. Despite Bendekahn's attempts to get northern-looking mounts, there was no mistaking the proud Alinar blood flowing through those horses' veins.

"And the men?" Andrald pursued with thumping heart. "What were they like?"

"Dark eyes, dark hair—dark souls too, by the looks of them," remarked Clane with a shudder. "And skin as fair as mine or yours." He plucked his plump arm, which was too pallid to be merely fair. He looked as if someone had white-washed him as a child, and it had never worn off.

"It gave me the creeps just to look at them," continued Clane, with another overly exaggerated shudder. "But I can't be too picky about who I serve, so I fed them and put them up for night just like all my customers."

He paused to catch his breath, then continued thoughtfully, "They were kind of secretive, though. Not big talkers; at least, not to anyone but each other. They'd bend over their supper plates and whisper like anything 'till midnight, when I had to come over and tell them to clear off so I can get to bed myself. They'd glare at me right hard when I told them that, but they marched up to their beds, even if they didn't say a word as to whether they liked their supper or not. Did that every time."

"When did they leave?" Andrald asked, his excitement now tinging his voice. He could no longer restrain it. These had to be Lance's fellow highwaymen. They had stolen the horses a week ago, and on the mounts, they could have easily gotten here in two or three days.

"Why, they haven't left at all!" Clane exclaimed, wringing his rag nervously in his hands. "In fact, they should be down here any minute now to get their supper."

36

wo glowing orbs burned like bright orange lanterns above Lance's head—watching. Pearl fangs gleamed in the torchlight—poised.

Lance was taunting, monologuing. What he said, Engrelin did not know. The sneering voice whined like a distant insect.

In petrified horror, Engrelin watched a long, lithe tail flick behind the huge taegr perching on a ledge high above Lance. The cat crouched lower to the rock, coiling for its deadly spring. Its flaming eyes marked Lance's every move. Engrelin shut his eyes briefly, hardly daring to breathe. When he opened them, he could make out the cat's tan head, its fangs bared in a silent snarl. The taegr had spotted its prey.

Nothing would stop it now.

"You're not even listening to me, are you?" Lance screamed.

Engrelin's gaze snapped back to Lance only just in time. Lance hurled his rock. Engrelin ducked. The rock whizzed past and splintered against the boulder behind him. As shards of rock rained down on Engrelin, a blood-curdling scream split the air.

Lance hesitated and glanced behind his shoulder. Engrelin saw his eyes widen with fear, caught a glimpse of the taegr flying through the air. Springing up, Engrelin dashed desperately forward. His shoulder rammed into Lance's middle, sending him flying back to smash against a near boulder. As Lance slumped motionless to the floor, the taegr thudded to the ground, right where Lance had stood only moments before. Staggering from the momentum, Engrelin caught Lance by the shoulder and dragged him to safety behind a boulder.

The taegr's hideous scream of rage filled the air, echoing off the cavern walls and resounding painfully in Engrelin's ears. Lance was safe, for now. But only Lance…

Scrambling up the boulder, Engrelin peered over the edge, letting only his eyes slip above the jagged top. His breath caught in his throat.

Though evidently young, the taegr was huge. Nearly eight feet long, counting its swishing tail, and at least four feet tall at its shoulder. Pacing back and forth, it swung its sleek, powerful head, searching for its missing quarry. Engrelin's hand tightened over Arrian's grip, which would have been slippery with his sweat if it had not been wrapped in leather. He ran his other hand nervously through his hair. He'd dropped his torch to grab Lance. Still burning, it lay near the boulder he and Lance hid behind. It was likely the only reason the taegr hadn't already followed him back here to tear them to shreds.

But no such fire burned in front of Elvera.

"Engrelin?" the girl whispered frantically from across the cave.

Dropping low, the taegr slunk across the cave floor towards the boulder Elvera had scrambled onto. It wasn't nearly high enough to escape the taegr's reach. Almost nothing was.

Engrelin dropped to the ground on the opposite side of his boulder, in full view of the great cat, if it would only turn to see him.

"Engrelin!" Elvera shrieked hysterically, clawing her way across the top of her rock away from the stalking taegr. The taegr took its time, its eyes riveted to its prey.

Engrelin dropped into a loose crouch and shuffled carefully over to the burning torch. Meanwhile the taegr, growling softly, had reached the base of Elvera's rock. It bent low, belly brushing the ground, tensing to spring.

"Engrelin!!!!!" Elvera screamed. "Help! Someone! Get it away from me!!!"

With an incoherent shout, Engrelin sprang forward. The taegr whipped around to meet his attack. Catching up the burning brand, Engrelin thrust it into the cat's face.

Screaming and snarling, batting the thin air in an agony of pain and rage, it withdrew.

Engrelin backed away until his shoulder-blades touched the cool stone of the cavern wall. Across the cave, the taegr glared at him, its eyes luminous in its singed and bloody face. Engrelin held Arrian protectively in front of himself, nearly squinting to see past the sword's bright blue glow. In his other hand, he brandished the torch. But looking into the cat's wild eyes, Engrelin couldn't be sure which the creature hated more: the fire or its bearer.

Finally, the taegr bounded forward, closing the gap between itself and Engrelin in four lithe leaps. Engrelin whipped Arrian around quickly, meeting the charge with cold steel. The blade sank into the taegr's shoulder. Again, the shrieking taegr withdrew. Pacing and snarling and spitting, its blood dribbling onto the cave floor, the creature bared its fangs. Engrelin kept the tip of his blade even with the taegr as it paced back and forth. His jaw ached from clenching it so tightly.

The taegr jumped back, as if trying to break away. Engrelin jumped forward to pursue it. The taegr swiveled on its hind legs and lashed back with one giant paw. It struck Engrelin's side. Engrelin brought his sword crashing down on the head shooting forward to destroy him. Steel clove through bone and sinew. Uttering a final scream, the taegr's lifeless body hurtled forward against Engrelin. Both crumpled to the floor, the air stirring beside Engrelin as the taegr's carcass fell, the light in the creature's eyes extinguished.

Engrelin scooted away from the taegr, then winced at the sharp ache shooting from his side. He put his hand to it quickly but felt no wetness of blood or unevenness of bones. He slumped to the floor with relief, letting the torch and his sword fall from his hands. Arrian was crimson to the cross-hilt.

"Engrelin?" Elvera's quavering voice sounded through the pounding silence. She crept out from behind a boulder, clutching her wringing hands at her breast. "Are you hurt?"

"I don't think so," Engrelin replied. To assure her (and himself) he sat up and tested his limbs.

Elvera glanced at the taegr's carcass. "Is it…"

"Dead?" Engrelin finished. "Yes."

"Thank goodness," she murmured, her voice catching. "When I saw Lance killed, I thought you were dead for sure."

Engrelin looked at her sharply. "I didn't kill Lance," he said. "I only knocked him out of the way, and he hit his head hard because of it. He'll only be out for a few hours, probably."

Elvera's jaw dropped. "You didn't kill him!" she gasped. Her dark eyes flashed.

"Of course I didn't. Why would I?"

"He nearly bashed our heads open with those rocks!" Elvera exclaimed, throwing her arms wide.

He's done worse, thought Engrelin bitterly. He locked gazes with Elvera.

"How would you feel," he asked slowly, "if someone expected you to kill another person who you'd been friends with your whole life?"

"Had been," Elvera interjected, meeting this new aspect and promptly flinging it back in Engrelin's face. "Past tense. He's your enemy now."

Engrelin yanked himself to his feet. *So much for being considerate, Elvera.* As he crossed the cavern over to where Lance lay motionless, Engrelin wondered if Elvera knew just how infuriating she could be. Whining and complaining about him one moment, begging him to save her and worrying about him the next, then turning completely around and demanding that he kill a friend!

Engrelin wiped the blood from Arrian and held the dimly glowing blade over Lance as a light. He winced at the blood matting Lance's fair hair to one side of his head. He had saved Lance, but at a nasty price.

Not as terrible as it might have been, he reminded himself.

Laying his sword aside, Engrelin retrieved the still-burning torch and gingerly used it to melt snow in a wooden bowl. Elvera sulked nearby, sitting with her arms wrapped protectively around her pack as though it contained some precious treasure Engrelin might steal.

Engrelin returned to Lance's side and gently washed the head wound with the melted snow. Pulling his extra tunic out of his pack, Engrelin tore it into strips. Quickly, he wound some of the strips around

Lance's head in a crude bandage. Taking the retrieved rope from his pack, he bound Lance's hands loosely with it. He removed Lance's cloak and covered him with it like a blanket. Lance's pack, plumped up, served as his pillow.

Then Engrelin withdrew, sitting down heavily beside Elvera, lapsing deeper into an exhausted silence. Drowsiness threatened to overwhelm him. His head tipped back against the rough stone.

"Why did you do it?" Elvera burst out.

Engrelin jolted and turned his head to meet her confused yet defiant gaze. "Why what?" he asked.

"Why did you care for him like that after all he's done to us? To you! He's been a beast ever since he got here. And since he was attacking us—trying to kill us—it wouldn't have been wrong at all to kill him."

The salvo of words swamped Engrelin in silence for nearly a minute.

"You don't understand—" he began.

"Maybe you don't understand," Elvera snapped back. "You don't understand your duty, do you? You're supposed to be protecting me. And instead of coming to me first when that awful monster, thing—whatever that was—came out, you ran to Lance first! And before that, when he was throwing those rocks, you just stood there, doing nothing to stop him. What if…"

She shuddered and stared intently at the floor, as if it held some awful spectacle that horrified her, yet she couldn't help watching. "What if he tries that again?"

Engrelin didn't answer. He gazed down at the sword cradled in his lap. Its glow had died down. But it had started the moment he had entered the cave. It must have known about the taegr or Lance. Perhaps both. He had lifted it against a dumb beast bent on destroying them all. But to plunge it into a fellow man, once a good friend?

Engrelin grit his teeth. No matter how many times Lance would lift his hand against him, he couldn't destroy him. He just couldn't. He would exert himself to his utmost to prevent any more of Lance's escaping or threats, but he would give his all to let his friend live.

I must be warped somewhere, he mused. Surely someone who would want to give a killer a third chance had to be a little loopy. He'd give Lance a fourth chance if he could risk it. But he couldn't. He had to protect Elvera.

His thoughts drifted to the map stowed in his pocket. He let his head drop into his hands. Now he would have to employ that as well, bringing Elvera's hellfire and brimstone of opposition along with it. And what if he couldn't read the map as well as he thought he could? If he lost them all in this terribly wide world…

Compared to the rest of Ontaria, they were miniscule—less than that, even. It could easily swallow them, just as the blizzard raging outside had nearly done. They wouldn't always find a refuge. Engrelin's fingers tightened around his temples. Why had he ever thought that he could do this? He wasn't a leader like Averendier. Even if he had all the remarkable attributes in the world, they would do nothing; Elvera had no confidence in him, anyway. There was nothing he could give. Nothing…

And yet.

Engrelin gently took Elvera's hand, placing his hand palm up inside hers.

"What are you doing?" Elvera demanded, making to pull her hand away, but Engrelin held it firmly. She stared in angry puzzlement at Engrelin's hand, crisscrossed with the red and white lines of his still-healing wounds and developing scars.

"You know how I got this?" he asked.

"No," Elvera shoved his hand back into his lap. This time, Engrelin let her. "It looks pretty recent, though," she added.

Engrelin nodded towards Lance. "Him."

Elvera curled her arms back around her pack. "I'd noticed the bandage before," she said. "I should have known he did it, since the first time I saw it was the morning out horses had been stolen."

She scowled fiercely, glaring at Engrelin out of the corner of her eye as if she couldn't bear to look him full in the face. "But why show it to me?" she demanded. "Don't you realize it sets me dead against him?"

"But that's not what I meant," Engrelin said. "I got these fighting for myself, for my life alone." He motioned to the healing lacerations covering his right hand. "But to protect yours, I'll suffer ten times as much. Like you said, it's my duty, and it comes before everything else. I'm going to lead you home the best way I know. I'll defend you whenever I must. But I don't want you to ever doubt any decisions I make about you, or Lance, or anything else we stumble across."

Elvera's face remained set in a cast of disdain as she gazed into the darkness, refusing to even look at him. Engrelin sighed and ran his hand through his hair.

"I'll always do my best to protect you from horse thieves, blizzards, taegrs—even Lance," he concluded softly, staring down at Arrian.

"Words mean nothing until you prove them with actions," Elvera scoffed, quoting someone Engrelin had never heard. "'Easily spoken, easily broken.'"

Engrelin's hand clenched around Arrian's gemstone pommel. The setting gleamed in the torchlight as if it were the true Stirling, the South star, fallen from the sky to be chained within a blade. The celestial body that had guided travelers and seafarers alike from the dawn of time now lay at Engrelin's fingertips. If only he could unlock its secret—stand an unmovable beacon for ages to come, confidently guiding home all who laid their trust in him.

He placed his injured hand on Arrian's naked blade, like a soldier taking a vow. His eyes scanned up and down the blade, searching wearily the inscription curving down the blood-groove that he had gazed upon many a time.

"Elvera, I have nothing else to offer but my life," he murmured, head bowed. "Don't tell me whether that's sufficient or not," he added. "I'll sell it dearly."

Elvera was silent.

37

Andrald stumbled back a step as the weight of Clane's words crashed down on him. Lance's highwaymen were here? And they would be down in the dining room in just a few minutes. Were the princesses endangered by their presence? Who knew what kind of rogues Lance had associated with!

"Are you sure?" he demanded, gripping the edge of the counter tightly.

"Never can be quite sure about anything with them," Clane answered. He gave the shining countertop a final flourish before stuffing the rag back into his apron pocket. "They're shifty. Don't like being around other people. Every night, they come down to take their supper when all other respectable people are in their beds. All other meals they have sent up to their rooms. But I just received their order through one of my little girls. I figure they think it's safe to come down with the storm blowing, shutting most folks out."

"Do you know how long they intend on staying?" Andrald asked.

"They never said when they intended on leaving, so no. I don't. I wouldn't be surprised if they came down here some time to offer to buy the rooms they're staying in right now so that they can live out the rest of their lives in them. But," his eyes shifted to the shuttered windows, "this storm is more than just shutting people out. As long as it's blowing, I can guarantee those men will be here."

At that moment, a young girl stuck her head out the kitchen door. Her eyes widened when they came to rest on Andrald. Nervously, she tucked a stray strand of her red hair beneath her kerchief. Mumbling something to Clane, she retreated into the kitchen.

"That's your tea," Clane announced. He turned and lurched into the kitchen after the girl.

Andrald lingered at the counter a few seconds longer, thoughtfully chewing the inside of his cheek. Slowly, he walked to the table where the girls were sitting. They looked as if they already knew danger lurked nearby. Isalinia held her head in her hands, while Lilac stared distantly into the fire. She smiled when Andrald approached. Though wan, the sight of it relieved Andrald slightly.

"Supper'll be here soon," he said, climbing into the bench across from Isalinia. He perched on the edge of his seat, keeping one eye on the girls and the other on the darkened doorway in the corner of the room—the door through which Averendier had gone, and from which the thieves would soon emerge. If only Engrelin were here with them. He might have identified the men.

Isalinia lifted her head, glanced at Andrald, and nodded to him, as if she had only just realized his presence. Her fingertips dug into her temples, her golden hair spilling over her shoulders. Andrald frowned with pity. The poor thing was taking her sister's disappearance hard. How much worse would she feel if she ever stumbled upon the truths behind the whole journey?

"Here," said a timid voice at Lilac's elbow. Lilac tore herself out of her many thoughts and glanced down to see a dirt-streaked face with its small owner. The little serving girl slid a heavy tray laden with a tea service and a steaming pie onto the table in front of Lilac. Lilac couldn't help wondering if the tray weighed more than the mite of a girl who had carried it.

"Thank you," Lilac said, offering the girl a smile.

The girl didn't answer. She only stared blankly at Lilac for a moment, then slipped silently back across the room and into the kitchen.

Lilac sighed and straightened on the bench. Andrald was already plunging deep into the tray. He handed her a teacup on a saucer and a plate holding a thick wedge of pie. The flaky golden crust enclosed a tender brown meat weeping gravy onto the plate. It smelled delicious. Lilac whispered a blessing to herself and took a cautious bite. As the warmth of the pie spread through her, she scrunched her shoulders and smiled.

"Like it?" Andrald asked as he served Isalinia.

"Mm-hmm," Lilac murmured.

"Sparrow pie is one of my favorites," Andrald continued. Picking up a large coffee pot (actually filled with tea), he poured the fragrant liquid into the girls' cups, then into his own.

Isalinia nearly choked on the bite of pie she had just taken. Swallowing hastily, she eyed the slice on her plate. "Sparrow pie?" she repeated. Picking up her fork, she warily poked the slice on her plate. Gravy trickled out and pooled on her plate. Ever so slightly, the bridge of Isalinia's nose crinkled.

"Do you mean those little brown birds that are always hopping around?" she inquired. "We're eating those?"

"Yep," Andrald answered. He spooned a large portion of the pie onto his plate. "It's delicious."

Isalinia remained unconvincedly skeptical. "I'd hardly think they're big enough to eat," she commented, poking the slice of pie again. "I couldn't imagine picking all the meat off the bones."

"Oh, they don't," Andrald replied through a mouthful. "That's why it's so cheap and easy. Just pluck off the feathers, take off the head and feet, gut it, and cook it in the pie. The bones disintegrate when they're cooked, so no worries about poking yourself on them. They're as soft as the meat."

Isalinia turned a subtle shade of green. Lilac coughed once or twice to avoid gagging.

Andrald, perhaps finding something amiss in their silence, looked up quickly. "It's just the same as eating chicken," he assured them.

"Only…with disintegrated bones," Lilac pointed out quietly.

Andrald shrugged amiably. "Yep, pretty much. But like I said, you don't notice them. They're all mushy now."

Isalinia brought her cup quickly to her mouth and sipped long and quietly, hiding her grimace behind the cup's rim. Lilac nearly smiled and returned her attention to the pie. Well, if a bone hadn't poked her in the first bite, likely one never would. And it was quite good…for northern food.

During the midst of the meal, Averendier rejoined them, an unfamiliar sag in his shoulders.

"I got us two rooms," he said, sinking onto the bench beside Andrald. One for us, and one for you girls."

Lilac served Averendier a large wedge of pie. He accepted it with a small smile and a nod.

"We'll stay here until the weather clears up," Averendier continued. "With Lance, Elvera, and Engrelin missing, I don't want to get split up any further. No matter what, we're going to stick together."

"Averendier," Andrald interrupted seriously, "about that…" With a twitch of his finger, he beckoned for his brother's ear. Frowning, Averendier leaned closer to his brother.

Lilac watched them, a deep, unexplainable twist in her gut, as they talked in harsh undertones to one another. Whatever news Andrald had for his brother couldn't be good. Averendier's lips pressed tightly together, he nodded curtly at intervals. Lilac hesitated over her supper, her fingertips barely brushing her saucer. Her ears strained to catch a single discernable word from the boys' mutterings, her violet eyes riveted to them. Averendier was scowling now, crushing a cloth napkin in his clenched fist. His eyes were frighteningly intense.

His eyes. Lilac stopped eavesdropping for a moment to contemplate them. She'd never seen anything quite like them in Alinar, where nearly everyone she had known—save her father and herself—had dark eyes varying from mouse brown to almost black. Averendier's were a clear, steady gray, like the sky just before the sun rose. Yet not so jubilant. They held such gravity. Anyone would be justified in looking twice at them.

Averendier's gaze shifted to meet hers. Lilac dropped her eyes quickly, struggling to ignore the heat stinging her cheeks and neck. Desperately, she snatched up her cup and took a long gulp from it, tilting the cup unreasonably high to hide her face. If only her face wasn't as red as it felt! She'd been caught staring at someone—practically gaping! She, the future queen of Alinar. How many times had her mother instructed her not to do just that?

Lilac drew a deep breath to smooth her ruffled nerves. She ventured a glance at Averendier. He was talking to his brother again, taking no notice of her. Lilac let her breath ease out with relief. Maybe he would let it slide. She set her earthenware cup back onto its saucer, missing the delicate *chink* of porcelain against porcelain. But why had she even expected it, in such a crude place as this?

Out of the corner of her eye, she saw Andrald nudge Averendier's arm hard. He jerked his head, motioning towards something. Both twisted slightly around to glimpse over their shoulders.

Following their gazes, Lilac almost instantly locked eyes with a man standing in the shadowy back doorway.

He had been watching her, dark eyes glinting with something like malice. This time, Lilac didn't look away. The man's gaze was a challenge, a gauntlet cast down, crying to be taken up. Her heart stuttered warningly as their stares stretched over several taut seconds. Something about his eyes was wrong. Really, really wrong. What, Lilac couldn't place, but it sent shivers trembling up her spine. His eyes narrowed as his stare turned to a glare, vicious and hateful. Lilac wouldn't have been surprised if the man strode forward to take her in his hands and snap her in half.

Finally, the man tore his gaze from Lilac's to stare at Isalinia, who had pushed her empty plate towards the table's center and again clutched her head in her hands. Just like the man, Lilac narrowed her eyes. Indignation overcame apprehension. She felt her muscles tightening. Bristling. That...*man* was glaring at *her* sister.

The deep call to protect resonated through Lilac like a trumpet blast. Purposefully, she shifted down the bench to sit closer to her younger sibling. She deliberately turned her face away from the sinister man. In the corner of her vision, she saw the man's eyes snap back onto herself. His eyes pressed like brands against her back. Another involuntary shudder nearly overtook her. Shrugging the sensation away, Lilac placed a gentle hand on her sister's shoulder.

"What's wrong?" she asked softly. Taking one of her sister's flaxen locks in hand, she let it slide through the cracks between her fingers.

Isalinia drew a shuddering breath and straightened a little on the bench.

"I'm all right." She offered Lilac a weary smile. "Just tired, I guess."

"We could go up to our rooms, if you'd like." Lilac suggested. "I'm sure Averendier wouldn't mind if we retired early."

Isalinia shook her head, brushing her loose hair back behind her shoulders. "Soon, Lilac. Let them finish." She tipped her head towards the brothers, who were whispering once again.

Lilac nodded. She still kept a close watch on the dark man from under her lashes. Another man, looking much like the first, had joined him. Together, they strode over to the service counter and quibbled for several minutes with the tavern keeper, who nodded and swiped nervously at the countertop all the while. Then they both crossed the room and seated themselves at the table just behind Averendier and Andrald, in the princesses' full view, and in full view of the princesses. At this choice of seating, Lilac stiffened. When would Averendier finish and take them to their rooms?

Lilac sipped her tea (now lukewarm) and watched the men over the cup's thick rim. They were hunched over their plates and conversing in close whispers. Occasionally, they shot a glance in her direction. Lilac set her cup down firmly, determined not to appear worried. Turning to Isalinia, she attempted to coax her sister into a conversation. But always, watched the men out of the corner of her eye. To her relief, they didn't seem to intend to do more than talk and stare.

The little red-headed servant who had served the girls earlier now approached the table where the two men sat. She held a tray carefully in both hands as she crept along (it seemed as if she couldn't move faster than a creep). One of the men snatched two bottles off the tray the moment it was in reach. Instantly, their attention swung onto the serving girl. Leaning forward, they whispered harshly to her. Though Lilac strained and strained to hear what they said, she couldn't catch a coherent word. Their expressions alone told her their message was anything but gentle.

The little girl gradually shrunk away from them. But before she could get out of reach, one of the men grabbed her wrist and pressed something into her palm. The girl jerked her hand free, her fingers closed tightly over whatever the men had given her. She shot a frightened glance at Lilac and fled back into the kitchen, jamming her closed fist into her pocket as she ran.

Lilac glanced at Averendier, who, in turn, frowned deeply, his troubled eyes resting on the closed kitchen door. So he had been watching also. Lilac's forehead creased. Maybe he would be willing to discuss it later.

Still frowning, Averendier rose to his feet.

"I think we should be getting to bed now," he said quietly. "It's been a long day, for all of us."

Releasing the breath she hadn't realized she had been holding, Lilac rose and followed her companions to the darkened doorway, (which she assumed must lead to the rented rooms). The sear of the men's eyes bored into her back. She shot a glance over her shoulder, only to clash with their hard, menacing gazes.

Lilac turned her head and held herself erect as she passed into a narrow, cramped hallway, which stretched on into many doors and darkness. Directly to her left was a staircase. Averendier immediately climbed the stairs. Grasping her long skirts, Lilac ascended behind her friends.

At the head of the stairs, Lilac paused and pressed her back against the rough wall, her heart thudding painfully against her ribs. Slowly, she flexed her cramped hands. Looking down, she realized she had clenched her skirts in such tight fists, two large, wrinkled splotches stretched across the front of her skirt.

Isalinia, who had mounted the stairs behind her, touched her sister's arm.

"Lilac, are you all right?" she asked.

Lilac glanced back to see Isalinia's concerned face.

"I think Averendier's waiting for us," Isalinia reminded gently. "Shouldn't we keep going?"

Lilac nodded and moved away from the wall, sucking a deep breath into her lungs as she did. She pressed her slick, clammy hands together. Nothing could make her shake the memory of those eyes. Nothing.

38

Andrald *sighed heavily and rolled onto his side, careful not to* bump into Averendier, who was sharing the narrow bed with him. His brother's soft snores filled the air—Averendier rarely snored, unless he was extremely tired. Andrald attempted to curl into a tighter ball. He had always managed to sleep like a rock anywhere he was, even on a violently pitching ship caught in a gale. The day's events had drained him just as much as they had Averendier. So why couldn't he fall asleep?

Groaning under his breath, Andrald turned onto his stomach and propped his chin on his rather flat pillow. Probably thousands of other heads lying on it night after night had made it that way. Andrald pushed himself up onto one elbow and eyed the pillow distastefully. Like *that* made him want to sleep more.

He had to stop thinking before he ended up sleeping outside in the snow. Trying not to contemplate how many people had slept in the bed before him, Andrald shifted his position again. The bed was hard and lumpy beneath him and smelled of dust and stale sweat.

Eventually, he stretched out on his back, staring up at the dark ceiling and occasionally twiddling his fingers.

Minutes or hours later, Andrald heard someone stirring in the next room, where the princesses were staying. He swiveled up onto both elbows and listened.

The walls were paper-thin. Every sound was distinct, as if it was taking place right in front of him. Someone shuffled around for several seconds. A grunt, closely followed by a muffled thump, as if someone were shoving their feet into a pair of tight shoes. Skirts swished faintly. A door latch clicked, and a door badly in need of oiling protested being eased open. Footsteps tapped along the wooden floorboards, growing fainter as their maker moved down the hallway.

The girls had no reason to leave their room. Not at this hour. They had everything they needed in there. Moreover, they should know better than to wander around in a strange place without an escort.

Swinging his legs out of bed, Andrald groped in the darkness for his shoes, thanking himself that he had thought to sleep in his clothes (due to the room's lack of heating). He jammed his feet into his shoes and, grabbing his short sword off a chair, buckled it around his waist. He crept over to the door, rested his hand on the knob, and hesitated. Tentatively, he glanced back at his slumbering brother.

"Averendier?" he whispered.

Averendier's only answer was a tired snore.

Andrald shook his head at himself. He probably wouldn't need his brother anyway. For all he knew, one of the girls could be sleepwalking.

With this thought, Andrald slipped out of his room and into the hallway.

At first, he couldn't see his hand stretched out in front of his face. The darkness prevailing in the hallway enveloped him, pressing painfully against his eyes and blotting out all noise but the whisper of his own breath. No one was there. Whichever princess had left her room must have gone downstairs. Why?

Andrald felt his way down the darkened stairway, his hands fumbling along the uneven walls. At the bottom of the stairs, he paused and glanced down the long, narrow hallway that stretched away to his left. Something seemed to shift in the shadows. Andrald froze and squinted. Nothing moved. Not one shadow left its corner. He shook his head at himself. His eyes were playing tricks. Who would be up at this hour?

Immediately, he frowned at himself. He was, for one.

Just to be sure, he walked up and down the hall once, but he neither saw nor ran into anyone.

Andrald groped his way into the main dining area. A little light still permeated the room from the faintly glowing embers nestled in the ashes of the nearly dead fire. Shadows cloaked the tables and chairs. The wind rattled the shutters slightly. All else was dead silent.

A faint breeze brushed Andrald's neck. He rubbed the back of it, almost absently. Then he turned. Where had that come from?

The sound of a door softly closing lead him back into the dark hallway. The door at its end hung slightly ajar. Andrald crossed the hallway and thrust his head through outdoors.

The storm had blown itself out, leaving huge drifts piled up against the tavern's walls. A cold wind still blew, briskly nipping Andrald's cheeks. Most of the clouds had rolled back from the sky, permitting the sliver of moon to shine coldly down onto the virgin snow. It shed its beams onto a lightly trodden path beginning at Andrald's feet. The footprints ruffled the snow from the back doorstep, across the barnyard, and to the stable door several yards away. A slice of light spilled out of the slightly open door, casting a golden line onto the snow.

Who would be out in the barn in the middle of a night like this? Thieves or vagabonds? Andrald's gut wrenched. Surely, not a princess...

He shuffled forward through the deep snow, which reached halfway up his calves in the sheltered barnyard. It stabbed up his quickly numbing legs. Andrald winced against the bitter cold, but kept his eyes fixed on the barn door.

The mutter of voices floated to meet him. The snow crunching under his feet sounded loud in comparison. The hushed voices grew more distinct as he neared the partially open door. Andrald involuntarily sucked in a breath. Holding it, he peered cautiously through the crack into the barn.

After walking in total darkness, it took his eyes a moment to adjust to the lanternlight. Gradually, he made out six shadows; three horses, and three people. Two of the people were dark haired men. Black cloaks with suspiciously red lining hung down their backs. Andrald's throat tightened at the sight of them. He had known about the highwaymen, but this…

The third person was a girl. Her hair hung down in a golden wash, gleaming in the lanternlight. One of the men was pressing something to her back, something which glinted silver. Andrald's heart lurched sickeningly. A knife. They were holding a knife to the girl's back. His hand crept down to clench his sword's icy hilt. Was that one of the princesses? And why would they—

Andrald hurriedly corrected himself. Not they. Him. Only one man stood in the barn, the one holding the knife to the girl's back. But he could have sworn there had been two just now, as there had been in the dining room that night. Unless.

Swift, crunching footsteps sounded behind him. Andrald jerked around.

Too late. Pain exploded from the side of his head. Sparks scattered across the snowy landscape. Blackness followed in their wake.

39

he snow dwindled to the occasional white flake drifting down from the darkened heavens. Then nothing.

Engrelin, standing in the cave mouth, smiled as he watched the storm end. The bitter north wind swiftly shredded the leaden clouds and drove them over the inky horizon, leaving the sky above Engrelin studded with stars. The sickle moon grinned down from its lofty perch. The rugged cliff face was awash in the ghostly sheen. The world was cold and indifferent towards him. But his smile wasn't a thing of mirth or joy. It was a promise. A promise to keep going, to push on, to never let the sun set on his discouragement and anger. Not that it had risen yet either...

An amused smile replaced the grim, and Engrelin tipped his head back to rest it wearily against the icy stone.

He still couldn't believe Elvera had remained unmoved by his assurances and promises. At least she had relented to Engrelin's leadership, so long as Lance was kept as far away from her as possible. Engrelin didn't see how it would work, since they would be traveling together. But he'd promised to do his utmost, and then some, to maintain peace between them. What more could be done than that?

Elvera had had many options. Lance could be left in the cave. They could set him free and let him go his own way. They could turn him over to the authorities.

Engrelin didn't think any were good options. If left behind in the cave, Lance would freeze to death. If released, he might rejoin his gang of highwaymen, and goodness only knew what havoc they would wreak. As to turning him over to the authorities…

Engrelin still hesitated. He had promised Averendier that if Lance caused any more trouble, he would turn Lance in. But Lance hadn't meant to drag Elvera into danger. He didn't have any particular menace towards her other than the wonderful reactions she had shown to his taunts on the way to Hyke's Crossing. He had just wanted to be free.

Unless Lance got hostile beyond the inevitable arguments and insults, Engrelin was going to keep him close. Engrelin's fingers groped in his pocket until they found his worn string of rosary beads.

Lance was still unconscious. It was help from heaven that he had remained so for so long. Judging from the size of the lump on Lance's head, Engrelin doubted he would wake up any time soon. He was guiltily glad—now he had time to breathe fresh air and think. The snow was deeper than he had hoped. In order to get anywhere, he would have to break a path for Lance and Elvera to walk through. Doing it for an entire day would get very old very quickly. It would be exhausting, but far better than spending the rest of the winter in a cave with Lance, Elvera, and a taegr carcass.

Engrelin sighed and shoved his hands under his arms for warmth. It would be Elvera's first encounter with snow. She would be completely unaccustomed to traveling through it. But if they found a dry place to sleep at night, she wouldn't be worse for the wear.

His biggest fear was Elvera's attitude towards the whole thing. A whole day of unchanging scenery, difficult walking, nothing to do but follow and talk…

Engrelin felt he could deal with any talk or complaints if Lance didn't egg her on or irritate her further. He seemed to be an expert at that. Maybe—big maybe—he would remember his promise to be civil to the girls and leave her alone.

Engrelin slouched against the rock. The snow sifted memories through him as fine and delicate and beautiful as the crystal flakes. Winters back home had always been long and hard, but they rang with their own flavor of pleasantness. His grandmother, mother, and Reigna would busy themselves by knitting and weaving warm clothing. Elmera would tumble on the floor with one of her many kittens. Engrelin, along with his father and brothers, would make arrows or mend their snowshoes. Just an hour before dusk, they would all tromp outside to tend the livestock.

Engrelin glanced back into the dark cave, flickering orange with the fire he had scraped up. This was the last place he could have pictured himself this winter!

But day marches through the snow would only be unpleasant if they chose to make it so. The days would only be dampened by complaints if they were uttered. He would have to work hard to keep Lance and Elvera cheerful and safe until they reached Elstar. It would take at least a week to get there. Once in Elstar, they would be reunited with the others. Everything would smooth out then.

Gradually, the sky lightened along the eastern horizon and the stars faded. The remaining ribbons of clouds were hemmed with the rose and gold of the sunrise. Engrelin caught sight of the last bright blue glimmers of Arrian, the south star, as it, too, quivered into the backdrop of morning sky.

Smiling—truly smiling now—Engrelin ran his hand through his hair. Wordless prayer slid through his heart as he watched the flaming rim of sun peer over the distant mountains. Golden beams spilled down the mountainside and flooded the valley. Engrelin threw his head back to soak in a few moments' blissful warmth after his frigid vigil. Then he turned and disappeared in the cave's cold darkness.

40

L ilac rolled over in her bed and stretched luxuriously, reveling *at* the way her body sank into the straw tick instead of meeting stubborn lumps and roots. When had she last slept in a real bed? Weeks, maybe even months.

"Isalinia," she murmured drowsily to her sister, who had slept beside her. "If this storm keeps on for a few days, I'm going to be spoiled."

There was no reply.

Lilac pushed herself up onto both elbows and dug the sleep furiously out of her eyes.

"Isalinia?" She stared at the empty space beside her. Almost uncomprehendingly, her eyes swept the cold sheets. Panic pumping through her, she shot glances around the small, bare room.

Her sister was nowhere to be seen.

Throwing back the covers, Lilac jumped out of the low bed. She winced when her bare feet hit the cold floorboards, but she doggedly bent and pulled her pack from under the bed. Feverishly, she drew on her clothes. She was quite unaccustomed to her heavy woolen skirts, and the buckle on the belt that held them all in place turned contrary and all but refused to buckle. Likewise, her boots refused to button. Lilac blew out of the corner of mouth. If only she could jerk the top two buttons in place and make and end of it! But she painstakingly wrestled the dozens of buttons through their loops.

After running her hairbrush hastily through her hair, Lilac braided it and pinned the long, golden coils around her head. Finally, she caught her cloak up off the back of a chair, whirled it around her shoulders, and rushed out of the room.

She had not taken half a step into the hallway when she ran slap-bang into Averendier, who still fumbled with his cloak clasp.

"I'm sorry!" she exclaimed with a nervous laugh. A familiar blush burned her cheeks.

"You're fine," said Averendier distractedly.

"Averendier, Isalinia wasn't in the room when I woke," Lilac pursued anxiously. "Do you know where she is?"

Averendier met her gaze sharply. Dread sapped all the moisture from Lilac's mouth. For the first time since she had met Averendier, Lilac was seeing fear in his eyes.

"Isalinia is gone too?" he said, almost in disbelief.

"What do you mean, gone *too*?" Lilac asked.

"Andrald wasn't in bed this morning either," Averendier answered. His brow furrowed. "His cloak and his sword are gone as well."

"Do you think they went downstairs together?" asked Lilac. She wanted to feel relieved by this possibility. But something twisting deep within her told her it wasn't so easy.

"They might have," Averendier consented with a nod. "But I don't think Andrald would have gone anywhere without telling me first. And I certainly don't think Isalinia would have left you without telling you." He looked questioningly at Lilac. "Did she?"

"Not that I remember," said Lilac, head bowed. Ruthlessly, she picked her brain for something to reason away Averendier's statements.

"Maybe they didn't want to disturb us," she offered, even while knowing it was a lame excuse. "We did wake up late."

They can't have been gone too long, she nearly added. The words were on her lips when she recalled, with a surge of renewed fear, the cold patch on the sheet beside her which should have been warm from her sister's slumbering body.

Averendier did not even try to smile. "Well, your Highness, let's go look downstairs. If they're there, they're there. If they're not…" He his broad shoulders. "We'll just have to face it." He clasped Lilac's arm briefly. "Let's just pray for the best."

Lilac glanced briefly down at his hand. It was large, and crossed with several small scars, but gentle in touch. A hand she could trust.

"And how will we face the worst?" she asked quietly. It seemed her voice had grown less tremulous, as if Averendier's strength had flowed into her through a mere touch.

"We'll start by searching for them," Averendier replied, withdrawing his hand. "The storm blew itself out last night. We'll look all over the village if we have to."

A few moments later, Lilac stood with Averendier at the hallway doorway. Anxiously, she scanned the dining room. The card players of last night were there again, talking over full plates. Several other people sat scattered along the benches, but Lilac did not recognize any of them. Isalinia and Andrald were nowhere to be seen. And, she realized with a churning sense of dread, neither were the dark men from last night.

Clenching her woolen skirt in her hands, she looked up at Averendier. He was surveying the room with such an unmoved expression, she wondered if he even saw anything.

"Averendier, the dark men from last night. They're not here," she murmured.

"I know," Averendier answered. "I didn't expect to see them. They eat their breakfasts in their rooms."

Lilac stared at him. "How do you know that?"

Averendier didn't answer. Instead, he marched determinedly up to the serving counter. To Lilac's amusement, anyone who saw Averendier striding towards them scrambled to get out of his way. Lilac followed in the clear wake he left, hiding her smile behind a mask of sobriety. Averendier looked either very angry or very, very imposing.

Probably both, she mused as she watched the fat tavern keeper shrink back as Averendier approached the counter.

"Clane, may I have a word with you?" Averendier asked, his voice both coolly polite and severely unrefusable.

"What do you need?" Clane gulped. He mopped a few droplets of water off the counter with a tattered rag. Lilac couldn't help but notice the man's eyes weren't on Averendier or the counter but fixed on Averendier's sword.

"Just an answer or two," Averendier replied.

"Been handing out too many answers lately," Clane grumbled. "I could get tired of this real fast." In a louder voice, he continued, "Answer to what questions?"

"A young man came up to talk to you last night. He looked kind of like me. Blond hair, gray eyes—"

"Sword?" Clane interjected, flailing his rag towards Averendier's weapon. "Looked like that one?"

Averendier nodded. "Yes. Exactly like this one."

"You must mean Adrian," said Clane, his voice twinging with nervousness. He bent intently to scrub some stubborn speck on the countertop invisible to Lilac.

"Yes, I do," Averendier said. Lilac noticed he let his hand, subtly but pointedly, drop to grasp his sword's hilt. "I'm looking for him. Have you seen him this morning?"

Lilac looked questioningly at Averendier. Adrian? He must mean Andrald, of course. But why the alias?

Clane leaned back on his heels and shook his head, jiggling his double-chins. "Can't say I have," he said. "Not head nor tail of him since he came and ordered supper for your lot last night."

Averendier spun away from the counter. Though his face wasn't marked with the slightest hints of frustration or disappointment, Lilac knew he felt both as keenly as herself. She trailed after Averendier as he strode back towards the hallway, scattering the people in front of him with his mere silence. Lilac fairly skipped to keep up with his long strides.

"Are we going to look around town now?" she asked, once they had entered the hallway and were safe from prying eyes.

"No, I want to check the barn first." Averendier said. "But," he added, turning his head to look at her, "if it does come to looking around town, I want you to stay here while I search. I don't want you going missing as well."

Lilac wanted to protest, but the awfulness of his words turned her lips to putty. What *had* happened to her sisters? Elvera first, and now dear Isalinia…

And what about Andrald, Engrelin, and—yes, even Lance? They had all gone off to who knew where. She couldn't blame Averendier for wanting to keep her in one safe place where he knew he would be able to find her. But logic did not quench her desire to join the hunt. After all, they were looking for *her* sisters.

And could she not disappear just as easily as they? For goodness sake, Isalinia had been right there in the bed beside her, as had Andrald with his brother! How had she and Averendier failed to notice their siblings' departures?

Averendier led her out the tavern's back door, closing it firmly behind them. behind them. Lilac stepped over the threshold into a world of whiteness. The snow glistened purely around her, a carpet of diamonds laid by some kind spirit. It came nearly to the top of her buttoned boots and soaked through the hem of her skirt. Lilac bent, scooped a little snow up in her hand, and worked it between her fingers. A cold, almost painful thrill traveled up her arm. Her fingers red with cold, she let the half-melted dollop plop back into the snow. It left an indent where it fell. Lilac looked swiftly away and around. At any other time, she would have gloried in this all-encompassing northern miracle. But not now.

Her gaze returned to the ground, where several different sets of footprints paraded from where she and Averendier stood by the tavern's back door to a barn close by. Her frown deepened.

"Someone's been here since last night," she noted, straightening.

Averendier glanced at the prints. "Someone has to take care of the horses," he answered. "It's probably just the stable hands."

Straightening his shoulders, Averendier followed the trodden path to the barn.

The snow in front of the barn door was badly trampled. Lilac noticed Averendier studied one print more intently that the rest before he flung the barn's double doors open.

A cry of surprise greeted them from within. A servant girl—the same who had served them the night before—stood in one of the empty stalls. Her mouth hung open with fright, her hands clenched close to her thin chest. Lilac thought she glimpsed a flash of gold between the girl's fingers.

The girl's darting eyes fell on the figures in the doorway. She visibly slumped. With relief?

"Oh…" she murmured, sinking onto an overturned crate, "I thought…I thought…"

She shook her head, her red hair straggling against her cheeks. "But they're gone now," she whispered to herself, her fingers tightening around whatever it was she held. "They're gone…I'm safe."

Safe? A little puzzled line appeared on Lilac's forehead.

"Safe?" said Averendier, echoing Lilac's thoughts. "From whom or what?"

The little girl started violently, her glistening eyelashes fluttering above indignant eyes. "You needn't know!" she exclaimed. "You can't know. You didn't see them! You didn't hear them! They didn't threaten you…" Terror froze her features as she realized she had gone further than she had intended.

Averendier pierced her with a look.

Ducking her head into her apron, the girl burst into tears.

Lilac reprimanded Averendier with a look, then crouched beside the frantically weeping girl. She put a gentle hand on her shoulder.

"No need to cry," she soothed. "We won't hurt you."

"You won't, but he might!" the girl sobbed, gesturing wildly toward Averendier.

"No, no. He won't lay a finger on you. Will you, Averendier?" She shot him a meaningful look which he did not catch. The little girl absorbed all his attention.

"I won't if she stops that," he said, his voice hard.

Lilac frowned disapprovingly at him. But the little girl slowly dropped her apron from her face, her eyes peeping fearfully above tear-stained cheeks. She looked as if she had been crying for longer than a few seconds. As she moved, something fell out of her hand and thudded to the floor.

"What's this?" Averendier demanded. Stooping, he deftly scooped the thing off the floor. In the sunlight streaming through the open doorway, the thing Averendier held shone a rich gold. It was circular and hung from a stout gold chain. Something like a folded bit of paper jutted out one side.

Crying out angrily, the girl jumped up and snatched at Averendier's hand. Lifting his hand out of reach, Averendier gently but firmly pushed the girl back onto the crate.

"It's mine, I found it!" exclaimed the girl, knitting her hands into fists.

Averendier flipped open what seemed to be a lid on the object, not noticing the tiny slip of paper that fluttered from it to the barn floor. "It has my brother's name inscribed on the inside."

Lilac's heart jumped into her throat. Andrald had been here!

"How was I supposed to know?" the girl mumbled, hanging her head. "I can't read."

Averendier's expression softened a little. "All right. I'll let you go on that one. But I do want to know where you found it."

The girl glanced fearfully at him, as if unsure that was all he would require of her. Seeming satisfied that it was, she pointed with a trembling finger to the empty stall she had been standing inside when they had arrived.

"It was in there, hanging on an old nail," she said shakily.

Averendier glanced at the stall, then turned back to her. "Who were you talking about earlier?" he asked. "People who you are now safe from?"

"Bad men," the girl replied. A shudder convulsed her thin frame. "Very bad men who pay girls like me to do their nasty work."

"What kind of work?"

"Sneaking," the girl whispered wearily. She drew her apron back over her face. "And spying. I didn't know why at first. But I know now."

"Why did they want you to do that?" Lilac asked. She touched the girl's arm tenderly, though she sensed the ominous threat looming behind the quavering voice. "Don't be afraid to tell us. No matter what you've done, we won't hurt you."

The girl shivered. "Spying so they can take people away. They wanted to steal people. Who wants to steal *people*?"

Lilac started, her eyes flashing to Averendier. Could she possibly mean…

"What people?" Averendier asked earnestly. He took a quick step closer to the quivering girl.

The girl pulled her apron away from her face and drew a long, shivering breath. "The men came down here last night," she said. "And they took a girl with long, pretty hair, like yours." She timidly reached out to stroke Lilac's coiled braids.

Lilac's heart wrenched. She couldn't possibly mean anyone but Isalinia. And the men had to be the ones who had watched them so intently and so maliciously the previous night. But why would they take her sister? Did they even know who she was?

The little girl still watched Averendier fearfully. The brooding of his eyes struck her with renewed terror—to her, he looked like some terrible giant who might fell her with one wrathful blow. She lurched onto her knees before him.

"I didn't mean to hurt anyone!" she cried desperately. "I really didn't!"

Averendier took her up gently and set her back down on the crate. "Where did they take the girl?" he asked.

The girl shook her head sorrowfully. "I don't know. They paid me, and they took her. They're gone now. You'll never find her." She stood, clenching her apron and staring dazedly about herself. "I'd…better get back to work," she whispered faintly. "I…need to get back to work."

Averendier nodded and took a step back to let the girl pass. Without a parting glance, the girl shuffled through the snow and into the tavern.

Together, Averendier and Lilac stared after the retreating figure until the tavern door shut, blocking all view of her forlorn figure.

"Averendier—"

"You'd better come upstairs with me," Averendier interrupted abruptly. Turning sharply on his heel, he marched out of the barn. Lilac, frowning, started to follow when something small and white lying on the floor caught her attention. Cautiously, she picked it up.

It was the piece of paper that had fallen out of Andrald's compass. In one corner, Averendier's name was printed in tiny, round letters.

Guiltily, Lilac closed her fingers tightly over it and hurried to follow Averendier back upstairs.

Once in the privacy of her room, Lilac barred the door. Guilt hammering in her chest, she unfolded the note. Quickly, she scanned the hurriedly scrawled message.

As she neared the last line, potent terror seized her. Dropping the paper swiftly, as if it had stung her, Lilac retreated several steps. The note drifted lightly to the floor.

"Oh, no," she murmured. Andrald's words raced through her mind. "No, no, no…"

41

*A*fternoon sunlight and shadow slanted across the snow, their patterns of light and dark shifting with each breath of wind. They wavered and danced over a line of trodden snow which three passing horses had churned. The path curved gently over the crest of a hill, dipping beyond it and out of sight.

But Andrald could hear the low hum of voices; he knew he was close. His horse (which he had borrowed from the tavern stable the moment he had regained consciousness) pranced nervously beneath him, likely sensing the danger Andrald had been pushing it towards. Its gray body gleamed with sweat from the gallop over the snow—a run abruptly cut short by distant voices.

Still breathing heavily, Andrald reached down to loosen his sword in its sheath. All day, he had been riding, striving to reach the kidnapped princess and her abductors before the winter sun set. Now, glowing with the warmth of the ride, he was bursting to act. All he needed was a plan.

Slipping from his horse's back, Andrald wrapped the reins around the lower branches of a tree. Sticking to the spidery shadows of the winter-bare trees, he crept up the hill's summit. There, he eased himself onto his stomach and peered over the edge.

Just below, at the hill's foot, three horses stood in the snow, three riders astride their backs. Two were men in dark red cloaks, their scarlet hoods pulled far over their heads, casting their faces in spectral shadow.

The other was the princess; her hands bound behind her back with rope, her head held high. The breeze played gently with her golden hair, rippling it about her face. She was astride Engrelin's old mount, Glorien. A thick rope stretched from the stallion's bridle to her captor's saddle horn, binding the two horses securely together. Andrald nearly whistled, impressed. For traveling like that, they had covered an incredible distance—they presently stood thirty miles from the tavern, and the sun still hovered at the horizon.

Andrald smiled. He had pursued them all day across snow-covered terrain without ever spotting them. Now they were here, within his grasp.

The men were arguing. Andrald had only to glance at the setting sun to know the reason for their conflict. Still, he inched closer to the ridge's edge, straining to listen.

"…Risking pursuit," he thought he heard one growl. "We'll have to push on through the night."

"But the horses need resting," the other retorted. "It's cruel to push them any further."

"Cruel? It's crueler to feel a rope around your neck. If we get caught, we'll be hung for kidnapping."

"But if we keep pushing, the horses will be too tired to run if we're spotted."

"We most certainly will have to turn tail if we stay…"

On and on they fought. Their argument didn't seem close to ending. All the better.

He gazed thoughtfully down. Anxiety cramped his stomach. Gritting his teeth, he crawled away, back the way he had come. He couldn't afford to let anything go wrong. At least he had the element of surprise.

"Surprise over the rise," he murmured to himself. Despite the situation, he smiled. It would make a good title for a ballad.

Seconds later, mounted on his gray horse, he galloped around the hill. As he broke from the last snowy curve, he yelled incoherently. He saw the kidnapper's heads snap up in surprise, their heels kick instinctively into their mounts' sides. Then he was upon them.

He drew his sword as he charged towards the bound princess. Still yelling, he sliced the rope stretched taut between the captor's horse and his prisoner's. Snorting, Glorien backed away from Andrald's swinging blade. Sheathing his sword, Andrald pulled his horse up beside the startled stallion and fumbled desperately at the princess' bonds.

"*Ymosod*!" The men screamed behind him. Giving up on the ropes, Andrald smacked Glorien's flanks, sending the horse spurting away. He jerked his gray horse back just in time to dodge a slice intended to take his head off. He threw his own blade up to catch the next swing; steel clashed against steel with a resounding *clang*. Andrald wheeled his horse in front of his enemy's mount. Crying out fiercely, Andrald swung his sword to meet its mark. The man toppled from his horse, crumpling into a heap on the snow, his crimson cloak pooling around him like a wash of blood. Andrald quickly looked away. Instantly, his eyes fell on the other man.

Hood thrown back, the man silently stalked the princess, who was guiding the horse away from the scene with her knees. Sucking in a quick breath, Andrald spurred his mount forward, striving to quickly close the gap between the man and himself.

The man struck his short whip against Glorien's flanks. Screaming, the stallion reared up onto his hind legs. The princess spilled out of her saddle into the snow. The enemy was only a few yards away.

Time ground to a halt. The red-cloaked man drew his sword—the motion lasted an eternity. Andrald bent low over his galloping horse's neck. He tried to pray—tried desperately. But no words would surface. Nothing could penetrate the internal scream reverberating through him.

The terrible sword fell. Andrald wanted to squeeze his eyes shut against the horrific product of that swing. But it was his duty to watch. Even if it was only to see her die, he must watch.

The black-hilted sword flew from its master's hand and buried itself deep in the snow. Both kidnapper and rescuer stared stupidly at it.

For snow was all it had struck.

Pale but triumphant, the princess looked up from where she had rolled to the side at the last moment. A glimmer of hope stole into Andrald's heart. Standing in his stirrups, Andrald nudged his horse between the princess and her assailant. He stopped low and snatched the man's discarded sword out of the snow. Balancing it in his free hand, Andrald pointed it at his opponent's neck.

The man's eyes darted from the princess, to his fallen comrade, and finally to Andrald, who wielded two swords in his hands, one silver and one crimson.

"Surrender if you value your life," commanded Andrald, lowering his voice threateningly.

"Surrender?" the man sneered. He dropped one hand to adjust his stirrup. "Tirendria never surrenders. We'll be up to our knees in blood, and still we'll fight to the last man, until all Ontaria is under Vendar's rule. If there's any surrendering to be done, you will do it."

The man straightened in his saddle. His wrist flicked. A searing pain shot through Andrald's left arm. Crying out in anger and pain, he dropped the man's sword, letting it fall into the snow beneath him beside a newly stained dagger.

The man shook his fist at his awry throw. "This time!" he yelled. Digging his heels into his horse's sides, he galloped away over the snow.

Andrald watched him leave, his horse's hooves tossing puffs of loose snow into the air. Andrald's tight grip on his weapon didn't loosen until the man crested a distant hill and slid out of sight.

Andrald jumped from his saddle and stooped over the princess stretched out on the ground.

"Are you all right?" he asked as he fumbled with the knots pinning her wrists behind her back.

"Fine," the girl replied, smiling up at him. In the wan light, he saw she was Isalinia. She flexed her sore wrists as the ropes fell away from them. "No broken bones, I think. Thank goodness for all this snow."

She looked up again, then gasped quietly, pressing one hand against her mouth. "You're hurt!" she exclaimed. She reached out and gently touched his slashed sleeve.

Andrald grimaced as her slender fingers traced his wound, sending another stab of pain up his arm and into his shoulder.

"It's nothing—hardly a scratch," he said. He pulled her hand away.

"You're lucky," Isalinia murmured. "He was aiming for your heart."

"*I'm* lucky?" Andrald seized her hands and pulled her to her feet. "What about you? Just an hour ago, you were as good as dead."

Isalinia's eyes widened. "For a while, I didn't think anyone would come," she admitted. "But then I knew you or someone else would find me."

"Especially to get you from those fiends," Andrald muttered. The man's bold declaration that he was a Tirendrian had shaken him. If the man was what he claimed, did he know who Isalinia was? If so, they were in more trouble than she could ever dream. But he could never tell her about the danger.

"I'm sorry it took me so long to reach you," Andrald said. "I was delayed."

"I know," Isalinia returned soberly. "I saw."

"Well," Andrald said, forcing his voice to be more cheerful, "one good thing came out of this."

"What's that?"

"We got two of our horses back."

"Two?" Isalinia blinked. Then her eyes clouded. "Oh, that other man. Did you really kill him, Andrald?"

A surge of unexpected grief and even guilt swept over Andrald. He turned to view the figure stretched out over snow stained red with blood.

"God forgive me," he murmured. He crossed himself slowly. "I didn't know what else to do."

Beside him, Isalinia murmured a prayer in Alinar.

Andrald seized her arm, overcome just as quickly with a urgency.

"We don't have time for this," he said. "We have to get out of here while we still can." He wiped his sword on the snow, dried it on his trousers, and rammed it into its sheath.

"But we can't just leave him lying there!" gasped Isalinia, horrified.

"Even if we tried, we couldn't bury him. The ground is frozen solid," Andrald answered sadly. Marking the girl's stricken expression, he continued, "That other man will be back soon, probably with some of his thug friends. They'll take care of him." He caught the fallen man's horse by the halter and held it steady while Isalinia mounted. "Meanwhile, we'll want to put as many miles as we can between us."

"Are we going back to the others?" Isalinia asked.

"We're heading back to the tavern, yes. I borrowed a horse from their stable to come find you." Andrald tucked the Tirendrian's sword and dagger into her saddle bag. The girl's eyes widened.

"I hope you won't need them, but just in case, they're here," Andrald assured. He tied the saddle bag shut.

"I'll pray," Isalinia replied with a little shiver.

Andrald nodded thoughtfully as he tied his gray mount's halter to the pommel on Glorien's saddle. Then he mounted the palomino.

"On to the tavern?" he said. He turned Glorien southwards.

A twilight gloom was stealing over the snow, but Isalinia flashed him a brave smile as she nudged her horse forward.

"So, answer one question for me," said Andrald, after riding in silence for several miles. The shadows had long ago deepened to murk around them. "Why did you go down to the barn last night, all alone?"

Isalinia looked pleadingly at him. "Must I?"

"I'd like to know," Andrald replied.

Isalinia sighed. "I'll tell," she said. "But it's embarrassing." Lacing her fingers around her saddle's pommel, she continued, "Do you remember that last night, you were talking to that tavern-keeper about the horses?"

Andrald jolted in his saddle as if he'd been struck by lightning. "You heard that?!"

Isalinia nodded. "Nearly every word. You weren't keeping your voices down, you know."

Andrald shook his head slowly. *When I think I'm keeping secrets...*

"I heard you talking to Averendier about it as well—"

"You have sharp ears," Andrald muttered.

"—and though I heard you mention you thought the men were some of Lance's highwaymen, I didn't think much of it. I was just really excited our horses were down there."

"So you had to go and see them for yourself," Andrald chuckled.

"Don't laugh!" Isalinia admonished, though laughter tinged her own voice. "I can't tell you now why I thought it was a good idea. But I waited until the snow stopped falling, then went down to see them. I was disappointed mine wasn't one of them."

"I'm sure it's fine, wherever it is," Andrald said. "Your father's horses aren't something to abuse. It'll be treasured just as much as Engrelin's and Elvera's." He patted Glorien's neck as he spoke, though something in him twisted as he finally allowed himself to think about his missing cousin and the princess. Where could they possibly be now… and were they all right? He frowned, then realized Isalinia was looking expectantly at him.

"What? I'm sorry, did you say something?" he asked, glancing at her. Something beyond her shoulder caught his eye.

"I said—"

"Shh!" Andrald commanded, pulling Glorien to a halt.

"Andrald, what is it?" Isalinia whispered, leaning far over her horse's neck.

Andrald didn't answer. He peered intently towards the line of trees to their left. He saw the faint, scarlet flickers of a distant fire.

"A campfire?" Isalinia queried.

Andrald nodded slowly, his chest tightening. "That's what it looks like."

"Do you think it's…" Isalinia's tapering silence said more than words ever could.

"It has to be." Andrald affirmed. "Who else would be camping on a night like this?"

"We should go," Isalinia murmured. "Before they see us."

Gently, Andrald pressed his knees into Glorien's sides. The stallion started forward at a cautious walk. "They'll see our horse's prints," he muttered.

"When they do, it'll be morning, and we'll be long gone by then," Isalinia reminded.

Andrald nodded. But he was still uneasy.

42

Are we ever going to stop?" Elvera moaned. She pulled her cloak tighter around her shivering shoulders. "We've been walking for *forever*."

Engrelin paused and sighed, running his hand through his damp hair. Damp, like the rest of him, from all the snow he'd plowed through for the past ten hours. He glanced back at Elvera, noting her purple lips, chapped cheeks, and red-tipped nose

"We can't stop," he said, his voice froggy with exhaustion. He frowned at himself. He had to get it sounding better if he wanted to lift Elvera's spirits. Not that he could help her much. Elvera seemed determined to make her day as difficult as possible—for herself and those around her.

"We'll freeze to death," he added. As if that would cheer her up.

"I'd rather freeze then stumble on like this," Elvera returned. "Besides, I heard people get warm before they freeze."

"Feel warm," Engrelin corrected. Didn't she understand he and Lance were just as tired as she? Walking for hours was one thing, breaking a path through thigh-high snow another. He felt as if all his energy had leeched into the snow, leaving him slumped and shaken and cold. Just thinking about it made him want to sit down.

But there was a time and a place for rest, and that wasn't anywhere close. Gritting his teeth, Engrelin turned and plowed forward another few steps, trampling the snow underfoot, forming a rough path for his companions to walk through.

"If we don't stop soon, I'll freeze solid!" Elvera pleaded.

Engrelin paused and turned again. "And if we do stop? What then?"

"What an interesting choice," Lance murmured.

Shuddering, Elvera drew her cloak up to her cheeks.

The sun inched closer and closer to the horizon. The miserable day drew to a close with a brave display of the sun sinking steadily and showily behind the mountains. The snow shimmered with color, transformed from a sea of diamond to a red and maroon desert. Engrelin watched the change half-heartedly, trudging with his head down and shoulders bent to meet the brisk, bitter wind the twilight brought. He thrust his swollen hands under his arms to warm them.

"Sun's setting," Lance announced.

"Mm-hmm," Engrelin murmured.

"Aren't we going to find somewhere to camp for the night?" Lance asked, cocking his head.

"Not here." Engrelin grunted as he shoved his body through an especially high drift.

"You expect us to walk all night?!" Elvera shrilled.

Pausing for breath, Engrelin wiped his arm wearily across his face, smearing wet snow across it.

"No, we're going to stop eventually," he said. "But not until we find shelter. We can't plop down in the snow whenever we get tired, unless you enjoy the prospect of turning into an icicle overnight."

"An Elvera-cicle," Lance snickered.

Engrelin shot him a warning look.

"What kind of shelter?" asked Elvera, for once ignoring Lance's comment.

"I'm looking for some trees," Engrelin replied. "If we find a wood thick enough, the ground beneath will be snow-free. We can bed down there. Besides, we need wood for our fire."

"You have sticks in your pack. You could use those," Elvera stated.

"Those sticks are my emergency store," said Engrelin. "For torches only."

They pushed further still, wrapped in belligerent silence. The darkness deepened by the second. Engrelin struggled on. He could hardly think straight. Why had he ever thought as a kid that snow was fun to romp around in? Here, there was no warm home to rush into when things reached their coldest. No change of clothes after the snow, melting against his body, soaked through the layers of leather and wool into his bones. Only to push on across this seemingly endless plain of snow, with no other hope for comfort but the meager shelter trees might provide.

Engrelin stumbled over a drift. He glanced down and corrected himself. Not a drift. A log, half-buried in the snow. And that could only mean…

"Look!" Elvera cried, her voice sudden and piercing. She pointed ahead, flapping her other hand wildly in the air.

Engrelin's eyes followed her point. His shoulders slumped with relief. Only a few yards ahead of them, at the crest of a gentle slope, loomed the shadowy wall of a forest.

"Make for it," he ordered.

A few more minutes of struggling through the snow, and they broke into the deep shadows and shallow snow beneath the trees' welcomingly outstretched arms.

Sighing happily, Elvera reached up to brush against one of the lower hanging branches. "Ow!" she exclaimed, jerking her hand away. "What kind of tree is that!" she gasped. "It ran me through!"

"No wonder. It's made of needles!" Lance jeered.

Elvera snorted and turned to Engrelin. He nodded slowly.

"In a way, Elvera, he's right. They're reghun needles. They're the tree's leaves. See?" Reaching up, Engrelin carefully bent down a branch that wasn't covered so thickly with snow. "It's a good thing too. The needles trap the snow up in the branches. The ground deeper in should be clean and dry."

Elvera glanced at the branch and shrugged indifferently. "I see," she said. "But how are we going to get in there? It's like a wall." She waved her hand at the ranks of towering conifers.

"Easy," Engrelin answered. He let the branch swish back up into place. "The branches don't grow so thickly inside. It'll be open once we get through the first few yards. No snow, and piles of reghun needles to make our beds on."

"What! Beds of these things?" Elvera jumped away from the trees as if they had bitten her.

Engrelin sighed and motioned to the forest. "Just go in and see for yourself."

Elvera shrank back. "Me first?" she asked timidly.

"I'll be right behind you the whole way," Engrelin assured.

"But what if another one of those…" She shuddered again. "What if one of those taegr things are in there?"

"It's not likely," Engrelin said. "They'll all be holed up in their caves because of the snow, just like the one we met."

"But what if—"

"If I go first, you're going to have to go in front of Lance," Engrelin said, his voice hardening to an edge. "You want that?"

Elvera glanced over her shoulder at Lance, who stood as still and as silent as a wooden pole. A perfect picture of innocence.

"No-ooo," Elvera said slowly. "I'll go in front."

"Just be careful of the needles!" Lance called out. "Hit one too hard and it'll go straight through you!"

Snorting in disbelief, Elvera flounced her way into the woods.

That was fast, Engrelin thought. He made sure that Lance was following close behind him before plunging into the dense branches after Elvera. He ducked a swinging branch Elvera had pushed aside only to be whacked smartly on the arm by another recoiling branch. He rubbed the tender spot on his arm. *And she thought pricking her finger hurt!*

After enduring many thrashing, prickly branches, the three finally broke out into a gloriously clear area along the forest floor. Not one flake of snow rested on the ground. In its place was a carpet of golden-brown reghun needles.

Elvera sighed contentedly. "This *is* nice," she said.

"That it is." Engrelin grunted, struggling to release himself from his pack.

"Don't you think we should go further in?" Lance asked.

"Of course not!" Elvera exclaimed, gaping at him. "Right here is perfectly fine."

Engrelin barely heard them as he vehemently shrugged his shoulders. Why couldn't he get his pack off?

"There's more protection, further in," Lance declared.

"And more animals. Isn't that right, Engrelin?"

"Uh-huh," murmured Engrelin absently, still tugging at his pack's straps. What was wrong with this thing? It had never done this before.

He let one hand drift down his chest. It closed over the cold metal of the chest buckle that connected the shoulder straps and held them in place. Engrelin nearly growled aloud. How could he have forgotten those?

"Besides, there's no snow here, and I'm sure there's plenty of wood lying around," Elvera continued. "There's nothing else we need."

"Well, you certainly have learned a lot on this trip."

"That's enough," Engrelin ordered. He nearly spoiled the silencing effect of his tone by sighing under his breath as his pack finally slid from his aching shoulders. "Now, Elvera, if you're okay with being alone for a few minutes, I'm going to take Lance with me to find some firewood."

"Me? Alone? Here!" Elvera quavered.

"'I'll leave a torch with you," Engrelin assured. He bent and fished one of the torches out of his pack.

"Still…"

"Might as well lug her with us," Lance scoffed. "If we don't, we'll come back to find her in a dead faint."

"That's what you think," Elvera returned haughtily, straightening. "I'm no coward. I'm going to stay right here, all alone, and guard the things while you two are gone." She jabbed her finger emphatically at the empty space beside her. "Right here. And I'll remain conscious."

A tiny spark sprang from steel and flint. A flicker. Then their faces were illuminated in the new blaze the torch flung forth.

Engrelin handed Elvera the torch. "Are you sure you'll be all right?" he asked.

"I'm sure," she answered firmly. She brandished the flaming torch like a sword. "I'm standing right here." Her rigid posture and arched eyebrows added, *let anyone dare defy me.*

The corner of Engrelin's mouth tugged into what might have been a smile. Dipping his head briefly, he brushed it away.

"We'll only be gone a few minutes," he said. He took Lance by the arm and steered him away. "Meanwhile," he added in a growl, "we're going to have a little chat."

"Thank goodness you're back," Elvera breathed. The torch drooped in her hand.

Engrelin didn't answer—he merely dumped his armload of wood into a jumbled heap on the ground.

"If you get that built into a nice fire, I'll fix us something warm to eat," she added.

"Emphasis on warm," interjected Lance.

Engrelin silently sat Lance down at the foot of a tree so the boy could rest his back against the trunk. Then he set wordlessly to building the fire, his mind drifting back over the past few minutes spent collecting fuel in the dark woods. Lance had said nothing during the entire walk and lecture. Who knew if he was going to hold his tongue as Engrelin had ordered him to!

"I hope you'll keep that going all night," Lance commented, eyeing Engrelin as he worked.

"I hope so too," replied Engrelin stiffly.

"He should." Elvera rummaged through her things. "We have quite the supply," she added, almost to herself.

"Supply of what?" Lance asked.

Engrelin's little pile of reghun needles and twigs sparked to life in a burst of flame. He might have smiled if he hadn't been listening. The lecture he had just delivered to Lance seemed to have fallen by the wayside.

"Oh. I thought you might mean something else," Lance remarked, shrugging.

"Like what?" Elvera drew a wooden bowl out of her pack, inspected it, frowned, and dropped it back into her pack. She resumed her rummaging, all her things clattering loudly together. What could she possibly have in there to make so much noise?

"Food. We're pretty short of it, you know," Lance said.

Engrelin's gaze snapped onto Lance, who just as quickly looked away.

Elvera shrugged. "It doesn't matter," she said. She drew a small metal pot out of her pack and set it on the ground. "We'll get whatever supplies we need when we get back with the others. Don't you remember?"

"Oh, yes, I remember," said Lance. "But what makes you think we're going back?"

"Common sense," Elvera snorted. "If you even understand what that means." She measured something out into the pot and set it beside the now steadily burning fire. "I mean, what's stopping us from going back?"

"What indeed," Lance agreed. His gaze slanted onto Engrelin.

Engrelin held his silence, his mind in turmoil. Elvera didn't know about the map in his pocket. He wasn't ready to tell her about it yet, especially after how miserably the day had passed. Lance…Lance shouldn't have known. But somehow he did, unless he was merely trying to spite Elvera and had no real idea of what he was saying. Engrelin pinched his lips tightly together. Knowing Lance, he probably knew. Somehow, he had learned about the maps.

Elvera was agonizingly quiet. If she had at least flared up at Lance's words, Engrelin would have had to explain the map, and he could put that ordeal behind himself. But her silence infected him, and all he could do was pace around camp, as if by wearing himself down further, he could improve their situation in some way.

Elvera finished baking what looked like flat cornbread cakes (though Engrelin was sure that wasn't what they were—she had admitted to never having eaten cornbread in her life). He untied Lance's hands so that Lance could eat, but he shook his head when Elvera offered him one of the cakes.

"You're not going to eat?" Elvera asked, drawing her hand back and looking slightly offended. "Is there something wrong with it?"

"No," Engrelin answered. "I'm just not hungry."

"You should be," Elvera pointed out. "You haven't eaten since this morning."

Engrelin paused in his pacing. Yes, she was right—he should be hungry. Starving, in fact. Humanly speaking, he should have been half-dead with exhaustion. He couldn't remember the last time he had slept, much less slept well. Two, three days, maybe? A whole week?

And yet here he was, not only on his feet, but rejecting the food that might enable him to keep watch tonight. His shoulders sagged at the thought. Another night of wakefulness and watching. And how many more?

He scrubbed a hand across his face. He couldn't do this. Averendier's plan was wrong. Staying up all night, then monitoring Lance and Elvera while breaking a path through deep snow was inconceivable.

He wouldn't have done it unless he'd been sure I could handle it.

A low sound beyond the trees nudged Engrelin out of his thoughts. He glanced over at Elvera. She was frozen, staring off the way they had come, her pale lips slightly parted. She had heard it too. It had been faint, but still…

Stooping, Engrelin bound Lance's hands. He placed a warning finger on his lips. Then he crept away from camp, back through the trees, following the noise. It was still there—the sough and crunch of snow being trodden underfoot.

At the wood's edge, he peered through the screen of reghun branches. At the same time, the sound stopped.

Not a hundred yards from where Engrelin crouched, two people sat on horseback. Instinctively, he ducked, his breath catching in his throat. Who were they? Had they seen the fire?

Cautiously, he peeked back out. The two riders were leaning towards each other, bent in discussion. A few wisps of muttered words tantalized Engrelin's ears, but nothing stood out coherently.

One of them glanced towards the woods. They seemed to be looking directly at Engrelin—directly through him. Their eyes glinted in the moonlight. Engrelin looked over his shoulder, following the man's gaze to the blossoming glow of the fire. Engrelin's hands knotted into fists.

No, not here. Whoever you are, stop anywhere but here.

As if they had heard him, the two riders straightened. Clucking softly to their horses, they guided them away over the snowy hills. Engrelin watched them until they fell out of sight behind a rise. Slowly, he released the breath he hadn't realized he'd been holding. He waited a few seconds, watching to make sure they didn't return before he slipped back through the trees to their camp.

"It's all right," Engrelin called as he approached the fire. He crouched down next to it and stretched his stiff fingers towards the warmth. In the dim light, he saw his hands were shaking with fatigue. Hastily, he stood and stuffed them into his pockets.

Elvera (who Engrelin had assumed, until now, to have turned into a statue) now slumped with relief. "What was it?" she asked shakily.

"You mean 'who'," Engrelin corrected. "Two people on horses. They're gone now."

"Maybe it was some of your friends looking for you. Engrelin, why did you have to go and scare them away?" Lance exclaimed mockingly.

Engrelin stiffened. "It wasn't anyone we know," he answered tightly.

Elvera's head jerked up, indignance flashing in her eyes. "And why not?" she demanded. "I think it's likely they're looking for us."

"No, Elvera," Engrelin said, his mouth as dry as the rustling reghun needles beneath him. "No one is going to be looking for us. We're on our own."

"The idea," Elvera sniffed. "Really, Engrelin. Lance comes up with better ones than that."

Engrelin stared at her. Did she think he was joking?

"Elvera, I'm not kidding," he said. "I'm dead serious. No one is looking for us. We're on our own from here."

"And why won't they?" Elvera demanded.

"Because Averendier won't let them," Engrelin replied.

"You're joking."

"I'm not."

For a fleeting moment, Elvera looked desperately small and scared. Then her dark eyes narrowed to slits and she shuffled to her feet.

"I see. You're in league with Lance, aren't you? You're kidnapping me, aren't you!" Her voice rose to fever pitch. "You're taking me away from my sisters! That's what you planned to do this whole time, wasn't it?"

"No!" Engrelin exclaimed, flinging his hands out. "I'm not kidnapping you! Whatever gave you that idea?"

"Then what *are* you doing?" Elvera demanded, arms akimbo.

"I'm taking you and Lance back to Monaria, just as we always intended."

"I don't believe you," Elvera spat. "I'm not going to listen to you anymore."

"What? How else do you plan to survive out here?" Engrelin threw his arm out, motioning to the darkness and trees pressing in from all sides.

"I don't want you. I want Averendier."

"You can't have him," Engrelin replied.

"And why not?"

"Because he doesn't know where we are, and I have no idea where he is."

"We do know," Elvera said. "Back at the tavern."

"By the time we get back there, they might have already left. We will waste time backtracking," Engrelin explained. "It's best to push on by ourselves."

Elvera fairly snarled.

"But I do know where they're going," Engrelin continued.

"Where? And how would you know?" Elvera snapped.

"We came up with a plan together a little while ago, in case we got separated," Engrelin explained. "We're going to meet up in Elstar. It's the capitol of Northern Florenth."

"How far is it?"

Engrelin raked his hand through his hair. "On foot, about a week," he admitted.

"A week!" Elvera wailed. "How am I going to survive a week with you and Lance?"

"By trying to cooperate," Engrelin said starkly. "You really don't have a choice."

Elvera's eyes blazed. "I hate you!" she hissed venomously.

"My thoughts exactly," Lance agreed.

Engrelin whirled quickly. "You stay out of this, Lance Smith."

Lance slouched and grumbled.

Turning back to Elvera, Engrelin pursued, "Your feelings can't be helped either. Just remember that you being here is your fault."

"My fault!" Elvera gasped angrily. "How is it my fault?"

"You followed me instead of going back to town like I told you to."

"If *you* hadn't let Lance escape, I wouldn't have followed you," Elvera retorted.

"If he hadn't run away, I wouldn't have had to hunt him down," Engrelin barked back.

"I never would have run away if you hadn't captured me," Lance returned.

Engrelin whipped around to face Lance. "And I wouldn't have had to capture you if you hadn't tried…hadn't…"

"I never would have tried to kill you if you hadn't done what you did back home," Lance yelled.

Engrelin clutched his head. "What is that supposed to mean?"

Smiling spitefully, Lance leaned back against the tree. "I'll never tell you while you're alive."

"Like I can hear you when I'm dead."

"Exactly."

Engrelin's hands slowly curled into fists. "Fine," he said, his voice low and searing as a blue ember. "If this is the way you both want it…fine."

Elvera only stared at him. Lance's smug expression shifted to a frown, and he squirmed uncomfortably, as if he just realized he was sitting on something wet.

"That's all you're going to say?" he asked. "Fine?"

Engrelin considered a moment. What more was there to say? Whether they liked it or not, they were stuck with each other. No amount of arguing would spirit them back to their group. Nothing was left to do but walk to Elstar during the day, rest at night, and pray they made it safely home.

"Yes, Lance," he said. "That's all. Now go to sleep, both of you. We leave for Elstar at first light."

To his utter shock, they both obeyed. Lance slumped instantly onto his side (in what must have been an exceedingly uncomfortable position), contriving sleep. Elvera scowled at both him and Engrelin in turn but jerked her blanket out of her pack and curled up in it close to the fire. Engrelin watched them. He groped in his pocket until his hand closed over the folded map.

43

Lilac *tugged her hairbrush though her hair, then began plaiting it in complicated knots for probably the fiftieth time that morning.* Sighing heavily, she let go of the braid's end and watched it quickly unravel at the bottom. Her gaze drifted from it to Andrald's note lying open on the bed beside her. She had read it so many times in the past few hours, she knew every line by heart.

That almost made it worse.

She didn't have to read it to start the dreadful parade of those words through her mind. Those awful words! One particular paragraph dragged its feet, gleefully tormenting her.

"…If I can find the princess, I will do my best to rescue her. Please don't be upset with my leaving without telling you—you need to stay here with the other one and guard her. Don't wait for me until Elstar. Just pray, for the sake of Ontaria, that I succeed. But if I don't…"

Lilac released a frustrated sigh and stood, clenching her hands at her sides, as if that would relieve her cramping stomach. How could Averendier keep such a secret from her? If they had gotten separated, even before now, each was to go his own way, and meet up at some far-away city. If Averendier hadn't impressed upon her the necessity of her staying put in her room, Lilac would be out right now, searching for her sisters.

But she had foolishly promised to remain in her room until Averendier told her she could leave.

That had been early that morning. Now, the sun had nearly reached its zenith. Imprisonment settled more heavily on Lilac's shoulders. If only she knew what was taking Averendier so long!

A light knock brushed against the door. It creaked open. Lilac spun to face the newcomer. Through the doorway thrust a tangle of red hair above a tear-smeared face. Relieved (though more than a little disappointed it wasn't Averendier), Lilac gave the girl a quick smile.

A hesitant grin spread over the girl's dirty face as she slipped the rest of the way into the room, balancing a tray on one arm. With an expert flick of her heel, she shut the door behind herself.

"I hope I'm not intruding or nothing," she said quickly. "I'm just bringing you some dinner."

"No, you're fine." Lilac motioned to a small table near the door. "You may set it there. Thank you."

The girl curtsied clumsily and slid the laden tray onto the table. "I'll be bringing your supper later," she said. "Your man told me to."

Lilac blushed to the roots of her hairs. "He's just a guide," she said quickly.

"Of course." The girl nodded, turning to leave.

"Wait," Lilac called, starting forward after her.

The girl paused with one foot in the hallway. "Yes ma'am?" she quavered.

"What is your name?" Lilac asked.

"Fern, ma'am," said the girl, dropping another curtsey.

"It's very pretty. Thank you." Lilac nodded her dismissal.

Fern backed out of the room and closed the door quietly behind herself. Lilac heard the girl's bare feet pattering as she scrambled across the hall and down the stairs. The smile left Lilac's lips as she listened. Fern was afraid of her—she seemed afraid of everyone. Her thoughts returned to the two dark men who had stolen her sister, and her frown deepened.

Minutes dragged into hours, persisting in wearing out their welcome and Lilac's patience. She ate her dinner, sat awhile in silence, coiled her loose braid back around her head, sat some more. Afternoon sunshine slanted through her small window, playing golden beams across her floor.

Still no Averendier.

Lilac moved over to her small window, watching the hustle and bustle of the stable boys in the stable yard below. They tramped contentedly through their chores, cloaks waving in the wind, not at all bothered by the snow lying thick on the ground. They floundered in it, making rifts and holes with their high boots. A couple boys tackled each other to the ground and rolled around, flattening the snow beneath them.

A rider swept into the stable yard, a black cloak lined with startling scarlet flying out behind him like a pair of outspread wings. The stable boys scattered wildly to get out of the way of the horse's flashing hooves as the creature thundered up to the stable door. The rider pulled his mount up so quickly, the foam around its mouth turned red. As the man jerked with the sudden halt, his cloak hood fell back from his head. Lilac gasped.

He was none other than the man who had watched her last night!

Questions flooded her brain. What was he doing here? Where was the other man? What had happened to her sister?

Lilac watched the man jump easily from the horse's back. Another shot of recognition coursed through her.

"Starlight!" she exclaimed, staring wide-eyed at the white horse. She pressed one hand against the windowpane, as if she could reach right through the glass to seize her sister's horse. Not only had the men taken her sister, but they had also stolen her sister's horse!

In agony, Lilac watched the man throw several harsh (and unprintable) orders at the stable boys, strike one of the boys so hard he spun down into the snow, then stalk into the tavern.

An icy thrill of terror wrapped its coils around Lilac's chest, squeezing until she could hardly breathe. It pulled her away from the window and into the nearest corner, where no one outside could possibly see her. One of those men had returned. Why? Had he come back for her?

Cautiously, she peered back out of the window, looking down at the terrified boys leading Starlight into the barn. Another helped his fallen comrade off the ground, pressing a checkered handkerchief to the boy's bloody nose and glancing over his shoulder to make sure the man wasn't coming back. No doubt that horse would be the best treated in the village today.

Turning away from the window, Lilac flung herself out on her bed. To further torture herself, she snatched up Andrald's note and read it over to herself, despite having already memorized it.

Some time must have passed before a soft knock sounded on the door. Lilac sprang to open it. *Please, let it be Averendier*, she prayed.

She tore the door open, revealing Fern standing shyly in the hallway. Lilac's shoulders wilted.

"Hello," she said, pulling a smile for the girl's sake.

Fern smiled for the first time Lilac could remember.

"Hi," she returned timidly. "I came to tell you your supper is ready and hot and waiting in the other room with Mr. What's-his-name. He asked me to come fetch you, if you don't mind. He says he wants to dine private with you tonight."

Relief washed over Lilac. Finally, Averendier was back.

"Thank you," she said. "I'll come."

Offering another shy smile, Fern bobbed her head and tripped down the hallway.

Lilac shut the door, checked herself quickly in the mirror, then hesitated. She cast a quick glance at the note lying placidly on her bed. Grimly, she picked it up and folded it small enough to fit smugly in her palm. Her hand clenched around the note, Lilac walked across the hall to Averendier's room and knocked on the door.

"Come in," Averendier called.

Lilac drew a deep, steadying breath, and entered.

Averendier was sitting on the edge of his bed, beside which he had pulled a table. At the opposite side of the table stood the room's only chair. Beside the supper dishes lay Andrald's compass Averendier's forehead was creased, but the lines smoothed when he met Lilac's gaze.

"Please, sit down." Averendier motioned to the chair. "I'm sorry we have to eat here, but I thought it would be best to lay low."

"Thank you," Lilac said stiffly as she lowered herself into the chair.

Averendier handed her a full plate. Together, they said grace. When it was finished, Lilac picked up her fork and worked on the food, an appetite she hadn't realized she'd had rolling through her. Watching

Averendier under her lashes, she watched him push his food around his plate instead of forking it into his mouth. Beneath the table, her left hand clenched tightly around Andrald's note.

"When are we leaving?" she asked finally.

She'd accidentally caught Averendier with a forkful of food hovering inches from his mouth (likely the first that meal to have gotten that far). He set the fork carefully back onto his plate.

"I'm hoping tomorrow," he said. "I'm sorry it's been taking so long. All that searching, and I only found one horse that I could buy."

"You don't need to find another one," Lilac said quickly. "One of those men came back just now. I saw him out my window."

Averendier's eyebrows shot up. "I didn't think any of us would see those horses again," he said quietly. "It'll help, though, with Elstar a week away."

He sighed heavily and pushed his plate to the center of the table. "Lilac, there's something I have to explain—"

"No need," Lilac cut in. She dropped the folded note on the table. "This explained everything."

Averendier picked up the note and scanned its contents. When he finished reading, he tucked the paper into his pocket. "Where did you find this?" he asked slowly.

"In the barn. It fell out of Andrald's compass when you took it from Fern. I found it on the floor just before we left."

Lilac drew a deep breath to steady her shaking voice. "Why didn't you tell me about your plan? We aren't going to be looking for each other?"

Averendier shook his head. "It'd be like looking for a needle in a haystack," he said. "Only harder."

"So you arranged a meeting place instead?" Lilac asked. It was brilliant, actually. So why couldn't she submit herself to the idea?

Because I've never been alone with a stranger in all my life. Because I'm afraid for my sisters. Because…because I know he still isn't telling me the whole truth.

Lilac bit her lip. And as long as Averendier was the keeper of that secret, she would never know more than this. She would only hold bits and pieces of the puzzle, never gaining the links to fit it all logically together.

"None of us will get desperately lost if we have a set place to meet up," Averendier explained. Obviously, he had already worked everything out in his head. Lilac had once marveled at his ability. Now it was the most frustrating thing she had ever known.

A sudden doubt struck a fearful chord in her heart.

"But what if none of the others show up?" Lilac asked. "Will they just wander aimlessly, searching for help, for the rest of their lives?"

Averendier's lips set in a grim line. "If no one shows up, we'll have to continue without them. I have a duty to all of you, but, since you're the heir to the Alinar throne, my foremost duty is to you. I must get you to Monaria. Right now, your sisters are out of my hands."

Out of his hands! What had happened to the brave young man willing to plunge into a raging blizzard for his companions' sake—for her sake?

"But what about your brother and cousin?" she faltered. "And Elvera and Isalinia? Andrald didn't even know if Isalinia was alive when he went after her. And now one of the men who captured her has returned. What does that mean?"

Averendier's expression softened a moment before he averted his eyes and stared fixedly at the table.

"I want to help them, Lilac," he said. "But I can't. I don't even know where they are. I promised your father that I would take you three to Monaria. And if I can't manage to take all of you, I will at least get one there safely."

He lifted his eyes to hers a moment; they brimmed with such defeat that everything within Lilac twisted. He had been...expecting something like this to happen, or he wouldn't have planned for it.

These are more than mere highwaymen who are after us. They're something worse—far worse. Why won't he tell me what?

The door across the room burst open and Fern rushed in, eyes wide, hands wringing her tattered apron.

"They're back!" she cried. "The men! Only this time, they're five of them!"

Lilac sprang to her feet, gasping, "Five!"

"Are you sure?" Averendier demanded sharply.

"I'm very sure," Fern answered earnestly. "They were all in the same room, dark haired, with those red-lined cloaks. Only…" The bridge of her nose wrinkled with puzzlement. "One of them had a gray cloak, and a nasty looking bird on his shoulder."

"Gray?" Averendier repeated. "That's strange. I know the others have just turned their cloaks inside-out, not very cleverly, I might add. Only Tirendrians dare to wear red cloaks."

"But the bird," Fern persisted. "It looked just like a hawk or something, like what snatches the chickens. 'Bout this big." She measured a length with her hands.

Surprise flitted across Averendier's face. "A falcon? That's new."

"Anything else?" Lilac asked.

Fern shook her head. Then she nodded, glancing timidly at Lilac. "Are you leaving soon?" she asked. Without waiting for his answer, she continued, "Whenever you do leave, will you take me with you? My house is just on the edge of town, and you can leave me there. Just please don't leave me here with these men. Goodness knows they don't have a drop of mercy in their souls. They'll make me work for them again. Please take me!"

Averendier looked questioningly at Lilac. She returned the glance sparking with command. Sighing, Averendier turned back to Fern.

"All right, you may come with us," he relented.

Fern opened her mouth to speak, but Averendier silenced her with an uplifted hand.

"We will, as long as you promise to be quiet about it. We leave at midnight. Be ready, or we go on without you."

"I won't get left, sir. Thank you!" Fern exclaimed blissfully. She darted over to Lilac to squeeze her in a quick hug. Then she rushed out of the room, wiping her wet face on the corner of her apron.

"Do you think we should trust her?" Lilac asked quietly.

Averendier turned to her, brow puckered. "She's not trying anything. We'll be safe taking her away from here. But on that note, you should probably go get some rest. We'll be riding through the night."

With a wan smile and a nod, Lilac returned to her room.

The moon was a sliver of silver shining coldly in the star-sprinkled sky. Tiny lights twinkled wherever the moonbeams touched the snow. Silence blanketed all. The only suggestions of sound were the stirring tree branches and the loose snow scudding along the wind-swept ground.

Midnight struck. Muffled sounds followed, seeming loud and distinct in the deep silence. A crossbar scraped. Metal jingled. The barn door creaked open and shut. Hooves pattered on the snow.

While the rest of the world lay wrapped deep in slumber, three people who had dared disturb the quiet mounted their horses. An admiral's son on a heavy draft horse stood beside an heiress and a scullery maid on their majestic Alinar mare.

Yet there was a fourth being awake that frosty night. A tall man, dark-haired with streaks of gray, leaned out of an open window. Silently, he watched the trio's departure. Beside him, a falcon dug its talons into the windowsill, its harsh voice silent, as if it knew its master's orders.

To wait. To watch. Then, to strike.

44

*H*ow much longer?" *Isalinia asked. Her voice shook in time* with her horse's jostling steps.

"An hour, maybe two," Andrald answered, though he wondered whether he should have answered at all. He'd learned something about Isalinia over the past forty-eight hours, something he would rather have not known.

"I'm glad, though. More time to enjoy this glorious morning!"

Andrald grinned at her sidelong. According to her, the glory of the morning wasn't the only notable thing that day. The sun was delightfully warm, the snow dazzlingly bright, the air crisp, and the sky peacock blue.

"But, of course, it will be nice to get back with the others," Isalinia continued.

Andrald frowned. She didn't know anything about the note he had left, telling Averendier to go on without him. She was not prepared for the empty rooms awaiting them, nor the missing faces. To her knowledge, the map in his pocket was non-existent. He was only backtracking to return the gray horse he had borrowed from Clane's stable.

"Then on to the north!" Isalinia sang out, oblivious of the shadow that had descended upon Andrald. "Let this snow try and stand in our way!" She playfully shook her fist at the countryside and smiled brightly at Andrald.

Andrald smiled back—he never brooded over anything for long, even if it deserved to be brooded over. Besides, smiles and laughter were highly contagious.

Thankfully, he thought, *talking isn't, or I'll have become a regular prattler by the time we get back to the others.*

"Even the horses are excited. I mean, just look at Glorien!"

Andrald patted his mount's satiny neck. "I think he's just happy to have a Tirendrian off his back," he said.

Isalinia snorted indignantly. "Of course he is! What horse wouldn't be? I know how it was. And I only had to spend a day with them—he had a whole week of captivity!"

"They probably treated him better," Andrald observed, "seeing as though the horses had to carry them."

"True," Isalinia consented. "In fact, they were arguing about just that before you rescued me. You should have heard them go on!"

"Mm-hmm."

"And imagine how it must have been for me, to have to sit there listening to them talking, not knowing when or if they were ever going to stop…"

"Oh, I can imagine," Andrald said, lips quirking.

"I'm glad you came to break it up."

"So am I."

Isalinia looked at him askance. "You know, you're awfully quiet today, Andrald. You usually talk a lot more."

"I do?" Andrald looked at her with surprise. Then he shrugged. "I guess I just can't find much to talk about right now."

"Nothing to talk about?" Isalinia flung her arms out wide. "Look around you! There's plenty!"

Andrald winced. *Why did I say that?*

"What I meant to say is we could spend our time better singing than talking," he added, stumbling over his words in his haste. Anything to escape another speech about the countryside's magnificence (or spectacular-ity, or awe-inspiring-ness, or…).

"If you'd like," said Isalinia, bobbing her head pleasantly. "It was nice last time. Would you like to start?"

"Sure." Andrald contemplated a moment (not before sending up a silent prayer of thanks for his ear's salvation), then sang a short ballad a sailor from the *Dermain's Folly* had taught him.

Isalinia smiled as she listened (though, oddly enough, her smile seemed to tilt more towards a grimace at times. Andrald wondered if she was getting a little saddle sore).

And so they sang their way until Isalinia rose in her stirrups and pointed ahead. "Look, isn't that it?" she asked, interrupting Andrald during one of his most boisterous shanties.

Andrald nodded, a lump lodging itself in the back of his throat (and not because his song had been interrupted). He was silent amid Isalinia's renewed fount of chattering as they rode up to the stable. The moment they dismounted inside the stable, he turned to Isalinia.

"Are we going to go find the others now?" she asked. However, once she saw Andrald's grave expression, a worried line etched itself between her eyebrows.

"No," he said. He shoved his hands deep into his pockets. "They aren't here, Isalinia."

"What!" Her eyes widened. "How do you know that? We haven't even been inside."

"We made a plan, a while back," Andrald began heavily. He continued to explain, as gently as he could, the route they and the others would take. As he spoke, and Isalinia realized she would only be separated from her sisters for a week, the lines of worry on her face smoothed.

"But," she said, when Andrald had finished, "if you knew about this plan, why did we come all the way back here?"

Andrald patted the flanks of the gray horse, now securely in its stall. "I had to borrow this fellow from here to come after you fast enough," he explained. "I couldn't just keep him, so back we came. And now…" He pulled a small pouch out of his pocket and bounced it lightly in his hand. "…I just have to tide Clane over with something before we leave. He's probably been wondering this whole time who took his horse."

They entered the tavern through its back door. Once inside, Andrald heard two raised voices garbling over one another. As they walked into the dining room, he put one arm protectively in front of Isalinia.

Immediately, he spotted Clane. The tavern keeper was splayed out over his spotless counter. A Northern Florenthian soldier held him by the collar of his tunic, shaking him vigorously.

"I have shackles in my belt!" the soldier was threatening. "And if you don't talk, they're going around your wrists this instant!"

"I've answered too many questions lately," spluttered Clane. Perspiration poured down his flushed face. His eyes were locked on the quiver bristling with arrows that protruded over the soldier's shoulder.

"And that's the problem," said the soldier disgustedly. "They're always the wrong answers. Here's the one you should have given to those men: no. A nice, even no. You knew exactly who they were."

"I didn't—" Clane gasped.

"Don't even try lying like that. You knew." The soldier twisted Calne's tunic in a tight fist, cutting off any protest the man might have given. "They were criminals. Tirendrians, at that. A double folly! Don't you know the penalty for treason?"

"I...I didn't...know who they were!" Clane gurgled. "They didn't give me names... or anything when they signed in. They just asked for food... and a room!"

"But I'm sure they gave you a fat purse when they checked out," growled the soldier. Nonetheless, he released Clane, letting him slide partway off the counter. Andrald marveled that the soldier had managed to hold the man's bulk for so long.

"I don't know how you manage to slip your beefy hands out of the fetters they deserve. But when I finally get you under lock and key, I'll request to be your guard. Your innocent pleas might snare anyone unaccustomed to them."

"You're too kind, Jedrick," grumbled Clane, rubbing his sore neck.

"Oh, I'm not finished with you yet," Jedrick warned. "I'm going to get one of my superiors to come and turn this place inside-out."

"You can't do that," Clane snarled. He wet his rubbery lips, his eyes darting from Jedrick's face to his numerous weapons.

"Oh, I have the authority," returned Jedrick. "And this time, I'll prove to this town what a worm you are."

"Worm!" scoffed Clane indignantly, drawing himself as straight as possible.

Jedrick's angry expression screwed in mock apology. "I'm sorry, I forgot. You're too fat to be a worm. 'Grub' would be more fitting."

Spluttering, Clane glanced to either side, as if to ensure no one had heard the insult. His beady eyes locked with Andrald's a moment. He jabbed an accusatory finger at the boy.

"There! I have witnesses!" he triumphantly exclaimed.

Jedrick glanced at Isalinia and Andrald, before turning back to Clane. "Witnesses to what?" he asked. "Calling you names? I'm sorry, did that hurt? But I've taken and dealt quite a bit of that in my time as a soldier, and I haven't seen a body booked for it yet. I *have* seen quite a few arrested for harboring criminals, especially kidnappers and murderers."

"Kidnappers?" Andrald stepped forward. "Do you mean the Tirendrians that were here?"

"*Were* here, and skedaddled just an hour ago? Yes." Jedrick spat to one side, his narrowed eyes roving over the newcomers. "But who are you to ask?" he demanded.

"We?" Taking Isalinia's wrist, which was coiled around and around with cruel, red rope burn, Andrald held it out for the soldier to see. "She's the victim of the kidnapping."

"I could have told you that from your arm alone," replied Jedrick, gesturing to Andrald's bloody, slashed sleeve.

Andrald glanced down at his wounded arm. "It looks worse than it is," he answered dismissively.

"Hmm." Jedrick grunted. "Cuts and rope burn can be gotten easily enough, though. Are you sure you aren't just trying to defend this wretch?"

"Defending?" Andrald smiled and jerked his head towards Clane, who cowered behind his counter. "I wouldn't feel safe with him if he lay dead next to me."

"That's nice," muttered Clane.

The soldier looked Andrald quickly up and down. "Huh," he said finally. "You two must be the ones he was talking about."

"He?"

"Well, if you are, you'll understand my token." Rummaging in his pocket, Jedrick withdrew something that glinted gold in the light streaming through the tavern's windows. Nestled in Jedrick's outstretched had was Andrald's compass. Andrald stared at it.

"The man who gave it to me, what did he look like?" Jedrick challenged. "If you can tell me, then the compass is yours, and I'll let you go your way."

"He looked just like me," Andrald replied. "Only taller, much taller. Name's Austain."

Jedrick nodded. "Right. That's right." He shoved the compass into Andrald's hand. "He swung by last night, told me there were some Tirendrians here that I needed to exterminate. But apparently—" he withered Clane with a glare— "they've left already, and no one has any idea where they're headed."

No one, except me.

Aloud, Andrald only said, "Thanks."

He turned to leave, then paused and strode back over to the counter. He tossed a few coins down in front of Clane. "Thanks for loaning the gray," he said.

Leaving Clane gaping, Andrald and Isalinia hurried back to the stable, where they mounted Glorien and Isalinia's horse, Snowstar. And they were off, out of Hyke's crossing and down the road. Soon they were but two dots on the hill's crest, dipping out of sight.

Also a pinprick, high above their heads, a falcon circled. It dipped once on the air current before it, too, floated out of sight.

45

Berwyn *stopped scrubbing the pot long enough to tuck a stray* strand of her brown hair back behind her ear. Beside her, Lednora paced back and forth, wringing her hands and murmuring frantically to herself. Finally, unable to bear it any longer, Berwyn clattered the pot onto a table to dry and straightened to look Lednora in the eye.

"This is enough," she said sternly. "Rumors or no rumors, I'm not going to have every helper in my kitchen fall to pieces. Especially you—I need you!"

Even as she said it, the persistent little voice in the back of Berwyn's mind whispered frantically, "But they're not rumors! They're true! They're real! It's going to happen!" Angrily, she shook it away.

"I know!" gasped Lednora. She snatched up a crude clay cup and took a long sip from it. She spluttered, and golden liquid trickled down her chin. "Too hot," she groaned.

"I've warned you about that," Berwyn reminded. Frowning, she peered into Lednora's cup. "And look! It's hardly even steeped! You can't expect it to have any effect when it isn't potent enough to do more than burn your mouth!"

"I'm sorry, Berwyn," Lednora whispered. A single tear slid down her cheek. She withdrew a step, twisting a corner of her tattered apron around her fingers.

Berwyn took a step closer to the girl. "No, I'm sorry," she said. "I just haven't been myself recently. Who can be in this place?" She thrust her hands out towards the kitchen's controlled chaos.

A few of her helpers, most of them older than she, looked at her askance, but they never ceased working, not even for a moment. Berwyn sighed inwardly, her shoulders drooping. How could she ever get them to believe she wouldn't report even the longest pause to Lord Rees? Even if she could find the words to explain her feelings, would they believe her?

Damien would know how to make them understand.

She shook her head at herself. Ever since meeting Damien that day on the road to the creek, his words had haunted her actions. She had even gone so far as to sitting up and joining the men's meetings at night. She still wasn't sure of Damien's plan. But neither did she want to seem content with her life in Kepspell—to despair of rescue or release. Especially while her father was in the thick of things.

She bit her inner lip. She had promised herself she would never think of Damien or his wild schemes while she worked. Something might slip out; then she wouldn't be able to do anything but regret.

Lednora hugged her sides fiercely. "You're not the only one who feels that way, Berwyn," she said quietly. "Do you think all of us have become as heartless as Warwick and Rees?"

"No," Berwyn admitted. "But sometimes it does feel like I'm the only one chafing under this slavery."

"Would the rumors be flying like they are if you were?" Lednora demanded, a shade too loud for comfort. Several workers darted glances in the girls' direction. Berwyn lowered her hands subtly, motioning for Lednora to quiet down. Lednora bent closer to Berwyn to continue. "The men, I've heard them planning. They want to—"

Berwyn pressed her fingers against Lednora's lips. "Not one more word. You want every soldier in this place breathing down our necks?"

Lednora shrank back, her sudden boldness shriveling into the fear relentlessly consuming her. "Oh, Berwyn! Do you think anyone heard me? Am I going to get all of us killed?"

Berwyn sighed softly and pushed the teacup across the table towards her helper. "Drink," she ordered. "Or the first person to die will be you—of hysterics."

Lednora's head jerked up, and she stared down into her tea a moment. A shy smile broke out on her face.

"You never can be serious, can you?" she wondered aloud, in a dreamy manner that made Berwyn shift uncomfortably. "The world will be crumbling around your ears, and you'll face it with a brave smile. But," she added, looking seriously at Berwyn, "it can't hold you up forever. Tears and sorrow are bitter to drink, but we must weep if we are to live. Things are coming, Berwyn. Freedom demands a bitter toll from those that seek her. We have to be prepared to smile, to cry, or none of us will be able to bear it."

She stared off distantly for a few moments, then picked up her cup and brought it to her lips. Instantly, she doubled up, choking.

"Still too hot," she spluttered.

Berwyn chuckled, rather nervously, and put an arm around Lednora's shoulders. "You all right?" she asked.

"Fine," Lednora croaked. The strange look on her face was gone. "Just don't expect me to drink any more of that."

Berwyn smiled briefly and slid the cup away. "I won't."

"*I'm sure Lednora is right*, Dad. And if Damien does carry out his plan..." Sighing, Berwyn let her head drop against her father's shoulder as they walked slowly through the twilight to their cabin. "Call me every sort of coward, but his ideas give me chills. All the danger and death they involve!"

Doctor Sirman said nothing; he only dragged his steps through the dirty snow clotting the path.

"And she thinks she's the one who's always scared, and turns to me for help. I don't deserve it, Dad. I'm probably twice as sick over this whole thing as she is."

"She is worried, Berwyn, but not because she fears what might happen, as you do," replied Doctor Sirman slowly, running his hand over his short, graying hair. It had grown longer during his imprisonment, hiding the tips of his ears and straggling down his forehead. "She fears what she knows. She witnessed many terrible things in Eastern Florenth before she was brought here.

"But you, Berwyn..." He turned his head to survey her, almost sadly. "You fear the unknown. I won't say it isn't a healthy fear. Most fear is healthy, or it wouldn't be permitted into our souls. Fear of God, Fear of evil. Even Damien Peterson fears."

He paused and took Berwyn by the shoulders, holding her an arm's length out in front of him. She winced and forced herself to meet her father's gaze. It was stern but sorrowful.

"Never do I ever want to hear my little girl calling herself a coward," he said severely. "What makes you think you are?"

Berwyn looked away. "I...I don't know," she stammered. "I just...*feel* cowardly. I don't know."

Her father's hands tightened on her shoulders. "You survived the attack on Fort Starr, didn't you? Helped to hide and destroy hospital records instead of concealing yourself from the enemy? And here, you've borne Warwick and Rees. You've handled that kitchen better than either of them thought you could. You've hidden many of your helpers' transgressions, even knowing you would be punished for it along with them were they discovered. And all through it, you've continued to heal the others."

He gave her one long, level look before drawing her against him in a strong embrace.

"I'm proud of you for all the places you have been brave," he murmured in her ear. "Bravery isn't just a thing for leaders, like Damien. Neither is it always there, like knowledge, a store just waiting to be dipped into whenever you want. Courage doesn't wash out fear or banish it forever from your heart. It's something we bring ourselves to by fighting, by doing what we know is necessary and right, even when our heart is in our throat and we're ready to die of terror. Courage—" he laid a hand on her chest— "is a choice. It's saying 'no' to fear and pushing on despite it. It's something I firmly believe is in you, Wren. It'll just take the right time to bring it out."

Berwyn gripped her father's shoulders, her face buried against his chest. She wanted to agree with him, yearned to do so with all her heart. So why this deep, gnawing emptiness within her that seemed to make her ring hollow? What if she didn't contain all the strength her father thought she did?

Pulling away, Berwyn gazed worriedly into her father's face. "But, Dad," she began, "what if—"

She was cut off by a distant shout—harsh, surprised, and commanding. Berwyn clung to her father's arm as more shouts rose in one hearty roar, like the crashing of breakers against a rocky shore.

"Dad, what is it?" she asked, darting fearful glances into the twilight. She thought she saw distant shapes moving in the fields.

Before her father could reply, the big brass alarm bell tolled. With loud, demanding crashes, it called the Tirendrian soldiers to arms.

As it continued ringing, the shouts were punctuated with screams— pitiful cries of pain that pierced to the core of Berwyn's being. She shuddered.

Doctor Sirman, without another word to his daughter, shook her off his arm and ran toward the commotion.

"Dad, no!" she screamed, stumbling after him. "Come back, don't go. Please, don't go!"

She caught the hem of his cloak and pulled back. But the weak clasp holding it at his throat snapped, leaving Berwyn with the cloak in her hands.

"I have to go!" Doctor Sirman yelled back to her. The intensifying clamor nearly drowned his voice. "Come with me, Wren. We'll face it together. They need us!"

Berwyn stood stock still, wavering, watching with a shattered heart her father running to his certain doom.

Dropping the cloak in a heap beside the path, she clenched her skirts and fled after him. Her breath shredded to sobs in her lungs, she ran, hurling herself after her father, a fleet, brown arrow hurtling towards that clash of voices and arms—the clamor of death itself, sending all scampering after it.

Just ahead of her, her father dodged around several toolsheds hulking silent in the darkness. Gasping, Berwyn staggered after him. She nearly stumbled over Lednora, who was crumpled on the ground, sobbing. Berwyn skidded to a halt and bent over her.

"Lednora! What's wrong?" she cried.

Lednora didn't look up, only rocked herself back and forth on the frozen ground and moaned.

"Lednora!" Berwyn shook her friend vigorously by the shoulder. "Lednora, are you hurt? Please, answer me!"

"Please, help them," Lendora moaned. "It's awful. Please, Berwyn. Help them, not me."

She was awfully right. Berwyn forced herself to straighten and take in her surroundings.

The fields, only just that afternoon rippling with the fresh, green sprigs of wheat, were black with a writhing, screaming mass of men. Tirendrian soldiers, with their swords and crossbows, shot and cut down anyone in their way. The prisoners of Kepspell fought back with whatever hoe, pick, shovel, axe, or weapon they had seized in their rebellion. Some valiantly sprang at their attackers, their bare fists their only defense. Blood sprayed across the dirt, watering the crop of hatred and revolt. Over the collective roar of anger, pain, and defiance, that terrible bell tolled its condemnation.

Berwyn nearly crumpled to her knees, sick. Already, so many lay dead. In just a few short minutes, they had been cut down. How precious few broke away and into the woods! How pitiably few compared to the numerous laying in a thick carpet of death upon the ground.

But she couldn't just stand here, watching them fall. Stumbling forward, her hand moved to lift the flap of her satchel. She had to help—to heal! She scanned the tumult for her father. She could not see him anywhere. She saw only red—the wounded and the dead, those fighting on, soaked with their own blood and that of their comrades and enemies, the bright scarlet of the Tirendrian's tunics and cloaks. The trampled snow lay crimson beneath their feet.

"Dad!" she screamed. The screams and crash of bows swirled around her, trampling her voice. She cast about wildly. If she could not find him, she must still tend someone, anyone!

Faint and sick, she rushed to the first person she saw stretched out on the ground. She stooped to check the man's pulse, to feel for life within him. Her eyes fell on his face. She stumbled back, a scream strangling in her throat.

Under that mask of blood and pain was the unmistakable face of Damien Peterson.

There was no pulse.

The fight around her was thinning—a general rout ensued the captives' vain attempt to break their bonds. Berwyn hurried through the midst of it all, nimbly dodging blows, hurriedly helping those she could, eyes always searching. Searching for the one face that would steady her and light the flame of courage in her heart where only coldness and sick emptiness weighed.

Finally, in that whirlpool of flame and red and darkness, she caught a glimpse of him— a gray figure stark and cool against the heat of the fight. But the sight gave her no comfort. A pained cry broke from Berwyn's lips. She dashed forward.

She ran to where he stood, bent nearly double, his arms pinioned behind his back by two soldiers. A third stood before him, preparing to run his sword through her father.

Screaming with rage, Berwyn pounced on the soldier lunging forward for the blow. She swung her satchel with all her might into the man's face.

The soldier staggered back, one hand pressed against his face. Then he whirled on her. Drawing himself to his full stocky height, the soldier pulled his hand away from his face. The buckle of Berwyn's satchel had cut a bloody trench across his right check and up over his temple.

Everything within Berwyn froze. Her father's pleas were distant, feeble echoes in her ears. She could not move. Could not breathe. Could not think.

Lord Warwick, his bleeding face contorted with rage, seized her by the arm and yanked her towards him, his sword raised. Something like a thunderbolt flashed through Berwyn—searing, flaming pain, swiftly followed by darkness.

Heavy, cutting throbs rent Berwyn's skull in two. She moaned and stirred, striving to lift one feeble hand to rub the pain out of her eyes.

"You're awake," said someone, close by.

Berwyn started, then shivered. She forced her leaden eyelids open.

Warwick bent over her, his face lurid in the light the kitchen fires cast. Berwyn nearly sat up. Kitchen fire! What was she doing in the kitchen? And why was Warwick here?

He turned, and she saw the fresh cut disfiguring his left cheek. Then she remembered and shuddered even more.

"I thought you would sleep forever, Miss Sirman," continued Warwick. His face was very close to her own. To Berwyn, squinting through her pain, it seemed unnaturally large. She reached back to touch her head; her hand came away sticky with blood.

"However, it gave me time to move your things into here," said Warwick. "Yours and your father's. *He* certainly doesn't need them anymore."

Berwyn stared and stared at him, numb with rage and grief. How could he put it so lightly? What was he doing her with her anyway? And why was she in the kitchen, and not her hut?

"What…what am I doing here?" she asked, her lips thick and heavy, her words drawling.

Warwick smiled down on her, maliciously and almost pityingly, yet with a relish that would have made Berwyn squirm if she'd had the strength.

"You forget already?" He drew back, as if surprised. "I did hit you hard. You should know better than to attack a Tirendrian officer like that. What if I *was* sticking your father full of holes? He was a rebel leader. He got what he deserved."

Berwyn's mouth screwed. How she wanted to scream and scream! But her lips and throat would not obey her. She could only use her eyes to burn this man stooping before her, until his own flashed to the challenge.

"Why…didn't you kill me…too?" she gritted.

"We already had to kill so many—we would have been short of staff," Warwick replied. "Don't think I stayed my blade out of kindness. You were defending your father, and not attacking me out of pure malice. For that, and that reason alone, we are letting you live. But you will live here, in the kitchen, working by day, sleeping by night."

He rose, towering over Berwyn and her pallet on the floor. Wincing, she pushed herself up onto one elbow.

"Never, from this point on, will you leave this building," he growled, "unless it is to the kitchen's outbuildings. You will sleep here, fix meals here, eat here. This is your home. If you ever break these rules, you will be run through without mercy. A guard will be posted here at the kitchen door at night to see that you obey."

Seizing her wrist, he wrenched up and yanked Berwyn up off the pallet. She cried out, more startled than pained, as he lifted her to her feet.

"Stand when I'm talking to you!" he barked. Warwick drew her close, closer than she ever wanted to be to him, forcing her to look him straight in his dark, sparking eyes. Hateful eyes, devouring her soul.

"I now have the power to let you live or to kill you as I see fit," he said, his voice mulling over each word, relishing them. "For now, I chose the former. But if you disobey me once, tread on the slightest rebel ground…"

He paused, his dark eyes darting over her face, searching for fear behind the misery. And it was there. Stark, paralyzing terror, as tight around Berwyn's heart as his hand around her wrist.

He smiled, ever so slightly, and flung her back. Too weak to catch herself, Berwyn fell into a table full of drying wooden dishes. She fell with them to the floor, her whole body convulsing with terror.

Warwick gazed coldly down on her a moment.

"You had better clean up that mess you made, Miss Sirman," he said. "Then go to bed. It wouldn't do for you to disobey me now."

He walked away several steps and paused at the kitchen door. "Until tomorrow," he said. Laughing quietly at the terrified look she gave him, Warwick stepped out into the night, slamming the door behind him.

46

E ngrelin pressed the heels of his hands against his eyes, as if he could shove all the weariness out of them. But it persisted, as it had for so long. He had to blink several times before he could see clearly again.

Not that there was much to see. The tiny crescent moon overhead shone faintly. The collage of stars gleamed coldly down. From where Engrelin sat slumped against a tree trunk, he could just barely see through the canopy of branches arching over him, a patch of midnight sky. And in that patch, a blue star twinkled.

Arrian.

Despite his exhaustion, Engrelin smiled. Bitter and grim perhaps, but a smile nonetheless. To him, it seemed when Lamar had given him the sword, he had inherited the star with it. There at his belt hung the weapon, there in the sky hung his guide. As long as he had the one at his side, and the other at his back, he would be able to protect Lance and Elvera and lead them safely northwards. Tipping his head back, he gazed gratefully up at the twinkling blue light.

Thanks a lot, for sticking through this with me.

Arrian twinkled back its welcome. Engrelin sighed and scrubbed a hand across his face. Now he was talking to stars. What next?

At least he didn't have to please it, like Elvera and Lance. Among her many frustrating stunts over the past week, the girl had refused to eat any of the meat Engrelin had caught on the road. (Lance, as usual, had sided with Elvera and refused to eat the meat as well.) He'd stopped hunting. Whatever he might have caught would have been wasted. Engrelin still had quite a few dried strips of it stowed away in his pack.

He stifled a groan in his hand. Lance grew more and more difficult to handle with each passing day. He never agreed with Engrelin, and only occasionally with Elvera (and only when she opposed Engrelin). Lance refused to get up when told and lagged throughout the day's march. It was a wonder that they had gotten so far in a week.

Engrelin hugged his knees to his chest. It was getting harder and harder to rein in his own tongue and temper. He pressed his forehead against his knees. Why had he been the one stranded with the two difficult people in the group? It ought to have been Averendier. Elvera might actually have listened to him, and he would have been able to keep Lance at bay. Yes, it should have been Averendier.

Immediately, Engrelin jerked the thought aside, struggling to bury with it the self-pity threatening to overwhelm him. No, he couldn't wish this on his cousin. On anyone. This would drive the calmest person insane.

But Elstar was only a few miles away. The thought was like a drowning man's first breath above water. At that moment, Elstar meant to him all the relief and friendliness in the world. If he only pushed through one more day…

If. Smiling wryly, he stiffly lowered himself to the ground, tucking one arm under his head to cushion it. This whole journey, ever since they had left Bryn, had been chock full of *if*'s. One way or another, they had all turned out well in the end. Why wouldn't this work just as well?

Why not? he thought thickly, letting his heavy eyelids sink shut. His whole body ached from exertion and lack of sleep. Except for the occasional doze snatched here and there, he hadn't slept at all. Now he might manage to get some in before—

"Psst! Engrelin?"

Someone grabbed his shoulder and shook it. Slowly, Engrelin forced his eyes open a crack. Blearily, he squinted up at the form bending over him. A stray lock of black hair swept against his check. He brushed it away and scrubbed his forehead hard.

"Elvera?" This was new. Despite his sleepless nights, Engrelin had always been the first one awake each morning. "Is something wrong?"

"No," Elvera answered. "I was just wondering if we're going to leave soon."

"Leave? Now?" Engrelin pushed himself up on one elbow. "But I can hardly see a thing."

"It's getting lighter over there, somewhere," replied Elvera. She waved towards the murky east. Engrelin's mouth twisted doubtfully. If there was any lightening of dawn, he couldn't see it.

"Besides," Elvera added, "you're always screaming for us to get up. If we're going to reach Elstar by this afternoon, we might as well get going now."

Oh, that's really what this is all about, Engrelin inwardly grumbled. There went his last chance for any sleep. Elvera would not leave him alone until he was up. Sitting up slowly, Engrelin ran his hand through his hair, rumpling it impossibly. He drew a deep breath, wincing as the sharp winter air cut his lungs.

"Lance is not going to like this," he warned as he struggled to his feet. He swayed uncertainly and reached out to the tree to steady himself.

"You mean *you're* not happy," Elvera snapped. "I don't care how you feel. We're getting up and going, right now." She flounced away to pull some sort of breakfast together.

Sighing, Engrelin fumbled to fasten his cloak clasp at his throat. There had to be some way to sweeten her dour personality. Hopefully, meeting back up with her sisters would make her more amiable. It seemed like nothing he did helped—being cheery, ignoring her, or even agreeing with her. Yet again, she seemed to have sworn enmity against him the moment she had set her dark, spiteful eyes on him. He couldn't do much more than wait and hope her mood would blow over.

"Breakfast is ready right over here," Elvera yelled through the predawn. "Get it now or go hungry!"

Hunched cozily beneath his thick cloak, Lance groaned. He rolled over into a more comfortable position.

"Stop shouting," he muttered. "It's the middle of the night. Can't a fellow get any sleep?"

"For your information, it's morning. The sun is up," snipped Elvera, not truthfully. She clattered several of her belongings together.

Lance's whole body jerked rigidly upright. He scowled blackly at the princess.

"And yes, I have to shout," she added, nose in the air. "It's the only way to get anything I say through either of your skulls."

"Oh, whatever." Lance curled back up, setting his back to Elvera.

Gritting his teeth, Engrelin strode over to where Elvera crouched at her meal preparations.

"Do you have to talk like that this early?" he demanded, an edge to his voice. "He's going to be a huge pain for the rest of the day."

"Why should I bother?" Elvera shrugged. "He's not my problem."

Engrelin sucked in a sharp breath. *Because it would make things a whole lot easier right now.*

Elvera picked up a bowl and offered it to him. "Here, eat this."

Eat it! Engrelin pressed his lips tightly together. Eating was the last thing on his mind right now. His stomach was hopelessly tangling.

Elvera glared at him. "What? Is it not good enough for you?"

"No—" Engrelin began. He dealt himself a mental slap. "I mean, yes, it's good enough for me, but I don't want it right now, thanks. I still have some of that rabbit left to finish off."

"Eating food like that, it's no wonder you've lost your appetite for good things," sniffed Elvera. She turned her back to him.

You really want to know what's making me lose my appetite—and my sanity—right now? The words hovered tantalizingly on Engrelin's lips, but he only clamped his mouth shut and stalked away to rouse Lance. Forget the rabbit.

After more difficulties, Engrelin finally managed to get his little group up and moving. Anxious to rejoin her sisters, Elvera was fairly cooperative that morning. Lance also behaved well (for Lance). Engrelin had to threaten only once to leave him behind before the sullen prisoner rose for the day. Shouldering their packs, the three set off through trees, working their way through the brush and branches to the road.

"Ouch!" Elvera exclaimed. "That branch just hit me!" She promptly yanked her skirt free of a clinging thorn vine.

Lance smirked. "Welcome to the North," he intoned sarcastically. "Home of needle trees, swinging branches, and skirt-snagging vines."

Huffing, Elvera freed herself and marched determinedly forward, only to trip on an exposed root and pitch headlong into a spiny devil's walking stick. While Lance snickered, Engrelin bent to help Elvera to her feet.

"You all right?" he asked the princess, quickly surveying her few scratches.

Elvera jerked her hand out of his. "Get off," she hissed. "I'm fine, and I don't need your help." Lightly sprinkled with snow, Elvera plunged forward along the broken path, her head high. Engrelin turned his head just long enough to catch Lance's smirk. Jaw tight, he pushed on after Elvera.

They soon broke out of the trees. The road stretched out in front of them. The passing of many feet and carts had worn muddy, slushy ruts on either side of the road. Engrelin guided his charges to the one side of the road, where some solid snow remained. For hours they tramped down the road, each step bringing them closer and closer to their companions.

As noon approached, Engrelin broke up yet another of Lance and Elvera's petty arguments and steered them off the road and into a copse of trees to eat a hurried dinner.

"We've got about six more miles to go," he said, after a few moment's silence (in which Lance and Elvera glared at each other openly). "Maybe less. That's about a two hour's walk."

"Two hours!" Elvera groaned. "That's ages! My feet are already killing me."

"You're the early bird," said Lance, raising his hands, which had been untied so that he could eat. (He still hadn't forgiven the girl for being roused early.)

"We wouldn't be this close right now if I hadn't," Elvera sniffed in reply.

"Two hours or two hundred," Engrelin interjected, "all that matters is getting there safely."

"No one is safe with him around," retorted Elvera, flinging her hands at Lance. Exasperated, she turned on Engrelin. "So much for protecting me. You've left his hands untied, for goodness sake!"

"Hey, I'm not doing anything!" protested Lance. He held his empty hands up.

Engrelin swallowed a mouthful of dried meat before he answered. "He can't eat with his hands tied." He took a concluding bite of biscuit.

"Feed him yourself," Elvera retorted.

His face contorted with disgust, Lance took a step away from the princess. "What is wrong with you?" he demanded incredulously. "If anyone tried that, I'd…I'd bite their fingers off!"

"Which is exactly why I haven't tried it," concluded Engrelin.

"Better Engrelin's fingers than mine," Elvera snorted, slapping her hands onto her hips. "Though, Lance, if you feel like biting things off, why don't you start with your tongue? Then I wouldn't have to listen to you blabber."

"I'd just write what I wanted to say," returned Lance. He smiled side-long at Engrelin. "Though, with your edu—"

Engrelin squeezed Lance's arm hard, cutting him off mind-word.

"Not one word about that, Lance," he whispered harshly. "Not. One. Word. Or I'll gag you for real."

"You're too kind," Lance muttered. "So saintly."

The muscles in Engrelin's jaw tightened. "I never wanted any of this, and you know that," he muttered, as he wrapped the ropes back around Lance's wrists. "Besides," he added, "there's a limit to how far anyone will let their prisoners go." Throwing Lance's cloak over his bound hands, he nudged him towards the road. "It's time to move on now."

Though she complained excessively, Elvera pushed bravely through the last two miles to Elstar. Lance was a different story. Someone must have pushed a defiance pill into his food when Engrelin wasn't looking. Lance dragged his feet with each step, waded through the slushy ruts, and once stood stock still at the roadside to contemplate a fallen branch half-submerged in snow. Blood boiling, Engrelin stalked over to Lance and yanked him out of his meditation on rotting wood.

"Do you have to do this?" Engrelin demanded, exasperated.

Throwing his head back, Lance dragged against Engrelin's grip as he was propelled forward. "Yes," he muttered.

Engrelin scowled. For the rest of the walk, he had to march behind Lance and give him a prompting shove every five steps.

By late afternoon, Engrelin caught glimpses of the city's tall, thatched roofs. The battlements of Wilelm's fortress towered over all. They began to pass people on the road so frequently, Engrelin pulled his group into a thicket for some quick instructions.

"Stay close to me," he said. "This place is huge. Don't ask anyone any questions, and don't answer if anyone asks you." Engrelin eyed Lance and Elvera levelly, hoping they were listening.

"When will we get something to eat?" Elvera whined. "I'm starving."

Lance stared at her. "We just ate."

"Soon," Engrelin interrupted. "We'll eat soon, Elvera. But I want to look around a bit first. After that, we'll find a tavern to eat at and spend the night in. If we can't find a suitable one, I know someone who lives near here. We might stay with them, though it's a long walk."

"As long as I don't have to sleep in the streets like a beggar," Elvera grumbled.

Had he just imagined it, or had Elvera just agreed with him? Engrelin stared at Elvera a moment, his mouth quirking in a small smile. He'd begun to think it was impossible.

"One more thing," he added, frowning at Lance. "No backtalk, messing around, or arguing with Elvera. Do not do anything that will cause a scene."

Lance opened his mouth to retort. Engrelin silenced him with an uplifted hand.

"If you do attract attention, and get yourself arrested," he warned, "don't blame me."

Lance tensed, an all too familiar gleam in his eyes. "Fine," he muttered, hanging his head. Then, so quietly that Engrelin barely heard him, "But you'll pay for it. Later."

47

You call this a capital?" Elvera demanded. She took odd, sideways steps to match Engrelin's weaving gait through the people clotting the street.

"Yes," Engrelin answered, brushing his hair away from his forehead.

"Methicayn has marble arches over all the streets and gold gilding and reflection pools and—"

"Alinar isn't called 'the Jewel of Ontaria' for nothing," Engrelin agreed, cutting her short. He put a firm hand on Lance's shoulder as they passed through a knot of villagers, who were so caught up in a furious debate, they didn't notice the disturbance. Engrelin frowned deeply. "Not much gold and marble here," he muttered. "It's probably best if we shut our mouths about it."

"Nothing here but mud and reeds," put in Lance cheerfully.

"I'd noticed," Elvera observed dryly as she stepped around an icy puddle. "They're on top of all the homes. Why?"

"To keep the rain out," Engrelin said. Shouldn't that have been obvious?

Elvera snorted. "Even the poor in Alinar have tile or shingle roofs."

"Thatch is cheaper," Engrelin explained. "And easier to lay than tile."

"They catch fire easily," Lance added.

"Do these taverns have thatch roofs?" Elvera demanded suspiciously.

Engrelin inwardly bit his lip. "Yes, they do, but—"

"I won't sleep in one." Elvera glared at Engrelin. "Try catching me in a burning house ever."

"It'd be a beautiful thing to behold," mumbled Lance.

Elvera's eyes bulged.

Shaking his head, Engrelin led them onto a tavern's porch. "We've got to go in here," he said. "I have to ask about something."

Elvera squinted up at the roof. "Is that made of that thatch stuff?"

Engrelin restrained a sigh. "Yes, it is," he said. "But I promise you, it's not going to burn any time soon."

"You don't know that."

"I do. I lived ivv6rmmrfy   z n a house with a thatch roof all my life," Engrelin argued. "It never caught fire."

Elvera, not in the least convinced, marched smartly down the porch steps and back out into the street. Once safely on the cobblestones, she turned to face Engrelin.

"I'm not going in," she said.

"If you to stay out there, Lance will have to be with you," Engrelin threatened.

To his astonishment, Elvera lifted her head defiantly. "Fine," she said. "I'll stay out here with him."

Engrelin stared at her in dismay. He couldn't leave her out here with Lance! Yet he couldn't leave her outside alone. Who knew what she would do?

"I'll be an angel," Lance promised.

Engrelin fixed him with a look. "I know exactly how angelic you can be, Lance Smith," he growled. "And if you ever decide to move one inch out of your sanctity, I'm bundling you off to Wilelm's men for horse theft and attempted murder."

Lance's smirk shifted to a frown; he scuffed his feet on the floorboards. "I'll wait with her by the stairs," he muttered sullenly.

Reaching quickly under Lance's cloak, Engrelin tested by touch the tightness of his prisoner's bonds. Lance wouldn't be wriggling out of those any time soon. Still uneasy, he let Lance join Elvera on the street. Engrelin whispered a prayer under his breath.

Once inside, he approached the long serving counter, where the tavern-keeper stood, scribbling furiously inside an old ledger. The man glanced up when Engrelin entered, then looked back down.

"We're full," he said mechanically. "Sorry for the inconvenience."

"I don't want a room," Engrelin replied.

The man held up one finger, signaling Engrelin to wait. He was suddenly conscious of Arrian pressing against his left leg, as if it had grown heavier. As subtly as he could, Engrelin tucked his cloak around it. As he did, he noticed faint blue light seeping through the top of the leather sheath. He breathed a silent groan. *No, don't glow. Not again...*

Desperate to draw his attention from his sword, Engrelin glanced quickly around the dining area. Dark wooden beams stretched across the ceiling, supporting the rooms above. Sunlight streamed through the windows, sending ribbons of light through the large room and striping the rows of tables and benches, and a small portion of floor that had been cleared for dancing. The logs in the fireplace burned low. Despite the early hour, three men sat at a table close to the fire.

The plunk of the tavern-keeper setting his pen down on the counter recovered Engrelin's attention. The man seemed slightly disgruntled (no doubt because Engrelin had insisted on staying even when he had been told there were no vacancies). But when their eyes met, the look switched remarkably to one of subtle pleasure.

"Well now," said the man. Planting his palms down on the countertop, he leaned back. "What can I do for you?"

"I'm looking for a man," Engrelin replied. "He's very tall, blond, and gray eyed. Have you seen him?"

"Nope." The man shook his head, though his eyes never left Engrelin's face. "I couldn't tell, so many people come in and out of here."

"You'd know him," Engrelin insisted. "This guy has to duck doorways. Name's Austain."

"Nope," the man said again. He brushed a hand over his meticulously combed hair and swept his arm out, gesturing towards the men sitting at the table. "My turn to ask you a question," he said. "Any of them look familiar to you?"

Engrelin glanced at the men. They were all fair skinned, with jet-black hair. Two had their cloaks, strangely lined with dark red, slung over the bench beside them. They were streaked with weather stains. They'd been traveling a while. The other still wore his cloak, only his was gray. On his shoulder perched a falcon. It cocked its head and blinked its sharp eyes at Engrelin.

"No," Engrelin said slowly. "I've never seen any of them before."

"That's funny." The man looked at Engrelin askance and scratched behind one large, red ear. "They're looking for you."

Engrelin started and stared hard at the tavern-keeper. "Looking…for me," he echoed flatly.

The man shrugged. "That's what they told me. They asked me, just today, if I'd seen a northerner with brown hair and strange blue eyes. Now, you've got the hair, and the darkest blue eyes I've ever seen. Strangely dark, if I may say so."

Engrelin's heart rose in his throat and nearly choked him.

"They also said you carried a large sword." The man's gaze darted to Engrelin's waist. Engrelin nearly snatched Arrian's hilt, but he restrained his hand just in time. His heart hammered against his ribs. *Please, don't glow. Whatever you do, don't let him see you glow!*

"That's kind of a funny way to identify someone," Engrelin said with a short laugh (which he knew wasn't convincing). "Most of the people around here have some sort of knife or sword right now."

"True," the man admitted. The man spoke reluctantly, having seen the tip of Arrian's sheath poking from beneath Engrelin's cloak. Then he brightened. "But there's no harm in calling one of them over here to be sure."

Before Engrelin could protest, the tavern-keeper leaned past the counter and yelled, "Hey, Linford! Come over here a moment?"

The man in the gray cloak glanced up and climbed to his feet. After handing his falcon to one of his companions, he approached the counter, tugging a leather glove off his hand.

"Linford," said the tavern-keeper, motioning to Engrelin, "this young man has just approached me to ask about his…" he groped.

"My cousin," Engrelin said quickly. "Austain. I'm Aaron. I was supposed to meet my cousin around here yesterday." He forced himself to meet Linford's eerily serene gaze. "Maybe you've seen him, or heard him asking about me? He's tall and blond."

"No," Linford said quietly. His voice was low and pleasant, yet the sudden intensity that sprung up in his eyes sent a shiver slithering down Engrelin's spine. "I arrived just yesterday," Linford continued. "I must have missed him. I'm sorry."

"Rats," Engrelin muttered, looking down. A faint reminiscence tugged his memory. He couldn't place it, but he was sure he had heard Linford's voice before.

"Yes, about his cousin," the tavern-keeper cut in. "Anyway, Linford, I thought he might be the boy you were looking for."

Linford hesitated. Engrelin caught his breath and prayed deep in his heart.

"No," the man said finally, his answer gliding smoothly from his lips. "He's not quite it."

The look he gave Engrelin said otherwise.

"Too bad," murmured the tavern-keeper, his voice tinged with sincere regret. "It was a good shot, though." He shrugged to himself.

"It happens." Linford nodded, still watching Engrelin closely.

A floodgate of memories slammed open. Engrelin nearly expected Linford to comment on how headstrong lads Engrelin's age were. This man had been in Lance's company of highwaymen! More than highwaymen, he realized, thinking of the red-lined cloaks. Tirendrians.

There was no doubt Linford recognized him. And Lance stood just outside with Elvera. He had to get back out there!

The tavern-keeper, meanwhile, twitched his fingers impatiently. "Well," he said brusquely, "if there's anything I can help you with…"

Engrelin sprang on the opportunity. "Actually, there is something," he said.

The man bowed slightly. "I am here to serve."

"Could you give me a list of other taverns in the area?" Engrelin asked. "I want to look for my cousin and find a place to spend the night."

"Sure."

The man rattled off a score of names and directions, ticking them off on his spindly fingers as he spoke. Engrelin fished as many names out of the flood as he could. Even as he did, he watched Linford out of the corner of his eye. To Engrelin's satisfaction, Linford was absorbed with the tavern-keeper's list. He too was locking the mentioned tavern names away in his memory.

Listen away, Linford. Just try and find me.

"That's about it," the tavern-keeper concluded, folding his arms on the countertop.

"Thanks," Engrelin said. He added conspicuously, "Mind if I use the back way out?"

Smiling, the man threw his hands up. "By all means!"

"Thanks again," Engrelin said. He crossed the room at an even pace, heading for the unlit hallway that led to the back. Once inside the hallway, he flattened himself against the wall.

"Here it is, Ramon," he heard Linford whisper. Coin's clinked, passed from Linford's hands to Ramon's. Leather soles tapped against the floor as Linford returned to his table. Breathing thinly, Engrelin edged closer to the doorway, trusting the shadows to hide him.

"What should we do, Captain?" asked a hushed voice, close by.

"Wait a few minutes," Linford replied quietly. "Then go out through the back and pick up the boy's trail. We're not going to lose them this time."

Them. They knew about Elvera. Engrelin backed away from the doorway and quietly drew Arrian, just in case. Its blade shone bright blue. Engrelin muttered and shielded the glowing blade with his cloak. *Why won't you cut this out?* he wondered as he walked down the hallway. *And at the weirdest moments.* First in Lamar's rooms, then in the cave with the taegr and Lance. And now here?

Engrelin watched the sword closely. To his surprise, the farther down the hallway he moved, the dimmer the blade shone. Engrelin stopped and stood stock still. The blue light neither increased nor decreased. Frowning, Engrelin retraced a few steps. Immediately, the blade glowed more brightly. Engrelin stared down at Arrian. What was it doing? It had started glowing the moment he had stepped into a tavern, a tavern where the keeper had been bribed by a Tirendrian. Had it known…

It's just a sword, he told himself firmly, sheathing it as he walked out the back door. *It's not like it can sense danger or anything.*

But the doubt gnawed.

"What are we doing?" Elvera demanded. She stood in the doorway of the tavern room Engrelin had just rented.

Engrelin didn't respond. He pulled a few things out of his pack and stuffed them into his pockets before he set his pack down on the bed with finality. He'd probably never see it again. He couldn't risk coming back to retrieve it. Though he had rented this room in a tavern close to Wilelm's castle, it wasn't for sleeping in.

Even as he stood there, Linford's men were following Engrelin's weaving path of tavern visiting. They would end up here, find his name in the tavern's ledger, and come upstairs to trap them.

But they would find the rooms empty. By the time Linford realized what had happened, Engrelin's trail would have grown cold.

Or so he hoped.

"Engrelin, why rent this room and then keep looking around?" Elvera asked, her hands again set on her hips. It was her favorite position for her hands (aggravatingly enough).

Engrelin straightened. "Let's just have one last look for the others," he said quietly. "We won't be in town too long. The sun will set soon."

Elvera scowled. "Couldn't we just wait here for them to find us?"

"No," Engrelin replied starkly. Her words struck him as strangely foreboding. They had to get out of here. To walk around town for a while, then slip out the city gates before they closed and start down the road.

To visit Aunt Ruth.

Engrelin knew he couldn't tarry in town any longer, not with Linford on the prowl. Aunt Ruth could read. The books she kept standing neatly on shelves in her house were burned in Engrelin's memory. She could help him plot out the rest of his trip to Bryn.

His guilt nagged mercilessly. He could always ask Elvera for help. But even if she did agree to read the names of the towns on the map, it wouldn't be without a tongue lashing and a whole lot of criticism. Besides, she would ask too many questions. She didn't need to know the dark secrets lurking behind this journey. Or of Engrelin's illiteracy. She had little enough trust in him already.

Engrelin bit his lip and fingered the map in his pocket. At that moment, Lance and Elvera began bickering in the corridor outside the room. Engrelin shut his eyes briefly. And he had been aching so for the relief that today had promised…

Engrelin cast one final glance at his pack lying slumped on the bed before he exited the room, closing the door softly behind himself.

48

Lilac drew a deep breath, then sighed and settled further down in her saddle. The fresh, clean night air washed over her in refreshing waves. She gazed quietly around the moonlit landscape bobbing in her vision as Starlight trotted steadily beneath her. It was Lilac's third time riding through the night, but the thrill of it was still as fresh as the first. It was so quiet, so peaceful, so beautiful.

Of course, that was not why she loved it so dearly. That, she would never tell anyone. Smiling, she swept her gaze over the gently sloping hills, blanketed in thick, glistening snow. How strongly it resembled Alinar's dunes under the moonlight!

Her smile shifted to a frown. Her home and her sisters—both had been growing on her mind during the past week. Were Isalinia and Elvera all right? Had Andrald managed to rescue Isalinia? Would she ever see either of them again?

Lilac pressed her curved knuckles against her lips. She needed to stop torturing herself with these unanswerable questions. Unanswerable, at least, until they reached Elstar. And that was only a few hours' time. Yet coming face to face with the truth was almost more frightening than questions left unanswered. What if her fears proved more than mere fancy?

Starlight nickered softly, releasing steamy breath into the frosty air. Averendier's horse, Ymwroli, shook his great head and whinnied back.

Lilac patted her horse's neck to quiet it. Tonight, they were to ride in silence.

Again, Ymwroli raised his head and whinnied.

"Hush." Averendier's soft reprimand floated through the darkness, followed by a string of gentle, whispered nonsense. Lilac watched him wonderingly. Ymwroli, the horse Averendier had managed to purchase at Hyke's Crossing, was unlike any horse she had ever seen. Strong and tall, with a glistening brown coat and long white feathering fringing each hoof. Though gentle as a kitten, the horse was a giant. Lilac preferred to admire him from a distance.

"Lilac," Averendier whispered.

Lilac pulled her steed up beside Averendier's. "Yes?"

"See the moon rising?" he pointed.

Lilac glanced at the horizon and nodded. The sickle moon was just crowning the distant mountains. "Yes, I see," she said.

"Once it's overhead, we'll stop to eat," Averendier said. "Until then, we'll keep following the road."

Lilac looked out at the winding ribbon of road, most of it churned into a muddy slush by the passing of many people, animals, and carts.

"All right," she said softly.

Averendier clucked softly to Ymwroli and kicked his heels into the giant's sides. Lilac nudged Starlight forward and followed Averendier down the hillside.

Hour melted into hour beneath the star-filled sky as the horses trotted down the road. After a while, Starlight nickered with impatience. Lilac stroked the mare's neck soothingly. The pace was growing monotonous. She snuck a glance at Averendier, then looked straight ahead, veiling a smile. There was no one around that she could see—not a farm for miles. Why shouldn't they have a little fun?

As they rounded a bend in the road, Lilac kicked her heels against Starlight's sides. Whinnying with joy, her mount sprang into a canter. Lilac bent low over her horse's neck. She scrunched her shoulders as the wind whistled past. Her hair fell loose of its braid and streamed out behind her like a golden banner. The wind whipped through it, waving long strands about Lilac's face and mingling with Starlight's flying mane.

Out of the corner of her eye, Lilac saw Averendier urging Ymwroli into a gallop. Despite his size and seeming clumsiness, the huge horse flashed its hooves and surged forward with surprising grace and agility.

"Come on! We can't let them catch up, Starlight!" Lilac exclaimed in her mare's ear. As if her horse had understood her, Starlight burst forward, stretching out to her full speed.

Joy bubbled like a lively spring within Lilac as the countryside flashed by. She had wanted to do this for so long! To feel the air rushing past. To know that she was not merely riding, but flying— soaring down the road!

A shout of triumphant laughter rang out beside her. Averendier?

Lilac risked twisting her head around just as Ymwroli thundered up beside her. Their steeds galloped neck to neck, stretched out, straining, running, full flight! Lilac laughed and flashed Averendier a smile. His eyes sparkled back, brilliant with moonlight and exhilaration, smiling more than his grave lips ever would.

For several miles, they pounded down the road, until the horses finally tired and lagged. Lilac, completely out of breath, chuckled between gasps. Neither she nor Averendier said a word until the moon was high overhead and they slipped off their steeds to eat. One word would have shattered the spell the ride had woven over them.

"That was wonderful," Lilac breathed as she tethered Starlight to a tree branch.

Averendier glanced at her and just as quickly averted his eyes. "I'm glad you liked it," he returned quietly.

Lilac smiled and tilted her head back to gaze up at the moon for one long moment. Maybe some of the old tales were true—the moon was truly bewitching. No matter how stoic Averendier was now, she had heard him laugh, laugh for the pure joy of living. Her smile sweetened, and she locked the memory away deep in her heart.

Morning dawned, burgundy clouds burning against a backdrop of gold. Lilac saw something sparkling in the distance, mixing with the brilliancy of the sunrise.

"Averendier, what's that?" she asked, pointing.

Drawing up beside her, Averendier followed her gaze. "That's the river that runs through Elstar," he replied. "Wilelm's keep is on an island in the river's center. We're getting close."

"That sounds beautiful," Lilac murmured, her eyes fixed on the glittering distance.

Averendier smiled knowingly. "It is, in its own way," he said. "But I don't think this city is quite what you're expecting."

Averendier was right. As Lilac had read in several books, Elstar was the largest and grandest city in Northern Florenth. She had to admit, it *was* large. But this was nowhere near her idea of grand. Alinar was graced with open streets, elegant arches over walkways, and hidden gardens scattered tastefully throughout. Here, the sky was blotted out by the upper stories of buildings jutting out over the street. The roads were paved with rough stone. There wasn't a plant in sight, though empty window boxes suggested flowers during a warmer season. Mud, filth, and garbage lay underfoot. Ragged children and animals roamed freely about. Lilac clutched her skirt to keep it from dragging through the puddles and stepped around a hog rooting through a filthy rut.

"Shouldn't we have kept the horses?" she asked Averendier, who walked briskly beside her.

"No," he answered. "They're best in the livery for now. It's too crowded in the streets to ride them through."

"It would have raised us above all this muck," Lilac quietly observed.

Averendier pressed his lips in a tight line, as if raising himself above the crowd was the last thing he wanted to do. Lilac bit her lip, frustrated. He had his reasons, and she knew they must be good. So why didn't he tell her? It seemed no amount of gentle prodding would produce the answers she craved.

"Did you set up a specific meeting place here?" she asked, edging around her last comment.

"No." Averendier rubbed the back of his neck slowly. "We probably should have. But none of us know this place well. I'm better with coastal towns."

Lilac glanced swiftly at him. Never had he sounded so tired. She wanted to think it was because of all the night riding.

"We're just going to stop at every tavern we come across and ask about the others there," Averendier continued. "They're probably doing the same thing. If we're lucky, we'll run into each other."

If they were lucky. Lilac's mouth went as dry as the deserts of her homeland. Wasn't he sure of ever finding them? A huge knot tied itself in the back of her throat, securing the terrible question rising within her. Had he never expected reunion at all? Had he just been saying that to comfort her?

Frowning, Lilac glanced upwards. Painted signs swayed in front of each shop, each displaying an assortment of different symbols and designs. Hardly any of them contained any writing. How to know where to look first?

Averendier led her confidently down the street until they reached a building with a steaming teapot on its sign. Averendier veered off the street and into the building.

The light aroma of tea wafted inside the tavern. Lilac sniffed quietly. She could easily have drunk the air.

After glancing once around the room, Averendier made a beeline for the serving counter. Lilac glanced at the sign that hung precariously below the countertop. It read 'No Board' in large letters, with something in another language printed just above it. Lilac assumed it meant the same thing as the words below.

The man standing behind the counter clacked his fingernails impatiently on the countertop.

"What do you need?" he asked gruffly.

"Any chance you've met any men named Aaron, Everen, or Adrian?" Averendier asked.

The man flung his hands up in the air. "What are you taking me for, a busybody? I'm not asking every Tom who comes in here what his name is. As long as he pays me for what he eats, I couldn't care less."

"Thanks for your trouble," said Averendier, backing away from the counter. Lilac exited with the frowning Averendier.

"Are they all like that?" she asked, once they were outside.

Averendier glanced at her. "I've seen worse," he said. "But I've seen better."

They spent the whole morning wandering the streets of Elstar, entering each tavern they came across. But no matter the name of the place, the shape of the building they entered, or the assortment of food served within, their answers never varied. No. No one had heard or seen anyone named Aaron, Everen, or Adrian.

At noon, Averendier bought Lilac some dinner to tide her over, but her stomach was so knotted, she nearly lost anything she forced down her throat. Where were her sisters and the boys? Would they ever find one another in this massive city?

Towards sunset, Lilac found herself standing outside of a tavern Averendier had insisted on entering alone. (He hadn't given any reasons why, but the raucous music and laughter pouring out of the open door was explanation enough.) Lilac refrained from pointing out that if he was making her stay out, Engrelin or Andrald probably wouldn't have entered at all.

Sighing, she leaned up against the tavern's porch railing and watched the sun sink low behind Wilelm's fortress, turning the surrounding river deep vermillion. Wilelm's keep sulked gray and foreboding against the flaming sky. An impenetrable fortress, no doubt. But so cheerless. She couldn't see a living soul crossing the large arched bridge that spanned the river, though dozens of gray-clad soldiers milled in front of the gate and on the battlements, as if they expected an attack at any moment. A sudden chill coiled through Lilac.

The door behind her slammed. Lilac jumped and whirled. Averendier stalked down the tavern steps, scowling blackly. An explosion of boisterous laughter from the tavern trailed after him.

Lilac raised an eyebrow in question.

Averendier only shook his head, his face twisted with disgust. "No luck," he said shortly. "But even if they had been there, no one could tell me. Wasn't a man in there who wasn't stone drunk. I don't even know why I entered."

"Because neither of us want to miss finding them," Lilac answered quietly. "And we didn't. There must be other places we can try."

Averendier nodded and brushed his hand quickly over his hair. "There are. This city is bursting with taverns. And that's the problem."

Lilac tried to recall all the different places where they had inquired. At least seven taverns, along with four or five herbalists and grocers, and even a few liveries. They had walked giant circles around the city all day, and to no avail.

"Might as well try that one next," said Averendier. He motioned to another tavern just across the street from where they stood.

They crossed the road over to it much more easily than before; most of the people previously crowding the streets had already returned to their homes for the night.

Lilac hadn't realized how dark it had grown outside until she stepped into the lamp-lit tavern. She blinked in the seeming brightness as she followed Averendier across the room.

"Do you take board?" Averendier asked the man who was busily wiping down one of the long trestle tables that spanned the room.

"We're full," answered the man, flailing his rag at Averendier. It snapped smarty, spilling crumbs out onto the floor.

"I don't want a room," Averendier said. He took a step closer to the man, who had straightened and eyed him sharply.

"You're the second person to say that to me today," he said.

"I am?"

Lilac searched Averendier's face for any trace of excitement or interest, but there was none. Her own heart had taken a sudden dive into a pool of hope—she struggled to fish herself out of it. They hadn't found the others yet. The man could be talking about anyone. Maybe he was just irritated about all the people who entered his business asking about the availability of rooms even though they didn't intend to rent one.

"Sure as I'm alive, you're the second chap," the man continued. Dropping his rag onto the table, he wiped his hand on his apron and reached out to grasp Averendier's heartily. "You must be this Aaron's cousin. You've got the height."

Averendier looked blankly at the man, though Lilac noticed the muscles around his jaw had relaxed.

"Aaron?" the man suggested hopefully. "I know it's a common name, but it's the only one the boy gave me." When Averendier made no move of recognition, the man sighed. "He's young, average height, with peculiar dark blue eyes?"

Lilac's gaze sharpened on the man's face. Aaron was obviously Engrelin's alias. The man couldn't mean anyone but Engrelin—he had the darkest blue eyes she had ever seen, almost the color of navy silk, only brighter, more crystal. Did this mean Engrelin and Elvera had been here?

"So, you've finally found my cousin," Averendier said. "Is he here?"

"No, I'm afraid he left over an hour ago," the man replied, scratching behind one ear. "I didn't have room for him either. But he was asking about you—seemed mighty eager to find you. Took off like a shot once I told him about some of the other taverns in town."

"Was anyone with him?" Lilac asked anxiously. Her hopeful flutter was quickly slowing to a sickening churn.

"As far as I saw, he was alone," the man said.

Lilac clenched her skirt and said nothing.

Averendier glanced briefly at her. "Do you know where he went?" he asked the keeper.

"Like I said, I gave him the names and directions to some of the best taverns around town," the man answered. "But he left by the back door, so I couldn't say which he likely went to first."

"Which taverns did you suggest?" Averendier asked.

The man immediately rattled off a list of names, but Lilac hardly heard one. Engrelin, at least, had made it here. But what about Elvera? And Lance? Had something happened to them along the way? Were they lost, or... She couldn't bring herself to think of any other possibilities.

"Thank you," said Averendier, his voice cutting Lilac's dark thoughts blissfully short. She caught his eye, and he tipped his head towards the door.

"I hope you find him!" the man called after the retreating duo.

"We've already visited all but two of the taverns he listed," Averendier murmured to her as they walked back out into the twilight street. "If there's no sign of them at either, we'll just have to go back to the others and look again. But," he added, his voice softening as he gazed down on her, "we'll spend the night at the next place we come to, whether we find them or not. We can continue tomorrow."

Lilac bit her inner lip and found herself nodding submissively. Only two more taverns to check that they hadn't already visited. The thought should have been relieving. But in one hour, Engrelin could have gone to any number of the taverns, possibly even coming behind them! She wanted to dig her fingernails deep into her scalp. They could chase each other around this city forever and never cross paths.

By the time they reached their destination, the first star winked overhead. Dusk had settled heavily over Elstar. Lilac's hands worked nervously as she paused in the tavern doorway beside Averendier. Would they find Engrelin here? Or would she have to endure yet another night of torturous worrying?

She scanned the dining room quickly, and her heart sank down to her boots. If they were here, they certainly weren't eating.

Averendier touched her arm gently. "Let's get something to eat before we inquire," Averendier said. His face was lined with concern. Lilac realized her hands were trembling violently.

"I'm fine," she whispered, sucking in a deep breath.

But Averendier led her to one of the empty tables, sat her down, and left to order supper. He returned with a steaming bowl in each hand. The first whiff of the soup met Lilac's nostrils, and her stomach growled. Blushing, she accepted one of the bowls, all the while pressing one hand against her stomach, as if she could silence it with mere touch. Her stomach continued snarling. She hadn't realized how hungry she was. Her hands shook as she spread a napkin over her lap and picked up her spoon.

Their hunger unanimously decreed silence. The gentle hum of conversation, and the warmth from the large open fireplace, wrapped around Lilac's shoulders like a blanket. Lilac scrunched her shoulders slightly and waited for Averendier to sit down. After grace was said, neither spoke a word until the last drop of soup had been devoured. Lilac, despite her anxiety, polished the last bits of moisture from her bowl with a biscuit.

"Are you ready?" Averendier asked finally. He pushed his bowl towards the center of the table for the tavern-keeper or one of his assistants to collect.

Smiling, Lilac shoved her bowl to join Averendier's. She hurried alongside him to the counter, where the tavern-keeper stood clutching his enormous, shabby ledger in his hands. The man blinked up at Averendier through the tiny wire-rimmed spectacles perched on the end of his nose.

"Yes?" he asked. Lifting his peaked chin, he squinted at Averendier through one eye.

"Has a man named Aaron come here during the past few days?" Averendier asked. He gave a short description of his cousin.

The man pursed his lips and he set the ledger down on the counter. "Last name?" he asked.

"I only have the first," Averendier replied.

Brow knit, the man flipped furiously through the ledger. "Aaron, Aaron" he muttered to himself as he sifted through all manners of accounts. He turned the pages at a dizzying pace. Lilac stared. Going that fast, how could he read the pages, much less find one name?

The man thrust his finger down onto a page, slamming the loose pages down on either side. The book flopped open to a page scrawled with spidery writing.

"Did he take board?" he asked. "Today?"

"Likely," Averendier replied.

The man muttered. The pages flew. The book slammed open to another page, covered with the same crabby writing.

"Here it is." The man jabbed a tangle of words with his spindly finger. "Aaron, name standing alone. Took board only half an hour ago. Up the stairs, fifth room to the right."

In a sudden surge of rapture, Lilac nearly clapped her hands. They were here! They were actually here! She wanted to kiss the ledger and its keeper in one swoop.

Averendier, though outwardly perfectly unruffled, bore a tiny glimmer of hope or relief in his gray eyes. Lilac knew without seeing that her own shone like stars.

Please, let Elvera be here with Engrelin. Please.

The man hunched over his ledger, then cocked his bald head and squinted up at Averendier. "You can rent the room beside his, if you'd like. Sixth room to the right."

"I think we will." Averendier slid a few coins onto the counter and turned away, scanning the room beyond for the stairway.

The tavern-keeper looked down at the large amount of money on his counter. Blinking like a stunned bird, he slowly lifted his gaze to meet Lilac's.

"Does he want no change?"

Lilac glanced at Averendier. "I don't think so," she replied.

"He...he didn't even give me a name to put it under," the man whispered.

"Austain. Austain Peters." Lilac offered him a reassuring smile. "We're staying just one night."

The man nodded. He reached slowly for his pen, though his eyes were still fastened to the coins scattered across his counter. Leaving him agape, Lilac joined Averendier, who was waiting for her at the foot of the staircase.

"Engrelin?"

Again, Averendier knocked on the closed door. Lilac waited behind him, her knuckles pressed to her lips. She let her eyes sweep back and forth over the number carved crudely into the door frame. It was definitely five. Engrelin (and maybe Elvera?) were not downstairs. They had to be up here. This was undoubtably their room. So why didn't anyone answer?

Finally, Averendier gave up banging on the door and tried the handle. Under his touch, the door swung inward into a room gloomy with twilight.

Frowning, Lilac followed Averendier into the room (after he ducked the low doorway), a familiar lump in her throat.

A flicker of flame, and the room was bathed in the glow of a lamp. Averendier set it down on the small table beside the door where he had found it. Its warm light illuminated the inevitable.

The room was empty.

"They might still be out looking for us," Averendier suggested in answer to Lilac's unspoken question.

"This late in the evening?" she replied doubtfully.

Averendier was silent. He glanced around the room. Lilac followed his example. It was a tiny, cramped space, with room enough for a narrow bed (that might fit two bodies with a little squeezing), the small table, a lamp, and two straight backed chairs. A glass window had been carefully set into the wall behind the bed. Its shutters were latched, shutting out any view of the outside. Something dirty and brown slumped on the bed. Averendier picked the thing up and held it out in front of himself.

It was Engrelin's pack. The sight of it roused Lilac out of her stupor.

"So they were here," she murmured.

"Mm-hm." Averendier rummaged through the pack, nodding to himself as if checking things off a list. Then he closed it and tucked it under his arm. "Hopefully, this means they'll be coming back."

"Is it Engrelin's?" asked Lilac, just to be sure.

"Yes. And it has Lance's pack inside it as well."

Lilac's lips tightened. The pack was so shrunken, so limp. And Lance's was inside of it… She desperately hoped none of them had starved.

"We'll wait for them to come back," said Averendier. "Meanwhile, let's get some rest. If the others come back tonight, I'll have Engrelin and Lance in here with me. I'll send Elvera to you in the other room." Promptly, he escorted her to the room he had rented. It was identical to the room they had just left, only there was an extra window to the bed's right. In the doorway, Averendier hesitated.

"Are you sure you'll be all right?" he asked.

Lilac gave him a weary smile. "I'll manage," she said. Inwardly, she screamed for him to stay a little longer. The last thing she wanted was to be left alone in such a strange place, especially after the high hopes she had nursed throughout the day had been dashed to pieces at her feet. Her only consolation was that Elvera might join her sometime during the night. And even…dared she hope…she would see Isalinia too?

"I'm just a room away," said Averendier, edging out into the hallway. "Call out if you need anything." He shut the door behind himself.

Silently, Lilac stared at the door for several moments, willing it to open again to admit one of her sisters. Finally, she turned and shrugged out of her skirt and blouse. For the first time since leaving Clane's tavern, Lilac donned fresh clothes. Shivering in the cold that emanated from the walls and the cracks in the floorboards, Lilac brushed her snarled hair smooth. She shook with cold and fatigue, and the hairbrush often fell from her numb hands. Finally, she managed to plait her hair in one long braid. Her eyes remained riveted to the door.

Any moment now, one of them will be coming through. Any moment now. Just any moment...

Her eyelids drooped. Lilac jerked herself to semiconsciousness and collapsed onto the bed, not even bothering to draw the covers over herself. She curled up on her side, drawing thin, shuddering breaths. Never had she been so alone.

They might still be out looking for us. It's still evening.

No, no. It's night now.

Will you be all right alone?

Yes...

No. I'm not all right. Elvera needs me. Isalinia needs me. I...I need them.

No, I'm not all right.

Bang, bang.

What was that?!

Oh, the door. Opening and shutting. Over and over.

Averendier leaving me. Over and over.

I'm alone. All alone.

"Not anymore," a smooth voice whispered. "I'm here. I'm here..."

Gasping, Lilac shot up into a sitting position, her heart stuttering in her heaving chest.

Only a dream, she told herself fiercely. Her nerves, strung as tight as watch springs, unwound only a little.

For somewhere, something was banging. Opening and shutting. Over and over.

Shuddering, Lilac slipped out of bed. Exhaustion fought to glue her eyes shut. It was all she could to keep them open a slit as she fumbled across the room towards the sound.

Bang, bang.

She turned towards it, and her fingers found the frosty windowpane. Of course! In the darkness, she could just make out that one of the shutters outside that had come loose and was swinging against the tavern's side in the brisk wind. Lilac sighed with relief and shoved the window open.

A blast of icy wind rushed into the room. Reaching out, Lilac groped for the wildly swinging shutter.

"Close the window, your Highness."

The voice came from behind her. Lilac gasped and whirled, pressing her back against the wall. Her eyes darted frantically around the black room.

A pair of bright eyes stared at her from across the room. A scream rose to her throat. In an instant, the intruder nimbly cleared the bed and smoothly slid his hand over her mouth. Another hand, thin and cold and strong, grasped her wrists and twisted them behind her back. Warm, gentle breath crept down Lilac's neck. Her skin crawled as if someone had broken an ant's nest over her head. She squirmed in the man's grip. Her heart fluttered so violently she thought she was going to be sick.

"Isn't this a pleasant surprise?" murmured the voice. "I set my snare for a peasant, and I catch a princess."

Lilac recoiled, another gasp strangling in her throat. She tried to jerk away, struggled to tear herself from the man's awful grasp. But he only pulled her back towards him. He slid his hand from her mouth. Cold steel pressed against her throat. Lilac froze.

"There now, no running off," the man whispered, almost comfortingly. It sent another shiver coursing through Lilac. "I've had enough people slip out of my hands today."

"My sister," Lilac gritted through her clenched teeth. "What have you done to her?"

"Nothing," the man soothed. "I've done nothing yet. That fool of a farmer dragged her off before I could catch him. He will pay for it later. But all in good time! Don't worry. You sister will not be harmed, unless he resists."

Lilac didn't know whether she would scream or burst into tears. Knowing Engrelin, he wouldn't go down without a fight.

Elvera, what's going to happen to you?

A chilling chord struck her heart.

What's going to happen to me?

The man lowered his knife. He began binding Lilac's hands tightly behind her back.

"What are you going to do to me?" she asked. She twisted her wrists as the unfamiliar bracelets tightened around them. The man touched her hands, lightly yet firmly, to hold them still as he worked.

"Nothing, your Highness," he assured. "I have orders. I shall do nothing to you. Yet."

49

salinia canted her head and smiled slightly, though Andrald still detected the hints of a grimace tugging at her mouth. He never could understand why. Maybe she still wasn't used to the saddle, even after their weeks of traveling. *That must be it*, he decided.

"It was very…emotional," she commented, referring to the ballad Andrald had just finished singing—one he found truly heart-rending.

He grinned at her. "Thanks," he said. "It's one my mom always sings before my dad leaves for a voyage." His own words sent a sudden pang through him. Was his father even alive anymore? Last he had heard, he had been severely wounded in battle. How severely?

"It was nice," said Isalinia.

Andrald shook his dark thoughts away, silently sending up a prayer for his father. "Your turn," he said. He guided Glorien around a deep rut in the road.

Isalinia was quiet a moment. "I have one," she said at last, "but I don't know it in your language."

Andrald smiled. "Sing it anyway—I don't mind."

"All right then:

Naradria ekli e mossol riaf
Fo e ytuae revn nekor
Wno eth traeh fo Pirian,
Naidraug fo jectsu eutr.
Riaf erew eirth syad

Ni tresed adsn
Fo ytineres dednuoun
Thew no e rvir shna.
Eth shak fo rai
Erat enth tarap
Pirian efil nekha ni eltta.
Naradria, efil nekha ni ferig.
Deiru retheget edis eth srolvo yal
Thoed eirth rolvo tannac reves
Ron ssensselfil laust wyaa.
So elase fo eirth noitoved
Detinu
Dnafshu dna efwi
Ni eirth sevar wrge
Owt seshu fo der dna etiwh
Smassol fo eth tseur elva
Evirth mifa eirth tsu.
Suth si eth rethesh fo
Pirian dna Naradria
Mrfo dniw rethaew dna rai.
Eirth elvo rfo oen rethona."

"Pretty," Andrald commented simply. He couldn't think of anything else to say. Alinar was one language he hadn't learned well.

"It's more touching when one actually understands it," explained Isalinia sympathetically. "It's a beautiful story about two lovers who were—"

Andrald didn't need to hear any more. "A beautiful day to hear such beautiful story!" he interjected tactlessly.

Isalinia looked dubiously at the overcast sky. "It doesn't look like it'll be beautiful," she quietly observed. "It looks as it did before we had that big snowstorm."

Andrald was silent. He knew that all too well. What consolation could he offer against the pending storm? They were two or three days' ride from Elstar and, as far as he could see, were that far away from shelter.

"The air even tastes like it," Isalinia continued. "Do you think it might snow as heavily as last time?"

Andrald squinted up at the sky; it looked like swaths of gray cotton draped from horizon to horizon.

"I don't know," he said slowly. "You really can't tell some days. We might not get snow at all."

"It's going to drop bucketloads on our heads," Isalinia predicted.

Both lapsed into silence, swaying gently in rhythm with their steeds' steps. The silence hung over their heads like the dark clouds heralding the storm. Andrald shifted uneasily in his saddle, finding the quiet distasteful and unsettling after the constant singing that had kept their spirits up over the past week. Isalinia attempted to hum a short tune, but it tapered off into nothing.

Something hissed past Andrald's ear. He jerked on the reins, yanking Glorien to a halt. Another arrow whizzed past and sank into a nearby tree. Andrald threw a wild glance over his shoulder. He saw several shadowy figures weaving through the trees behind him.

"They've found us!" Isalinia cried. Even as she spoke, an arrow ripped through her skirt's hem.

"Head for the woods!" Andrald whispered as if he were shouting. He pointed to a slight gap in the forest ahead.

Isalinia obediently kicked Snowstar. Both horses sprang into the gap. Andrald lagged behind Isalinia, ducking low branches and trailing vines that threatened to snatch him off Glorien's back.

Shouts rang out behind them. Andrald bent lower over Glorien's neck. Now was not the time to fall off his horse.

Or was it?

They were several hundred yards into the thick evergreens. The tree's fluffy branches still hid the pursuers from view. Andrald jumped from Glorien's back, landed on his feet, and slapped the stallion's flanks. Snorting, ears pinned back, Glorien spurted riderless into the tangled trees.

Isalinia reined Snowstar in. "Are you crazy?" she exclaimed.

"Jump off and let her go!" Andrald answered.

"What! Why?"

"Just do it!"

An arrow tore through the vines and embedded in Andrald's arm. Gasping with pain, Andrald grasped the shaft protruding from his arm.

Seeing it, Isalinia literally jumped off her horse's back, landing hard on her hands and knees. Andrald rushed over to her, yanked her to her feet, and slapped Snowstar back into a gallop. Together, the two stumbled into the thickets, running in the opposite direction the horses had taken. As they charged through brush and clearings, Andrald grit his teeth and jerked the arrow out of his arm. He wrapped his belt tightly above the wound. All the while, thorns and brambles tore his clothes and skin. Beside him, Isalinia sobbed for breath.

Finally, he pulled Isalinia into a shallow cave scooped out of a mountainside. Inside, they both slumped against the wall, gasping for breath. A few snowflakes drifted past the cave mouth.

"Did…did we lose them?" Isalinia panted.

"I…I don't…know," Andrald returned, clutching his injured arm. "I was hoping…they would follow…the horses."

"I'm hoping…that too," Isalinia wheezed. She squeezed her sides tightly, as if that would help her breathe better. She offered Andrald a weak smile. "I'm glad you sent them off."

"I'm glad…you jumped," Andrald said. "But we probably won't see them…ever again."

"I know," Isalinia returned. "But at least—" She broke off and glanced up at the cave ceiling.

"What?" Andrald followed her gaze.

"Don't you hear it?" Isalinia whispered.

"No."

"Listen."

In the silence that followed, all Andrald heard was the wind moaning outside the cave and the snow swishing against the rocks.

"No," he began slowly, "I don't—"

"There it is again!" Isalinia clutched Andrald's arm.

Andrald cried out sharply, and Isalinia jumped back.

"Are you all right?" she asked.

Andrald clamped his bloody arm to his side and drew several deep breaths. "It's nothing," he murmured.

Even as he said it, he heard a scraping sound overhead, like rocks grating against one another. Warily, he drew his sword, balancing it in his good hand.

"What is it?" Isalinia asked, glancing from side to side. "Is it them?"

"I don't know," Andrald whispered. His arm throbbing in time with his thudding heart, Andrald crept toward the cave entrance. He stepped out into the swirling snow.

The figure standing in the sweeping storm whirled quickly toward Andrald. In his hands he clutched a bow, its arrow notched, its deadly point directed at Andrald's heart.

Andrald never had the chance to cry out.

50

Engrelin stifled a groan in the hand he dragged across his mouth. "Can't you two just quit it?" he demanded.

"No," replied Lance and Elvera in sour unison. They scowled at each other.

Apparently they can both disagree with me unless they do so at the exact same time. Engrelin lifted his eyes imploringly to the cloud-clotted sky. Would this never end?

"I still don't understand why we didn't wait for the others back in Elstar," muttered Elvera, crossing her arms over her chest.

"We just couldn't," Engrelin replied shortly. He detoured around a branch that had fallen across the road.

"May I also remind you that I've been the only one carrying a pack for…since…"

"Since early last night and now its evening again," Lance prompted.

"Exactly."

"No, you may not remind me," said Engrelin flatly.

"And my back hurts," Elvera added.

"I would offer to carry it for you," Lance proposed, "but as my hands are cruelly bound behind my back, I am physically unable to assist you in your trials." Lance sighed dramatically and tilted a smile toward Engrelin.

Maybe gagging Lance wasn't such a bad idea after all. Engrelin kicked a chunk of ice, sending it skittering off the road.

"Would you like me to carry your pack for you?" he asked at last.

"No!" Elvera fiercely clutched her pack straps, as if she expected Engrelin to tear it from her back. "I would never trust you with my things!"

"And yet you would let Lance carry it."

"Of course not!" Elvera's eyes bugged with disbelief. "Are you nuts? I wouldn't trust him with a horse I didn't like."

"Thanks for the lovely compliment," returned Lance cheerfully.

"If you don't want help, stop complaining," Engrelin said.

"I just want to make sure you know how much I suffer for your stupid ideas," Elvera retorted primly, smoothing the front of her dress.

Consider me aware. Engrelin slowly ruffled his hair. His eyes passed back and forth across the woods lining the road. Any minute now, he would find it.

They approached a lane branching from the main road—a lane that he had been down only once, but the welcome waiting for him and his group at the end of it would be as warm as if he had walked down the lane a hundred times. Smiling to himself, Engrelin veered onto the lane, pleasantly surprised that Lance and Elvera followed him uncomplainingly.

Snow blanketed Aunt Ruth's garden. Clusters of crimson holly berries glinted through the ice. Several snowdrops wagged their heads above the crust of snow. As they approached the house, Engrelin looked back at Lance and Elvera. They glared back.

"Please try and look like you're somewhat happy you're here," he commented. "You don't want to walk into someone's house looking like a couple sourpusses." As he spoke, he dropped and untied Lance's hands. Then he moved forward again to lead them to the house.

"Lance?" he heard Elvera hiss. "What's a puss?"

"Huh. As if you didn't know," Lance snorted.

"I don't. Am I supposed to?"

"I only assumed—"

"Stop assuming and just tell me what it is," Elvera snipped.

Lance heaved a sigh. "It's a cat," he relented.

"A taegr?!"

"No, idiot. A little cat. Hardly bigger than a possum."

"What's a possum?"

"It's—oh, forget it," Lance grumbled. "No use trying to instruct ignorance incarnate."

Elvera spluttered indignantly.

Chuckling under his breath, Engrelin mounted the porch steps. After checking to make sure Lance and Elvera were still behind him, he rapped on the house's door. His half-frozen fingers tingle painfully. Behind him, Lance and Elvera fell silent. A few seconds passed, with no response. Engrelin knocked again.

From within the house, footsteps drew near. The latch snapped open, and the door creaked two inches inward.

"How can I help you?" asked Aunt Ruth's muffled voice. It still sounded as pleasant as Engrelin remembered it, but he thought he detected a hint of apprehension. Or even fear. Why else would she be holding the door almost completely shut?

"I'm Engrelin Peterson, ma'am," Engrelin murmured. He dragged one hand through his unruly brown hair while a flush tingled up and down his neck. Behind him, Lance snickered softly. Engrelin almost couldn't blame him. What kind of a fool had he been to expect that an elderly widow would help him, much less allow him to impose on her hospitality? He should have asked Elvera for help, no matter what uproar or shame might have ensued.

This is what Averendier would have done, if he were in a pickle like this.

Engrelin drew a deep breath and squared his shoulders, trying to convince himself of it.

"I'm Austinian's nephew," he tried again. "I was here about two months ago with Averendier and Andrald."

Had it really been two months ago? It felt more like two centuries.

The door immediately swung all the way inward, revealing short, smiling Aunt Ruth.

"I remember you now," she said. She pressed Engrelin in a quick hug. She glanced beyond Engrelin, and her eyes clouded. "But where are your cousins?" she asked. "And who are these two?"

Engrelin shut his eyes and prayed that Lance was behaving himself. When he turned and opened them, he saw Lance standing respectfully under the widow's gaze, like a soldier under inspection. And, unlike a soldier before his peer, he was smiling.

"This is Lance, and this is Elvera," Engrelin said, motioning to them in turn. Lance bobbed his head, breaking into a wider smile. It sent vivid recollections of happier times tearing through Engrelin's mind. He shifted his gaze to Elvera, who barely managed a lip twitch. At least she was *trying* to look less like a sullen toddler.

"They've been traveling with me for a while," Engrelin explained. "I was with Averendier and Andrald, but we got separated along the way."

"Separated by what?" Aunt Ruth asked, her brow puckering with concern.

"A large blizzard," said Lance quickly.

Engrelin glanced at Lance, but Lance was looking earnestly at Aunt Ruth. Well, it was mostly true. But Lance had jumped on his response a little too swiftly. Would Aunt Ruth guess Lance was the real reason they were no longer with Averendier and Andrald?

But Aunt Ruth only smiled and turned back towards the door. "Speaking of blizzards," she said, "here comes more snow! Please, come inside. Make yourselves at home. I'll have supper on the table in just a moment."

Engrelin held the door open for Aunt Ruth as she bustled inside. Once she passed into the house, Elvera scowled and jabbed her elbow sharply into Lance's middle.

"Blizzard, really?! You're the reason I'm not in dependable hands right now! That, and Engrelin."

Lance smirked but said nothing. He strode through the door, swinging his arms to emphasize his freedom. Elvera screwed up her face, as if she had just bitten into a lemon, and flounced into the house as well.

Engrelin put one foot through the doorway, then hesitated and turned to look outside. Snowflakes streaked across the garden. Little waves of snow already skittered across the porch's worn floorboards. They had arrived not a moment too soon.

But, with Linford possibly on his trail, should he have brought them here at all?

The snow will stop them, he thought. Icy fear stabbed his stomach. Unable to convince himself, Engrelin let the door swing shut. He latched it tightly. The sound seemed to echo in the narrow, tidy hall. Voices, animated with cheer and the house's inviting warmth, spilled from the kitchen's open doorway. Engrelin moved towards it, his throat tight.

He paused in the doorway to watch Elvera and Lance, who were—wonder of wonders!—chatting pleasantly with Aunt Ruth as she bustled about the kitchen preparing supper. Elvera was even smiling! Engrelin frowned. They seemed so happy. Had he been doing something wrong all of this journey, and even before that? Could he have stopped everything, from Walche's vengeance, his exile, Elvera's first glares, and—worst of all—Lance's betrayal? Had it all happened because he wasn't getting something straight?

He shook his head at himself. No, he couldn't think of anything he could have done. It was better to stop thinking along that line. Nonetheless, guilt hung like a rock in his stomach. He wasn't doing well now, likely endangering Aunt Ruth by coming here. He should have swallowed his pride and dread and just asked Elvera.

Engrelin glanced at the kitchen windows, rattled in their frames by the howling wind. Too late for second guesses now. They were sealed in.

"Engrelin? Sit down, young man!" Aunt Ruth called. "Don't just stand in the doorway watching."

"Are you sure you don't need help with anything?" Engrelin asked.

Aunt Ruth waved a dripping spoon dismissively. "I wouldn't be telling you to sit if I did," she said. "Take a seat!"

Nodding, Engrelin slid into the seat next to Lance, who shot him a dangerous glare.

"Hope you don't mind eating in the kitchen tonight," Aunt Ruth continued, as she ladled soup into thick ceramic bowls. "I usually close the dining room up for the winter—I don't often get visitors around now. Besides, it's quite cozy in here with the fire." She set the steaming bowl on the table before them all.

"The kitchen's fine for us," Engrelin said. "We're just grateful for the shelter."

"And the hot food," Lance added impishly.

Aunt Ruth beamed. She led them in a short grace before she too sat and dove into her bowl like her guests. All but Engrelin. He just stirred his soup around with a spoon and stared down at the chunks of fresh vegetables floating in the bowl, willing himself to be hungry and failing utterly. His stomach was in too many knots to conceivably hold food.

"Where are you three headed?" Aunt Ruth asked as she refilled Lance's bowl.

"Bryn, Monaria," Engrelin answered.

Aunt Ruth cocked an eyebrow. "Isn't it a little late in the year to be skipping across the countryside?" she asked.

It was the first skeptical look he had ever seen her give anyone. It only seemed to make things worse.

"I need to be home in time for the planting season," Engrelin said, dodging the question. "I have family I want to get back to."

A faint gleam of reminiscence flashed in the woman's eyes, and she quickly diverted the subject. Engrelin ground his teeth and stared angrily into his bowl. Out of everything in the world, he hated to be pitied.

A goggle-eyed stare from Elvera told Engrelin just how blackly he was scowling. Quickly, he scrubbed a hand across his face, as if he could wipe his resentment away like crumbs.

Gradually, the pleasant murmur of voices and the security of the walls around him lulled his tattered nerves. The trembling shutters shut out any view of the cold, bitter world beyond Aunt Ruth's kitchen. For the moment, they were safe. What soup he forced himself to eat warmed his lips into a smile, even if it was small.

"Now," said Aunt Ruth finally, as she cleared the last dish from the table. "Shall I show you to your rooms?"

Engrelin's smile faded; his shoulders tensed in all too familiar knots.

"If you'd like, you can take Lance and Elvera back, Aunt Ruth," he said. "There's still something I'd like to talk to you about."

"We can always discuss it in the morning when you're fresh. I know how tired one can be after getting off the road…" Aunt Ruth voice faded as she noticed the urgency in Engrelin's gaze. She sighed. "All right, dear. But let me show these other two to their rooms first. I'll be right back."

Looking troubled, Aunt Ruth hustled Lance and Elvera out of the kitchen. As she left, Elvera threw an angry, probing glance over her shoulder, as if she knew she could unlock all Engrelin's secrets with a final look.

Engrelin was glad she couldn't.

Though the snow howled through the clearings and ripped down the roads, it sifted finely through the sieve of evergreen branches, powdering those standing below. It would have been impossible to see them until you stumbled into them, so well did the tree's shadows cloak them. The men were not concerned with secrecy, however. They were not there to hide.

Flint and steel crackled together. Sparks flew, illuminating one man's face for split seconds. His companions stood in a semi-circle around him, impatiently watching the man bent over a pile of pine needles, tools in hand.

"Hurry up, Craig," one muttered. "We don't have all night."

"Wind's scattering them," retorted Craig. He clashed the flint and steel vigorously together, but to no avail. "They don't have time to catch. We may have to wait for the wind to die down a bit."

The other gritted his teeth. "We need the wind for this work," he said. "You have to get one spark to catch. Just one. It's all we'll need."

Craig peered up into his companion's face, expressionless in shadow. "Want this to work? Give me a hand. Crouch down beside me and block the wind."

Without complaint, the man dropped to his knees and bent his back to the wind.

A tiny glow sprung up within the needles. A wisp of smoke slithered skyward. Craig dropped his tools. He gathered the thinly smoking needles in his cupped hands and blew on them gently, holding them within the shelter of his companion's body. After a few blows, the needles smoked. They flared to life in his hands. Amid his companion's soft cheers, Craig set the needles within a firepit they had previously prepared. The flames licked eagerly at the kindling.

"Torches ready?"

The rasp and slap of cudgels sliding through rough hands answered unanimously. The leader of the group, now discernable in the fire's steadily growing light, smiled as he looked out over his men. One by one, they dipped the pitch-soaked ends of the sticks into the fire, shielding their faces from the acrid smoke as the pitch smoked and burned.

"Remember," said the leader as the last man lit his torch, "we're not here to capture anyone. We're just destroying a place they consider a safe spot, in case any of them break through Linford's barrier."

"You don't think any of them are in there?" asked one of the men. His voice betrayed his disappointment. He, for one, had anticipated a night of sport, perhaps even honor.

The leader shook his head. "No. they would have had to travel a night and a day without rest to get here by now. No—" He shook his head again. "Only the widow's in there. We were merely sent here as a precaution. A tactical precaution, you might say."

Looking pleased with himself at this clever way of describing their mission of sabotage and arson, the man lifted his torch level with his head and gazed out through the screen of trees at the outbuildings lying wrapped in snowy peace. He motioned to Craig, who scuffed fresh dirt over the newly made fire. The leader waited until the last newly glowing ember was buried beneath the forest loam.

He motioned to the clearing. "Move in," he commanded.

51

E ngrelin sat waiting at Aunt Ruth's dining room table a moment, fingering the blue and white checkered tablecloth and staring at the shuttered window. Shoving his chair back, he moved over to the window, pushed it open, and unlatched one the of the shutters. Night had fully fallen—the swirling white flakes were stark against the blackness. He slid the window closed, not bothering to fasten the shutter. Sighing heavily, he let the lace curtain fall back into place. The snow must stop by morning. Having to sit here and wait while possible Tirendrians were on his trail was going to drive him batty.

"I'm open for business," said a voice behind him.

Engrelin whirled sharply, snatching for Arrian's hilt. His darting gaze fell on Aunt Ruth, her hand pressed over her mouth in surprise. His ears burning, Engrelin released the hilt. Spreading his hands palm-down on the table, he leaned forward.

"You can read, *ei*?" he asked in *cymraeg*.

"*Ei*, I can," Aunt Ruth replied. Looking even more puzzled, she pulled out a chair and sat down at the table across from Engrelin. He was relieved she didn't ask him why he had changed languages. Though he knew Lance could understand what he said, Elvera could not. She was the only one he didn't want hearing what he said.

"Why do you ask?" Aunt Ruth asked.

Engrelin drew the map out of his pocket and spread it out on the table, smoothing the soft, damaged corners flat.

"This is the only thing I have to show me our way home." He whispered, even though it wasn't necessary. "But I can't read." His voice tightened with embarrassment. "I can decipher the landmarks on maps, but I'm not sure where exactly I should follow them to. If you could point out and mark the major cities on the way to the Pwynt, I think I could find the rest of the way on my own."

Aunt Ruth glanced swiftly at him. "I thought you were going to Bryn," she said.

Engrelin nodded slowly. "After the Pwynt." He shook his head slightly at the question in Aunt Ruth's eyes.

Aunt Ruth nodded as if he had spoken aloud and bent over the map he pushed towards her.

"It's a good map—very detailed," she commented, perching a slender pair of glasses on the tip of her nose. She fetched a pencil from a jar, returning to bend over the map once again. Her pencil's sharp point hovered over the northern regions of Ontaria.

"We're here," she began, circling the sketched fortress representing Elstar. "The Pwynt is here." Her pencil glided up to scratch a large x over another fortress positioned near a peninsula along the Northern Sea. "The most major cities you will have to pass through in Monaria are Duraig, Arivan, and Cilcy, here, here, and here." She circled the three cities, which were stretched in an almost perfect line from Elstar to the distant Pwynt.

Aunt Ruth proceeded to explain a few smaller landmarks that would lead Engrelin from one city to the next, since the roads, winding around mountains, never traveled in a straight line.

"And I assume," she added, peering at Engrelin over the rims of her glasses, "that unless you want to brave the *Anailwch*, you'll be passing through Tirendria's tip?"

"Unfortunately, yes." Engrelin's fingers curled with frustration, bunching the tablecloth in his fists. He dearly hoped Zacara had been right when she said Vendar would be directing his attention elsewhere.

"Did you take the old bridge last time?" Aunt Ruth asked, tapping the blue ink river with the end of her pencil.

"Yes."

"There's no telling whether or not that ancient hunk still stands," the widow observed. "But you'll make it across the creek. If the old bridge is out, there's another a mile downstream. It's further into Tirendria, but there's no other way across." She drew a line further down the creek. "I doubt it's in better condition that the first," she said. "And it's guarded like the other."

"Thanks." Engrelin's gut twisted at the thought of having to smuggle Elvera over the border without Averendier's help.

"That's about it, unless you have more questions," Aunt Ruth concluded, sitting back in her chair.

"Thanks," Engrelin said. He folded the map and stuffed it back into his pocket. "*Nos da.*" He stepped away to leave. But Aunt Ruth grabbed his arm and pulled him back to the table.

"Engrelin, you guard her well," she whispered, locking Engrelin's gaze with hers. "Don't let anything happen to her. The fate of all Ontaria is in your hands."

Engrelin jerked back, his heart stuttering a startled staccato. Was it that obvious?

"How do you know?" he demanded tersely.

"I wish I could say it was her manner alone," Aunt Ruth said. "But there were inquiries going 'round today, for her."

"Did they say who she was?" Engrelin demanded breathlessly.

"No."

"Then how do you know she's—"

"Hush." Aunt Ruth pressed a stern forefinger against his lips. "Others around here understand *cymraeg*, perhaps." She smiled and straightened her shoulders. "But I am better informed than most. After all, I am the mother-in-law of the Monarian admiral."

"So they didn't say exactly who she was?" Engrelin asked. Small relief even if they hadn't.

"No," Aunt Ruth said. "Only fools would. But the moment I saw her with you, I knew. She certainly doesn't carry herself like a peasant, even if she does sulk." The widow's eyes brightened with understanding and sympathy.

Engrelin's fingers curled around Arrian's hilt, and he turned away to the window. On the other side of the glass, the storm still raged.

Beyond it, he thought he saw a tiny orange glow bobbing. Frowning, Engrelin moved over the window and peered out into the night.

"But is there any other way that I can help you?" Aunt Ruth continued. "Provisions maybe?"

It took Engrelin a moment to comprehend what she had said. He glanced at her, then back out the window.

"I don't want to raid your pantry in the middle of winter," he murmured.

The orange dot seemed to have multiplied. Half a dozen drifted through the snow, but the flakes fell so thick and fast, he could discern nothing more than the light itself.

A gentle hand fell on his shoulder. "Now, you ought to know that my cellar is busting at the seams, and there's plenty to spare. The neighbors all pay me for my quilts in food, and…"

One of the dots seemed to swell, larger and larger, until it took up the whole window, as if it were hurtling towards it.

Because it was.

Engrelin jerked back and flung himself over Aunt Ruth. As they fell, Engrelin twisted sharply, putting himself between the widow and the ground.

Just as his shoulder blades hit the floor, A sharp crack and tinkle of broken glass filled the air.
A split second later, the flaming torch sailed into the kitchen. Hitting the floor, it showered sparks on to Engrelin and Aunt Ruth.

Engrelin struggled upright, snatched up the burning brand, and flung it back out the window. He slammed shut the loose shutter and latched it tightly. But even in his frantic haste, he hesitated a second before banging the shutters closed to catch a glimpse of the outside, and the inevitable truth.

The house was surrounded.

Engrelin whirled to help Aunt Ruth off the floor. She trembled so violently, she could hardly stand. Engrelin half-carried her to the nearest chair.

"The place is surrounded," Engrelin said as he splashed a basin of water over the scorched and smoking floorboards. "Is there any other way out?"

Aunt Ruth stared glassily at him a moment, until the sound of another window shattering somewhere in the house made her start. She shook her head.

"No, not that—wait, yes!" She sparked to life in an instant and sprang over to one corner of the kitchen. Kneeling on the floor, she yanked open a trap door.

"This is the cellar," she explained, shouting now over the yells and the brittle breaking of windows. "There's an old passage starting down here which leads into the woods. We used it to haul wood and keep it dry during the winter. I haven't been in it for years, but it should still be passable."

Engrelin opened his mouth to respond. He was cut short by a terrified scream. He and Aunt Ruth exchanged looks.

"I'll be back!" he called. Turning, Engrelin charged down the passage which led to the guest bedrooms, following the shrill screams to one of the doors.

He rammed his shoulder against the door, snapping the lock. The door sprang open as if it were spring-loaded, revealing Elvera. She stood in the center of her room, petrified, shrieking at the top of her lungs. Flames greedily consumed the curtains fluttering around her shattered window. More crept up the walls. The carpet she stood upon soldered at the edges. Engrelin took this all in one glance before he rushed into the room and seized Elvera's shoulders.

Elvera screamed louder and flailed violently in his arms. But when she twisted completely around and saw Engrelin, she slumped.

"It…it came through the…the window," she chattered, trembling from head to toe.

"At least have the brains to get out of the room before you go up with it!" Engrelin exclaimed. He dragged her out of the room. She blubbered in a soft, weary way.

However, just as Engrelin yanked her through the doorway, she latched onto the doorframe (which wasn't burning yet).

"Come on!" Engrelin urged, tugging her away. "Do you want to burn to death?"

Elvera whimpered at the suggestion but clung stubbornly. "My pack," she whispered. "It's still in there."

Engrelin glanced back into the room, now roiling with smoke. "It's too late, we're just going to have to leave it," he said.

"I'm not going to leave without it!" Elvera exclaimed, clawing his arm frantically. "Go back in and get it!"

"I can't—"

"I'm not leaving!"

Engrelin grabbed her and shoved her to the floor in the hallway. "Stay here," he ordered. And he darted back into the burning room.

Shielding his face with his bent arm, Engrelin cast about the room. Smoke and heat billowed into his face. Through the haze, he spotted Elvera's pack lying on her bed. He grabbed the packs straps and flung it across the room out into the hallway. That instant, the mattress roared up into flames. Engrelin staggered out of the room.

Elvera still cowered in the hallway, clutching her pack tightly to her chest. The orange of the flames danced in her wide, dark eyes.

"What are you still in here for?" Engrelin blazed, shouting above the fire's growing growl. "Get into the kitchen now!"

Whimpering, Elvera scurried down the hallway. Engrelin ran close at his heels. Running feet pounded behind him. Engrelin twisted around to see Lance dashing towards them. Engrelin nearly started. Wasn't Lance going to use this opportunity to escape?

When they rushed into the kitchen, they found it still untainted by fire. But it was empty. Engrelin skidded to a stop and cast about wildly for Aunt Ruth. Where had she gone?

"Engrelin, what are we waiting for?" Elvera asked. Still clinging to Engrelin's arm, she sank to her knees as if she were melting. If he didn't act soon, she might just.

"Get down in the cellar and stay down there," Engrelin ordered, peeling her fingers off his arm. He pointed across the room to the open trap door. "Stay there and wait for me."

Elvera stared wide-eyed at Lance. "With him?"

"Yes, with him!"

"But I—"

The shutters covering the kitchen window began to shiver and smoke, flames creeping up inside the cracks. The torch Engrelin had flung outside hadn't gone far enough.

"Just get in there!"

Elvera needed no second prompting. She flew across the kitchen and down into the cellar.

Engrelin grabbed Lance's shoulder. "And you—"

"I'm not going to hurt her, Engrelin," Lance said. He gripped Engrelin's hands tightly and slid if off his shoulder. "Just trust me. You go."

The sincerity caught Engrelin off guard. But there was no time for questions or even wonder. The flames burning the shutter were creeping down the wall. Lance sprang down into the cellar. Engrelin turned in a slow circle in the middle of the kitchen, struggling to decide which way he should go. The strange house seemed bigger than ever, the crashing of glass more distinct, the roar of flames more ravenous, the shouts outside more discernable. Finally, he simply rushed forward into a hallway he had never been down, and which didn't seem to be in as much danger of burning as the others.

"Aunt Ruth!" he shouted as he charged down one hallway after another. Never had he realized what labyrinths large houses could be! He rammed his shoulder into every closed door he came across, breaking them open, until his right shoulder and arm must have been one large bruise. The roar of flames stalked him hungrily through the house, drawing closer with the precious second that ticked by. Panic arched through Engrelin. If he didn't find Aunt Ruth soon, the window fire would consume the kitchen. There would be no way out for him but through one of the windows. Elvera and Lance, ignorant of the tunnel, would be trapped. Aunt Ruth would die.

Through the black haze, Engrelin's smarting, groping eyes fell on a door at the end of the hallway—a dead end. It hung slightly ajar. Engrelin staggered in, and nearly sprawled over the large bed that stood close to the door.

On the bed, unconscious, slumped Aunt Ruth.

Engrelin checked the widow over quickly. She didn't seem hurt. The window in this room was astonishingly still whole, though the shutters were flung wide. Beyond it, Engrelin saw the blazing fury that had once been Aunt Ruth's barn. Guilt clamped over his chest and throat. This was all his fault. If he had only stayed away, and asked Elvera for help…

Gently, he lifted Aunt Ruth's limp form in his arms, along with the quilt she had lain on. Something slid to the floor and thudded at Engrelin's feet. He glanced down to see a thick, leather-bound book. On the cover, inscribed in gold, were the only two words Engrelin could ever recognize: *Sanctaidd Beibl*. Beside it, two golden rings were scattered on the carpet. Stooping awkwardly, Engrelin picked up the bible and the rings and tucked them in the quilt with the widow. Bundling her more securely in his arms, Engrelin stepped into the hallway.

A wave of intense heat rolled over him, bringing smoky tears to his eyes and singeing his skin. Hastily, Engrelin drew a loose portion of the quilt more tightly over Aunt Ruth to shield her from the heat and flames and smoke writhing through the air.

Move and hurry.

Engrelin took one step forward, and then another, squinting against the smoke blowing in his face. As he moved down the hallway, the heat only intensified. Sweat poured down his forehead and dripped into his eyes. Unimaginable, that there could be such heat!

He stumbled quickly down the hallway, Aunt Ruth's head bumping gently against his damp shoulder. Engrelin glanced down at her, readjusted his grip, and turned a corner.

Flames engulfed him.

52

erwyn stirred, then shivered, pulling her thin blanket tighter around her shoulders. Why was it so cold? The thought wandered through her numb brain for several minutes before she gathered the mental and physical strength to lever herself up on one elbow and look around the dark kitchen. Tonight, it seemed darker than ever before. Her bleary eyes took several seconds to focus on the open fireplace across the room. She saw the faintest reddish-orange glow gleaming amid yesterday's gray ashes.

With a groan, she pulled herself upright. She'd forgotten to bank the embers. Another glance showed her that the smaller fireplace she usually relied on for nightly warmth had long since died out. She had no choice but to rise and start a fire with the embers she had left before they too grew cold. What a delay dead embers would cause in the morning!

She shivered as her ragged stocking feet crept across the paved floor towards the fire. Her trembling hand groped in the darkness of the tinder box for some wood shavings. It only scraped the bare, dusty bottom of the wooden crate. Berwyn sank back on her heels, staring dumbly into the crate. What would she start the fire with if she had no shavings?

She rose and cast about the dark kitchen. She would never dare tear up any of the rags or towels—it seemed Rees kept track of even those. She didn't dare get in trouble now. She couldn't go out to the woodshed at night (she could hear her guard snoring as he slumbered instead keeping watch outside the kitchen door). Berwyn stooped and swept the floor with her bare hands, feeling nothing but dust and the bare rock. What she would have given for a few leaves or pine needles!

Finding nothing she could use and hesitant to tear even a strip from her own garments, Berwyn sank wearily onto her pallet, drawing her knees up close to her chest and tipping her head back against the wall. How could she have been so stupid as to go to sleep without first banking the fire? Exhaustion, the only excuse, was not good in her eyes. She was always tired. She couldn't do this every night, cause a delay to their already early mornings. Warwick wanted the breakfasts served on time for the men so that the women and children's shift could come in quickly enough for both groups to get to work promptly. Berwyn was sure he would seize any opportunity to finish what he had started during the revolt.

The thought made Berwyn shudder and shift, rustling the straw in the pallet beneath her.

The straw. Berwyn froze, bunching the straw beneath the rough canvas in her hands. If only there was some way to tear into her pallet to get a little of the straw so that she could light the fire without reducing the little comfort it provided her.

Unless she used her father's old bedding instead.

Everything within Berwyn turned cold at the idea. She had never touched the pallet and pillow Warwick had so mockingly dragged into the kitchen after her father's death. Her "inheritance," as he cruelly referred to it. But surely it would be all right if she just took a little straw. Her father would understand.

Berwyn pulled the pillow out of the cabinet in which she had hidden it and retrieved a knife. Biting her lip, she slitted the crude stiches along one hem, just enough to reach inside and grab a handful of straw. She brought the pillow over to the fireplace, uncovered the last few red embers, and reached into the pillow.

Her hand closed over dry, crackling straw, and something else. Something thin and hard. Berwyn quickly drew it out and dumped the fistful into her lap. But it was too dark to identify anything. She cast some of the straw onto the embers. As they flared up, Berwyn picked up the object and held it close to the fire.

Her father's pipe.

Berwyn's shoulders shook with suppressed tears. She couldn't cry aloud—she might wake the soldier leaning against the door outside. What was her father's pipe doing in there? It still smelled faintly of the root he had smoked in place of tobacco. Now, however, the thin stem and wide bowl were sealed with wax—drippings from the tallow candles issued in Kepspell. Why had he sealed it?

Having reduced the meager handful of straw to ashes, the embers sank down to brood. Laying the pipe aside, Berwyn reached into the pillow again and pulled out more straw, throwing it out on the fire. Her hand brushed against a soft, fine fabric within the pillow. Afire with curiosity, she let her fingertips linger on it. But the fire had to be built up before the embers died.

She took some splinters of wood and then some larger logs from the wood box and piled them on top of the cheerily leaping flames. Topping it off with a final handful of straw, she reached into the pillow once again, groping for the fabric. Instead, her hand tangled around something cold and clinging. Startled, she jerked her hand back, only to find it entwined in a gold chain.

Berwyn stared with disbelief at the slender, rich chain wrapped around her fingers and the oval-shaped emerald, a little bigger than her thumbnail, which hung from it in a golden setting.

She had seen it once before when she was little. She remembered clinging to her father's legs, waiting for him to explain what was wrong, when she had noticed the green glint in his hands.

"Just something I gave your mother on our wedding day," he had briefly explained. He would say no more about it. But Berwyn, little as she was, had understood her father wept for the woman who had died only a week after Berwyn's birth. She had been frightened then, frightened at this glimpse of the sorrow her father carried in his heart. But she had also, through her father's grief, realized that this woman who had brought her into the world must have been truly wonderful, truly lovable and good for her father to weep so bitterly over her death.

Berwyn held the jewel up to the firelight, smiling sadly to herself as the flames glistered on the inscription scrolling across the back of the stone: Wrenn. Her mother's name. Berwyn turned the stone over and over in her hands, watching it gleam. Reaching back, she clasped the slender chain around her neck and tucked the jewel well beneath the neck of her blouse. She would wear it always.

More curious than ever, Berwyn resumed her attention to the pillow. What else had her father stowed in here?

Her groping hand found a few more wisps of straw, and the fine, almost silky fabric she had felt earlier. Her forehead puckered as she cut the slit a little wider and drew the folded piece of fabric out. The pillow seemed deflated once the entirety of the fabric lay in her lap.

Her fingers explored the smooth fabric a moment. It felt rich, but old—worn in places, repaired in others. A curiously shaped patch, almost like a point, made her run her fingertips over it several times. What was this?

Standing, she let the fabric ripple out of its folds, stretching it out in front of her and allowing it to pool at her feet. It was immense, rectangular, and dark green in color. Berwyn caught a glimpse of gold against the dark background. Gasping in surprise, she took several hurried steps away from the fire, her fingers tightening around the edges of the fabric. This was the last thing she wanted to burn. This was the *it* of which her father and his companions had whispered.

This was no ordinary piece of fabric.

53

Engrelin *clutched Aunt Ruth's body tighter to himself. Wicked* orange and blue flames devoured the walls and ceiling around him. He could hardly gasp one breath through the smothering heat and smoke. At any moment, the whole house would collapse on top of him and Aunt Ruth. Could he still reach the cellar?

All this flashed through his mind in the fraction of a second. For that fraction of a second, he hesitated, struggling for breath and feeling the flames brush eagerly forward. His shoulders tensed.

And he charged on.

Every running step he took seemed to stretch out, as if someone had fastened lead weights to the soles of his shoes. Around him, the flames seized fragments of the walls and ceiling and hurled them to the floor, showering sparks and glowing embers onto Engrelin's arms and shoulders. The floorboards crackled and split ominously beneath his pounding feet.

Finally, he ducked under the sagging kitchen doorway. The shouts from the men outside greeted his ears. How close would they dare to get to the house? Would they come inside, or were they content to let the fire claim their victims?

Engrelin's eyes frantically swept the smoldering floor. The cellar door was shut, but still there, uncovered. He staggered towards it, dodging pieces of ceiling that threatened to fall on his head. His trembling hand fumbled at the cut-out handle on the trap door. He shifted Aunt Ruth's growing weight to one arm. The burning roof growled and splintered. Engrelin's slick fingers finally found their hold, and he tore the door open.

One corner of the room buckled and crashed in. The whole kitchen swayed, raining embers down onto Engrelin and Aunt Ruth. Engrelin leaped into the cellar, carrying the limp widow with him.

Hardly had he begun to shut the door, when, with a terrible roar, the whole kitchen collapsed. Debris plummeted down, crashing against the door and slamming it shut. The force flung Engrelin off the ladder, his arms still tight around Aunt Ruth. The cellar's earthen walls trembled with the shock. A corner of the wood floor above cracked, letting hellish light glare into the cellar.

Engrelin lay where he fell, coughing. He wiped his streaming eyes on his blackened sleeve and swallowed repeatedly to sooth his burning throat. Very gently, he sat up and uncovered Aunt Ruth. The quilt was scorched in many different places, but the woman herself was unscathed.

"Engrelin, what are you doing?" Elvera asked, coming up behind him. "The floor's wood—it'll come down on our heads any minute! I can't believe it didn't just now."

"What, he's not dead?" Lance exclaimed from somewhere in the darkness.

Engrelin looked up at the sound. He had half-expected to find Lance gone.

"Sorry to disappoint you," he said, "but no."

Roused by the voices, Aunt Ruth stirred. Still wiping his watery eyes clear, Engrelin crouched beside her.

"Ma'am, are you all right?" he asked.

Aunt Ruth raised herself on one elbow and rubbed the back of her head. Then she gasped sharply, her hands darting to the floor, groping. "The *Beibl*!" she cried softly. "And my rings!"

Engrelin took the things out of the quilt and pressed them into her hands. "Here."

Aunt Ruth clutched her treasures to her chest; her whole body shook violently. A muffled sob broke through the semi-darkness. Engrelin put a supportive hand on her shoulder—what else could he do? Pity and guilt were tearing him to shreds. Why, oh why had he ever come here?

"I'm all right," Aunt Ruth said finally, drawing a tremulous breath. "I made an absolute fool of myself, running off and putting you all in danger. But when I saw the barn…" She tapered off, and in the reddish light, Engrelin saw several more tears slip down her cheeks. He groped for her hands and squeezed them. What other consolation could he try to offer? Her house, everything she owned, was now gone.

"Aunt Ruth," he whispered huskily, "I'm truly sorry. But we need to get out of here. The floor won't hold up forever. I need you to show me where the tunnel is."

"Help me up," Aunt Ruth ordered.

Once she was on her feet, with Engrelin's hand still resting on her shoulder, she shuffled over to a stack of tall, empty baskets. "Behind there," she said.

Engrelin dragged the baskets away. Carved into the wall was a space even blacker than the cellar.

"Be careful—the ceiling's low," Aunt Ruth warned. She stepped into the tunnel. Elvera followed her quickly. Lance, moving towards the entrance, stumbled into Engrelin, and clutched his waist to keep from falling.

"Sorry, can't see a thing in here," muttered Lance once he had righted himself. "And you're no help. You're a better wall than a door, Engrelin."

Engrelin, too tired to argue or even retort, stepped aside and let Lance pass through into the tunnel. After dragging the baskets back into place, he followed his companions into the tunnel.

The darkness pressed painfully against Engrelin's eyes. He kept one hand on Lance's shoulder, using it as a guide, since the tunnel walls were too wet and crumbly to feel along. Stagnant water pooled here and there along the sloping floor. Something tangled around Engrelin's ankles. He stumbled forward. He pulled it away (it might have been a rope, slimy from the mud and wet) and pushed on. Despite stooping low, his head occasionally brushed the tunnel's roof, sending little cold clods raining down onto his head and shoulders.

They crept through the black tunnel for what seemed like hours, breathing heavily and slipping in the mud underfoot. Finally, they stepped out into open air, among the final few snowflakes petering down from the leaden sky.

The woods were cool and dark—not like the tunnel, but fresh and soothing after their brushes with fire and the difficult journey. The storm had been furious, but brief, and had nearly spent itself. In the distance, the flames of Aunt Ruth's home and barn leaped to kiss the sky. The foursome stood silent for several minutes, watching the house burn.

"I'm so sorry," Engrelin whispered, his eyes fixed on the curling flames. "I never should have come here."

"No—" Aunt Ruth began. She caught Engrelin's expression. Her lips tightened. "This wasn't your fault or mine," she said quietly. "It was them. Don't let yourself or anyone else say otherwise."

Engrelin clenched his teeth and averted his gaze, directing it back to the burning wreck that had once been the widow's house. He clamped his hand tightly around Arrian's hilt. He was on this journey to protect and preserve life. Why did he only end up hurting himself or someone else in the process?

I wasn't meant for this, for any of it. Why did they have to choose me?

"I'm going to make sure you get somewhere safe," he said firmly.

"But you—"

"You think I'm going to let your house burn down, then leave you in the woods?" Engrelin demanded, turning on her sharply.

Aunt Ruth gazed at him a moment, then sighed and bowed her head in a nod. "I have a cousin, only a mile from here, who would take me in.. If you want to escort me there—"

"It's not a want, it's a must," Engrelin interjected tightly.

Aunt Ruth nodded again. She motioned to the woods. "This way."

Turning her back to her destroyed home, the elderly widow walked away, clutching her *Beibl* tightly to her chest. Engrelin, following behind Lance and Elvera, fingered the map in his pocket. All of this because of a map? Because of his pride and his dread of Elvera's anger?

He wanted to turn around, run back to the site of the fire, and toss the map on top of it all.

But if he did that, he would have no guide to help him finish his journey, and that would be yet another mistake on his part.

Still, as he strode through the snow-flecked night, striving to do at least one thing right, he burned the map to flaking ashes in his heart.

"*Will you be all right* from here?" Engrelin asked.

"We're not even ten yards from the front door." Aunt Ruth chuckled softly. Engrelin wondered how she could even think of laughing, after all that had happened to her that night.

"I think I'll be fine."

"I'll be watching from here, just to be sure," Engrelin said, motioning to the thicket they crouched in.

Aunt Ruth's expression sobered. She reached out to give Engrelin's hand a squeeze, but when he pulled his hand away, she grasped his elbow instead.

"Remember what I said, Engrelin," she whispered. "I'll be fine. You worry about that girl."

Engrelin didn't answer. With a sigh, Aunt Ruth left the brush. She walked up a path of crushed shells up to the house. Silently, Engrelin watched her walk up the porch steps and knock on the door. Her relative answered and ushered her inside. Engrelin sighed inwardly and pushed his hair back off his forehead. She, at least, was safe.

Elvera plucked Engrelin's sleeve. "Engrelin?" she whispered. "Can we go now?"

Engrelin gave the house a final look before turning. "Yes, we can go now."

Elvera scrambled out of the thicket and onto the path, clutching her long skirts. Engrelin grabbed Lance and pulled him up to the path where Elvera stood staring and shivering, her cloak's hood drawn far over her head.

"Where are we going now?" she asked.

"North," Engrelin replied shortly. He started down the path back towards the main road, propelling Lance in front of him.

Elvera snorted. "Where north?"

"Monaria, through Tirendria."

"How far away is Tirendria?" asked Elvera, panting as she struggled to keep up with Engrelin's long strides.

"Didn't you listen to Averendier's plans?" Engrelin asked, looking at her askance.

Elvera only glared.

"Only a few hours' walk," Engrelin relented. "You'll know we're there when we cross an old bridge."

Elvera nodded and pulled her cloak tighter around her shoulders. Engrelin glanced at her sidelong, concerned despite his irritation. He nearly sprawled over Lance, who had stopped abruptly in front of him for no reason than to anger Engrelin.

So the night wore on. The drifting snowflakes petered out, leaving the sky murky with clouds.

Just as dawn stained the horizon, Engrelin led his group off the road and into a copse of reghun trees which screened them from view while spreading a golden, snow-free carpet on the ground. They were only a mile away from the bridge and Tirendria. It was a bad place to stop. but Engrelin had stumbled frequently over the last few hours, more asleep than awake. If he didn't stop and sit down, he would drop dead. Besides, he reasoned, it would be wise to rest before they reached the most dangerous stage of their journey.

Lance threw himself to the ground immediately. Elvera, sniffing delicately, settled herself down far away from him.

"You'd think he hadn't slept in ages," she commented to Engrelin.

Engrelin glanced over at Lance, who was snoring softly, seemingly already plunged deep in slumber. He frowned. He hadn't slept, truly slept, in what seemed like years. Through his weary brain paraded the list of sleepless nights he had suffered since the loss of his family. Elvera's and Lance's figures blurred. Engrelin shook his head and fiercely rubbed his eyes, which stubbornly persisted in only opening halfway. He had to keep some sort of watch, he thought drowsily. They were so close to Tirendria. What if the Tirendrians decided to patrol the road this far south and discovered them?

Engrelin clenched his jaw and grasped Arrian's hilt. Not while he still drew breath.

Breath that was steadily deepening. His legs threatened to buckle beneath him. Engrelin sank down at the base of reghun tree and propped his back against the jagged back, oblivious of the way it tore his clothes and scratched his neck.

Elvera's smudgy figure remained in his sight until he fell into an uneasy sleep, his fingers still clutching his sword.

54

Engrelin clenched both hands tightly around Arrian's hilt. But they were so slick with sweat, he could hardly hold his sword at all. Gritting his teeth, he grasped it tighter, so tight his fingers ached. But he couldn't drop it now, not when he needed it so badly.

In the pitch darkness around him, a snake twisted in some dark, serpentine dance. Engrelin wouldn't have known it was there if it hadn't been for the reddish gleam of the creature's eyes and the brilliant radiance Arrian threw out.

A sharp hiss behind him. Engrelin whirled, swinging Arrian in his wake as both weapon and torch. The serpent quickly darted out of the blade's path. It hissed, almost derisively, flicking its blood-red tongue between its fangs.

"Ffarmwr," the creature whispered, low and sinister. "Just drop it. What need do you have for that thing? It's a tool for warriors and men. You're just a boy."

Scowling, Engrelin drew his blade close to his body, mistrusting the snake's delicate weave. His gaze latched onto the creature's glittering eyes.

"I can't give it up," he said. "Who else would carry it?"

The serpent chuckled, opening its mouth wide to display its cruel fangs, which somehow seemed larger than they had before.

Because they were. The serpent seemed to be swelling. Growing. Engrelin stepped back. The creature, only able to rear itself to

Engrelin's waist before, now swung its head high over Engrelin's. Its lips curled in a cruel leer. Engrelin took another step back and bumped into a clammy, unseen wall behind him. His mouth dried, his heart kicked up several gears. There was no escape.

"Give it to me," hissed the giant snake, lowering its great head level with Engrelin's. Its slender tongue still darted in and out, this time inches from Engrelin's face. "You never wanted to be the bearer in the first place, did you?"

Engrelin didn't answer, but he shifted his hold on his sword, clutching the grip with both hands.

"Let me have it," the serpent coaxed. "Lay it down, and never worry about it or its mission ever again. *I* shall become the *Arweddwr gon Arrian*, as you were intended to be. I will bury the sword in the darkness, and it will be forgotten by all. The prophecy shall fail. And I..." The creature's large, gleaming gaze drifted far beyond the dark wall at Engrelin's back. It seemed now to be talking to just itself, to have forgotten Engrelin was standing in front of it. "...I shall live."

Prophecy? Engrelin wondered. He closed his eyes for a moment, still seeing through the thin skin of his eyelids Arrian's blue glow. It, at least, was prepared to meet the dangers before it. A thrill ran up Engrelin's fingers and into his shoulder. It urged him to do the same.

"I won't drop it," he said, opening his eyes to see the serpent gazing intently in his face.

The creature stared unblinkingly at Engrelin. A low, discontented growl rumbled through the darkness.

"That was unwise," it growled. "Unwise indeed. Give it up while you still have the chance."

"Never."

A bellow of rage erupted from the creature's throat. The serpent's head shot forward, fangs bared, mouth gaping. Engrelin jumped swiftly, desperately, to one side and drove Arrian upward. The blade pierced the creature's head, just below its jaw.

Uttering a shrill, nether-worldly shriek, the creature writhed backwards. Engrelin jerked Arrian free and sprang clear of the writhing serpent. As the snake's screams faded, Engrelin became conscious of a wetness on his hands. He looked down. Dark blood dribbled off his hands—the serpent's blood. Arrian's brilliancy was coated with it. Engrelin's stomach lurched.

Out of the darkness, the serpent's sinuous voice drifted. "Murderer."

"No!"

Engrelin jerked awake, gasping for breath, his heart galloping in his chest. The darkness gave way to cloudy, mid-day gloom. The reghun copse materialized. The chamber was gone. The Serpent was gone.

But his hands were still wet.

Engrelin closed his eyes briefly, but when he looked down, he realized his hands were only sweaty from having grasped Arrian so hard for so long. The sword was sheathed. He drew it a couple inches out of its scabbard, just to be sure. The blade was clean, though it glinted the palest blue.

Engrelin heard someone snickering. His gaze jerked up to meet Elvera's. The girl, still lounging on the needle-strewn ground, vainly tried to hide her laughter behind her hand.

"That was the funniest thing I've ever seen," she chortled. "My sisters never talked in their sleep."

"Well, this is the first and last time," Engrelin grumbled. The princess' mocking eyes had instantly extinguished the surface terror of the dream, clearing his head enough for a good mental flogging. How could he have fallen asleep when the slightest thing gone wrong could have plunged them all to ruin?

Engrelin dragged himself to his feet, then reached out to steady himself against the tree. The sleep he *had* gotten hadn't done him any good. He actually felt worse.

"Well, it was interesting at the moment," said Elvera. "More interesting than Lance." She jerked her head at Lance, who was sprawled out on his back, his head hanging back and his mouth gaping wide. Obnoxious snores rumbled in his throat.

Elvera plugged her ears with her fingers and made a face. "Not funny."

Despite himself, Engrelin chuckled. Lance was snoring so uproariously, there was no doubting he was wide awake. His chest heaved with his exaggerated breaths.

Just as quickly as it had come, Engrelin's smile vanished. Lance's arms were spread wide. He had forgotten to tie him up! Engrelin fumbled in his pocket for the length of rope he had stored there the previous night.

His fingers met nothing but his ragged lining of his pocket. Engrelin let his breath hiss sharply between his clenched teeth. Of course, when Lance had smashed against him in the cellar. He must have reached into Engrelin's pocket and pulled out the rope. Where else could it have gone?

Lance had pulled it out and…had dropped it in the tunnel. Engrelin's eyes narrowed to dangerous slits. The thing he had tripped over in the tunnel had been nothing other than his own rope. Maybe he could still…

His eyes darted to Lance's waist, and he ground his teeth so hard it hurt. Lance, at his own convenience, had ditched his belt as well.

Furious, Engrelin seized the hem of his cloak. Tearing several strips from the bottom, he tried to splice them together. But the fabric was so rotten by months of travel, it fell apart in his hands. Engrelin threw them to the ground in frustration. He had nothing else but his own belt to use. He jerked his belt from his waist and strode over to where Lance lay. Engrelin shook him.

"What do you want?" Lance demanded, swatting Engrelin away (and confirming the fact that he had been feigning sleep for a while). His icy-blue eyes opened, fixing Engrelin in their angry glare. The light in them shifted at once to resilience once he saw the burning, restrained rage in Engrelin's eyes and the thick belt he twisted in his hands.

"What are you going to do to me now?" Lance grumbled.

"Nothing to hurt you," Engrelin replied. "Just stand up."

Grudgingly, Lance obeyed. He flinched when Engrelin first touched him, but only growled when Engrelin twisted the belt around his wrists. Engrelin ignored him and continued to fasten the belt as tightly as he could. It was too thick to be drawn very tight, but Engrelin knew it would hold Lance for a while, at least until he could think of something better. The last thing he needed while he was so exhausted was an unrestrained Lance.

"How far away are we from the bridge?" Elvera asked. She moved towards Engrelin, giving Lance a wide berth.

"About an hour or so, the way we're going," Engrelin answered. He took a step back to scrutinize his work. He bit the inside of his cheek hard. He just couldn't seem to get it right.

"What way is that?"

"Through the woods." Engrelin knew from experience it would be easier to slip past the guard house if they went far back into the woods and came around along the creek bank. He didn't want to put a single toe on the road until they were right in front of the bridge.

Elvera thrust out her lower lip but didn't protest. Engrelin turned away from Lance, refusing to let a sigh move beyond his chest. If he behaved as though the belt were secure, maybe Lance wouldn't think about escaping. He scrubbed a hand across his face. Big maybe.

"Don't worry," put in Lance cheerfully, his eyes gleaming. "We won't be swimming. Engrelin doesn't want to take the road, for fear we'll become human targets. Isn't that right?"

"No, it isn't," Engrelin said in a low voice. He inwardly cringed as he bent to retrieve his sword. Since his belt was around Lance's hands, he had no way to carry it comfortably. Engrelin finally punched the clasps on the scabbard through the neck of his cloak. Arrian rested beneath the cloak, against his back, the pommel jutting out.

Lance sneered. Elvera's eyes darted between the two, as if she did not know who to believe. Engrelin forced a reassuring smile.

"No one would hurt a princess," he said.

It was a blatant lie, and he wouldn't have blamed Elvera if she had sniffed and told him so outright. She said nothing at all, though her eyes grew wider. She shut them, her glittering lashes a dark line against her warm skin. She hugged her sides tightly, as if she could only hold herself together by brute strength.

Lance's words settled over them like a dark cloud as they set off through the woods. Lance seemed to have even scared himself, he crept along so quietly. Engrelin kept imagining he heard footsteps behind him. Every time he looked over his shoulder, Tirendrian red seemed to flicker through the tangled trees. It took him moments to realize it was only his imagination. Still, the next time it might not be mere fancy. It might be the last thing he ever saw in Ontaria.

Elvera clung to him like a burr, jolting at the slightest sounds, from the wind rattling the branches to a clod of snow falling to the ground. By the time they reached the creek, Engrelin was sure the sight of her own shadow would have stopped her heart.

Reaching the creek bank didn't help anything in the slightest, even if they did make good progress. The woods hemming the bank in were far too thick to wrestle through, especially for Elvera. The narrow strip of clear ground on which they were able to walk hung a precarious ten feet above the gurgling water. The snow had buried all indications of the weak spots in the bank; there was no warning as to when they would step on thin ground and fall through. After stepping into several sinkholes, Elvera clung to Engrelin's arm and had to be dragged along. Every time her foot sank more than two inches into the snow, she went into fits of frantic screaming that made even Lance cringe.

"Can't you shut her up?" he demanded in a loud whisper after Engrelin had fished Elvera out of a terrifying pit six inches deep.

Engrelin shot Lance a furious, helpless look and turned to try to comfort the princess. He reached out to take her hand, but she only snatched hers. She stared at his scarred right hand with horror or something else which Engrelin couldn't quite place.

"We're almost there," Engrelin said. He took a few steps forward to coax her on, as he might have with an uncertain animal. "We're already come this far."

Elvera tore her eyes from his hand to his face. Just as quickly, she looked away, beginning a nod. It ended in a gape, as if her jaw's muscles had quit her completely.

"Engrelin?" she quivered.

"The holes aren't that deep," Engrelin said, with an edge. He had detected the slight dip in the snow which might be another hole.

"Engrelin?"

"What?"

"The bridge is gone."

Engrelin swiveled quickly, following Elvera's stare. Sure enough, the road was only a few yards behind him. But there was no bridge over the creek flowing sluggishly between its high banks. A single rotten post stood near shore. Fastened to it by a single bent nail was a single rotting board.

Lance stood behind them and stared into the water. "What now, genius?"

Engrelin reached feverishly into his pocket, drew out the limp map, and held it in front of himself. The bridge Aunt Ruth had drawn out for him was roughly a mile downstream. One mile, passed as the afternoon had?

"There's another crossing, a mile downstream," he said for his companions' benefit, without taking his eyes from the map. "It'll only take—"

A piercing scream shattered his sentence. A hand wildly snatched Engrelin's map, tearing it in two. Through the halves, Engrelin saw Elvera tumble back over the lip of the bank. He lunged for her, letting the pieces of the map flutter forgotten onto the ground.

But it was Lance who reached her first. Lance who, with one jerk, tore his hands free from Engrelin's belt and slammed down beside the bank, arms outstretched. One hand grabbed Elvera's mid-air. The other latched onto Engrelin's cloak clasp, pulling Engrelin down with him. Elvera's scream was cut off for a few seconds, as if someone had punched her in the stomach. She continued shrieking, louder than before.

"Lance, get off me!" Engrelin exclaimed, tearing Lance's hand away from his chest. He felt his cloak loosen around his shoulders.

"I don't want you to fall in too," Lance grunted.

Engrelin ventured a cautious glance over the bank. The frightened princess dangled with her feet two yards above the water, her eyes rolling with fright as she clung to Lance's arm.

"Engrelin, a little help?" Lance demanded through his grit teeth. "I don't know if she weighs this much, or her pack, but it hurts."

Elvera's mouth gaped wide, her eyes flashed, her lips flapped. But she could only croak hoarsely.

Dropping down onto his stomach, Engrelin reached over the bank. "Grab my hand," he called down.

Elvera dug her fingernails into Engrelin's palm. She hung a deadweight in the boys' arms, offering no assistance. The bank, slick with mud and snow, only let them scoot back a few inches at a time without slipping. Several times, Engrelin's heart nearly deserted him as he felt Elvera's sweaty hand slipping out of his.

"I can't swim," Elvera mumbled, her eyes screwed tightly shut. "Don't drop me."

"We won't," Lance promised, so firmly Engrelin looked at him sidelong. He thought Lance couldn't have cared less if Elvera had ever dropped dead in her tracks. But now…

Just when Engrelin thought his burning arms wouldn't hold out for another second, they dragged Elvera on top of the bank. She sank into a sodden, miserable heap at their feet.

"Anything broken?" Engrelin asked anxiously, struggling to his feet. His cloak and sword slid from his shoulders to the ground with a muffled *thump*.

"I'm fine," Elvera sniffed, drawing her shoulders stiffly upright. Still, she shook like a wet leaf caught in the wind.

Lance put a hand on Engrelin's shoulder. Engrelin locked eyes with Lance, then straightened and clasped his hand. "Thanks for catching her," he said awkwardly.

Lance nodded. "I didn't want her to fall in," he said. "Only you."

A sudden, vicious light sprang into Lance's eyes. Engrelin yanked away. But Lance pulled him back, straight into his flying fist.

Engrelin reeled back from the blow, his hand darting to his waist for his sword. His hand closed over empty air. At the same moment, he stepped backwards into nothing.

55

If only, by shutting her eyes, Lilac could also block out the vivid scenes of the past few days. All night, they had been plaguing her, chasing away any sleep she might have gotten.

That night at the tavern, the man, after reassuring her that he wouldn't draw so much as a bead of blood from her body, had bound Lilac securely to one of the ladder-backed chairs. He had hardly finished when a falcon had flown into the room through the window (which the man had reopened) to light upon the man's wrist.

At that moment, someone had knocked on the door. The man had opened it and held a conversation in confidential whispered with whomever had been in the hallway. Lilac had strained against her bonds to hear what the men were saying.

"Captain Linford, should we get rid of the boy?"

"No," the Captain had answered. "Bring him. He is the admiral's son. We can't just throw something like that away. If anything, he'll fetch a good ransom."

Lilac's insides had frozen. But though she had strained until the ropes cut cruel abrasions into her wrists, she distinguished nothing more from the men's mutterings.

Finally, the door had closed and the man, Linford, walked slowly over to her, gently stroking the bird still perched on his arm. The falcon eyed her, flexing its hooked beak.

"Preparations are being made at Reing for your visit, Your Highness," Linford had said softly. The calmness—even kindness—of his voice disoriented Lilac more than cruelty or threats.

He had pulled a table up beside Lilac and sat in the chair across from her. After spreading a piece of paper out on the table and pulling a pencil out of his pocket, he had continued, "I must write those there so they will be prepared for our arrival. They'll be so pleased to hear you have accepted our invitation."

Indignation had burned part of Lilac's fear away. She said quietly but firmly, "Captain, I did not accept anything. You're forcing me to come with you."

"True," the captain had nodded and looked up briefly from his letter. His eyes had shone with something akin to pity. "But I'm sure, if you had been given the choice, you would have found it hard to resist. But never fear. The invitation has been extended to your sisters. Soon you will once again enjoy one another's company."

Lilac had pressed her lips into a tight line, worry gnawing at her stomach. What was going to happen to her sisters? To *herself*?

Isalinia, Elvera, please be anywhere but this city, she had desperately prayed. More than ever, she longed to know where they were. Perhaps it was good she didn't.

Hard scuffling had broken out in the room beside hers, followed by silence, one more menacing than ever before. Lilac had found herself holding her breath until a knock had sounded on the door. Linford had finished rolling his letter into a tight tube. He shoved it into a cylindrical container on the falcon's leg before he acknowledged the person in the hall. Finally, the door had opened a crack.

"He's out, finally," a disgruntled voice had grunted.

"Good." Bringing the falcon to the window, Linford had launched it into the night. Lilac had heard the beating of the bird's wings as it shot away. Linford had closed the window and turned to Lilac.

"And now, Your Highness, we have quite the walk ahead of us. I suggest you get out of that chair." He had proceeded to release her from the chair, but left her hands bound in front of her.

The walk had been a terrible one. All that night and through the following day, they had marched. Linford had only let them halt once, and only when the snow blew so thickly, they couldn't see where they were going. They had camped for the night, even after the storm had passed.

Lilac sighed and turned onto her side, wincing at the hardness of the ground she had collapsed onto hours before. Hours before, and still not one wink of sleep. They might as well have kept marching. Her arms, still bound in front of her, ached horribly. Painfully, she flexed her tingling fingers and shivered in the brutal north wind that tore through the trees with no thought to the miserable creatures huddling against it.

"You're awake, finally."

Lilac flinched, then turned her head towards the voice.

Linford crouched beside her, seeming to materialize out of the thin air.

"I want to get an early start today," the man continued quietly. "I see no use in keeping His Majesty waiting any longer than he must. That is, if it's all right with you, Your Highness." He raised one eyebrow questioningly.

Lilac groped for an answer. Did he actually want her opinion? Or was he simply mocking her with her helplessness in the situation?

Linford nodded slowly, as if she had answered him. "Whenever you are ready," he said, before he straightened and strode away.

Lilac let her breath out in relief and glanced wearily around herself. Three men within Linford's company milled about. Averendier was sitting bound against a nearby tree; the blood crusted to one side of his head was the only indication to the struggle that night in the tavern. One of the men stood in front of him, talking and occasionally shoving his prisoner against the tree. They seemed not in the least daunted by the fact that Averendier, when standing, towered a head over the tallest among them. Linford did not seem to care what brutality they exercised on this prisoner.

Lilac strained unconsciously against her bonds. If only she could break free and rush to his assistance! But even if she were untied, what could be done to stop them while Linford was around?

"Trying to get away, Your Highness?"

It was if she had summoned him with her thoughts. Lilac shuddered, closed her eyes, and willed Linford away. Always, he lingered near, ready to sap every drop of courage from her soul.

"I'm afraid it doesn't work that way," he continued. Reaching down, he loosened the ropes and slipped them off her slender wrists. "There. All you had to do was ask for them to be removed."

Lilac stared down at her raw wrists. A scream welled within her. But she uttered not a sound and resisted the powerful urge to chafe her wrists.

Linford took her shoulders and pulled her to her feet. At his touch, Lilac froze. The moment she was on her feet, she swiveled and slapped Linford sharply across the face.

"How dare you touch me!" she exclaimed, eyes flashing. "I can get up myself."

The tips of Linford's ears grew scarlet. Briefly, he reached up to touch the red handprint splayed across his cheek. Gently—ever so gently! —he took Lilac's wrists and again bound them in front of her. When he spoke, his voice hadn't lost an ounce of eerie calm.

"You must get accustomed to it, I'm afraid," he practically crooned. "You're not in Alinar anymore, Your Highness."

Lilac clamped her lips shut over a retort. Her hand still stung from the blow it had delivered. Justice must come later. Right now, for Alinar, she needed to stay alive.

Soon, Linford signaled for his group to move on. The weary tramp resumed. Lilac held herself straight as she marched down the little-used path. Linford tramped ceaselessly beside her.

However, as the hours dragged by, she stumbled on the rugged trail. Always, Linford's hand shot out to catch her before she hit the ground. Each time, Lilac numbed more and more to his touch. Not that she ever said anything to him. She was too tired for that. Too tired. Exhausted. Absolutely exhausted.

Lilac's vision blurred. Her foot snagged on a root hidden beneath the snow and she lurched forward. Linford, grabbing her arm at the last moment, gently helped her back to her feet. They both stood still a moment, Lilac staring dumbly down at the blood trickling down her leg from her badly skinned knee. The bottom of her long woolen skirt, completely soaked through, clung persistently to her trembling legs. She shivered and couldn't stop shivering.

Wordlessly, Linford took her hands in his and cut her bonds, letting the ropes fall into the snow at Lilac's feet. He slung one of her arms over his shoulder, slipping his own supporting limb across her back. Lilac shied for the fleetest of moments. But the deadweight of her body prevented her from moving. All she could do was lean against him with troubled gratitude.

"Does this help, Your Highness?" Linford asked quietly as they moved on. In his strange way, he was mocking her feebleness.

Lilac no longer had the strength to care. She simply leaned against him and dragged herself on.

56

ance's laughter still resounding in his ears, Engrelin tumbled back into the creek. The water swirled closed over his head. He plummeted down, down into the paralyzingly cold water. His lungs crushed against his ribs, screaming for air. Desperately, Engrelin struck out, fighting the downward momentum of his fall over the bank. Up and up and up. His clothes wrapped him in their sodden folds, bent on dragging him into the murky depths. Engrelin tried to tear himself free, but as he tore at his jerkin's laces, he sunk further. He left his clothes be and struggled upwards. Up and up and up. His lungs seared his chest. He had to breath water or die of the pain. Up and up.

His head broke the surface. Alternately, he gasped and choked on the sweet air and the water lapping into his open mouth. His floating body knocked against something slimy but solid. Still gasping and choking, he clung to it with all his remaining strength. He leaned his forehead against the thing; it was splintery against his wet skin. A board.

Engrelin pressed the water out of his eyes and looked about him. Not just any board. The board to the vanished bridge. In the crawling current, he had hardly drifted twenty yards from where he had fallen in!

Engrelin rested against the board for a few seconds, his breath steadying. The water rippled apologetically past, caressing his shoulders with little icy waves. Finally, Engrelin lifted his head to look up at the bank rising to his left. It was slippery with mud, but he thought he could see several indentations and ledges that he might cling to and scramble his way back to the top. The worst that could happen to him was falling back into the water, which had already proven to be quite free of rocks. It was deep. The only thing he had to fear from it was freezing.

Clenching his teeth to keep them from chattering, Engrelin pulled himself to the foot of the bank. The water swirling around him no longer felt cold, but white hot against his skin. Engrelin dug his fingers into the bank's earthen side and winced. Hopefully, his numb fingers would hold onto the outcroppings tight enough.

Cautiously, as silently as he could, Engrelin tested the first slab of rock jutting out from the bank, slowly lowering more and more of his weight onto it. It held. He gritted his teeth and heaved himself up onto it. The next outcropping also held, as did the next. He inched higher and higher, clinging to each handhold with all the strength his swollen fingers would allow.

Higher still, almost to the top, he wormed his way onto a difficult, narrow ledge, which hardly stuck two inches out of the mud. As he pressed himself against the bank to rest a moment, he thought he heard soft sobbing. Elvera? Engrelin shook himself to action and continued climbing.

"Would you just *stop*?"

Lance's voice, so terrifyingly close, stopped Engrelin short just before he lifted his head over the edge of the embankment. He stooped back down and pressed himself against the cool earth. Lance must have brought Elvera to the road. But why?

Elvera sniffed hard for several moments. But she could not seem to restrain herself. The tears flowed, wrenching Engrelin's heart. But he did not move. Showing himself now, wet and weak and weaponless, would be nothing short of suicide.

"Come on, get up," Lance ordered impatiently.

"I'm tired," Elvera sobbed in reply. The girl's skirts ruffled limply across the snow.

"Why don't you come with me? You can rest soon."

"Why did you push Engrelin in?" Elvera returned.

"I pushed you," said Lance.

"But you caught me," Elvera said. "And you didn't even intend to get my toes wet. You just wanted a chance to get Engrelin's sword before he fell in."

"True," Lance sighed melodramatically. "I couldn't have him resurrecting with that thing, though it might have made him sink faster. But it worked anyway, didn't it?"

"You're a monster," Elvera muttered miserably.

"You know, that's the nicest thing you've ever said to me," Lance returned, apparently in too good a mood to pass up yet another opportunity to banter with the princess.

"All right." Elvera's voice, though laced with tears, was strictly determined. "Run me through with it. Finish me off, just like you always wanted to."

Engrelin dug his nails into the bank. *Don't say stuff like that! Don't you realize there's still hope?*

But Lance only laughed. "I wouldn't kill you, even if I could pick up Engrelin's sword."

"And why can't you?"

Engrelin pictured all too well the expression that Elvera must be wearing.

"Because you're such a weakling? Thank you for finally admitting it."

Lance's breath hissed audibly from between his teeth. "For your information, I've always been stronger than him. But," he smoothly continued, "it's not a matter of strength. It's will. The sword just won't let me pick it up."

"If I were a sword, I wouldn't let you touch me either," Elvera snorted.

"It isn't about likes or dislikes either," said Lance, as if he were a scholar explaining something to an ignorant pupil, or a farmer explaining a variety of vegetable.

"Then what is it?"

"Oh, you just wouldn't understand," returned Lance, brushing her off in a way that said he himself did not understand.

"No, I suppose I wouldn't," Elvera returned. Something sugar-sweet crept into her tone, something that made Engrelin shift his position uncomfortably. Why wouldn't she keep her mouth shut and move on so he could climb up and help her?

"There are quite a few things I haven't understood in the past few months. Maybe you could clear some up for me?"

"Maybe," answered Lance tersely, suddenly wary, as he very well might be.

"You pushed me in to unclasp Engrelin's cloak..."

"Yes."

"To get Engrelin's sword..."

"Yes."

"Even though you couldn't use the sword yourself..."

"Yes."

"So you pushed Engrelin in to get him away from his sword *and* from me..."

"Right again," Lance said. "Honestly, I'm shocked. I think you just used your brains. I was beginning to wonder when you would figure it all out."

Elvera snorted derisively. "At least I have brains," she said. "But why," she pursued, plunging through Lance's angry silence, "were you Engrelin's prisoner in the first place?"

Engrelin's breath caught in his throat.

"Didn't he tell you?" Lance sneered. "I tried to steal your precious horses."

"But he seemed to have known you before that," Elvera persisted. "Did he?"

"Don't even remind me of that," Lance growled.

"Why not?"

"Why?" Lance echoed angrily. He stared down at the girl sitting in the middle of the snowy road. "He's responsible for hundreds of people's deaths. He even tried to kill me!"

"Him?" Elvera's shrill laughter grated against Lance's ears. "I was the one who wanted to kill you. But he wouldn't do it, even after all you did!"

"He just didn't want you to realize who he really was," Lance retorted. He paced up and down, churning the snow beneath his feet to a muddy slush. Elvera watched him silently, confused, not knowing the thoughts rushing through Lance.

Fort Starr. The slaughter of hundreds. His family's death. Traeth Euriad. Averendier. Engrelin.

"My father said he was a farmer."

Elvera's voice pierced through the thick wall of memories swarming Lance's brain. He glanced at her, then acknowledged her words with a curt nod.

"He was," he said. "But that doesn't make him any less guilty."

"Of what?"

"Fort Starr," Lance replied, as if she should know all. She should know. Everyone should know of what had happened that past summer, of all the lives cruelly twisted or wiped out.

"Is Engrelin a Tirendrian?" Elvera pertly demanded.

"No." Lance laughed, low and bitter. "He's worse. He's a Peterson."

"A Peterson?" The girl was clearly confused. As if she didn't know. Didn't know who the Petersons were! Everyone knew who they were. Everyone knew that the attack was a Peterson's fault. All the Petersons' faults.

"Engrelin's uncle could have saved those at Fort Starr," Lance exclaimed, flinging his arms out. "But he didn't. He just sat back and watched the slaughter. He arrived in time to clean up the mess. He…"

Lance ranted on and on, using such lurid description that Elvera shuddered. Every little point, every element of the attack was turned over and scrutinized. Lance felt as if he were talking to a stone wall. Elvera just sat there and shuddered. Lance continued to tell her of his reception of the awful news. Of Engrelin's impassiveness to it all. His protection of his cousin. Protecting Averendier, as if he deserved it!

Lance turned away, tears threatening his eyes and burning his throat. As if she cared what had happened to him and to others after Fort Starr. Her family hadn't been on the island. She didn't have any reason to care.

But he did. He cared desperately. Why else was he here?

"So…you hate Engrelin for something he didn't do," Elvera murmured in Lance's silence.

Lance whirled on her, his face working. Yet when he spoke, his voice was startlingly cold. "Engrelin is every bit as responsible as his uncle," he said. "You don't believe me, do you?"

Elvera bowed her head.

"Why don't you ask a few people from Bryn why Engrelin left home? Ask them why he left his sister and his grandmother alone to come here. Ask him why he came even though he didn't *want* to!"

"I…I don't think I want to know," Elvera whispered brokenly.

"He left because a royal order, issued by our king, told him to. Him, Averendier, Andrald, and his uncle. They all had to leave Monaria, under royal order. They're practically exiles. Criminals. Murderers!" He screamed the last, bending over the unresponsive girl. "Murderers, do you hear me?!"

Elvera burst into tears. They streamed down her face, leaving streaks through the mud that adorned her cheeks. Her shoulders convulsed.

Lance watched her, taking a small satisfaction in seeing her thus. No one, no one knew how it felt until it happened to them. They could cry all they wanted, but they wouldn't truly know. To be betrayed by your best friend…

He turned away, his hand traveling up to touch his shoulder.

"But…but what about the Tirendrians?" Elvera gasped behind him. "Why blame Engrelin for all this when they're the ones responsible. Look at yourself! You're helping them. You're one of them!"

Lance whirled viciously around and swung his fist back, as if to strike her. "Shut up!" he growled. "And don't breath a word about that again."

Elvera shrank back and whimpered in response.

Slowly, Engrelin brought his eyes over the lip of the bank. Lance and Elvera were close by. Elvera slumped in a forlorn heap on the ground. Lance towered over her, one hand balled in a fist. Even closer to Engrelin than they, tangled in Engrelin's cloak, Arrian's gemstone pommel gleamed, urging him to come and take it up.

Engrelin threw another furtive glance at Lance, whose back was turned. It was now or never.

Quietly, Engrelin pulled himself onto the bank. Still crouching, he crept forward to retrieve his sword. His eyes never left Lance.

"We should move on now," Elvera muttered, beginning to drag herself to her feet.

"No, stay down," Lance replied, shoving her back to the ground. "We might as well wait here."

"Wait? For what?"

"Our escorts."

Engrelin's gaze sharpened on Lance's back. Escorts?!

"Aren't you enough?" Elvera demanded.

"No," said Lance. "I can't get you to Reing on my own."

Engrelin watched Elvera recoil; he quickly adjusted to this new blow. Hadn't he expected it?

He had to get her away from there. Now.

At that moment, Elvera threw a despairing glance in his direction. Their eyes met. She froze. Her eyes widened. Her lips parted in a gape. Engrelin's whole body tingled with fear.

Look away! he mouthed.

"What are you staring at?" Lance demanded. "Soldiers? Get used to it, you'll be seeing a lot—" He began turning.

Engrelin didn't wait to see Lance's reaction. He ran. Lance charged to meet him. At the last moment, Engrelin dropped into a roll, passing beneath Lance's outstretched arms. He caught Arrian by the hilt and sprang back to his feet. He now stood between Elvera and Lance. Arrian blazed blue in his hands.

"You again!" Lance yelled, his face contorted with hideous rage. "Why I didn't kill you that first night after you left Bryn, I'll never know."

"Because it was Walche, and not you, who attacked me, Lance," Engrelin answered quietly. "I may have shot you in the shoulder, but at the time, I had no idea it was you."

Lance flung back his head. "Fine," he growled. "Kill me. Follow the blood-soaked footsteps of your beloved uncle."

Engrelin flinched. "I'm not going to kill you," he said.

Elvera laughed hysterically.

Lance shot her a glare. "Why not?" he demanded.

Engrelin met Lance's gaze, forcing himself to swallow the lump rising in his throat. "Your life isn't mine to take," he said quietly. *Because I love you,* brawd. *Can't you see that?*

Lance stared at him, for once scrambling for a retort.

"Engrelin," Elvera said suddenly behind him, "why don't you just let me die?"

"*What?*" Engrelin turned partially towards her, still keeping a watchful eye on Lance.

Elvera dragged herself to her knees; her eyelashes glistened with tears.

"I knew, all along, this was going to happen," she murmured thickly. "Why do you keep dragging it out?"

Engrelin stared dumbly at her. She had known…her death? What could she possibly mean? She didn't know about Vendar's letters to her father…did she?

He opened his mouth to ask. But the voice they heard wasn't his.

"All of you, remain where you are if you value your lives."

57

D read thrilled through Engrelin. He closed his eyes briefly. They were here. Too soon. His fingers tightened around Arrian's grip. Its blade shone a brighter blue than before.

Slowly, Engrelin turned.

At least a dozen soldiers, in bright military red, stood in a semicircle behind Lance. One, taller than all the others, seemed to have one eye that was darker than the other. He wore an equally dark scowl.

"Drop your sword," this man growled.

"No," Engrelin gritted.

The man cocked one eyebrow with surprise. The men gathered around him glanced at one another.

"I'm telling you," the man repeated, his voice an even, razor blade of anger, "to put your weapon down."

"And I'm telling you I won't," Engrelin retorted. He shifted his grip, feeling the cold gemstone setting of Arrian's pommel. He heard someone moving behind him. He spun.

A soldier was reaching out to grasp Elvera's arm and drag her away. With an enraged cry, Engrelin sprang forward. The soldier leaped back, avoiding losing his head by mere inches. He fell back in a graceless wave of arms and legs. Engrelin advanced. He found himself in a circle of soldiers. They moved slowly, blades pointed inward, like the spokes on a wheel.

Engrelin sprang into their midst, driving them back with Arrian's broad strokes. He had to get them away from Elvera. He had to! The steel curving dangerously around him gave no room for despair or anxiety in his heart. A fierce, inexplicable rage and vigor flowed through him, lending him strength from some unknown source. A blade darted dangerously toward his torso—Arrian swept around and shattered the offending sword in fragments that scattered onto the snow. Another sword glanced off his shoulder. Engrelin sprang forward and away, deeper into the whirling circle of red.

Red. Red everywhere. Red on the soldier's wickedly flashing blades. Red upon Arrian's mortal, flawless blue. Red tunics, weaving in and out and around him. Or was it blood?

Engrelin stumbled. He viciously righted himself in time to catch a stroke. He grasped the offender's arm and shoved him back, following the soldier's retreat with a straight, deadly thrust. The Tirendrian fell, leaving a gap in the hoard. Through that gap, Engrelin glimpsed Elvera. He froze.

"Halt!" ordered the leader simultaneously.

The soldiers around Engrelin who could tucked their swords away, though their hands hovered over the hilts. Several were unable to move; the snow beneath them was stained scarlet. Engrelin stood where he had stopped, his gaze riveted on the leader. He held Elvera's wrists behind her back in one strong hand. With the other, he held a knife to her throat. The man's eyes were not on the princess or Engrelin. They drifted over the bodies on the ground. He did not seem surprised or even angry. Simply contemptuous, as if he thought he could have done better.

"Impressive," he remarked flatly.

Engrelin refused to look down. A sick lump settled in his stomach. *Horrific.*

"But now that you've had your fun," the man continued, "Put your sword down, boy."

Engrelin stood stock still, tightly clutching his bloodstained sword.

"That's Cuthrell speaking, boy," one of the soldiers behind Engrelin murmured, just loudly enough for him to hear. "You'd better obey."

I won't. I can't, Engrelin thought, his heart thudding in icy stabs.

Cuthrell scowled at Engrelin. "If you don't put that weapon down now…"

Engrelin stood rigid, uncertain, his hands clinging to Arrian's grip as to a lifeline.

"I'm not going to wait forever," said Cuthrell.

When Engrelin didn't answer, the man took the knife and grazed a thin line across the pit of Elvera's throat. The girl went whiter than the snow, her lips parting in a silent scream.

"Don't touch her!" Engrelin exclaimed, lunging forward. One of the soldiers caught him by the arm and jerked him back.

Cuthrell placed the point of the knife against Elvera's throat. "This will all stop, when you put down that sword," he said evenly. "If you don't, I will kill her."

Engrelin's jaw snapped shut. He couldn't just give up like this. He couldn't. Without Arrian, they stood no chance.

Even as he thought it, enough blood welled in Elvera's cut to send a droplet of blood trickling down her neck. Engrelin bit the inside of his cheek. He had no choice. He had to.

Slowly, ever so deliberately, he bent and laid Arrian in the snow, point outward: a temporary surrender.

Instantly, someone buffeted him on the back, throwing Engrelin to his knees. Before he had time to straighten, a soldier seized his arms and wrenched them behind his back. Engrelin grimaced. The snow soaked through the knees of his trousers.

Handing Elvera off to Lance, Cuthrell strode up to Engrelin.

"You know, I'm surprised," he said. "There aren't many who would dream of challenging a Tirendrian patrol. Anyone who has met the end they deserve."

Grasping Engrelin's chin, Cuthrell jerked the boy's head back, forcing him to look him in the face. Engrelin saw why the man's eyes had looked different from each other. One was normal, but the other was missing entirely. It had been replaced by a dark glass ball that stared vacantly out. A cruel scar ran from the man's hairline to his jaw, passing through his left eye and the socket holding the glass ball.

"I'm surprised you even made the effort, knowing how it would end," continued Cuthrell. He bent closer still, so that his hot breath stirred Engrelin's limp hair over his forehead. "I had intended to kill you and dump your corpse in the river. But seeing what you can do, I think you should come with us. Yes?"

Engrelin didn't answer. He didn't think the man expected one. His eyes were on Elvera, whom Lance was leading towards the creek bank.

The soldier holding Engrelin twisted the boy's arms savagely and dug his knees into his spine. "Answer the captain," he hissed.

Squinting through his numerous pains, Engrelin curtly nodded.

"Good." Cuthrell straightened. "We're heading downstream, to a little place where you and the princess can wait for your fate to be determined."

He eyed Engrelin a moment longer before whirling sharply to speak with his officers.

"How many did we lose?" Engrelin heard him demand.

"Four, sir," was the nervous reply. "Keneil's hurt, but he'll push through. Harper's pretty bad, though."

"Five out of commission?" Cuthrell growled. He glared at Engrelin over his shoulder. Engrelin met the look steadily. His guard cuffed him sharply. "Cut that out," he snapped.

Brimming with anger and indignation, Engrelin fixed his eyes on the ground. He needed to stay calm and keep his head. They weren't beaten yet. He would find a way to get them out of this. Somehow.

The soldiers cleared the bodies of their dead and wounded comrades away. Engrelin watched their work silently. He didn't see Linford or his soldiers among the patrol. How had they known he, Lance, and Elvera would be here?

His searching eyes fell on Lance guarding Elvera, far out of the soldiers' way.

Of course, Lance. He must have snuck off while Engrelin had slept. Engrelin ground his teeth. The one moment when it was crucial to stay awake, and he had fallen asleep!

The fact that he hadn't slept for days before that morning never crossed Engrelin's mind as a worthy excuse, or as any excuse at all. His mistake, his halt, had brought all this about. Otherwise, they might have been on their way through Tirendria right now, as free people. He bowed his head. The grip on his arms did not lessen in the slightest.

The mutterings and preparations around Engrelin ceased to be as he formulated plan after plan of escape. They all proved futile when Cuthrell stalked over to him and roughly ordered him to rise.

Engrelin struggled onto one knee, but the soldier behind him gave him a hard shove, spilling him forward into the snow.

Blowing out of one corner of his mouth, Cuthrell grasped Engrelin's shoulders and jerked the boy to his feet. He accepted a length of hempen rope from one of his men and yanked Engrelin's hands out in front of him.

As he wound the rope around Engrelin's wrists, he said, "You're going to help my men pole downstream, to pay for your work here."

Engrelin nodded tightly, pressing his lips shut over all the bitter words crowding to them. For Elvera's sake alone, he needed to remain silent.

"However, your hands will remain bound the entire way," Cuthrell continued. "Just in case you decide to fall in and swim to shore. We'd have to help you along with a few arrows if you did. We don't want things to get too uncomfortable, do we?" His good eye searched Engrelin's face. For what?

"No," Engrelin said through his teeth. "We wouldn't."

"Good." Cuthrell pulled the ropes tight—too tight. They cut brutally into Engrelin's wrists, the skin on either side of them puckering. Engrelin winced. Cuthrell nodded with satisfaction, finished the bonds off with a complicated knot and dropped the boy's hands.

Engrelin subtly flexed his tingling fingers. How did they expect him to pole a boat down a creek when he could hardly move his fingers?

"Failure to obey our orders will receive swift and severe punishment," said Cuthrell. He took a step back, looked Engrelin up and down, and frowned, obviously disappointed with what he saw.

Cuthrell shoved Engrelin forward. "Now get in the boat."

Engrelin scanned the area around, but he saw no water craft anywhere. "Where is it?" he asked.

Cuthrell delivered a cuff that made Engrelin's ears ring.

"I don't want to hear any questions out of you—not so much as a peep. Do you hear?" he growled. "Don't let me catch you saying a word ever."

Engrelin blinked to clear his head. Such violence in answer to a reasonable question let a little despair creep into his soul. How long would he and Elvera be at this man's mercy?

The soldiers lowered a ladder over the creek bank, into the boat, Engrelin presumed. Lance shoved Elvera down the ladder. Engrelin bit his lip until the tang of blood filled his mouth. He had to keep quiet. He was no use to Elvera dead.

Cuthrell led Engrelin off to one side while the soldiers struggled to load Arrian into the boat. The sword had, by now, stopped glowing. But it jumped out of the soldier's arms every few feet they carried it. Finally, one of the soldiers got the idea to tie ropes around the weapon and drag it to the boat without touching it. This way (though still muttering about the sword's weight) the soldiers carried it into the boat.

The moment the weapon clanged into the boat's bottom, Cuthrell led Engrelin over to the bank. At their approach, Lance popped his head over the bank's edge.

"Ready to depart, Captain?" he asked.

Cuthrell gave him a withering look.

Lance blanched slightly but didn't look away.

"Yes, I'm ready," Cuthrell answered. He shoved Engrelin towards the ladder. "Get in."

Engrelin climbed slowly and painfully down the ladder. Cuthrell followed nimbly, flanked by two of his soldiers. Just two. If only it had been that way from the start.

Engrelin stood in the middle of the boat, trying not to shiver. His sopping clothes were plastered to his skin like wet paper. In the boat's bow, Elvera huddled. Lance stood watchfully over her, though he didn't refrain from offering Engrelin a sardonic smile. They both knew how fruitless the careful watch was. Elvera had admitted she couldn't swim. That eliminated every chance they had for escape. Engrelin never could, never would leave her.

Cuthrell's harsh voice sliced through Engrelin's thoughts. "Boy, you will be poling."

Grasping one of Engrelin's shoulders, Cuthrell steered the boy to one side of the boat. "You'll keep the backs of your legs against this bench." He patted the low bench behind Engrelin. Engrelin barely resisted telling Cuthrell he already knew how to pole. He had lived almost all this life beside a creek!

"This creek is narrow most of the way, so you'll be using a pole, not oars." Cuthrell drew a long, heavy pole out of the boat's flat bottom. Dipping one end into the creek, he shoved the other into Engrelin's bound hands. "This one is yours. I expect to see you using it."

He punctuated his words with a piercing glare. Engrelin glared back. For a moment, he thought the captain was going to strike him again. But Cuthrell speared him with a furious look before swiveling away.

A soldier took up a pole on the boat's port side and shoved it into the water. Cuthrell pulled down the rope ladder, then cut the ropes that had been holding the boat to the bank. The boat gently drifted into the current.

"Poles in!" Cuthrell shouted.

Engrelin and the other soldier dug their poles into the creek's muddy bottom, propelling the craft forward. Engrelin clenched his teeth as sharp pains stabbed down his arms from his bound wrists. Because of the ropes, he had to hold the pole awkwardly; it was so clumsy in his hands that he nearly dropped it several times.

"His Majesty never waits!" Cuthrell exclaimed from where he held the rudder. "Faster!"

Grinding his teeth, Engrelin obeyed.

58

Lilac gazed down into the shallow valley, her eyes following Linford's men as they silently slipped lower. She and Linford stood on the valley's brink, watching the soldiers' advance. Lilac searched among the men for Averendier, but she saw no sign of him. Yet she knew he was there, somewhere.

"What are they doing?" she asked Linford. Like snakes, the men below wove in and out of the trees, closing in on a cluster of buildings in the valley below.

Linford's black eyes shone with satisfaction. "They're fulfilling my orders," he answered. He canted his head towards the distant house. "Just watch, Your Highness."

Lilac's gut twisted. The last thing she wanted to do was watch.

But she would have to. It was the only way she would get an answer.

The soldiers were so far away now, they looked like little red dolls creeping towards a set of dolls' houses. One marched ahead of the others. Drawing his sword, he strode up to the door and smashed the sword hilt repeatedly against it. Even though Lilac couldn't hear the metal crashing against the wood, she winced.

"What do you want from these people?" she demanded, turning to Linford.

A small smile formed on his lips. He never seemed to mind her questions. He listened to them and answered as if she were a small child asking about the most foolish and obvious of things.

"Your Highness, did you not see the creek yonder?" Linford pointed into the valley.

No, she had not. Reluctantly, Lilac followed Linford's point. Her eyes fell on the gray ribbon of water flowing through the valley's bottom. Out of the corner of her eye, she saw the house door burst open, one hinge snapping as it did, nearly crushing the man struggling to emerge from the house.

"We need a boat," Linford continued calmly. "Reing, where I am taking you, is on the other side of the creek."

Down in the valley, Linford's soldier screamed at the man who had answered the door. A few harsh words drifted all the way up to Lilac's ears. They burned with the profanity. She clamped down on her lower lip.

Do we need it that badly? she wondered.

The man of the house was now on his knees, his hands stretched imploringly up towards the soldier who towered menacingly over him. The groveling repulsed Lilac—not the action itself, but to whom the man relented.

"It's orders, Your Highness," Linford said softly, so perfectly mirroring Lilac's thoughts that she shuddered.

Orders, she thought bitterly. *If his commanding officer told him to chop his own head off, he'd do it for orders' sake.*

More movement down in the valley caught her attention. She looked back down only just in time to see the man struggling to his feet. Linford's soldier whipped his sword out of its sheath. With brutal swiftness, the soldier drove it through the man.

Lilac staggered back with horror, her hands flying up to cover her mouth and heart. *Dear God, did they just kill him?*

Below, the soldier jerked his bloody sword out of the man's prone form. Casually, he wiped the blade clean on the front of his tunic. He rammed his sword back into its sheath and motioned to his companions. Without a backwards glance, the soldiers moved to a collection of sheds, leaving the man in a pool of blood on his own doorstep.

And Lilac could only stare. All this…for a boat? To take *her* somewhere. Was she that important to Linford and his men that they could take lives so carelessly to hurry her journey? She wiped her hands on her skirt, as if they were stained with the man's blood.

"Something bothering you, Your Highness?" asked Linford. The hint of amusement in his voice stoked Lilac's rage.

"What your soldiers just did to that man…" she whispered, her chest heaving. "It was brutal. Unjust. It was—"

"Nothing," Linford smoothly interjected. "He wasn't of any importance to us or to you."

Of no importance! Lilac itched to scream at him, box his ears, scratch that imperturbable face of his, do something—anything!—to vent the fury swelling within her. That man down there had probably been a father. What would his wife and children do without him in this wilderness?

"Why?" Her anger cut out any tremor that might have blemished her voice. "What did he do to deserve death?"

"Ever the inquisitive." Linford chuckled gently, shaking his head. "Perhaps it can be best said that fear is my keenest weapon, and I don't sprinkle it lightly. His death will instill fear throughout the rest of this region of Northern Florenth. If they like their heads on their shoulders, no one will oppose our passage."

Lilac's anger was too great for words. She clamped her mouth shut, grinding her teeth until the muscles in her jaw cramped. Through a red haze, she watched the Tirendrian soldiers drag a long boat out of a shed and lower it into a creek.

"It's time to go down now, Your Highness." Linford offered Lilac his arm. When she didn't move, he gently took her wrist. Lilac's stomach flopped like a beached fish. Down the valley was the last place she wanted to go.

"Captain Linford!" a voice called from behind him. "Wait!"

Linford put a hand on Lilac's shoulder, silently commanding her to stand still.

"Yes?" he asked. "What is it?"

"I just received a message from a Lance Smith and Captain Cuthrell at border patrol," the unseen messenger gasped. "They answer your commands and are glad to tell you they will be keeping a keen eye on all the routes over the border. We're confident we'll catch the two that slipped through your fingers."

Lilac jolted. Lance! Did that mean…

"Very well. Is that all?"

"Yes sir."

"Then carry on, soldier."

As the crunch of the messenger's running footsteps faded, Linford turned to Lilac, a smile wavering on his lips. Lilac stared at him, her hands curling into fists. She felt as if someone had just kicked her in the stomach.

"Well, well, Your Highness," said he, his voice as smooth as satin. "On to Reing. And who knows? Your sisters may already be there, waiting for you."

59

Sleep lay a heavy fog in Berwyn's mind when she heard the kitchen door slam open. Some scuffling. A sickening thud. And the door banged shut. She clawed at her gritty eyes, struggling to clear them. Warwick had informed her she was going to have a new assistant to train soon, but she hadn't expected them this early in the morning.

Gradually, the sleep crawled from her eyes. Through the shadows, she spotted a young man leaning against the kitchen door. He was pressing one hand over his mouth (he must have hurt it in his fall). Berwyn sighed and sat up, smoothing her hair behind her shoulders.

"Wait just a moment," she said, climbing stiffly off her pallet. She had slept in her clothes, so all she had to do was straighten them quickly. Her quick rising seemed to startle the young man for a moment. The table standing in the kitchen's center must have blocked his view of her from where he stood.

He watched her silently as she stuffed several sticks and pieces of wood onto the banked ashes in the fireplace. A cheery little flame leaped up into the darkness, sending light and shadow flitting across the kitchen's rough board walls. After running her fingers through her hair and untangling her pendant's chain, she turned to the boy.

"Want something for that cut?" she asked.

He stared at her but didn't answer. Berwyn turned anyway and fished a rag out of a drawer, wet it, and held it out to him.

He lowered his hand to take it, nodding his thanks. Berwyn's eyes widened and her hand shook momentarily. He was…

No, it couldn't be. Damien Peterson was dead.

But she wouldn't have mistaken those dark blue eyes anywhere.

Berwyn watched him with a puzzled frown as he self-consciously pressed the rag to his bleeding mouth.

The boy glanced at Berwyn uncomfortably, then looked down at the floor. He explained thickly, "Warwick sent me here to be…trained."

"Yes, I know," Berwyn said. "He told me."

The boy shifted against the door. "It's not that bad," he continued. "The lip, I mean. If that's what you're wondering."

Berwyn shook her head to rouse herself. "No. It's not that. I'm sorry. It's just…well, I am a doctor…but I guess that doesn't have anything to do with it." She bit her lip and averted her gaze from the boy's confused eyes. "I mean, you look like someone I knew…but he's dead. I'm sorry."

The boy's face clouded. "You mean Damien?" he asked, with some difficulty.

Berwyn looked up sharply. "He's dead," she repeated.

"Yes," the boy nodded. "But I'm not."

"So you're his brother?" Anger flickered within Berwyn, though she couldn't place why.

"Yes," the boy said again. "I'm Ouen."

Berwyn fiddled with the pendant at her neck to restrain her hand. Damien's brother. It was almost as bad as being Damien himself. They had both schemed constantly. They were both responsible for her father's death.

"Why did Warwick send you here?" she heard herself asking.

"He said that you needed help. He said several of your assistants had either been killed or ran away during the revolt," Ouen answered slowly.

"And whose fault was that?" Berwyn demanded sharply.

Ouen looked down. "They were good people," he said. "They were willing."

"Are you saying I'm not?"

Ouen glanced up at her. "I'm not suggesting anything of the sort," he said. "Unless you're guilty, Miss Sirman?"

Berwyn's hand tightened around her pendant.

"My brother spoke highly of you," Ouen continued, dropping his eyes to the floor once again. "He said you had spirit, but fear holds you back."

"So now I'm a coward?"

"That wasn't—"

"Is this how you get all these helpless people to join your mad schemes?" Berwyn asked. "By insulting them and telling them that your way is the only way that isn't directed by fear? And where are they now?" She threw out her arms, motioning to the empty kitchen. "Gone! All gone, in one night. And all you care is about getting more courage, more victims, so you can try it again."

"Miss Sirman," Ouen murmured, reaching forward to gently touch her arm. "I understand your hurt more than you—"

"No, you don't!" Berwyn exclaimed. She shoved his shoulder, pushing him back.

Face ashen, Ouen grasped his shoulder and sank back against the door.

"Berwyn," he whispered, "one of these days, you're going to realize the bitterness and grief and fear you have let into your life. And it's no one's fault…but your own."

"How bad is it?" Berwyn asked, stepping forward.

He gave her a look.

"Not me," she added hurriedly. "Your shoulder."

Ouen watched her sidelong a moment. Then he sighed and let his hand drop. "Not really bad," he said. "I've had it a little while."

"I can see that," said Berwyn. Inwardly, she berated herself. How could she have struck an injured person? She should have noticed he was hurt from the moment he had walked into the room. *But I was too busy fuming at him.* She shook her head at herself. The Petersons deserved all the anger they received. But that didn't mean she should leave any of them to suffer.

"Have a seat and let me look at it," she said, pulling up one of the kitchen's rickety stools.

Obediently, Ouen sank down onto it. Berwyn peeled his tunic, stiff with dried blood, away from his shoulders. At the sight of the wound, she drew a sharp breath. She touched it tentatively. Below the wound, livid bruises and weals crisscrossed his back—marks only a lash could cut. Quickly, she looked away.

"It's on the verge of infection," she said slowly. "I'm going to have to burn it clean."

"Burn it out?" Ouen eyed her suspiciously. "I came here to be trained as an assistant, not get lectured and branded."

"You'll be leaving this place feet first in a week if I don't," Berwyn warned.

Ouen slouched. "Make it quick," he said hoarsely.

Berwyn pulled a slender rod out of her satchel and shoved the end into the coals to heat.

"For a brave and daring Peterson, I'm surprised," she said. "If other men have to endure death, why can't you take this easily?"

Ouen looked at her sharply. "Miss Sirman, I'm tempted to think you just want to do this out of revenge," he said quietly.

Berwyn flushed deep scarlet. "I'm not," she mumbled, turning the glowing rod over in her hands. "I hate doing this kind of thing."

"But you feel you must do it, for my sake." Ouen nodded. "What if my brother and I felt that we were doing the right thing for the people here, even if it caused ourselves and others pain and discomfort. Do you know what it's like to know you're sending someone to their death?"

"Then don't do it," Berwyn returned bluntly.

Ouen smiled sadly. "Then I, like you, would be leaving the people in this place to sicken, rot, and die. Miss Sirman, there are more sicknesses than bodily ones. We need to get out of here before our minds and hearts are infected. Poisoned, like many. Not with indoctrination, or even their beliefs, but fear alone."

Berwyn's hands shook. "But you saw what happened! There's no escaping this place alive."

"In a large group, maybe so," Ouen agreed. "That's the mistake Damien and I made. But if a few of us escaped with intelligence and managed to get back to Monaria, we could bring a whole army back here, an army big enough for the large-scale liberation this place needs."

Berwyn probed the white-hot rod into his wound. Ouen gasped sharply and shut his eyes, gritting his teeth until she was finished. Fetching a jar of salve, she smeared it over his torn back.

"So you have another plan," she said.

"I do. Near the end of this month, Vendar will have his annual festival at Reing. Most of the soldiers who guard this place will be gone. It would be the perfect time for a few people to slip out unnoticed." Ouen winced as Berwyn wrapped an herb-stuffed bandage around his shoulder. "If you're willing, Berwyn," he added, "I would like to take you along."

Berwyn finished winding the bandage around his shoulder in silence and turned to wash the salve off her hands. Go with Ouen? A Peterson?

Her mind drifted to the thing hidden away in her satchel. She reached inside and fingered it a moment. Slowly, she turned back to Ouen.

"I would like to come," she said. "But under one condition."

Ouen raised an eyebrow.

"There's an assistant here in my kitchen, Lednora. I want her to come with us."

A slow smile spread across Ouen's face. "Then it's settled. I'll let you know when I'm ready."

Berwyn nodded and turned away again, feeling strangely light.

60

The harsh thud of boot-nails striking the wooden bottom of the boat pounded Engrelin's ears, rattling into the back of his skull. He grit his teeth over a moan and pressed the heels of his hands against his heavy eyelids.

No, not yet. Please, I'm not ready.

"Get up!" Cuthrell punctuated his words with a hard kick, driven into the prostrate boy's chest.

Engrelin coughed hollowly, fighting to lift himself from the boat's damp bottom.

"I said get up!"

The blow, catching Engrelin just beneath the ribs, forced a groan between his cracked lips. He struggled into the sitting position and shoved Cuthrell away, still blinking the weariness from his eyes. If it weren't for Elvera, he would have tried more than a shove.

"I'm up, I'm up," he muttered, scrubbing his bound hands across his face.

A rough hand seized his jerkin and pulled him to his feet, bringing him inches from Cuthrell's snarling face. The captain's glass eye grotesquely reflected the waxing moon.

"Did you just say something?" Cuthrell demanded.

Engrelin bit his lip and looked away. The captain backhanded him across the face and shoved him over to his all-too-familiar bench.

"I thought you had. Resting time's up. Get back to work."

Engrelin tried to get a good grip on the pole Keneil handed to him, but his fingers were so numb he hardly knew whether he held it or not. Over the past few days, he had refused to see what the brutal ropes had done to his hands. The painful thrills occasionally spearing through the numbness were knowledge enough.

Besides, aching limbs were the last of his and Elvera's worries. Admitting to the misery of even the slightest things was unthinkable. He had to focus his mental capacities on escape.

Cuthrell struck Engrelin on the shoulder (Engrelin often wondered how the captain managed to exercise his brutality while keeping the boat balanced, but he did).

"Stop daydreaming and use your pole!" he barked. "Do you think we have all night? I want to reach Reing by dawn."

Dawn. Engrelin nearly dropped the pole; it had suddenly gained ten times its normal weight. Could he hold out until dawn? He glanced quickly up at his wrists. Just as quickly, he looked away. In the moonlight, the rope glistened black.

As he mechanically dipped the pole in and out of the water, back and forth, his gaze wandered to the boat's bow, where Elvera still huddled. No one would have dreamed of striking *her* if she had spoken. Yet she hadn't uttered so much as a moan since she had boarded the ship three days ago. Just now, she sat with her back against the boat's side, her legs drawn up to her chest. Her hair, spilling loose down her back, obscured most of her face. Her hands dangled in her lap, free from any restraint.

Engrelin turned away to cough into the crook of his arm, struggling to muffle the sound while still gripping the heavy pole. He had dropped the pole once, and that had been enough. No one on the boat seemed to pay him any heed when the fit subsided and he paused poling long enough to throw his head back and gulp in the fresh air. The frigid air tore like broken icicles through him, making him catch his breath. Engrelin coughed again, but more quietly this time. Nonetheless, Cuthrell and his soldiers left him alone for this, as they had the past days. It seemed the only sound he was permitted to make without reprisal.

The night wore on. Fog rolled in and hung in swaths above the water. The mist settled refreshingly against Engrelin's face, though it further dampened his clothes. He lifted his head to meet it as a friend. It seemed to wash away some of the confusion from his muddled brain.

Engrelin glanced now and then in Elvera's direction, never too long, lest they think he was seriously contemplating diving overboard with her. Yet what was the point of watching? If Cuthrell or Lance decided to do something to her, he was next to powerless to stop them. Even if his hands were free, he was in no condition for a fight.

The reality settled heavily in his throat. He swallowed it quickly and looked down at his pole and the black water swirling around it as he moved it back and forth. The only thing he could do right now was this…and what consolation was that? He was only speeding Elvera and himself to whatever awful fate the future held.

Once the light came, perhaps, things would be clearer. Perhaps then, he would have a plan.

But dawn must come with the light. It slipped slowly into the sky, a hesitant smudge of gray and blue on the horizon. And with the dawn, so also must come Reing. A grim fortress, a sullen black hulk against the cold daybreak. In the gloaming still lingering below the trees, the creek's water seemed the same color as the fortress it slipped past; there was hardly any distinguishing where one ended and the other began.

"Make for the right." Cuthrell's voice cut through the gloom.

As Keniel turned the rudder, Cuthrell roused Lance, who had been sleeping in the bottom of the boat. He took his post beside Elvera, who looked alive for the first time in days, and seemed to be contemplating a swift end by pitching herself headlong out of the boat. Lance took a precautionary grip on her arm just as the boat glided up beside a dock which seemed to have materialized out of the fog. Engrelin searched the place for even the glimmer of a torch but saw nothing but murk and fog.

One of the soldiers sprang to the starboard side to secure it to one of the dock pilings. Leaning wearily on his pole, Engrelin watched Elvera struggle up a slippery ladder and onto the dock. She was a splotch of crimson against all the drab grays and blacks of water, land, and sky.

"Come on." Cuthrell's sharp cuff jolted Engrelin forward. "Get out."

After tucking his pole into the boat's bottom, Engrelin clambered up onto the dock on infuriatingly trembling legs. They threatened to buckle beneath him as he stood beside Elvera on the slick dock. While Cuthrell and Keneil climbed out of the boat, Engrelin let his gaze sweep upwards, scanning the sky for he knew not what. They came to rest on the smallest patch of gray sky through a rent in the clouds. In that tear, the pinpoint of Arrian glittered blue. Finally, a light. A small, relieved smile brushed Engrelin's lips.

"What are you smiling at?"

Engrelin jerked his eyes back down to see Cuthrell glowing in front of him.

"Is it against some rule to smile?" The words slipped from his mouth before he quite knew what he was doing. Would he soon be commanded not to breathe?

If possible, Cuthrell's expression darkened. It was the only warning Engrelin received before the captain smashed his fist into Engrelin's mouth. Knocked off balance, Engrelin stumbled back, only to be caught in the harsh, unfriendly arms of Keneil. The man shoved him back upright, close to the captain's face.

"Did I say you could speak?" he demanded, seizing Engrelin's wrists.

"You asked a question," Engrelin mumbled, hanging his head. He didn't dare reach up to brush away the stream of blood that tickled his lip. He did, however, sneak a swift upward glance at the sky. Arrian was gone. His light was gone. His shoulders slumped.

"You must learn to submit," Cuthrell growled, his hands picking at the swollen knots binding Engrelin's hands fast. "You think I'm bad? Just wait until you meet some of the people in here. They won't bat an eye at slitting your throat for your impertinence. I have a mind to do it myself."

Cuthrell ripped the stiff ropes from Engrelin's wrists. Engrelin clenched his teeth over a cry. Thin scarlet rivulets ran from the abrasions encircling his wrists.

"Boy, you're to go with Keneil," Cuthrell said. "Obey him without question. He'll report to me if you've been insolent."

As he spoke, the captain jerked Engrelin's hands behind his back. Engrelin barely restrained a gasp as cold shackles closed over his raw, torn flesh. What was the point in switching them in the first place? Iron or rope, it didn't make a difference. Thread would have held him fast.

"He's to level eight, cell eleven," said Cuthrell, shoving Engrelin towards Keneil. To Lance, the captain added, "She's to level one, cell three."

Engrelin glanced at Elvera but didn't have time to glimpse her face before Keneil shoved him into motion to stumble across the mist-slick dock towards a barely visible doorway. Engrelin squinted. They needed a lantern or something. Behind him, he heard Lance following with Elvera.

Engrelin had the sudden, overwhelming urge to break free. To rescue Elvera in one triumphant blow, or die trying. If he could only get his hands free—

The prison door slammed shut behind him. Engrelin cringed in the sudden curtain of darkness. It pressed in on all sides, stifling, crushing. He gasped in a breath, only to choke on it.

Keniel struck him, urging him on into the darkness.

61

So, *this was Reing.*

Lilac gazed up at the fortress, swathed in fog. It seemed to grow as the boat drew closer. The stone walls loomed over the water, casting a faint shadow in the pale morning light. Lilac barely resisted a shudder. This was where Linford was taking her. For what? And why?

"Almost there," said Linford beside her.

Lilac started at the suddenness of his voice. Pressing the heels of her hands against the boat's rub rail, she cast a glance over her shoulder at Averendier. A stout pole in his hands, he was helping propel the boat down the creek. He looked up, and their eyes met briefly. Averendier gave her a short nod, then looked away again. But Lilac had seen the determination in his eyes. For him, the fight had only just begun.

The boat bumped up against a dock piling. Lilac swayed and clutched the side of the boat to steady herself as one of the soldiers reached to secure the boat to the dock with rope.

Linford climbed up onto the deck. Turning back, he extended his hand to Lilac.

"You next, Your Highness."

Lilac stared at his hand a moment. Take that monster's hand? Not while she drew breath.

She firmly gripped the ladder rung in her hands and pulled herself up.

Linford's soft chuckle filled Lilac's ears as she scrambled up onto the dock. Heat creeping up her cheeks, she held her head high. She moved off to one side while the other men piled out of the boat. She no longer needed an arm to lean on; three days of resting on the boat had given her time to regain some strength.

As the last man pulled himself onto the dock, Lilac felt Linford's thin, strong hand clasp over her wrist. She looked up to meet his unsettlingly quiet gaze.

"Stay with me, Your Highness," he said. "We're heading in. We wouldn't want you to get lost in a place like this."

Fighting a shudder, Lilac looked away. But the feel of Linford's skin against her own burned.

"Linford?" said a harsh voice from behind them.

Lilac turned her head to see a large man walking across the dock towards them, flanked by a limping soldier. A brutal scar slashed through the man's left eye and down his cheek.

Beside her, Linford stiffened. "Cuthrell," he returned smoothly, outwardly calm if not inwardly. "I thought you were posted on the border."

Cuthrell sighed dramatically and swept an arm towards a small boat tied to one side of the dock. "I was," he said. "But I happened upon a little bit of luck and had to bring it here."

"I see," said Linford, nodding carefully.

Lilac's breath thinned. This man had been on the border? Was he the man who had sent Linford the message about her siblings? Was the luck…people? Her sisters? A huge knot in the back of her throat choked back the terrible questions that burned her mind. Were either, or both, of her sisters here?

"But we can talk later," said Cuthrell. "You need to lock this girl up. Level one, cell three. That's where the captain wants them."

Linford's hand tightened around Lilac's wrist. "That's where I'll go," he said. He offered Cuthrell a parting bow, then led Lilac over to a doorway gaping in the high, sheer rock walls of Reing. He plunged unhesitatingly into the prison corridors.

The stench of sweat and blood and unwashed bodies hit Lilac in a wave, and she barely refrained from gagging. The damp, heavy air pressed down and around her like a wet, musty blanket. Dim torches burned here and there in iron holders along the walls. They cast more shadow than light.

"You're a lucky prisoner here, Your Highness," Linford told her as they hurried through the dark, winding passages. "Being of royal blood, you will be kept on the first level: the only level of Reing above ground and ventilated."

Lilac didn't reply; she was too busy trying to breathe through just her mouth. She clutched her skirts in her free hand, carrying them above the stagnant water pooling in the passageway. Somewhere deep in the darkness, she heard water dripping steadily.

"There are ten levels to Reing," Linford continued, as if touring her around some palace or gallery. "The lower the level, the worse the conditions."

He paused just long enough to take one of the torches out of a holder before pressing on. The torch cast a weak circle of light around them as they walked. On the edges of it, Lilac saw iron bars stretching from floor to ceiling, forming cells which looked little better than cages. A few eyes gleamed out at her from behind the bars. Lilac shuddered and fixed her eyes on the floor, which was never level, but always slanted one way or another. Though she tried to hide from her eyes the horror around her, her ears could not shut out the moans and mutters drifting past in varying degrees of despair.

Linford led her up and down countless staircases, which sometimes were a few steps only, and other times wound several flights up or down. Lilac's head spun with the enormity of the place. Once, she drew too close to a wall and her hand grazed against it. She yanked it away, caked with grime. Revulsion choking inside her, she scrubbed her hand off on her skirt. She scowled. This was no prison. This was a maw of suffering and filth that men were cast into, never to be seen again, never to walk on grass or soil or to look up at the sky.

And she, daughter of Bendekahn and the heiress to an ancient throne...she was here. Why?

Someone shuffled in the passage ahead. A grunt broke through the stifling air. Lifting his torch high, Linford squinted into the darkness.

"Having trouble?" he called.

Lilac's eyes narrowed until she could just barely make out the silhouette of a man against the even deeper darkness behind him. He was doubled over, dragging something.

"That prisoner resisting?" Linford demanded.

Prisoner! Lilac's eyes widened as she and Linford drew closer. The torch cast a reddish gleam onto the soldier and the form he was dragging. It was the limp young man, his head bent so that she couldn't see his face. His dark hair was damp and tangled, blood and dirt were smeared across his tattered garments. Lilac stopped where she was and stared, too horrified to go any closer.

"He was," said the soldier. He grunted again, trying to get a better grip on the inert body. "He was pretty bad when we first got him. So Cuthrell—the captain—I mean, tried to break him on the way here. I guess…" His voice grew awkward, though whether it was from shame or caution at the expression that had passed over Linford's face, Lilac knew not. "I guess he went a little too far. The kid blacked out on me a couple minutes ago. I've been trying to get him down to level eight."

The torch cast weird shadows on Linford's face, disfiguring his frown. "I'll have to speak to Cuthrell about this," he said slowly.

Cuthrell. Lilac remembered now. The scarred man they had just passed on the docks. Had this been his luck? Lilac couldn't help but feel relieved. It wasn't either of her sisters. The feeling twisted to pity as her eyes wandered over the boy, and she realized dark blood trickled down his hands from the pair of shackles clamped around his wrists. How could men treat one another this way?

"Did you say level eight?" asked Linford.

"Yes. Level eight, cell eleven," the soldier promptly replied.

"That's pretty far."

"Yes sir, it is."

"When you get to level three, ask for help."

"Yes sir."

"Carry on," Linford commanded.

The soldier, unable to salute, bowed slightly before continuing his slow journey down the corridor, dragging rather than carrying his unconscious prisoner behind him.

Lilac barely felt Linford tugging her further into the passages. Her mind had been torn back three days, to the valley where Linford's men had stolen the boat. The peasant, ruthlessly and needlessly run through. His wife, rushing to the door to stand there in shock, her hands pressed over her moth and heart. A child, so little its chubby legs seemed unable to support it, had clung to her skirts. Lilac had hardly been able to look at the awful sight. In an instant, woman and child had become widow and orphan.

And Linford had dismissed it as nothing. Lilac supposed the misery of the prisoner she had just witnessed was nothing. The darkness and dirt the prisoners of Reing lived and died in was nothing.

And yet he treated her as a something.

"Level two," Linford announced, his soft voice slicing through her thoughts like a small, sharp blade. Lilac realized that the air around her had thinned to an almost breathable state.

They ascended yet another staircase, this one spiral and much longer than any they had yet mounted. At its head, Lilac found herself blinking in the weak light flowed through a barred window. From there, Linford led her down a much cleaner, much broader hallway than those below. The cells here actually had walls of stone, with a grate door, as opposed to the cages on the lower levels. White-hot guilt stabbed through Lilac. She was to live here, while everyone below rotted in blackness and grime?

Linford steered her towards one of the grate doors.

"Level one, cell three, Your Highness." He said it almost cheerfully. Taking a key off a nail in the wall, he thrust it into the lock and pulled the door open. The soft hum of voices faded. Lilac realized it had been coming from within the cell. Her cell. She clenched handfuls of her skirt. Who was in there?

Linford pushed her into the cell, closing the door gently behind her. Lilac spun and clutched the iron bars.

But Linford was already gone. She heard other voices close by, down the hallway.

One was quiet and grave. Not Linford's, but still extremely familiar. Lilac clenched the bars tighter and pressed her forehead against them, straining her ears. *Averendier, is that you?*

A door slammed with the metallic rattling of bars. Pattering footsteps retreated down the corridor. Then silence.

If Averendier had been there, he was gone now. Lilac slumped against the door.

"Another new one?" whispered a voice behind her.

Lilac froze, her heart thudding against her ribs.

"Second one today," another replied. "Haven't they been busy?" The voice was tinged with scorn, but it wasn't exactly unpleasant.

"Where do you think she's from?" asked the first voice.

"Monaria, probably. Last I heard, they hadn't been gotten yet."

"No, look at how blond her hair is. Probably Eastern Florenth."

"No, they executed them last year. Remember?"

"Oh, yes. Poor Auletea." The first girl sighed sadly.

Lilac turned. Two pairs of bright eyes met hers: one brown, one green. Their owners were both girls about Lilac's own age, perhaps younger. Their dresses, though wrecked by prison life, still bore a nobility that matched the bearing of their wearers. The girls sat side by side upon a bench which hung from chains on the wall, as friends might do on any normal bench in a garden on a pleasant afternoon.

"I hope we didn't scare you," said the girl with the green eyes. She brushed some of her black hair away from her face.

"No, you were fine," Lilac answered, smiling. "It was actually quite pleasant to hear you both."

The girls flashed sympathetic, knowing smiles.

"What country are you from?" the other girl asked, rather timidly.

"Alinar," Lilac replied. A familiar ache tugged in her chest.

The girls exchanged puzzled glances. "Alinar?" the green-eyed girl repeated. "But, if you're from Alinar, then where did she come from?"

She? Lilac's eyes darted to one corner. Her heart leaped. There, splayed desolately out on a bench, was a girl clad in bright red, her dark hair spilling loose almost to the floor.

"Elvera!"

62

At Lilac's cry, Elvera lifted her head and stared up at her sister, her eyes round with joy. "Lilac?" she quavered.

Lilac smiled down at her, supreme joy swelling in her breast.

Elvera raised herself on one elbow, face lit. It disappeared immediately, overcast with shadow. She crumpled back onto the bench, burying her face in her hands.

"No," she moaned. "Not you too."

Lilac knelt beside her sister and smoothed the dark, tangled locks from Elvera's forehead. "Yes, me too," she said gently, the catch in her throat making her voice tremble.

"I wish…I wish you weren't," gasped Elvera through gulping sobs. She looked up wearily. "Where's Isalinia?"

Lilac frowned. "I don't know," she answered.

"What do you mean?" Elvera sat up. "I thought she was with you."

Lilac shook her head slowly. "No, I haven't seen her since that village where we all got separated," she said. "We don't know where Andrald is either. Isalinia was kidnapped, and Andrald went after her."

"*We* don't know? You mean you and Averendier, right?" Elvera's eyes narrowed to accusatory slits. "Those boys are responsible for this, all three of them. They're the reason we were brought here."

Lilac gasped and pressed her fingers against Elvera's lips. "How could you say such a thing?" she whispered earnestly, searching her sister's face. "Father never would have let us come with them if he thought they meant us harm!"

"He didn't know," Elvera retorted. She flung her arms wide, motioning to the cell they were in. "Isn't this proof enough?"

Lilac drew back as if her sister had slapped her. Was this the joyful reunion she had always imagined? To return to her sister's side, only to discover someone as bitter as a veteran nursing old wounds?

"It's all Engrelin's fault," Elvera continued spitefully. "He fell asleep when he was supposed to be guarding Lance. So Lance snuck off, got the Tirendrians, and brought them to us. Lance told me all about it on the way here. And Engrelin *let* them capture us. He hardly fought at all!"

"I'd heard, on my way here, that Lance had escaped," Lilac said carefully. "I was hoping you weren't with him," she added in a low voice.

"Well, I was," Elvera burst out angrily. "The whole time, I was. Engrelin wouldn't let Lance out of his sight while he was awake. He wouldn't even kill him when he should have! And then Engrelin fell asleep, right on the Tirendrian border, when I needed him most! That's plain proof he isn't on our side."

Lilac frowned and nearly put a hand to her head. Elvera's logic was dizzying.

"And where is Engrelin now?" she asked. Surely, he couldn't have fallen far from Elvera's fate. If only Elvera could see that...

Lilac's thoughts drifted to the prisoner she had passed on her way up. She brushed the persistent memory away. Surely, he couldn't be suffering to that extent. Surely. And Averendier?

Elvera sullenly muttered something. It sounded like numbers.

"What was that?" Lilac asked.

Elvera lifted her head, her dark eyes snapping with defiance. "Where's Averendier right now?" she challenged. "Or Andrald? What did he do with Isalinia?"

Lilac faltered. She watched with pity and horror the twisted triumph burning in Elvera's eyes at her hesitation. What had happened to her sister?

"This Averendier," said the green-eyed girl. "Was he highborn? If so, he will probably be in one of the cells on this level."

Lilac turned eagerly to the girl. "He was," she said, with a sudden sparkling hope. "How do you know?"

The girl smiled sadly. "Because my brothers are here as well," she said. She pressed her hands up against the wall closest to the cell door, indicating her brothers were on the other side. "Derin and Jayce, of Western Florenth. And I'm Vivian."

"My brothers are here too," said the other girl, twining her light brown hair nervously around her fingers. "At least, some of them. Wilelm and Wilory. And I'm Eileen, of Northern Florenth."

"All of you, here?" Lilac asked in astonishment. "But why?"

Vivian and Eileen looked at her wonderingly. Vivian said slowly, "You are Bendekahn's daughter, aren't you?"

"Yes."

"And yet…You don't know that we're being held hostage here?"

"Hostages!" The word thrilled through Lilac like an electric shock. Through her mist of surprise, she heard herself asking, "Why?"

Vivian's expression of surprise deepened. "Weren't you told?" she asked incredulously. "If any of our fathers lift a finger to help Monaria, we will be killed."

63

arkness. Pain, despair, identity, existence, ceasing to be. All darkness, and darkness only.

Sensation, perhaps. He seemed to be sliding forward. Dragging slowly and uselessly and endlessly on. It did not matter how long it would take him to get to wherever it was he must reach, or when he would stop. The darkness swallowed time. Time no longer mattered. Time no longer was. Darkness only.

Rest. Resting on what could not be seen, imprisoned by what could not be discerned.

Cold. Chills that drifted along the nothingness. Shapeless, malicious cold.

Dampness? Yes, dampness, the source of which was not known. Dampness that must fled but could not be escaped. Dampness increasing, intensifying, filling mouth and lungs—

He couldn't breathe. Gasping, he wrenched himself free from something's grasp and fell a few inches to the floor. He choked violently, heard the spatter of water on the floor beneath him. Air, sweet air! Heaving, he forced himself to breathe. In and out. In and out.

"Stupid boy."

The darkness took on a voice, low and thin. He winced and let himself sink the rest of the way to the floor, pressing his cheek against the clammy stones. Dampness and cold. Tingling cold. Vague pain wandering through his skull.

"Come on." A shadowy form bent over him, shook him lightly, claws latched onto his shoulder. "You must drink the rest."

Why? What did it matter whether he drank or not? He moved his lips, battling to force his question beyond his lips. A low voice moaned, a voice he knew could not be his own.

"Come on."

He was rolled over onto his back, to stare up into the fathomless depths of the ceiling and the blackness against the blackness hovering above him.

"You must drink it."

Why couldn't he be left alone? All he wanted to do was sleep.

Talons reached between his head and the floor, forcing his head up. Everything lurched and dropped. He closed his eyes and prayed desperately for it all to end, to stop, to leave him to lie in peaceful darkness.

But it was not to be. Something was pressed to his lips, the voice again urged. He could not resist. Could not even move. Lethargy pinned him where he lay.

"Come now." Again, the voice wound through the night. "Drink, and then we will talk."

"Thir!"

The exclamation, so loud, so sharp, made him cringe. An ache sprang out of the nothingness, an ache that made him shut his eyes all the tighter and ignore the shadow clutching him and the strange voice rebuking it.

"How many timeth muth you be told?" demanded the voice in a strange lisp. "Do not torment or quethion the prithonerth. My lord?"

The shadow's silence stretched on.

"You do not do well to interrupt me, Florenthian," it hissed at last.

"And it doeth not do you well, Lord Reeth, to contradict the orderth King Vendar himthelf hath given me," returned the lisp gravely. "No one ith to touch or even thpeak to thith prithoner unleth he himthelf give permithion."

"And how do you know whether he has given me permission or not?" asked the shadow cunningly.

"The king tellth me when he gives permithion or no," replied the lisp, unruffled. "Would you like me to go to him and athk if you were permitted?"

He heard the shadow mutter something, the tone sent shimmers of horror through him.

"Come out, my lord," commanded the lisp, "and I will let thith be forgotten onthe."

A rustle. The talons released him, letting him fall back onto the cold floor. The shadow drifted past, out of his sight. A groan, a metallic clatter, and all was still, all was dark. A faint tapping, like footsteps, sank into the silence.

And he was alone.

He sighed, then shivered, staring aimlessly into the darkness. Something had just happened, he knew. Voices had spoken. It had seemed important. But he could not recall one word of it now. That had faded with their presence.

He only knew that he was needed. Needed badly. He tried to sit up. Only, after hours of exertions, he found himself in the same position as before, lying on his back, gazing up into the darkness above, his eyes roving in the darkness around. He was needed, but for what, he hadn't the faintest idea. Not the faintest.

Everything was faint, after all. Surreal. Cobwebs of what might have been fell away. All was blank.

Another jolt coursed through him. Again, he strove to sit up. Again, he found himself in the same position. He breathed thinly, fingers seeming to grope, yet laying heavy and still.

He was needed for something. Something. Something was. He was something. He had a name. What was it? Did he have a name?

Did it matter? Did anything matter? Was anything real? Was anything anything at all?

There was darkness. Darkness above, darkness around, darkness below.

Darkness, and darkness only.

Darkness absolute.

64

For a moment, *Lance could not force his lips to move. Guilt* hammered in his chest and tightened like a clamp around his throat.

The Captain sat back in his chair, his piercing eyes fixed on Lance's face. "It's just as I told you," he said coldly. "We did it nearly a month ago." He cocked one eyebrow with suspicion. "Are you displeased with me, Smith?"

Displeased? Oh no. That was not it at all. Lance glared at the Captain, who smiled at him with something like petty amusement. Did he find entertainment in this sort of thing? Lance's hands curled around the arms of his chair.

"How could you do that?" he demanded. "She was just a little girl."

"She wouldn't have been for long," replied the Captain. "The only safe Peterson is a dead one. It was best to do it while we had the time to waste on small missions."

Lance's stomach reeled. He clenched the arms of the chair harder to steady himself. All he could see was her face. All he could hear was her laughter. Out of all her attributes, all he remembered was her youth. She had been so young, so innocent, so helpless!

And they'd just killed her.

But that wasn't the worst. He had *told* them about her. He was the reason she was dead. Her blood was on his hands.

I had to tell them. It'll all come out for the good.

He had told himself this a thousand times over. But now not even he was sure he was right to think that.

"I'm surprised, Smith." The Captain's blunt voice butted through Lance's dark struggles. "I thought you would have wanted this."

"Wanted what?!" Lance jumped to his feet so quickly, his chair crashed onto its side. Behind him, the office door banged open and boots tapped anxiously across the floor.

"One peasant girl, and all this?" said the Captain disapprovingly. "One life. It's nothing compared to the hundreds taken in battle."

Lance leaned forward over the Captain's desk, gripping its edge so tightly his knuckles showed white. "You know that out of all this wretched world holds, I only want one thing," he spat. His throat felt as if it had been ripped in two.

"And what was that?" The Captain's eyes gleamed mockingly.

"You know," said Lance, his breath escaping in a growl. "You said, that if I brought you even one of the princesses, you would tell me where my mother was. You said you knew."

"Yes. I did say that, didn't I?" The Captain shook his head. "Shameful business, Smith. I think, by now, you would have figured out for yourself." He, too, bent over the desk—so close to Lance he felt the man's breath on his forehead as he spoke.

"She's in her grave."

Lance's eyes burned with a sudden rush of tears. He glared into the Captain's wickedly sparkling eyes for one moment longer before he reared back and struck the man hard across the face.

As the Captain stumbled back, Lance sprang forward to continue his punishment. But strong hands from behind latched onto him, pinning his arms behind his back. The fight oozed out of Lance as quickly as it had risen. All he had done, the lies he had lived on, had all been for this moment.

They had all been for nothing.

Regaining his composure, the Captain strode around the desk and planted himself inches from Lance's face.

"If you want to join your precious mother that badly," he snarled, "keep it up." He slapped Lance's chin up so that the sullen boy would look him in the face. "I can arrange that meeting pretty quickly." He patted the sheathed sword at his side.

Lance glowered and said nothing. He almost wished the Captain would kill him so he could be done with this cursed world forever. There was nothing left to live for.

"No? Very well. Terry here—" he motioned behind Lance to the soldier who held him prisoner "—is going to take you down to level eight. You can join that poor friend of yours." He chuckled, malevolence throwing a wild light into his eyes. "It's too bad he had to be so difficult, and a Peterson." He chuckled again, looking Lance's wretched figure up and down. "But since the Smiths are next to the Petersons in honor, why shouldn't it be the same with shame?"

Lance's heart wrenched with the painful combination of guilt and hatred. *No, not Engrelin. I'd rather be chained to a lunatic in complete darkness than be in the same cell as him. Especially now…*

His mouth tightened into an iron line, bitterly sealing the scowl on his face.

"Take him away," ordered the Captain, flinging his hand disgustedly towards the door.

Lance barely had enough time to shoot a hail of wrathful darts in the Captain's direction before the office door shut between them. Lance and his guard walked down the hallway, descended a steep staircase, and were lost in torchlit darkness.

Lance's shoulders drooped as he trudged down the dank, pitch-black corridors: passageways that he, only an hour ago, had walked as a free man. The cool touch of shackles reminded him that was never again to be, forever and ever.

So be it.

After a while, Terry said, almost wistfully, "It's a pity you blew up on the Captain like that. Since he's the superior officer here, he says and does what he likes, and you've just got to flow with it sometimes. You could become quite useful to him."

Lance stiffened. So he was just a tool now.

Terry was wrong. He had stopped being useful to the Captain the moment he had dragged Elvera into Cuthrell's hands. Since then, the

Captain had been looking for a way to get rid of him. And he, Lance, had played into his hands.

Lance scowled at his own incompetence. The Captain cared little enough to let him crawl into one of Reing's dark holes to die. He was only an insignificant drop in this ocean of prisoners.

"I'm getting what I deserve," he muttered bitterly.

"Hardly!" Terry exclaimed. "Hitting him was just a blunder. He might still pull you out of this mess. There are many ways to serve."

Something in Terry's words made Lance shudder. "I don't want to serve," he said vehemently. "Not him, not anyone!"

Even as the words left his mouth, he realized he was wrong. There still was One to whom he wanted to be faithful. But after all he had done, would he still be welcome?

"Suit yourself." Terry's voice shrugged. "Just remember what you're losing."

"Not much." He'd long lost everything he put value in: his faith, his family, his friends. What did it matter if he died as well?

"I must say, though," Terry continued, talking on in his small, high voice for the sake of talking, "the guy you're being put up with will be glad of the company. If he's awake, that is. Feeble sort of fellow. The ones Cuthrell brings in always are. Plumb worn out. When he was brought in, he conked out even before they reached the upper staircase. Didn't they tell you?"

Through his strangling guilt, Lance managed to shake his head. The past month, especially the days spent on the boat, flashed vividly before his mind's eye. All the hatred and abuse he had slathered on Engrelin, someone he had once considered his most loyal friend! His heart ached to repeal all that had been said and done, to see Engrelin well and strong.

But even if Engrelin did live, would he ever forgive Lance for all that he had done to him? His thoughts tore back to his conversation with the Captain. An unbidden sob tore his chest, and he ducked his head.

However, Terry didn't seem to have heard it at all. He only continued, in a confidential tone, "Though I dare say he's lucky. There are some brought here who don't even reach their cells alive, just drop stone dead along the way." Lance felt the burn of Terry's wondering stare on his back. "There is a way to avoid that," he said slowly.

Lance lifted his head and retained his stubborn silence. Terry sighed, pulling Lance to a halt. Lance heard him fumbling with his shackles and a set of keys. An opening door grated and groaned. Dimly, he could see bars stretching from floor to ceiling in a wall to his left.

"This is yours," said Terry simply. He pushed Lance forward into the cell, which was so dimly lit the boy could hardly see a thing.

Probably all the better.

Behind him, the door clanked shut and the key screeched in the lock. Terry whispered something. It fell unheeded on Lance's deaf ears. Then Terry pattered away the way he had come. Lance still stood inside the door, petrified, staring across the cell at the figure huddled on the floor in one corner. He knew who it was. He dared not move, lest he be aware of his presence.

A cough rasped in the stillness, hollow and deep. Still, Lance stood staring. He had seen so many people like that in his life. All his siblings, lost to pestilence. Both his parents, lost to Tirendrians. Now it was his own destiny to die.

So why was he so horrified? Shouldn't he be familiar with this by now? Hadn't he been the hand to wield death to so many precious to himself? What did it matter if the awful litany increased?

His thoughts drifted and warped, and still he stood. Finally, as if someone had tied a string around his waist and was pulling it, he crossed the cramped cell in small, unwilling steps until he stood beside his inert companion.

"Engrelin?" His voice faltered through the darkness, cutting through Engrelin's labored gasps for life. Lance fell to his knees and with trembling hands pushed Engrelin's straggling hair back from his forehead. Lance rested his palms there a moment, as if taking that long to comprehend the heat. One of his brothers had felt like that before he died. His pulse had also been erratic. Lance reached to take Engrelin's pulse. His hand closed over hot flesh, torn and swollen by rough hempen ropes. Guilt surged up in waves and broke over Lance, bowing his shoulders.

"This is all my fault," he whispered fiercely. "All my fault."

His hands shaking with urgency, Lance tore several strips from the bottom of his tunic and carefully bandaged the bloody wrists. Jerking his cloak from his shoulders, he spread it out on the floor. As gently and carefully as he could, he transferred Engrelin onto it. His friend was completely limp in his arms. He stirred slightly and mumbled, ending with the wracking cough Lance had heard when he had first entered the cell. Lance winced and lowered Engrelin onto the improvised blanket.

What to do now? Lance hovered uncertainly over Engrelin. This former friend was all he had left in the world. And now he too was slipping away from him. *Dying.* What power did he have to stop it? He, who had hurried it along in the first place?

Lance pressed one of Engrelin's' clammy hands to his trembling lips. His breath came in shallow gasps, shaking his strong frame.

"Oh God!" he whispered imploringly. The prayer screaming inside him could never be put into human words, even if he were given all eternity to do it. *God, please. Not him too. Please. Please help me. I...I don't know what to do.*

65

Lilac tossed restlessly on the hard bench. *It bored into her back and shoulder blades.* Shivering, she tugged her cloak tighter around her body. But the thick wool did not cut the chills that wafted through the non-glazed window and seemed to emanate from the walls. Sighing softly, Lilac sat up on the bench and clutched her dully aching head in her hands.

How long had she been here? Three, four days? It felt like years. In the tiny cell, each hour dragged its feet.

At least she had Vivian and Eileen to help break the monotony of prison life. But the ever-present fact that they were prisoners—worse, hostages—crushed out any life that might have entered their conversations.

Lilac clenched handfuls of her skirt. If the freedom crying out within her were given a voice, it would shout so loudly the walls of Reing would crumble in its wake.

But such a thing did not exist. The solid wall around her would remain solid. She was stuck. For how much longer?

"Can't sleep either?" asked Vivian.

Lilac lifted her head out of her hands and offered Vivian a weary smile. "Not really. Sorry if I'm keeping you awake."

Vivian smirked. "Really, Lilac. I've been here months, and I haven't gotten a good night's sleep yet."

On cue, Elvera, though unconscious, whimpered loudly. Lilac's gaze snapped onto her. Even through the gloom she saw Elvera's troubled face as she tossed through yet another nightmare. How much longer would her sleepless nights last? Another week? A year? Always?

A terrible thought occurred to her. How much longer did she have before she, too, became like her sister—embittered, despairing of all hope?

It cut like a knife to her heart, and she shuddered. Vivian glanced at Elvera a moment before bringing her gaze to meet Lilac's.

"We have to face facts," said Vivian slowly but firmly, as if she had lifted a hatch and peeked into Lilac's mind. "We're never going to leave this place alive unless Tirendria wins the war or our parents lay siege to the prison." She sighed and laced her fingers in her lap. "Either way, we don't have much of a chance."

"But we can't give up!" Lilac exclaimed.

Vivian's head snapped up. "I'm not," she said fiercely, punching one fist into her open palm. "Anything is possible, especially when we have the Lord on our side. I'm not going to lose faith in Him yet."

"Neither am I," said Lilac. It was almost a breath of relief. "I just wish we could find a way out without trying to force through the impossible."

Vivian grinned and glared imposingly at the encompassing stone walls. "Impossible escape, start being possible," she commanded.

Lilac suppressed a chuckle behind her hand. Vivian threw her a twinkling smile.

"But," Vivian pursued, sobering, "to be serious, I—"

Footsteps sounded in the corridor outside the girls' cell. Both froze, their insides curdling with sudden fear. Eillen, asleep until then, shot upright on her bench, as if a crossbow bolt had slammed into the wall above her head. Her timid gaze darted to the grate door.

"It's too early for Brutis' rounds again," she said, moving closer to Vivian. "An officer, maybe? Just making…his rounds?"

Vivian didn't have time to reply. A key turned in the lock with a terrifyingly precise *click*. The door clattered open. Lilac startled and shut her eyes. What was someone doing, coming to their cell in the middle of the night? It had to be something bad. Had one of their fathers—

A hand closed around her wrist. Lilac's eyes flew open. Her heart galloped so wildly in her chest, she was sure everyone in the cell could hear it. Everyone…including Linford, who stood holding her wrist with a gentle impatience as if she should have anticipated his visit.

"Lilac of Alinar, you must come with me," he said quietly.

Lilac stood, scanning the man's face for any betrayal of malevolence or pity. But his mask was perfectly painted—not one drop of recognition did he show, as if he had never seen her until that moment.

Without another word, Linford released her wrist and motioned to the grate door. Lilac followed him out into the corridor. Dread sapped her mouth dry as she hurried after him down the brightly lit hallway.

"Who summoned me?" she asked Linford, who strode casually and effortlessly along, as if he had all the time in the world to watch Lilac die of fear and suspense.

"His Majesty, Vendar, King of Tirendria," Linford answered formally.

The King? Cold sweat trickled down Lilac's back. Her father had agreed to help Monaria. She was going to her own execution, cloaked in the sinister darkness of the night. She was going to be quietly put away, never to see Vivian or Eileen or Elvera ever again. Or Averendier. She would just vanish.

Yet as she watched the hallway gradually change around her, a little confused line stretched between her eyebrows. The grate doors were replaced by solid wooden ones, beside which hung brass plaques etched with writing in a language she had never seen before. This definitely wasn't a scaffold; nor a torture chamber. Where was Linford taking her?

"You're to enter here, Your Highness," said Linford. He led Lilac over to a dim doorway and gently pushed her inside, shutting the door softly behind her.

In the seeming darkness after the hallway's glare, Lilac squinted. From across the room, three pairs of eyes stared back at her.

The men stood behind a desk which, besides two chairs, was the only piece of furniture in the small room. One man was an average looking Tirendrian soldier in a red tunic. The second was swathed in dark robes and stared unsettlingly at her out from under a large hood. The third—

Everything in Lilac froze. And burned. She took a step back, hardly restraining a scream. He was undoubtably the King of Tirendria. Everything, from the circlet on his head, the embroidered tunic on his back, the authoritative posture in which he held himself, said so.

He was Vendar. The person responsible for her ignominious capture and imprisonment. The monster guilty of a thousand atrocities.

The man who was her father.

66

Through his bleary haze, he thought he heard someone crying close by. He stirred, listening intently. Now someone mumbled occasionally. Someone must be in the cell with him.

It occurred to Engrelin that he could make that logical conclusion. It filled him an absurd sense of pleasure. Someone was in the cell with him, he could recall his own name, he could flex his fingers if he tried... The list would go on forever if he let it. He was master of himself again, not a drifting nothingness. Even the darkness seemed to have dissipated somewhat. A faint red light gleamed beyond the thin skin of his eyelids.

Another voice, steady and low, drifted over the undercurrent of weeping. Two new cellmates? For a moment, Engrelin was tempted to open his eyes. But the persistent crying changed his mind. Whoever it was, they probably wanted to be left alone.

He sighed, then coughed and gingerly shifted onto his other side. He could now do that too. He was going to live after all. He settled quietly, but instead of pressing against the clammy stones beneath, his cheek met something warm and rough. Engrelin jolted with surprise. Was he in a bed?

Bit by bit, he forced his gritty eyes open. They protested like windows with swollen frames. Slowly, the thick stone walls around him formed out of the gloom; massive block upon massive block, stretching up and up until lost in darkness. Engrelin's surge of surprise slipped back into disappointment. He was still in the cell. Only now he could see everything around himself. He frowned thoughtfully. Had one of the soldiers left a lantern lying around?

A bright beam flashed in his eyes. Squinting painfully, Engrelin flung up one hand to shade them. The light, which he had longed to see for so long, now hurt.

"I'm sorry—I know it's bright," said a gentle voice. It lilted in Engrelin's ears like the most beautiful hymn ever composed. He hadn't heard a kind word since…Aunt Ruth.

"I'm not used to this darkness like you are," the man continued. He set the lantern down on the floor, so it did not shine so fully on Engrelin's face.

Still squinting, Engrelin lowered his hand. The man, unusually short, bent over him.

"I'm glad to find you awake, though," said the man. "Your companion tells me you've been out of it for quite some time."

"Have I?" Engrelin asked, with difficulty. His jaw felt rusty, out of practice. He bit his lip against the way his voice faltered. But the man had his curiosity piqued. So there *was* another person in here with them.

"You have." The light shifted, and Engrelin realized the man wasn't short, only kneeling beside him. The man wore a long red military cloak over his black robe.

"But the fever has nearly broken now," the man said, pushing his hand onto Engrelin's forehead. The hand was cool and rough and gentle. "Thank the Lord. I'm told you've had a close shave. It seems you have quite the road ahead of you. You're not ready to leave this world. Not yet."

You can't pole down a creek in sopping wet clothes during the middle of winter and expect to stay well, Engrelin thought wryly. He leaned slightly forward. The light glinted off the man's cloak clasp, which was rather strangely shaped. No…not a clasp… Engrelin squinted harder.

A crucifix, dangling from a silver chain around the man's neck. That, and the black robe…

"You're a priest?" Engrelin asked incredulously. It ended in a harsh cough, which he vainly tried to stifle in his arm. Sharp little aches still shot through his chest.

The priest laughed softly and put a gentle, firm hand on Engrelin's shoulder to steady him. "Yes, I am," he admitted. "That took you a while, didn't it?"

"Yes—but how did you get here, Father?"

Engrelin tipped his head back, trying to glimpse the passageway behind him. He only saw bars stretching from floor to ceiling, and a soldier in military scarlet standing beyond.

Engrelin looked back at the smiling priest. "Do they actually let you in here?"

"Some do, in secret," the priest answered. "To visit the faithful here."

The light flickered over his face, briefly illuminating the kind smile smoothing the creases on his brow and deepening the crow's feet at the corners of his eyes. "I was wondering…"

"Confession, Father," said Engrelin earnestly, catching the priest's hand in his, as if he feared the priest might leave him before administering the sacrament. This might be the last chance, in all this short life, that he might have to receive it.

The priest nodded and said, "I'll give you a few minutes to prepare."

Over the next few minutes, Engrelin poured his heart out to the priest. All the trouble and frustration of the past few months were packed into bundles of faults and delivered to the healer of souls. The priest listened patiently, then gave his gentle advice and absolution. Finally, to Engrelin's supreme surprise and joy, the priest drew out of a small case a tiny, round piece of bread. The Bread.

In the most unimaginable of places, Engrelin knelt in the darkness of Reing to receive the Lord of all.

"You can always find Him, no matter where you are," said the priest quietly as he helped Engrelin back onto the floor to rest. "You simply must look. Seek—"

"And ye shall find." Engrelin smiled as he levered down onto his elbows. "I know, Father."

"But now that you have the strength and the Food for your journey, I want you to remember this. You have many things on your hands. The princess, for one. Ensuring her safety is a promise you must live up to. You must help her out of here. But find help. Do not try to take this all upon yourself. This is not something any man should take on alone. Attempted alone, it will not succeed."

Engrelin nodded, a little uncertainly. "I know, Father. But—"

"You'll find friends in the most unexpected places, I think," said the priest, cutting Engrelin short. "Remember this also: It's not too late to forgive. It never is."

Engrelin's frown deepened. What did he mean by that?

"I have to leave you now." The priest climbed to his feet. "Take up the cross you have been given to bear, Engrelin. Do not let any lingering feebleness from your illness discourage you from action. The strength you need flows strongest when our body is weakest. Strength is more than muscle or ability. Remember?"

Engrelin smiled faintly. "I will, Father."

"And," the priest added as he picked up the lantern and shielded the flame from hitting Engrelin's face, "You must get your sword back. It is yours to bear. It means more to Ontaria than any of us realize."

"I...I will," Engrelin promised quietly, though he wondered how he would carry out such a promise. How did the priest know about Arrian, anyway?

But before he could ask, the priest lifted his hand in blessing. He hurried out of the cell, his lantern sending strange beams of light dancing along the walls. The Tirendrian guard, who had been standing stoically in the corridor all the while, moved to lock the door, then led the priest down the corridor.

"There ith one more on level thix." The soldier's voice slid back through the darkness that gradually strengthened with the lantern's retreat.

Engrelin almost sat up to stare after them. He'd heard that voice somewhere. Somehow it was connected with the past few days. But he had been too sick to care what went on around him, much less hear people talking, hadn't he?

What rank could that man possibly hold which would allow him to smuggle a priest into Reing?

Without the priest's lantern, the only light was the distant glow of a torch, allowing only shadows to be seen. The keen chill and damp, which Engrelin had forgotten in the priest's presence, crept back into the air and clung to his perpetually damp clothing. The silence was broken only by the distant dripping of water and the softest sobbing, so low Engrelin hardly heard it. He sighed and drooped back to the floor, hugging his sides loosely and staring up into the seemingly endless ceiling. Whoever shared the darkness with him could talk to him when they felt like it. He wanted to be left alone to think. And plan.

He had a lot of planning to do. There were so many things he would need to escape. Clothes to replace his wrecked ones, food, and weapons (how he was going to get his hands on even a kitchen knife, he hadn't the faintest idea). He must figure out how to get himself out of his cell, and Elvera out of hers. He scowled. He couldn't just steal keys. He would have to pick the locks on both. With what? And where in this place was Elvera's cell? If only there was a way to know exactly where she was before he broke out so he could plan that part ahead of time…

Engrelin sat up and clutched his head in his hands. This was going to take a lot of thinking. Maybe too much for just him. The priest was right. He needed help. But how to get it swiftly? Elvera's fate hung constantly on the brink of a precipice, poised to tumble down to destruction at any moment.

The soft sound of someone shuffling towards him distracted Engrelin. He glanced to the side to see a dark figure creeping slowly towards him. Engrelin sighed and ran a hand through his damp hair, bracing himself for the outpouring of some woe-ridden story.

"Engrelin?"

Engrelin started. His eyes narrowed. There was something frighteningly familiar about that voice. Something…

"Lance?" He spoke the name slowly, unbelievingly. "Lance, what are you doing down here?"

"I'm a prisoner, same as you," returned Lance shortly.

Engrelin stared at him, but through the gloom, he couldn't see the expression on Lance's face. Was this just another mockery?

"But…but why down here?" he asked again.

"I punched Reing's superior officer in the face," Lance replied curtly.

Engrelin didn't know whether to laugh or not. "And why did you do that?"

A hand grasped his, almost imploringly. "Please, Engrelin, don't ask that," Lance whispered brokenly. He drew his hand away just as quickly as it had come. "I'm here, okay? That's all that matters."

Engrelin touched his hand, and his fingers met bands of cloth wrapped around his wrists.

"Was this you?" he asked, holding out his thickly bandaged wrist. "And the blanket?"

"It's not a blanket, it's my cloak," Lance mumbled.

Engrelin fingered the wool beneath him thoughtfully. It was unbelievable. Simply false. It had to be.

He turned his head away, his eyes searching the darkness as if it could provide the answers he sought. During those three miserable days on the boat, Lance had made no move to make Engrelin comfortable or end Cuthrell's abuse. Instead, Lance had watched Cuthrell's actions with open approval. What, in the space of a week, had changed that? Had it even changed at all?

"Why didn't you keep it for yourself?" Engrelin asked.

"I was…nervous, that's all."

"Nervous?"

Lance drew a slow breath. "I thought you were dying," he said shortly.

"Oh." Not knowing what to say to that, still struggling with disbelief, Engrelin said nothing more. A slow smile quirked one corner of his mouth. "I'm not that wimpy, Lance."

Lance made the effort to laugh, clasping Engrelin's shoulder. Engrelin met him in the rough embrace, surprised to find Lance's whole body was shivering. He pulled away slowly.

"Lance, what's happened to you?" he murmured, almost to himself.

Lance was silent, slipping his hand away and sitting so still that he seemed hardly to be there at all.

"I got absolution from that priest, that's all," he said finally (and rather grouchily).

Absolution! It made absolutely no sense. The Lance of a week ago would have scoffed at even seeing a priest, much less have gone to confession!

"I mean," Engrelin said slowly, "Why did you turn back to us—to help me—in the first place?"

Lance's silence again stretched on. "If I tell you," he whispered, "will you forgive everything I've ever done to you?"

The words sent a shard of dread cutting through Engrelin. He had a terrible feeling, deep in his gut, that Lance was referring to something that had happened recently, something only he knew about. Something truly awful.

But the priest's words momentarily overrode Engrelin's fear. It wasn't too late to forgive. Never.

"I promise, Lance," he said quietly.

Lance's deep wavering sigh—of relief or dread—whispered through the darkness.

Light flashed into their cell. The grate door was flung open. Engrelin's head jerked up to see several Tirendrian soldiers crowded into the cell, their lanterns throwing pools of light helter-skelter. Engrelin briefly glimpsed Lance's grief-stricken expression.

Engrelin was jerked to his feet and shoved out of the cell, the guards following, leaving Lance behind in bitter darkness.

What now?

67

As Engrelin staggered between two of his guards, their hands cruel clamps around his arms, his mind worked furiously. What had Lance meant to tell him? And why would it have upset him so much. Not one word Lance had spoken gave Engrelin a clue as to what it was. He bit his lip in frustration. But it had to be bad. Really, really bad to make him turn like he had.

The cells and staircases of Reing passed him in a blur. The soldiers' cursing his lagging steps were distant whines. Blows were still felt, and more feeble than he knew, Engrelin sagged between them. But still he wondered, what had gotten Lance so worked up?

Engrelin was thrust through a doorway into a room. A room so brightly lit, he was momentarily blinded. One of the soldiers shoved down on his shoulders, buckling Engrelin's legs, his knees striking the floor with a sickening *crack*. As he bit back a cry of pain, the guard's hand grasped a handful of his hair and yanked back, forcing Engrelin to lift his head.

His eyes adjusted to the bright light, and by squinting he could pick out his surroundings. He was kneeling in the center of a bare, gray room in front of three men who surveyed them from their perspective chairs. Engrelin's eyes drifted over them, finally coming to rest on the figure farthest to the left. His lips parted in shock, recognition coursing through him.

It was none other than Newfield, the captain he had met in Elstar. Engrelin quickly ran the encounter in the library through his head. He should have known it when the man's mood switched so suddenly.

"Well," said the traitor, sitting forward, "What do you know? I think the wretch recognizes me."

Engrelin glared at the man, oblivious that the guard had finally released his painful hold on his hair.

"You think me a traitor," said Newfield flatly. He raised his eyebrows. "On the contrary, Engrelin Aaron Everen Peterson, if I had *actually* been one of Wilelm's advisors, you would have been correct. But this—" he motioned to the austere room "—this is my country."

Engrelin could only stare, the blood in his veins heating. He'd only known the man for a brief moment, and yet Newfield hadn't seemed terrible. He certainly never would have guessed the man was a traitor.

How many others have we laid our trust in only to have it broken?

The man sitting between the other two cleared his throat, bringing Engrelin's attention to him. For a moment, everything within Engrelin plummeted, for the man sitting before him was Bendekahn's. Even as he thought it, he realized the man's hair was brown, not blonde, and straighter than Bendekahn's. Engrelin breathed a small sigh of relief. A small one, for the likeness was still disturbing.

"Vendar," rasped the man on the right, "get on with it. We don't have all day. There are still festival plans to enact."

Engrelin glanced at the last man out of the corner of his eye and no more, barely resisting a shudder. The robe the man wore swallowed his body—all but his hands, which rested in his lap. They seemed composed of nothing more than bone and sinew with shriveled flesh stretched over them. His piercing yellow eyes, sunk deep in their sockets, glared out from under the shadow cast by the hood he wore pulled far over his forehead. Engrelin averted his eyes and fixed them on the elaborately carved leg of Vendar's chair. The man looked little better than a living corpse.

"Where is his sword?" asked Vendar suddenly.

"I put it in the *trysor*," the hooded man replied. "A petty piece. You wouldn't find much interest in it, Your Majesty."

Engrelin simmered. It was one thing for Vendar to possibly want his sword. It was another for this creep to slight Arrian.

"You said it was a Kingsword, Rees," said Vendar, turning angrily towards the man.

Rees mumbled something under his breath. Vendar drew back in his chair, letting the breath hiss out through his teeth. "His? It's not possible."

"As Your Majesty thinks," said Rees with a shrug.

Vendar brooded a moment until his eyes happened to brush over Engrelin's kneeling figure. He glanced at Newfield. "The charges?" he demanded.

Engrelin watched Newfield rustle a paper from a stack on the floor and smooth it out over one knee. Charges…against him?

"Murder of four, assault of two, theft and…kidnapping," Newfield read aloud. He glanced expectantly up at Vendar.

The words were branded in Engrelin's mind. It was preposterous!

"I haven't—" Engrelin began angrily, but a harsh kick from his guard cut him short.

Vendar leaned forward in his chair. "You were the one with the princess Elvera, weren't you? Or were my men mistaken?"

Engrelin stared blankly at him.

"I can't see how Bendekahn would have entrusted his daughter to the hands of a young, exiled orphan," Vendar added. "Or perhaps being of Aaron's line raised you a little higher than other peasants?"

The words stung like a blow. Engrelin drew his head back an inch, eyeing Vendar warily.

"I can see it as nothing other than kidnapping," concluded the Tirendrian king, sitting back.

"Seeing as though you planned to murder her, you could say I was rescuing her," Engrelin remarked dryly. His guard cuffed him.

"I'm in no mood to take any impertinence, young man," Vendar growled. He continued smoothly, "The sword you had was obviously stolen. How else would you have gotten it? And you killed four of my soldiers on the border and wounded two others. What do you think I brought you in to hear? A story?"

Comparatively, Engrelin wouldn't have minded one at that moment.

Vendar snatched the paper from Newfield and shook it. "A peasant who, after living his whole light on the same plot of dirt, is found on the Northern Florenthian border in possession of a princess and a priceless weapon. He claims to be carrying one to safety, having been entrusted with the other."

Crushing the paper in his fist, Vendar threw it down in front of Engrelin. "This sort of thing only happens in wives' tales," he said.

Engrelin stared down at the paper, his lips pressed in a tight, white frown. "I'm not a murderer, a kidnapper, or a thief," he said starkly.

"Then what?" Vendar snapped. "A hero? A prince in disguise?"

A small smile played over Engrelin's face. "Like you said—I'm a young, exiled orphan."

"You're a Peterson!" Vendar snarled. "An insolent one, at that." He lapsed into silence a moment, a silence during which everything inside Engrelin fluttered violently. Had they brought him here only to hurl lies at him?

"Who told you to bring the princess to Monaria?" Vendar asked abruptly. He sat forward in his chair, scooting it forward several inches.

Engrelin's mouth snapped shut.

"Well." Vendar sat back again (he seemed rather fond of doing so). "If no one told you to take her, you were obviously kidnapping her.

"I was told," Engrelin said sharply.

"By whom?"

"I can't say," Engrelin replied. He gave himself a mental slap. He shouldn't have said anything at all. Let them think he was a kidnapper. It didn't matter anyway—all four of them knew they were lying; the accusations were false.

"It's not that you can't. You won't," Vendar corrected. He sighed heavily and glanced at the men sitting beside him before continuing, "Perhaps we should tell you of the insolent and…uncooperative prisoner's fate."

"I already have an idea," Engrelin gritted.

"Then you must know of the festivities we hold here annually," Rees interjected smoothly. "An entire week dedicated solely to the celebration of our monarch's reign. It begins tomorrow."

Engrelin shrugged with affected indifference. He didn't need—didn't want—to know how they celebrated Tirendrian rule.

"At the end of the week," continued Rees, "A boat will leave our docks, carrying hostages with them."

Engrelin's gaze sharpened on the man's withered face. "Hostages?" he echoed.

The hints of a smile further disfigured Rees' face. "The children of Kings Wilelm and Jayce are some. But I think you will be most interested to hear that Bendekahn's daughters will be boarding the ship with them."

A wave of nausea swept through Engrelin, mingled with further dread and despair. Daughters? Did that mean…

"What does this have to do with me?" he demanded, struggling to maintain his impassivity. He had even less time than he thought.

"I thought you might like to know they are bound for Monaria, just as you had planned," said Rees. "Or, should I say, as Bendekahn planned?"

Engrelin's jaw spasmed, drawing a dark chuckle from Newfield.

"Didn't you know we already knew?" the Captain asked.

"Then what was the point in asking me all these questions or bringing me here in the first place?" Engrelin demanded.

"You are one of Aaron's last living descendants," Rees said coolly. "Your family is all but eradicated. Austinian is dying from battle wounds. We caught one of his sons on the border and killed him, along with one of Bendekahn's daughters. His oldest son is to board with the hostages. It's all a one-way trip for them. It will also be so for you."

Engrelin's heart plummeted. Andrald and Isalinia, dead? It just wasn't possible.

And these men had dragged him here just to torture him with this information? That just couldn't be. There had to be some other reason behind it. There had to be! Something behind this useless pain…

Engrelin's thoughts warped back to the boat. A strange numbness descended on him.

"What are they sailing there for?" he heard himself asking.

"Drowning, off the coast of Monaria," Newfield answered promptly.

Vendar nodded, his dark eyes shining. "Fitting, I find," he said quietly.

Fitting?! Engrelin's whole body tensed, his hands curling to fists at his sides. "Can you just kill them for no good reason?" he demanded. "Their deaths won't stop their fathers from joining Monaria's cause."

"I have my reasons, just as I had with your sister," Vendar said. "And I killed her."

Engrelin stared and stared, too numb to even think. "What?" he murmured. The word fell brokenly from his cracked and bleeding lips. He couldn't breathe, as if someone had kicked him in the gut.

Through the haze, Engrelin saw Vendar shaking his head with contrived sympathy.

"It's a pity you had to leave her alone like that, so out in the open. You know," he added, chuckling, "afterward, my men told me she persisted in holding onto a fiddle to the end. Said she'd promised to keep it until you got back. Poor girl. She kept her side of the bargain, but big brother couldn't keep his end and didn't save her. You should have stayed home, boy."

His grief screaming within him, Engrelin wrenched himself free of his guard and sprang at Vendar. He caught the man about the throat. Vendar's chair overturned, throwing them both to the floor in a tangle of blows and wood. Engrelin lost his grip on the king's throat. He began pummeling him instead, little heeding the blows he received in return. His guard waded into the fray. He flung Engrelin back. He fell against Vendar's chair, striking his head against the carved leg.

Stunned, Engrelin lay there a moment, his lips moving but not drawing breath. A few blows to the face brought him back to reality in time to receive a kick to the stomach. Weaker than even he knew, gasping with pain and anger, Engrelin was dragged back to his former position in the middle of the room. Through a mist of unshed tears, he saw Vendar reclaim his seat, his embroidered tunic torn, his face contorted with rage.

"Do you realize," the man hissed, "whose feet you are kneeling at?"

Engrelin lifted his eyes to glare at the man. "If I weren't being forced to," he said, "I would refuse to kneel."

Rees staggered to his feet, one arm stretched out before him, as if reaching to grasp something.

"Kill him!" he cried. His eyes were fixed to the far wall, his whole body rigid. "Kill him now, while we still have time! While we have the chance…" His eyes, still staring at the wall, widened, as if he viewed some awful spectacle.

"No, Rees," said Vendar, much to Engrelin's surprise. He had considered himself dead then and there.

Rising, the king took a few steps towards Engrelin until he loomed over his prisoner.

"I was going to lay you aside quietly," Vendar whispered, as if he was confiding some great secret to Engrelin's care. "You and your friend Lance. We have places here like your homes, farms, and forges, for people who agree to stay neutral and stay quiet.

"But not now. Not here. At the end of this week, just before your royal friends leave for Monaria, both you and Lance will die in front of the very people you have tried to hide and defend. We shall give them a taste of what is to come."

Engrelin made no answer. *Not everyone I was defending,* he thought wretchedly. *Not everyone I should have been defending…*

"Take him away," Vendar ordered, stepping back and flailing his hand in dismissal. He glanced down at Engrelin. "Until next week, Peterson."

The guard yanked Engrelin to his feet. He staggered out the door, his body seeming ten times heavier than before. He knew it wasn't the fight or even his recent illness that weighed him down.

"You ought to have killed him now," he heard Rees hiss behind him.

"Once the boy is through mourning his little sister, he won't have time to do anything," Vendar scoffed.

The door shut, plunging Engrelin in familiar darkness.

68

endar, her uncle?

It was better than being her father. Lilac closed her eyes and tipped her head back against the cold wall. She would never, never forget the feeling of absolute fear and horror than had gripped her after her first glimpse of Vendar. Half-blind as she had been from the brightly lit hall, Lilac hadn't seen at first that his hair was brown and less wavy, and his eyes dark—nothing like her father's fair features and violet eyes.

Nevertheless, the word *father* had slipped from her lips before she had time to recover her wits. Her voice had been the first to speak in that silent, menacing room.

A hooded man standing beside Vendar had leaned close to him to whisper, "Hengar must have raised her ignorant."

Even though Vendar had waved him off, Lilac's cheeks had grown warm. The question sprang up in her mind: Who was Hengar?

Vendar had plastered a smile on his face and turned to her. "I'm not your father, Lilac," he'd said gently. "I'm your uncle."

Lilac's wash of relief had drowned in a wave of revulsion. An uncle who lived off stolen lives, sown division, and broken treaties. A man drenched in innocent blood. Even in her cell, she shuddered and pressed the heels of her hands into her eyes. She was related to this man how? She wanted to believe he was lying—wanted desperately. But something terrible and true within her told her that he was not.

The meeting continued to play out in her mind. Vendar had seated himself in one of the chairs and had motioned for her to take the other. Lilac had barely sat down when Vendar had leaned forward, his eyes fixed expectantly on her.

"My dear girl," he'd said, "considering that you are my niece, I don't like to see you languishing in this prison like a common criminal. I would gladly withdraw you and your sister from it and welcome you into my home. But under one condition." He had leaned closer still. "I have been deeply considering naming you my heir."

Lilac had recoiled violently. The very thought! Even now, when merely reminiscing, her mouth filled with a bitter bile.

Vendar's sickly smile had broadened. "Don't act so surprised," he had admonished. "I never married, and I have no close relatives or anyone I deem worthy to inherit my throne. And, after all, you are my oldest niece." He chuckled and spread his arms wide. "And you've shown that you are more than capable."

Lilac wondered still what had made him think that. "But I'm already in line for another throne," she had quietly reminded him.

"You father's throne—bah!" Vendar had exclaimed in disgust. "What is that? I have armies unlike any on the face of Ontaria, Lilac." His voice had again changed to one of subtle pride. It had been almost cajoling. "Once I conquer Monaria, there will be no country in all the world able to withstand me! Withstand *us*," he had added softly. He had slid his heavy, jewel-encrusted sword into Lilac's lap.

"The whole world would be your inheritance. All you would have to do would be give up Alinar and come live with me." His dark eyes had searched hers penetratingly. "Think of it."

Lilac had stared down at the sword, everything in her churning. Of all the terrible things she had expected out of Vendar, becoming his heir was the very last. The worst.

Swallowing hard, she had pushed the sword back over to Vendar. "I'll think about it," she had promised, in a voice she had hardly recognized as her own. "But I need more time."

"Of course—there's no rush. Though the sooner you decide, the sooner we can set everything in motion." His dark eyes had gleamed like two chips of polished onyx. "When it comes to conquering the world, Lilac, every moment counts."

As the memory faded back into the gray walls of her cell, Lilac remembered Vivian was sitting on the bench across from her. The girl's stunning features were tight with deep thought; even the light in her eyes frowned.

"Your...uncle—or whatever you want to call him—I thought he'd chosen an heir a long time ago."

"Vivian!" Lilac exclaimed. "You don't think I'm actually going to accept the proposal, do you? Imagine being the queen of this place..." She shuddered again at the thought.

"I knew that!" Vivian looked up quickly, then fixed her eyes back on the floor, as if she drew all her answers from it. "But I thought I had heard rumors that several of Vendar's advisors were vying for some lord's son to be appointed. A distant relation, and only through Dermain's marriage to Elodina, who died decades ago. She was Vendar's mother." A scowl screwed her lips. "I wouldn't give the creature in question credit by calling him human. Warwick, I think his name was. He's the one who devised the plan to harness prisoners of war in towns to work for the army's benefit. It's disgusting, Lilac, little better than slavery."

Lilac frowned. "If he already had someone in mind, why did he ask me?" she wondered aloud.

"Maybe I heard wrong," said Vivian with a shrug. "It was just a rumor, after all. Maybe your uncle does want you to rule his kingdom after him. But if I were him, I wouldn't want to cross his brother's wrath."

"But he told me he had no..." Lilac's voice drifted, realizing who Vivian meant. Vendar was her uncle, so that made her father his brother. The likenesses were too strong for her to argue that it wasn't true. It was almost too horrible to possibly be true.

Why hadn't her father told her? He had never kept secrets from her! At least, as far as she had known. Which, she reflected, rising to pace the length of the cell, wasn't much. There was so much to the world that she had never known, things that she would rather have gone on without knowing.

"I need to get out of here and get answers," she muttered fiercely. She stepped over to the barred window and glared out at the misty morning.

"We all want that," said Vivian sympathetically. "But how? It's not like we can ask the guards for the keys. We're hostages, Lilac. What's more, the heirs to many kingdoms. We're worth more to them than we might think."

"That's exactly why we need to get out of here," Lilac said earnestly.

"What are you suggesting?" Vivian asked. Her eyes sparkled more brightly than Lilac had ever seen.

Lilac's gaze drifted over the creek that slipped silently past the fortress' feet. "To start," she said thoughtfully, "We'll need boats."

69

The guard shoved Engrelin back into his cell. Engrelin snatched one of the iron bars to steady himself as the grate door slammed shut. The guard's footsteps faded to silence. Engrelin slumped against the wall of bars and pressed his hands over his face. Elmera was dead? Why had he come all this way, only for Elmera to die…and for him to be condemned?

"Engrelin, is that you?" Lance drew up beside Engrelin and put a gentle hand on his arm.

Engrelin drew one last shuddering breath and let his hands drop. "Yeah, it's me," he said.

"I guess they told you?" Lance asked awkwardly. "About Elmera?"

Engrelin nodded and looked down, tears burning the back of his throat. "Yeah."

"I'm sorry, Engrelin. It's all my fault—I told them you had family," said Lance fiercely. "But I never dreamed they would—"

"Just forget it," Engrelin cut in, misery sharpening his voice. "There's nothing you or I can do about it. But the others—"

"What others? The princesses? Did Bendekahn—"

"As far as I know, Bendekahn's done nothing," Engrelin said. "But Vendar's planning to kill the girls anyway, along with any other royal hostages he has penned up here. He—" Engrelin hunched his shoulders "—he already killed Andrald and Isalinia on the border."

Lance was silent a moment; Engrelin saw, with eyes now thoroughly adjusted to the dark, Lance's hand moving up, down, then side to side, in a most reverent crossing.

"Are they going to kill Averendier as well?" he asked at last. "I know he and Lilac were brought here same the day we arrived."

"Yes," Engrelin answered. "And…and us too. I'm sorry, Lance. It was my fault this time. I…tackled Vendar to the floor."

"That trumps punching Newfield," Lance chuckled.

Engrelin said nothing. He flexed his bruised fingers a moment, recalling how it satisfying it had felt to drive them into Vendar's face. Guiltily, he shook the thought away.

In the awkward silence, Lance wedged his shoulder in between two of the cell's bars.

"So…how's Vendar planning to do it?" He said it casually, as if he were asking what they had eaten for dinner. Had it come to that? Engrelin shook his head at himself. They had both expected this for so long, how could he expect a different reaction?

"Drowning, off the coast of Monaria," he said tightly.

"No, I mean, what is he going to do with us?"

"Oh. We're supposed to be executed on the docks. It's Vendar's way of saying farewell."

"More like 'fare-badly,'" Lance muttered.

Engrelin's stomach twisted.

"So." Lance drew himself erect. "What's the plan?"

Engrelin shrugged. "I have no idea. We have to figure out some way to break out of our cells."

"Obviously."

"Oh, and we only have a week to figure all this out," Engrelin continued. "We'll be completely on our own. No counting on outside help, not even from the others. They'll have no idea what we're planning."

Lance mused silently a moment. "We won't need a map of this place," he said. "I've walked through here so many times, I know it like the back of my hand. It's a labyrinth, designed to confuse anyone trying to escape. If you take all the staircases leading up, one way or another, you're going to end up on the lowest level. And you must go all the way down to level ten to find the one staircase that leads to the top floor, where the hostages are."

"That's nice to know," said Engrelin. "You wouldn't also happen to know the exact cells everyone's being kept in, would you?"

"I do," said Lance, with a smudge of pride.

Engrelin smiled faintly, recalling the priest's advice to get help. Where would he be without Lance right now?

Well, he wouldn't exactly have ended up here without him either...

Engrelin shook his head. They were together here now. Lance had turned back, for whatever reason.

"We'll need provisions," Lance said. "That'll be easy. I know where the kitchens are. They hardly keep a single guard over them."

"So they should be perfectly clear at night," Engrelin mused.

Lance nodded. "Anything else?"

"Weapons," Engrelin said. The place at his left hip felt empty without Arrian's reassuring weight pressing against it.

"That'll be a bit tricky, Engrelin," said Lance uncertainly. "The armory is under guard, lock, and key day in and day out. There's no way we're getting in there uninvited."

"Do we just ask for an invitation?" asked Engrelin mildly.

Lance shook his head with silent laughter, then sobered. "You want your sword back, don't you." It was a statement, not a question.

Engrelin nodded. Arrian was the only thing he'd lost that he might have the chance to recover.

"I heard Rees mention where it was, but I can't remember exactly what he said. It was something in *cymraeg*."

"We might be able to find it," Lance said. "They might have a place for storing ancient weapons around here."

Despite himself, Engrelin smirked. "Sure. Because there are so many of those in the world."

Lance looked at him side-long. "And your forgot one thing," he said.

"What?"

"New clothes. I know you haven't had the chance to look in a mirror recently, but I thought you might like to know—"

"I'm a wreck?"

"Yeah, pretty much..." Lance grinned lopsidedly. "You need new everything. It looks ready to fall off at any moment."

"All right, new clothes," Engrelin said, lightly shoving Lance. "What else do you want? The keys to the king's treasury?"

"That would be nice," Lance reflected. "But I think the only keys we'll be needing are the ones to our cells. We could always pick the locks," he added hopefully.

"With what?"

"Right." Lance pursed his lips.

Engrelin scowled. There had to be some way to get out. Some way to get everyone away before they were all slaughtered!

"There ith a way," said a voice behind him.

Both boys gasped and whirled into a wash of lurid light. On the other side of the bars, his scarlet tunic startlingly bright in lanternlight, stood a Tirendrian officer. Engrelin's eyes dropped to the man's waist. From the officer's belt hung a ring so tightly packed with keys that their jagged ends stuck out in all directions. Engrelin's scowl darkened. Just as they were found out, here was the answer to their problem. He could have reached out and touched the keys if he'd dared.

"What are you doing here?" Lance demanded.

The officer waved his hand vaguely. "You thpeak very loud," he said.

"We'll quiet down, if that's what you want," Lance said angrily. "Not that it'll do any good now that you've heard us." He made a shooing motion.

Engrelin expected the officer to grin maliciously before stomping off to report to his superior officer that two prisoners were plotting a break. Why had they gotten so excited that they had stopped whispering?!

To his surprise, the officer set his lantern down at his feet. He gripped the cell bars in his hands.

"I not go tell my commander," said the man haltingly.

Lance's eyes nearly popped out of their sockets. "What?!"

"I want to help you," the soldier insisted.

"Help us?" Engrelin echoed doubtfully. "Why?"

"Becauth. I am a prithoner, like you. It would be my ethcape juth ath much ath yourth."

The soldier's lisp tugged Engrelin's memory. This was the man who had warded off Rees sometime during his illness. He had also been with the priest. Now he wanted to help them escape?

"Prisoner?" Lance repeated confusedly. "You're a Tirendrian officer."

The man smiled grimly, though not bitterly. "That doth not mean I am not a prithoner," he said. The lantern light shifted, casting an orangey glow on the man's light-blond hair. "I am altho far from my home."

"If you're a prisoner, what are you doing out there, instead in a cell?" Engrelin challenged. "And don't give me any flak about having just broken out. I saw you walking around here a week ago."

"No, I have not juth broken out," the man said. "The Tirendrianth have more than one way to keep prithoner people they do not like. They put me ath head offither of prithon level eight. I wath juth at my roundth when I hear your voitheth. Echoth carry far here." He waved at the ceiling.

Engrelin's cheeks prickled. "If you're so high-ranking, why risk helping us escape?"

The man's eyes burned into Engrelin like blue flames. "I rithk nothing," he said. "What ith rank compared to freedom? What honor can they give me to make thith home?" He motioned again to the dank darkness around him. "I want to be free juth ath you do. I want the king'th children to be free. For thith all, I will help you."

Engrelin and Lance exchanged wondering glances, their eyes flickering the same message: *He was with the priest—we should trust him.* Even if they hadn't seen him with the priest, his simple sincerity alone would have convinced them he was honest.

"All right, you're in," Engrelin said.

A smile beamed on the man's face. "Thank you," he murmured, bowing slightly. "I will not fail you."

"What's your name?" Lance asked.

"Here, they call me Captain Welric," the soldier answered. "But you must call me Welric only. To me, captain ith only another way to thay 'prithoner.' And thoon, God willing, I will be a free man."

"Do you really think we can trust him?" Lance asked Engrelin once Welric had retreated down the passageway to finish his rounds (but with the promise to come back as soon as he had finished his routine).

"Do we have any other choice?" Engrelin replied. He scrubbed a hand through his damp hair and sighed. "I honestly don't see any other way to do this. We need someone who can let us out of here." He tapped the iron bars, thick as his forearm.

Lance nodded thoughtfully and sank down against the cell wall. Engrelin joined him. He didn't realize until he sat down how dead tired he was, even after sleeping for who knew how long. Shutting his eyes, he tipped his head back against the clammy wall.

Instantly, painful memories flooded his bleary mind. He was too tired to push them away.

Elmera. So young, so frail, so sweet. The way she tossed her hair when she laughed. The many abandoned kittens she had patiently nursed back to health. How she had turned her nose up at Engrelin's attempts at meal-making. Somehow, he saw even that through a rose-tinted lens.

How she had cried when he left her behind!

He covered his face with his hands. At least while he while he planned, he could distract himself. Rest was becoming torment again.

"You all right, Engrelin?" Lance asked.

Engrelin didn't answer. Lance rested his hand on Engrelin's arm.

"What did they tell you about Elmera?"

Engrelin stiffened, as if bracing for a blow. "Not much," he answered huskily. "Just that's she's dead, and she still had my fiddle."

"Sweet little thing," Lance murmured. He sighed deeply. "I was hoping they might have told you more than they told me," he said. "Since you were her brother."

Engrelin lifted his head slowly. "Why did they tell you?" he asked, hoping to turn the discussion slightly away from Elmera. He wasn't ready to talk about her yet, not even with Lance.

"Right before—" Lance cleared his throat quickly. "The same day I punched Newfield."

"About her?"

"Partly." Lance said nothing for a long while. "It was for my mother, too," he said finally.

"Your mom? But I thought she was killed at Fort Starr."

"She…she was. Only, that's not what Newfield told me at Elstar. I was so desperate for news about her and Dad, Engrelin. I believed him."

Engrelin touched his temple a moment. "You saw Newfield in Elstar?"

"Yes. I followed you there, remember?"

"I know." Engrelin's fingers tensed, remembering the tautness of the bowstring between them. The bowstring he had released that first night away from Bryn. "Lance…" he groped. There wasn't any way to soften the question he needed to ask.

"Yes?" Engrelin felt Lance straightening beside him.

"What…what made you follow me in the first place?"

"I was wondering when you'd ask," Lance said. He sounded tired. Really tired. Engrelin bit his lip.

"I didn't mean—"

"You deserve to know," Lance cut in. He sighed heavily. "I'd like to blame Uncle. Or getting sick after hearing about Fort Starr. I haven't thought clearly since, not until I heard about Elmera. This was the last place I thought I'd recover. Talk about a healthy environment." He gestured around the prison. The two chuckled quietly but thoughtfully. Engrelin shifted slightly, realizing for the first time how filthy the cell was.

"I thought I hated you," Lance said.

You don't have to tell me that, Engrelin thought, though the confession filled him with indescribable relief.

"Maybe Uncle convinced me I did. Maybe I convinced myself. I don't know. Bryn had small love for the Petersons then. I don't think I believed it until I saw you push Uncle over in the forge that Sunday before you left."

"It must have looked pretty bad," Engrelin admitted.

"It convinced me," Lance said. "Enough to follow my uncle out of town Monday and sneak into your camp. I didn't know he meant to kill you, to pay you back for the insult Sunday. I'm glad now he didn't succeed, but then…" He sighed again. "You'd shot me. I know you didn't know who I was. But I was so hurt and furious I thought you *had* known and had shot me out of spite. And that's what my uncle told me."

A hand clenched Engrelin's chest and squeezed hard. "I'm so sorry, Lance," he whispered.

"It was my own fault for following you," Lance returned sharply. "I should have let that wound keep me home. Then I wouldn't have met Newfield in Elstar. He found me lurking around the castle walls, trying to figure out how to follow you in. He brought me inside and recruited me to follow you to Alinar and figure out what you were doing. When we learned, we were ordered to capture the princesses on the way to Monaria. We were supposed to attack just after you entered Tirendria. But I couldn't wait to get a crack at you, to pay for my shoulder and whatever else I'd accused you of."

Lance paused again, this time longer than before. Engrelin shared the silence. He doubted. Lance wanted any comments right now, forgiveness or other. So he just listened.

"We made a deal," said Lance in a low voice. "If I captured even one of the princesses and brought her here, Newfield would tell me where my mother was. He said he knew. I was fool to believe him…but I wanted to so badly. That's why I showed myself, that night in the cave. I could have hidden. But I hadn't meant to run far. I didn't think you'd follow me as far as you did. I had to come back to get a princess. I figured in the cave, with nowhere for you to run, was as good a chance as I'd get. Then that cat showed up."

He chuckled weakly. "I don't think I'll ever step into a cave again. I didn't want to in the first place. I saw paw prints by the creek. But I had to shelter…and I had to get Elvera." He laughed again, tiredly. "It's all sort of stupid, I guess, trying to get one girl and trade her in just to free another. I can't believe I tried it."

"There's always a chance some of them survived," Engrelin said. "It's not stupid to try to get them back."

"But it hurts too much to hope, just to be disappointed in the end. I'd rather live thinking they're dead. I…God, I just can't take it anymore. Seeing you in here was the last straw. I never had any friend but you—not a real friend—my whole life."

Engrelin clasped Lance's shoulder. "But it's over now," he said. "It's behind you. Forgiven and gone."

Lance gripped Engrelin's hand so tightly it hurt. Engrelin did not pull away.

"I wonder where Welric is," Lance muttered. "He should have been back by now."

"He'll come soon."

The boys sat in companionable silence until the key clanking in the lock announced Welric's return. Engrelin lifted his head in surprise. It was still pitch dark. Welric must have left his lantern behind.

"Welric?"

"Here, Arweddwr," Welric replied. "I have brought thomething for you both."

Welric shoved plates into the boys' hands.

"I am thorry it ith not much," Welric whispered. "But the cook would wonder about thieveth if I took more."

Engrelin's stomach cramped with sudden, painful complaint. He hadn't thought about food until now. When had he last eaten? By touch, he found the food on his plate: stale bread, rather dry meat, and a cup of rusty water. But he wolfed it down as if it were a Christ Mass dinner.

"Do not choke on it," said Welric, in a halting version of a jest.

Smiling wryly, Engrelin handed Welric his empty plate, inwardly wishing he was at home and could ask for seconds. What he had eaten had settled in his gut like a rock. He was hungrier than before he'd eaten.

"That wath quick," Welric muttered.

"He's hardly eaten anything in a week," Lance explained through a mouthful. "I'm surprised we can't see right through him."

"If I had known, I would have brought more, cook or no cook," said Welric mournfully.

"Don't bother," Engrelin said. "There's far more at stake than my stomach."

"Right. Though I do not think break and rethcue go well without it."

Engrelin's lips quirked. "True," he said. Then he sobered. "You heard all we said, right?" When Welric nodded, Engrelin added, "Do you have any ideas?"

Welric thought a moment. "One thing you may like," he said slowly. "I know of plathe where they take prithonerth' thingth. What you call it…Loot? *Trythor.*"

Engrelin's heart made a little leap. That was where Arrian was!

"If you like, I let you in to take what we might need for the journey," Welric offered.

"Yes," Engrelin agreed, hoping his excitement didn't show too plainly.

"Food, I can get mythelf. And I have the keyth." He jangled the ring of keys hanging from his belt.

"And I know what cells the hostages are being kept in," Lance said. "I can show you."

"Good. You two keep thinking. I muth go now." Welric rose, the dishes clattering slightly in his hands.

"So soon?" Lance got to his feet.

"I have dutieth," Welric explained. "Later, Lance, we can talk."

Engrelin also stood. "Is there anything we can do to thank you?" he asked.

"Arweddwr, you are letting me free," said Welric, gripping Engrelin's shoulder gratefully. "For me, that ith enough."

70

eart stuttering violently, blood pounding through his veins, breath rasping in his throat, Engrelin waited. Beside him, Lance's harsh breaths also shattered the silence. Engrelin was glad he couldn't see his friend's face. He was nervous enough.

A week had passed since his interview with Vendar. The festival ended tomorrow. If they didn't escape tonight, it would be the last night he, Lance, and all the other hostages spent in Ontaria.

Engrelin shut his eyes and pressed his forehead against the cold bars. His chest heaved under his tunic. He had to stop thinking.

"Where's Welric?" Lance whispered anxiously.

"Shh." Engrelin sent darting glances into the darkness. "Do you want someone to hear you?"

"I am here, Lanthe," said a voice from the darkness, so startlingly close that both boys jumped.

"Engrelin, Arweddwr, are you ready?"

"Yes," Engrelin whispered past the knot in his throat. Why did Welric keep calling him that? It was the same thing the serpent in his nightmares called itself. Or had wanted to call itself, at least.

"Welric, where's your lantern?" Lance asked.

"I did not bring one," answered Welric as he quietly swung the cell door open. "Too much light. I do not want to be theen."

"I thought you said everyone would be out celebrating." Engrelin stepped into the corridor, free at last of the cramped cell.

"Moth, yeth," Welric acknowledged. "But thome of uth had to be left to guard the prithonerth and other thingth." He put a firm hand on Engrelin's shoulder. "Do not worry tho much, Arweddwr. It ith God'th will, we will ethcape."

Engrelin reached up briefly to clasp the guard's hand. In Welric's broad, warm hand, he realized his own was clammy and trembling. Quickly, he withdrew it.

"To the Trysor?" Lance asked as he swung the grate door carefully shut. Even so, the heavy grate door twanged as it shut. Engrelin cringed. His eyes flashed across the dark passageway, searching for the glimmer of an exploring lantern.

"Yeth." Welric nodded decidedly. "Arweddwr?"

Engrelin sighed. He would have to ask Welric about that name soon before he went crazy wondering.

He motioned down the passageway, even though he knew neither of his companions could see his hands. "Lead the way, Welric."

The guard touched Engrelin's arm lightly in reply, then stepped forward and took the lead.

They quietly wound through the passages of level eight. The ground never ran evenly, but always slanted up or down for no apparent reason. In the utter darkness, it was impossible to navigate. Engrelin stuck out his left hand occasionally, reassuring himself with the feel of the grimy wall. Prisoners moaned and muttered in the cells the trio passed. Each time, Engrelin bit his lip so hard it drew blood. The tang of it mixed with bitter fear in his mouth. The slight noises tensed every muscle in his body for a run. But run where?

They're not going to find us, he tried to convince himself. *They're all celebrating right now. They won't find out we're missing until we're long gone.*

If it were true, it might have been comforting. But it was far from true. After all his scheming, Vendar wasn't going to brush the princesses to the back of his mind or lighten his guards just because of a party. If anything, their numbers may have been doubled. The thought made Engrelin's pace quicken.

He bumped up against Lance's back.

"What's wrong?" he hissed.

"Dead end," Lance returned. He grabbed Engrelin's hand and pressed it up against a clammy wall.

"Where's Welric?" Engrelin asked. Fear looped around his chest. "Welric?"

"Juth a moment." Welric's voice sounded muffled. Something scrabbled around in the darkness, then cracked, like a stuck latch being forced open. A sudden breath of fresh air struck Engrelin's face.

"It wath quite thtuck," Welric observed placidly. "We will go up now."

Engrelin took several steps forward until his groping foot struck a stair.

"The rail ith to the right," Welric called from behind them. "Juth follow the thtairth up. I mutht clothe thith door."

Engrelin's hand found a curved iron railing. Gripping it firmly, he ascended the first step. Cautiously, he felt for the next one and then the next. He heard the hidden door's latch snap and Welric's accustomed feet hurrying up the stairs.

"We mutht hurry," Welric urged. "They are long thtairth."

Engrelin and Lance labored behind Welric until they reached another blank wall. Engrelin felt all along its surface, but he couldn't find the handle.

"Like thith, Arweddwr." Welric brushed up against Engrelin's shoulder, pushing him slightly out of the way. Again, he heard a latch snap. The door opened, letting murky light floor the stairway. Engrelin flinched and threw his hands up in front of his eyes. Lance muttered behind him.

"Na," Welric scolded under his breath, holding up one hand. Engrelin saw, through somewhat adjusted eyes, that the door was only open a crack. Welric peered tentatively through it. His hand moved to the dagger at his belt.

"Wait here," he commanded. Without giving either boy time to ask why, Welric slipped through the crack and into the corridor, pulling the door almost shut behind him.

His footsteps padded on the smooth stone floor. Even with his ear pressed to the crack, Engrelin barely heard them. Something scuffled. A muffled, sickening sound, like poking a knife through a full wine skin. A groan, and the door opened all the way. Engrelin stepped into the hallway, followed by Lance.

Welric tucked his dagger into his belt. "We do not worry about guard at thtairth now," he said. "But there may thtill be thome on thith level. Come. Quietly."

Trying not to notice the stain on Welric's hand, Engrelin followed, though not before glancing at the twilight filtering through a barred window.

"Welric, I thought you said you wouldn't come to get us until after dark," he murmured.

Welric paused. "I would think it safeth, Arweddwr. but if you want to look in the Trythor, you will need light to thee with. And you could not bring a torch—a light in the window would bring attention to the room. Only the Lord Reeth ith thuppothed to be in the Trythor."

Engrelin nodded and focused again on making each step he took as silent as possible. Welric, safest because of his uniform, walked first, peered around every corner in the corridor. If the coast was clear, he motioned Engrelin and Lance forward. If it was not, he would hold up one hand. The boys crouched in the shadow of a doorway, waiting for the "all clear" signal. They never saw any of the guard. But the mere knowledge that they were here sent Engrelin's heart thudding against his ribs.

Finally, Welric stopped outside a door and fumbled with the lock. "Here," he whispered. He quietly swung the door inward on its perfectly oiled hinges. "I will thay out here and watch, ath you thaid. Go quickly, find what you need."

Wordlessly, Engrelin slipped inside the room, Lance at his heels. Once they were both inside, Welric closed the door behind them. The key clicked in the lock.

Lance let out a low whistle. "You'd think they'd put shelves in here or something," he murmured, toeing the nearest pile.

The room wasn't large, yet the heaps and heaps of things piled on the floor made it seem even smaller. There was no apparent rhyme or reason to anything. Some of the mounds rose to Engrelin's waist. There was hardly any room to walk.

"How are we supposed to find anything?" Lance asked.

"Dig," Engrelin replied. "I'll start on this end, you take the other. Just take whatever we need."

Engrelin bent to survey the things at his feet while Lance waded into the center of the mess. Clothing, jewelry, weapons, mess kits, and all sorts of odds and ends were jumbled on the floor. Engrelin picked up a sterling bracelet studded with amethyst and rubbed it slowly between his fingers. Who had once worn this? Were they even alive anymore? The thought chilled his fingers, and the bracelet slipped through them and back onto the floor.

It fell with a soft jingle next to a sword. Its naked blade shone a clean, cold blue. Heart thrilling with joy and anger, Engrelin gently picked up Arrian. Such a beautiful, ancient thing, and they had cast it on the ground like all this other trash? His hand tightened over his sword's hilt as he looked around for the scabbard.

Soon he found not only it, but also a sturdy bow and quiver. He belted Arrian on, slung the quiver over his shoulder, and rummaged around until he had found at least a dozen arrows that weren't cracked or splintered. These he stuffed into the quiver.

Looking up from his work, Lance smiled his approval. "You're beginning to look a little more like yourself," he said. "But you still need this." He handed Engrelin a jerkin, one of the very ones Lamar had given him. The Tirendrians must have found it at the inn in his pack and brought it here.

"Thanks." In return, Engrelin handed Lance two daggers he had found during his hunt for arrows.

Lance swung a short naval sword on its belt over his shoulder. Engrelin looked twice at the weapon.

"Lance, isn't that Averendier's?" he asked.

"I assume so. His name's on the hilt," Lance replied.

"Bet he'll be happy to have that back," Engrelin murmured. He turned to hunt for any clothing that wasn't of the silk or velvet variety which abounded in the *trysor*. Finally, he gathered the cornflower-blue tunic, a pair of brown trousers, and sturdy stockings and leather boots. These he donned quickly, stuffing his rotten, discarded clothing into a far corner of the room.

Someone knocked softly on the door. It opened, and Welric peered into the room.

"You are taking a long time," he whispered. His watery-blue eyes drifted over them. "Do you have everything you need?" he asked.

"Almost," Engrelin replied. "We'll be out in a moment."

Welric nodded and said, "That jewelry on the only thelf ith the hothageth. Bring it."

Engrelin glanced back at the shelf (the only one in the room). It was heaped with glittering piles of precious metal and gems. "All right."

Welric backed out into the hall and shut the door. Engrelin sighed softly through his teeth and looked down at a pile of clothing.

"I'll find a couple sturdy packs. One for weapons, one for clothes."

Lance waved him off. "Don't bother about me. I've already found what I need."

Engrelin located two packs in good condition. One, he gave to Lance, who had rustled up quite an assortment of weapons. He filled the other with clothing and the jewelry. During the hunt, he found a fawn-colored cloak, which he slung over his shoulders. Lance found a cloak as well. and soon the packs were too full to carry anything more. Slinging the packs on their shoulders, the boys exited the room.

Welric locked the door behind them. "We go down to dockth now," he said. "Come. There thould not be many guardth."

Welric's prediction proved correct. Not once did he flash the "stay back" signal to Engrelin and Lance. They plunged back into the dark staircase, down through the cell blocks, and out the same door through which Engrelin had first entered Reing.

"Where did all the guards go?" Lance asked once they were out in open air. It blew refreshingly into Engrelin's upturned face.

"More and more abandon their potht to join the fethival," Welric explained. "Hopefully, it will help uth get hothageth out."

Welric led them across the wooden dock. "The boat ith over here," he said. He pointed into the water. Engrelin barely distinguished the shape of a large rowboat sitting on the water. Twilight was deepening by the second. His unaccustomed eyes relaxed in the welcoming darkness.

"It's a little big," he commented as he lowered the packs into the boat's bottom.

Welric chuckled. "It theem big now, but when twelve people in, it ith not tho big any more. Bethide," he added, "I do not think we will be in thith boat for long. We will be out of Tirendria thoon. Then maybe, if war over, we all go home."

"Where is your home, Welric?" asked Lance. He grunted as he dropped the heavy packs into the boat.

"Eathtern Florenth, Lanthe," Welric promptly replied. "I wath brought here to be a tholdier when the Tirendrianth attacked. Before then I be with wife, two children." Despite the gloom, Engrelin saw the tender smile lighting Welric's face. It sent reminiscent pangs shooting through him. "Maybe three children now," Welric added. "My wife ready to have third baby when I left. If it live, maybe two yearth old now."

Engrelin peered down into the boat to hide the expression he felt pinching his face. "Welric, where's the food?" he asked.

"Down there," said Welric, pointing under one of the thwarts. "It ith not much, but it wath all I could find. Is it too little?"

"It'll do for now," Engrelin said, frowning. "We can hunt on the way if we must. But I'm not much of a fisherman."

"That ith eathy," said Welric. "Back home, I fithed every day."

At that moment, the heavy prison door crashed open. Light poured onto the dock. Engrelin shielded his eyes with his arm. Beyond it, he saw a swaying figure in the prison doorway, holding a torch aloft.

"Wha...whatt are ya...ya doin' here?" the soldier slurred. He lurched forward, clutching the doorway with his free hand.

Welric stepped forward. "I am moving thome prithonerth," he said, not untruthfully.

"Id...diot," the soldier drawled. "The special prisoners be...be going to...to holding house two, up hills, up...up streams." The drunken man flapped his hand towards the stream. "Weren't ya...ya told?"

"No," answered Welric shortly. "But I thank you for telling me."

Subtly, he touched Lance's and Engrelin's arms and motioned them towards the doorway. As they hurried past the intoxicated man (who seemed more interested in keeping himself on his feet than in the fugitives hurrying by), Engrelin prayed the soldier was too drunk to get curious and find the boat.

Quietly, the trio hurried through the labyrinth, back up to its first level. They encountered only one guard, and he was sprawled face down on the corridor floor. Welric stepped over him, the boys following suit. With each step he took, Engrelin's heart slammed against his chest all the harder. They were almost there. Almost.

Too soon than seemed possible, they had mounted the hidden staircase and were walking down the broad hallway that ran through Reing's first level.

"What cell, Lance?" Welric asked, fingering the ring of keys at his belt.

"Three and four," Lance answered promptly. "Over here."

They crowded around the grate doors. As Welric wrestled with the lock, Engrelin peered frowningly into the darkness of a cell beyond.

"I don't hear anyone in there," he said.

"They're here," Lance said emphatically. "They've got to be here!"

Engrelin heard Welric whisper something in another language. Then the man jerked the grate door open.

But Engrelin was sure now. With a punched-in-the-gut feeling, he ducked into the cell and glanced around once.

It was empty.

71

Crouched in the bottom of the boat beneath a protective canvas, Engrelin grimaced. The low thwart above him pressed into his spine, Arrian's pommel dug under his rubs, and the canvas trapped his and Lance's breath, stifling what little breath the excited boys managed to draw. Though Welric had assured them the trip upstream wouldn't take more than ten minutes, already it felt as if hours had dragged by, and Engrelin had yet to hear the tell-tale *thump* of the rub-rail striking against dock pilings.

"Engrelin?" Lance whispered breathlessly.

"Yeah?" Engrelin tried to shift and face Lance, but his sword only drove into his side all the harder.

"Where will we be taking the royal kids, after this?"

"To Monaria, I think. That was the original plan with Bendekahn's daughters. I don't think any other place is safe."

"After that, we'll go home, right?"

"I guess so. You can come with me to the farm, if you want to. I could use the help."

"I don't think I have a choice. I couldn't in good conscience let your poor grandmother live off your cooking."

Engrelin chuckled and shook his head. "Fair enough."

They were silent a moment. The only sound was the whisper of the water washing against the boat and the swish of Welric's pole pushing the boat along. "Why do you ask?"

"Just…wondering," answered Lance evasively.

Before Engrelin could press further, a warning thud sounded. The boat rocked slightly as it bumped against something.

"Just a moment, Captain," a rough voice said. "What are you carrying here?"

Engrelin's heart squeezed. His hand latched around Arrian's hilt. He hadn't counted on a water patrol.

"I am taking thupplieth to holding houthe two," said Welric carefully, but honestly.

"We'll see about that." The two boats scraped and rocked together. The speaker must be leaning forward. Willing himself to be small and still, Engrelin held his breath.

The canvas behind him, where the stores rested, was jerked back. Fresh air rushed past Engrelin. He didn't dare breathe it in.

"Parcels, parcels…" the patrolman muttered, striking the packs and packages with a long pole. It banged up against the side of the boat, jolting Engrelin's heart off beat each time.

"You're good. Carry on."

"Yeth thir." Welric said, his voice impassive. The boats scraped together one final time, and the rhythm of Welric's pole swishing through the water resumed.

Engrelin released Arrian's hilt. Lance's pale face swam dizzily in front of him. He shook his head to clear it, then realized he still hadn't released his breath. He let it out, drawing another slowly.

He and Lance said nothing until the boat bumped against dock pilings.

"We are here," Welric whispered above them, somewhere beyond the canvas. "I have tied the boat to the dock. Do not move. I will be back thoon."

"All right," Engrelin replied in the barest of whispers.

Welric's footsteps sounded hollowly across the dock, loud in the stillness. Engrelin's hand tightened over the crowbar that had sat beside him throughout the trip.

His plan was frail and likely to fail. They didn't even know whether the hostages were here.

What the drunken guard had said…special prisoners to holding house two.

Engrelin shut his eyes, praying that the man had been right, that the guards would leave their post under the guise that Welric had come to relieve them of their duty and permit them to join the festival. That the holding house was as old and possibly insecure as Welric thought. That it had windows.

That the hostages were actually inside.

The thousands of ways the plan could fail loomed before Engrelin, a wall as tall as Reing itself. He grit his teeth. It was simple. Simple, yet difficult. And so very dangerous.

Welric's footsteps announced his return, then rocked the boat. The canvas above the boys' heads was flung back. Engrelin blinked up at the moonlit sky and Welric's figure silhouetted against it.

"It ith time," Welric whispered. Reaching down, he pulled Engrelin to his feet.

"Already?" Lance said wonderingly as he crawled out from under a seat. He gratefully accepted Welric's assistance up. "The guards left their post that quickly?"

"They probably would have, if they had been there," Welric replied.

Engrelin's stomach dropped. "Do you mean the hostages…"

"They are in the building, thure enough," Welric assured him. "I could hear them thinging."

"Singing?" Lance echoed incredulously.

Welric shrugged. "I do not know why they thing. But the guardth are not there. That ith a good thing, yeth?" He climbed up onto the dock.

"I don't know," Engrelin said uncertainly. He looked at the nearby hill. It sloped gently, illuminated slightly by the moon (he certainly could have been happier without the moonlight). Crowning the hill was a small, square building, its stone walls silvery against the darkness.

"They could come back at any moment and find us. We're not doing the fastest thing in the world."

"I know that, Arweddwr," said Welric quietly. "But I think they abandoned their post to go the fethtival, as you planned. They probably will not return."

"At least, not sober," Lance muttered.

The skin on the back of Engrelin's neck crawled. Having the guards return would be bad—their returning drunk would be ten times worse. He sucked in a deep breath and prayed, however futilely, that the guards weren't drinking.

The three crept wordlessly up the hill. In the distance, the sounds of a wild festival rose and fell. Welric had explained that though usually held several miles away at Vendar's castle, the king had decided this year to hold it at Reing, for obvious reasons. He had soldiers to humor for the war ahead. He had the assured victory against his opponents in the form of nine young people, the children of kings and an admiral. Engrelin's hand tightened around the crowbar in his hand. There was no enemy in sight now, no immediate danger. Yet the tension of watching alone clamped tightly around his chest and throat. There was no more time to think, to plan, to wonder. Just to act.

Soon—too soon—they were slipping into the holding house's shadow, cast by the full moon. Welric rounded to the building's front to post guard in front of the heavy iron-bound door. Engrelin and Lance crept around to the back.

"I thought Welric said this thing has windows," croaked Lance, hoarse with anxiety.

"Back wall," Engrelin answered, somehow forcing the words through his dry lips.

They rounded the back corner of the building. There stood the window, three iron bars stretching vertically across it over a heavily glazed pane of glass. Engrelin's breath eased out with relief.

He locked eyes with Lance. Lance caught the look and nodded grimly, taking his place by the window and wrapping a sack around the lowest bar and holding it firmly there with both hands. Engrelin glanced at the fogged glass beyond the bars and slowly, very slowly, he slipped the crowbar under the sack-wrapped bar, shoving it far to overlap the next, careful all the while not to shatter the glass. Bracing himself, he tugged. The bar gave not an inch. Huffing impatiently, Engrelin yanked again. And again. Back and forth, back and forth. The bar trembled slightly, grated, and stubbornly clung in its mortar.

While Engrelin still tugged away, he noticed Lance cocking his head toward the window. He was smiling slightly. Engrelin heard faintly from within the holding house the girls' voices, faint but discernable even through the thick walls. Engrelin thought he could pick Lilac's out from among the others as they warbled:

> "Where choicest flowers can be found,
> Where fruitful branches grow
> Where lion and lamb together bound
> Where rivers gently flow..."

Engrelin felt a slipping thrill through his tool as the bar began to give. Wedging the crowbar in tighter, he yanked harder, excitement lending energy to his shaking arms.

> "Where weary travelers find their rest,
> Where—"

Crack!

At the sound, Lilac startled, the words on her lips dying. Beside her, Elvera screamed.

"What was that?" Vivian demanded.

Averendier strode over to the house's single window (from which the sound seemed to come). Derin and Jayce, two of the hostage princes, broken stones in hand, stopped trying to dig under the wall to watch Averendier. Eight pairs of eyes hung anxiously upon him. Lilac thought she saw motion beyond the window.

"What is it?" Vivian repeated, stepping beside Averendier. His dirt-caked hands hung loose at his sides.

"I don't believe it," he murmured.

Engrelin waved his hand in one final warning. No one screamed again, so they must have seen him. Lance tossed the bar they had broken off to the side.

The singing wasn't resumed. Anticipant silence reigned.

The boys attacked the second bar. This time, Lance wielded the crowbar. Engrelin held the iron bar wrapped with sacking to muffle the scrape of metal against metal. The second bar gave way easily against Lance's strength. Again the boys switched places.

Engrelin pulled steadily at the bar, his hopes rising within him. Rotten mortar crumbled onto the back of his hands. Arrian slapped his thigh rhythmically with each pull. Already, the bar inched out of the mortar.

"Almost there," Lance whispered, his eyes fixed intently on the bar.

Engrelin didn't even nod—he only tugged. Arrian tapped against his thigh. *Almost there. Almost there.*

"Midnight, and all ith well!" Welric's voice rang out loud and clear through the stillness.

In warning.

"Lance!" Engrelin hissed. He twisted his head around, twisting in all directions. "Can you see anything?"

Lance didn't even have to turn. Raucous laughter burst close by. The boys' eyes met.

All was not well.

"They're at the edge of the woods," Lance whispered hurriedly. "They look drunk. Maybe that'll buy us some time?"

Engrelin didn't answer. Gritting his teeth, jerked once more on the crowbar. The third and final window bar clattered to the ground. Lance snatched it up to pry the windowsill loose, but Engrelin caught his arm.

"Lance, we don't have time for that!" he exclaimed. "We're going to have to get them out another way."

"Wot's this about breaking someone out?" drawled a heavy voice beside them.

The stench of cheap beer hung in the air. Both boys spun to face their adversary, dark and shapeless in the night.

"Do something!" Lance cried. He lunged at the soldier.

Engrelin's heart bounding, he whirled back to the window. Drawing Arrian from its sheath, he plunged the glowing blade straight into the pane of fogged glass. Terrific crystal shards exploded in every direction. They caught Arrian's light and the pale moonbeams for a split second before showering to the earth. Nine pale faces gaped at

Engrelin from within the dark building. Quickly, Engrelin scraped the jagged glass from the windowpane with the crowbar. He motioned frantically for the hostages to climb out.

"Out here!" he whispered urgently. "Now!"

He stepped back from the window and collided into someone. Crying out fiercely, he spun, Arrian raised.

"Sheesh, Engrelin, it's just me!" Lance jumped beyond the blade's reach. He held a dripping knife away from his body. A resolved expression tightened his features. In answer to Engrelin's silent question, he jerked his chin towards a prone figure lying face-down in the snow. "He won't be bothering us again. God forgive me."

Engrelin rested his hand briefly on Lance's shoulder. "What about the others?" he asked.

"You're not going to believe it, but they're so loud, they didn't hear the window breaking. Can't you hear them talking to Welric?"

Both boys listened. Rising loudly over the crunch of broken glass beneath the fugitives' feet was the grumble of slurred voices, Welric's lisp barely discernable among them.

"We're all out," said Averendier suddenly behind them.

Engrelin turned and nodded to his cousin. It was near miraculous to have that tall, grave figure standing there!

But this was no time to revel over victory's mere beginnings.

"Good," Engrelin said. "Go down to the creek. A boat's waiting there. Get into it, all of you, and wait. Welric and I'll join you in a moment." His eyes drifted to the corner of the building that he knew the Tirendrians would soon round, perhaps to figure out what happened to their companion. "Lance, go with them."

Lance clasped Engrelin's arm briefly before turning and walking away, waving for the other hostages to join them. Engrelin ran his eyes over the group as they crept away down the hill. He edged towards the building's corner and pressed his back against the cold wall. Over his own thin breaths, Engrelin heard the Tirendrians' voices distinctly. His heart lodged in his throat as he listened to them argue with Welric over who had duty in front of the building. Could they be convinced that Welric had been sent there to guard?

A scream pierced the stillness. Engrelin's heart jolted, then quit him completely.

"What was that?" one of the Tirendrians barked. Another cursed loudly.

All at once, many feet stumbled heavily in the snow. Heavily, but quickly. Engrelin dashed from behind the building, down the hill towards the boat. In his rush of fear, he thought he could feel hot breath creeping down his neck. It only lent wings to his feet.

Down by the creek, the escaped prisoners were leaping into the boat. All but one. Lance ran back up the hill towards him, sword drawn.

He skidded to a stop beside Engrelin. They both turned to face the Tirendrians. As Engrelin had guessed, they had circled the building before they realized the prisoners had fled to the creek. Now they swarmed down the hillside, slipping from ice and drunkenness, and all the more terrible for it.

"What...do we do?" Lance panted, stooping to catch his breath. "Elvera...recognized me."

"Unfortunately," Engrelin muttered. Would that girl never stop wrecking everything? He glanced at the oncoming soldiers and his heart hitched up another gear. "Lance..." He stopped. He couldn't ask anyone to do this.

Lance hunched his shoulders, but smiled, baring his teeth slightly. "Why not?" he said softly, his eyes on the Tirendrians. "Let the others go. After all, what do we have to lose?"

72

W*ith a defiant shout, Lance charged back up the hill. Engrelin* ran after him, his boots digging deep into the snow, Arrian blazing blue in his right hand.

A few yards away from the soldiers, however, Engrelin dropped onto one knee, threw Arrian down. He tugged his bow and arrow out of his quiver. Not allowing himself time to think, he strung the bow, notched an arrow, and fired. One Tirendrian soldier cried out and dropped into the snow. He didn't rise. His comrades surged around him in an angry red wave.

His fingers slick, Engrelin reached back for another arrow. He let his breath hiss out when his fingers met only three feathered shafts. Only three arrows out of the dozen he had stuffed into his quiver. The rest must have spilled out in the boat on the way.

No time for disappointments. He fired again, sending this shaft into the heart of a soldier who had just clashed blades with Lance. Lance paused long enough to lift his sword in a grateful salute before plunging to meet the next foe.

Welric burst down the hill, his eyes as bright a blue as Arrian's blade. At the same time, Engrelin saw one of the hostage princes rush up from the creek. Engrelin thought for a moment he was going to be sick. The prince had to go back! Didn't he see they were fighting to give the others time to get away?

The anger and dread reverberating through Engrelin sent his final two shots awry. Growling with frustration, he tossed the bow aside. Snatching up Arrian, he ran full tilt up the hillside. Another prince followed closely at his heels.

Flashing blades and harsh yells surrounded Engrelin He couldn't take the time to survey the scene, or even to decide who was winning. He pounced on the nearest soldier, a hulk of a man battering Welric back and back. He blocked a stunning blow that might have taken Welric's head off. Roaring angrily, the soldier swung around to Engrelin. Engrelin knocked the man's blade aside and drove his own sword home.

He had not pulled Arrian free when something burned his arm like fire. Crying out, Engrelin jumped back. He narrowly missed the Tirendrian's blade as it darted in for a second hit. The man's face twisted with rage, he swung his sword again. Engrelin fended off the ringing blows, deafened to all but the ring of steel.

The soldier tripped on something buried in the snow, giving Engrelin the chance to dart in and slice the man's leg. The man screamed with pain and rage. He lurched back to his feet and smashed his blade against Engrelin's. A numb shock rattled up Engrelin's wrists. Recovering, he lunged forward. The edge of his blade met the flat of the Tirendrian's. They bound. Engrelin shoved hard, trying to push the enemy's blade aside and away. But the man, though drunk, had not spent the past two weeks convalescing in a cell.

"Trying to get me to give up?" panted the soldier. He was leaning forward, perspiration beading his forehead and he strove to win the bind.

Engrelin didn't answer—he was far too busy to banter.

"Engrelin!" someone yelled behind him. "Look out, he's got—"

Too late, Engrelin saw someone rushing up behind him. He lunged forward, knocking the Tirendrian and his sword back. The man stumbled. His sword swung wildly, narrowly missing Engrelin's head. Someone crashed into his back. A thud. A groan. Someone reeled against him, clutching his arm for a split second before slipping to the ground. Engrelin reached to catch whoever it was, then froze. Arrian nearly fell from his hand.

Lance lay deep in the crimson-stained snow, a dagger embedded deep in his chest.

Engrelin had not even the chance to cry out in anguish when he heard the swish of a blade cutting through air. He stumbled back. The second soldier—Lance's murderer—waded forward. Engrelin watched him come through a red haze. And plunged forward, driving the sword into the man's middle.

But there was still the other soldier. Engrelin heard him scrambling along the ground, groping for his sword. Engrelin whirled, his eyes scanning the ground for the man's weapon. It lay only a yard away. He rushed toward it.

The soldier reached it first. Scrambling forward on his hands and knees, he snatched it away just as Engrelin bent to retrieve it. He stuck it out. Engrelin tripped over it and went sprawling. He turned mid-fall, flinging Arrian up to catch the soldier's blade.

There was nothing to catch. Instead of attacking his vulnerable enemy, the soldier was gone. Engrelin jumped to his feet. Beyond the scuffle and fighting around him, he spotted a retreating figure. The soldier who had tripped him was running back up the hill, towards the holding house and the woods.

Towards the barracks and hundreds of other soldiers.

Engrelin hesitated only a moment to glance at Lance's prone body. Then he sprinted after the running soldier.

The soldier had a head start, but he was drunk. As he neared the top of the hill, he began stumbling. It wasn't until he reached the edge of the wood that he looked back. His and Engrelin's eyes met. The soldier cursed and sprang into the underbrush.

Engrelin tensed, sheathed his sword, and jumped after him.

Engrelin pumped his legs harder, following the man as he wove around tree trunks and crashed through thickets. Briers and vines tore Engrelin's skin and clothing. He held one arm crooked in front of his face to shield it as he ran.

The running soldier stopped, whirled, and charged back towards Engrelin. His sword hissed through the air and came in crunching contact with Engrelin's left shoulder. Screaming with pain, Engrelin snatched his sword out of its sheath and stumbled forward to block the man's next blow. It never came. His foot snagged on something. He bowled into the soldier, sending them both tumbling. Stars exploded in Engrelin's vision, followed by a wash of darkness.

Lilac could hardly believe what had just happened. One moment, they were singing for what they thought might be their last night.

The next, they were free.

Free. The words seemed to echo on the wind that streamed past her cheeks, whipping off the water's edge. She clambered into the boat behind her sister. Even as she climbed, she looked back onto land, where Vivian stood with Eileen, holding the sobbing girl. She had lost both of her brothers in the fight on the hillside.

A dagger of pian pierced her heart. How many more would have to die?

She ached to join them, but Vivian and Eileen had a bond that months of imprisonment together had forged. She wasn't about to impose on it now.

Elvera sat silent on the bench beside her, shivering in the cold, staring out into nothing. Lilac scooted closer to her, wrapping an arm around her hunched shoulders.

"We're going to make it," she whispered comfortingly, brushing the long strands of her sister's hair behind her ear.

Elvera shook her head. Her shoulders convulsed beneath the wool cloak. "It's all my fault," she whispered. "I shouldn't have…but he…I didn't know…"

Lilac drew her sister tight against herself. "It's over now," she soothed. "They're going to get us home."

"I gave us away," Elvera chattered, fighting back the knot in her voice.

Lilac swallowed past her constricting throat. "It's over," she repeated. "Everything…everything's going to be fine." Her arms tightened around her.

Elvera wept.

73

The first thing Engrelin was aware of was the pain. Sharp, acute thrills that tore the breath from his lungs. The stench of sweat and blood filled his nostrils. Sound ceased to exist save an incessant ringing in his ears.

I've died. Lance died, and I'm dead too.

He tried to shift his position and cringed. A soft moan escaped his lips. No, not dead. Most definitely not.

Slowly, he forced his heavy eyes open. The star-sprinkled sky swirled lazily over his head, making his stomach churn sickeningly. Gradually, the stars grew still. Engrelin shoved the Tirendrian's limp body off himself and struggled into a sitting position. Another wave of nausea swept through him. Engrelin put a hand to his head and felt a lump and the stickiness of half-dried blood. More blood flowed gently down his back and chest. His left arm hung limply from his torn shoulder.

Finally, the thought of his companions pushed through his pain and made him start. How long had he been out of it? What had happened? Were any of them still alive?

Clumsily, he tore strips from the dead Tirendrian's cloak and bound his useless arm across his chest. He staggered to his feet. His stomach lurched, and he reached out to cling to a tree for support (likely the self-same tree he had bashed his head against). When the nausea finally died down, he wiped Arrian's stained blade clean in the snow and rammed it into its sheath. Drawing a final, strengthening breath, he moved away from the tree and staggered back to the creek.

The pain and dizziness were relentless. Engrelin paused every few steps to rest against a tree. Only the thought of reaching the others kept him on his feet.

Finally, he broke out of the woods near the hill's foot. He nearly fell over Welric, who had been peering anxiously into the trees.

"Arweddwr!" Welric exclaimed joyfully. "Thank the Lord, you are thafe!" He gripped Engrelin's hand warmly, but quickly snatched it back when Engrelin grimaced. The older man quickly drew Engrelin out into the moonlight. He shook his head. "Thethe are bad. Very bad. You need a meddyg to thitch you up." He made a sewing motion.

Engrelin seized Welric's hand. "Maybe later," he said. "But for now, please don't tell anyone. We have enough to worry about."

Welric frowned. "I do not like it," he said slowly. "But maybe you are right." He reached to his shoulder and pulled loose Engrelin's cloak. "You muth have dropped thith during the fight," he said. "It will hide the blood."

Engrelin took the heavy cloak and held it in his good hand, feeling foolish and miserably useless.

Silently, Welric took it back and helped drape it over Engrelin's bent shoulders. Together, they started walking back to where the boat was.

"Welric, one thing," Engrelin said. "Why Arweddwr…"

"*Gon Arrian*?" The *cymraeg* words rolled off Welric's tongue like no others would. He nodded and looked at Engrelin quizzically. "Do you not carry a thword called Arrian?"

"Yes," Engrelin acknowledged. Even now, he couldn't shake off the memory of his dreams.

"Bethide," Welric continued, "One knowth thethe thingth when they thee them."

Engrelin's forehead wrinkled with confusion, but Welric offered no further explanation. He led Engrelin directly down to the creek, where Engrelin washed the blood off his face and hands and out of his hair.

"How many were hurt, Welric?" Engrelin asked finally, sitting back on his heels.

Welric shook his head slowly. "Bad thingth," he said sadly. "I am lucky. I hath only a cut on thith cheek, though it can thcar. You know Lanthe died." Welric smiled sympathetically when Engrelin started with surprise or pain. "I know. I thaw what he did. He wath your good fellow, Arweddwr. I am thorry."

Welric must have meant friend, Engrelin reflected as he dried his face on a corner of his cloak. He pressed it to his stinging eyes for a moment before letting it go. Why did they all have to die, and he never able to care for them? What good could come out of a war if everyone he loved was killed? Why was he being left behind?

Slowly, he got to his feet. "Why are any of us still here?" he wondered aloud.

He hadn't meant for Welric to hear, but the man did and nodded.

"We had to thtay long," he said sorrowfully, perhaps thinking Engrelin meant the wait for departure. "To bury Lanthe and two hothageth."

Engrelin stared. "Two princes dead?"

Welric nodded again and led Engrelin toward the boat. "Both young men, from Northern Florenth. It ith very thad." He was silent a moment, his arm tightening supportively around Engrelin's. "They died well, Arweddwr. 'Greater love hath no man.'"

But they shouldn't have died at all! You and Lance and I all stayed here to let them go free! Engrelin couldn't force the words past his numb lips. The sight—and the feel—of Lance falling dead against him played awfully through his memory.

"Avery!" Welric called. Engrelin lifted his head to see Averendier striding towards him, relief etched plainly on his face.

"Engrelin! Thank God, you're alive," Averendier breathed, folding Engrelin into a quick—but inevitably painful—embrace.

"Andy, ith it done?"

Averendier's jaw twitched. "Yes, we finished," Averendier said. "Jayce is smoothing everything over now. I wish we could do more."

Welric shook his head. "We have done all we could do. Now we muth leave, remember them in prayerth, before more tholdierth come."

"We'll get ready to go then," Averendier said.

Welric glanced questioningly at Engrelin. "Are you ready, Arweddwr?"

Engrelin let his gaze drift past Averendier to a thicket where one of the princes stood, using the flat of a blade to rustle snow and bracken over three gentle mounds. He wanted so badly to go there, to whisper at least one prayer.

But Welric was right. They had to leave now, or all death and pain would have been in vain.

With a pang, he remembered about Isalinia and Andrald. How would he ever tell Averendier and the princesses?

"I'm ready," he said quietly.

But I'll come back for you, Lance, he added silently. *One day. I'll bring you back to the farm, just like we planned. You don't belong here. I wish we could bring you now…If only you were still with us! Why did you have to shove me over, to take the dagger for me? I might have found a way to block it, to dodge it. Anything better than this. I might have saved you…*

Freedom's cost was almost too high to bear. Would even more of them have to die before Monaria could be reached?

Dear God, no…

"Engrelin?" Averendier prompted.

Engrelin sighed and looked away. "Yeah, I'm coming."

The surviving hostages were already in the longboat. Lilac sat straight as a pike on one of the thwarts, looking down the river, her eyes searching the rising mists. Always searching ahead. Lilac never seemed to look behind.

Yet she didn't know what painful things the past held. She couldn't know what equal pain the future could bring. Yet she looked ahead, with her chin raised, as if defying all—past, present, and to come.

If only it were that easy. Engrelin turned his back on Lance's grave, on Reing, and on Arrian, which gleamed in the early morning sky. He stepped into the boat that would take them home.

Epilogue

*B*erwyn, *are you ready?"*

Berwyn jumped at Ouen's whisper. She looked quickly up from the dishes she had been washing to see that the boy had cracked the kitchen door open and was peering in at her. Lednora, who had stayed after dark to help Berwyn with the monstrous stack of dishes, went pale as snow.

"What happened to the guard?" she asked fearfully.

"He's out." Ouen explained hurriedly. "Come on!"

Berwyn nearly dropped the plate she held. "Now?"

"It's the last night of the festival, like I told you," he answered. "It's now or never."

A chill ran up Berwyn's spine. Quickly, she turned and dried her trembling hands on a towel. Then she slung her satchel, and its precious contents, over her shoulder. Turning back to Ouen, she said, "I'm ready."

"Ready for what?" Lednora trembled.

Berwyn grabbed her hands. "No time to explain," she said. "I'll tell you as we go. Just know that everything's going to be all right as long as we listen to Ouen and do as he says."

Hand in hand, the girls slipped out the door where Ouen stood waiting. Berwyn's heart thumped in her chest as Ouen ran off into the dusk and they followed. Berwyn's pendant bounced against her chest.

I'm really doing this, she thought, hardly believing herself. The tang of dread filled her mouth. *Dear Lord, help us. We're going to die.*

"Your Majesty."

"Please, sit down."

Lamar obeyed, sinking into his chair. But he sat forward with his hands clasping his knees.

"Do you need something, Your Majesty?" he asked.

Bendekahn settled heavily in a chair. "Conversation, maybe. Or advice. You and Johanthan never can seem to separate the two."

Lamar laughed shortly. "I guess we never can see you differently than when we first knew you, even if you are king now."

"And maybe I don't mind the advice so much as I say," Bendekahn returned. He too sat forward. "I'm still not at rest about Johanthan's plan. I haven't received any word yet from Julian that the girls have arrived."

"You're too anxious," Lamar said. "If the weather stayed fair, they would have only just reached the Pwynt. It will take another two weeks for word to reach us."

"Still…" Bendekahn brushed his hand across his forehead. "I can't help thinking I made the wrong choice. Johnathan is worried too."

"You know he's stubborn as an ox until he gets what he wants, then frets about it the rest of his life even if it turns out well in the end. Look at you now. You're here because of him."

"Even though you gave him a hard time, yes. But this is different, Lamar," Bendekahn said earnestly. "These are my girls. I would have loved to talk to Zacara about this, but I don't want to until I have your opinion first."

"Opinion on what, Your Majesty?"

"About my sailing to Monaria."

Lamar looked doubtful. "Didn't you refuse to send your daughters by sea because it's frothing with pirates? And you haven't left Alinar since—"

Bendekahn held his hand up quickly. "Even here, Lamar," he warned.

Lamar sighed and took a deep breath. "You cannot sail. You'll get attacked on the way. And though I believe we could fight off any pirates, it's still risky. Ontaria needs you. You can't throw your life away."

"Ensuring my daughters' safety will never be throwing my life away," Bendekahn replied quietly, "though you speak well." He was silent a moment. "I will wait a month," he said. "And if I do not receive word before then that my daughters have reached Monaria safely, I shall immediately sail for the Pwynt."

Lamar stood. "Send Johnathan and myself instead, Your Majesty," he said. Surely—"

"You and Johnathan shall go," Bendekahn said. "And in a month's time, I will follow. In the meantime, I will clear the path a little. It's about time we purged our seas of piracy." He also stood. "Tell Johnathan, Lamar, that you two are to sail for Monaria tomorrow. I must tell Zacara."

Without another word, Bendekahn left the room.

Lamar bowed slightly to the empty doorway. "As you will have it, Your Majesty."

Geirfa

Arth wen—polar bear
Arweddwr—bearer
Arweddwr gon Arrian—bearer of Arrian
Bonesig—Lady (name of cow)
Brawd—brother
Ceffyl—horse
Cyllel—a farmer's everyday knife, about the length of a hunting knife
Dant y llew—Dandelion (name of cow)
Ei—yes
Firlas—a penny
Meddyg—physician, doctor
Nos da—good morning
Pryntawn da—good afternoon
Sanctaidd Beibl—Holy Bible
Traeth Euriad—Golden Shores (the name of the Peterson farm)
Trysor—treasury
Kitchen—kitchen
Yomosod—attack
Ystafell fyw—living room

Eowyn A. Stephenson

Acknowledgements

Wow. *Okay. Here goes! So many wonderful people put in the time and love and tears to make this book possible! I couldn't possibly say "the end" without mentioning them—*or else this story may never have come into your hands.

First and foremost, my big sister Beth. Wow. If you hadn't sat with me all those evenings and listened and fangirled…how many plot holes and spelling errors might still exist! You were the first member of the Ontaria fandom (if that ever becomes a thing). To Mary Cate Mateer—just…wow. I don't know where this would be without all our talks and just general squealing over each other's characters and all the crazy hard work you put into alpha reading. Thank you so much, bestie. To my Mom and Dad—though this is already dedicated to you all, I have to add something. If you never let me have free reign over my passion of writing, I never would have gotten this far. Thank you for that.

To all my Alpha readers: Elizabeth Stephenson, Mary Cate Mateer, Bennett Bauer, Seth Bauer…thank you. This would be very different without all of y'alls input and watchful eyes.

To all my Beta readers: you awesome ydubs people *tight hugs* Charissa Franklin, Karissa Franklin, Timothy Benefield, Ana Rattin, Amanda Ferguson, Lila Lemon, Joseph Beesley, Hannah Smith, Hannah Mollohan, and Evangelyn Wuchner. Even if all you did was read a couple chapters or read the whole thing and simply squeal—thank you so much. Y'all took so much time out of your lives to read my giant book.

My amazing copy editor: Laurel Scott. Thank you, thank you, thank you. You squeaked time in your busy schedule to work on some teen's story. It means so, so much to me. Thank you.

Bennett, you took time out of your busy college life to help me figure out the basics and formatting, and designed the logo for Lily Fields. Thank you.

And to all you readers…my deepest gratitude. You have taken a moment to peek into the worlds inside my heart. I hope it filled you with all the happiness a reader can receive from the written word. Thank you.

And a final thanks to my Heavenly Father. Without Him, I would not have been, nor would this story that He wrote on my heart.

May His blessing be on you all.

-Eowyn

About the Author

Eowyn has always loved writing stories, from the moment she drew her first picture book and printed her name and age conspicuously on the cover so that everyone who checked it out at the library would know how old she was when she wrote it. Now she writes her stories hoping they might touch people's hearts and imaginations with pure, wild adventures. She loves writing, listening to soundtracks, gardening, talking to her cockatiel or cat, drinking coffee and tea, curling up with books, the smell of libraries, and eating a lot of chocolate.

Eowyn A. Stephenson